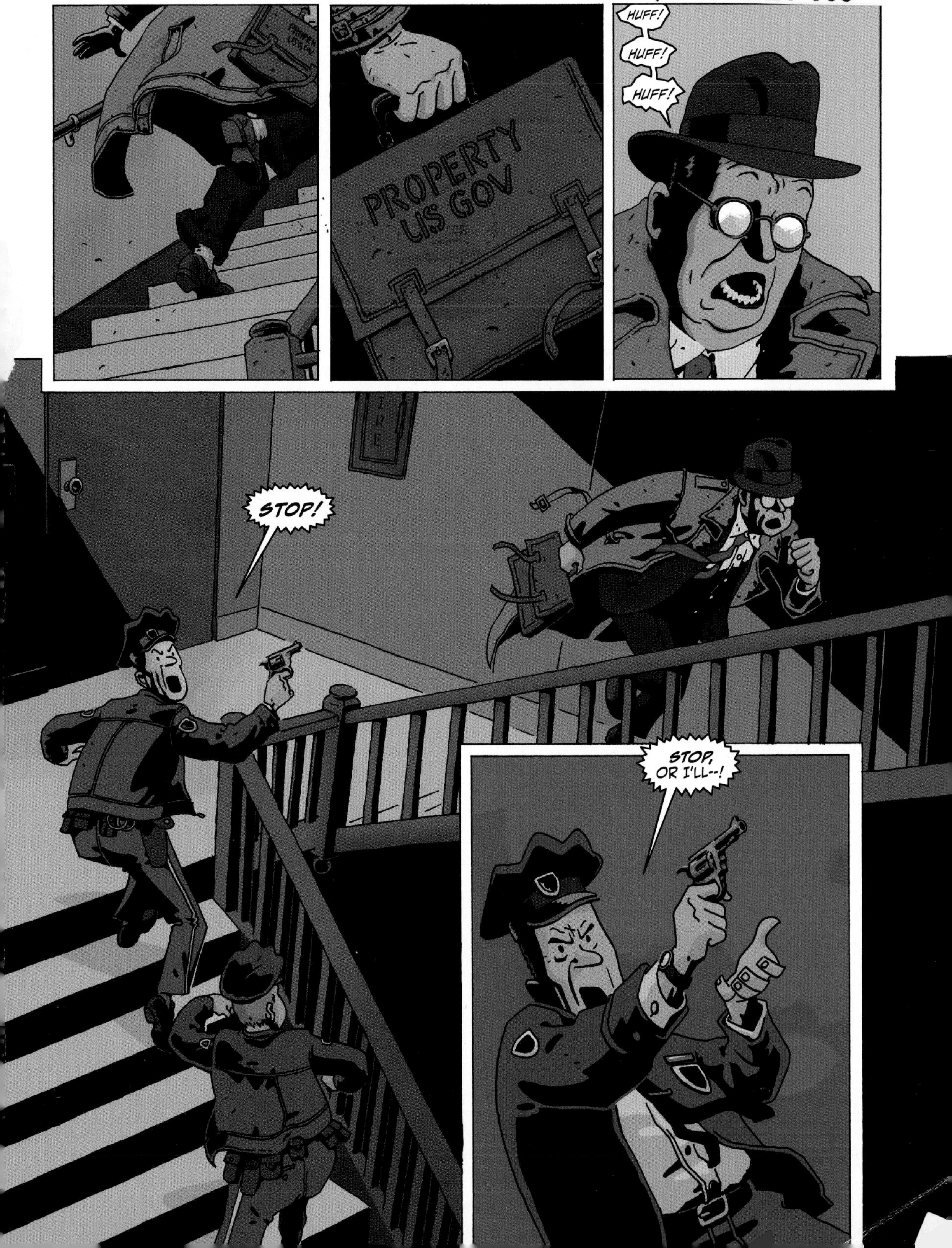
PROPERTY
U.S. GOV
HUFF!
HUFF!
HUFF!
STOP!
STOP, OR I'LL--!

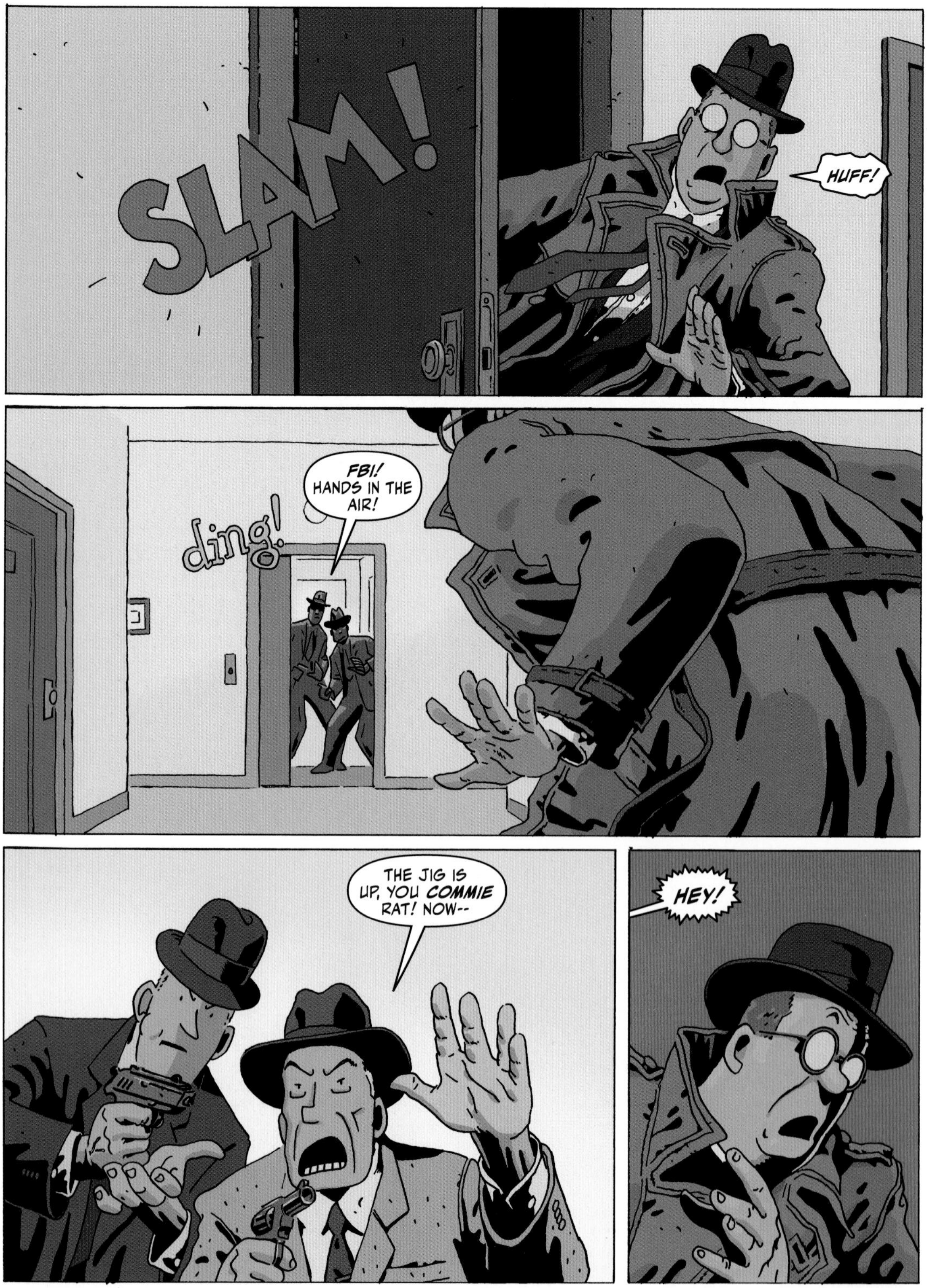
SLAM!
HUFF!
FBI! HANDS IN THE AIR!
ding!
THE JIG IS UP, YOU COMMIE RAT! NOW--
HEY!

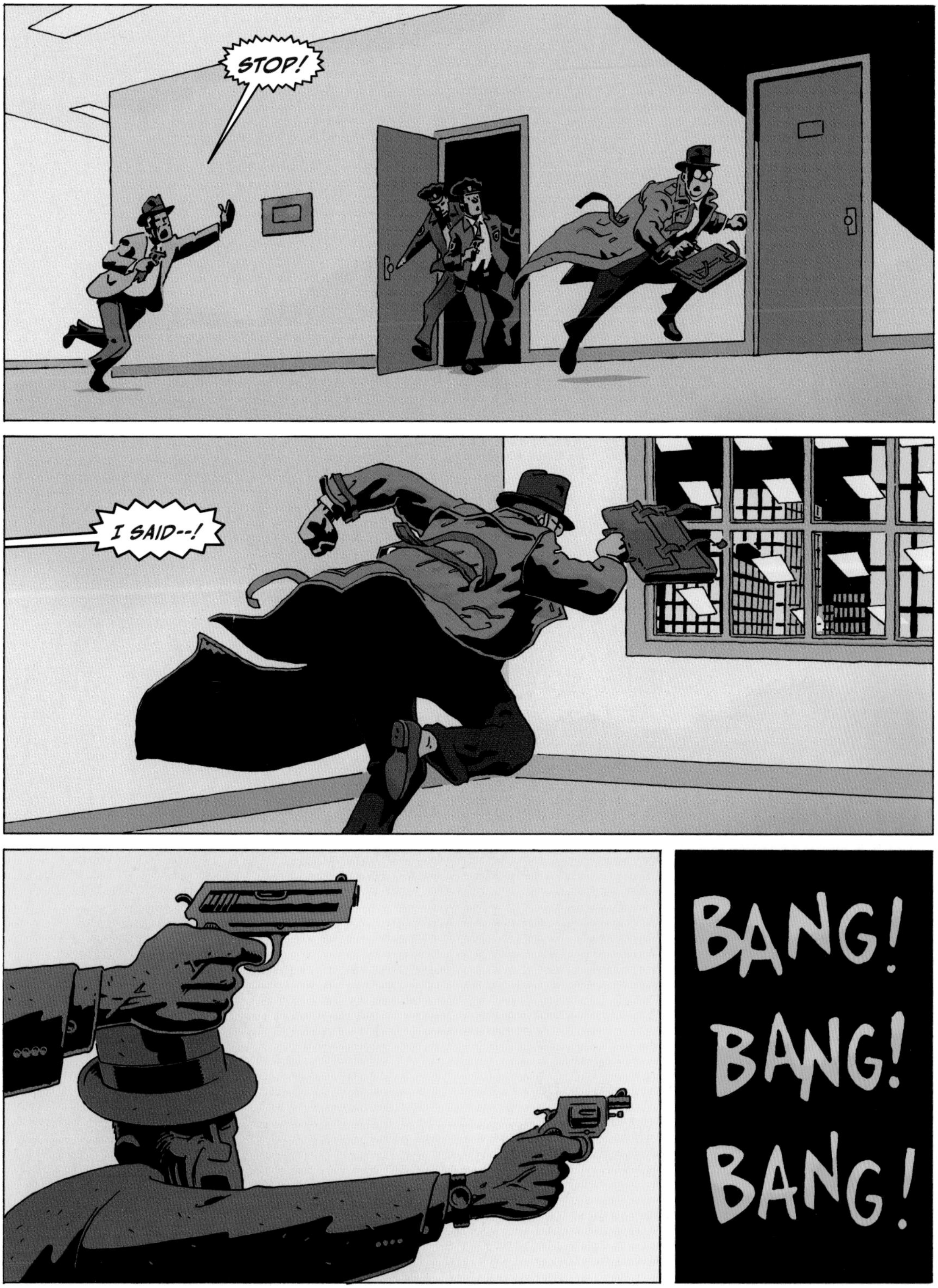
STOP!
I SAID--!
BANG!
BANG!
BANG!

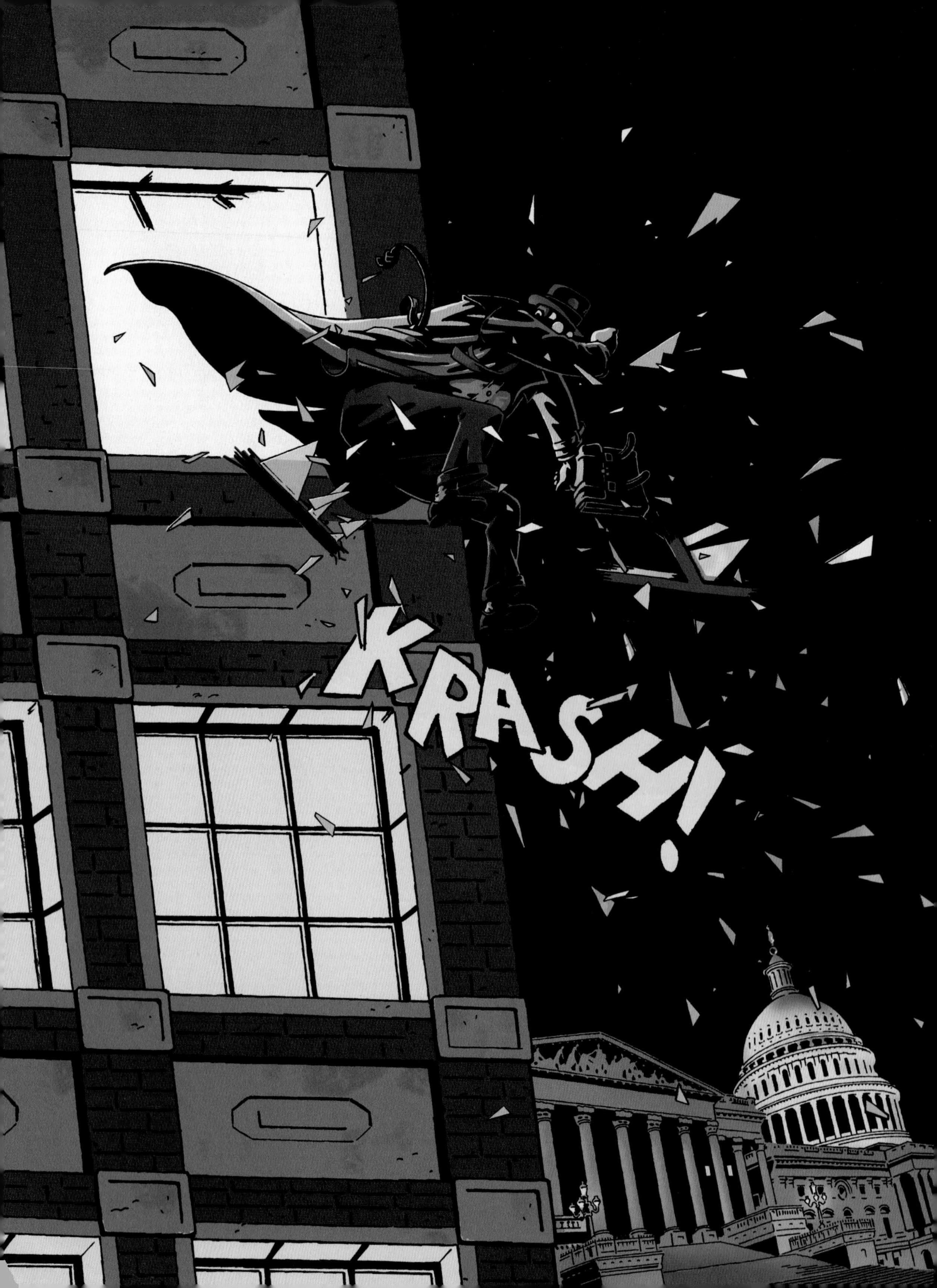
KRASH!

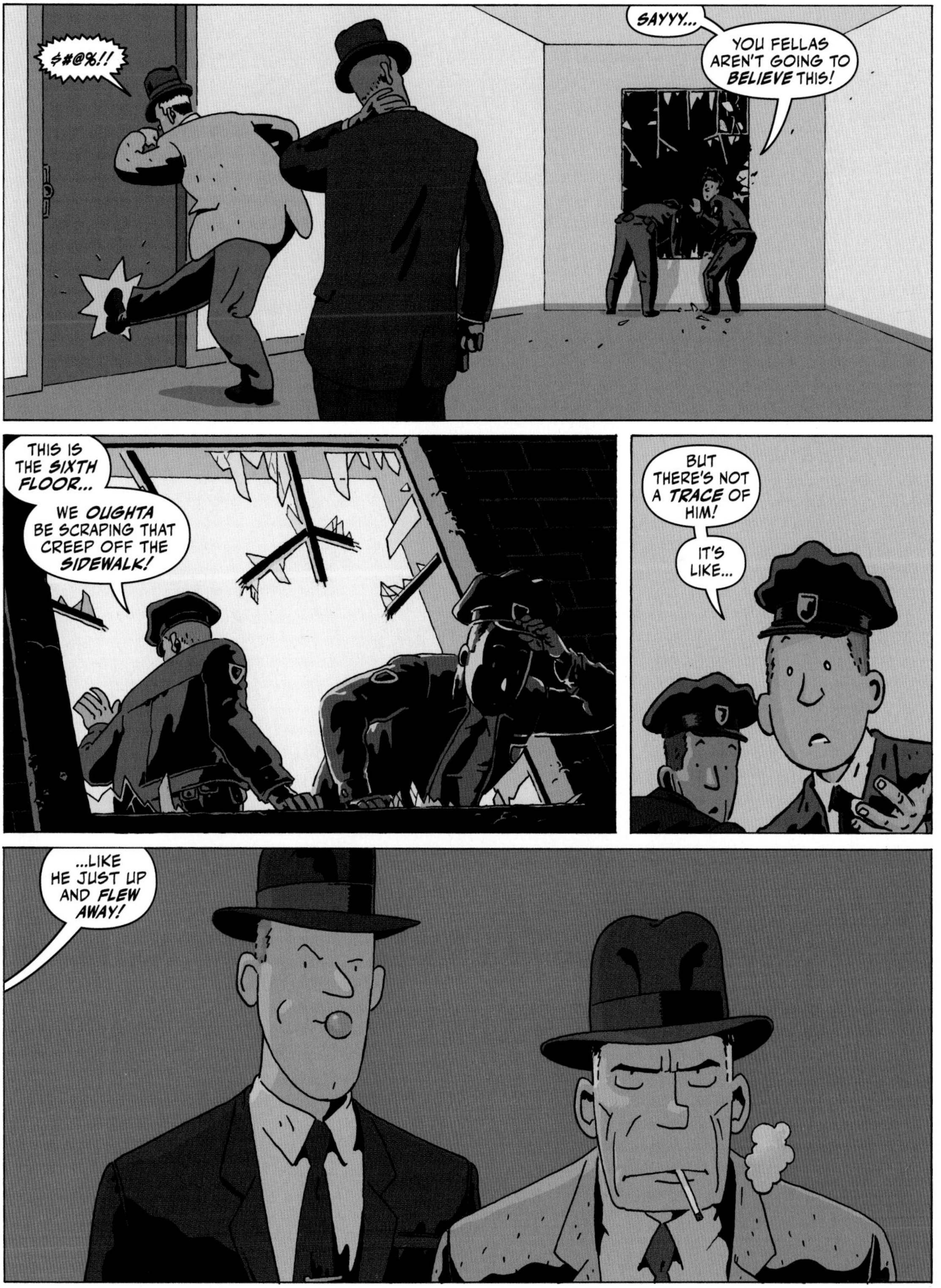
$#@%!!
SAYYY...
YOU FELLAS AREN'T GOING TO BELIEVE THIS!
THIS IS THE SIXTH FLOOR...
WE OUGHTA BE SCRAPING THAT CREEP OFF THE SIDEWALK!
BUT THERE'S NOT A TRACE OF HIM!
IT'S LIKE...
...LIKE HE JUST UP AND FLEW AWAY!

REDS

# SCARE

BY **LIAM FRANCIS WALSH**

An Imprint of
**SCHOLASTIC**

All rights reserved. Published by Graphix, an imprint of Scholastic Inc., *Publishers since 1920.*
SCHOLASTIC, GRAPHIX, and associated logos are trademarks and/or registered trademarks of Scholastic Inc.

The publisher does not have any control over and does not assume any
responsibility for author or third-party websites or their content.

Library of Congress Control Number: 2021937539

ISBN 978-1-338-16709-2 (hardcover)
ISBN 978-1-338-16708-5 (paperback)

10 9 8 7 6 5 4 3 2 1      22 23 24 25 26

Printed in China   62
First edition, April 2022

*Red Scare* was drawn with Pigma Micron pens (size 08) and a Pentel brush
pen on 14" x 17" paper and colored with Adobe Photoshop. The graphic novel was
lettered with Comicraft's Mighty Mouth font and Blambot's Billy the Flying Robot.

Edited by Adam Rau and David Saylor
Book design by Steve Ponzo
Creative Director: Phil Falco
Publisher: David Saylor

For Dora,
who carries my heart in her heart

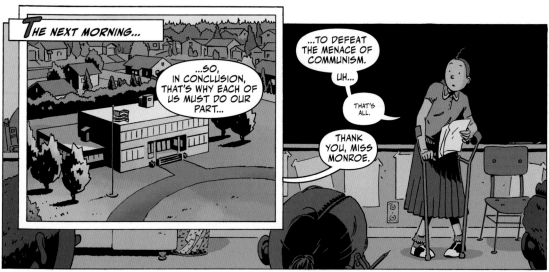

THE NEXT MORNING...

...SO, IN CONCLUSION, THAT'S WHY EACH OF US MUST DO OUR PART...

...TO DEFEAT THE MENACE OF COMMUNISM.

UH...

THAT'S ALL.

THANK YOU, MISS MONROE.

GOOD WORK, PEGGY. YOU MAY TAKE YOUR SEAT.

NOW THEN, UP NEXT WE HAVE...

LET'S SEE...

HEY, SKIP! YOU FORGOT YOUR LUNCH AGAIN, BUT I BROUGHT IT FOR YOU!

SO? WHAT DO YOU WANT, A MEDAL?

NO!

I-I JUST-- I...

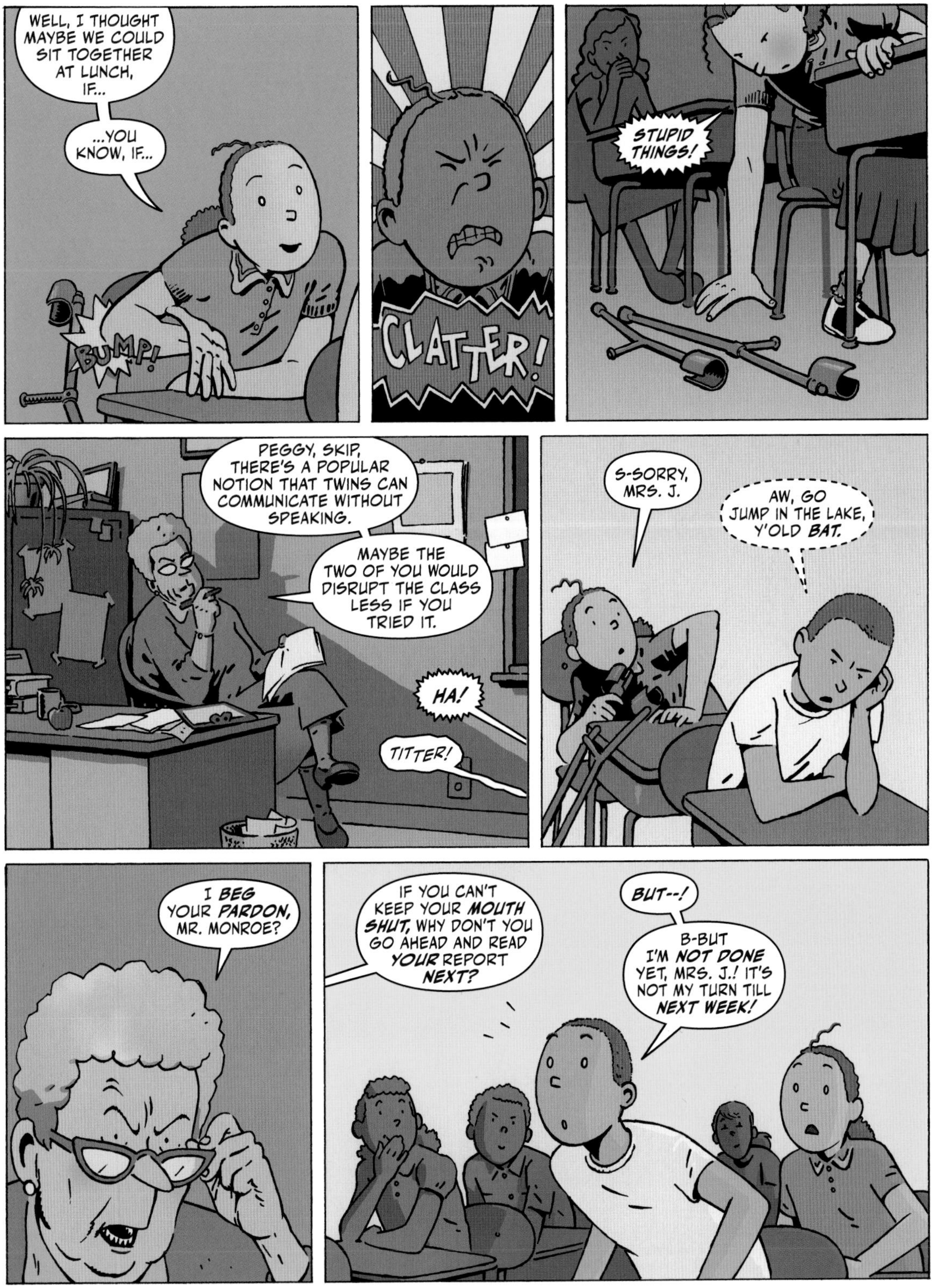
WELL, I THOUGHT MAYBE WE COULD SIT TOGETHER AT LUNCH, IF...
...YOU KNOW, IF...
BUMP!
CLATTER!
STUPID THINGS!
PEGGY, SKIP, THERE'S A POPULAR NOTION THAT TWINS CAN COMMUNICATE WITHOUT SPEAKING.
MAYBE THE TWO OF YOU WOULD DISRUPT THE CLASS LESS IF YOU TRIED IT.
HA!
TITTER!
S-SORRY, MRS. J.
AW, GO JUMP IN THE LAKE, Y'OLD BAT.
I BEG YOUR PARDON, MR. MONROE?
IF YOU CAN'T KEEP YOUR MOUTH SHUT, WHY DON'T YOU GO AHEAD AND READ YOUR REPORT NEXT?
BUT--!
B-BUT I'M NOT DONE YET, MRS. J.! IT'S NOT MY TURN TILL NEXT WEEK!

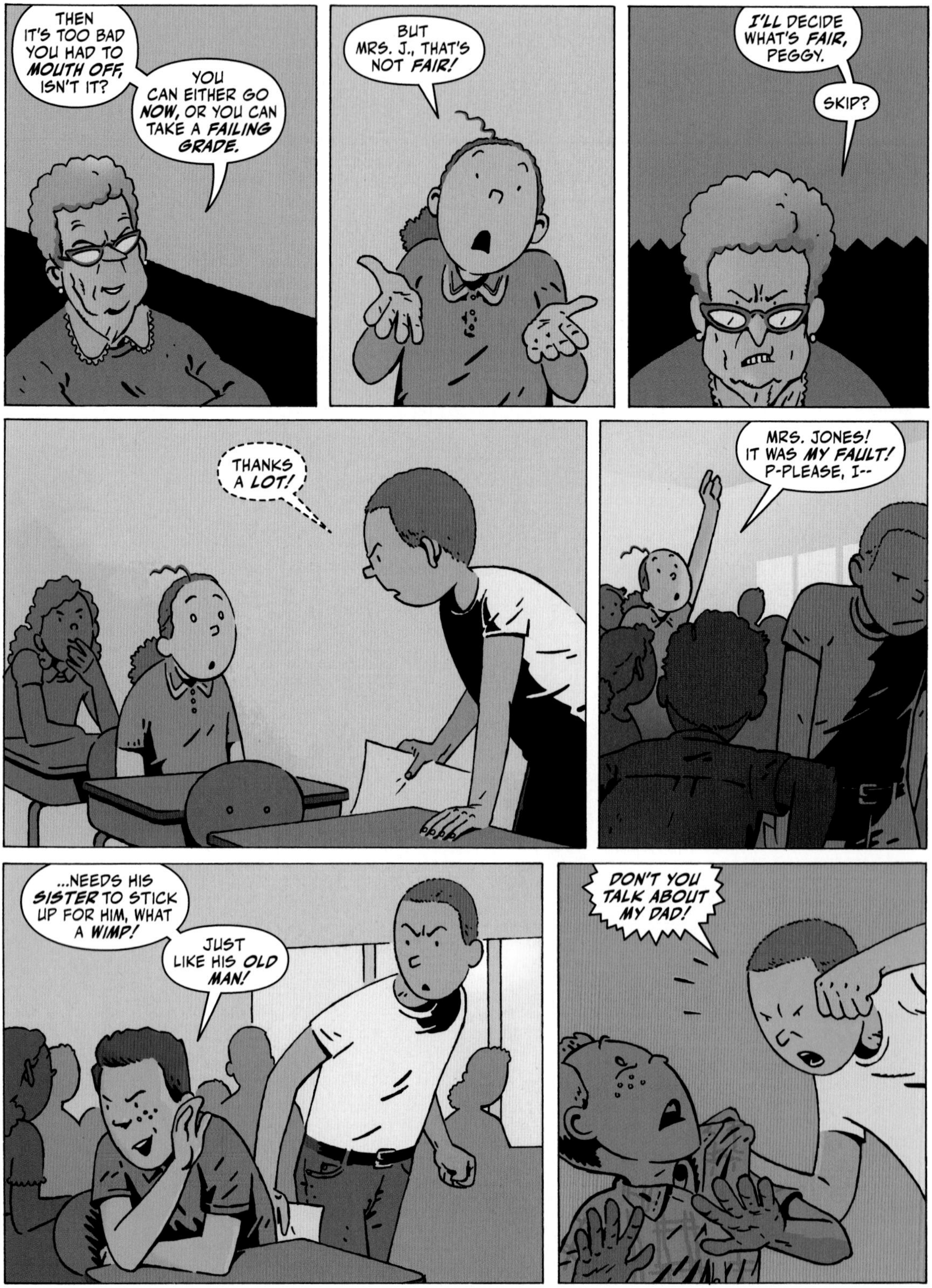
THEN IT'S TOO BAD YOU HAD TO MOUTH OFF, ISN'T IT?
YOU CAN EITHER GO NOW, OR YOU CAN TAKE A FAILING GRADE.
BUT MRS. J., THAT'S NOT FAIR!
I'LL DECIDE WHAT'S FAIR, PEGGY.
SKIP?
THANKS A LOT!
MRS. JONES! IT WAS MY FAULT! P-PLEASE, I--
...NEEDS HIS SISTER TO STICK UP FOR HIM, WHAT A WIMP!
JUST LIKE HIS OLD MAN!
DON'T YOU TALK ABOUT MY DAD!

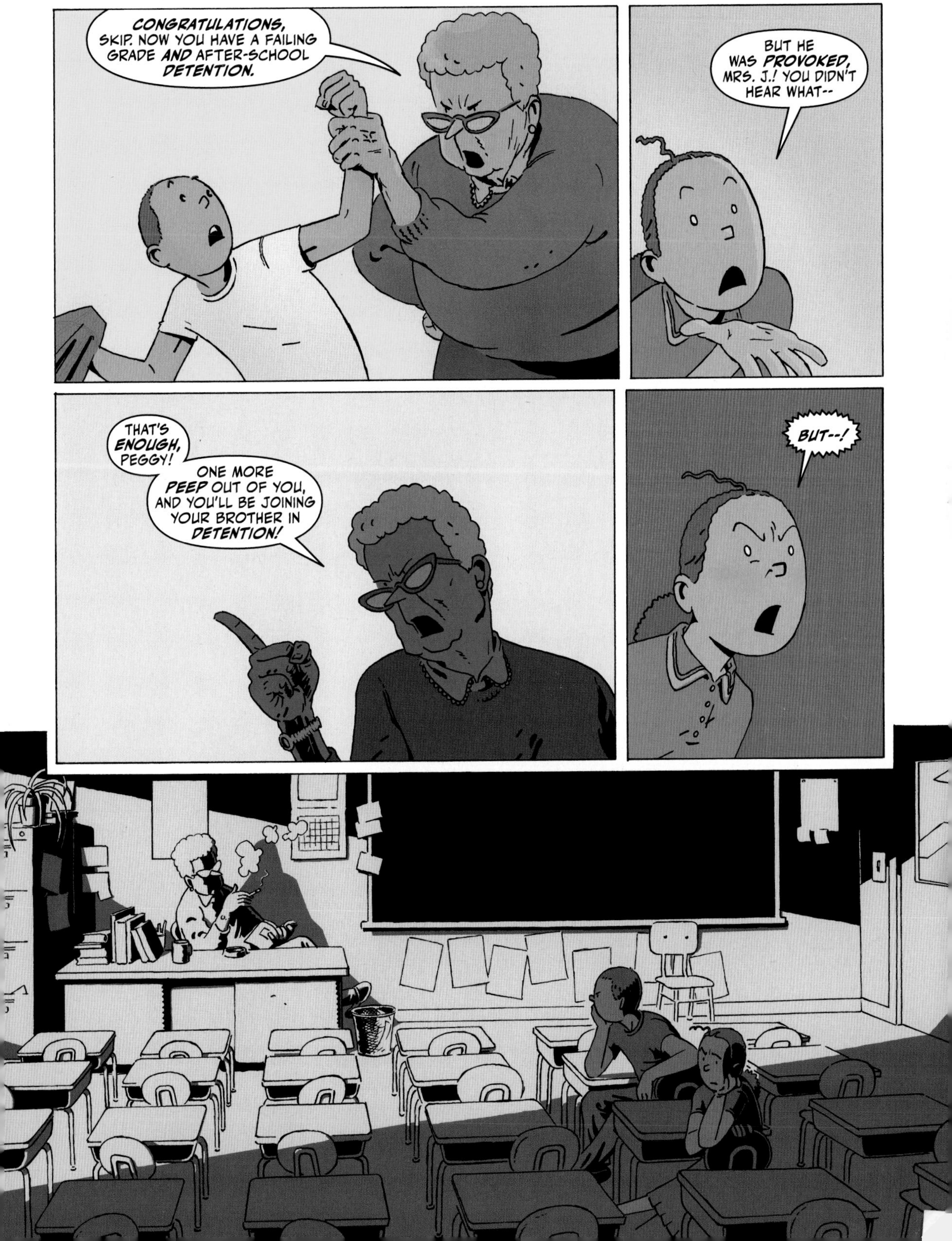
CONGRATULATIONS, SKIP. NOW YOU HAVE A FAILING GRADE AND AFTER-SCHOOL DETENTION.
BUT HE WAS PROVOKED, MRS. J.! YOU DIDN'T HEAR WHAT--
THAT'S ENOUGH, PEGGY!
ONE MORE PEEP OUT OF YOU, AND YOU'LL BE JOINING YOUR BROTHER IN DETENTION!
BUT--!

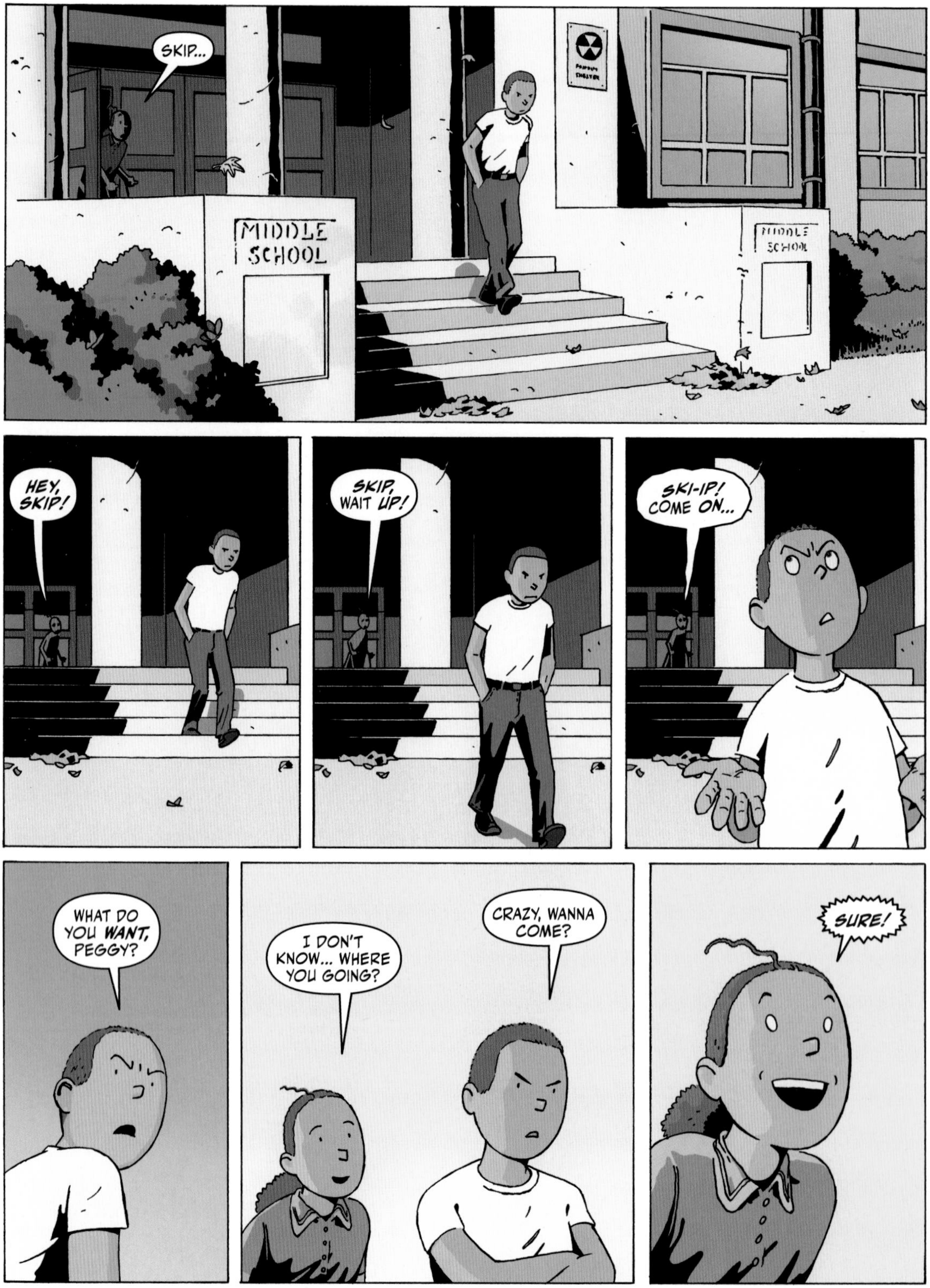
SKIP...
MIDDLE SCHOOL
MIDDLE SCHOOL
HEY, SKIP!
SKIP, WAIT UP!
SKI-IP! COME ON...
WHAT DO YOU WANT, PEGGY?
I DON'T KNOW... WHERE YOU GOING?
CRAZY, WANNA COME?
SURE!

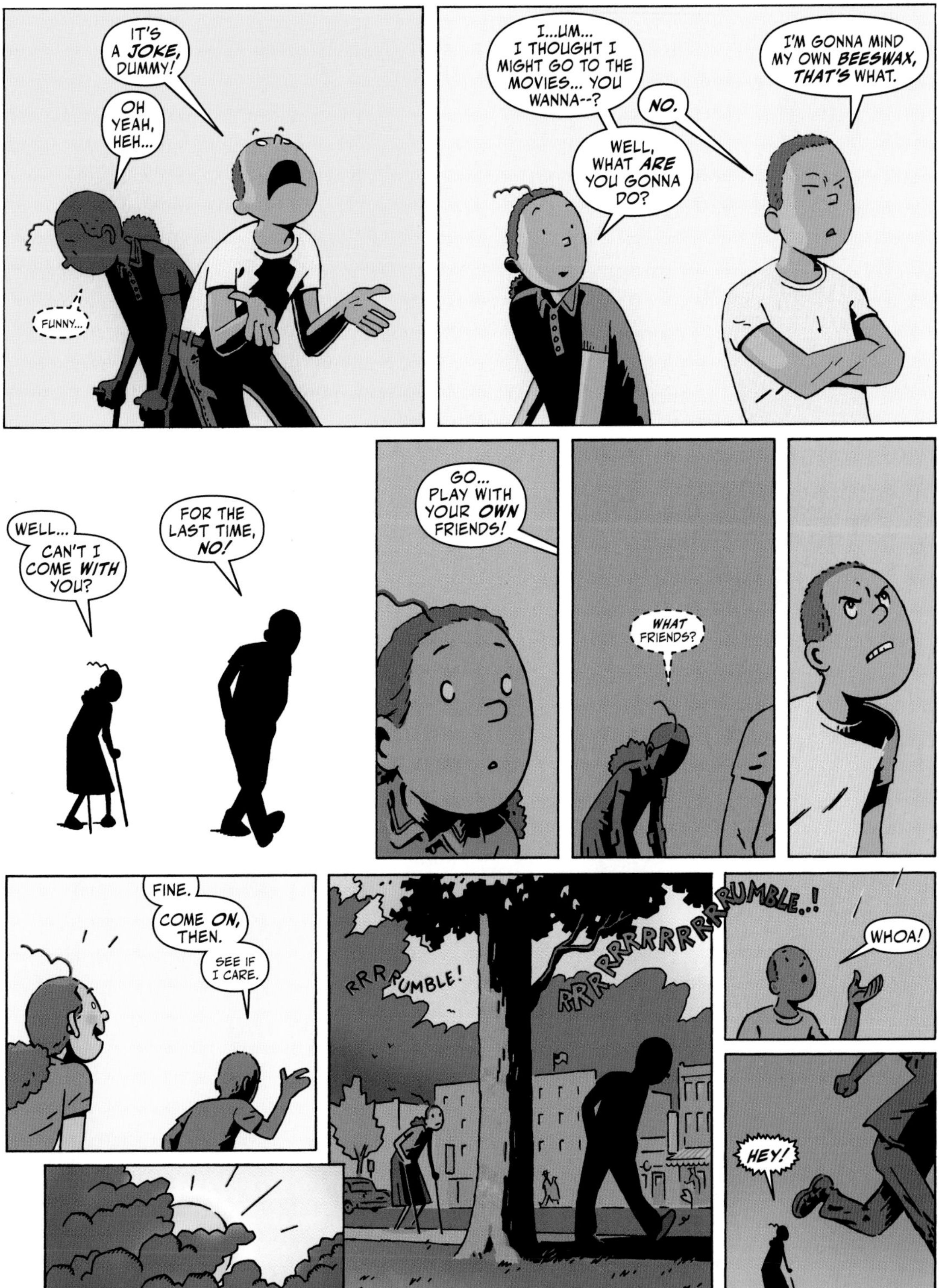
IT'S A JOKE, DUMMY!
OH YEAH, HEH...
FUNNY...
I...UM... I THOUGHT I MIGHT GO TO THE MOVIES... YOU WANNA--?
NO.
WELL, WHAT ARE YOU GONNA DO?
I'M GONNA MIND MY OWN BEESWAX, THAT'S WHAT.
WELL... CAN'T I COME WITH YOU?
FOR THE LAST TIME, NO!
GO... PLAY WITH YOUR OWN FRIENDS!
WHAT FRIENDS?
FINE.
COME ON, THEN.
SEE IF I CARE.
RRRRUMBLE!
RRRRRRRRRRRRRUMBLE..!
WHOA!
HEY!

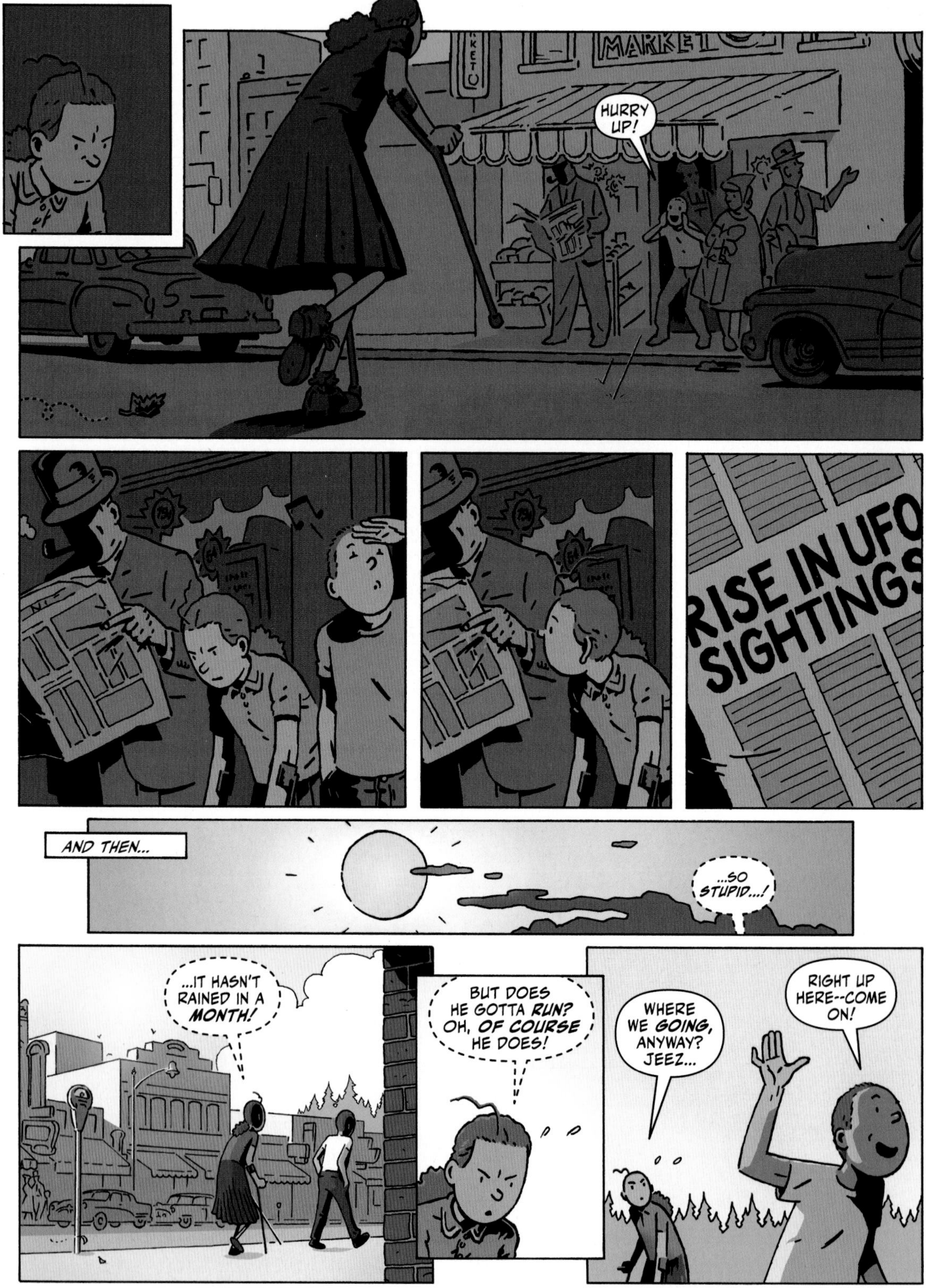
MARKET
HURRY UP!
RISE IN UFO SIGHTINGS
AND THEN...
...SO STUPID...!
...IT HASN'T RAINED IN A MONTH!
BUT DOES HE GOTTA RUN? OH, OF COURSE HE DOES!
WHERE WE GOING, ANYWAY? JEEZ...
RIGHT UP HERE--COME ON!

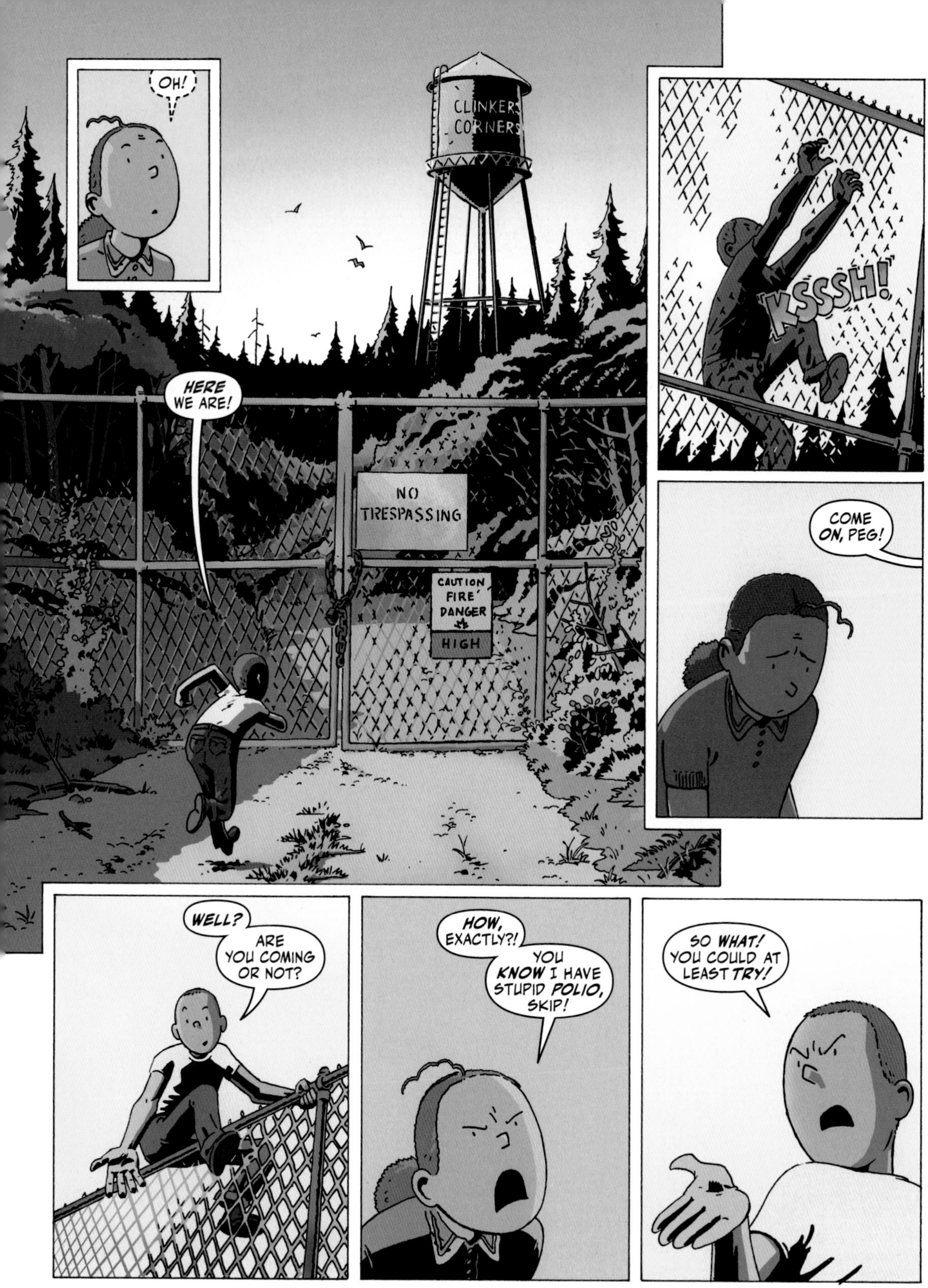
OH!
CLINKERS CORNERS
HERE WE ARE!
NO TRESPASSING
CAUTION FIRE DANGER
HIGH
KSSSH!
COME ON, PEG!
WELL?
ARE YOU COMING OR NOT?
HOW, EXACTLY?!
YOU KNOW I HAVE STUPID POLIO, SKIP!
SO WHAT! YOU COULD AT LEAST TRY!

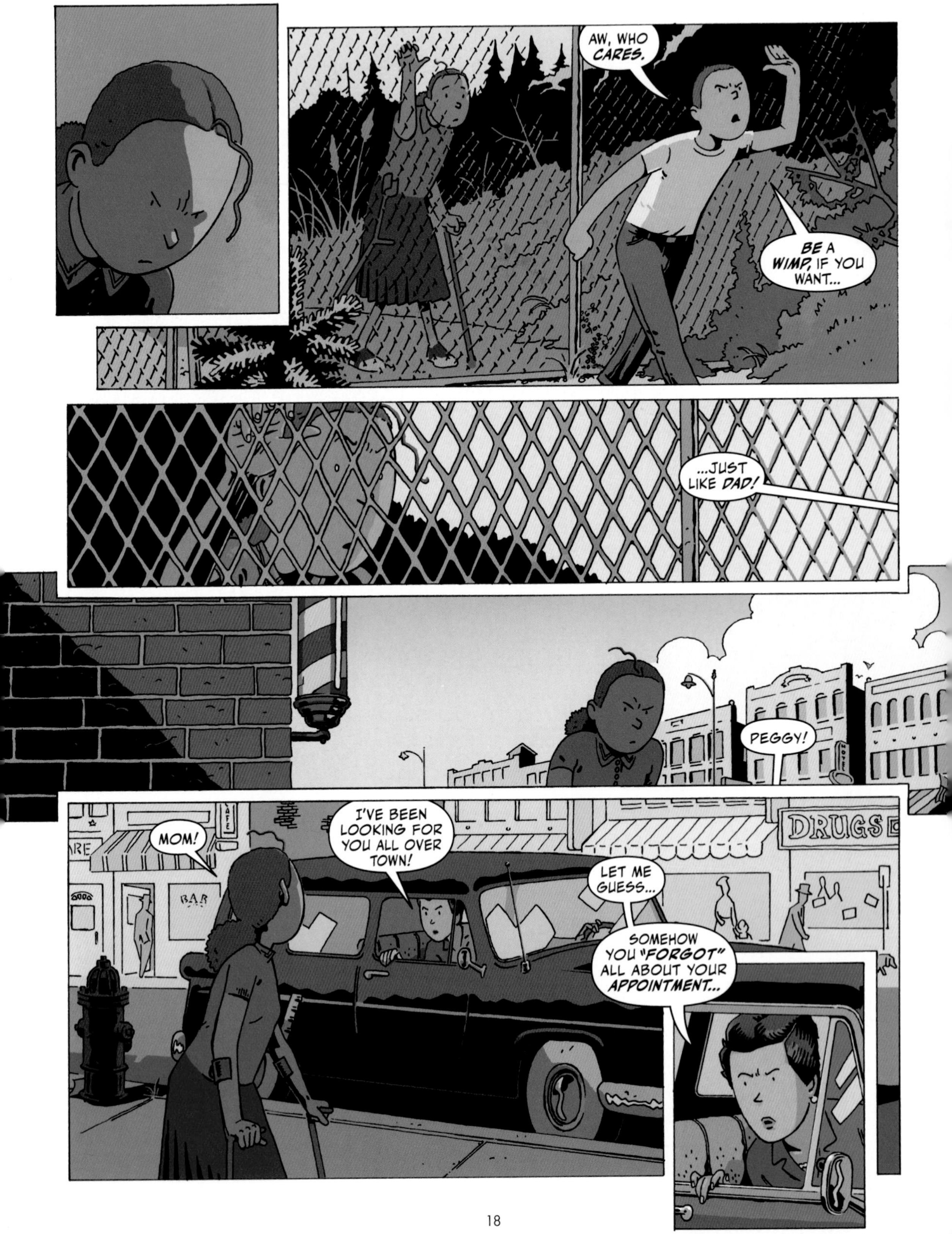
AW, WHO CARES.
BE A WIMP, IF YOU WANT...
...JUST LIKE DAD!
PEGGY!
MOM!
I'VE BEEN LOOKING FOR YOU ALL OVER TOWN!
LET ME GUESS...
SOMEHOW YOU "FORGOT" ALL ABOUT YOUR APPOINTMENT...
DRUGS
BAR
CAFE

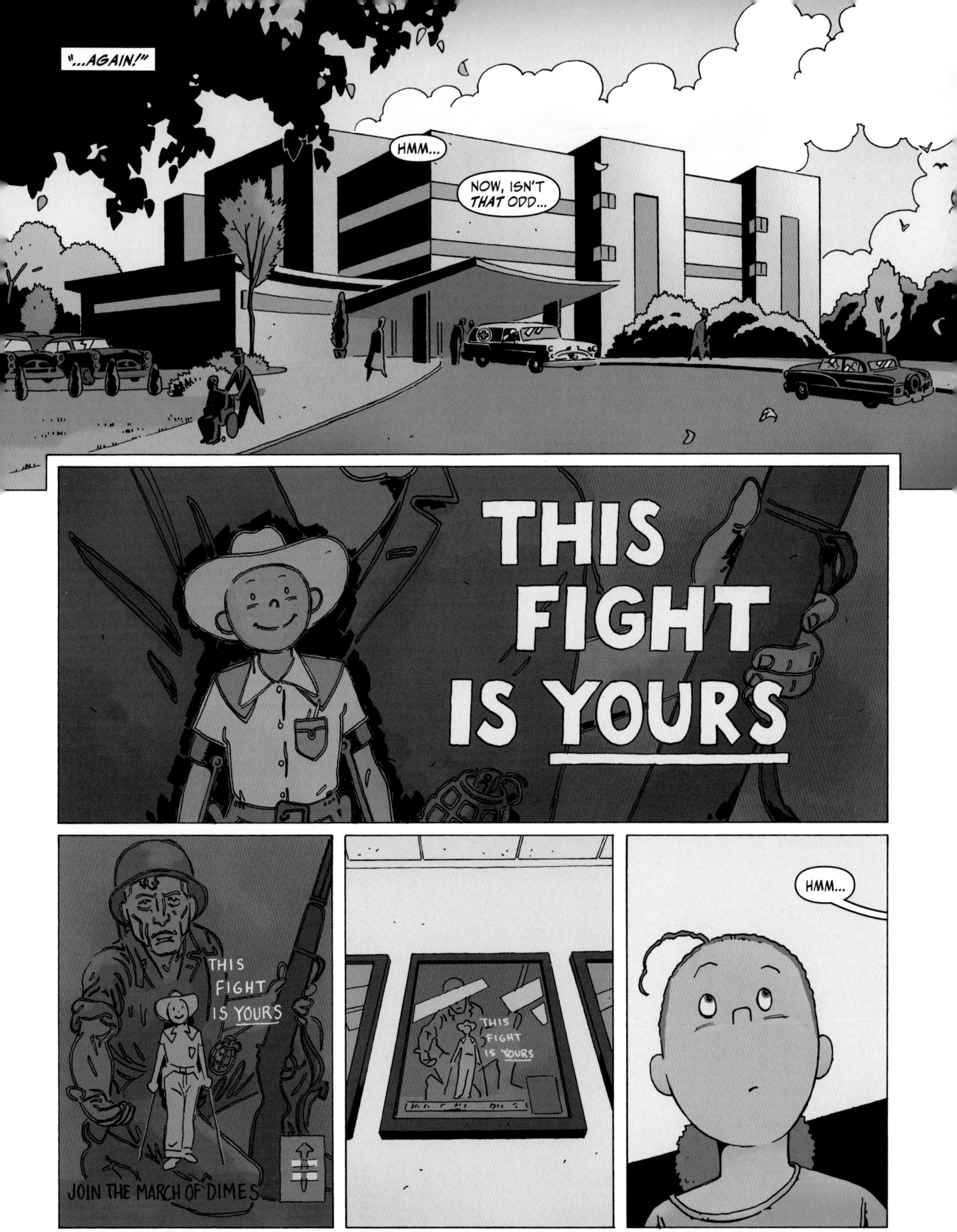
"...AGAIN!"
HMM...
NOW, ISN'T THAT ODD...
THIS FIGHT IS YOURS
THIS FIGHT IS YOURS
JOIN THE MARCH OF DIMES
THIS FIGHT IS YOURS
HMM...

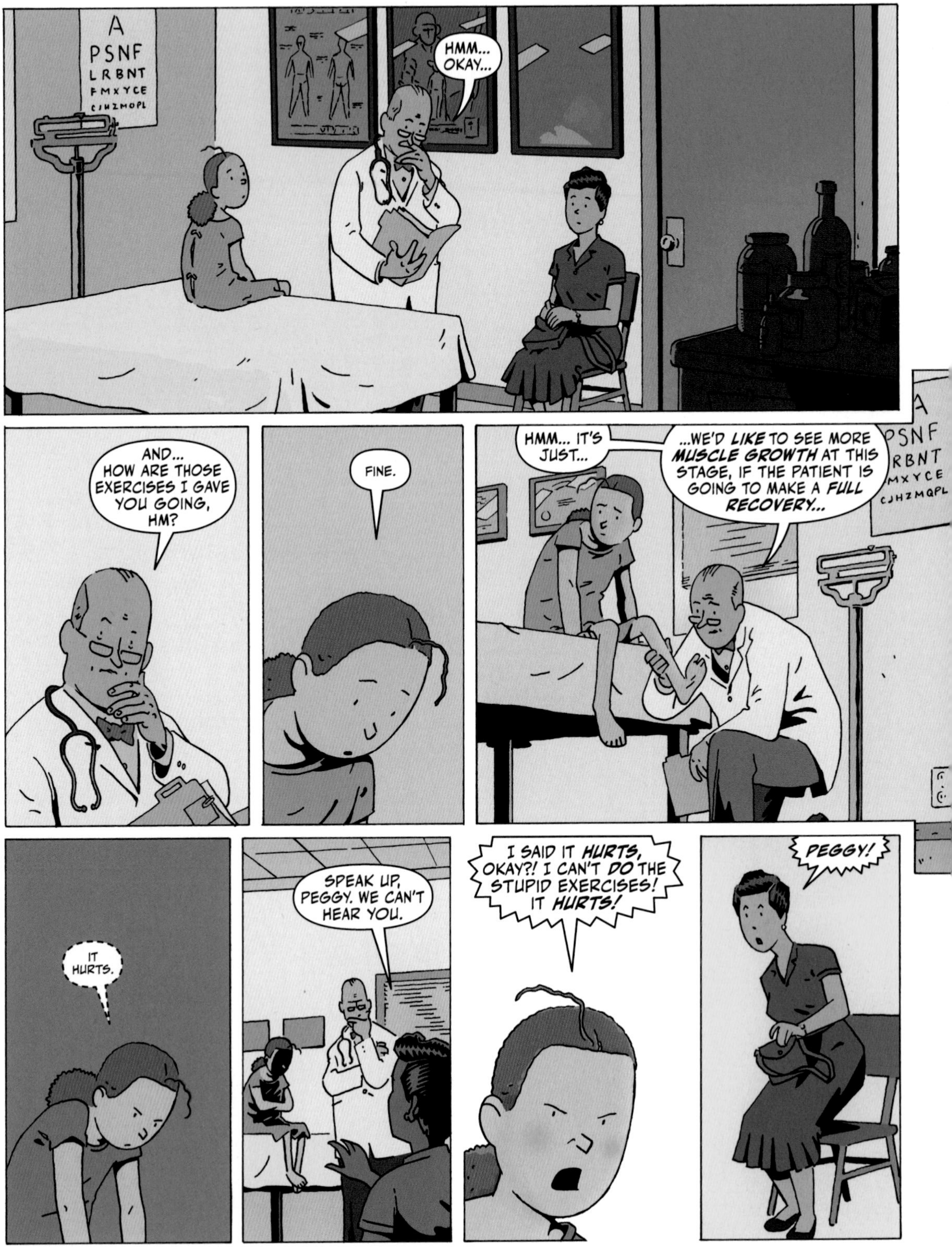
A
PSNF
LRBNT
FMXYCE
CJHZMOPL
HMM... OKAY...
AND... HOW ARE THOSE EXERCISES I GAVE YOU GOING, HM?
FINE.
HMM... IT'S JUST...
...WE'D LIKE TO SEE MORE MUSCLE GROWTH AT THIS STAGE, IF THE PATIENT IS GOING TO MAKE A FULL RECOVERY...
IT HURTS.
SPEAK UP, PEGGY. WE CAN'T HEAR YOU.
I SAID IT HURTS, OKAY?! I CAN'T DO THE STUPID EXERCISES! IT HURTS!
PEGGY!

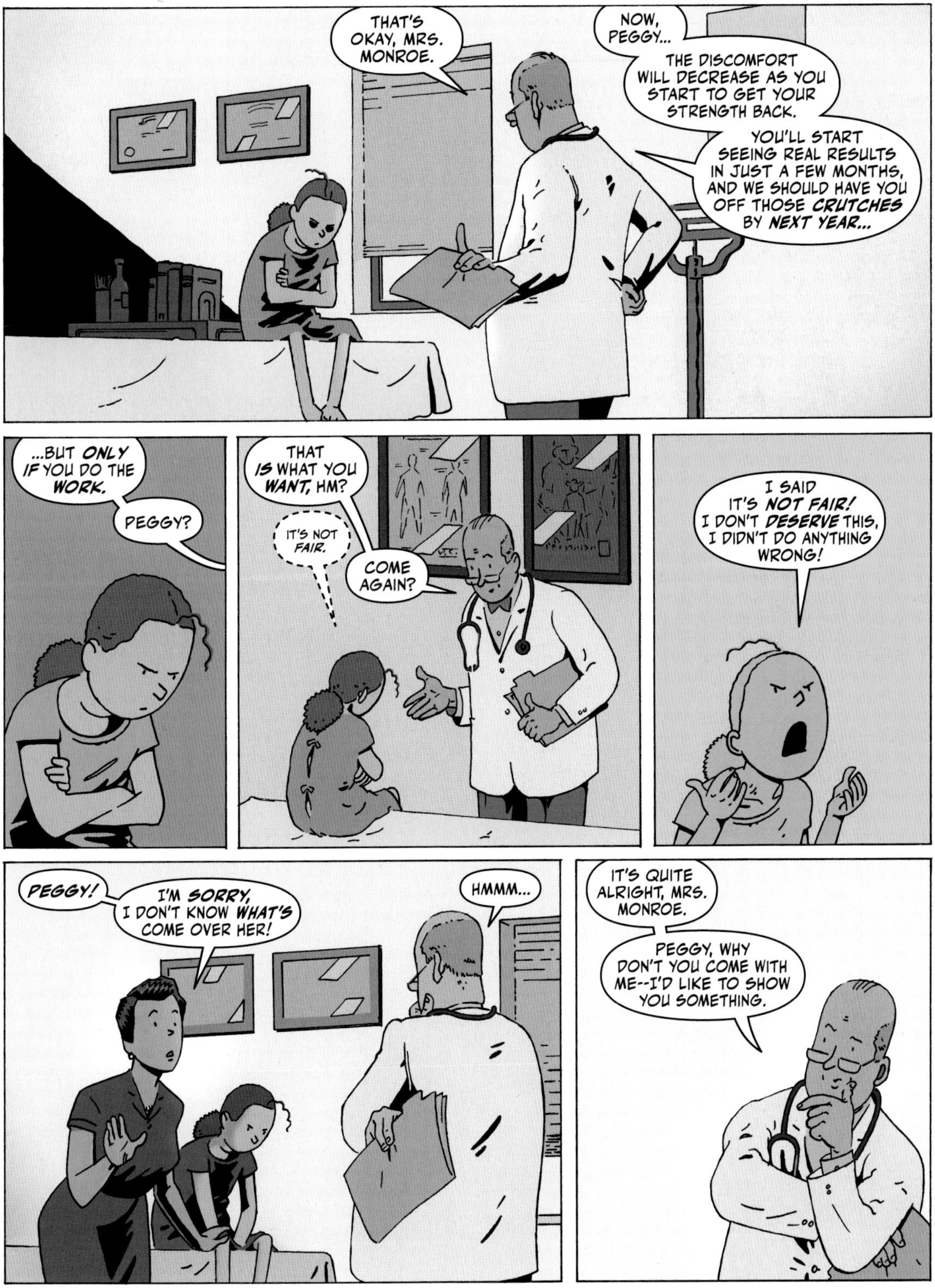
THAT'S OKAY, MRS. MONROE.
NOW, PEGGY...
THE DISCOMFORT WILL DECREASE AS YOU START TO GET YOUR STRENGTH BACK.
YOU'LL START SEEING REAL RESULTS IN JUST A FEW MONTHS, AND WE SHOULD HAVE YOU OFF THOSE CRUTCHES BY NEXT YEAR...
...BUT ONLY IF YOU DO THE WORK.
PEGGY?
THAT IS WHAT YOU WANT, HM?
IT'S NOT FAIR.
COME AGAIN?
I SAID IT'S NOT FAIR! I DON'T DESERVE THIS, I DIDN'T DO ANYTHING WRONG!
PEGGY!
I'M SORRY, I DON'T KNOW WHAT'S COME OVER HER!
HMMM...
IT'S QUITE ALRIGHT, MRS. MONROE.
PEGGY, WHY DON'T YOU COME WITH ME--I'D LIKE TO SHOW YOU SOMETHING.

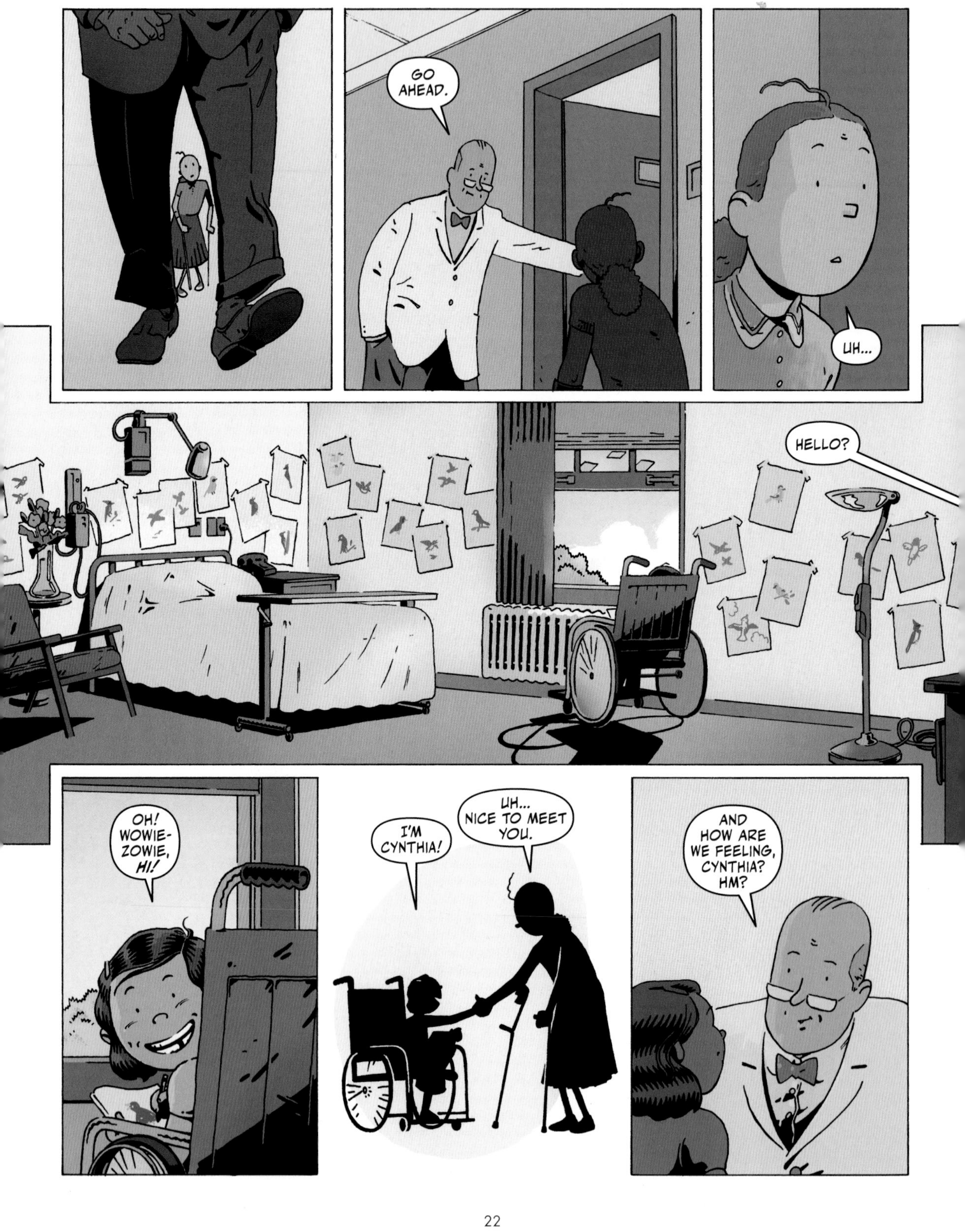
GO AHEAD.
UH...
HELLO?
OH! WOWIE-ZOWIE, HI!
I'M CYNTHIA!
UH... NICE TO MEET YOU.
AND HOW ARE WE FEELING, CYNTHIA? HM?

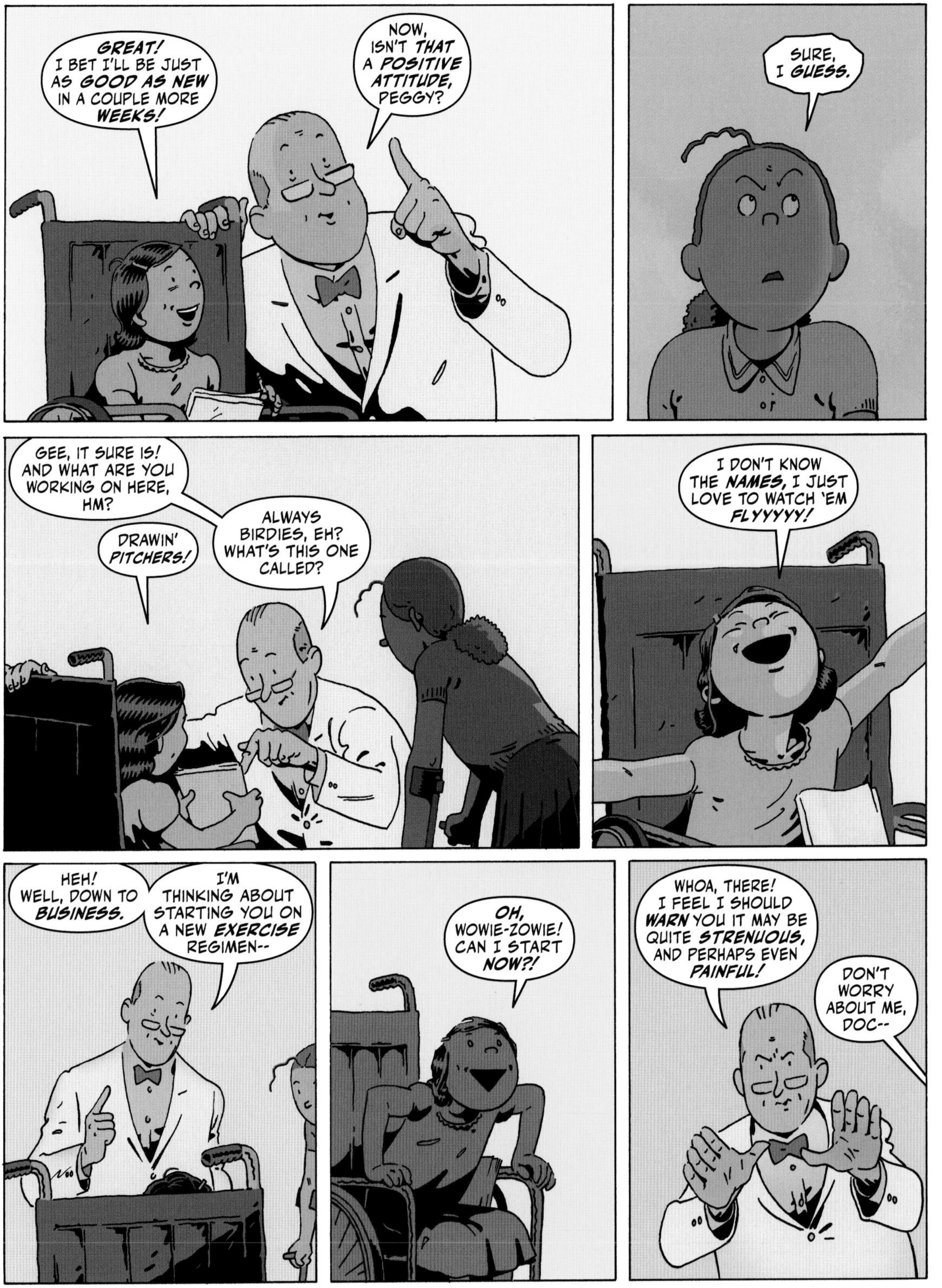
GREAT! I BET I'LL BE JUST AS GOOD AS NEW IN A COUPLE MORE WEEKS!
NOW, ISN'T THAT A POSITIVE ATTITUDE, PEGGY?
SURE, I GUESS.
GEE, IT SURE IS! AND WHAT ARE YOU WORKING ON HERE, HM?
DRAWIN' PITCHERS!
ALWAYS BIRDIES, EH? WHAT'S THIS ONE CALLED?
I DON'T KNOW THE NAMES, I JUST LOVE TO WATCH 'EM FLYYYYY!
HEH! WELL, DOWN TO BUSINESS.
I'M THINKING ABOUT STARTING YOU ON A NEW EXERCISE REGIMEN--
OH, WOWIE-ZOWIE! CAN I START NOW?!
WHOA, THERE! I FEEL I SHOULD WARN YOU IT MAY BE QUITE STRENUOUS, AND PERHAPS EVEN PAINFUL!
DON'T WORRY ABOUT ME, DOC--

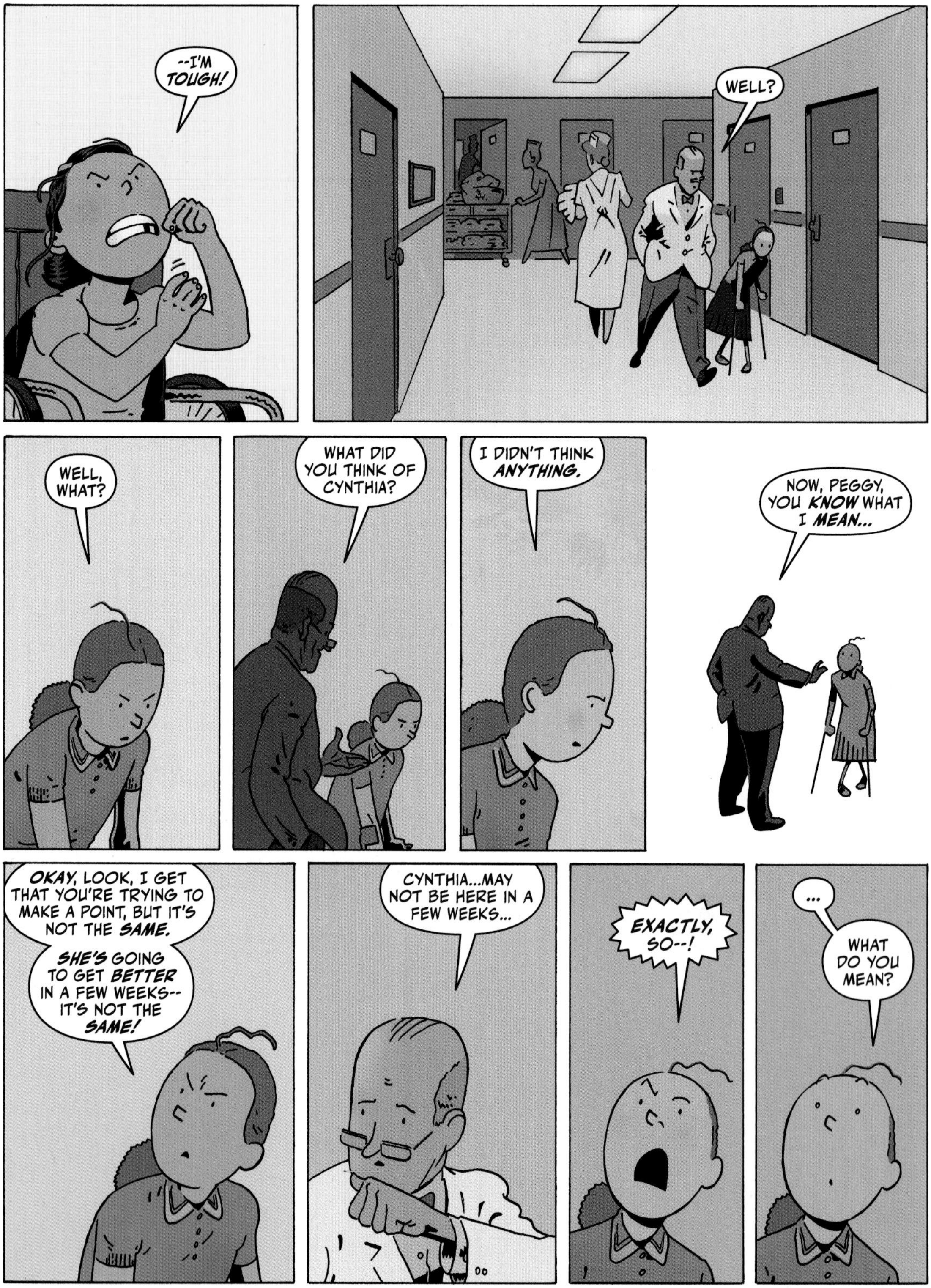
--I'M TOUGH!
WELL?
WELL, WHAT?
WHAT DID YOU THINK OF CYNTHIA?
I DIDN'T THINK ANYTHING.
NOW, PEGGY, YOU KNOW WHAT I MEAN...
OKAY, LOOK, I GET THAT YOU'RE TRYING TO MAKE A POINT, BUT IT'S NOT THE SAME.
SHE'S GOING TO GET BETTER IN A FEW WEEKS-- IT'S NOT THE SAME!
CYNTHIA...MAY NOT BE HERE IN A FEW WEEKS...
EXACTLY, SO--!
...
WHAT DO YOU MEAN?

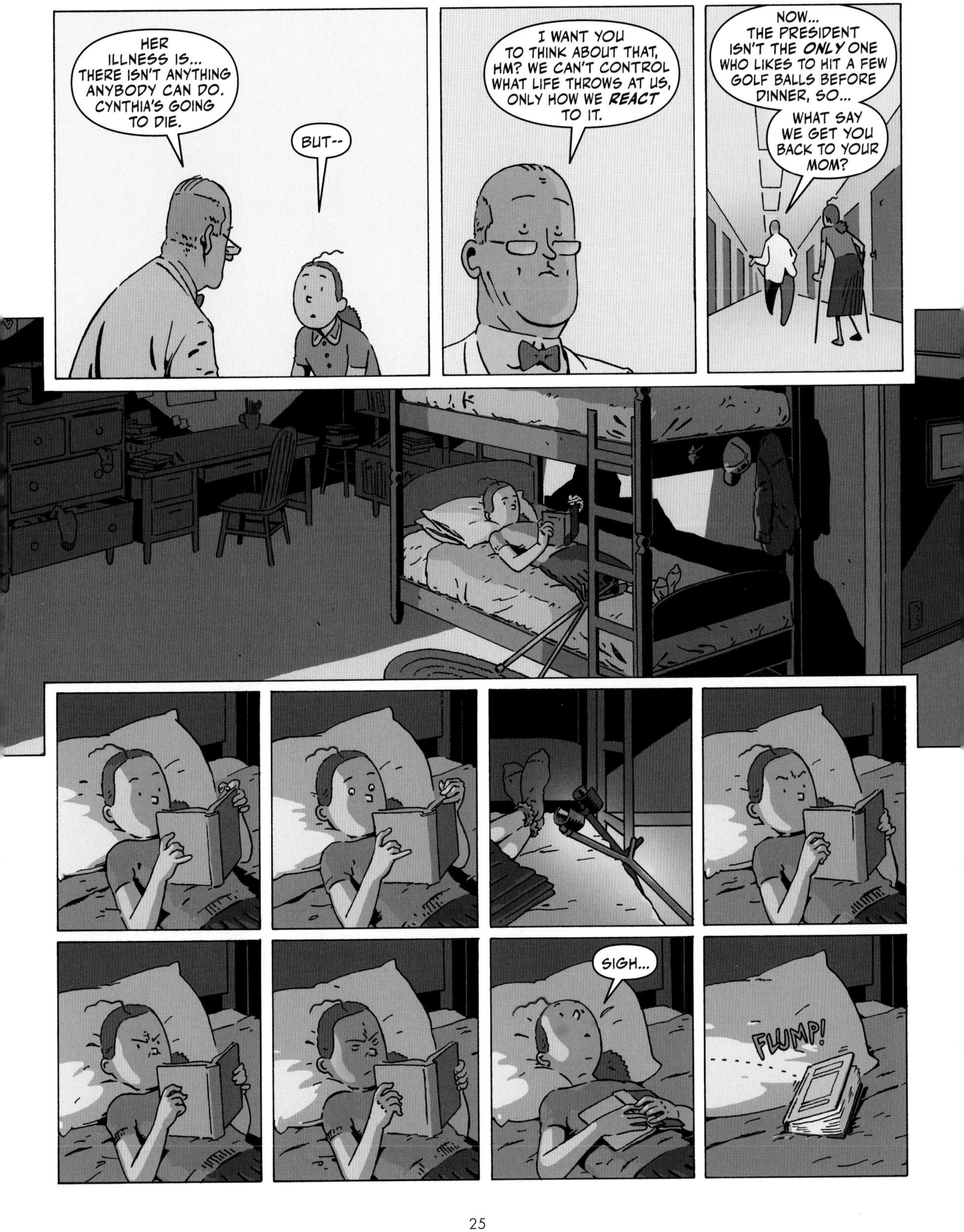
HER ILLNESS IS... THERE ISN'T ANYTHING ANYBODY CAN DO. CYNTHIA'S GOING TO DIE.
BUT--
I WANT YOU TO THINK ABOUT THAT, HM? WE CAN'T CONTROL WHAT LIFE THROWS AT US, ONLY HOW WE *REACT* TO IT.
NOW... THE PRESIDENT ISN'T THE *ONLY* ONE WHO LIKES TO HIT A FEW GOLF BALLS BEFORE DINNER, SO...
WHAT SAY WE GET YOU BACK TO YOUR MOM?
SIGH...
FLUMP!

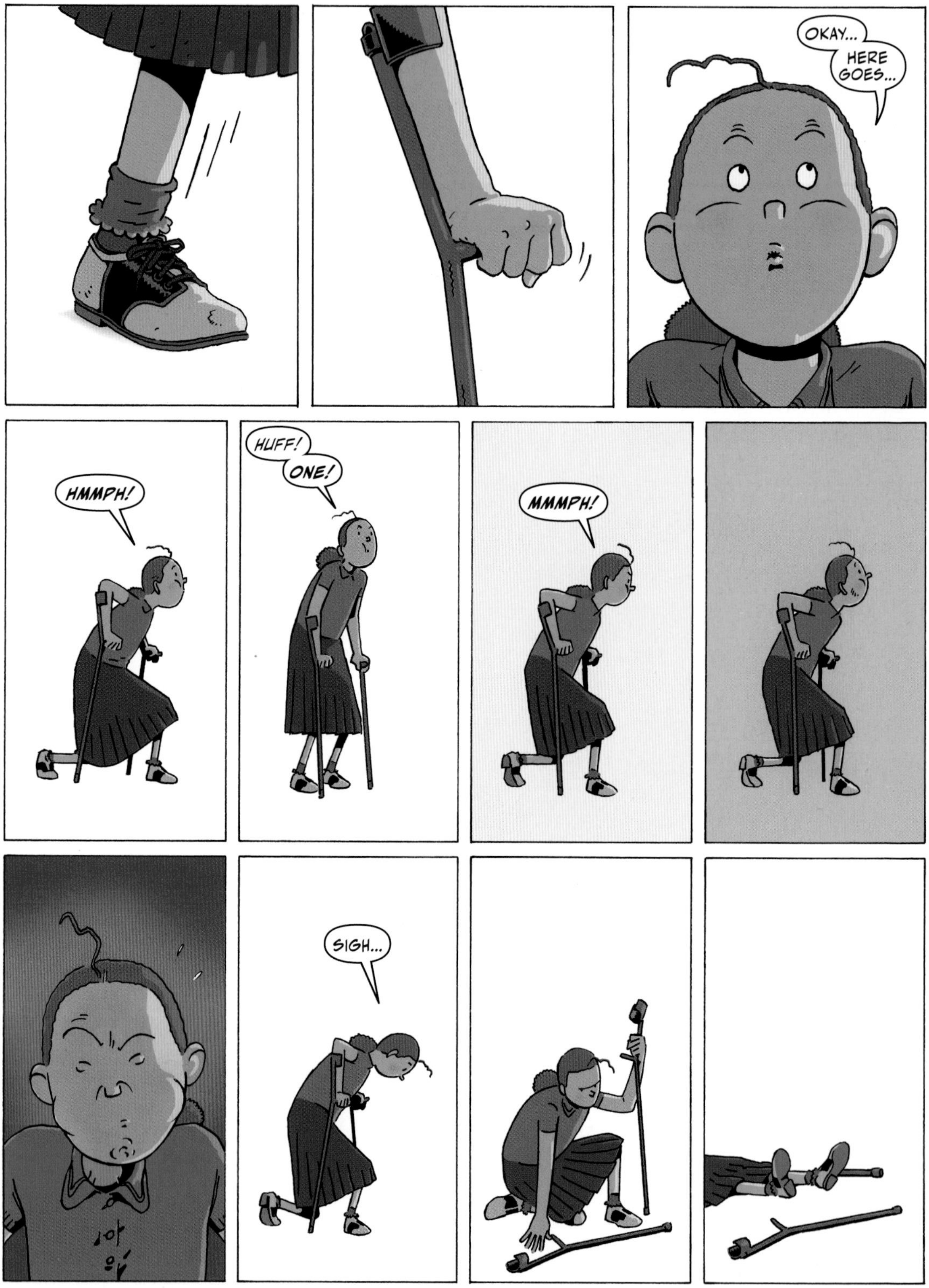
OKAY...
HERE GOES...
HMMPH!
HUFF!
ONE!
MMMPH!
SIGH...

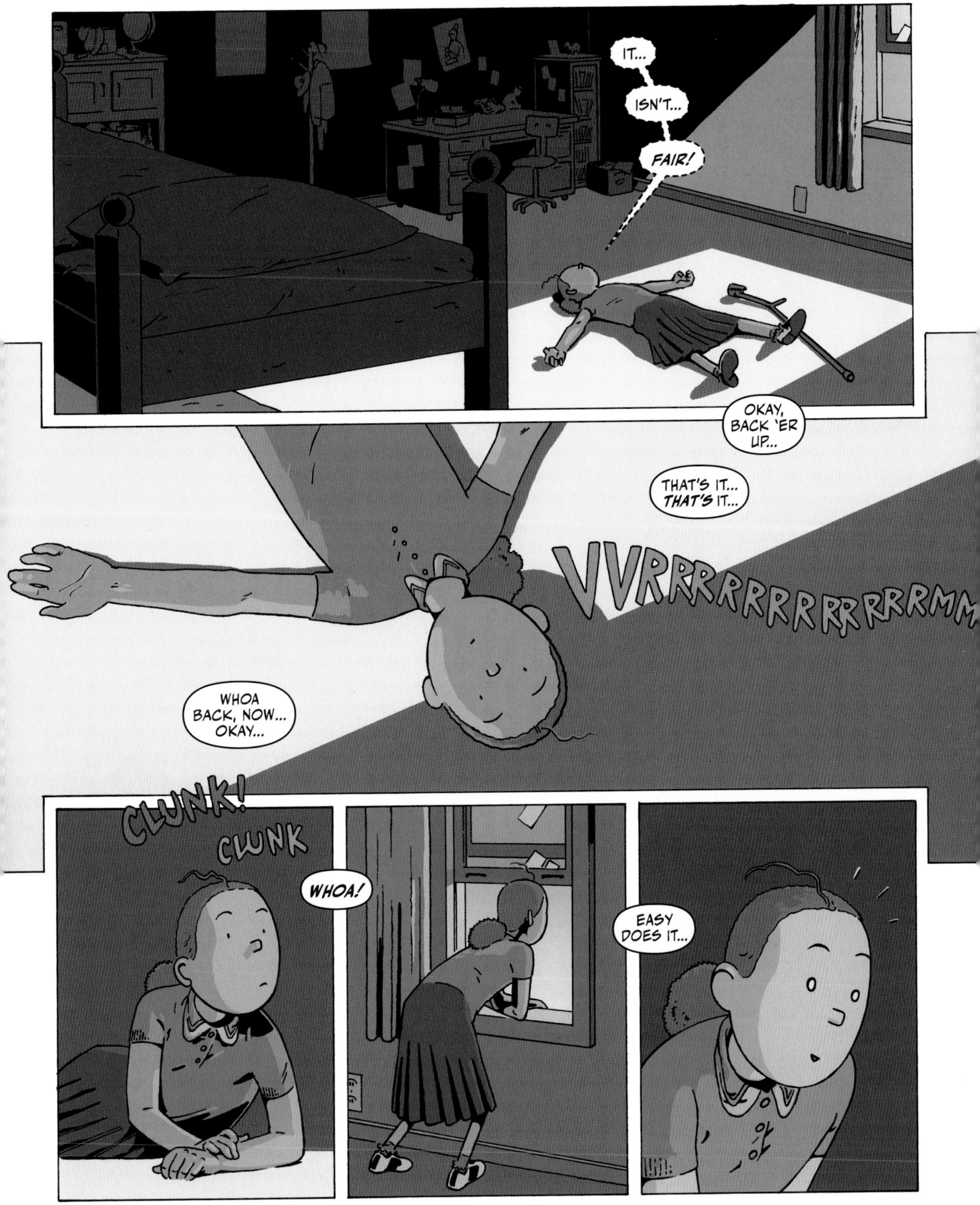
IT...
ISN'T...
FAIR!
OKAY, BACK 'ER UP...
THAT'S IT... THAT'S IT...
VVRRRRRRRRRRRRRMM
WHOA BACK, NOW... OKAY...
CLUNK!
CLUNK
WHOA!
EASY DOES IT...

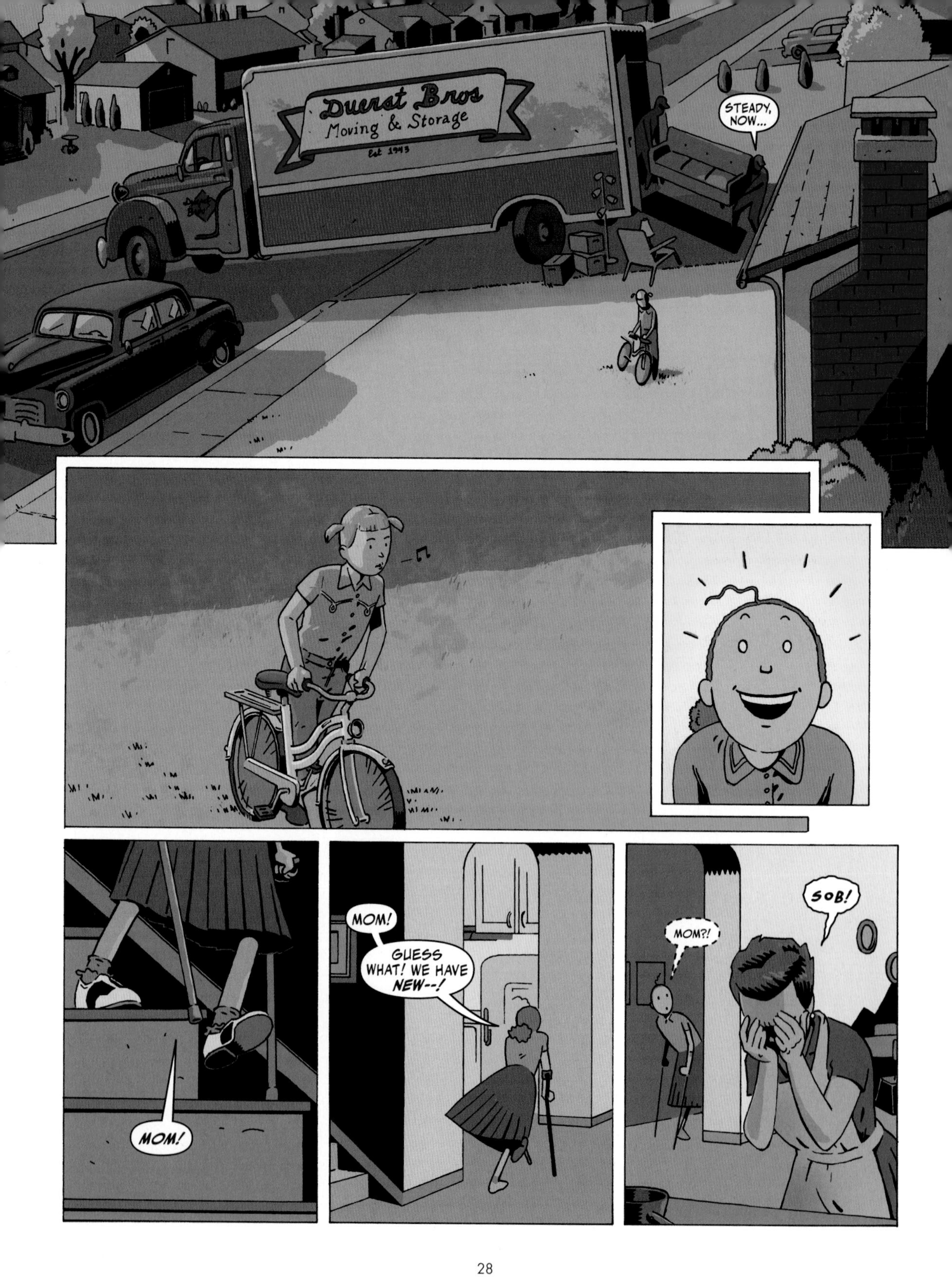
Duerst Bros
Moving & Storage
Est 1943
STEADY, NOW...
MOM!
MOM!
GUESS WHAT! WE HAVE NEW--!
MOM?!
SOB!

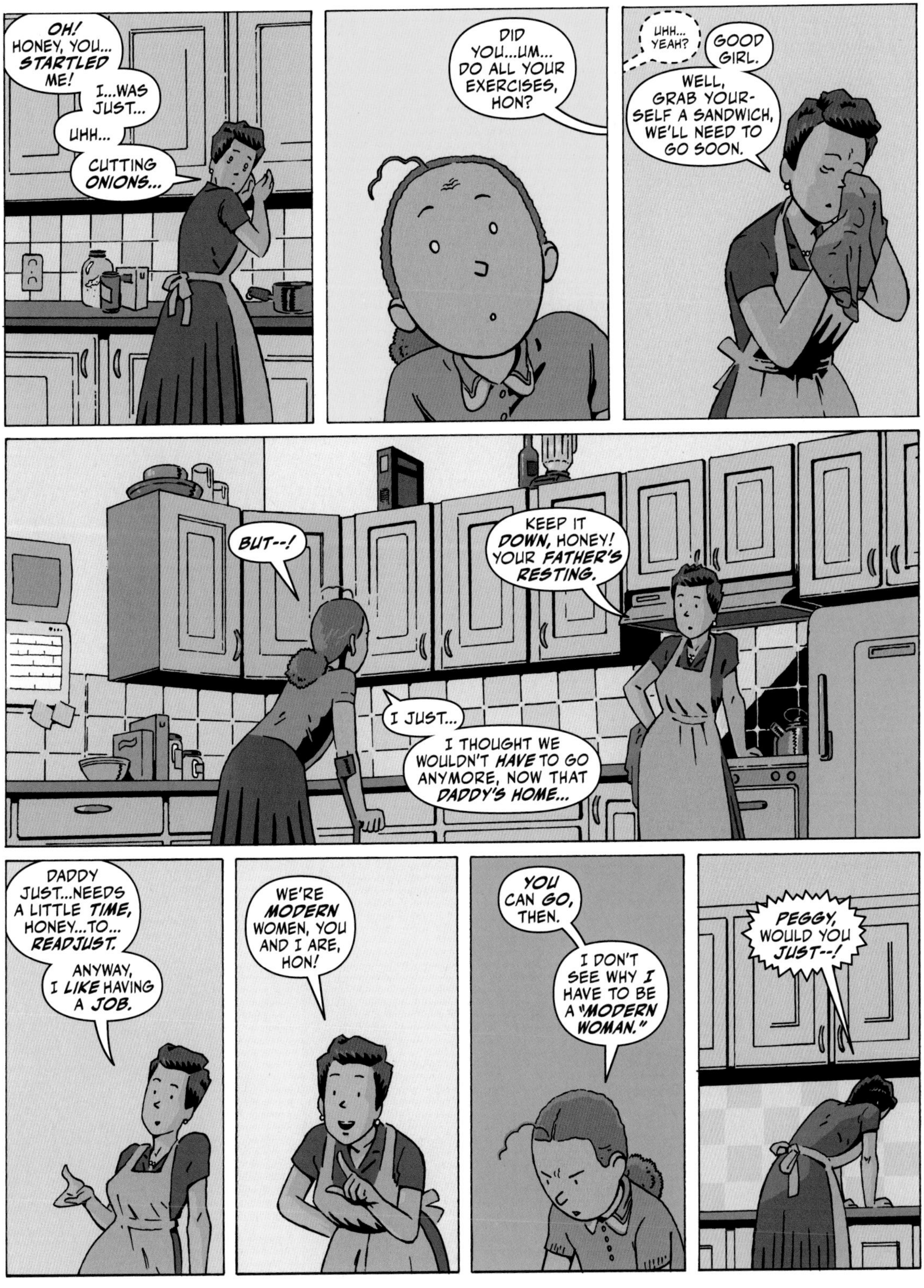
OH! HONEY, YOU... STARTLED ME!
I...WAS JUST...
UHH...
CUTTING ONIONS...
DID YOU...UM... DO ALL YOUR EXERCISES, HON?
UHH... YEAH?
GOOD GIRL.
WELL, GRAB YOUR-SELF A SANDWICH, WE'LL NEED TO GO SOON.
BUT--!
KEEP IT DOWN, HONEY! YOUR FATHER'S RESTING.
I JUST...
I THOUGHT WE WOULDN'T HAVE TO GO ANYMORE, NOW THAT DADDY'S HOME...
DADDY JUST...NEEDS A LITTLE TIME, HONEY...TO... READJUST.
ANYWAY, I LIKE HAVING A JOB.
WE'RE MODERN WOMEN, YOU AND I ARE, HON!
YOU CAN GO, THEN.
I DON'T SEE WHY I HAVE TO BE A "MODERN WOMAN."
PEGGY, WOULD YOU JUST--!

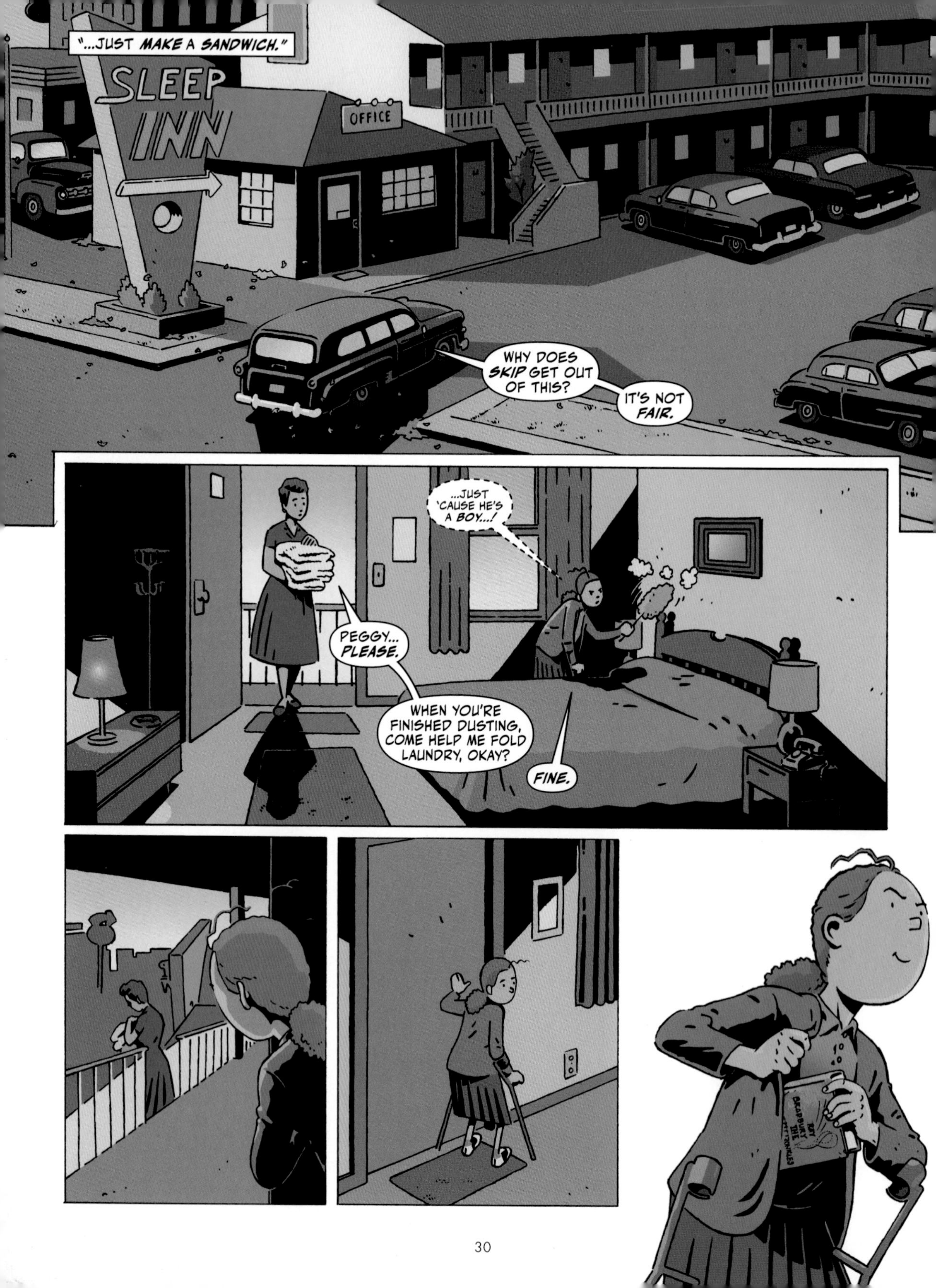
"...JUST MAKE A SANDWICH."
SLEEP INN
OFFICE
WHY DOES SKIP GET OUT OF THIS?
IT'S NOT FAIR.
...JUST 'CAUSE HE'S A BOY...!
PEGGY... PLEASE.
WHEN YOU'RE FINISHED DUSTING, COME HELP ME FOLD LAUNDRY, OKAY?
FINE.

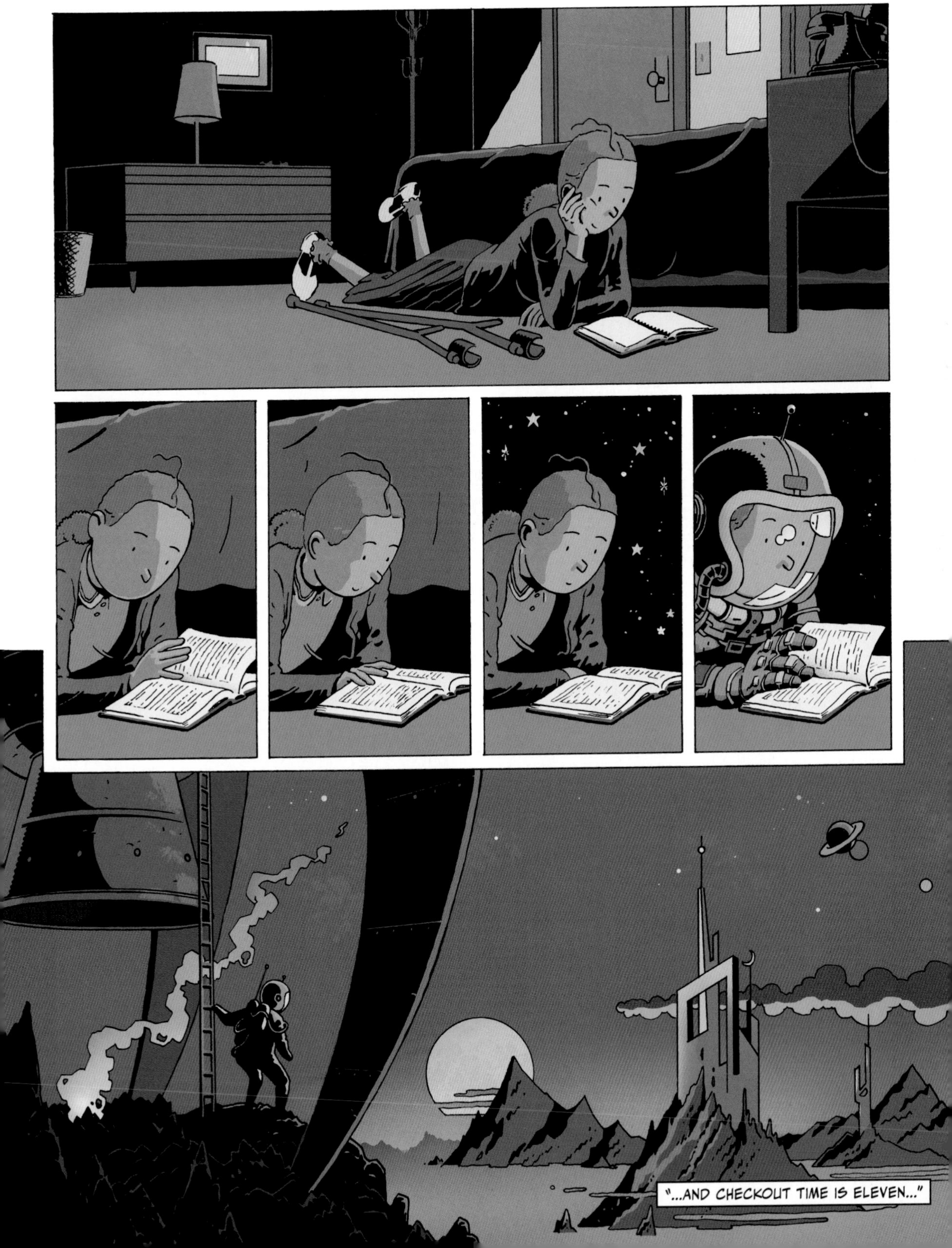
"...AND CHECKOUT TIME IS ELEVEN..."

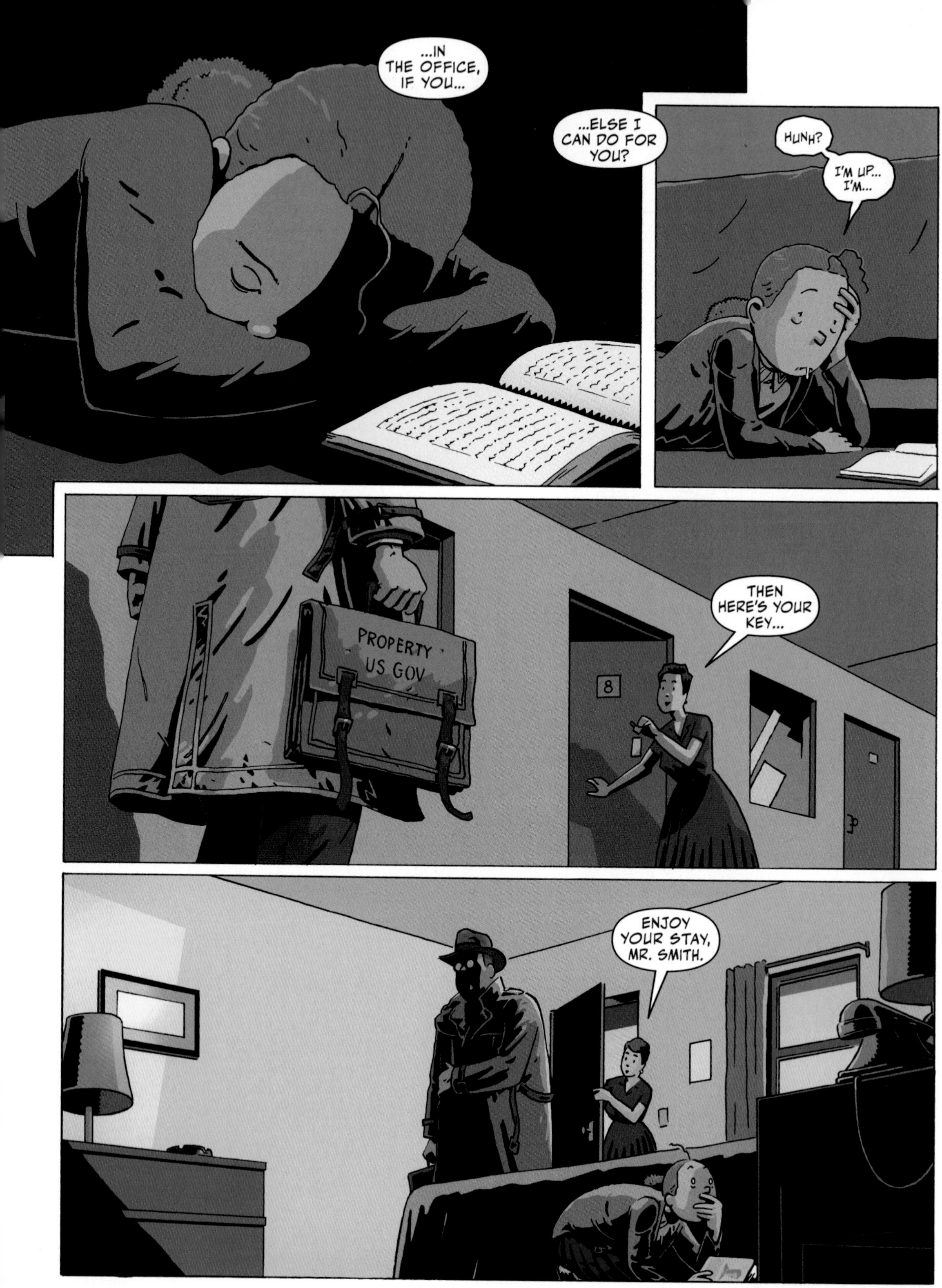
...IN THE OFFICE, IF YOU...
...ELSE I CAN DO FOR YOU?
HUNH?
I'M UP... I'M...
PROPERTY US GOV
8
THEN HERE'S YOUR KEY...
ENJOY YOUR STAY, MR. SMITH.

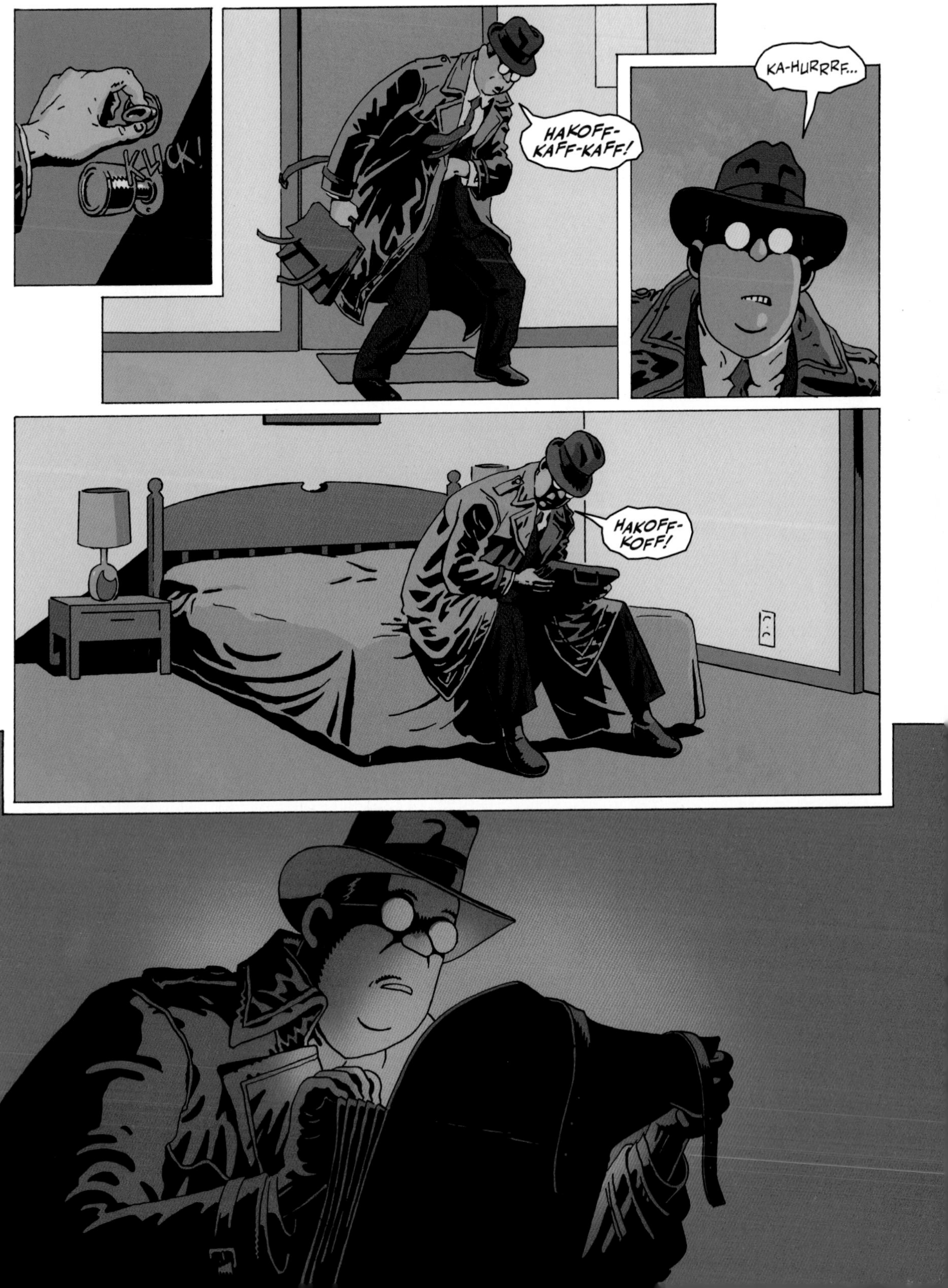
KLICK!
HAKOFF-KAFF-KAFF!
KA-HURRRF...
HAKOFF-KOFF!

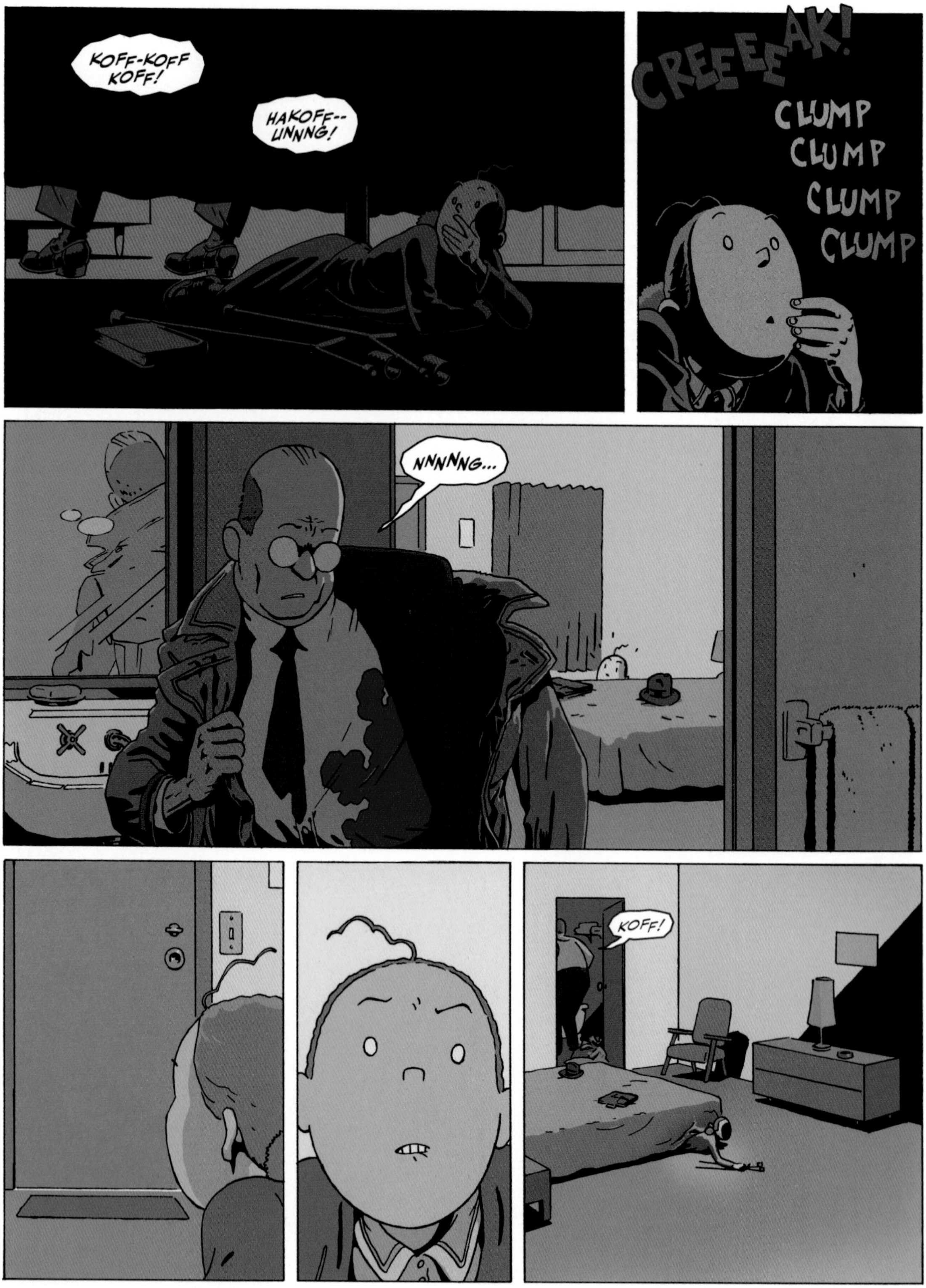
KOFF-KOFF KOFF!
HAKOFF-- UNNNG!
CREEEEAK!
CLUMP
CLUMP
CLUMP
CLUMP
NNNNNG...
KOFF!

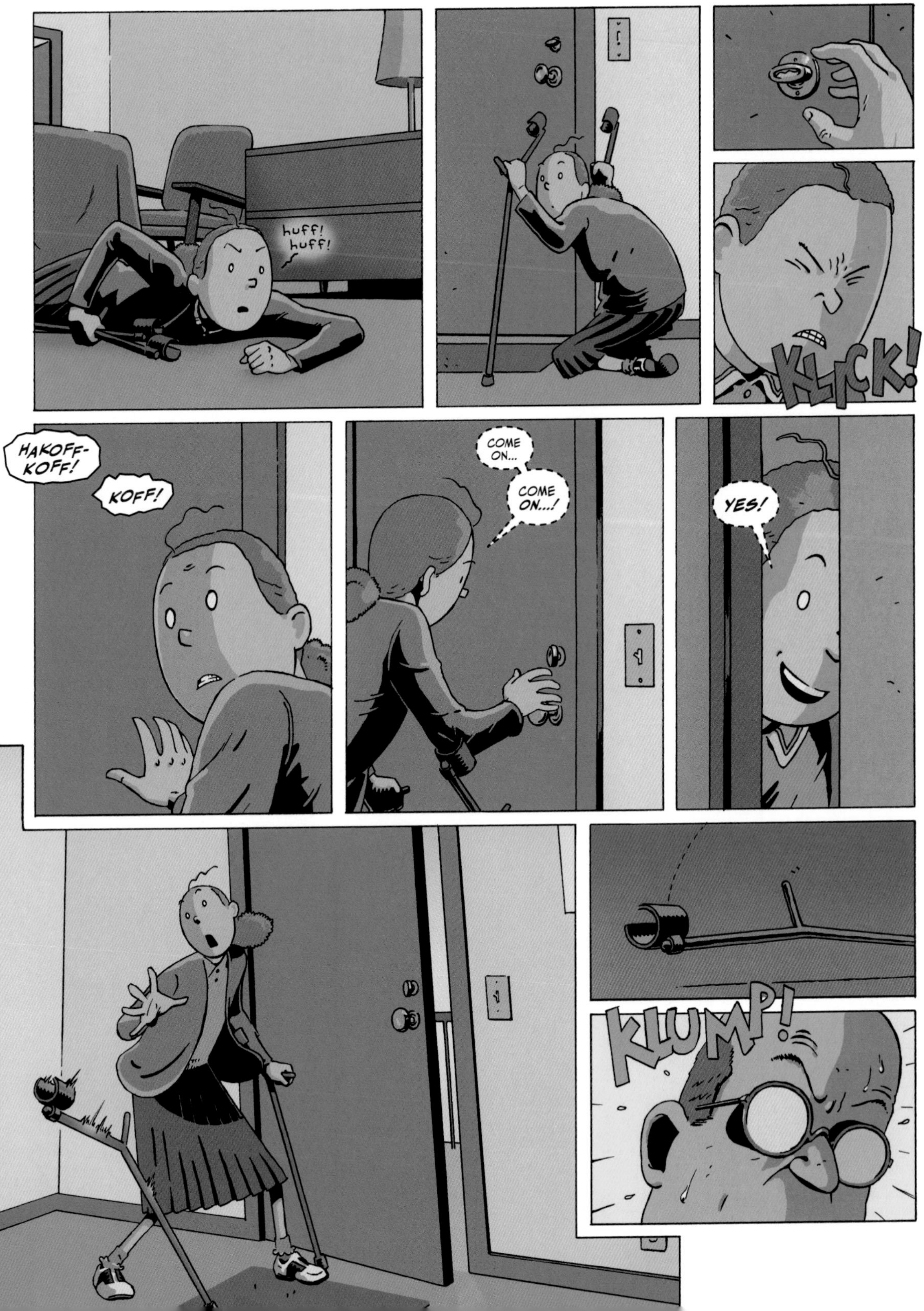
huff! huff!
KLICK!
HAKOFF-KOFF!
KOFF!
COME ON...
COME ON...!
YES!
KLUMP!

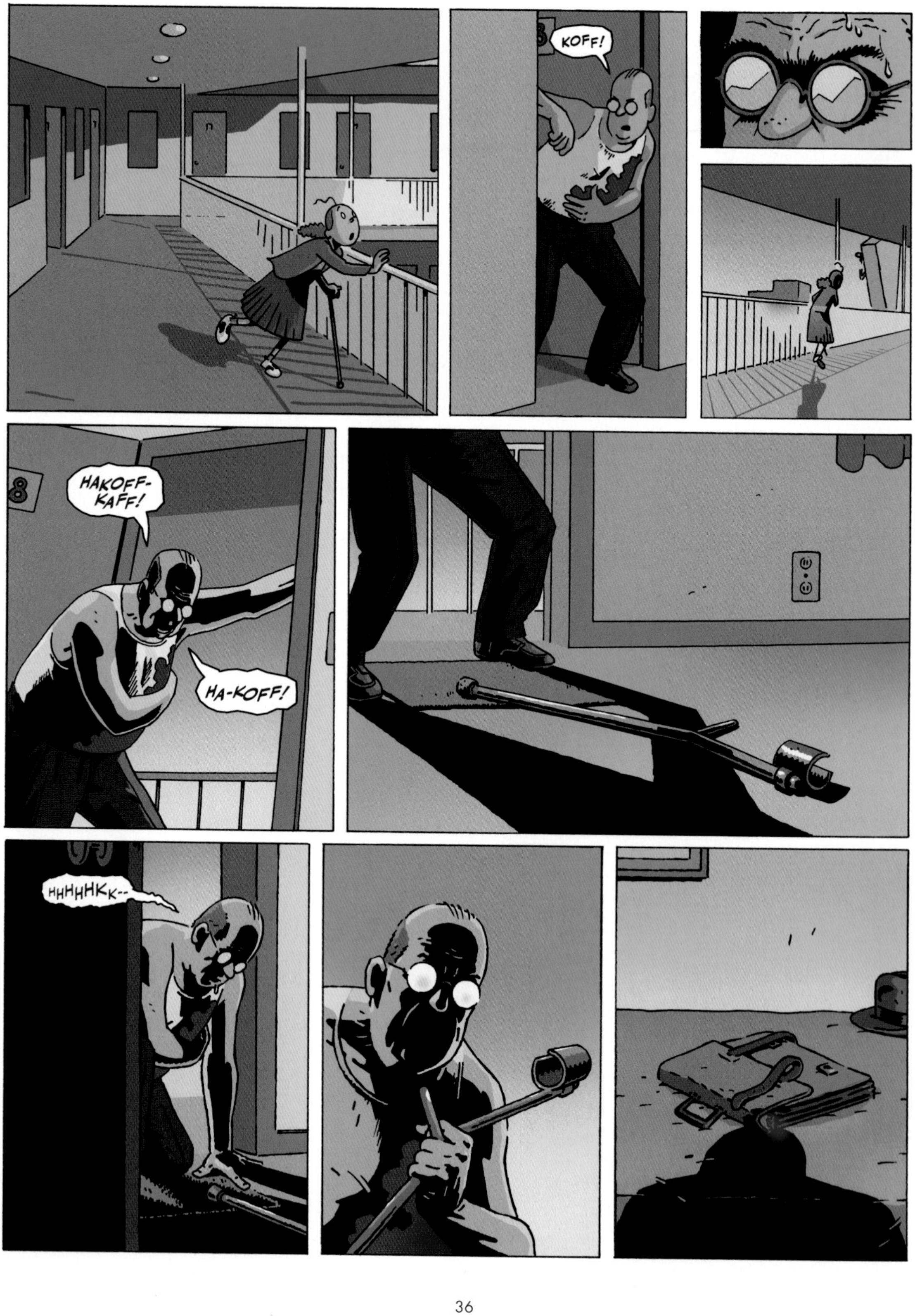
KOFF!
HAKOFF-KAFF!
HA-KOFF!
HHHHHKK--

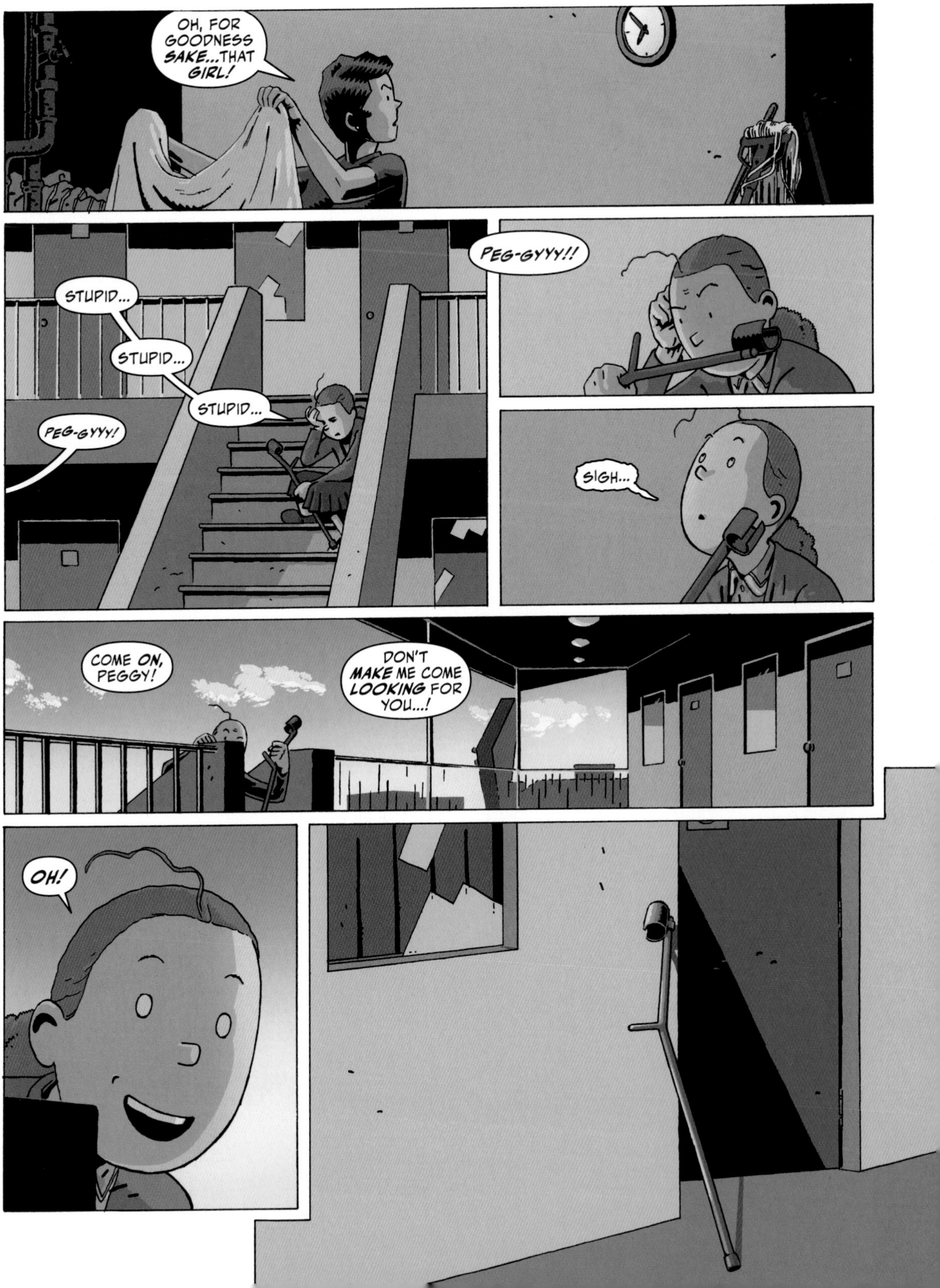
OH, FOR GOODNESS SAKE...THAT GIRL!
STUPID...
STUPID...
STUPID...
PEG-GYYY!
PEG-GYYY!!
SIGH...
COME ON, PEGGY!
DON'T MAKE ME COME LOOKING FOR YOU...!
OH!

AAAIEEEEEE

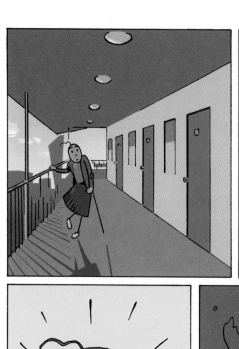

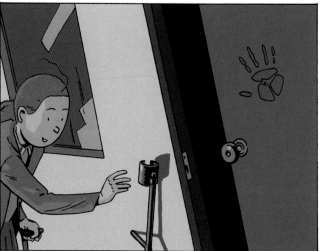

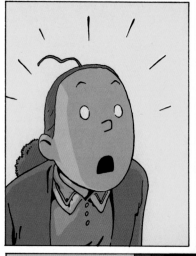

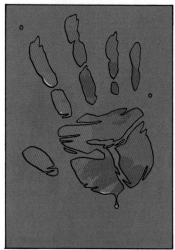

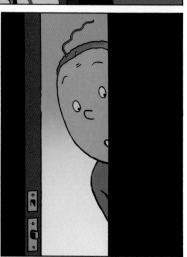

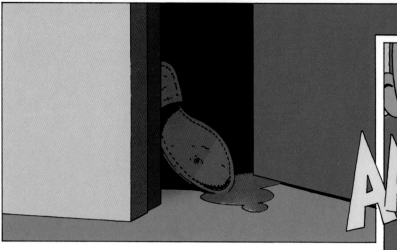

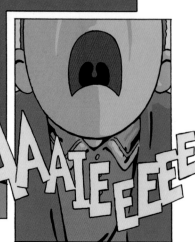

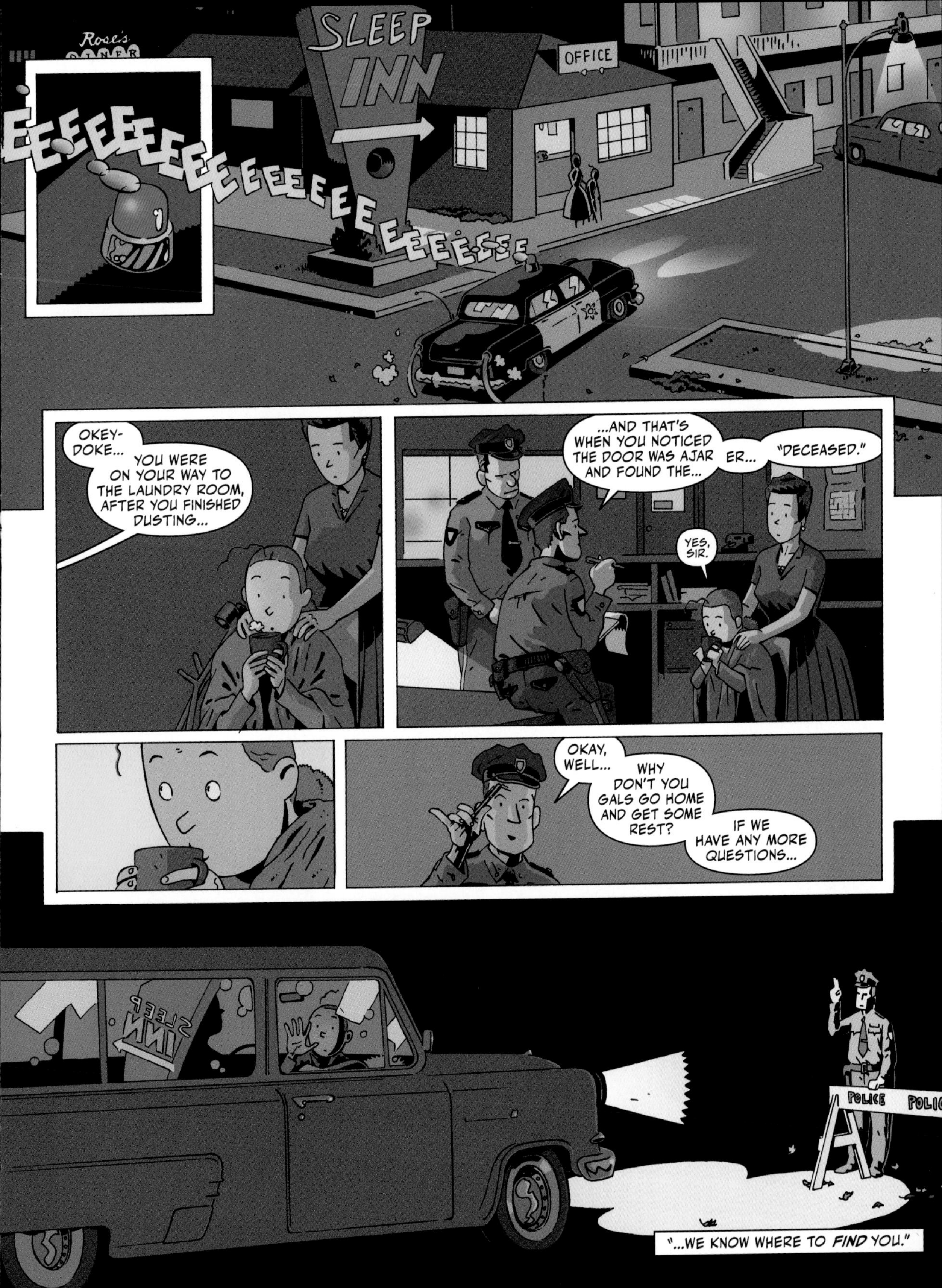

Rose's DINER
SLEEP INN
OFFICE
EEEEEEEEEEEEEEEEEEEEE
OKEY-DOKE...
YOU WERE ON YOUR WAY TO THE LAUNDRY ROOM, AFTER YOU FINISHED DUSTING...
...AND THAT'S WHEN YOU NOTICED THE DOOR WAS AJAR AND FOUND THE...
ER...
"DECEASED."
YES, SIR.
OKAY, WELL...
WHY DON'T YOU GALS GO HOME AND GET SOME REST?
IF WE HAVE ANY MORE QUESTIONS...
SLEEP INN
POLICE
POLIC
"...WE KNOW WHERE TO FIND YOU."

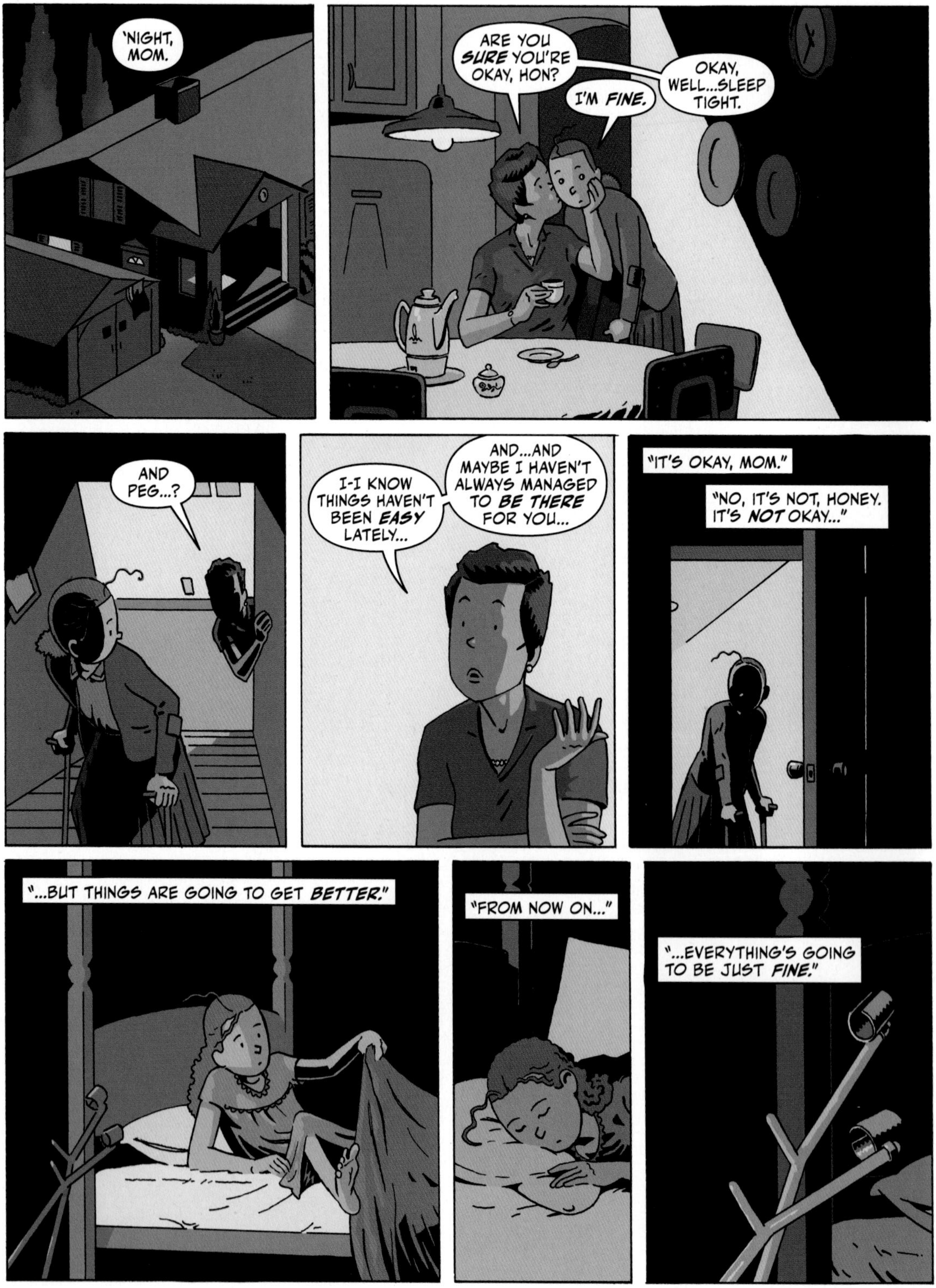
'NIGHT, MOM.
ARE YOU *SURE* YOU'RE OKAY, HON?
I'M *FINE.*
OKAY, WELL...SLEEP TIGHT.
AND PEG...?
I-I KNOW THINGS HAVEN'T BEEN *EASY* LATELY...
AND...AND MAYBE I HAVEN'T ALWAYS MANAGED TO *BE THERE* FOR YOU...
"IT'S OKAY, MOM."
"NO, IT'S NOT, HONEY. IT'S *NOT* OKAY..."
"...BUT THINGS ARE GOING TO GET *BETTER.*"
"FROM NOW ON..."
"...EVERYTHING'S GOING TO BE JUST *FINE.*"

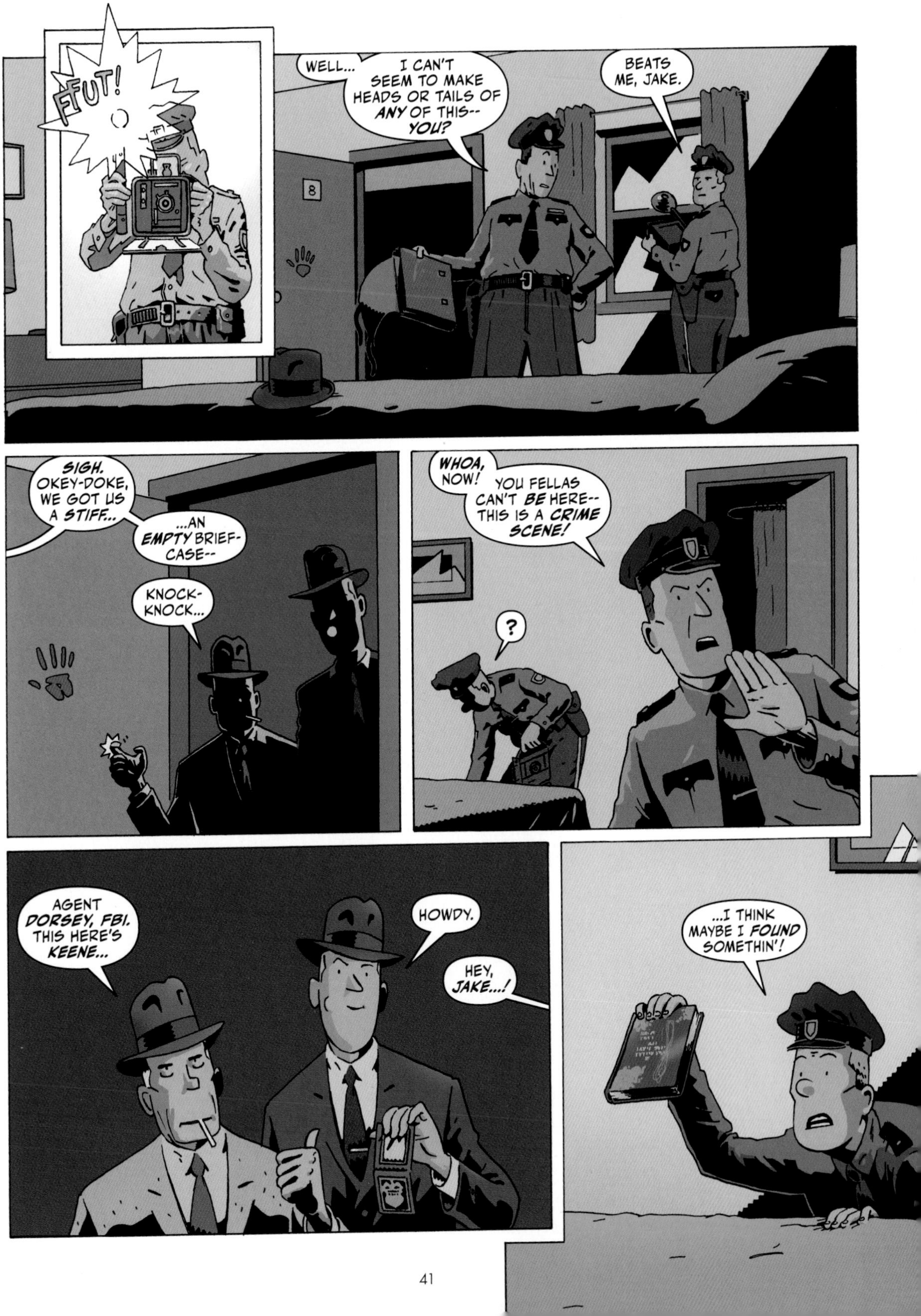

FFUT!
WELL...
I CAN'T SEEM TO MAKE HEADS OR TAILS OF ANY OF THIS-- YOU?
BEATS ME, JAKE.
SIGH. OKEY-DOKE, WE GOT US A STIFF...
...AN EMPTY BRIEF-CASE--
KNOCK-KNOCK...
WHOA, NOW!
YOU FELLAS CAN'T BE HERE-- THIS IS A CRIME SCENE!
?
AGENT DORSEY, FBI. THIS HERE'S KEENE...
HOWDY.
HEY, JAKE...!
...I THINK MAYBE I FOUND SOMETHIN'!

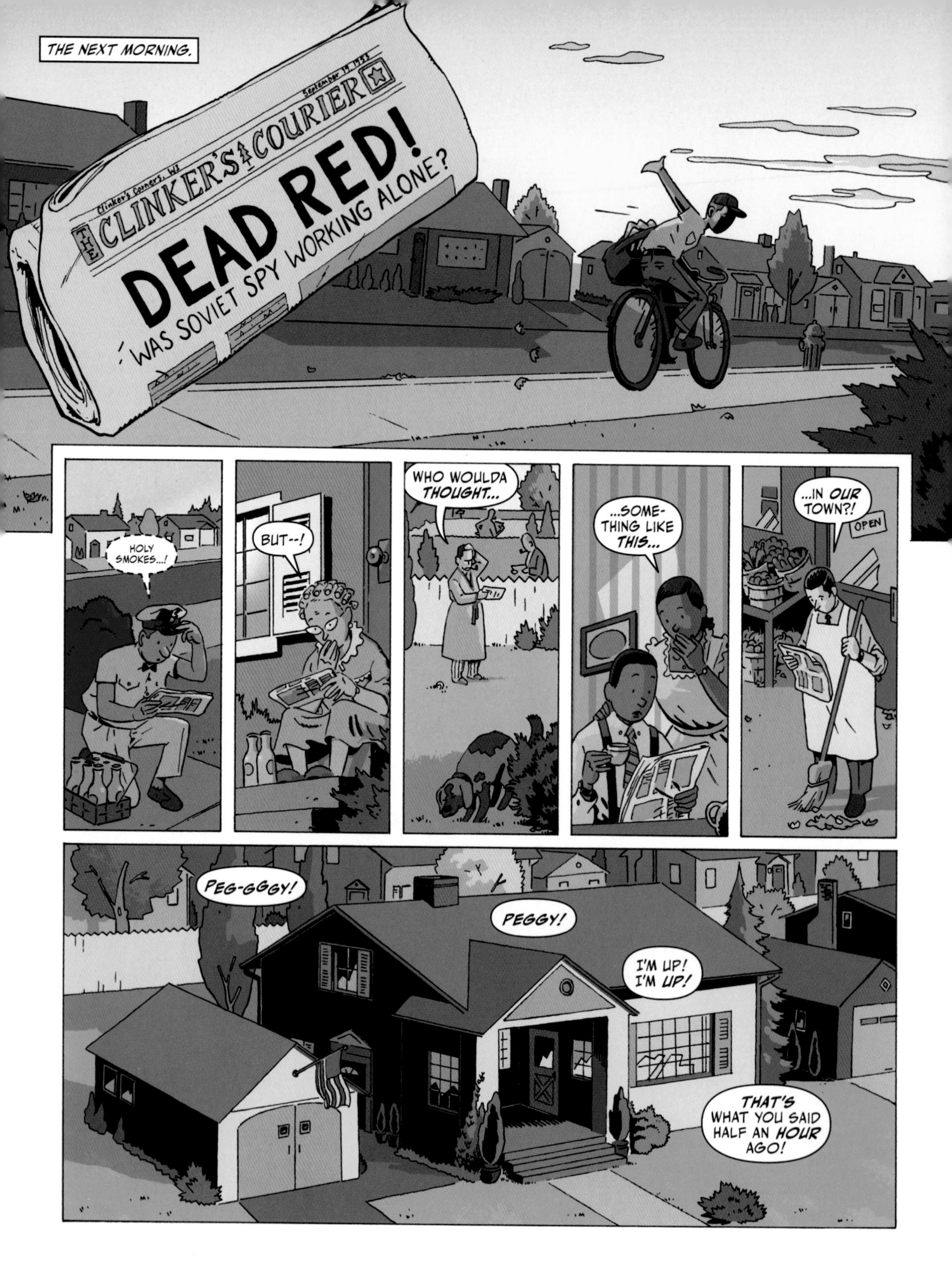
THE NEXT MORNING.
Clinker's Corners, WI
THE CLINKER'S COURIER
DEAD RED!
WAS SOVIET SPY WORKING ALONE?
HOLY SMOKES...!
BUT--!
WHO WOULDA THOUGHT...
...SOME-THING LIKE THIS...
...IN OUR TOWN?!
OPEN
PEG-GGGY!
PEGGY!
I'M UP! I'M UP!
THAT'S WHAT YOU SAID HALF AN HOUR AGO!

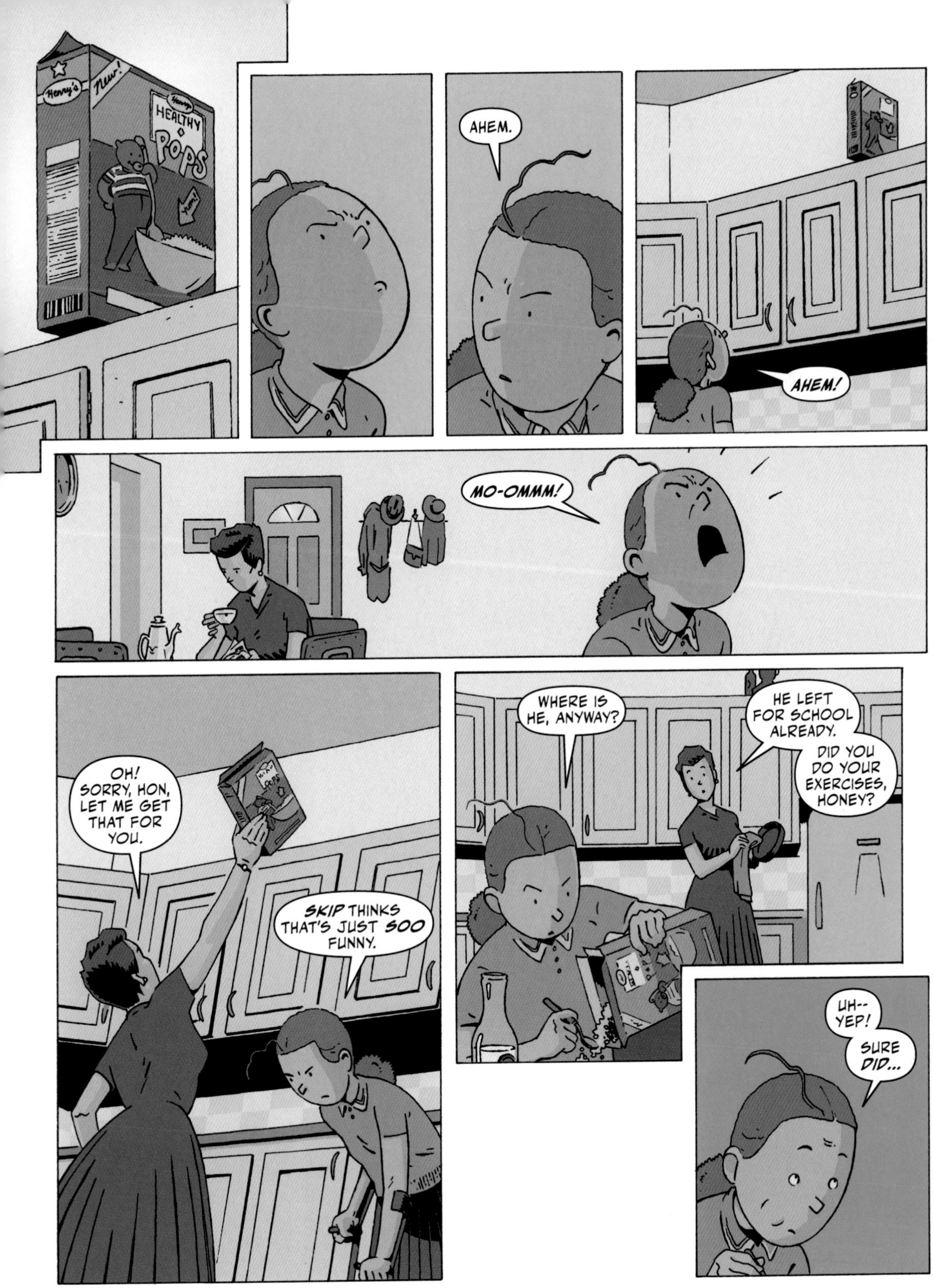
Henry's
New!
Henry's
HEALTHY
POPS
Yum!
AHEM.
AHEM!
MO-OMMM!
OH! SORRY, HON, LET ME GET THAT FOR YOU.
SKIP THINKS THAT'S JUST SOO FUNNY.
WHERE IS HE, ANYWAY?
HE LEFT FOR SCHOOL ALREADY.
DID YOU DO YOUR EXERCISES, HONEY?
UH-- YEP!
SURE DID...

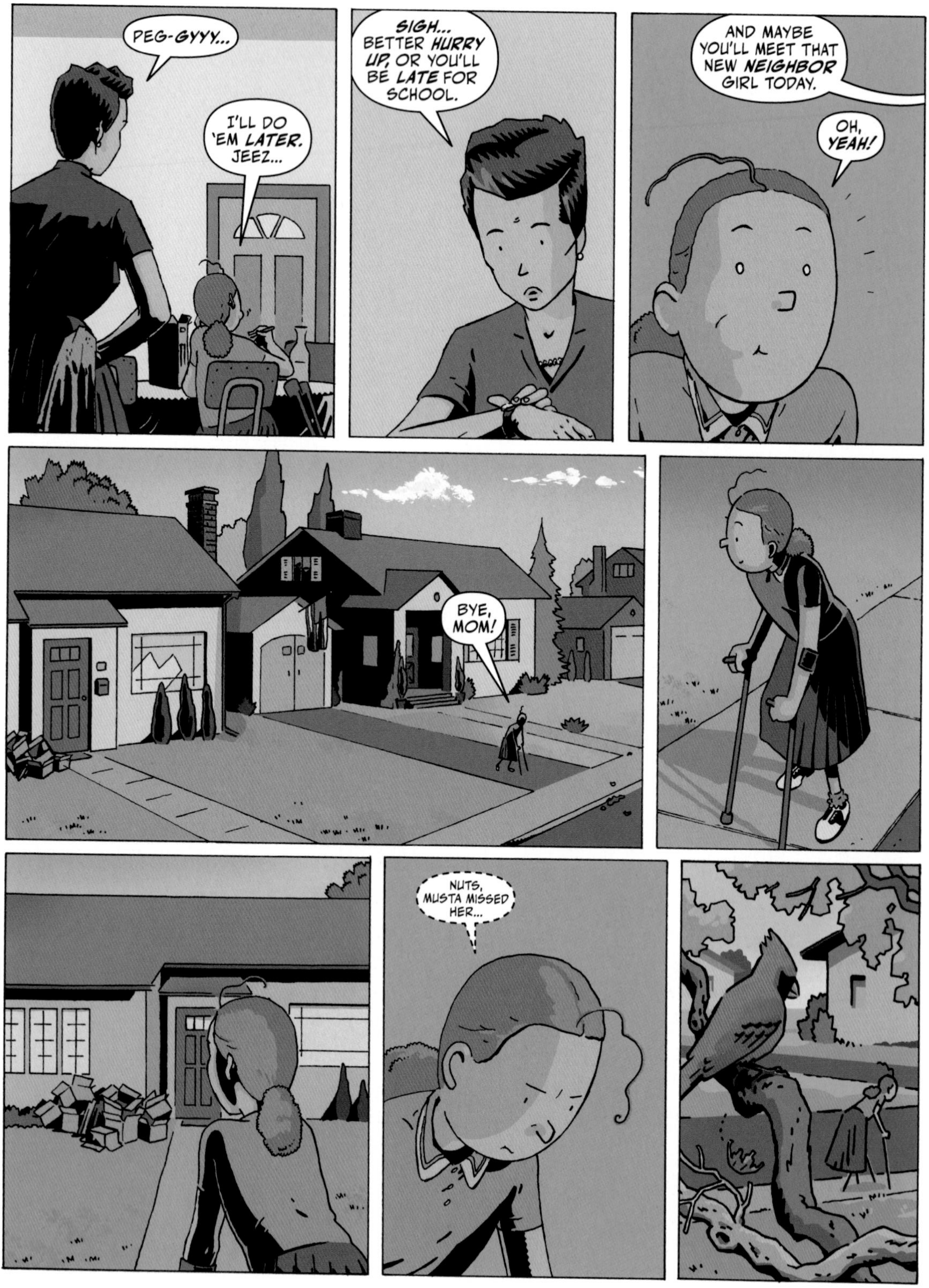
PEG-GYYY...
I'LL DO 'EM LATER. JEEZ...
SIGH... BETTER HURRY UP, OR YOU'LL BE LATE FOR SCHOOL.
AND MAYBE YOU'LL MEET THAT NEW NEIGHBOR GIRL TODAY.
OH, YEAH!
BYE, MOM!
NUTS, MUSTA MISSED HER...

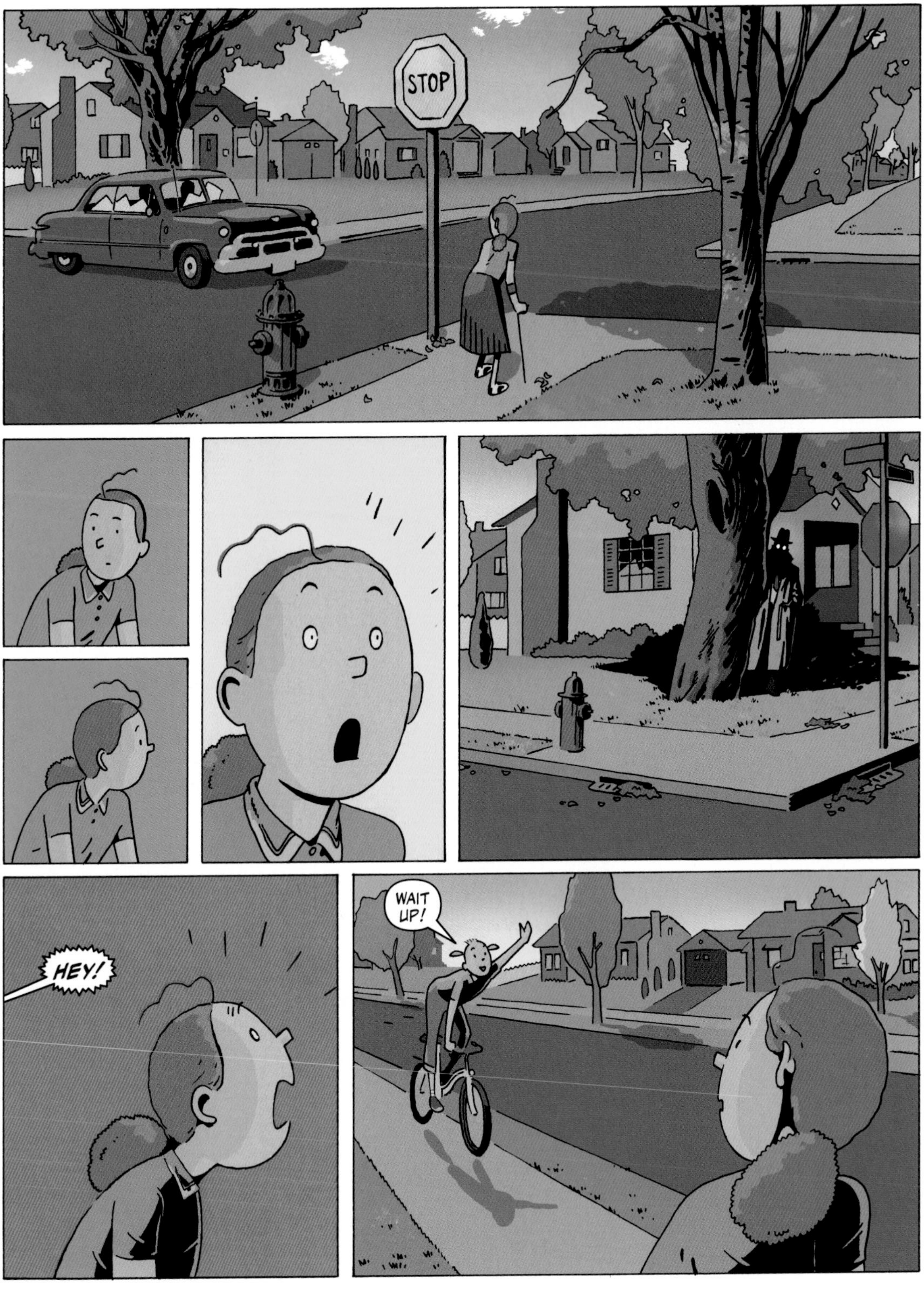
STOP
HEY!
WAIT UP!

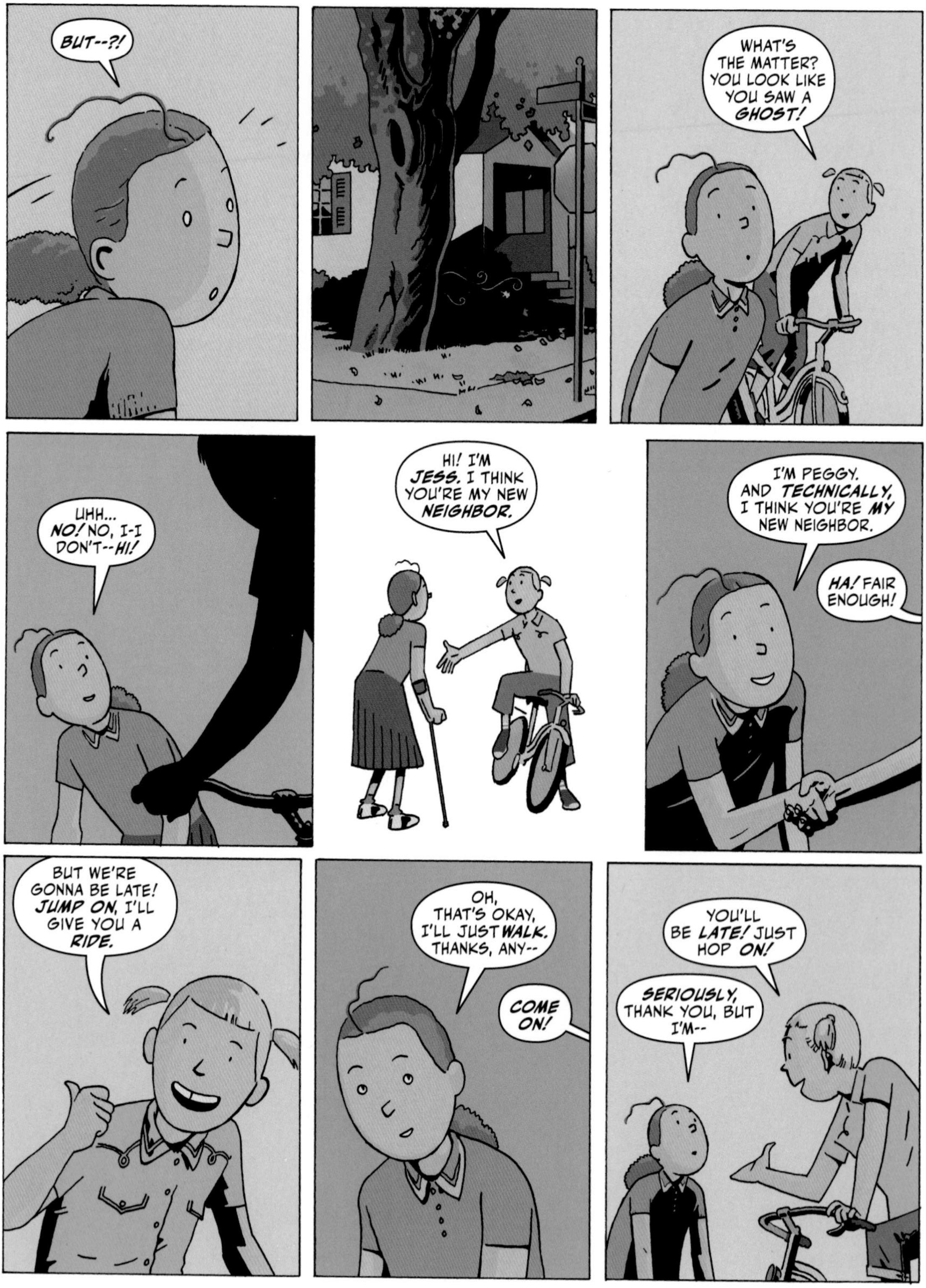
BUT--?!
WHAT'S THE MATTER? YOU LOOK LIKE YOU SAW A GHOST!
UHH... NO! NO, I-I DON'T--HI!
HI! I'M JESS. I THINK YOU'RE MY NEW NEIGHBOR.
I'M PEGGY. AND TECHNICALLY, I THINK YOU'RE MY NEW NEIGHBOR.
HA! FAIR ENOUGH!
BUT WE'RE GONNA BE LATE! JUMP ON, I'LL GIVE YOU A RIDE.
OH, THAT'S OKAY, I'LL JUST WALK. THANKS, ANY--
COME ON!
YOU'LL BE LATE! JUST HOP ON!
SERIOUSLY, THANK YOU, BUT I'M--

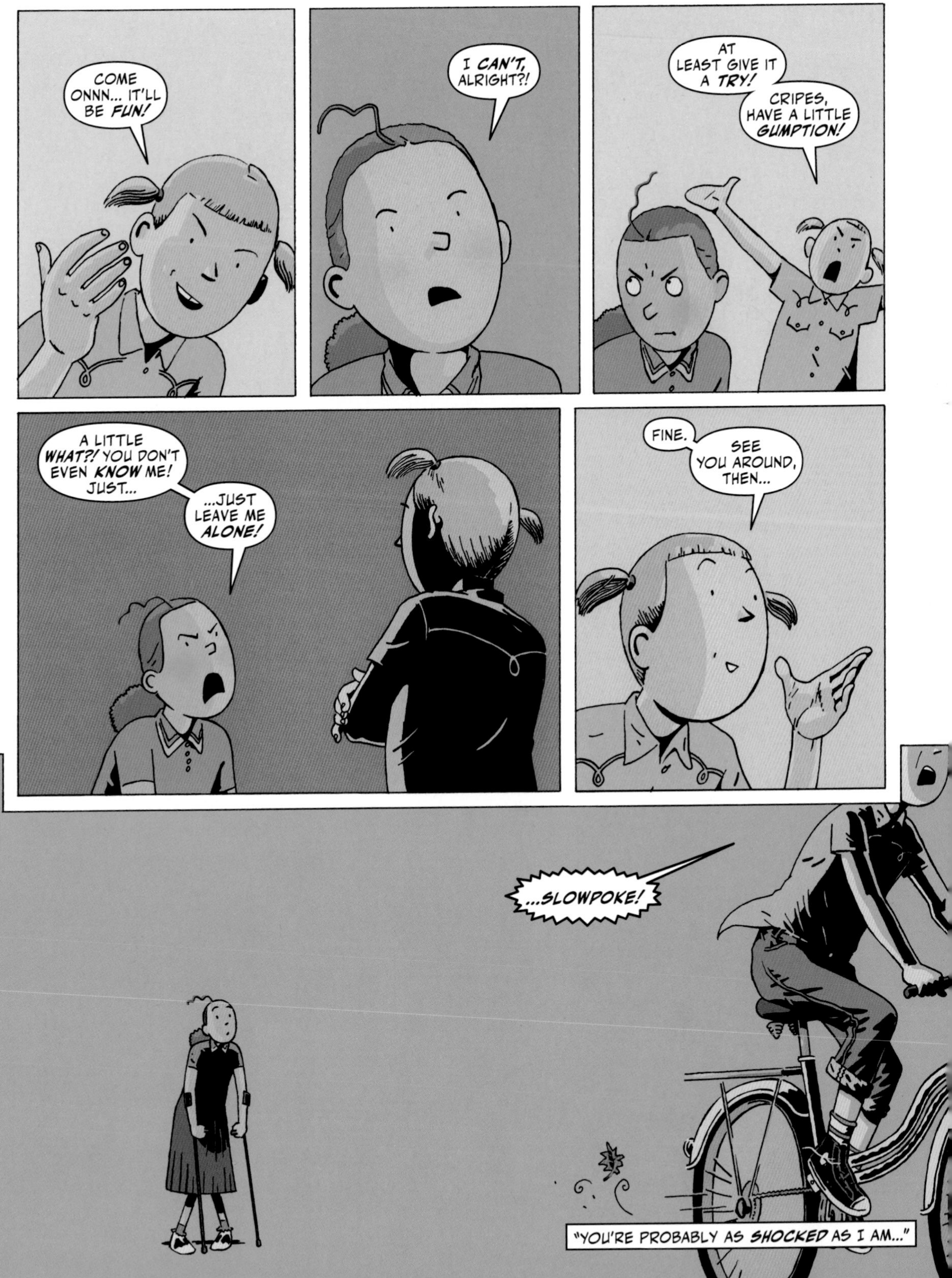
COME ONNN... IT'LL BE FUN!
I CAN'T, ALRIGHT?!
AT LEAST GIVE IT A TRY!
CRIPES, HAVE A LITTLE GUMPTION!
A LITTLE WHAT?! YOU DON'T EVEN KNOW ME! JUST...
...JUST LEAVE ME ALONE!
FINE.
SEE YOU AROUND, THEN...
...SLOWPOKE!
"YOU'RE PROBABLY AS SHOCKED AS I AM..."

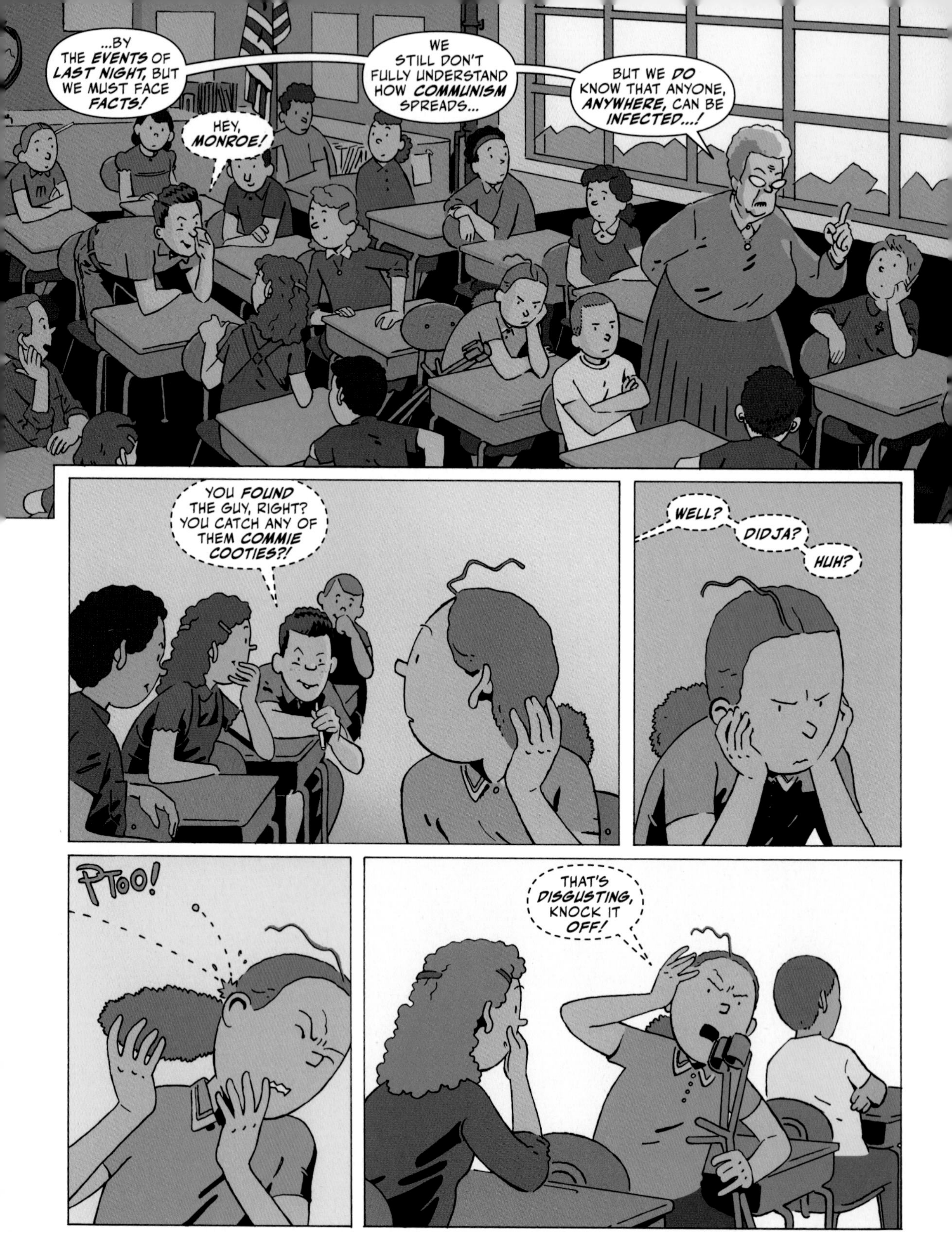
...BY THE EVENTS OF LAST NIGHT, BUT WE MUST FACE FACTS!
WE STILL DON'T FULLY UNDERSTAND HOW COMMUNISM SPREADS...
BUT WE DO KNOW THAT ANYONE, ANYWHERE, CAN BE INFECTED...!
HEY, MONROE!
YOU FOUND THE GUY, RIGHT? YOU CATCH ANY OF THEM COMMIE COOTIES?!
WELL?
DIDJA?
HUH?
PTOO!
THAT'S DISGUSTING, KNOCK IT OFF!

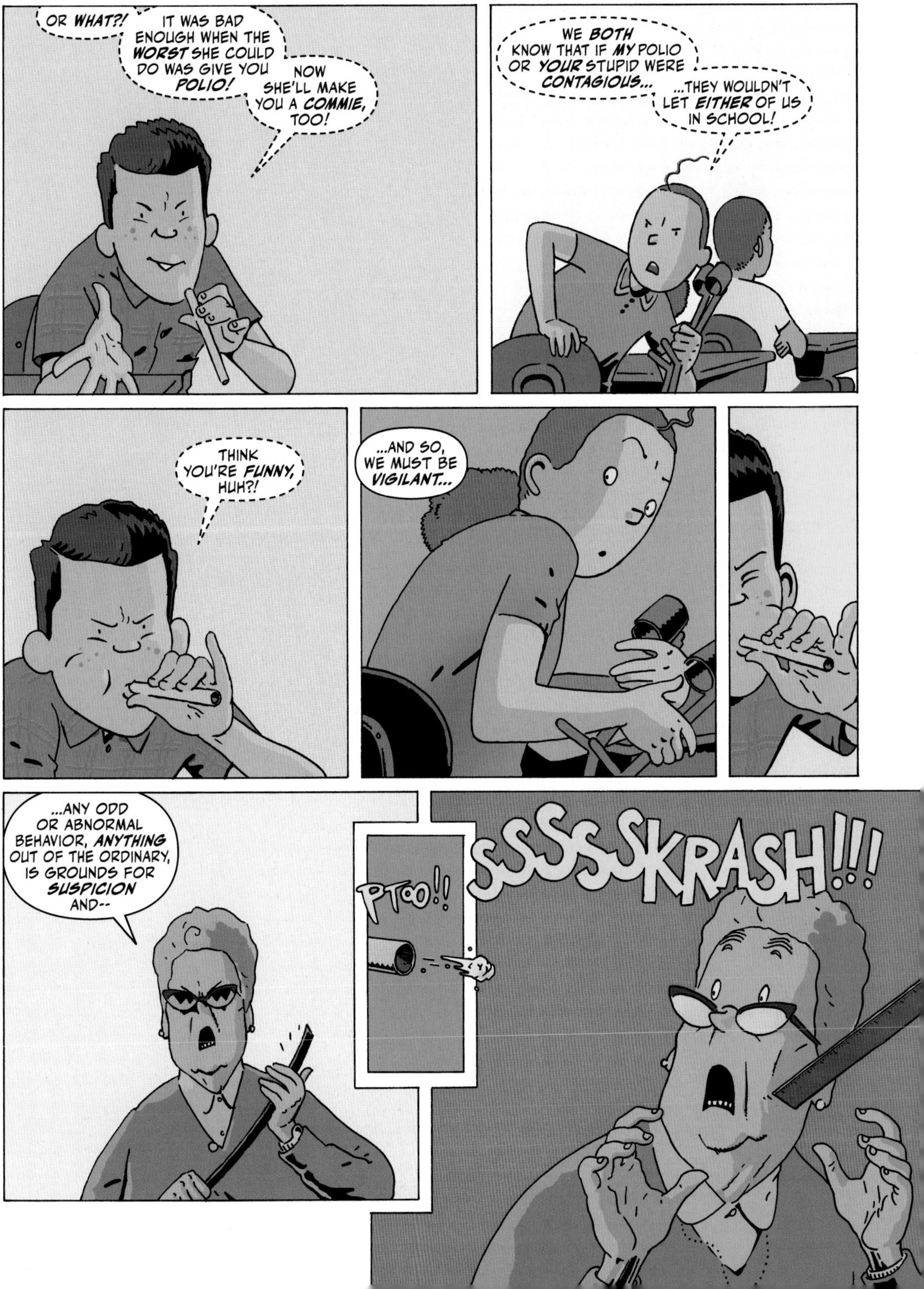
OR WHAT?!
IT WAS BAD ENOUGH WHEN THE WORST SHE COULD DO WAS GIVE YOU POLIO!
NOW SHE'LL MAKE YOU A COMMIE, TOO!
WE BOTH KNOW THAT IF MY POLIO OR YOUR STUPID WERE CONTAGIOUS...
...THEY WOULDN'T LET EITHER OF US IN SCHOOL!
THINK YOU'RE FUNNY, HUH?!
...AND SO, WE MUST BE VIGILANT...
...ANY ODD OR ABNORMAL BEHAVIOR, ANYTHING OUT OF THE ORDINARY, IS GROUNDS FOR SUSPICION AND--
PTOO!!
SSSSSKRASH!!!

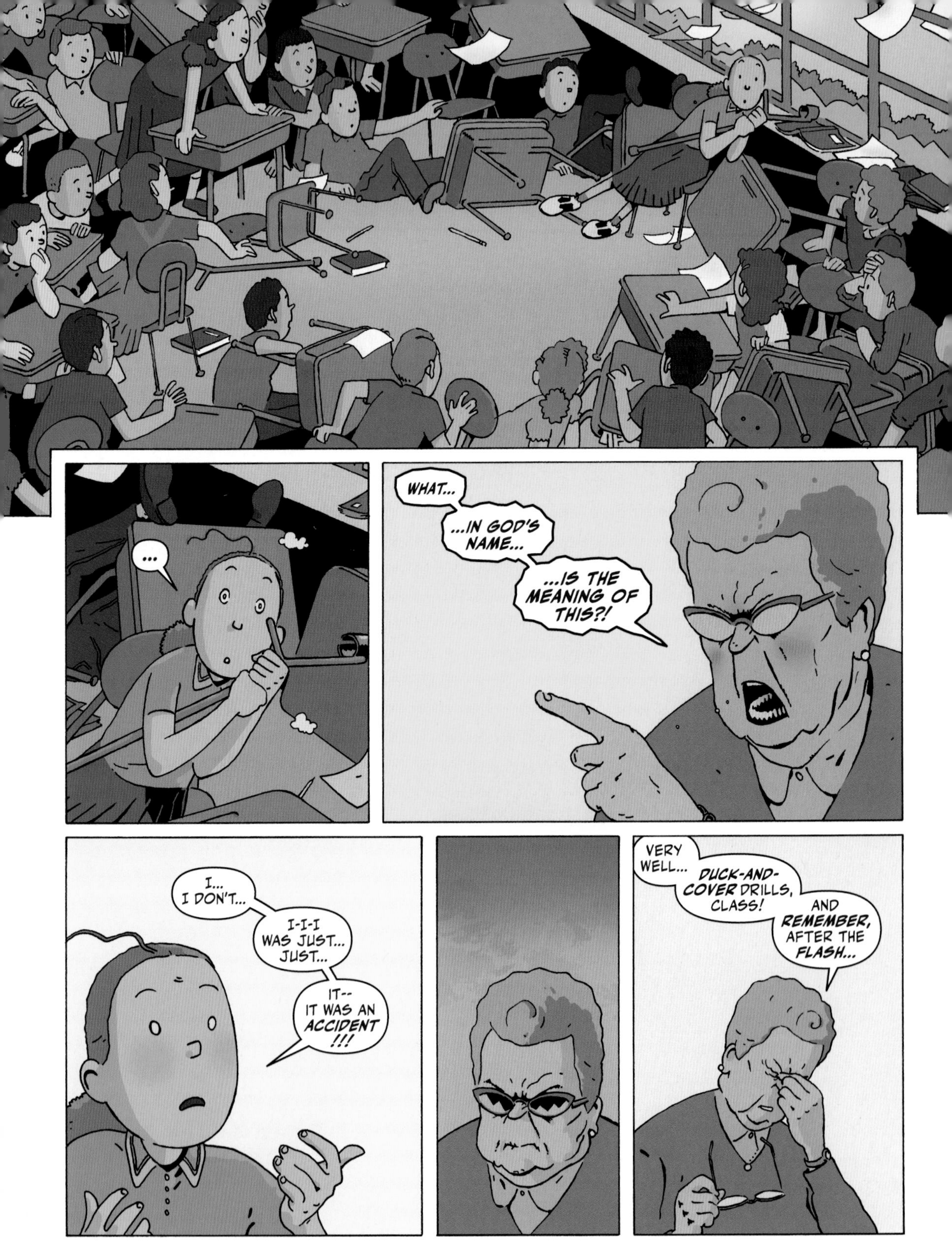
...
WHAT...
...IN GOD'S NAME...
...IS THE MEANING OF THIS?!
I... I DON'T...
I-I-I WAS JUST... JUST...
IT-- IT WAS AN ACCIDENT !!!
VERY WELL...
DUCK-AND-COVER DRILLS, CLASS!
AND REMEMBER, AFTER THE FLASH...

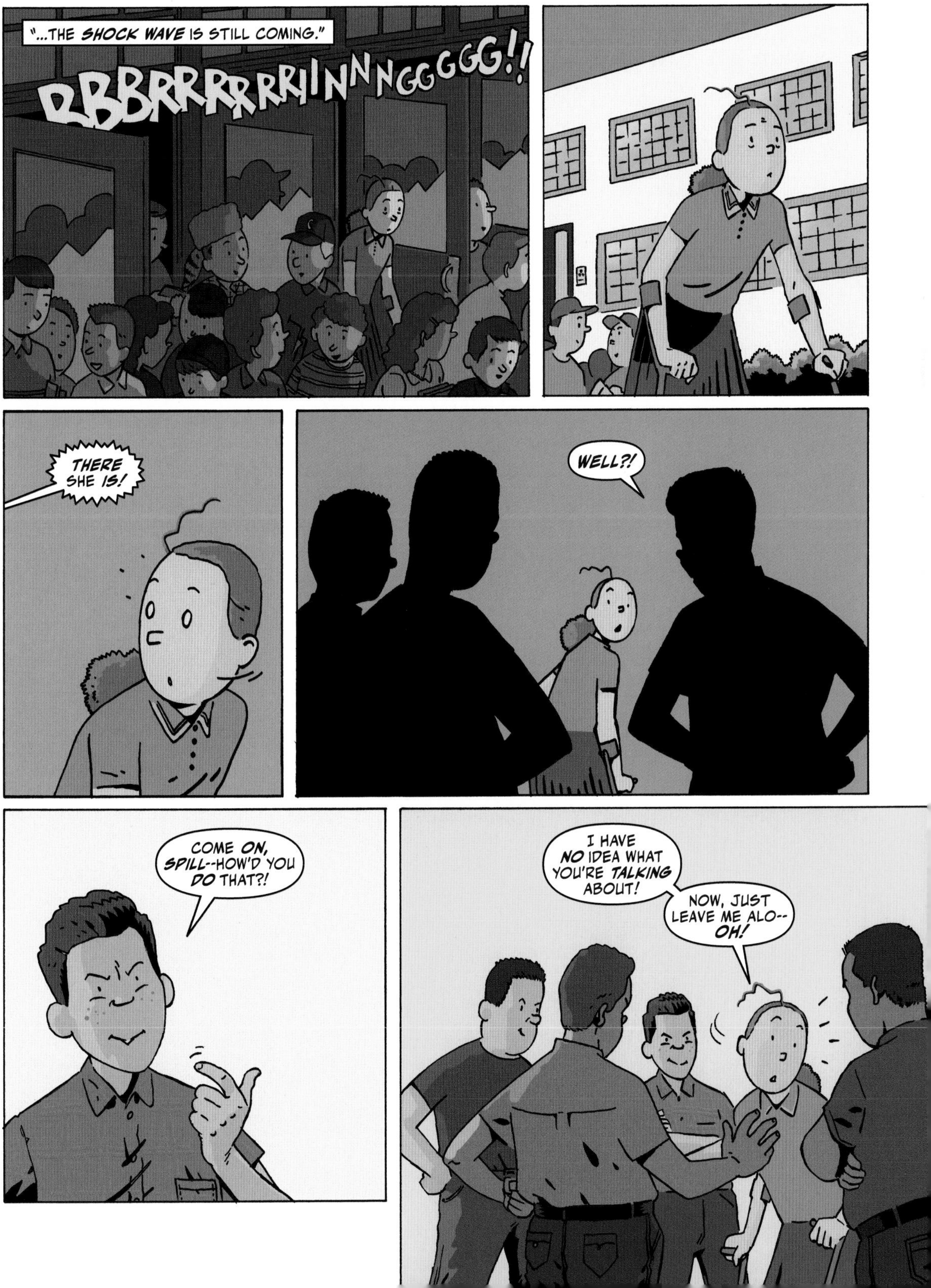
"...THE SHOCK WAVE IS STILL COMING."
BBBRRRRRRRIINNNGGGGG!!
THERE SHE IS!
WELL?!
COME ON, SPILL--HOW'D YOU DO THAT?!
I HAVE NO IDEA WHAT YOU'RE TALKING ABOUT!
NOW, JUST LEAVE ME ALO-- OH!

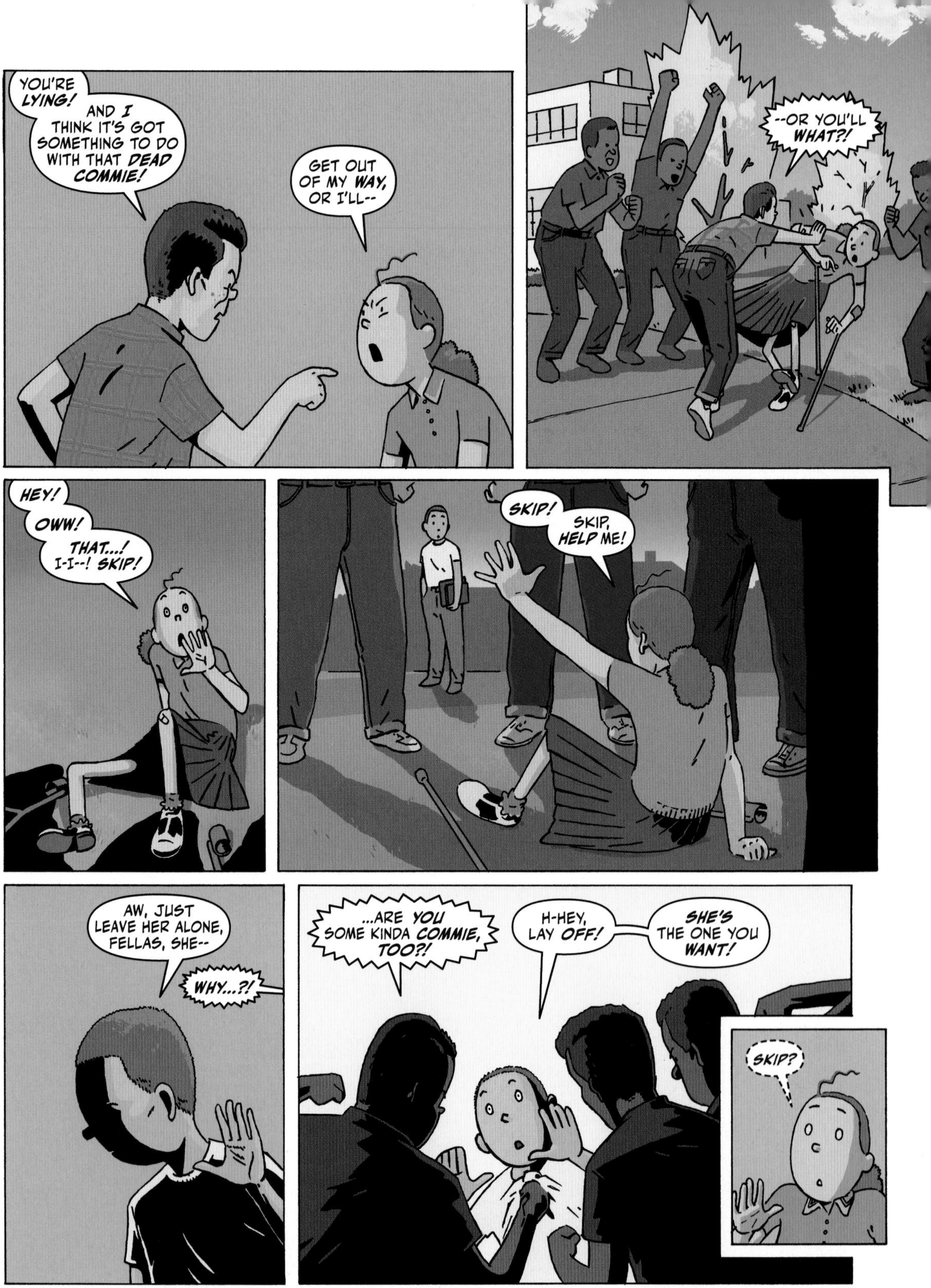
YOU'RE LYING!
AND I THINK IT'S GOT SOMETHING TO DO WITH THAT DEAD COMMIE!
GET OUT OF MY WAY, OR I'LL--
--OR YOU'LL WHAT?!
HEY!
OWW!
THAT...! I-I--! SKIP!
SKIP!
SKIP, HELP ME!
AW, JUST LEAVE HER ALONE, FELLAS, SHE--
WHY...?!
...ARE YOU SOME KINDA COMMIE, TOO?!
H-HEY, LAY OFF!
SHE'S THE ONE YOU WANT!
SKIP?

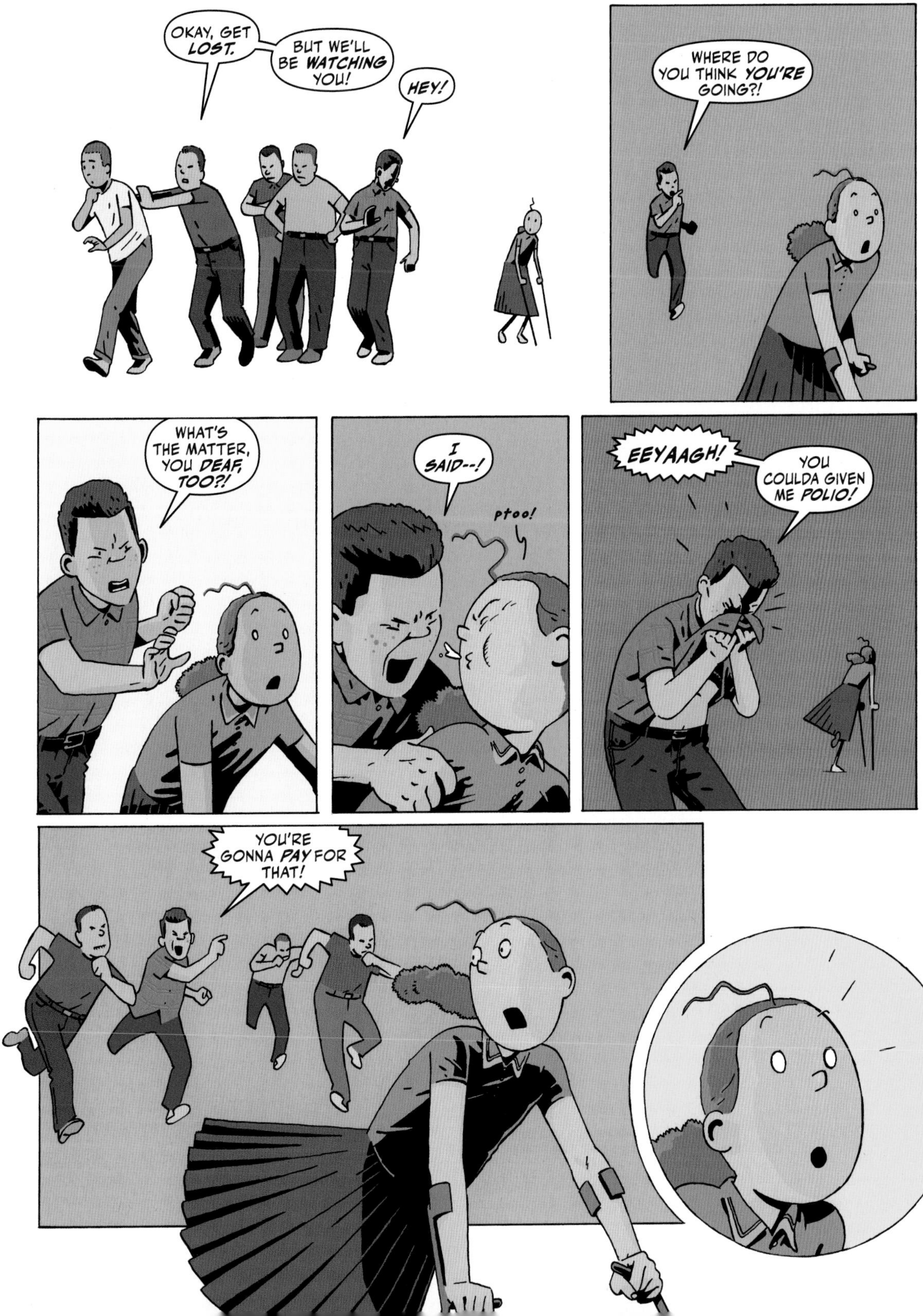
OKAY, GET LOST.
BUT WE'LL BE WATCHING YOU!
HEY!
WHERE DO YOU THINK YOU'RE GOING?!
WHAT'S THE MATTER, YOU DEAF, TOO?!
I SAID--!
ptoo!
EEYAAGH!
YOU COULDA GIVEN ME POLIO!
YOU'RE GONNA PAY FOR THAT!

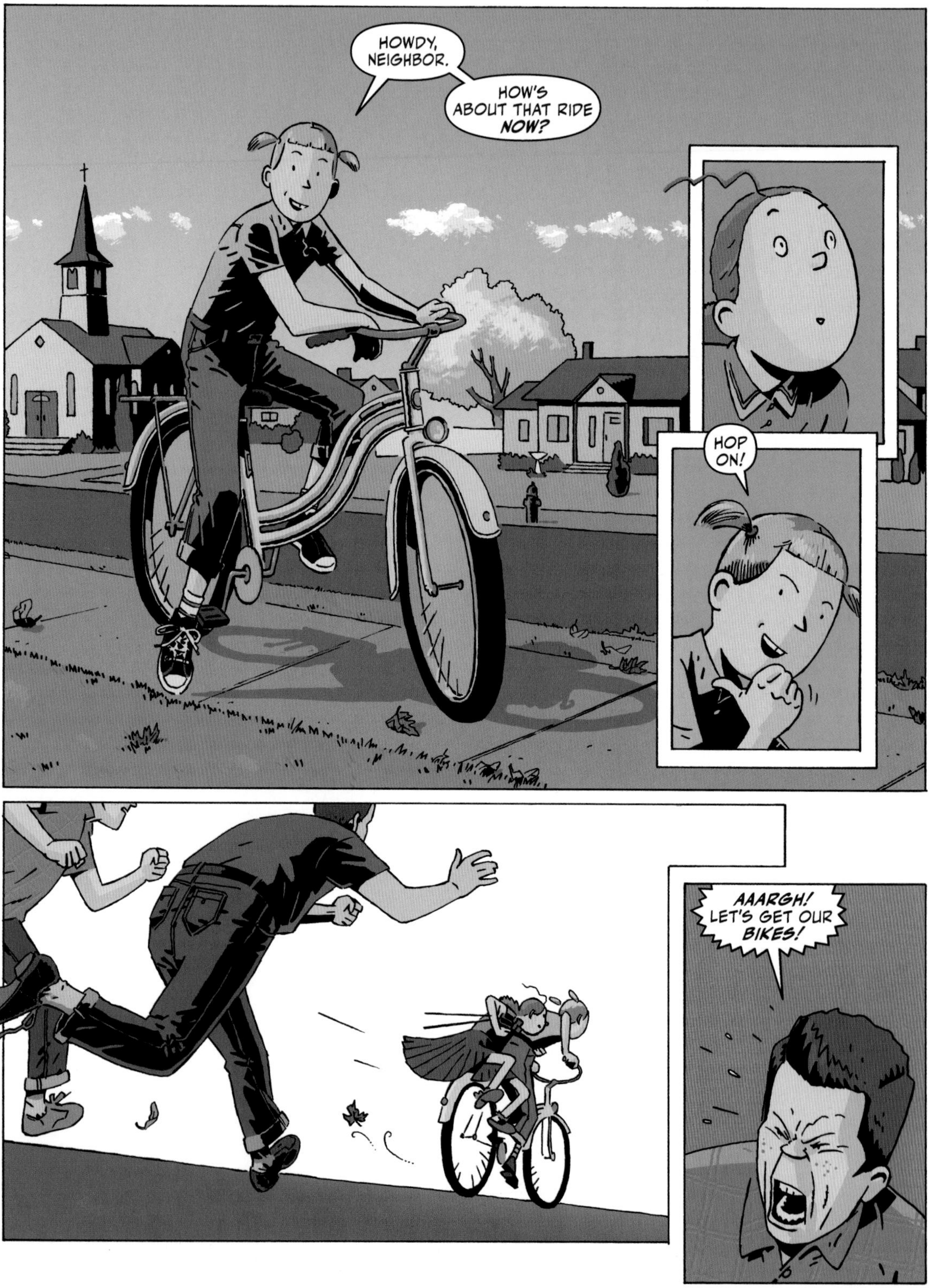
HOWDY, NEIGHBOR.
HOW'S ABOUT THAT RIDE *NOW?*
HOP ON!
*AAARGH!* LET'S GET OUR *BIKES!*

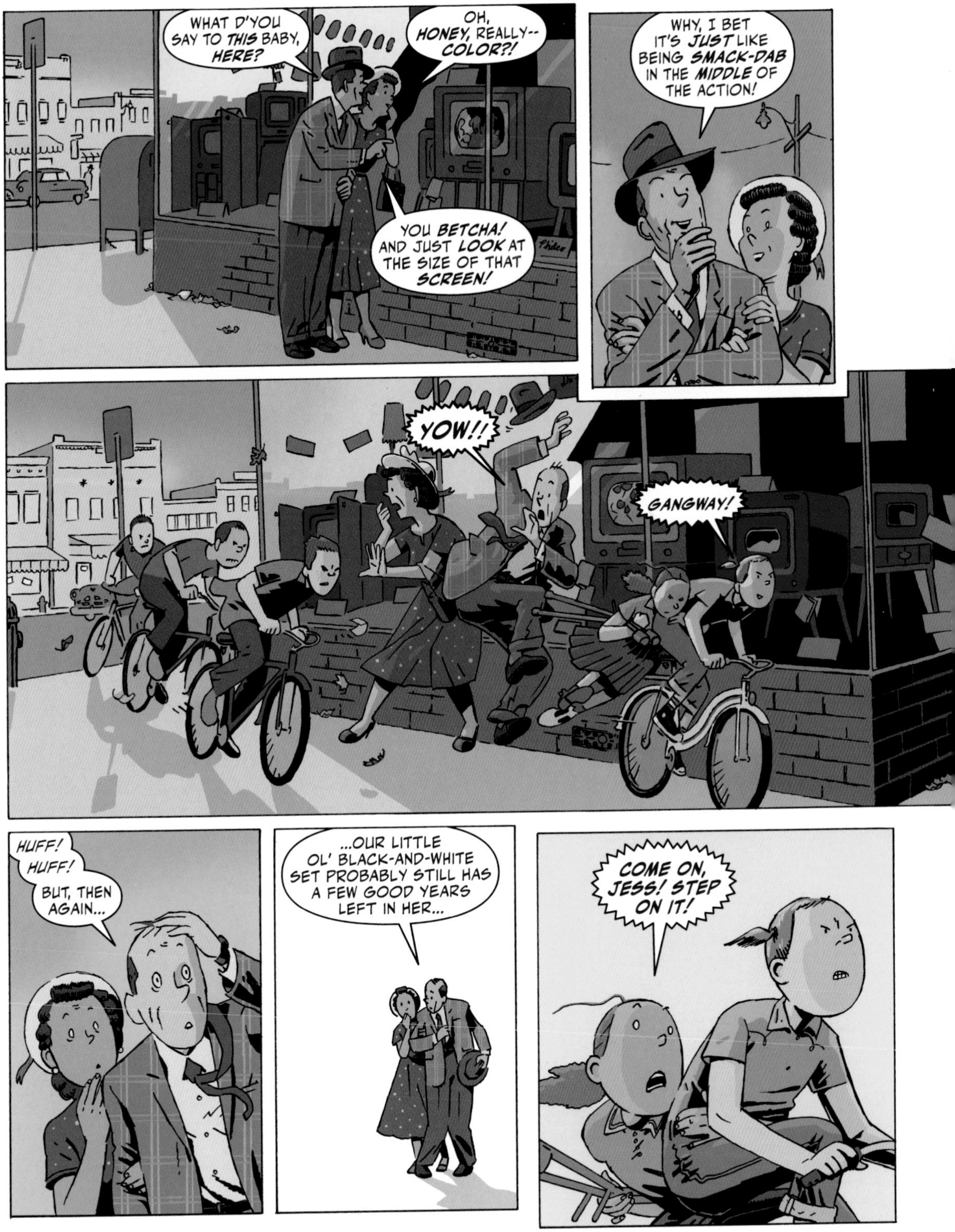
WHAT D'YOU SAY TO THIS BABY, HERE?
OH, HONEY, REALLY-- COLOR?!
YOU BETCHA! AND JUST LOOK AT THE SIZE OF THAT SCREEN!
Philco
WHY, I BET IT'S JUST LIKE BEING SMACK-DAB IN THE MIDDLE OF THE ACTION!
YOW!!
GANGWAY!
HUFF!
HUFF!
BUT, THEN AGAIN...
...OUR LITTLE OL' BLACK-AND-WHITE SET PROBABLY STILL HAS A FEW GOOD YEARS LEFT IN HER...
COME ON, JESS! STEP ON IT!

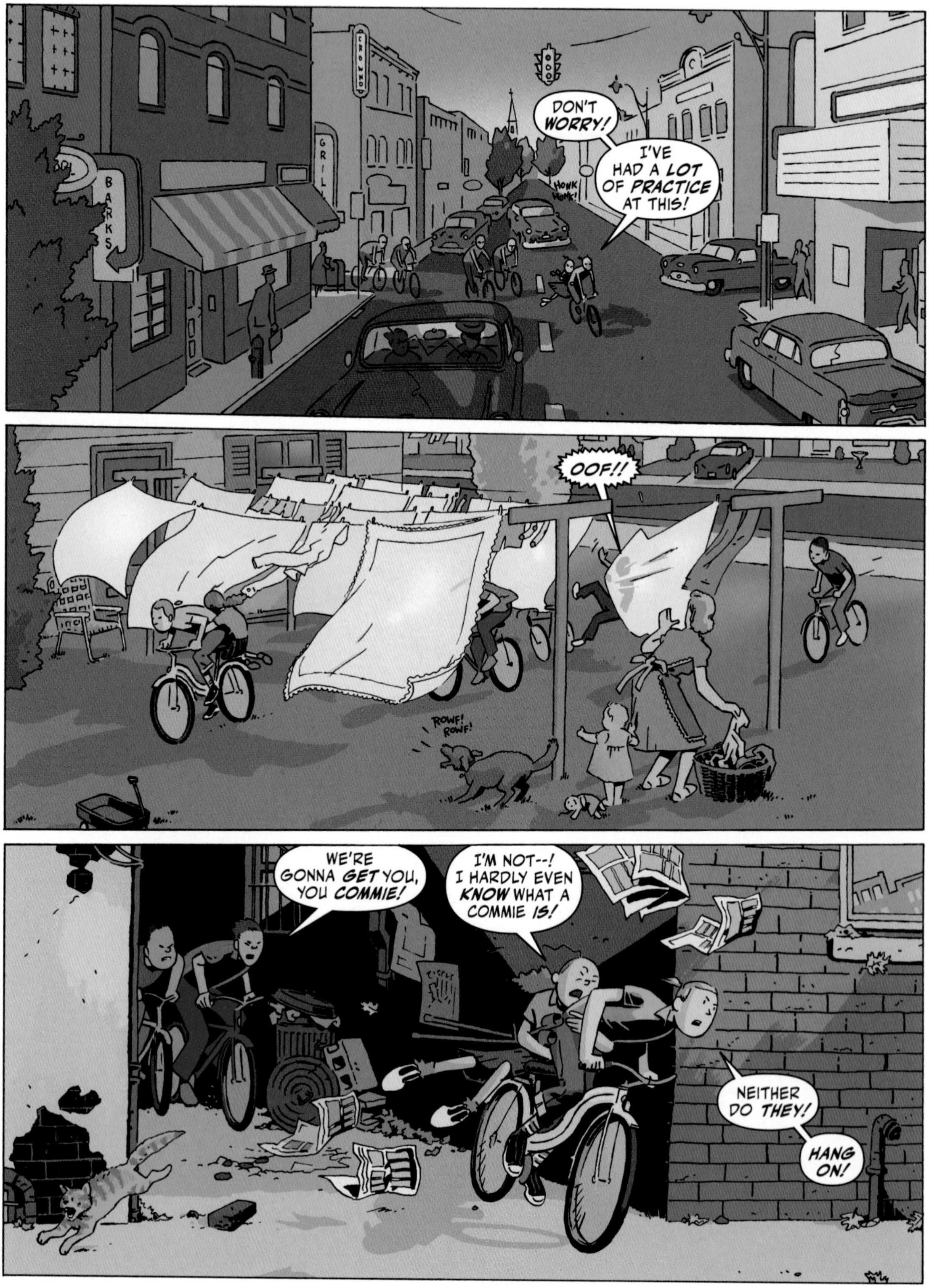
BARKS
HONK HONK
DON'T WORRY!
I'VE HAD A LOT OF PRACTICE AT THIS!
OOF!!
ROWF! ROWF!
WE'RE GONNA GET YOU, YOU COMMIE!
I'M NOT--! I HARDLY EVEN KNOW WHAT A COMMIE IS!
NEITHER DO THEY!
HANG ON!

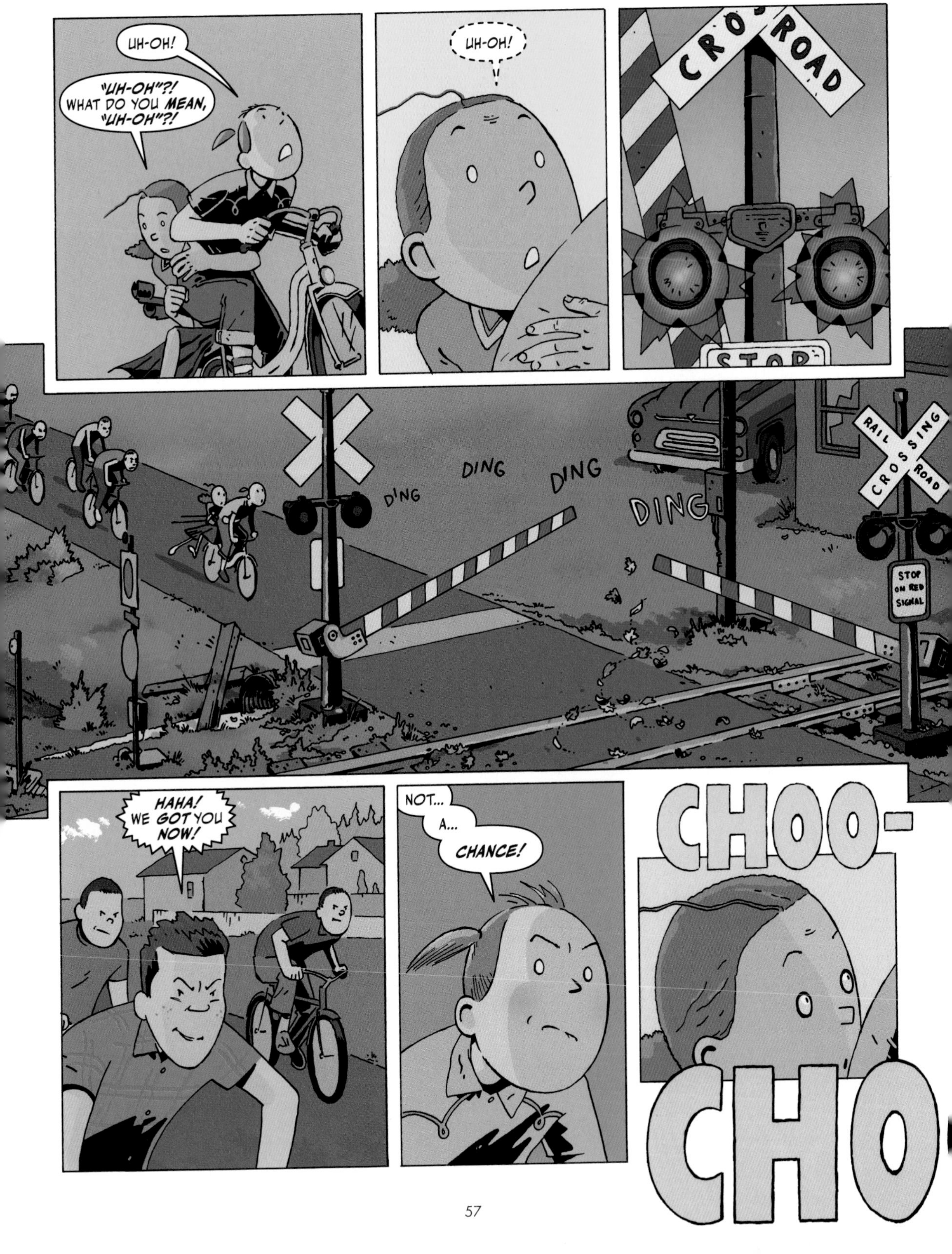
UH-OH!
"UH-OH"?! WHAT DO YOU MEAN, "UH-OH"?!
UH-OH!
CROSS ROAD
DING
DING
DING
DING
RAIL CROSSING ROAD
STOP ON RED SIGNAL
HAHA! WE GOT YOU NOW!
NOT...
A...
CHANCE!
CHOO-
CHO

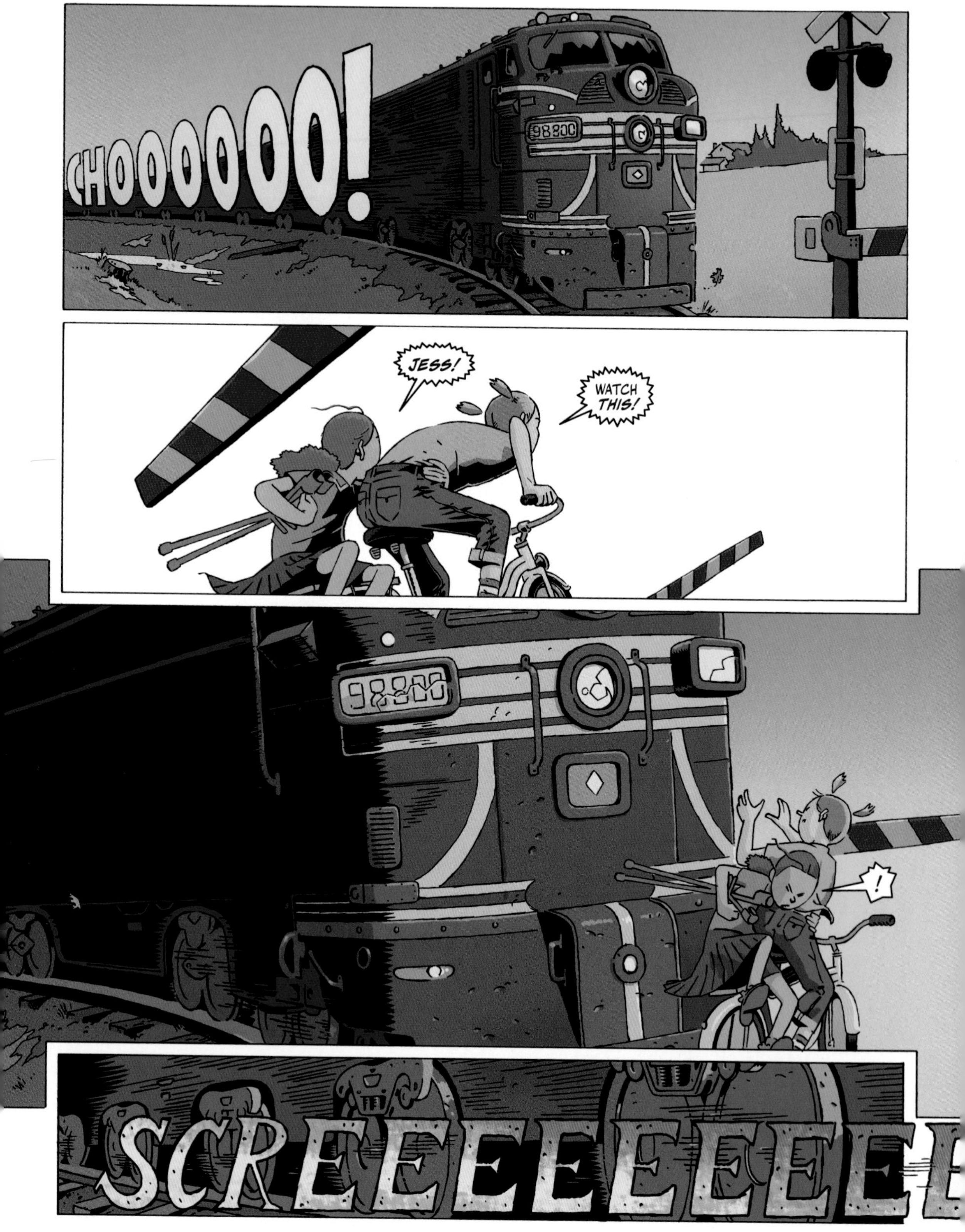
CHOOOOOO!
JESS!
WATCH THIS!
!
SCREEEEEEEEE

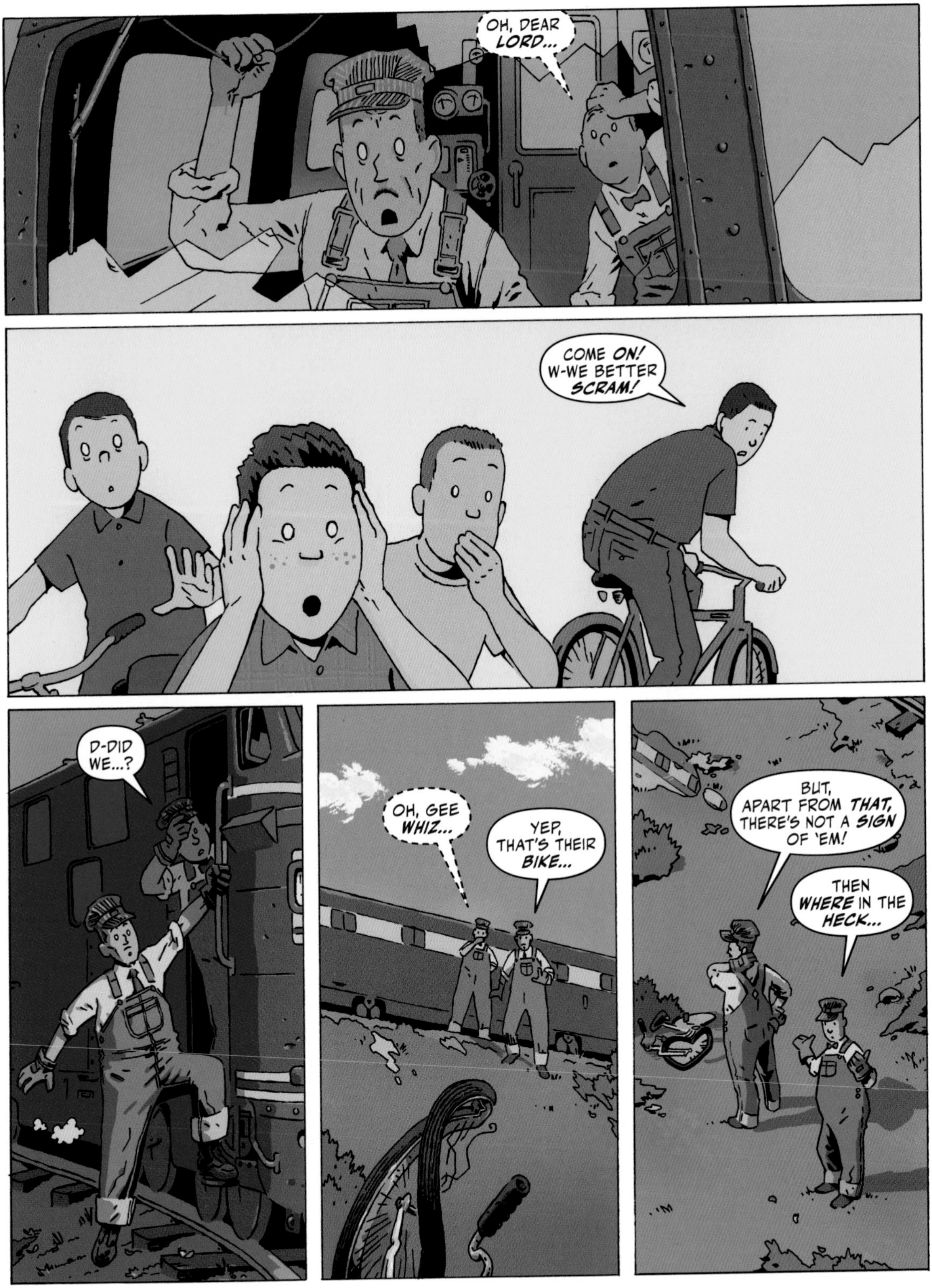
OH, DEAR LORD...
COME ON! W-WE BETTER SCRAM!
D-DID WE...?
OH, GEE WHIZ...
YEP, THAT'S THEIR BIKE...
BUT, APART FROM THAT, THERE'S NOT A SIGN OF 'EM!
THEN WHERE IN THE HECK...

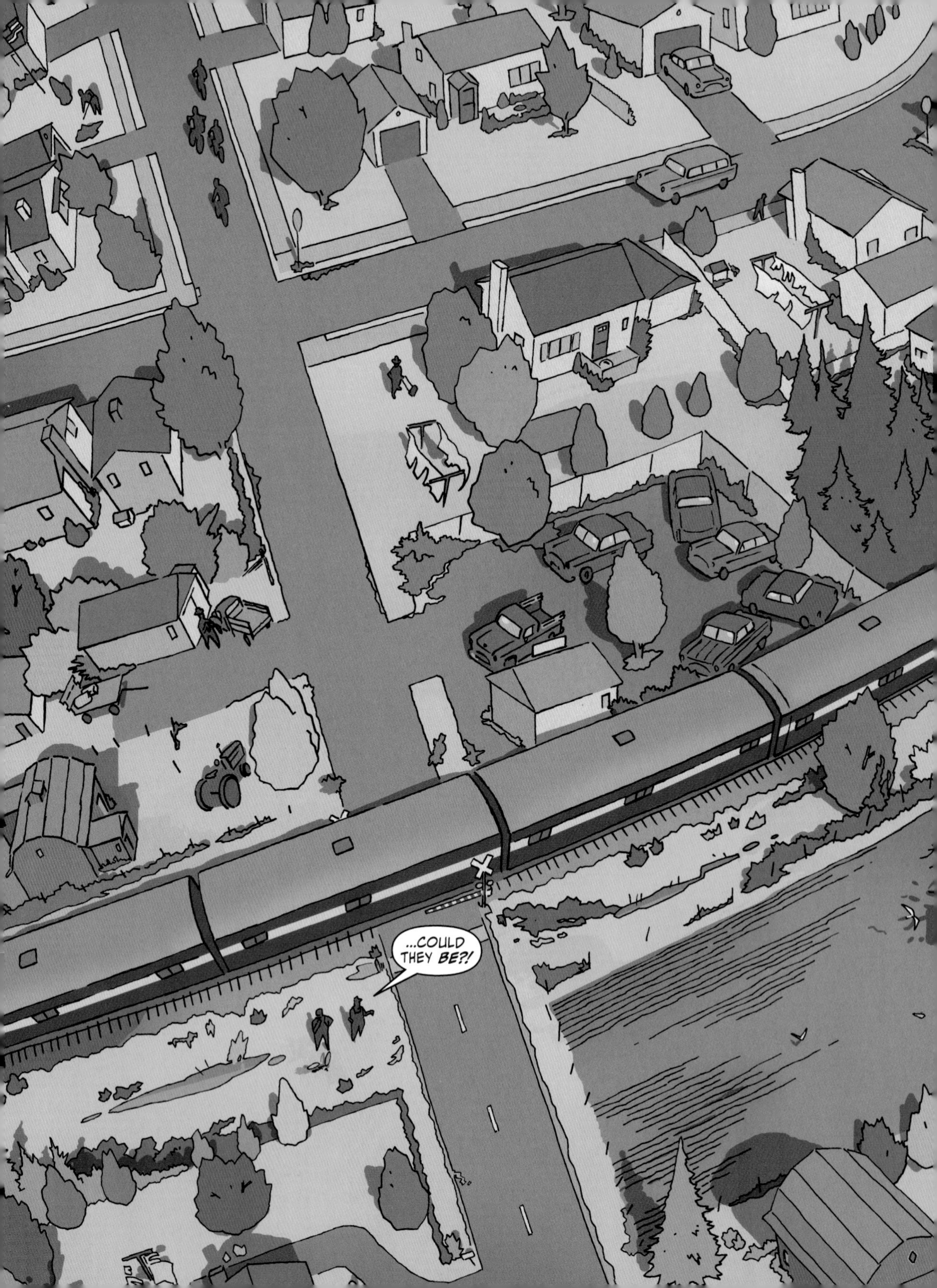
...COULD THEY *BE*?!

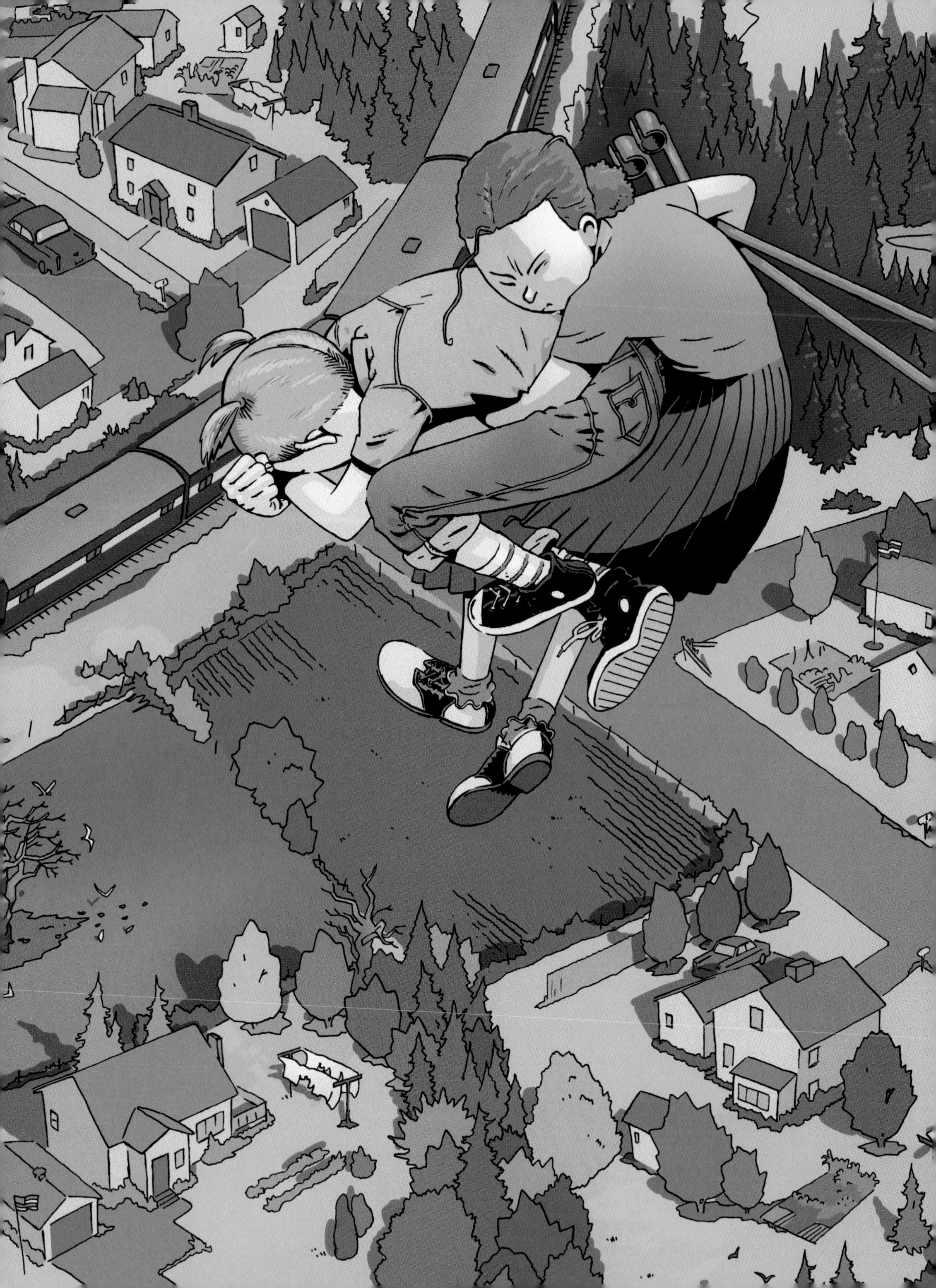

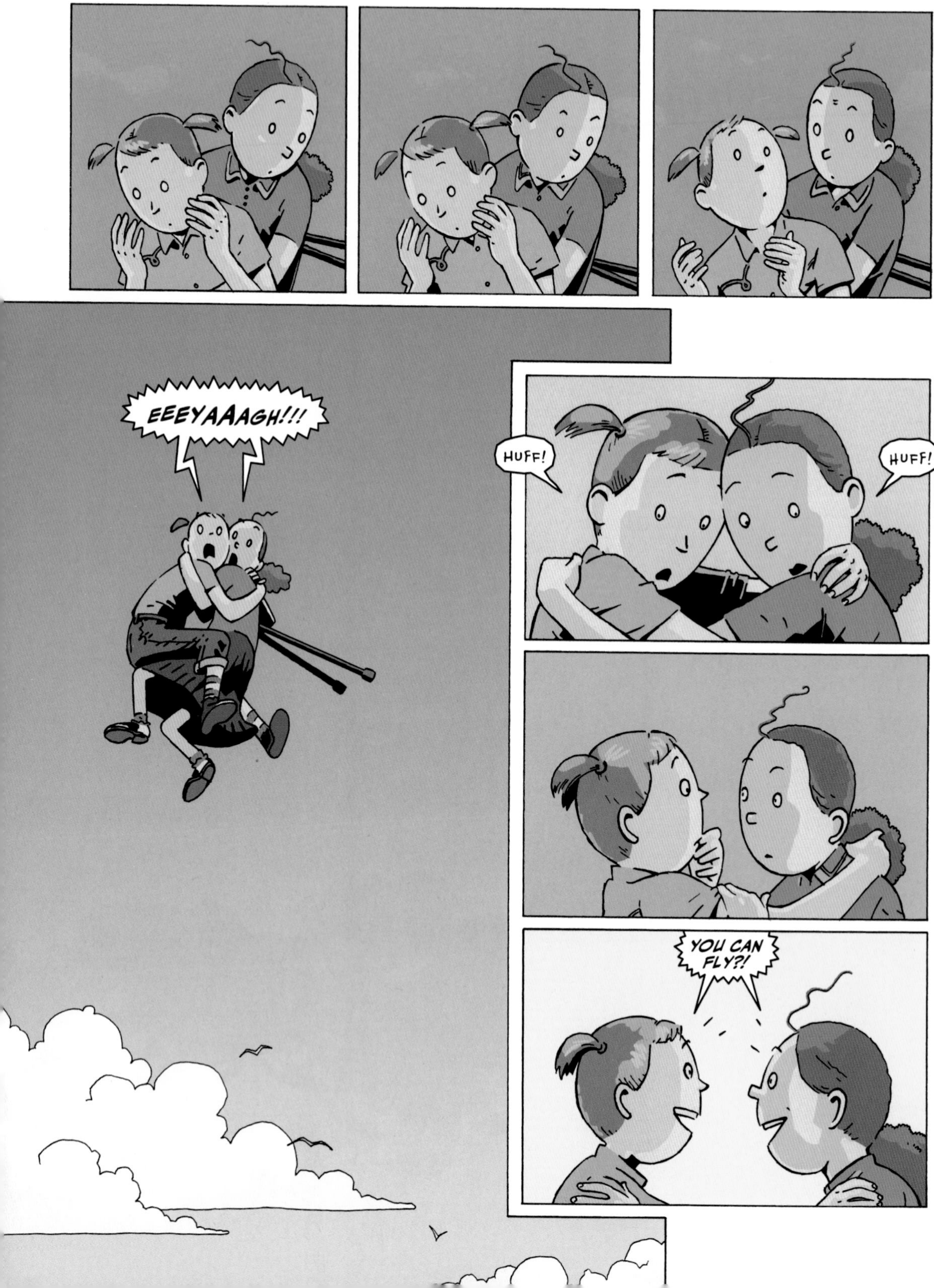
EEEYAAAGH!!!
HUFF!
HUFF!
YOU CAN FLY?!

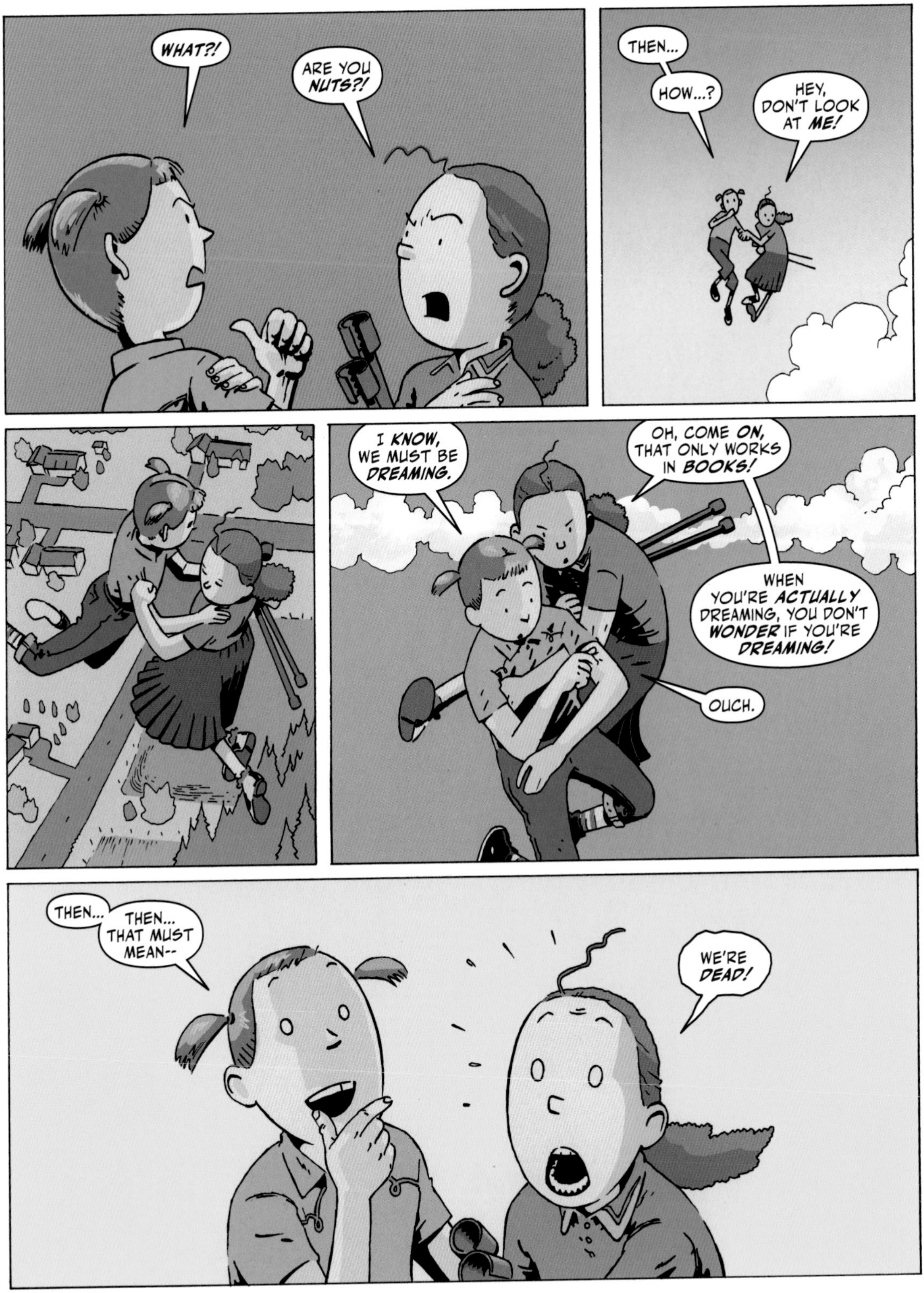
WHAT?!
ARE YOU NUTS?!
THEN...
HOW...?
HEY, DON'T LOOK AT ME!
I KNOW, WE MUST BE DREAMING.
OH, COME ON, THAT ONLY WORKS IN BOOKS!
WHEN YOU'RE ACTUALLY DREAMING, YOU DON'T WONDER IF YOU'RE DREAMING!
OUCH.
THEN...
THEN... THAT MUST MEAN--
WE'RE DEAD!

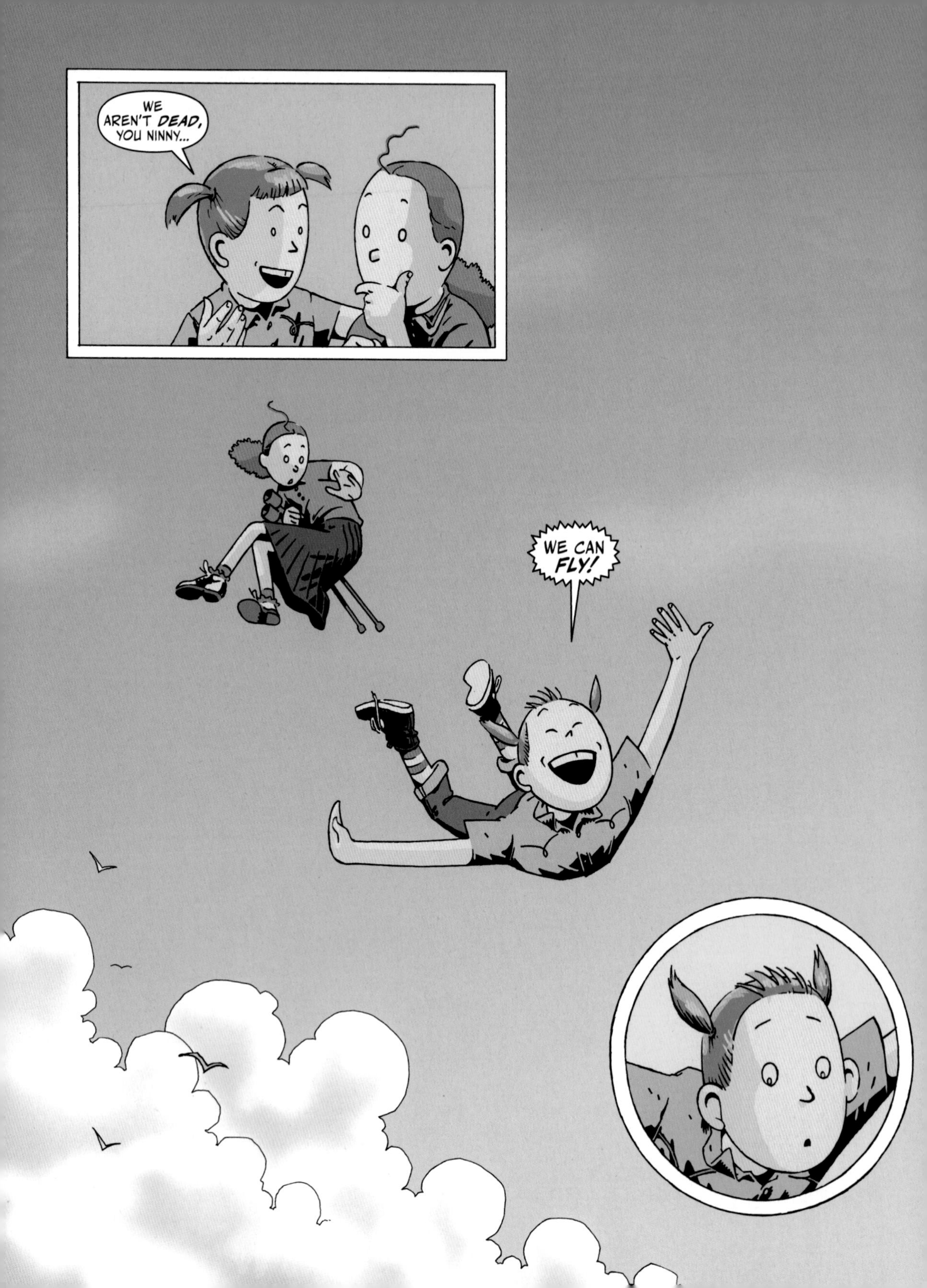
WE AREN'T DEAD, YOU NINNY...
WE CAN FLY!

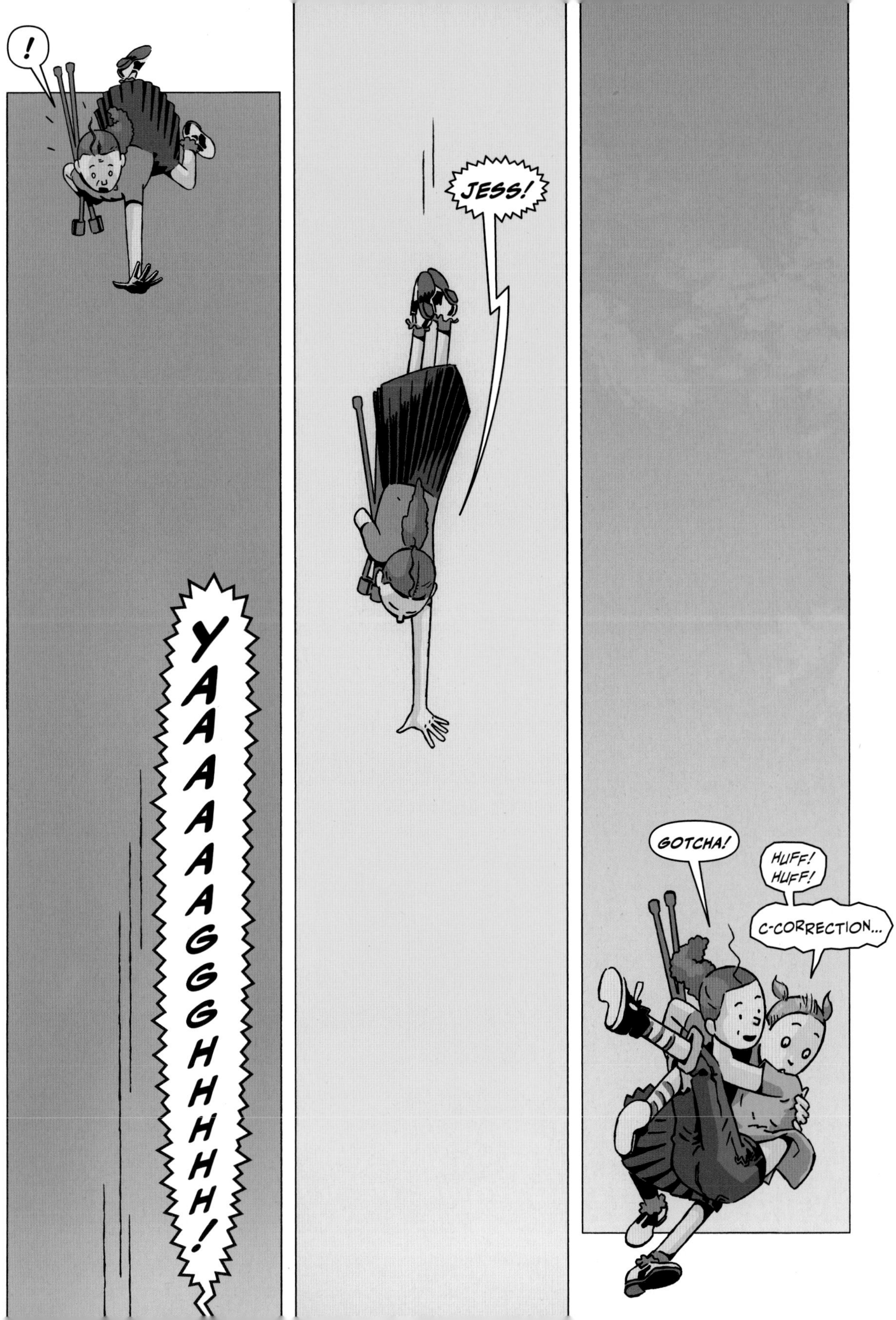
!
YAAAAAAAGGGHHHHHH!
JESS!
GOTCHA!
HUFF! HUFF!
C-CORRECTION...

...YOU CAN FLY!

B-BUT--I--HOW--?

"HOW" CAN WAIT. FIRST, GET US DOWN SOMEPLACE SAFE...

CLIN CORI

"...THEN WE'LL WORRY ABOUT HOW."

RATTLE RATTLE

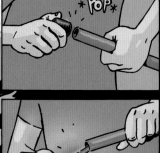

*POP*

WHERE IN THE WORLD DID YOU GET THAT?!

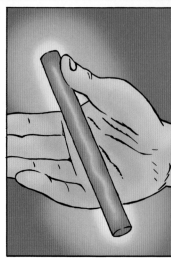

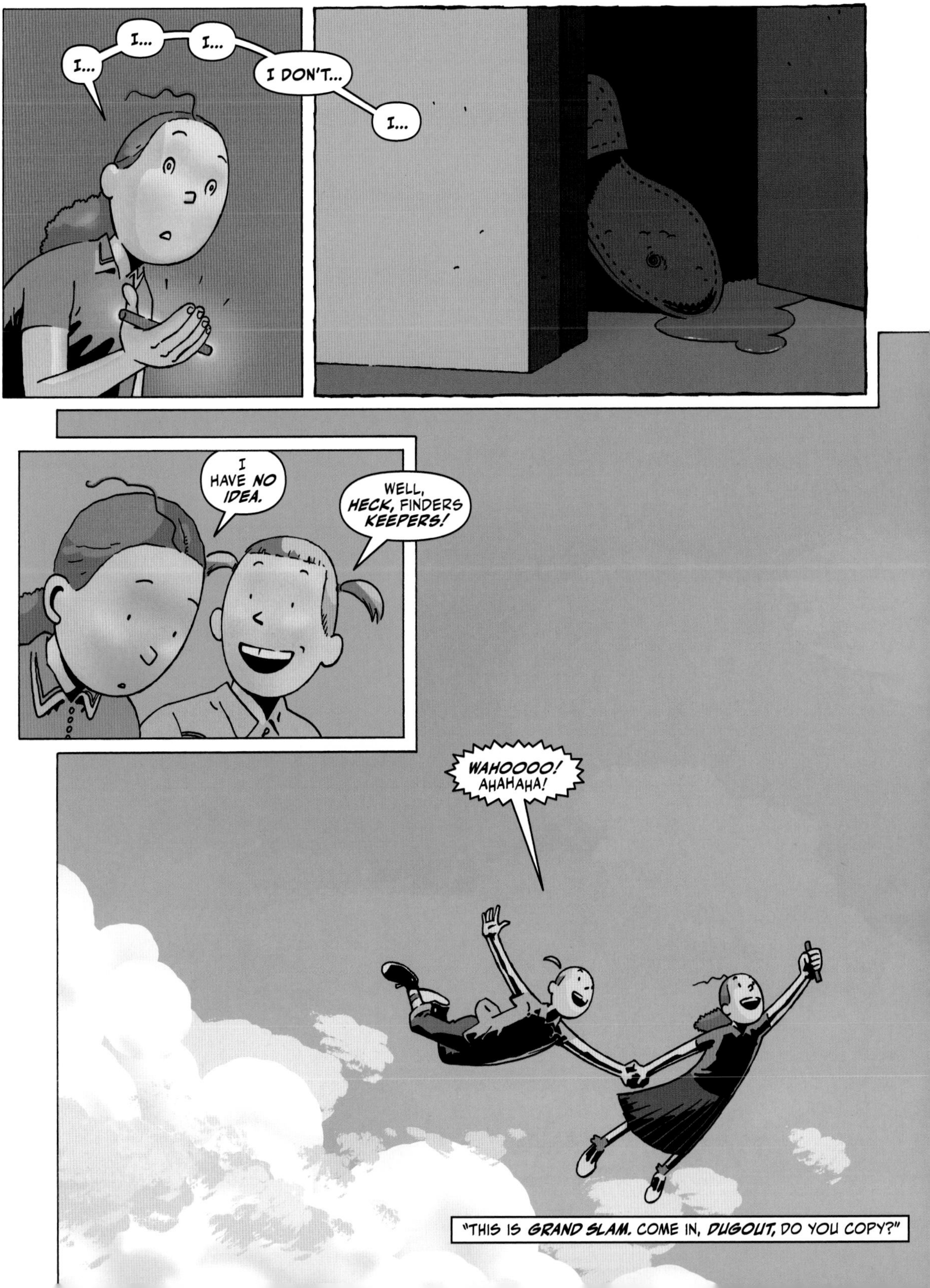
I...
I...
I...
I DON'T...
I...
I HAVE NO IDEA.
WELL, HECK, FINDERS KEEPERS!
WAHOOOO! AHAHAHA!
"THIS IS GRAND SLAM. COME IN, DUGOUT, DO YOU COPY?"

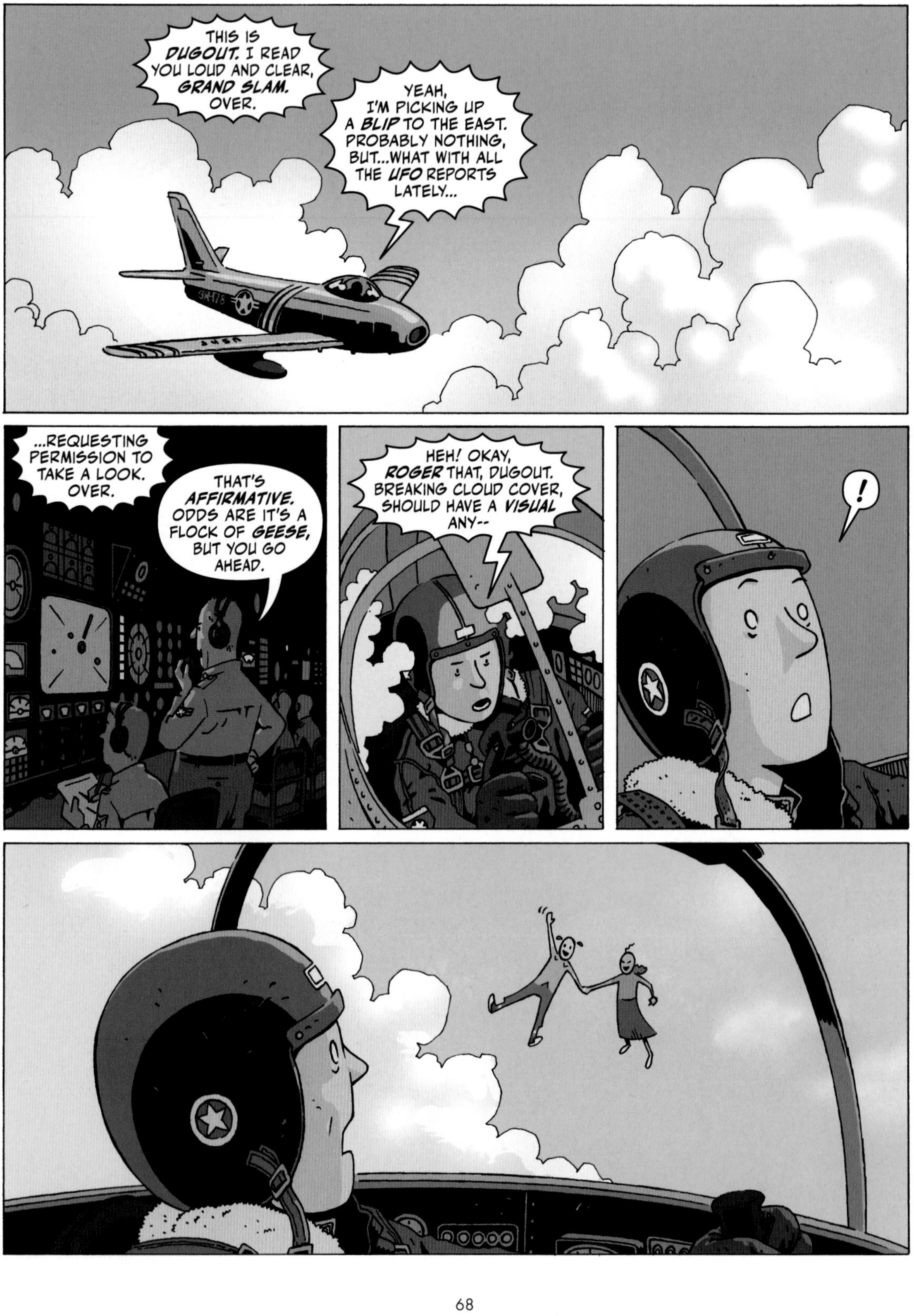
THIS IS DUGOUT. I READ YOU LOUD AND CLEAR, GRAND SLAM. OVER.
YEAH, I'M PICKING UP A BLIP TO THE EAST. PROBABLY NOTHING, BUT...WHAT WITH ALL THE UFO REPORTS LATELY...
...REQUESTING PERMISSION TO TAKE A LOOK. OVER.
THAT'S AFFIRMATIVE. ODDS ARE IT'S A FLOCK OF GEESE, BUT YOU GO AHEAD.
HEH! OKAY, ROGER THAT, DUGOUT. BREAKING CLOUD COVER, SHOULD HAVE A VISUAL ANY--
!

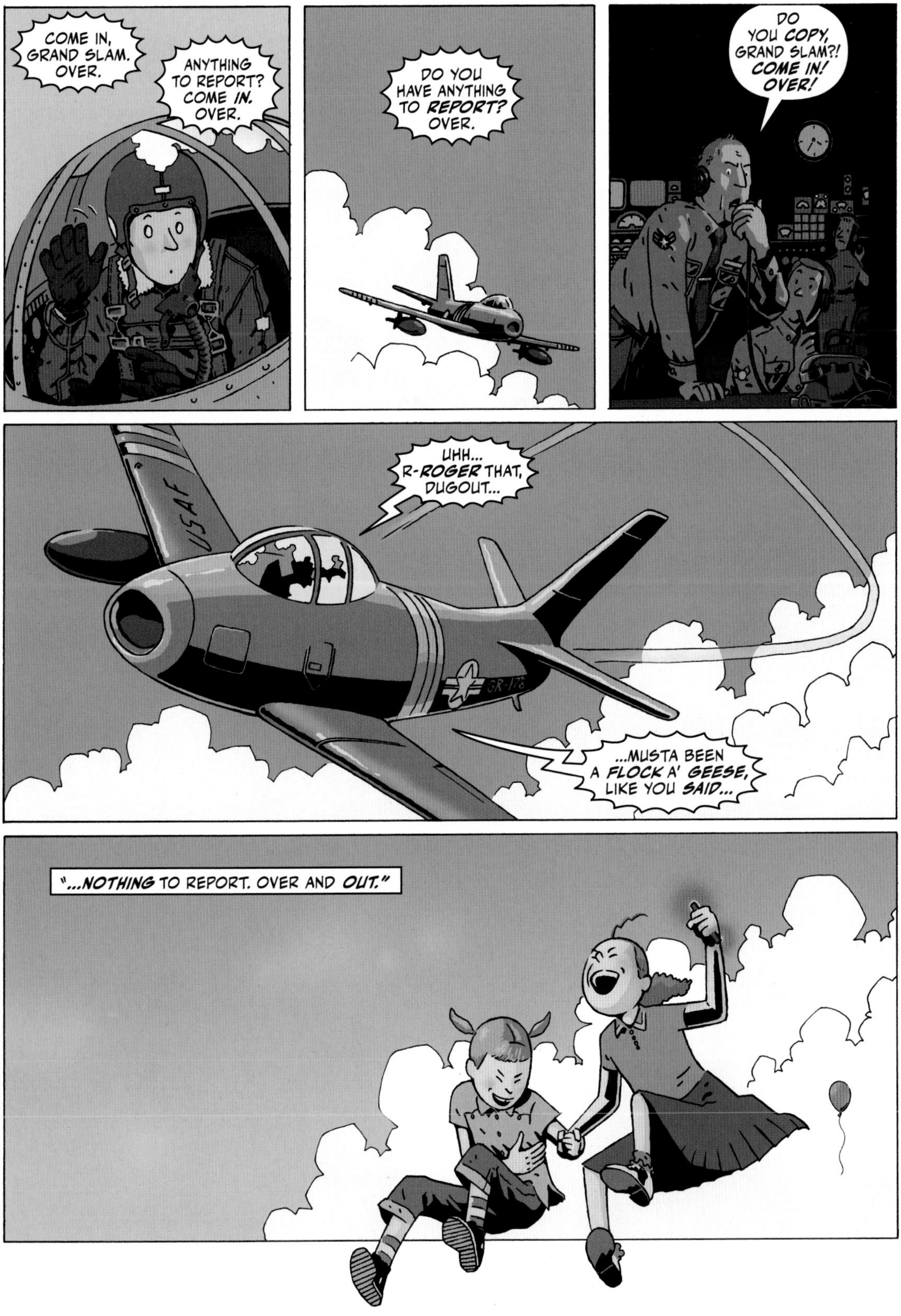
COME IN, GRAND SLAM. OVER.
ANYTHING TO REPORT? COME IN. OVER.
DO YOU HAVE ANYTHING TO REPORT? OVER.
DO YOU COPY, GRAND SLAM?! COME IN! OVER!
UHH... R-ROGER THAT, DUGOUT...
USAF
...MUSTA BEEN A FLOCK A' GEESE, LIKE YOU SAID...
"...NOTHING TO REPORT. OVER AND OUT."

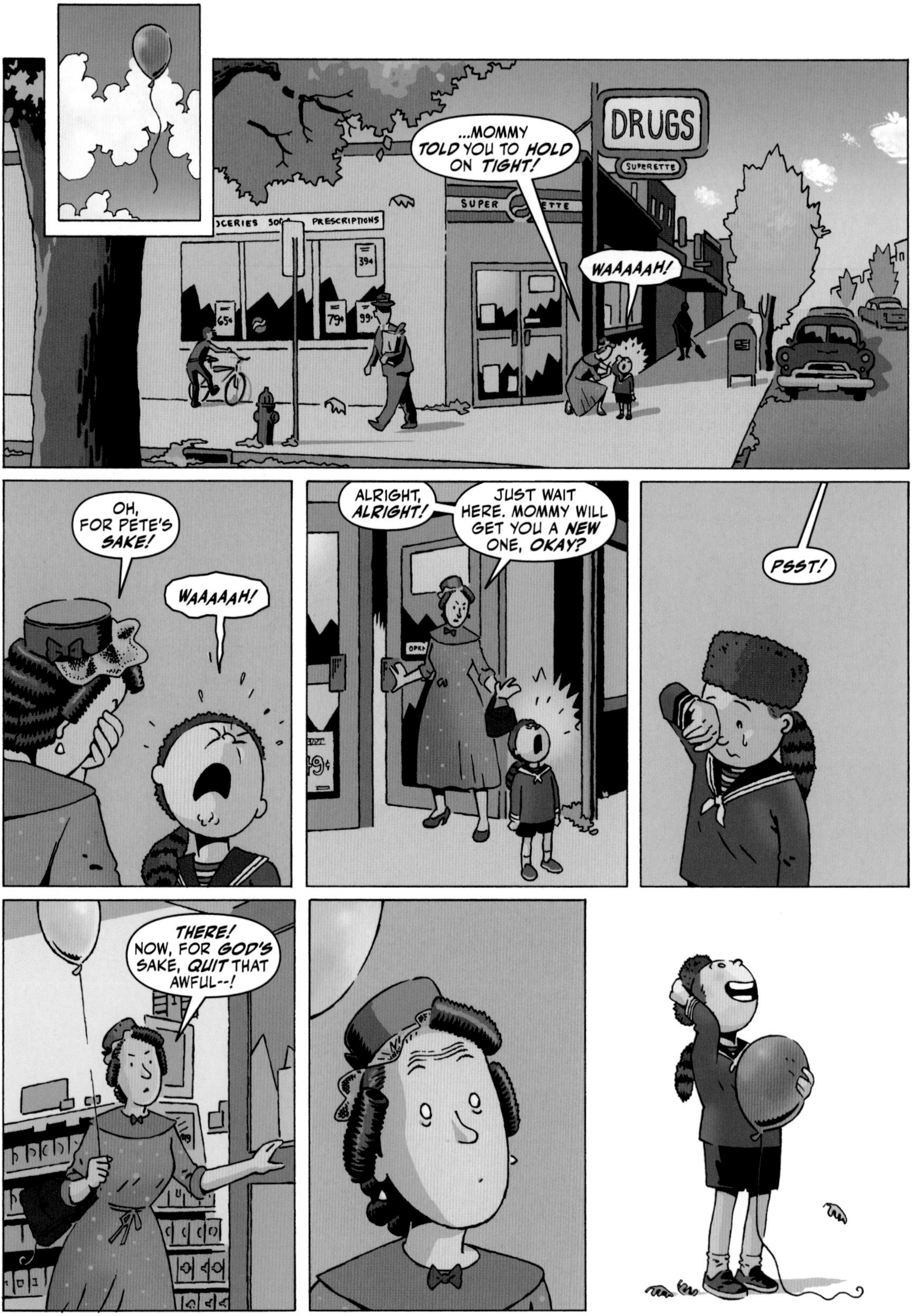
DRUGS
SUPERETTE
SUPER ETTE
CERIES SO PRESCRIPTIONS
39¢
65¢
79¢
99¢
...MOMMY TOLD YOU TO HOLD ON TIGHT!
WAAAAAH!
OH, FOR PETE'S SAKE!
WAAAAAH!
ALRIGHT, ALRIGHT!
JUST WAIT HERE. MOMMY WILL GET YOU A NEW ONE, OKAY?
PSST!
THERE! NOW, FOR GOD'S SAKE, QUIT THAT AWFUL--!

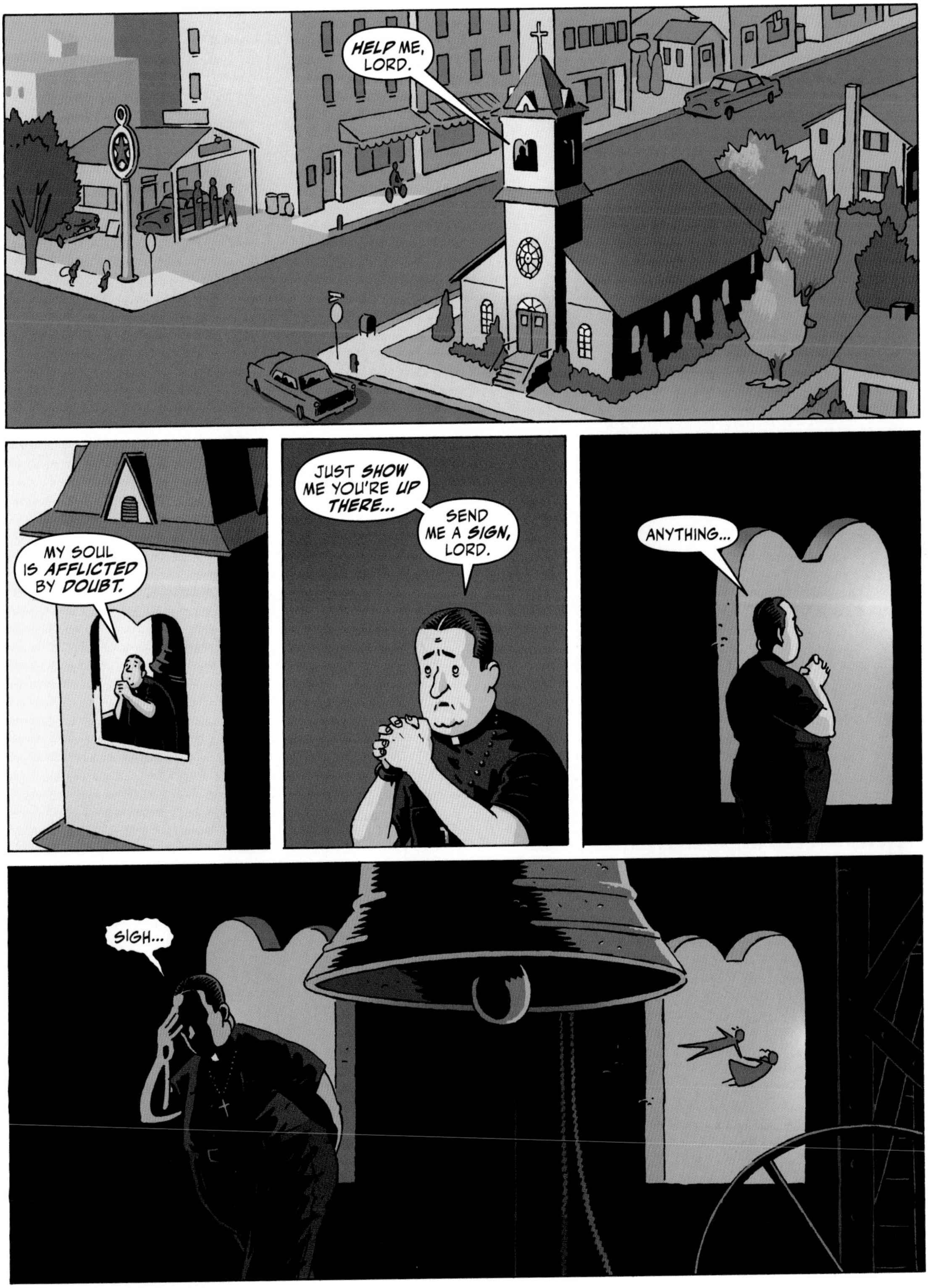
HELP ME, LORD.
MY SOUL IS AFFLICTED BY DOUBT.
JUST SHOW ME YOU'RE UP THERE...
SEND ME A SIGN, LORD.
ANYTHING...
SIGH...

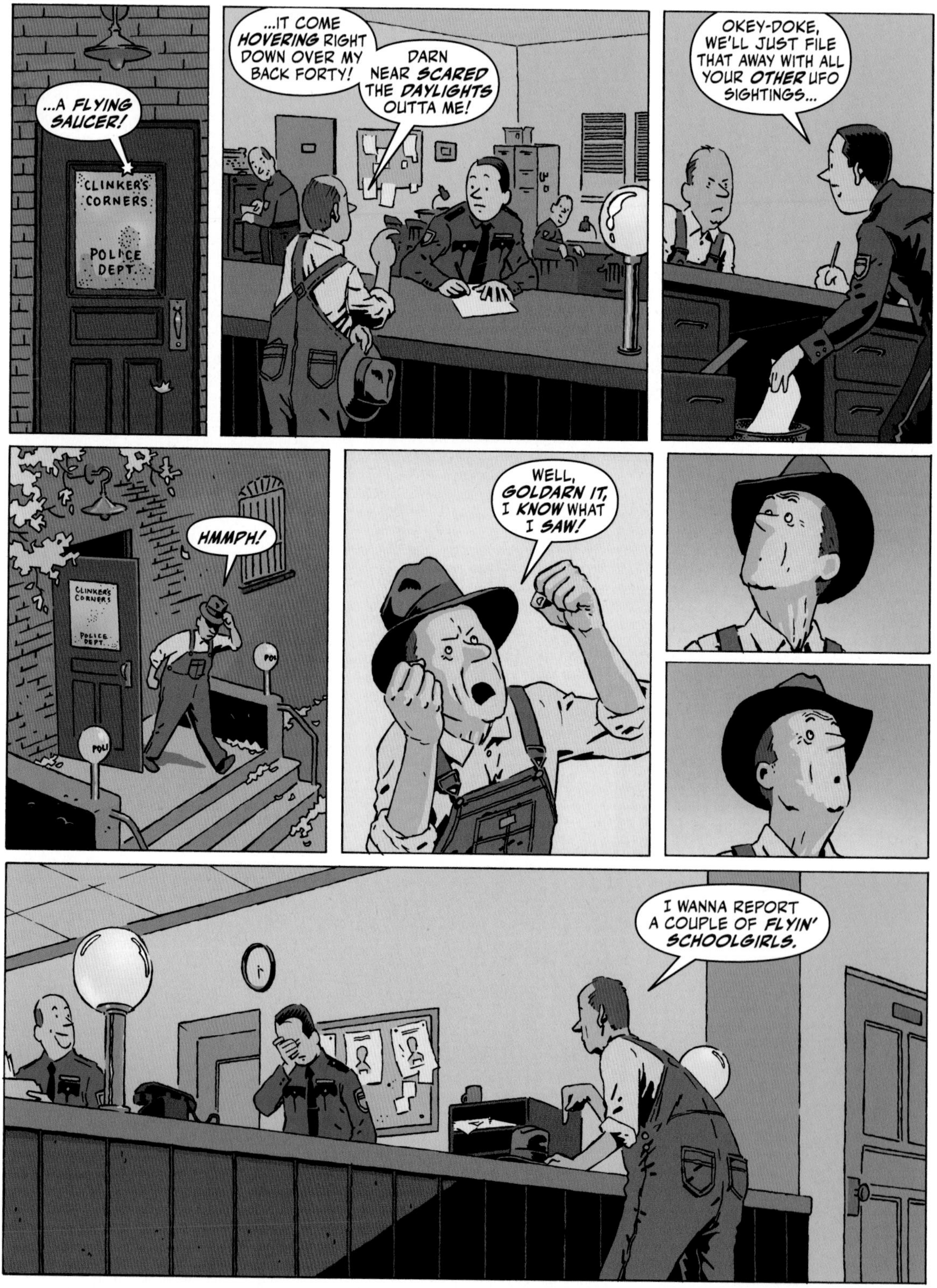
...A *FLYING SAUCER!*
CLINKER'S CORNERS POLICE DEPT.
...IT COME *HOVERING* RIGHT DOWN OVER MY BACK FORTY!
DARN NEAR *SCARED* THE *DAYLIGHTS* OUTTA ME!
OKEY-DOKE, WE'LL JUST FILE THAT AWAY WITH ALL YOUR *OTHER* UFO SIGHTINGS...
CLINKER'S CORNERS POLICE DEPT.
*HMMPH!*
WELL, *GOLDARN IT,* I *KNOW* WHAT I *SAW!*
I WANNA REPORT A COUPLE OF *FLYIN' SCHOOLGIRLS.*

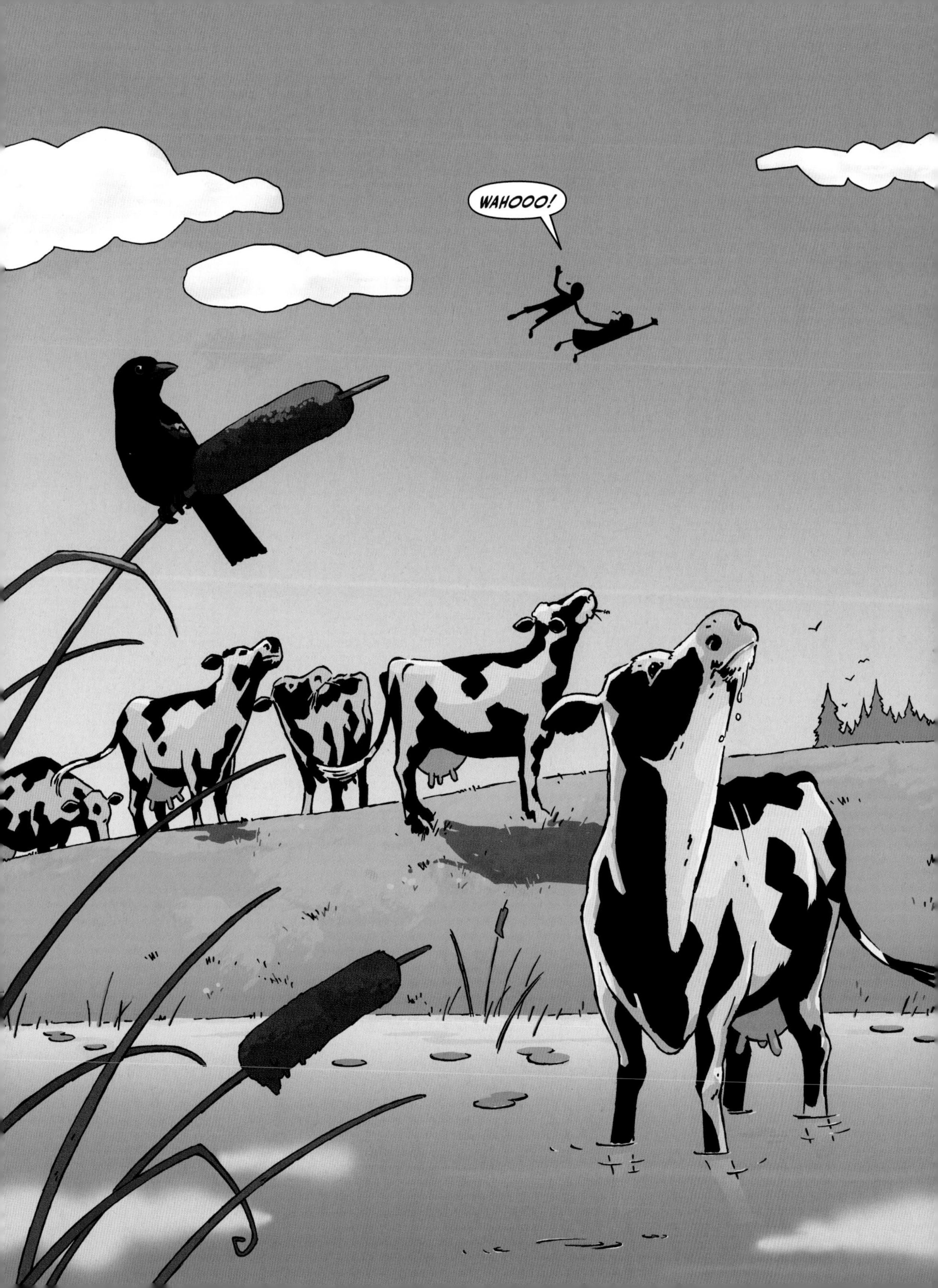
WAHOOO!

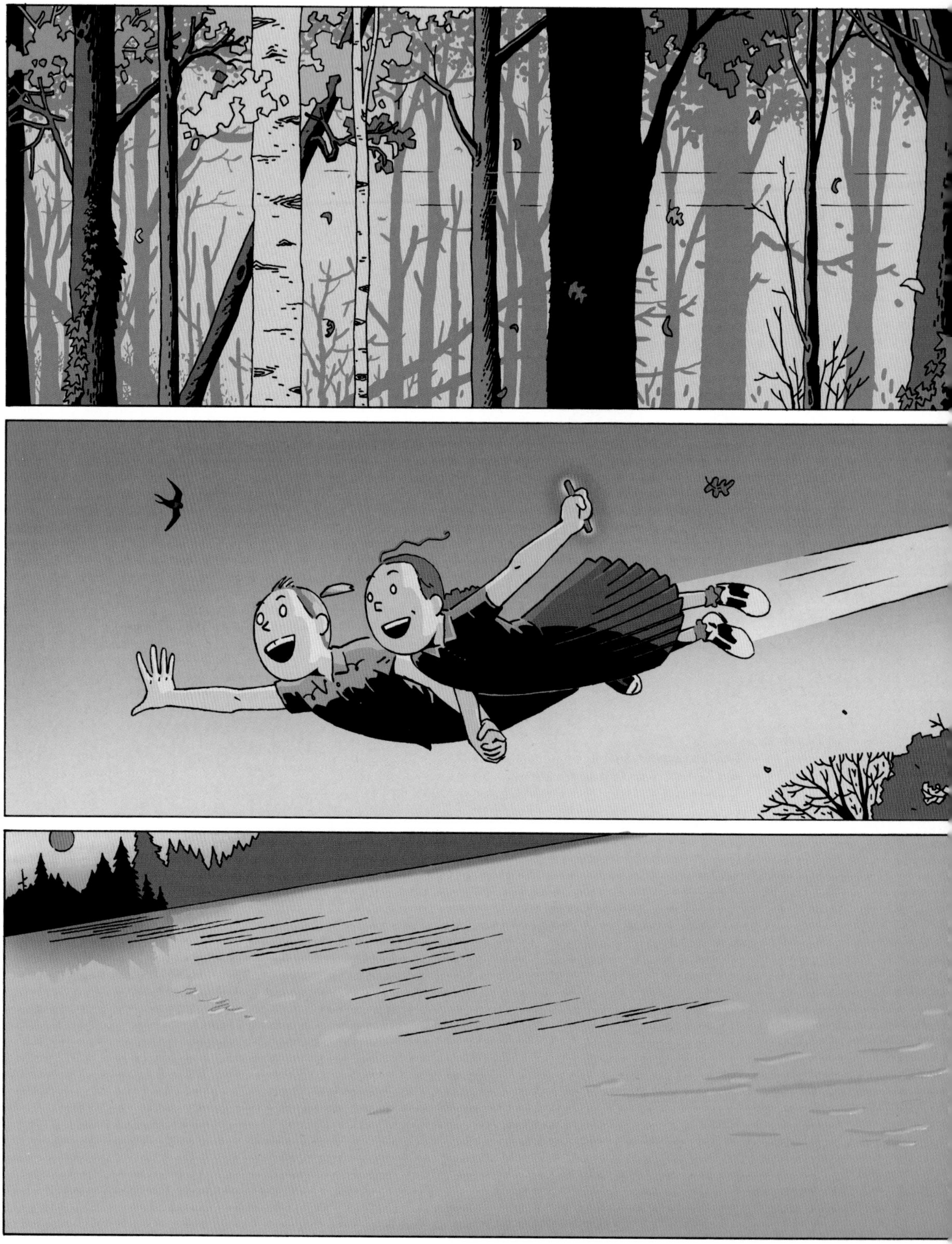

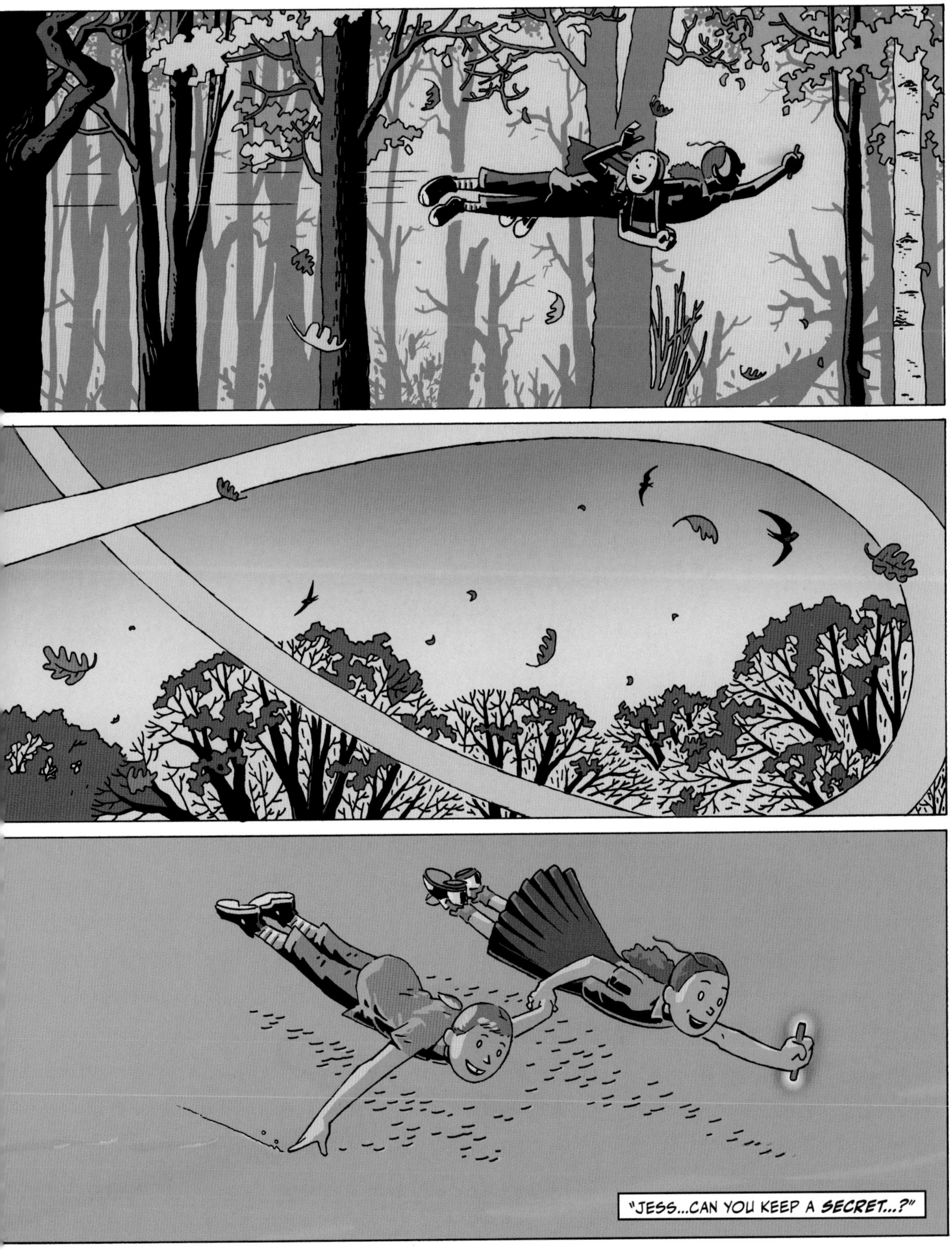
"JESS...CAN YOU KEEP A SECRET...?"

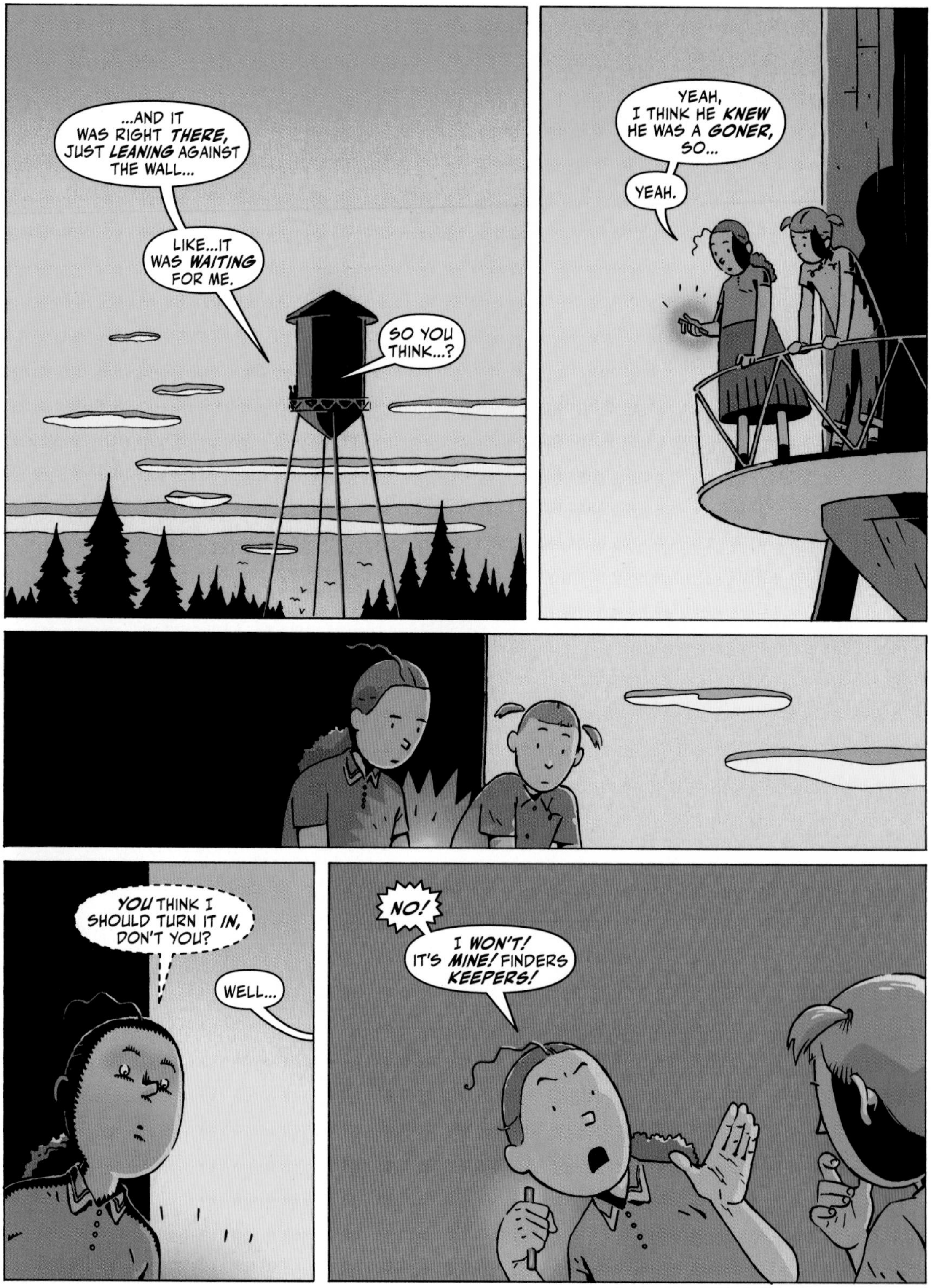
...AND IT WAS RIGHT THERE, JUST LEANING AGAINST THE WALL...
LIKE...IT WAS WAITING FOR ME.
SO YOU THINK...?
YEAH, I THINK HE KNEW HE WAS A GONER, SO...
YEAH.
YOU THINK I SHOULD TURN IT IN, DON'T YOU?
WELL...
NO!
I WON'T! IT'S MINE! FINDERS KEEPERS!

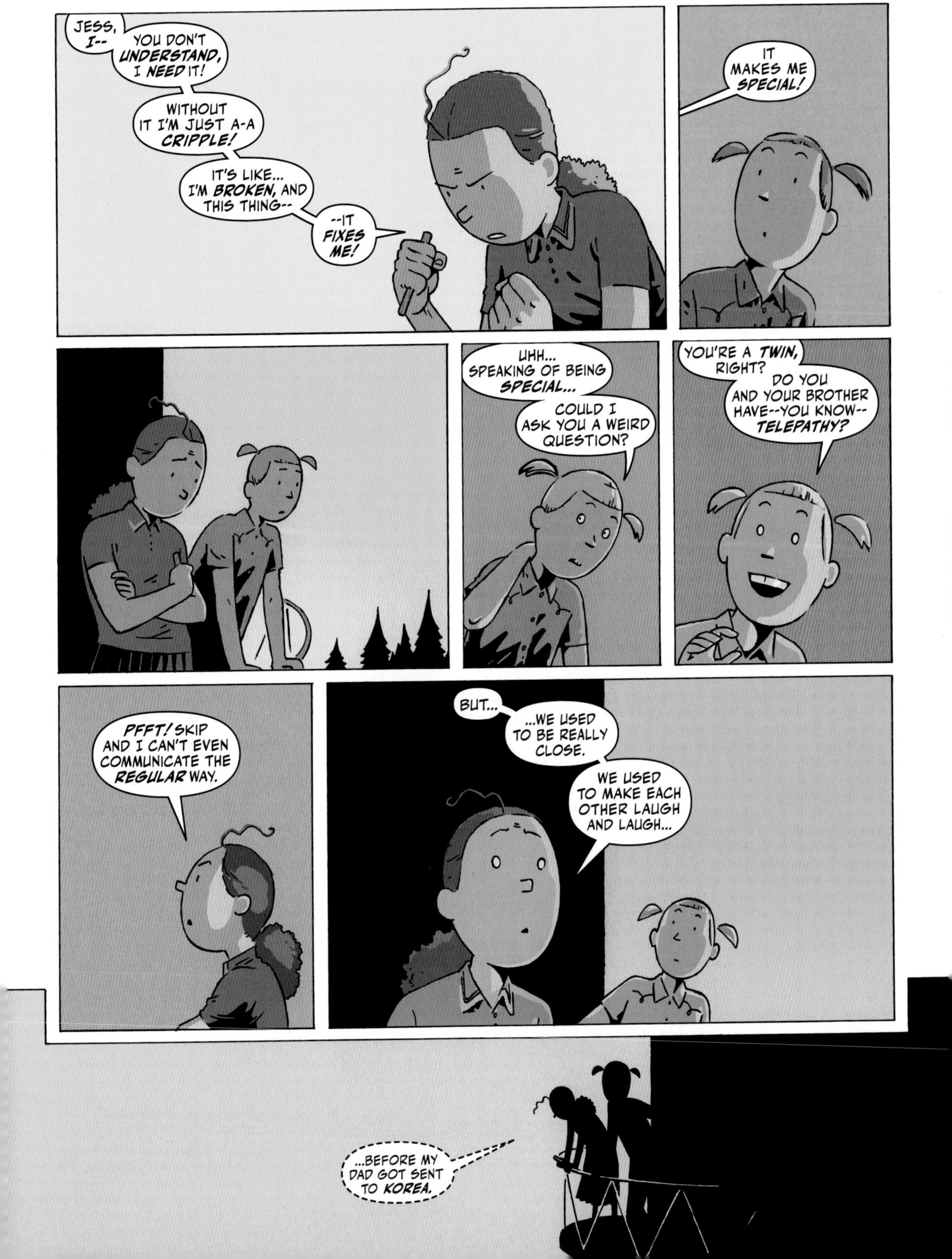
JESS, I--
YOU DON'T UNDERSTAND, I NEED IT!
WITHOUT IT I'M JUST A-A CRIPPLE!
IT'S LIKE... I'M BROKEN, AND THIS THING--
--IT FIXES ME!
IT MAKES ME SPECIAL!
UHH... SPEAKING OF BEING SPECIAL...
COULD I ASK YOU A WEIRD QUESTION?
YOU'RE A TWIN, RIGHT?
DO YOU AND YOUR BROTHER HAVE--YOU KNOW--TELEPATHY?
PFFT! SKIP AND I CAN'T EVEN COMMUNICATE THE REGULAR WAY.
BUT...
...WE USED TO BE REALLY CLOSE.
WE USED TO MAKE EACH OTHER LAUGH AND LAUGH...
...BEFORE MY DAD GOT SENT TO KOREA.

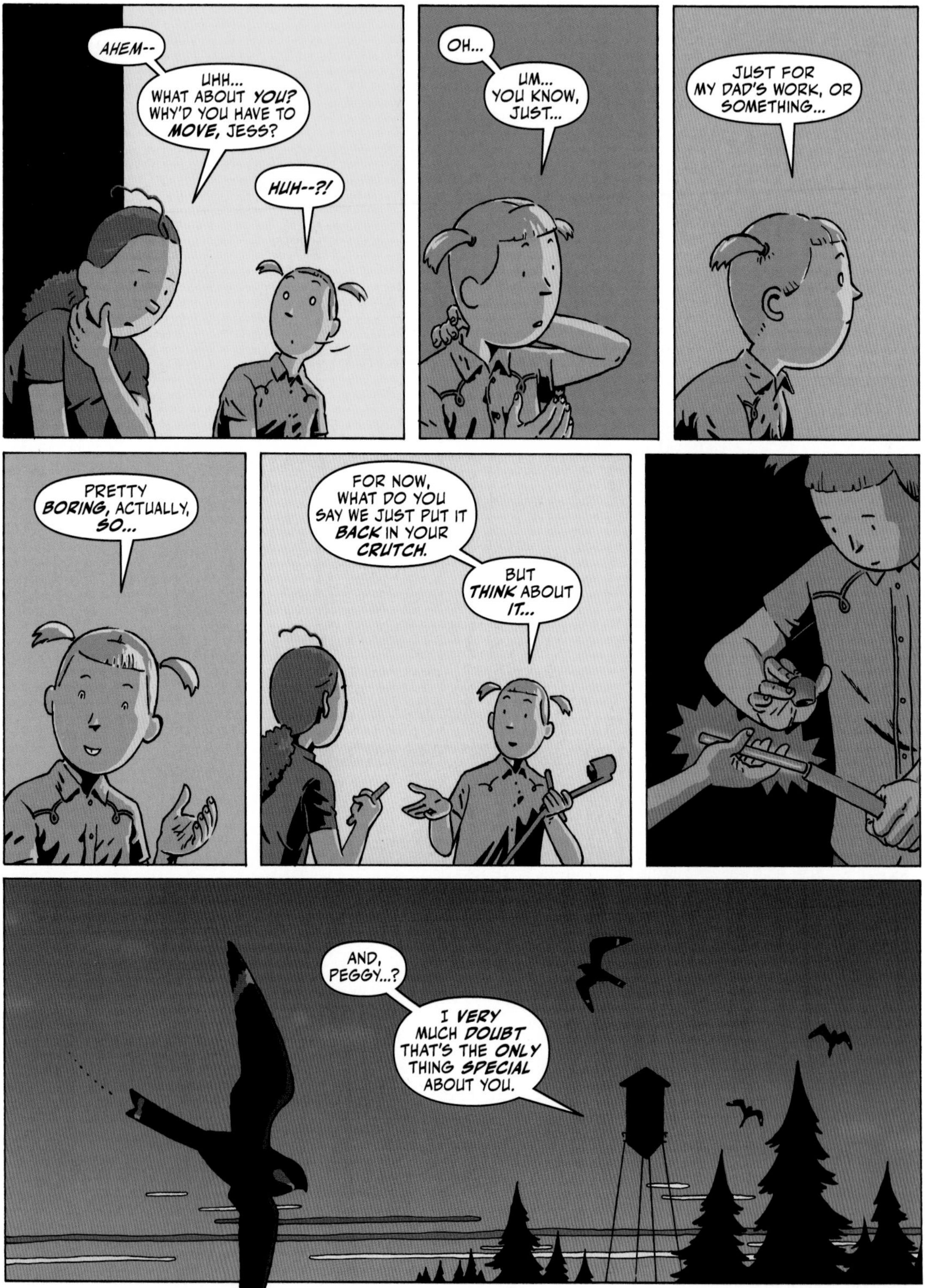
AHEM--
UHH... WHAT ABOUT YOU? WHY'D YOU HAVE TO MOVE, JESS?
HUH--?!
OH...
UM... YOU KNOW, JUST...
JUST FOR MY DAD'S WORK, OR SOMETHING...
PRETTY BORING, ACTUALLY, SO...
FOR NOW, WHAT DO YOU SAY WE JUST PUT IT BACK IN YOUR CRUTCH.
BUT THINK ABOUT IT...
AND, PEGGY...?
I VERY MUCH DOUBT THAT'S THE ONLY THING SPECIAL ABOUT YOU.

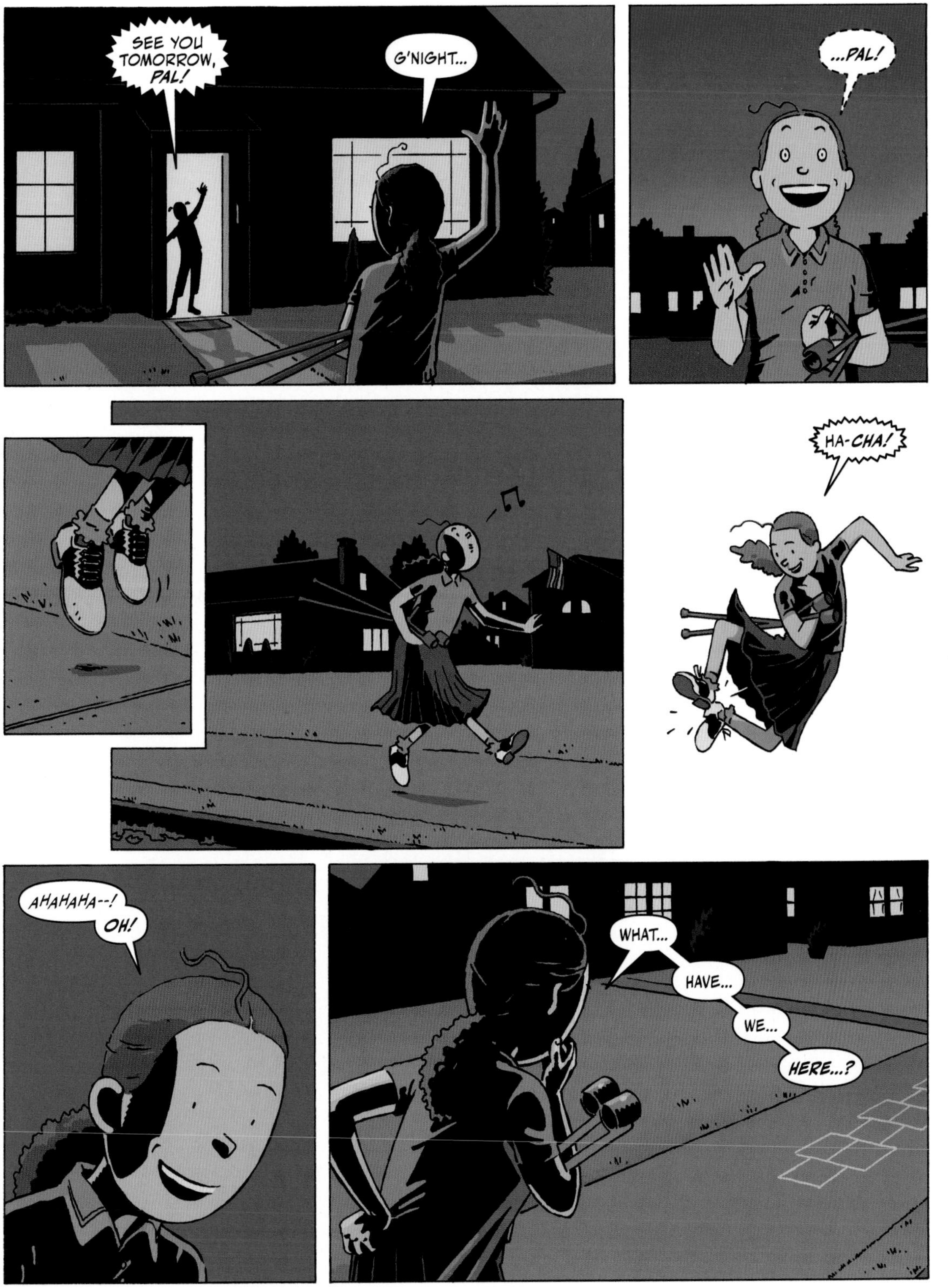
SEE YOU TOMORROW, PAL!
G'NIGHT...
...PAL!
HA-CHA!
AHAHAHA--! OH!
WHAT...
HAVE...
WE...
HERE...?

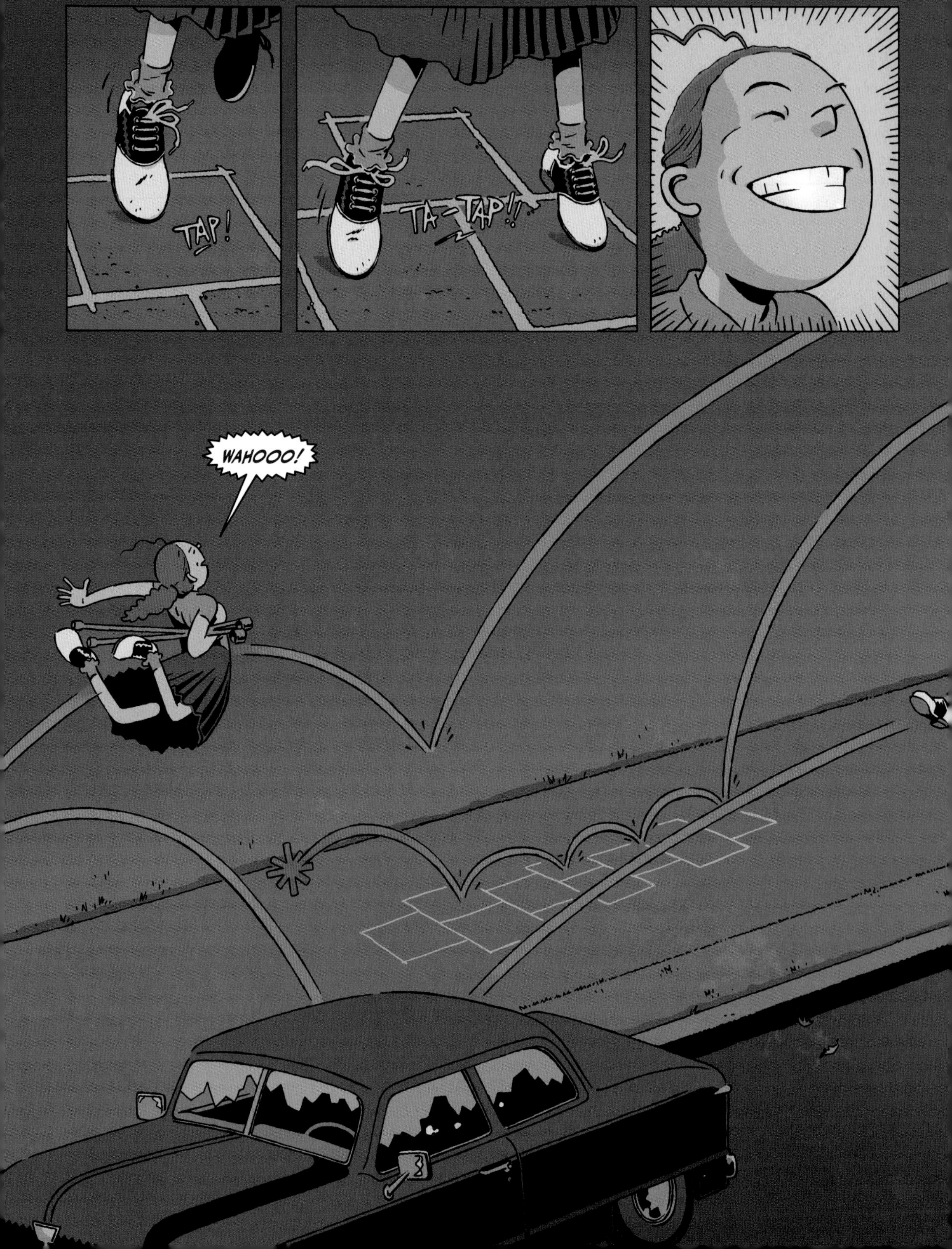
TAP!
TA-TAP!!
WAHOOO!

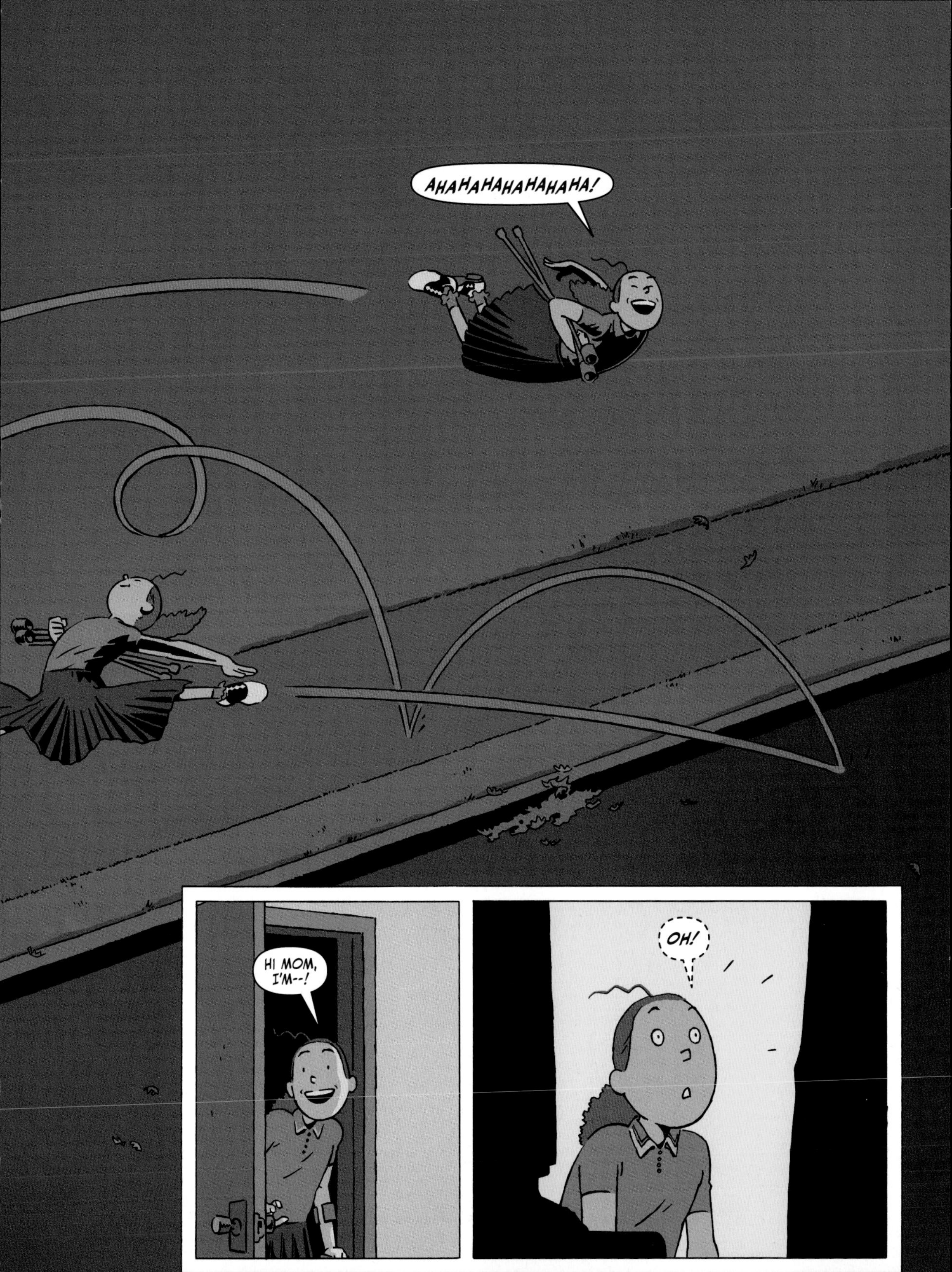
AHAHAHAHAHAHAHA!
HI MOM, I'M--!
OH!

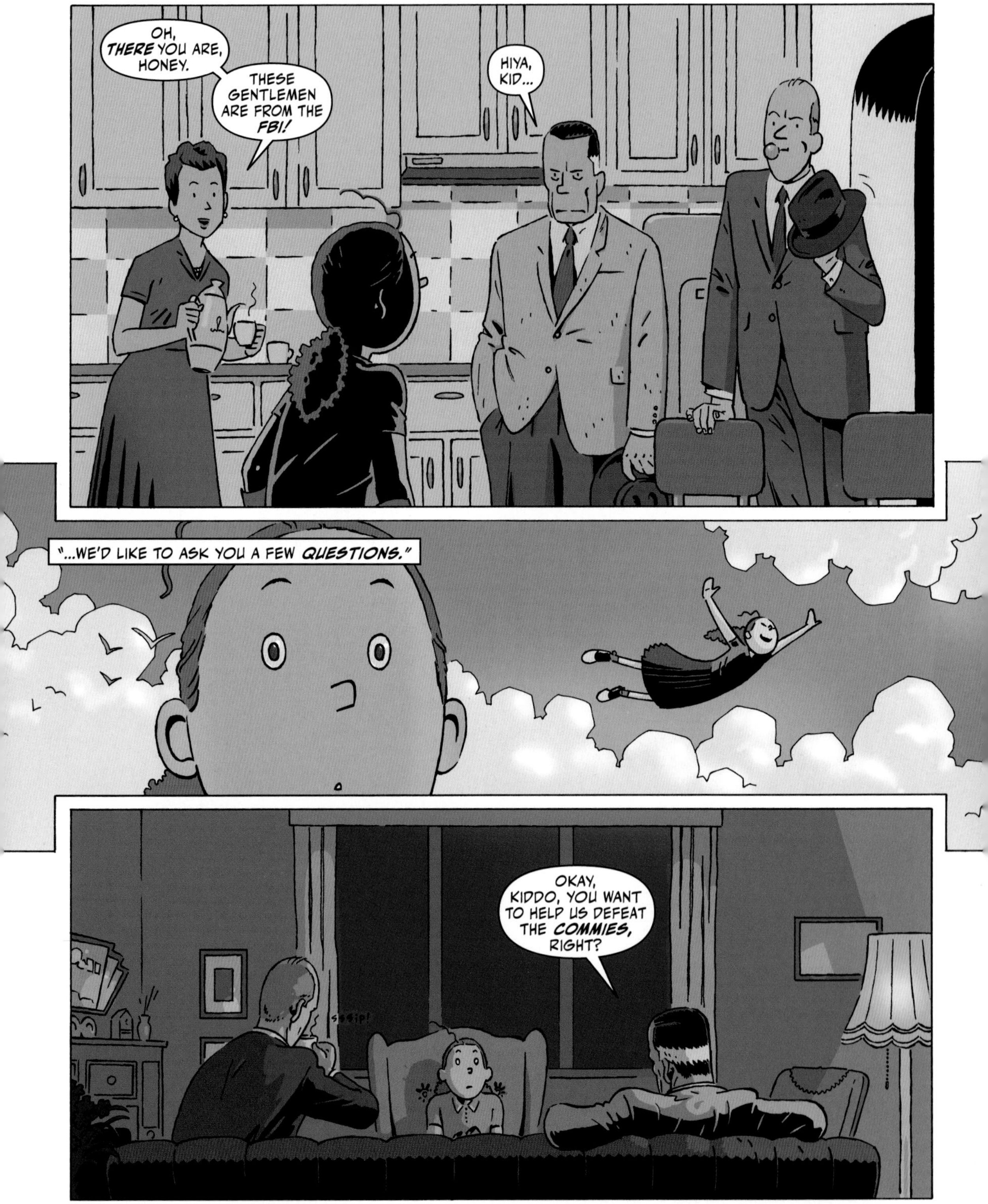
OH, THERE YOU ARE, HONEY.
THESE GENTLEMEN ARE FROM THE FBI!
HIYA, KID...
"...WE'D LIKE TO ASK YOU A FEW QUESTIONS."
SSSIP!
OKAY, KIDDO, YOU WANT TO HELP US DEFEAT THE COMMIES, RIGHT?

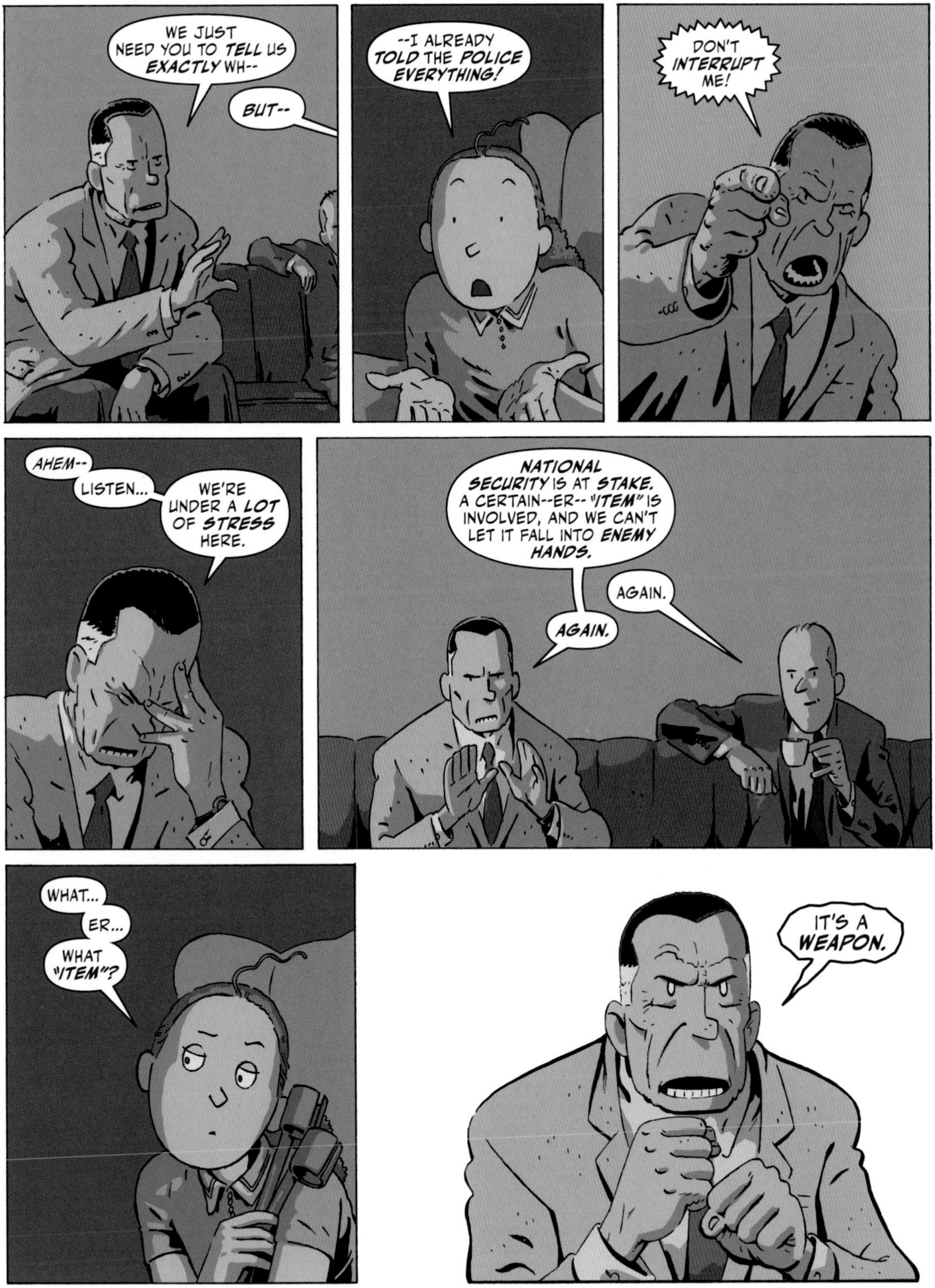
WE JUST NEED YOU TO TELL US EXACTLY WH--
BUT--
--I ALREADY TOLD THE POLICE EVERYTHING!
DON'T INTERRUPT ME!
AHEM--
LISTEN...
WE'RE UNDER A LOT OF STRESS HERE.
NATIONAL SECURITY IS AT STAKE. A CERTAIN--ER-- "ITEM" IS INVOLVED, AND WE CAN'T LET IT FALL INTO ENEMY HANDS.
AGAIN.
AGAIN.
WHAT...
ER...
WHAT "ITEM"?
IT'S A WEAPON.

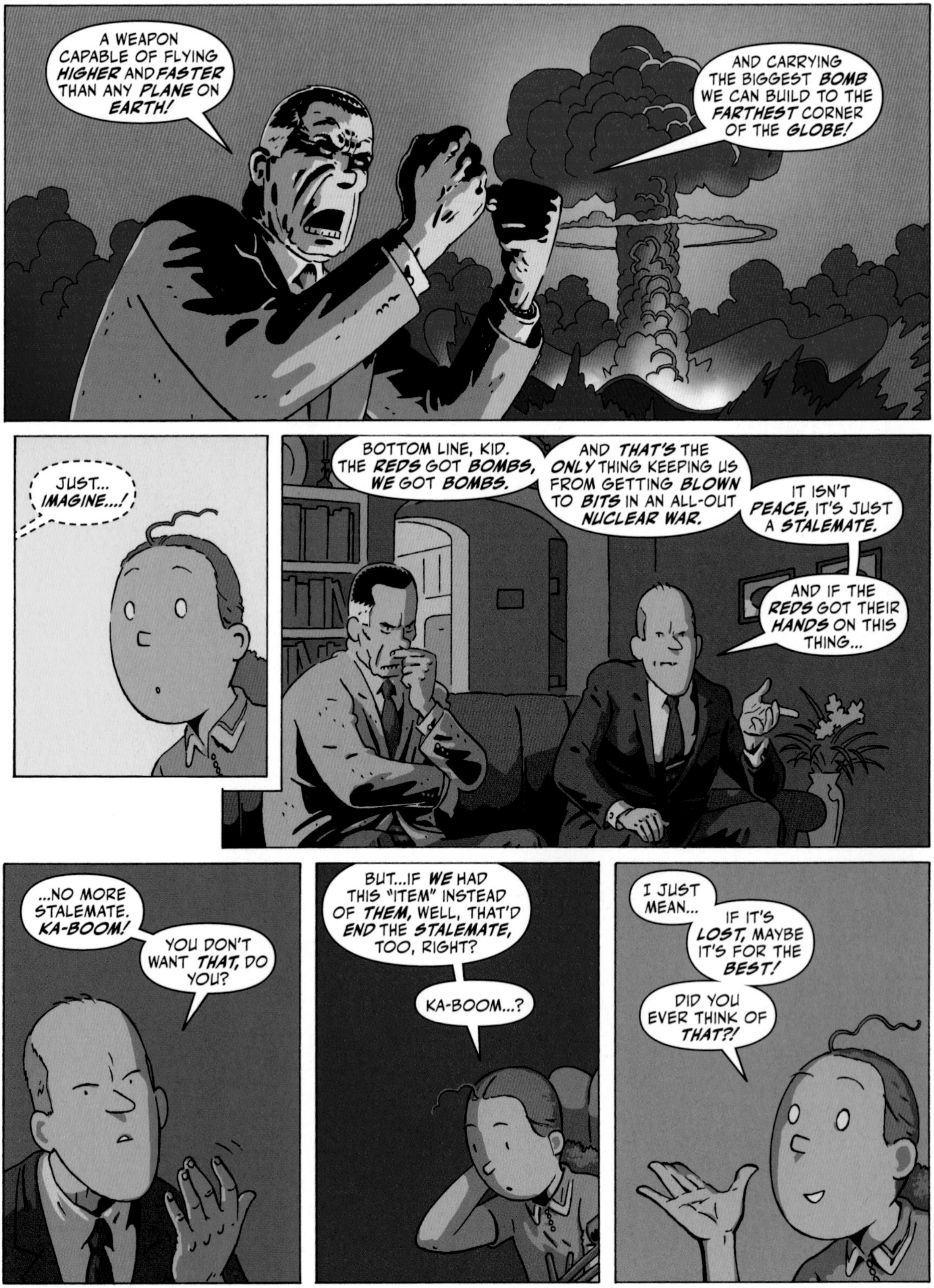
A WEAPON CAPABLE OF FLYING HIGHER AND FASTER THAN ANY PLANE ON EARTH!
AND CARRYING THE BIGGEST BOMB WE CAN BUILD TO THE FARTHEST CORNER OF THE GLOBE!
JUST... IMAGINE...!
BOTTOM LINE, KID. THE REDS GOT BOMBS, WE GOT BOMBS.
AND THAT'S THE ONLY THING KEEPING US FROM GETTING BLOWN TO BITS IN AN ALL-OUT NUCLEAR WAR.
IT ISN'T PEACE, IT'S JUST A STALEMATE.
AND IF THE REDS GOT THEIR HANDS ON THIS THING...
...NO MORE STALEMATE. KA-BOOM!
YOU DON'T WANT THAT, DO YOU?
BUT...IF WE HAD THIS "ITEM" INSTEAD OF THEM, WELL, THAT'D END THE STALEMATE, TOO, RIGHT?
KA-BOOM...?
I JUST MEAN...
IF IT'S LOST, MAYBE IT'S FOR THE BEST!
DID YOU EVER THINK OF THAT?!

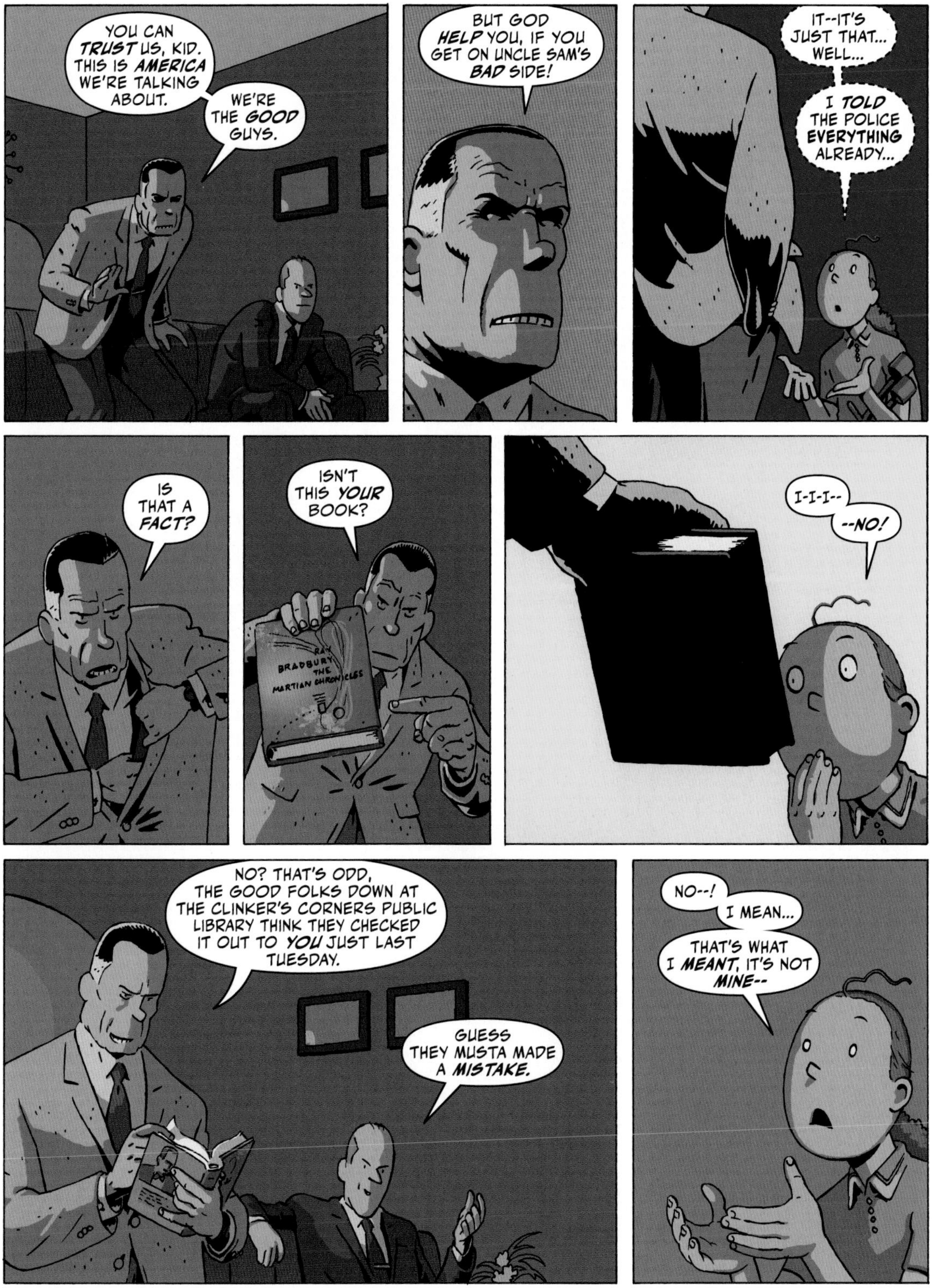
YOU CAN TRUST US, KID. THIS IS AMERICA WE'RE TALKING ABOUT.
WE'RE THE GOOD GUYS.
BUT GOD HELP YOU, IF YOU GET ON UNCLE SAM'S BAD SIDE!
IT--IT'S JUST THAT... WELL...
I TOLD THE POLICE EVERYTHING ALREADY...
IS THAT A FACT?
ISN'T THIS YOUR BOOK?
RAY BRADBURY THE MARTIAN CHRONICLES
I-I-I--
--NO!
NO? THAT'S ODD, THE GOOD FOLKS DOWN AT THE CLINKER'S CORNERS PUBLIC LIBRARY THINK THEY CHECKED IT OUT TO YOU JUST LAST TUESDAY.
GUESS THEY MUSTA MADE A MISTAKE.
NO--!
I MEAN...
THAT'S WHAT I MEANT, IT'S NOT MINE--

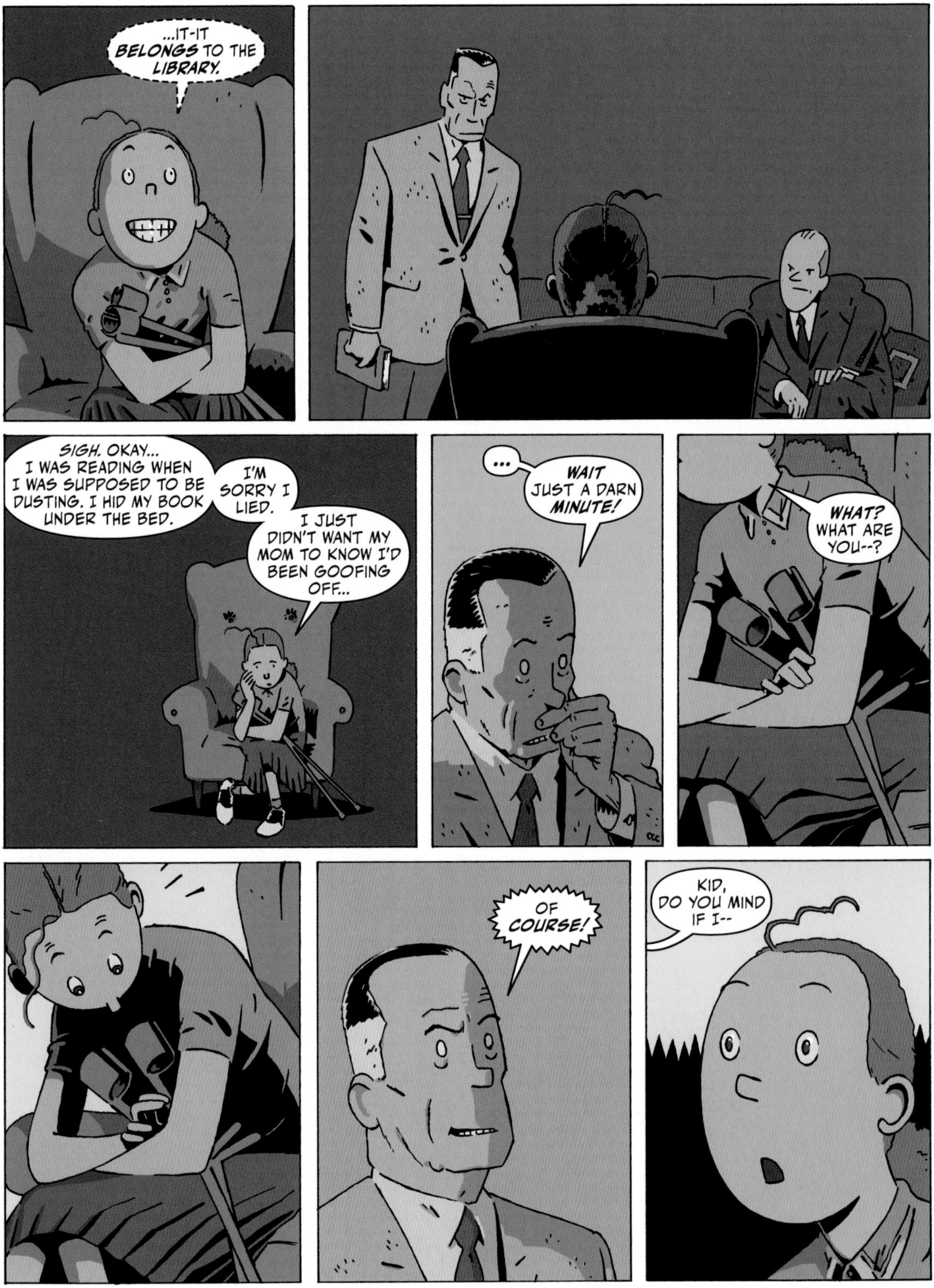

...IT-IT BELONGS TO THE LIBRARY.
SIGH. OKAY... I WAS READING WHEN I WAS SUPPOSED TO BE DUSTING. I HID MY BOOK UNDER THE BED.
I'M SORRY I LIED.
I JUST DIDN'T WANT MY MOM TO KNOW I'D BEEN GOOFING OFF...
...
WAIT JUST A DARN MINUTE!
WHAT? WHAT ARE YOU--?
OF COURSE!
KID, DO YOU MIND IF I--

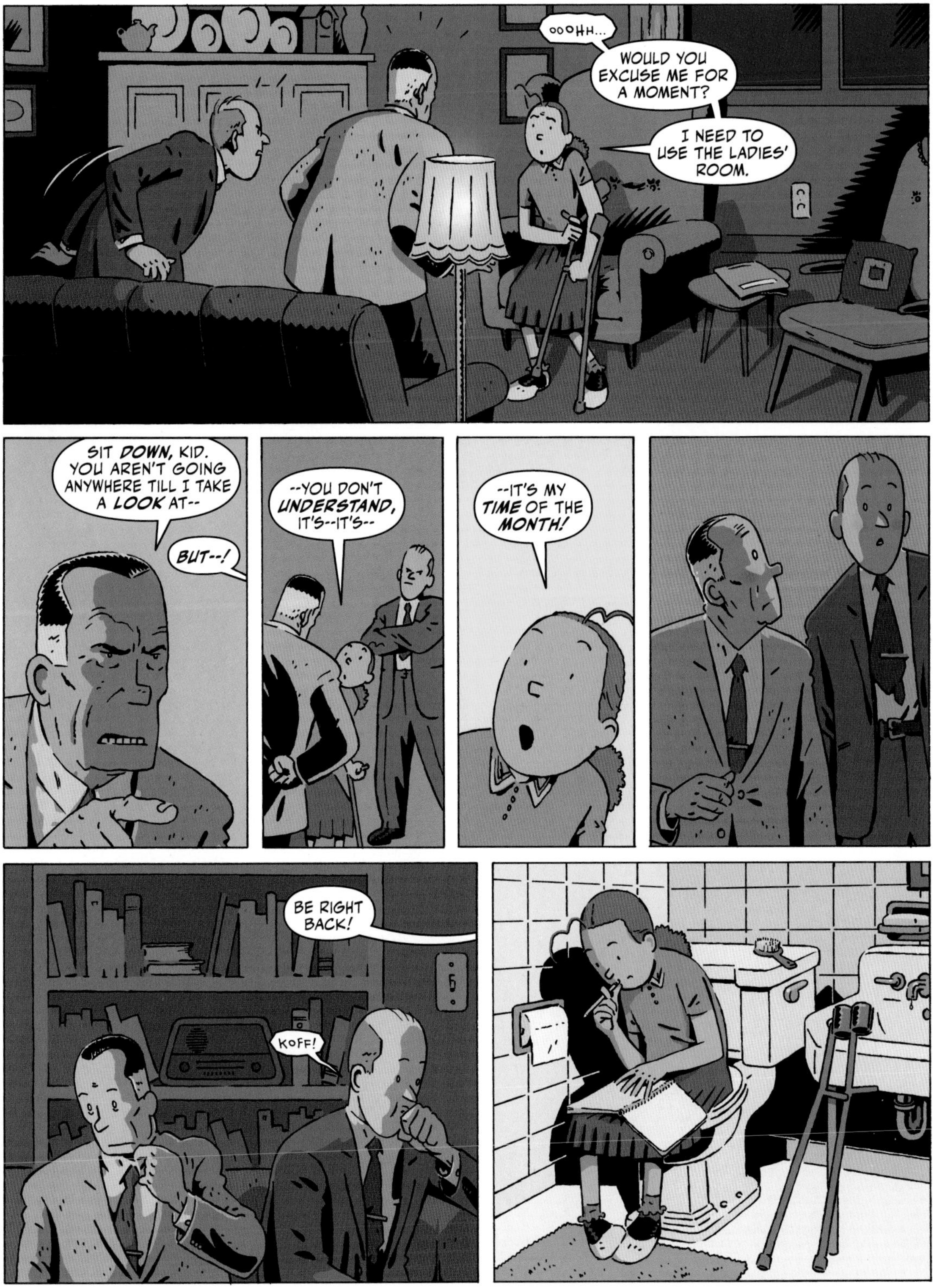
OOOHH...
WOULD YOU EXCUSE ME FOR A MOMENT?
I NEED TO USE THE LADIES' ROOM.
SIT DOWN, KID. YOU AREN'T GOING ANYWHERE TILL I TAKE A LOOK AT--
BUT--!
--YOU DON'T UNDERSTAND, IT'S--IT'S--
--IT'S MY TIME OF THE MONTH!
BE RIGHT BACK!
KOFF!

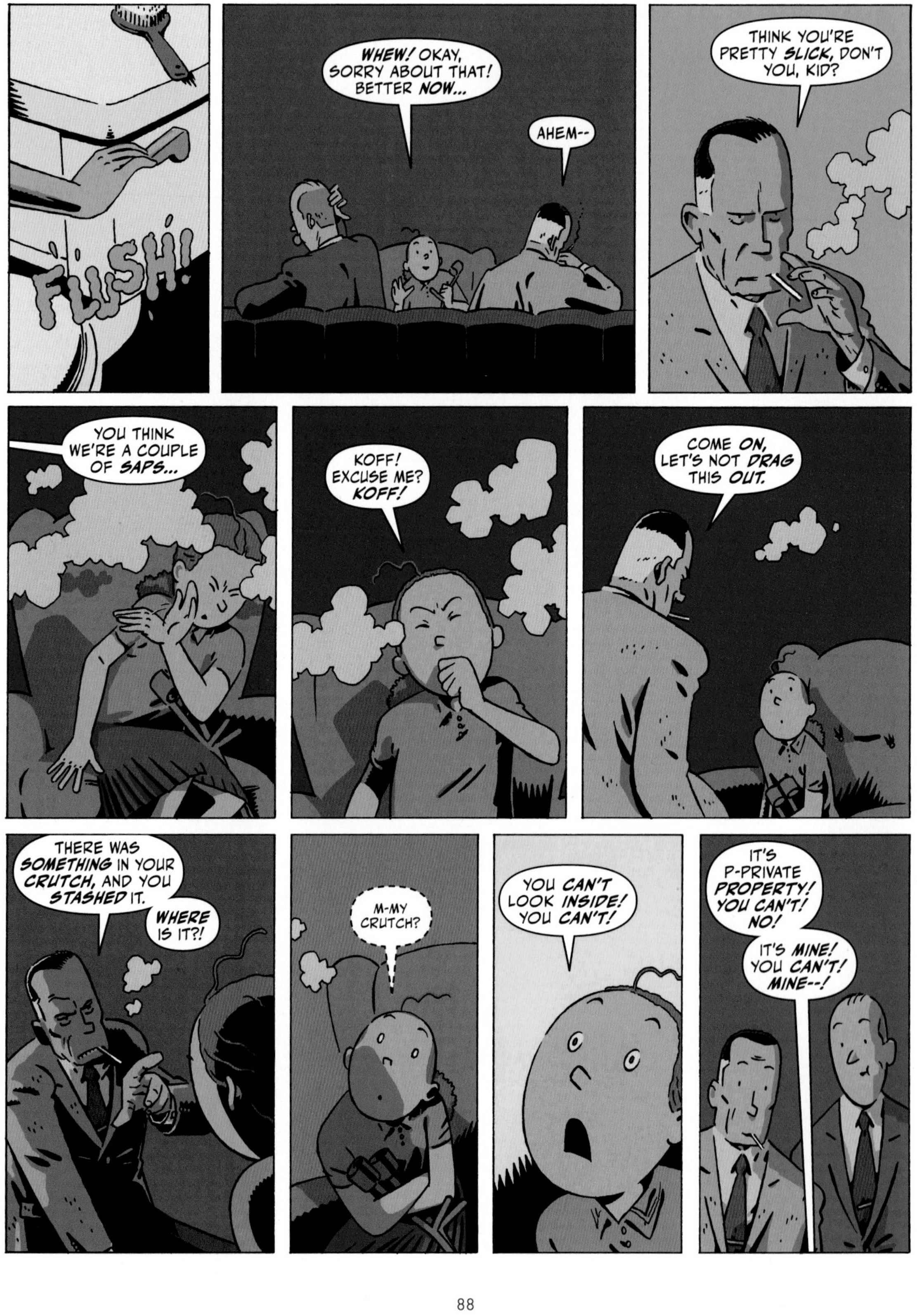
FLUSH!
WHEW! OKAY, SORRY ABOUT THAT! BETTER NOW...
AHEM--
THINK YOU'RE PRETTY SLICK, DON'T YOU, KID?
YOU THINK WE'RE A COUPLE OF SAPS...
KOFF! EXCUSE ME? KOFF!
COME ON, LET'S NOT DRAG THIS OUT.
THERE WAS SOMETHING IN YOUR CRUTCH, AND YOU STASHED IT.
WHERE IS IT?!
M-MY CRUTCH?
YOU CAN'T LOOK INSIDE! YOU CAN'T!
IT'S P-PRIVATE PROPERTY! YOU CAN'T! NO!
IT'S MINE! YOU CAN'T! MINE--!

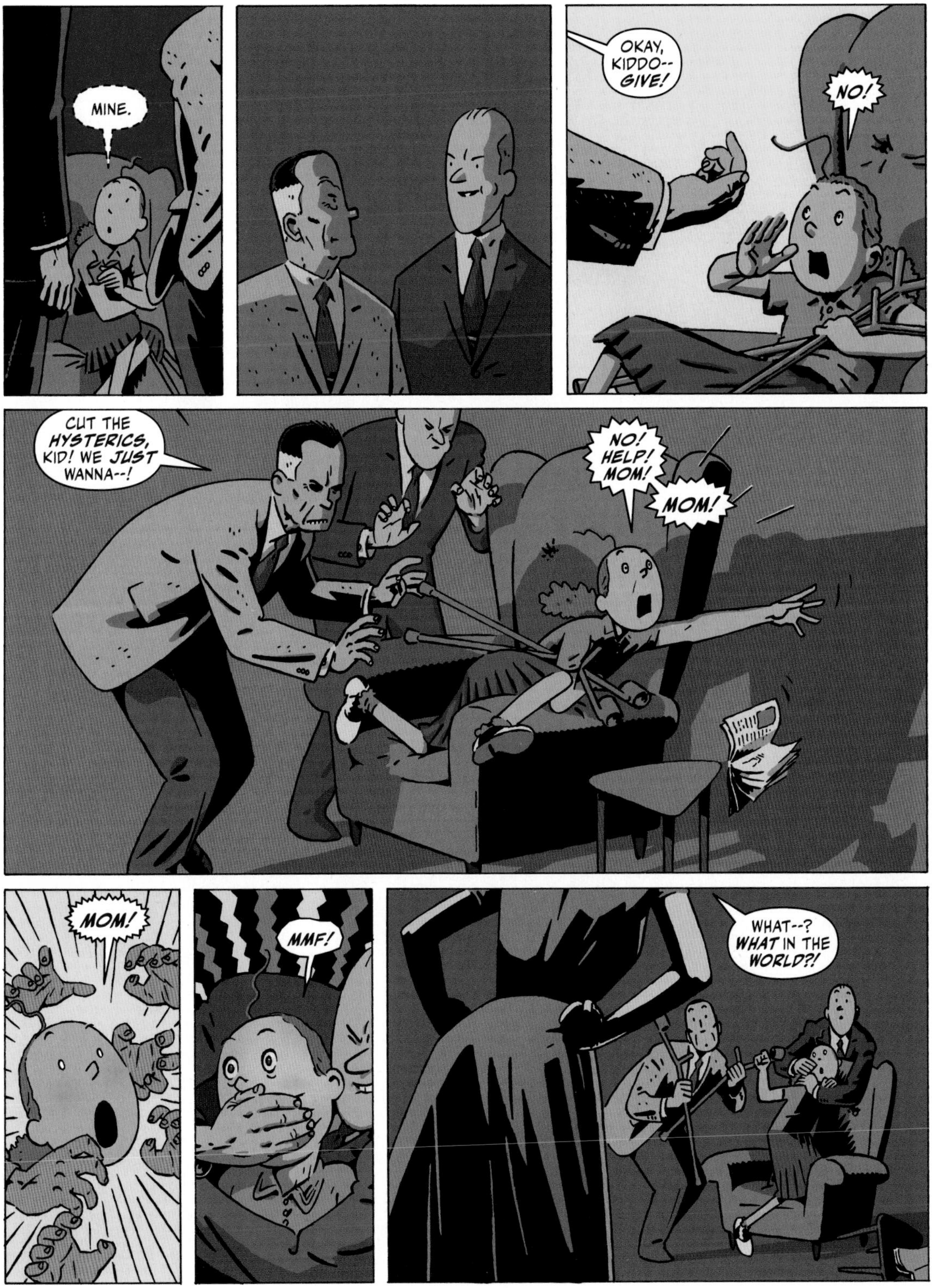
MINE.
OKAY, KIDDO-- GIVE!
NO!
CUT THE HYSTERICS, KID! WE JUST WANNA--!
NO! HELP! MOM!
MOM!
MOM!
MMF!
WHAT--? WHAT IN THE WORLD?!

ER... MA'AM, IF YOU'LL JUST LET US *EXPLAIN*...

DON'T *LISTEN* TO THEM, MOM! THEY--!

PEGGY, IT'S THESE MEN'S *JOB* TO KEEP US SAFE...

SO QUIT BEING *PIGHEADED* AND *COOPERATE!*

THANK YOU *VERY* MUCH...

BUT, *MOM*...!

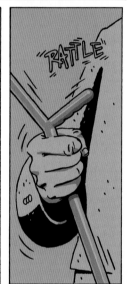

RATTLE

WELL, WELL, WELL, WELL...

POP!

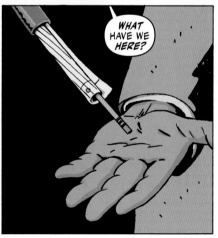

WHAT HAVE WE HERE?

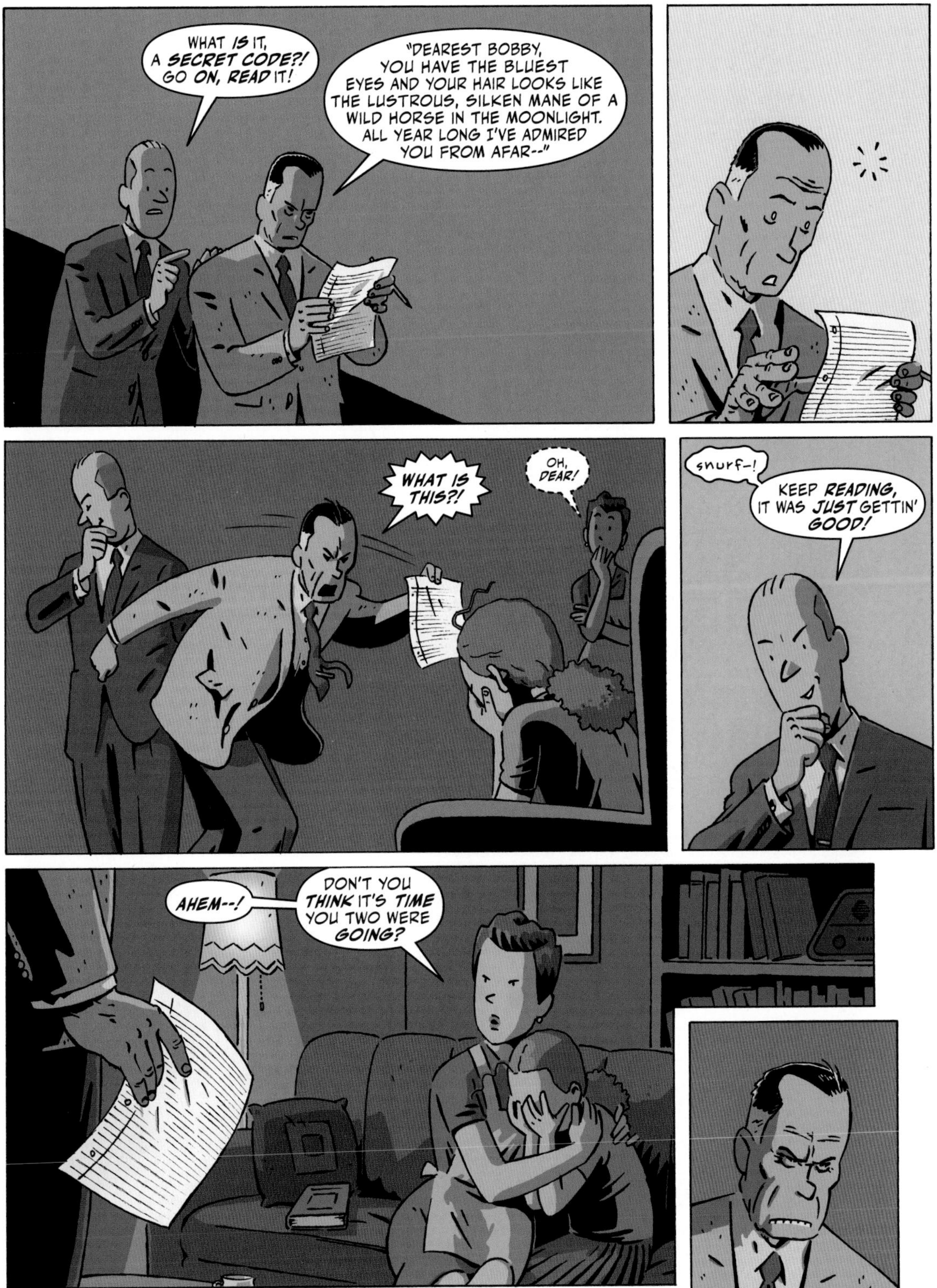
WHAT IS IT, A SECRET CODE?! GO ON, READ IT!
"DEAREST BOBBY, YOU HAVE THE BLUEST EYES AND YOUR HAIR LOOKS LIKE THE LUSTROUS, SILKEN MANE OF A WILD HORSE IN THE MOONLIGHT. ALL YEAR LONG I'VE ADMIRED YOU FROM AFAR--"
WHAT IS THIS?!
OH, DEAR!
snurf-!
KEEP READING, IT WAS JUST GETTIN' GOOD!
AHEM--!
DON'T YOU THINK IT'S TIME YOU TWO WERE GOING?

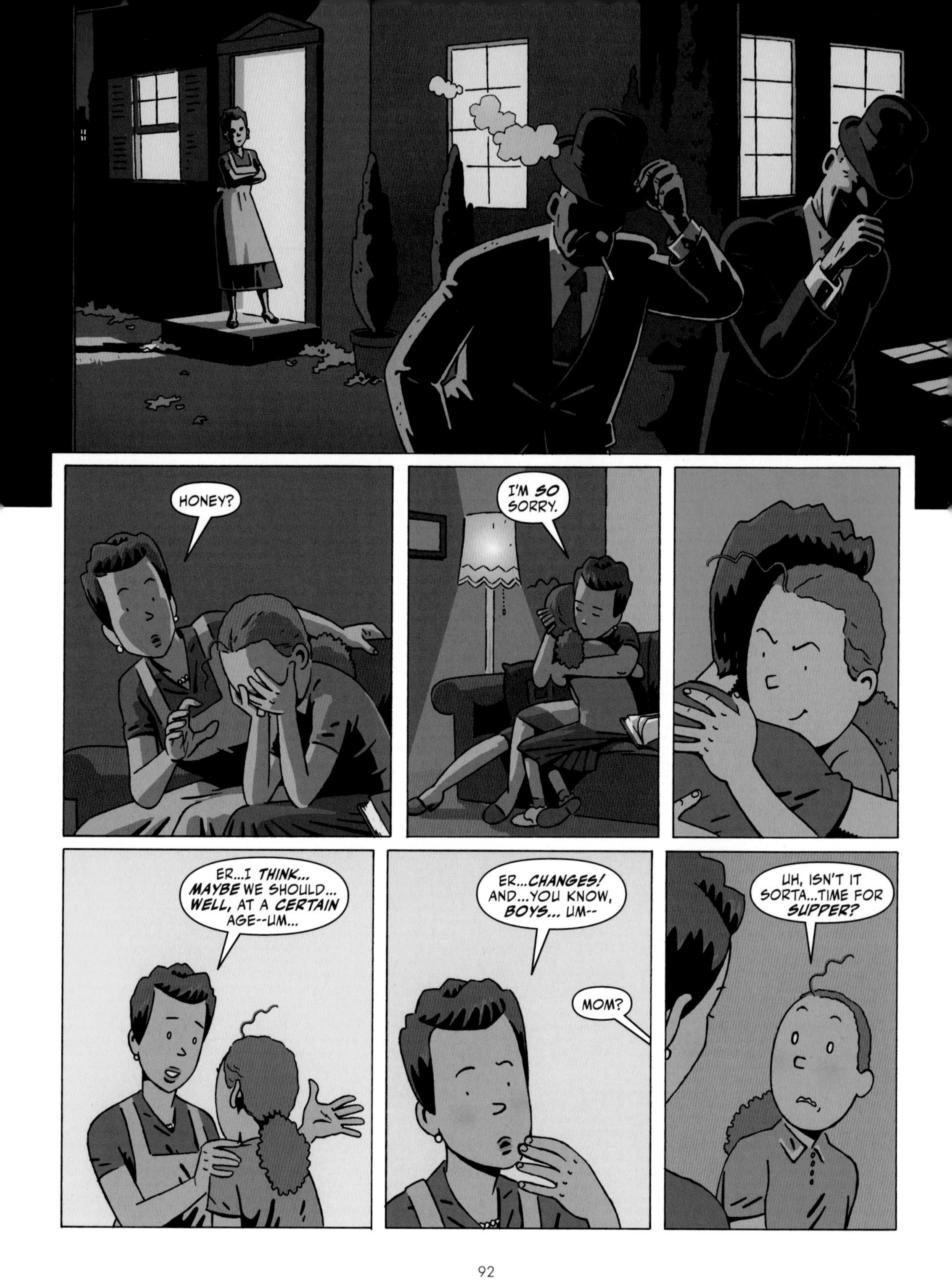
HONEY?
I'M SO SORRY.
ER...I THINK... MAYBE WE SHOULD... WELL, AT A CERTAIN AGE--UM...
ER...CHANGES! AND...YOU KNOW, BOYS... UM--
MOM?
UH, ISN'T IT SORTA...TIME FOR SUPPER?

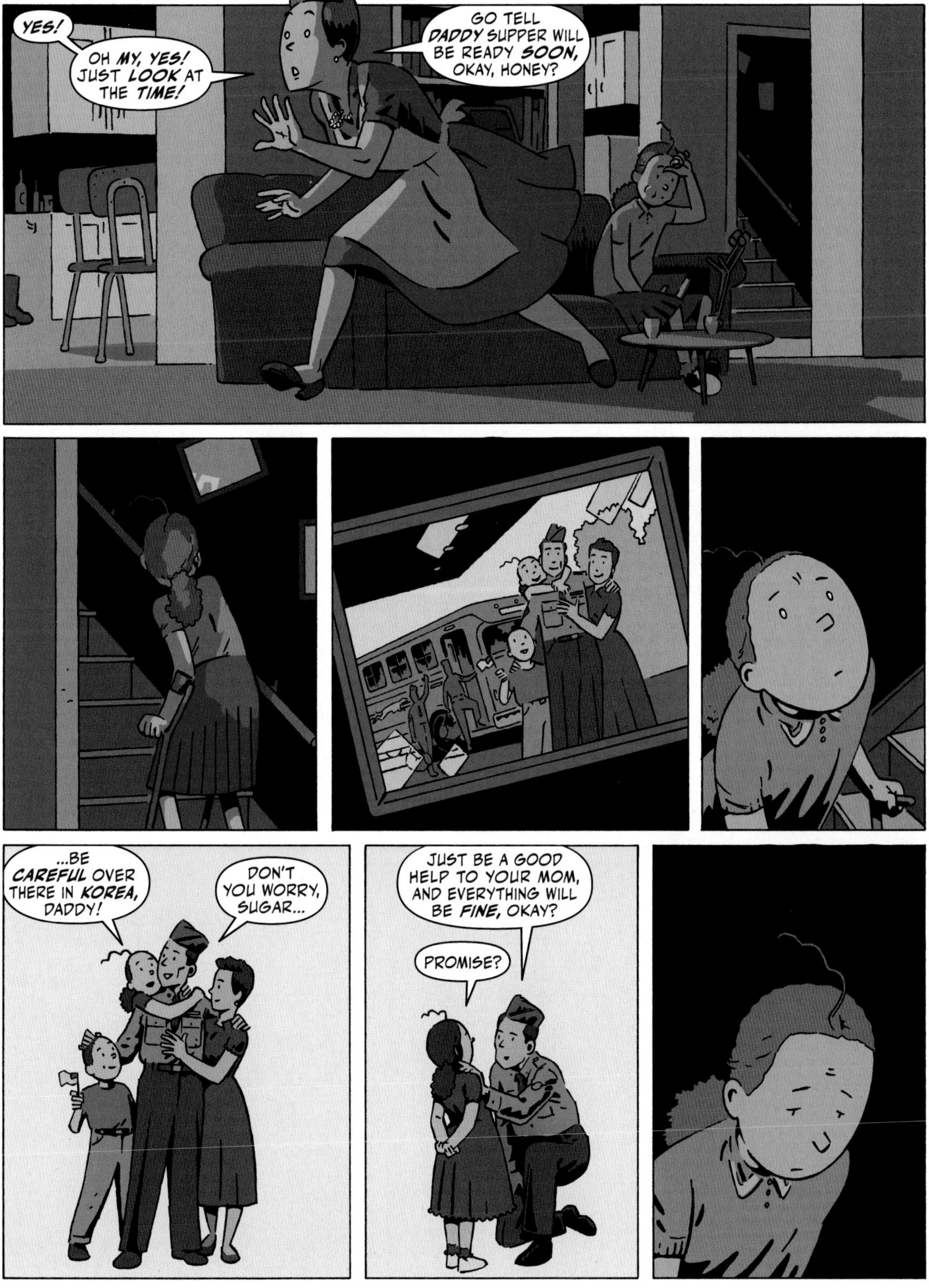
YES!
OH MY, YES! JUST LOOK AT THE TIME!
GO TELL DADDY SUPPER WILL BE READY SOON, OKAY, HONEY?
...BE CAREFUL OVER THERE IN KOREA, DADDY!
DON'T YOU WORRY, SUGAR...
JUST BE A GOOD HELP TO YOUR MOM, AND EVERYTHING WILL BE FINE, OKAY?
PROMISE?

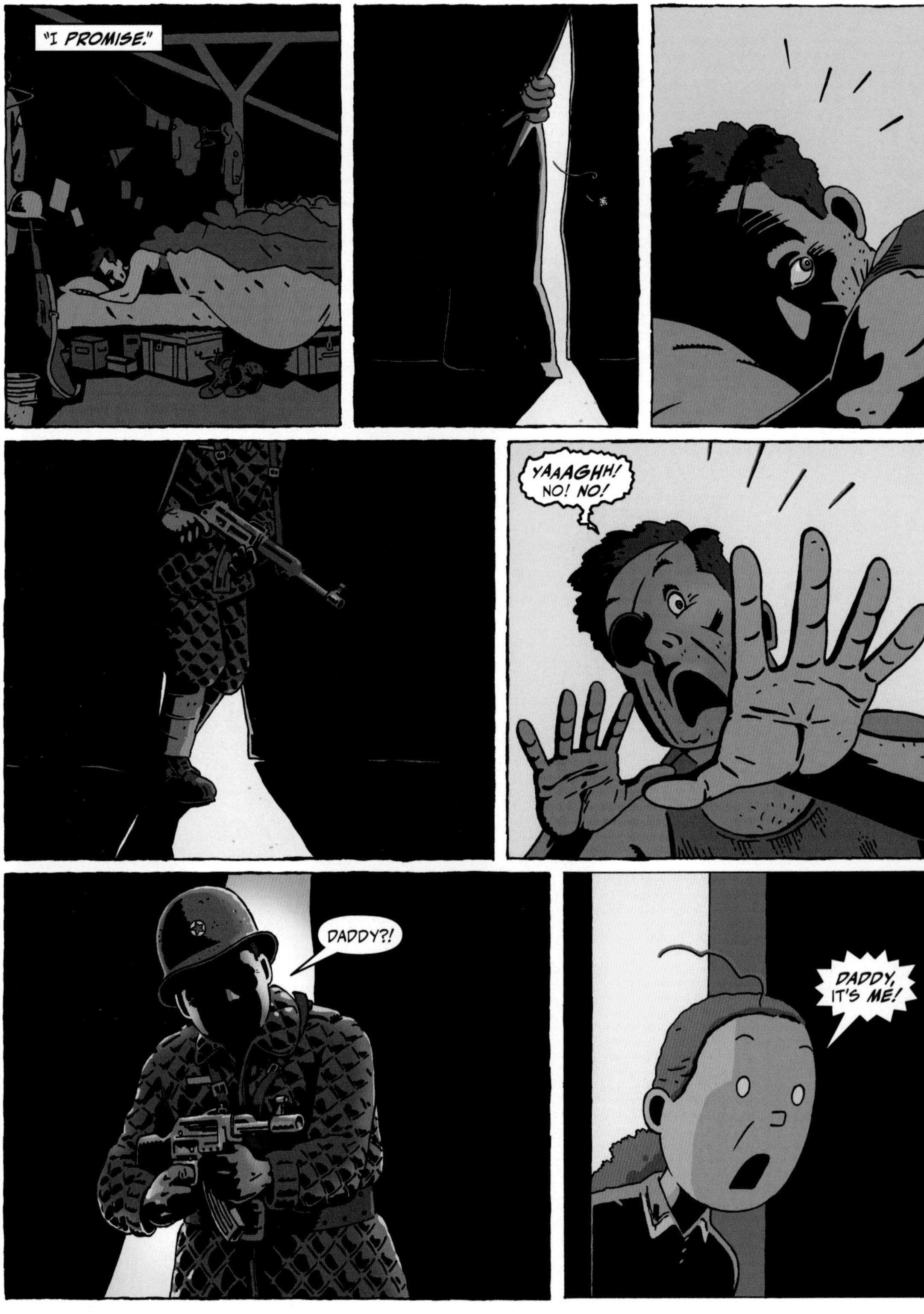
"I PROMISE."
YAAAGHH! NO! NO!
DADDY?!
DADDY, IT'S ME!

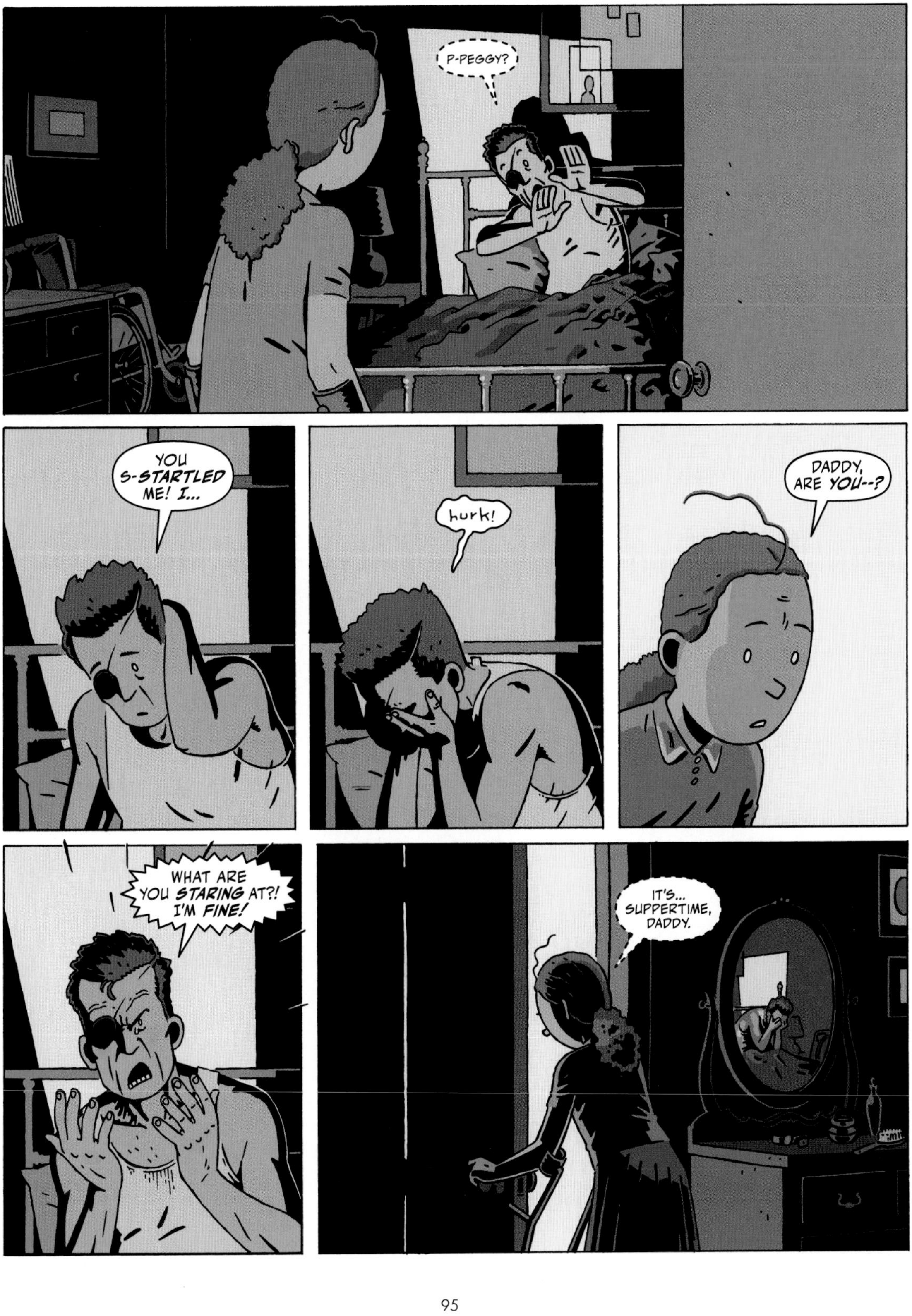
P-PEGGY?
YOU S-STARTLED ME! I...
hurk!
DADDY, ARE YOU--?
WHAT ARE YOU STARING AT?! I'M FINE!
IT'S... SUPPERTIME, DADDY.

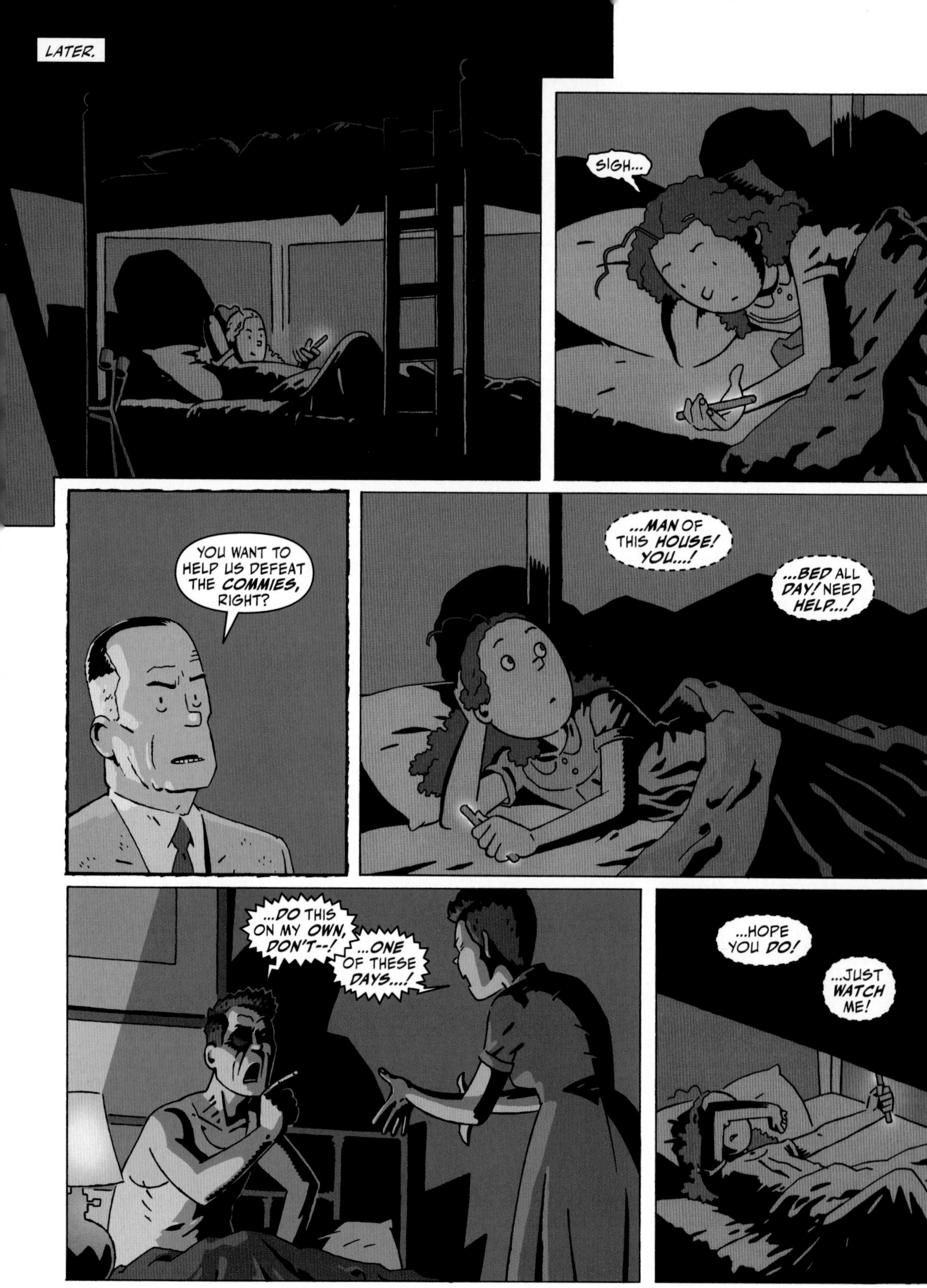
LATER.
SIGH...
YOU WANT TO HELP US DEFEAT THE COMMIES, RIGHT?
...MAN OF THIS HOUSE! YOU...!
...BED ALL DAY! NEED HELP...!
...DO THIS ON MY OWN, DON'T--!
...ONE OF THESE DAYS...!
...HOPE YOU DO!
...JUST WATCH ME!

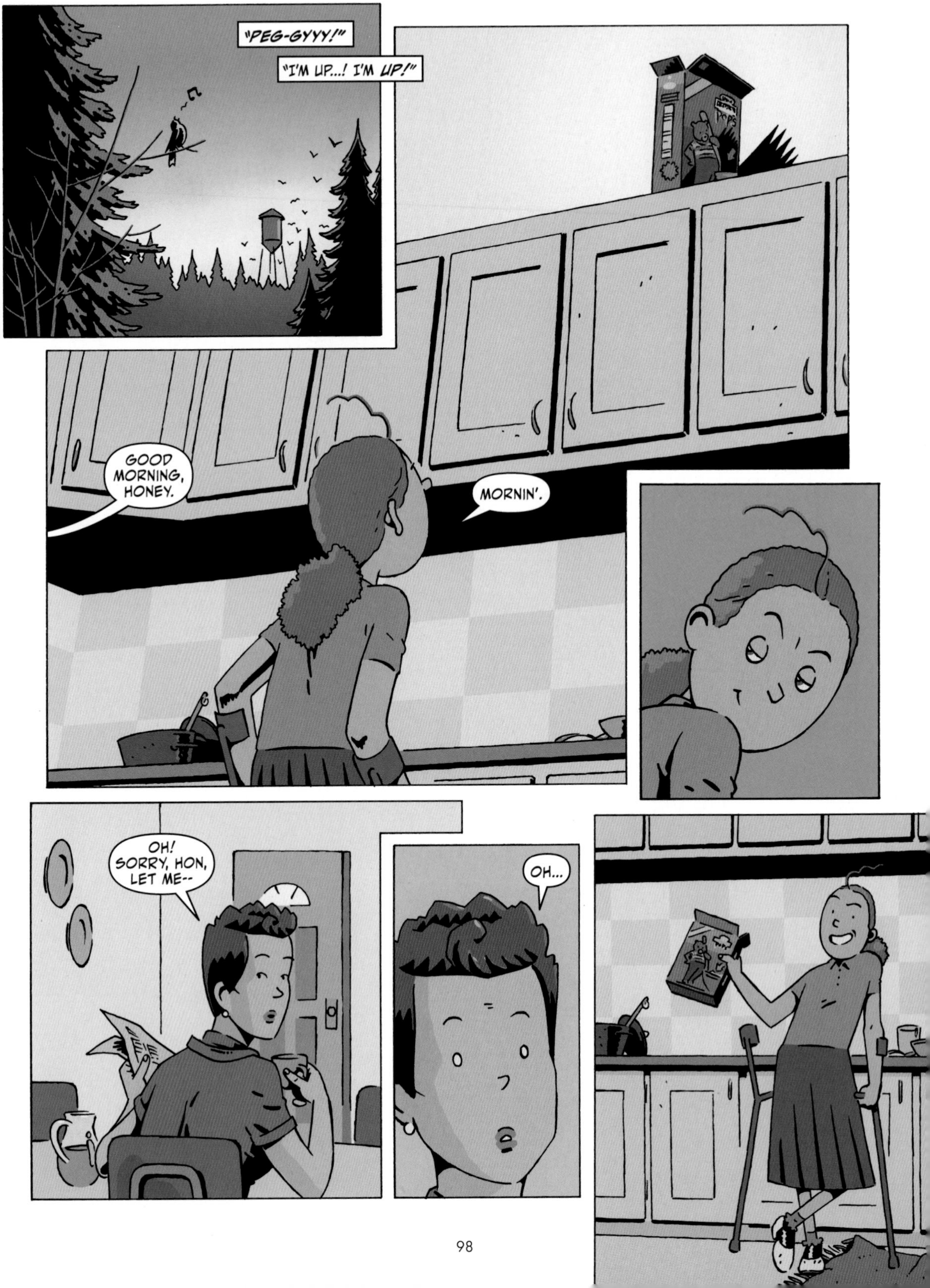
"PEG-GYYY!"
"I'M UP...! I'M UP!"
GOOD MORNING, HONEY.
MORNIN'.
OH! SORRY, HON, LET ME--
OH...

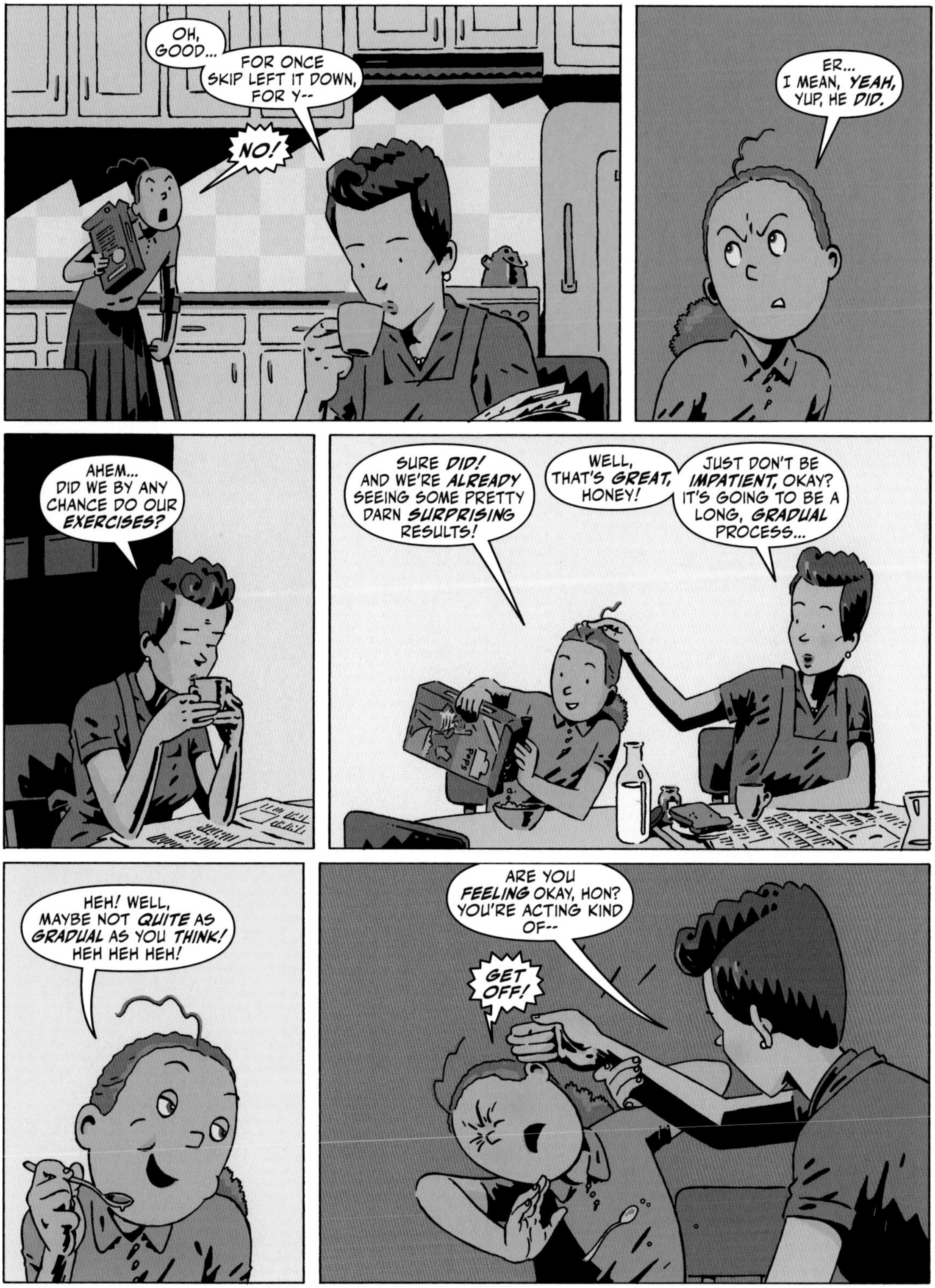
OH, GOOD...
FOR ONCE SKIP LEFT IT DOWN, FOR Y--
NO!
ER... I MEAN, YEAH, YUP, HE DID.
AHEM... DID WE BY ANY CHANCE DO OUR EXERCISES?
SURE DID! AND WE'RE ALREADY SEEING SOME PRETTY DARN SURPRISING RESULTS!
WELL, THAT'S GREAT, HONEY!
JUST DON'T BE IMPATIENT, OKAY? IT'S GOING TO BE A LONG, GRADUAL PROCESS...
HEH! WELL, MAYBE NOT QUITE AS GRADUAL AS YOU THINK! HEH HEH HEH!
ARE YOU FEELING OKAY, HON? YOU'RE ACTING KIND OF--
GET OFF!

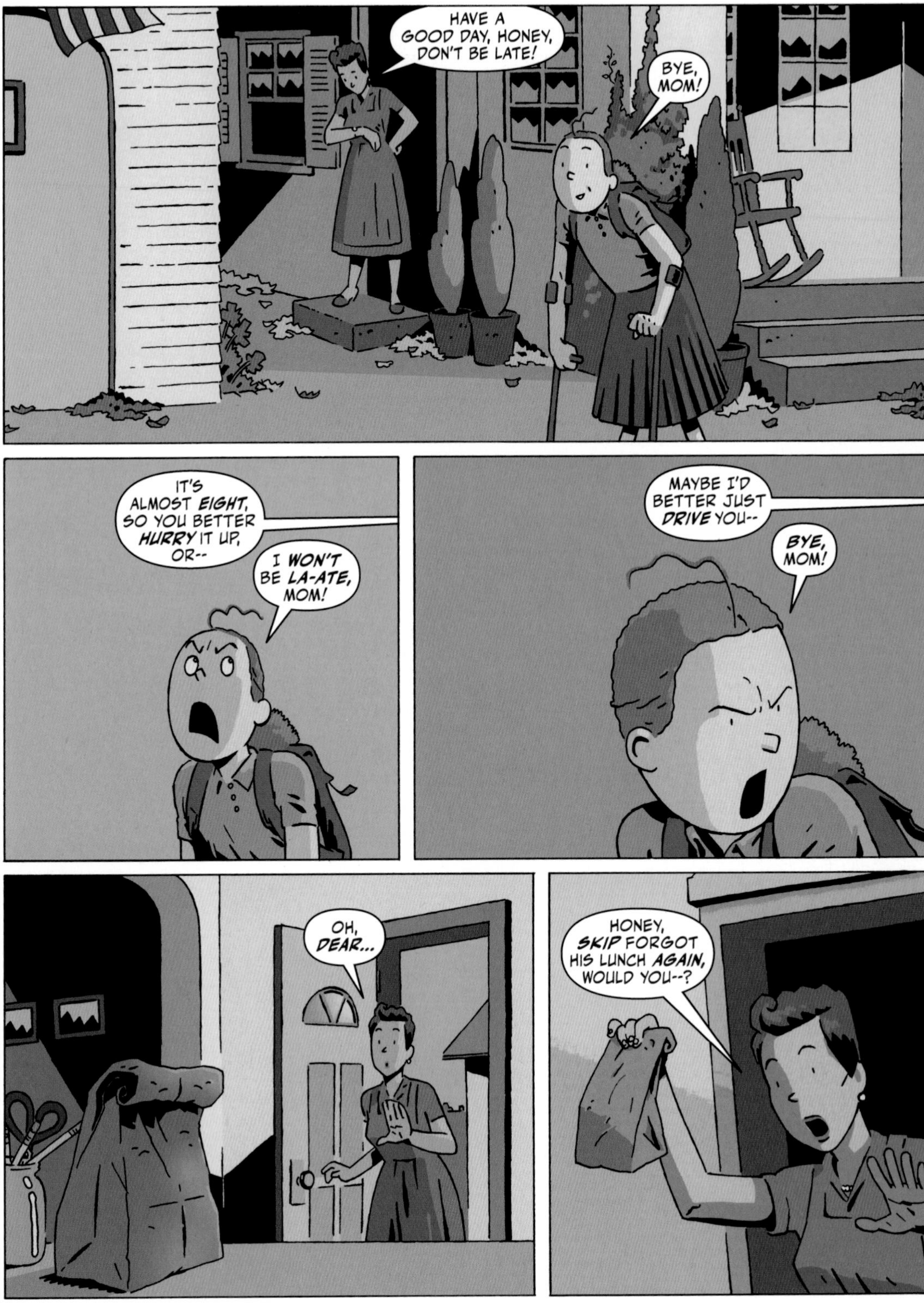
HAVE A GOOD DAY, HONEY, DON'T BE LATE!
BYE, MOM!
IT'S ALMOST *EIGHT*, SO YOU BETTER *HURRY* IT UP, OR--
I *WON'T* BE *LA-ATE*, MOM!
MAYBE I'D BETTER JUST *DRIVE* YOU--
*BYE*, MOM!
OH, *DEAR*...
HONEY, *SKIP* FORGOT HIS LUNCH *AGAIN*, WOULD YOU--?

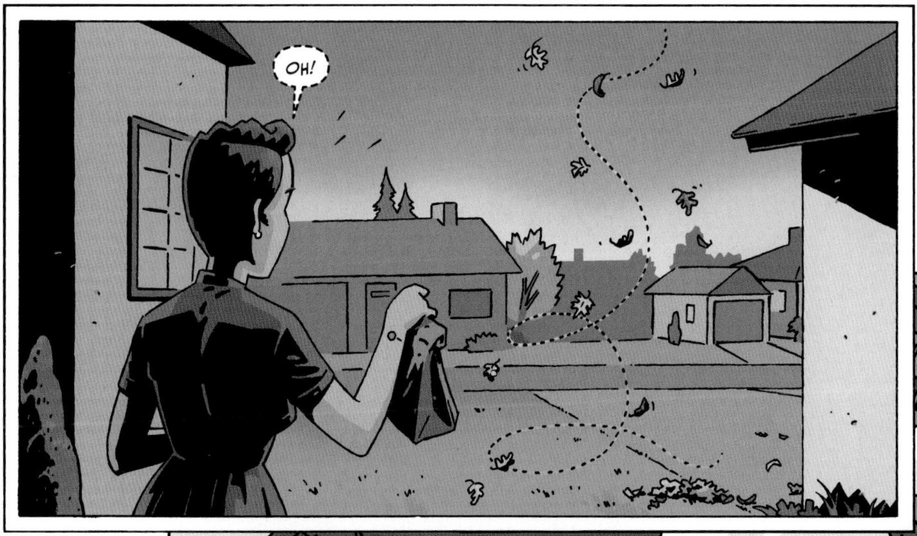
OH!

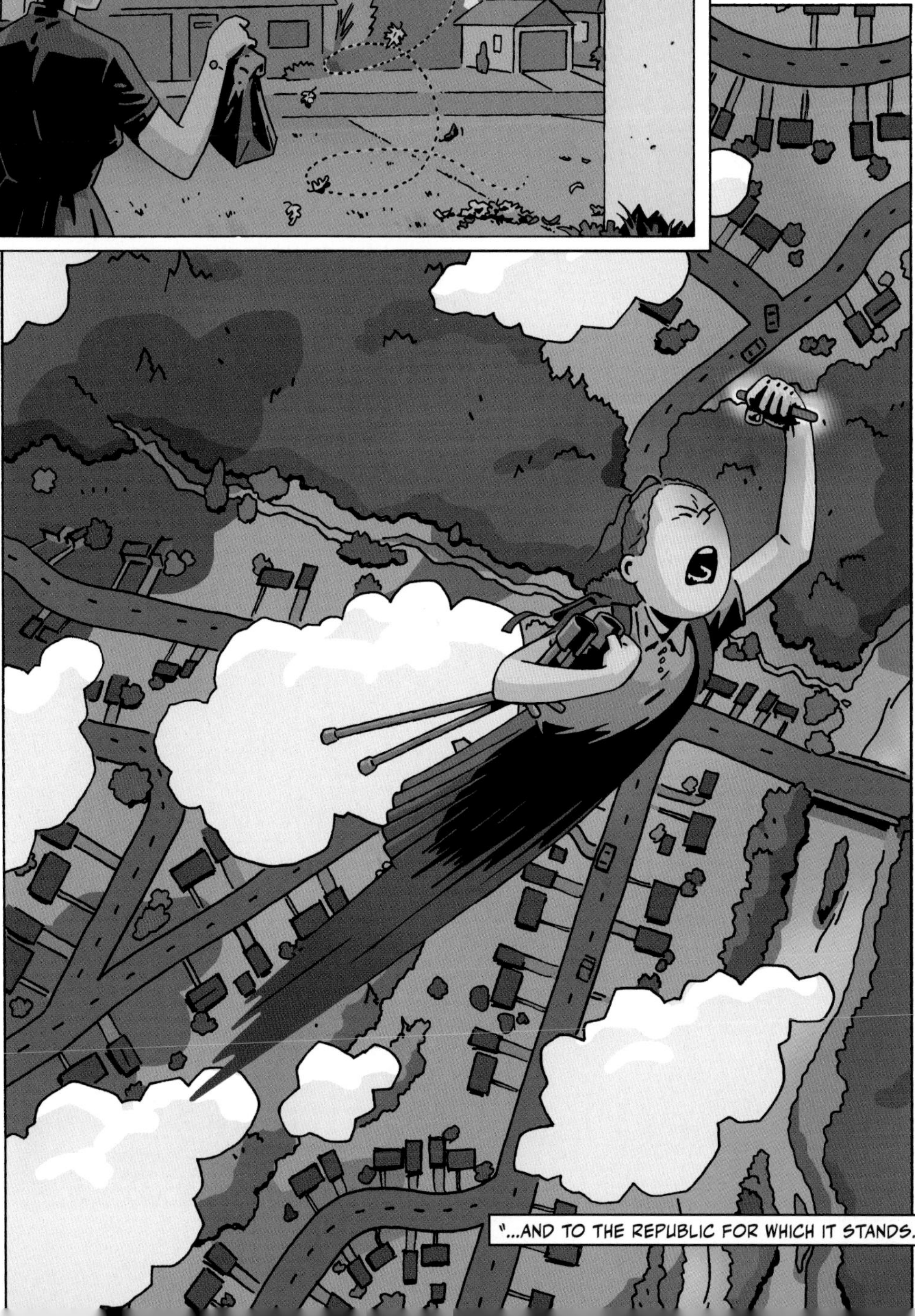
"...AND TO THE REPUBLIC FOR WHICH IT STANDS..."

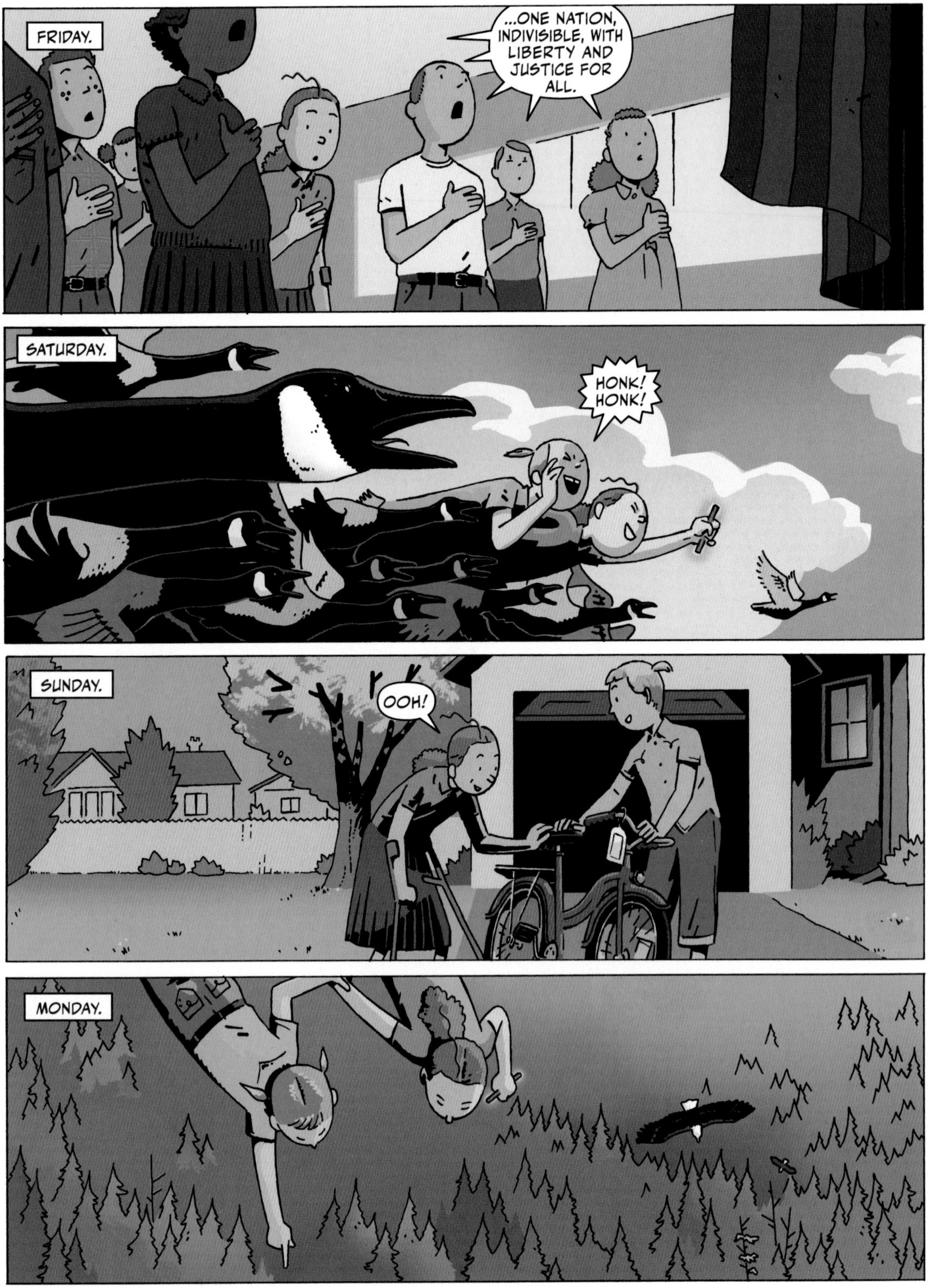
FRIDAY.
...ONE NATION, INDIVISIBLE, WITH LIBERTY AND JUSTICE FOR ALL.
SATURDAY.
HONK! HONK!
SUNDAY.
OOH!
MONDAY.

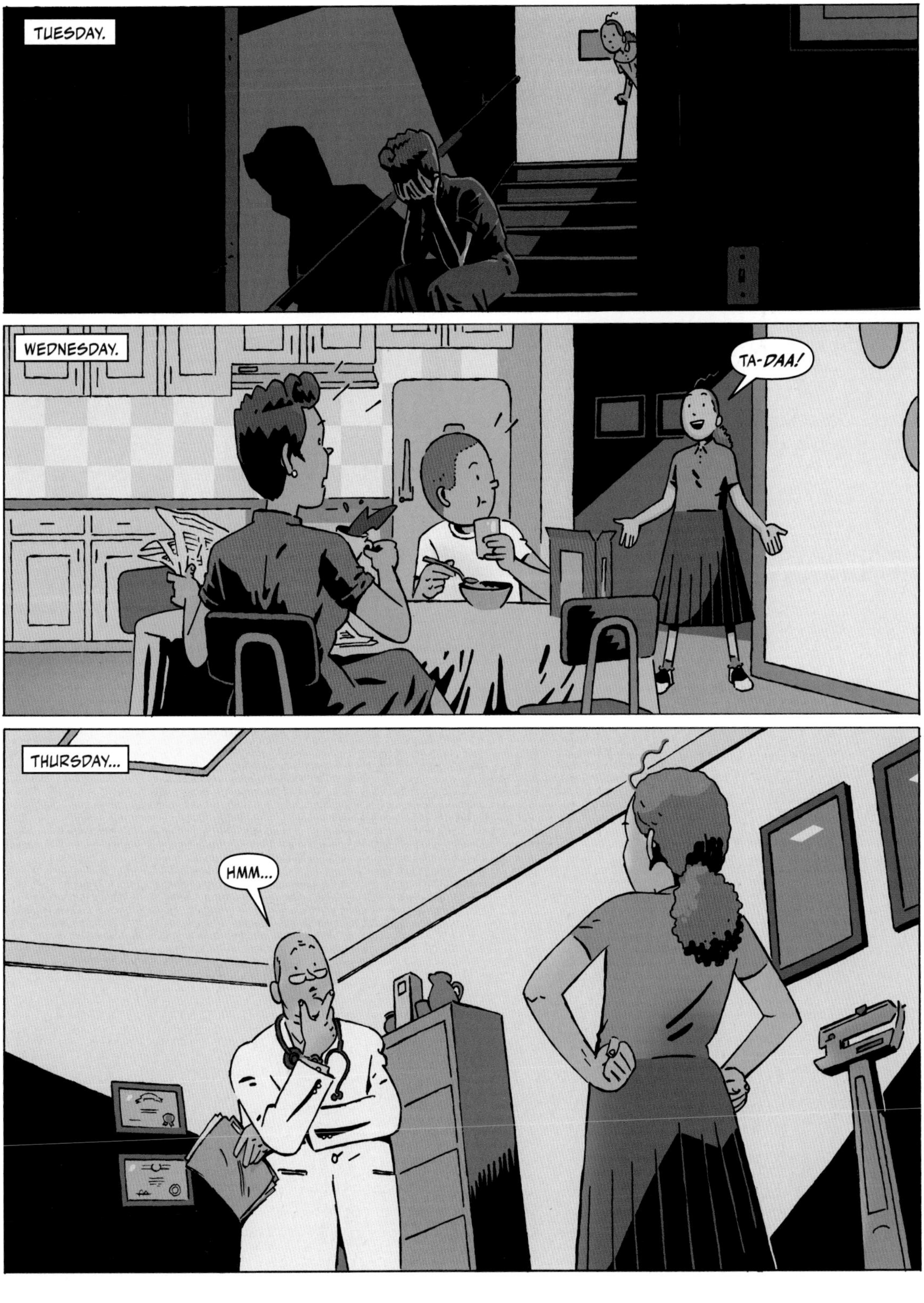
TUESDAY.
WEDNESDAY.
TA-DAA!
THURSDAY...
HMM...

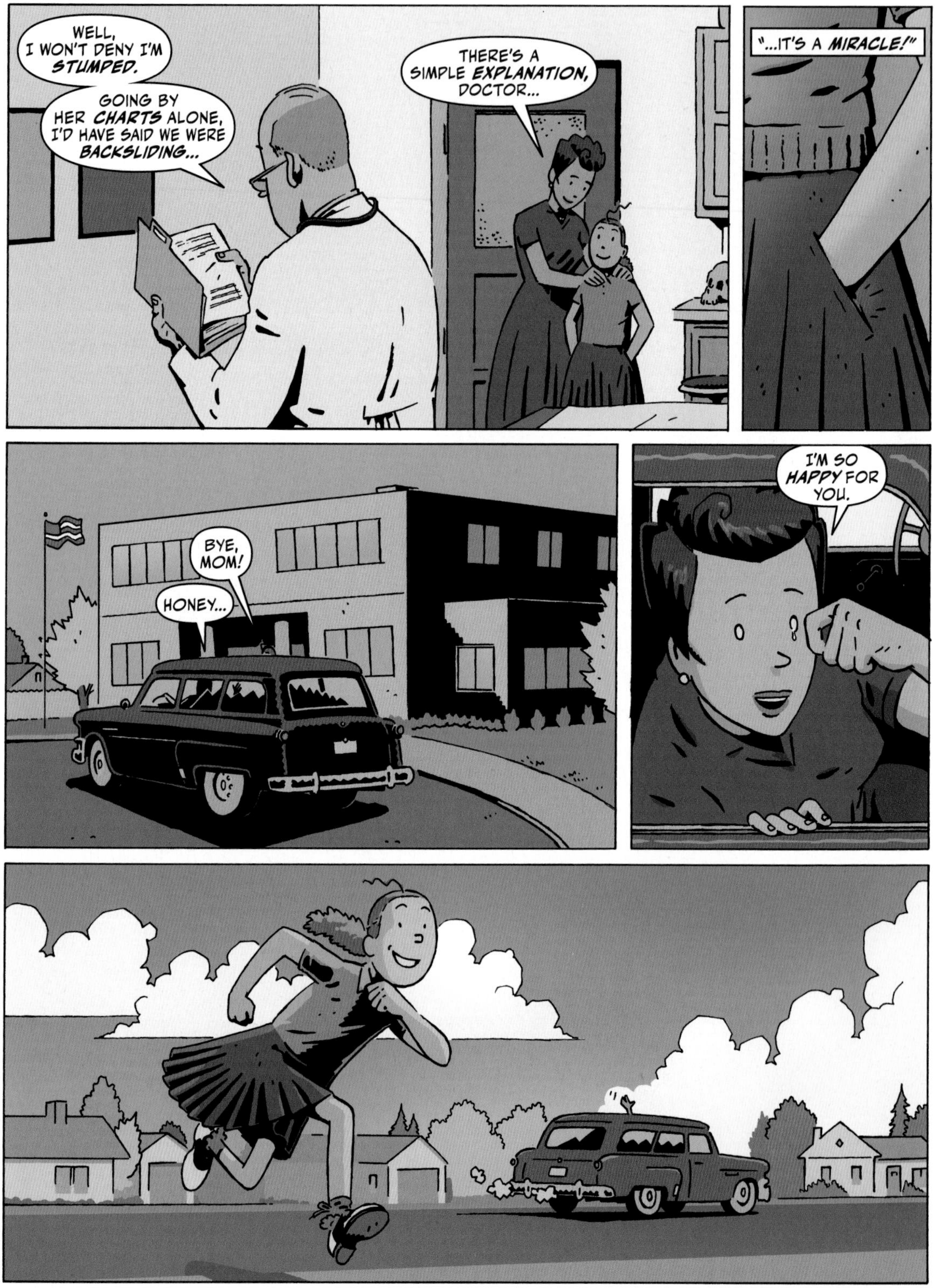
WELL, I WON'T DENY I'M STUMPED.
GOING BY HER CHARTS ALONE, I'D HAVE SAID WE WERE BACKSLIDING...
THERE'S A SIMPLE EXPLANATION, DOCTOR...
"...IT'S A MIRACLE!"
BYE, MOM!
HONEY...
I'M SO HAPPY FOR YOU.

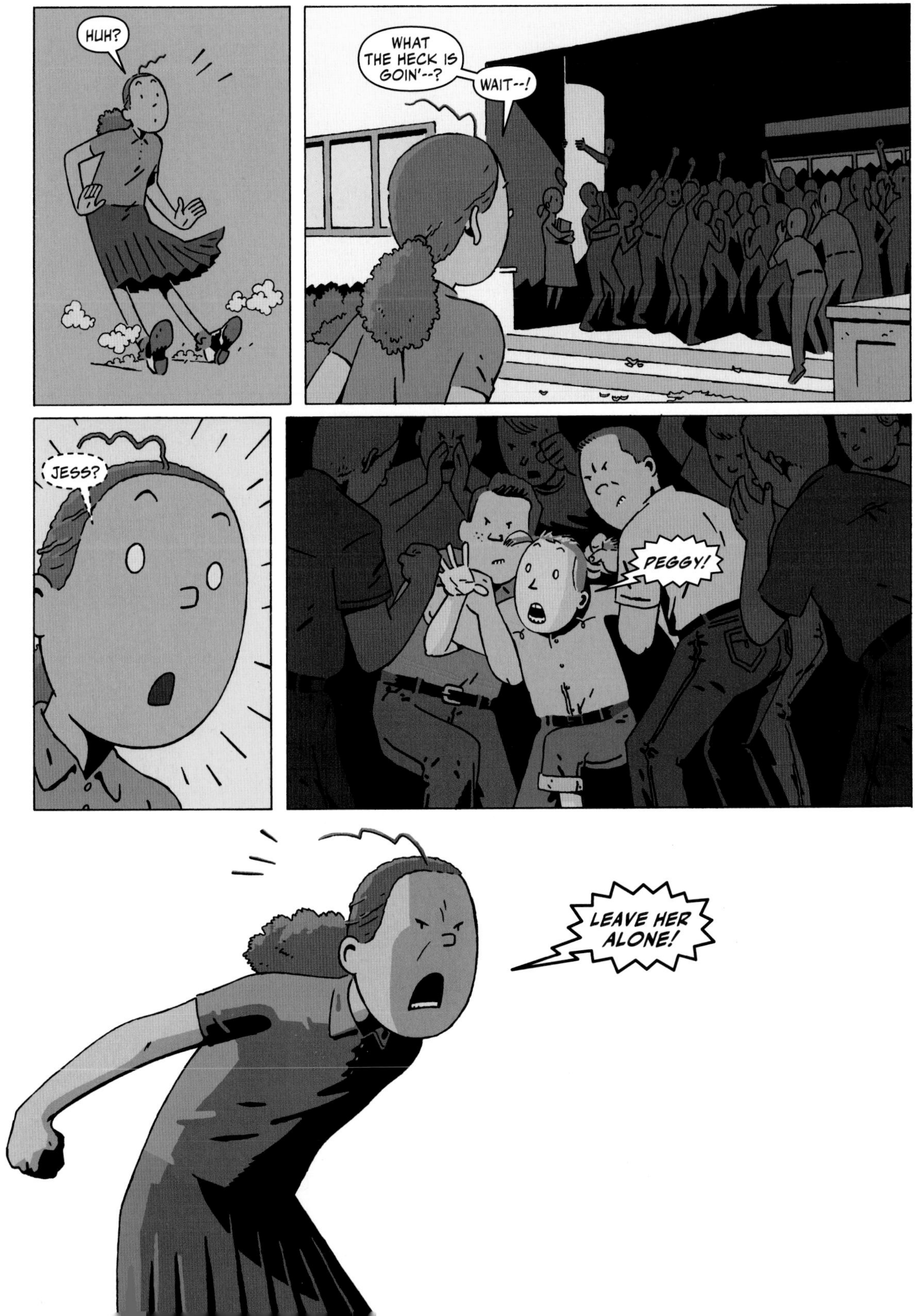
HUH?
WHAT THE HECK IS GOIN'--?
WAIT--!
JESS?
PEGGY!
LEAVE HER ALONE!

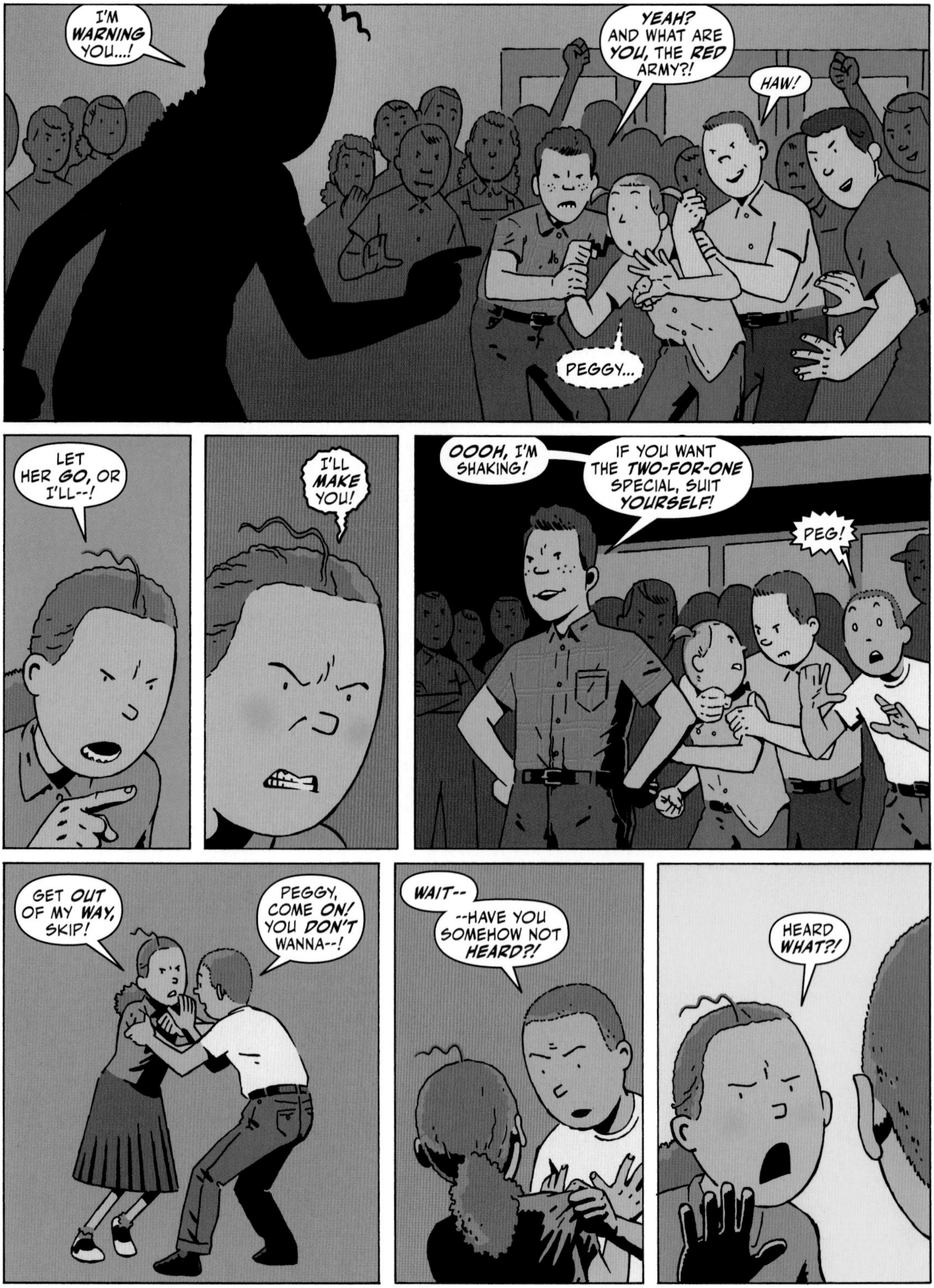
I'M WARNING YOU...!
YEAH? AND WHAT ARE YOU, THE RED ARMY?!
HAW!
PEGGY...
LET HER GO, OR I'LL--!
I'LL MAKE YOU!
OOOH, I'M SHAKING!
IF YOU WANT THE TWO-FOR-ONE SPECIAL, SUIT YOURSELF!
PEG!
GET OUT OF MY WAY, SKIP!
PEGGY, COME ON! YOU DON'T WANNA--!
WAIT--
--HAVE YOU SOMEHOW NOT HEARD?!
HEARD WHAT?!

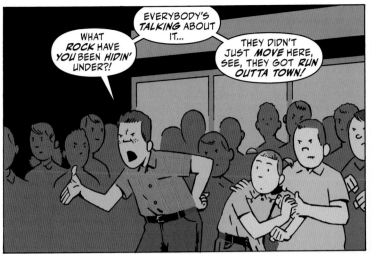

WHAT *ROCK* HAVE *YOU* BEEN *HIDIN'* UNDER?!

EVERYBODY'S *TALKING* ABOUT IT...

THEY DIDN'T JUST *MOVE* HERE, SEE, THEY GOT *RUN OUTTA TOWN!*

THEY'RE STINKIN' *COMMIES!*

YEAH, *RIGHT!*

*ASK HER!*

MY *DAD*... WHEN MY DAD WAS *YOUNGER*...HE... YEAH.

THERE'S NO *LAW* AGAINST IT!

BUT WHEN PEOPLE FOUND OUT, HE COULDN'T GET A *JOB* ANYMORE...

*THAT'S* WHY WE *MOVED.*

MAYBE... I SHOULD'VE *TOLD* YOU... SORRY...

...PAL?

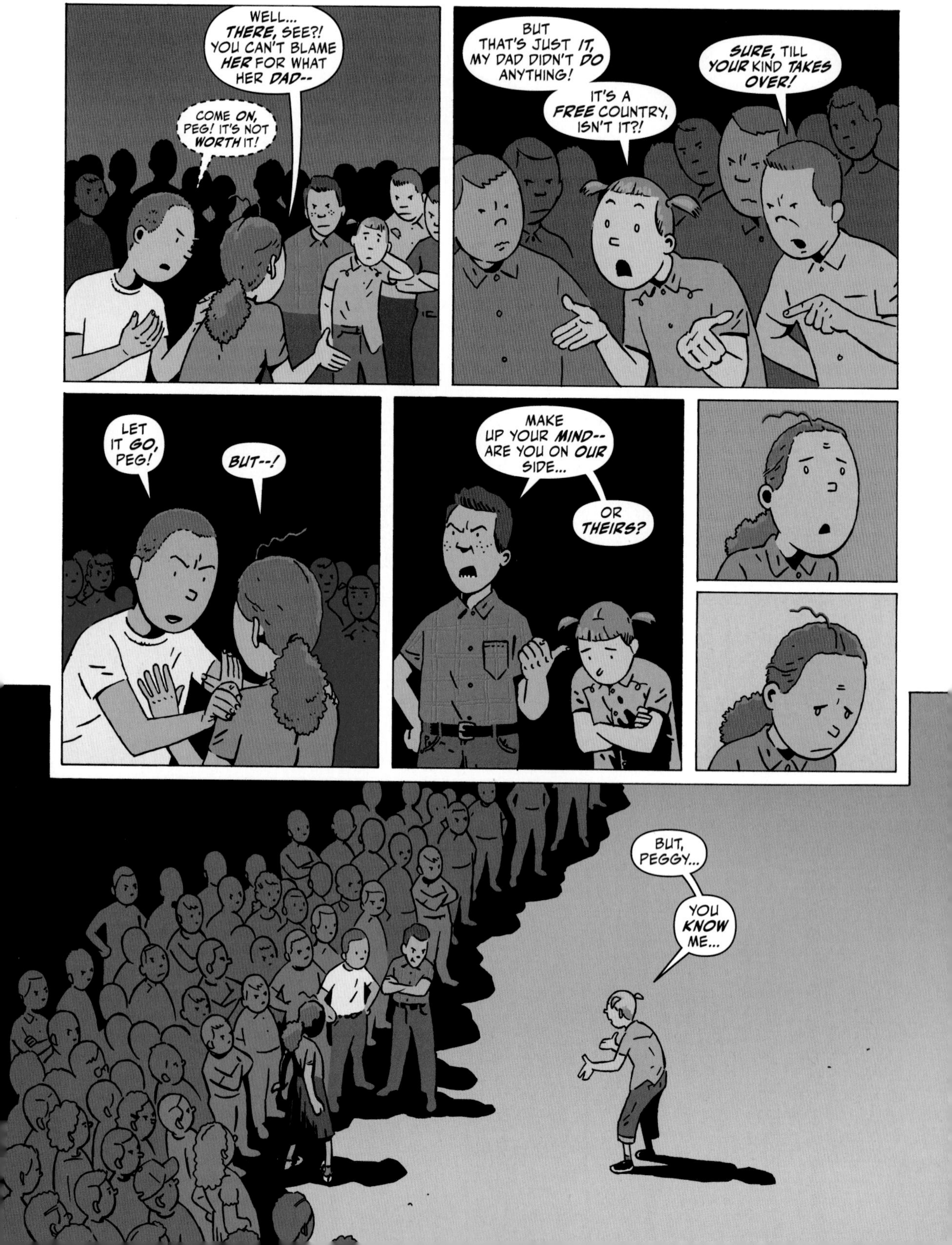
WELL... THERE, SEE?! YOU CAN'T BLAME HER FOR WHAT HER DAD--
COME ON, PEG! IT'S NOT WORTH IT!
BUT THAT'S JUST IT, MY DAD DIDN'T DO ANYTHING!
IT'S A FREE COUNTRY, ISN'T IT?!
SURE, TILL YOUR KIND TAKES OVER!
LET IT GO, PEG!
BUT--!
MAKE UP YOUR MIND-- ARE YOU ON OUR SIDE...
OR THEIRS?
BUT, PEGGY...
YOU KNOW ME...

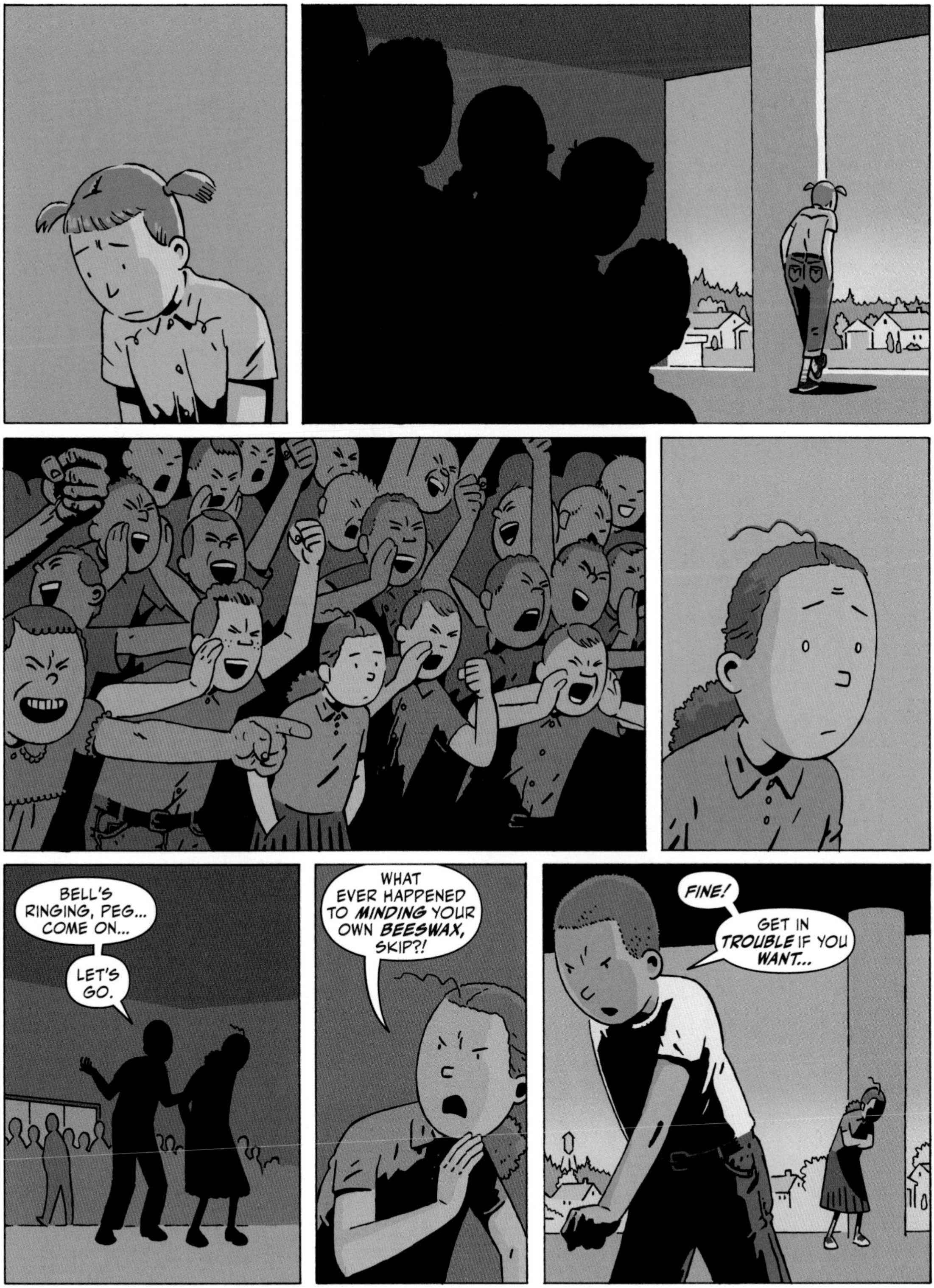
BELL'S RINGING, PEG... COME ON...
LET'S GO.
WHAT EVER HAPPENED TO MINDING YOUR OWN BEESWAX, SKIP?!
FINE!
GET IN TROUBLE IF YOU WANT...

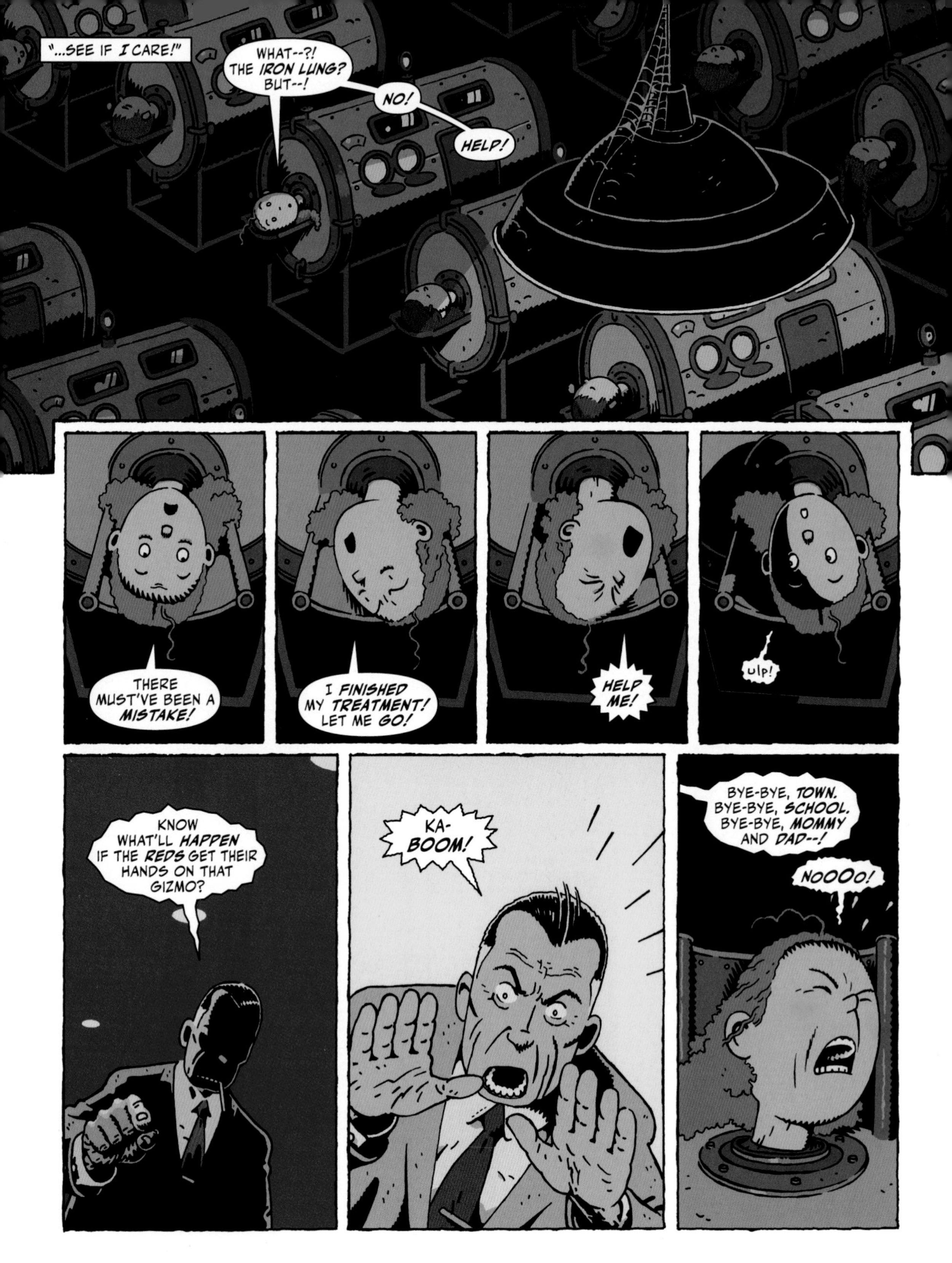
"...SEE IF I CARE!"
WHAT--?! THE IRON LUNG? BUT--!
NO!
HELP!
THERE MUST'VE BEEN A MISTAKE!
I FINISHED MY TREATMENT! LET ME GO!
HELP ME!
ulp!
KNOW WHAT'LL HAPPEN IF THE REDS GET THEIR HANDS ON THAT GIZMO?
KA-BOOM!
BYE-BYE, TOWN. BYE-BYE, SCHOOL. BYE-BYE, MOMMY AND DAD--!
NOOOO!

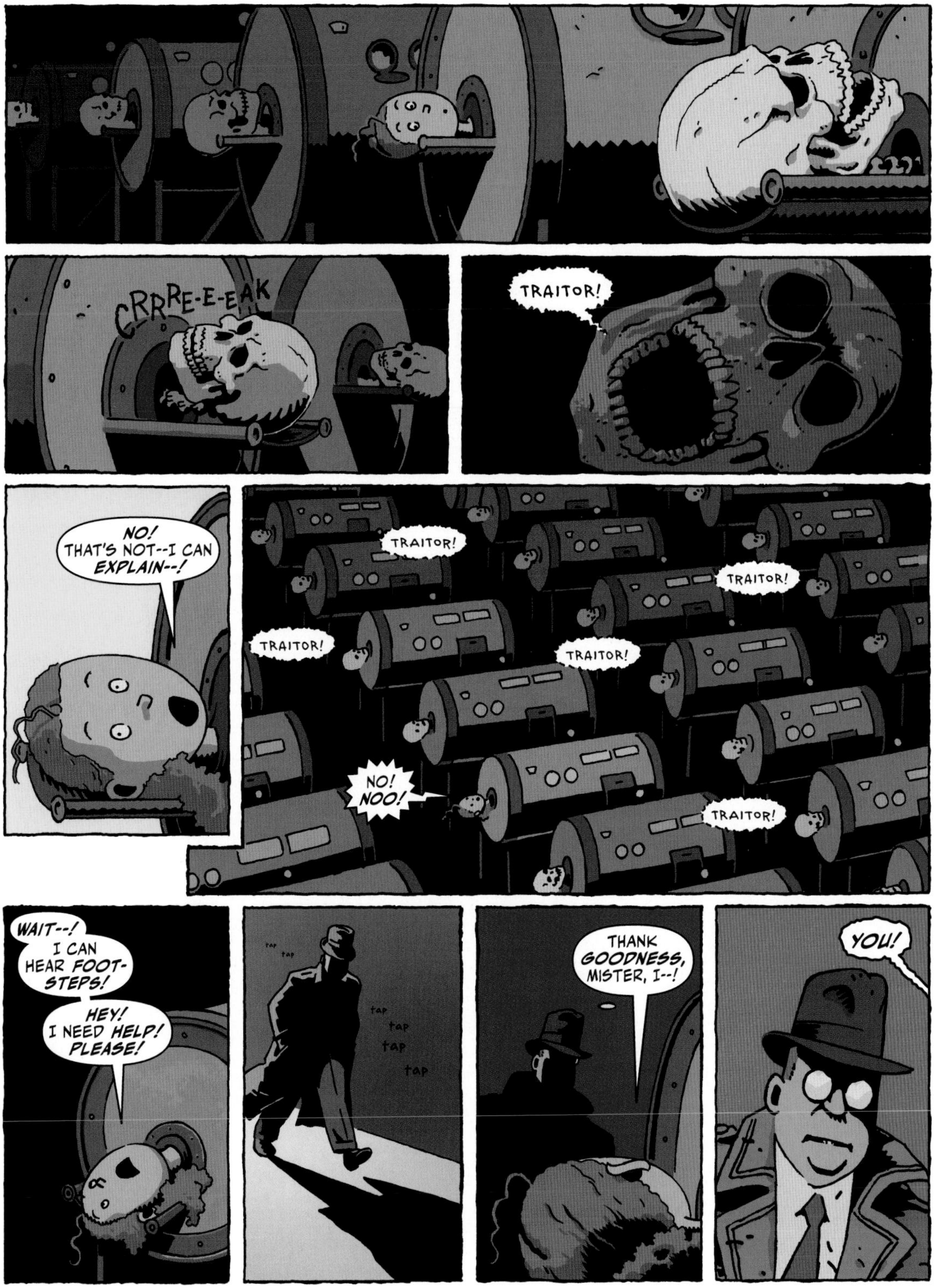
CRRRE-E-EAK
TRAITOR!
NO! THAT'S NOT--I CAN EXPLAIN--!
TRAITOR!
TRAITOR!
TRAITOR!
TRAITOR!
NO! NOO!
TRAITOR!
WAIT--! I CAN HEAR FOOT-STEPS!
HEY! I NEED HELP! PLEASE!
tap tap
tap tap tap tap
THANK GOODNESS, MISTER, I--!
YOU!

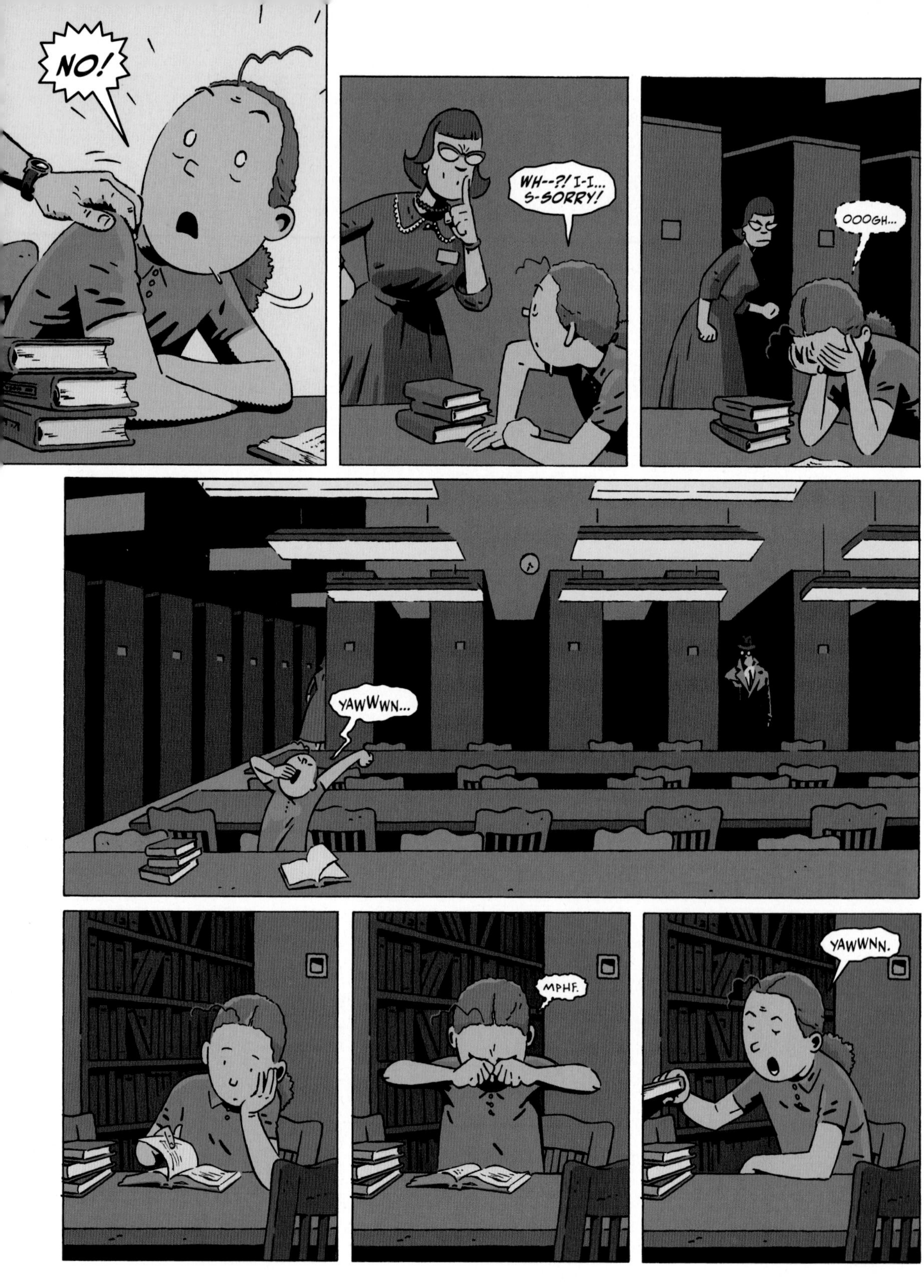
NO!
WH--?! I-I... S-SORRY!
OOOGH...
YAWWWN...
MPHF.
YAWWNN.

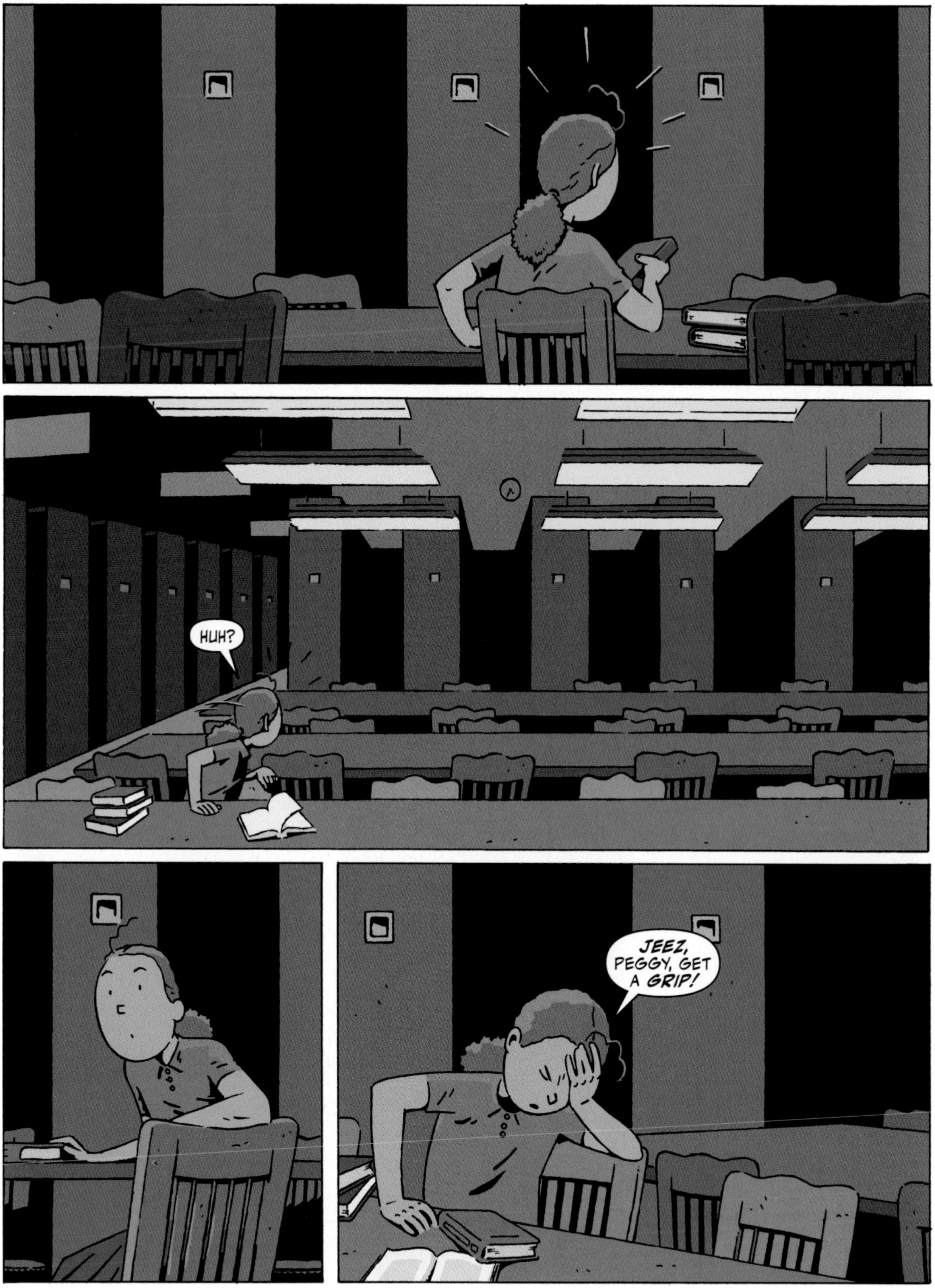
HUH?
JEEZ, PEGGY, GET A GRIP!

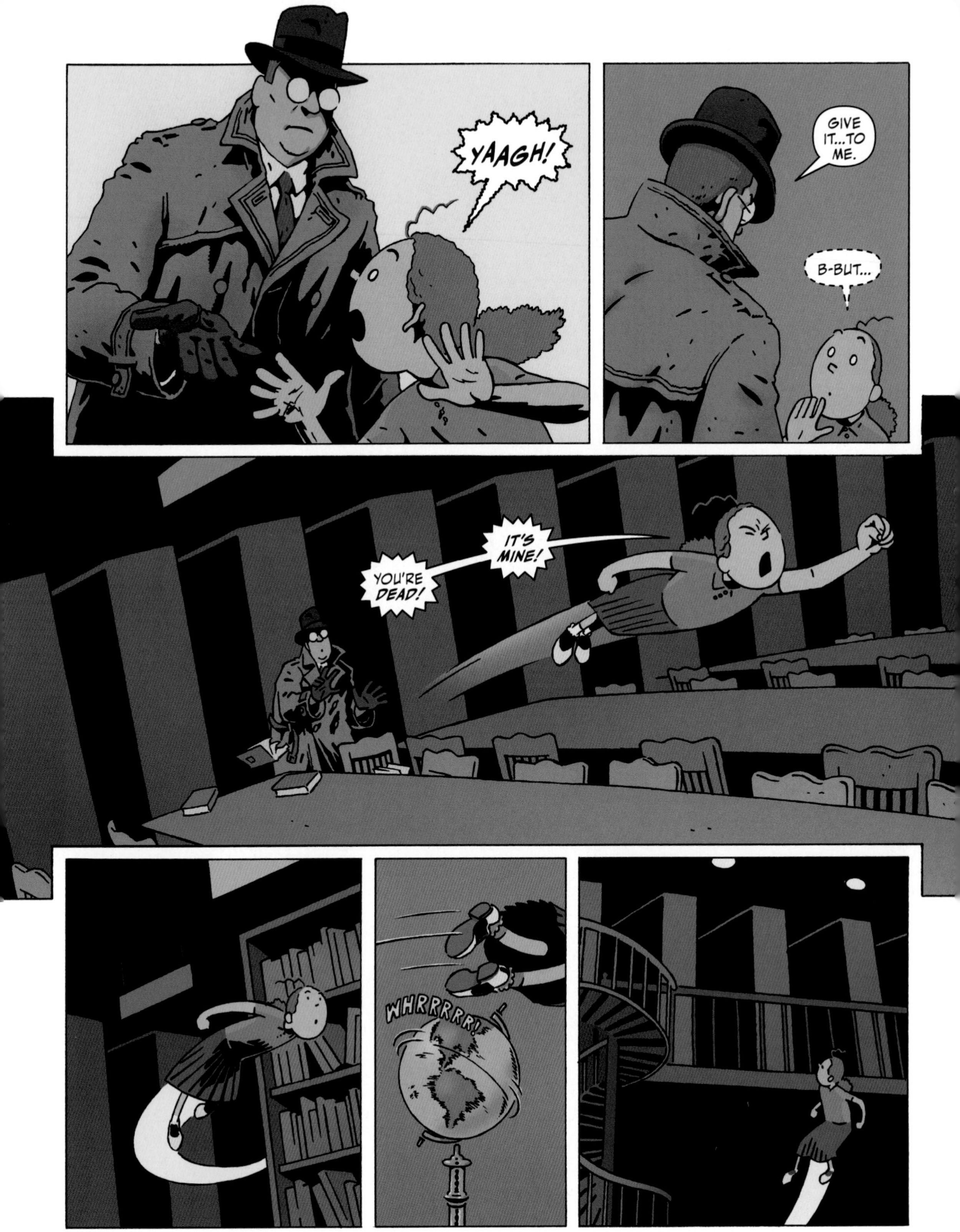

YAAGH!
GIVE IT...TO ME.
B-BUT...
IT'S MINE!
YOU'RE DEAD!
WHRRRRRR!

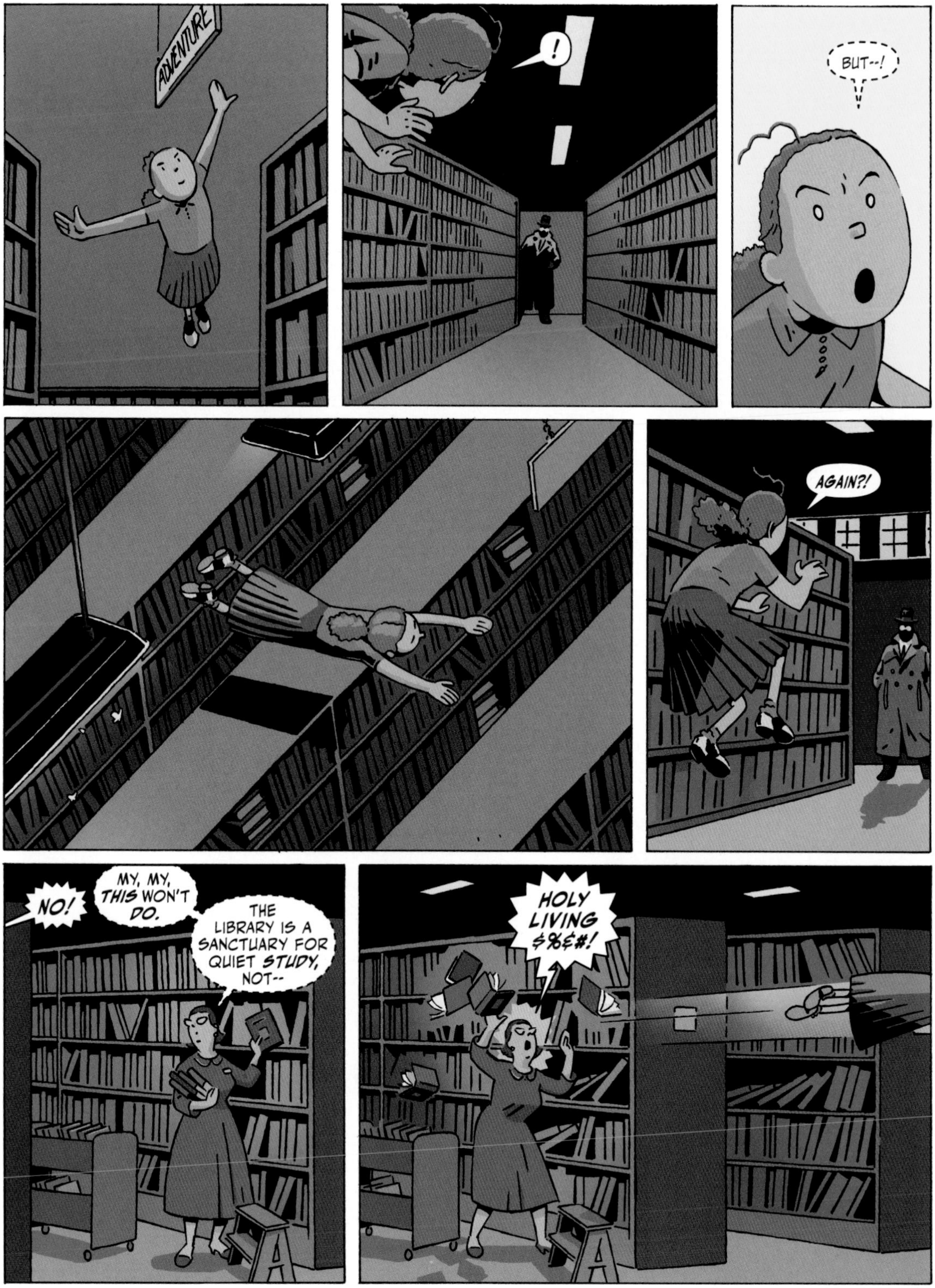
ADVENTURE
!
BUT--!
AGAIN?!
NO!
MY, MY, THIS WON'T DO.
THE LIBRARY IS A SANCTUARY FOR QUIET STUDY, NOT--
HOLY LIVING $%¢#!

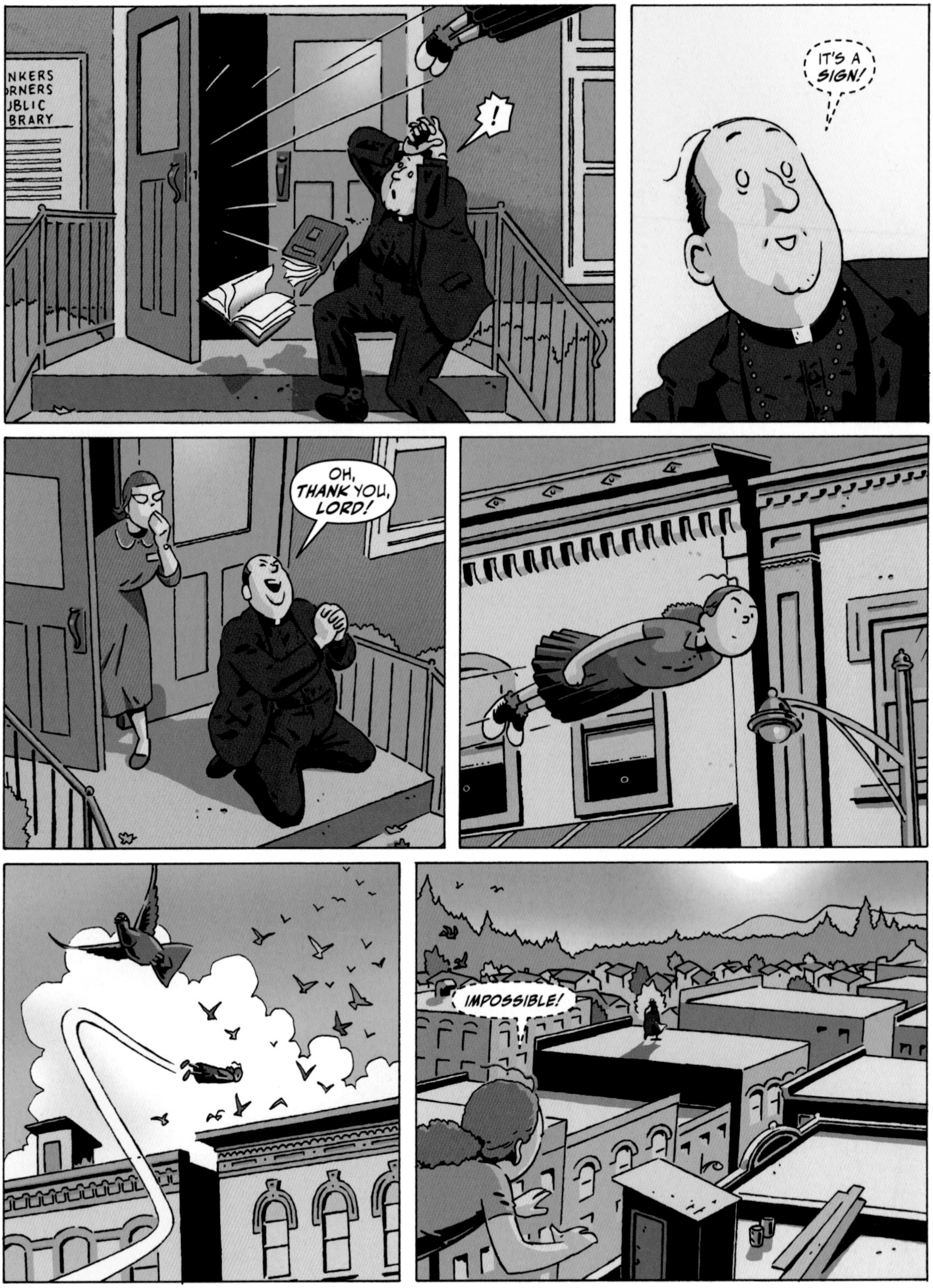
NKERS
ORNERS
UBLIC
BRARY
!
IT'S A SIGN!
OH, THANK YOU, LORD!
IMPOSSIBLE!

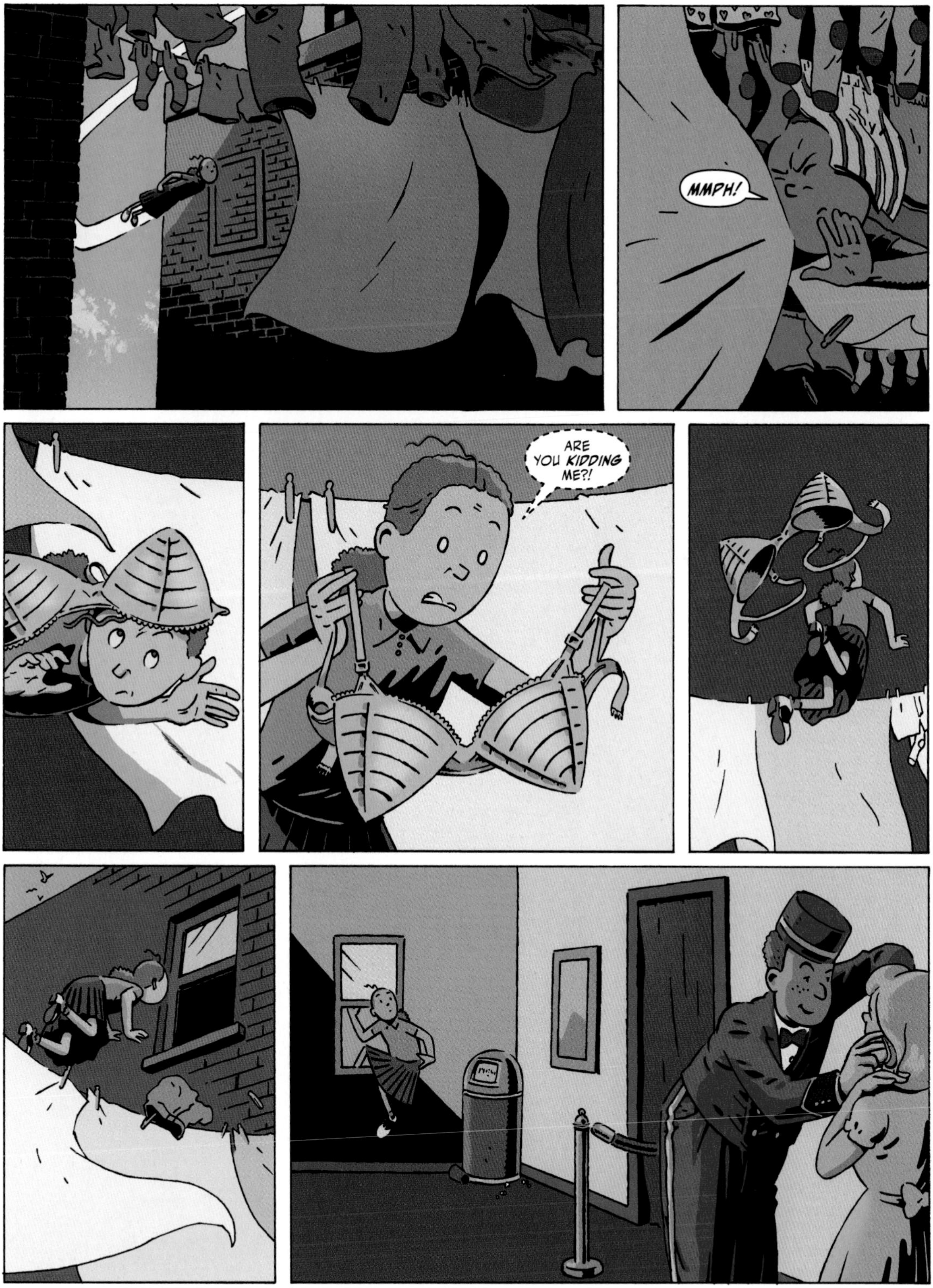
MMPH!
ARE YOU KIDDING ME?!

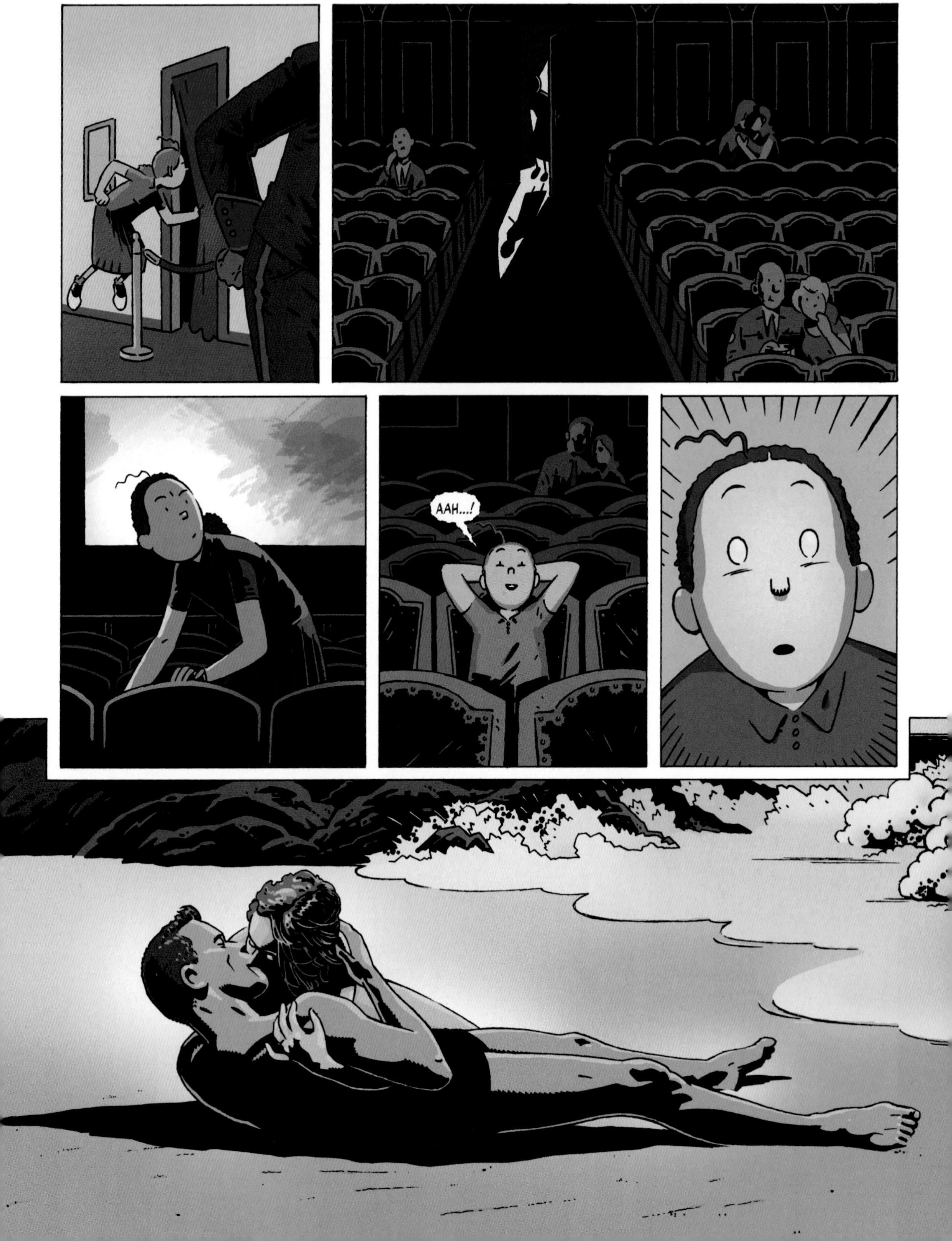
AAH...!

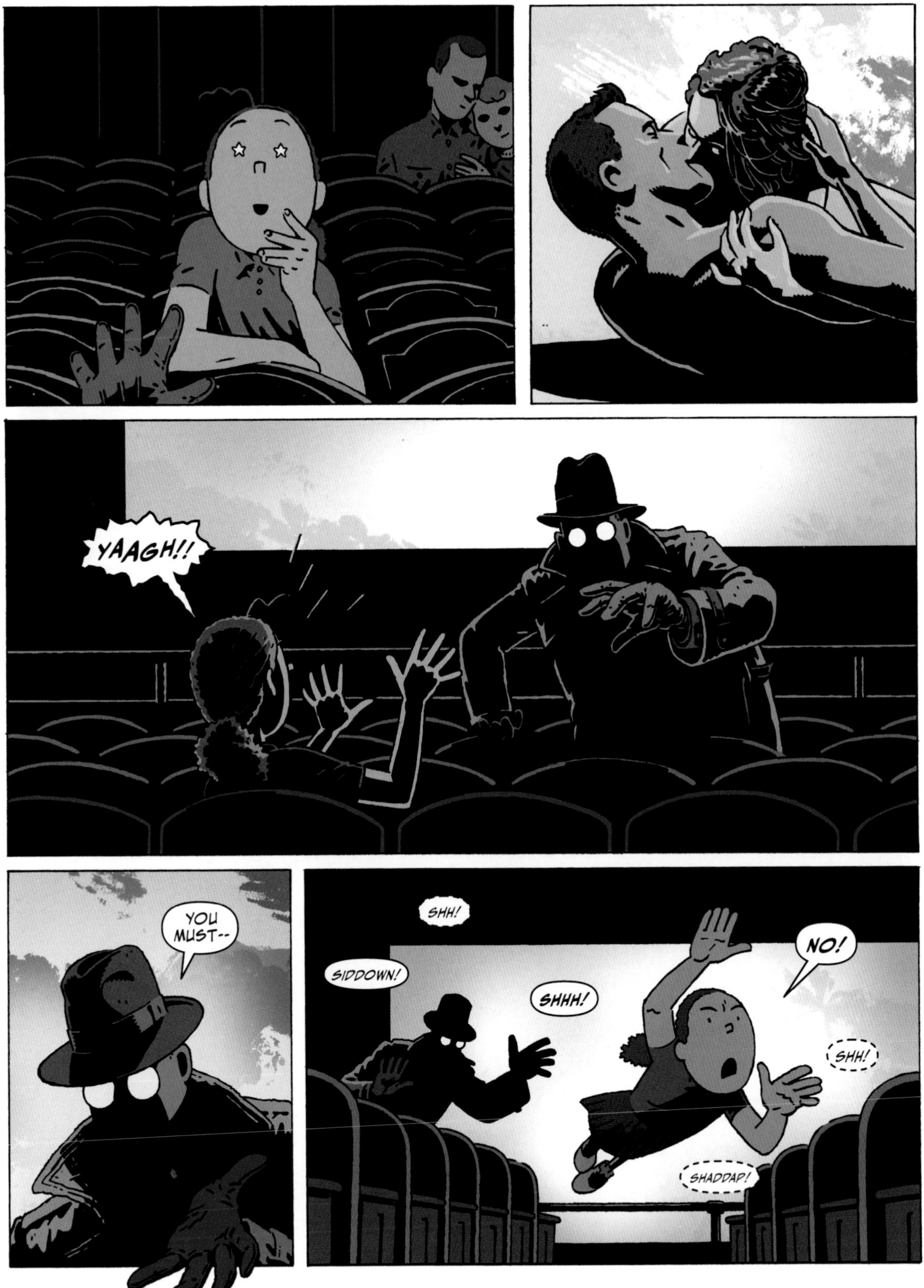
YAAGH!!
YOU MUST--
SHH!
SIDDOWN!
SHHH!
NO!
SHH!
SHADDAP!

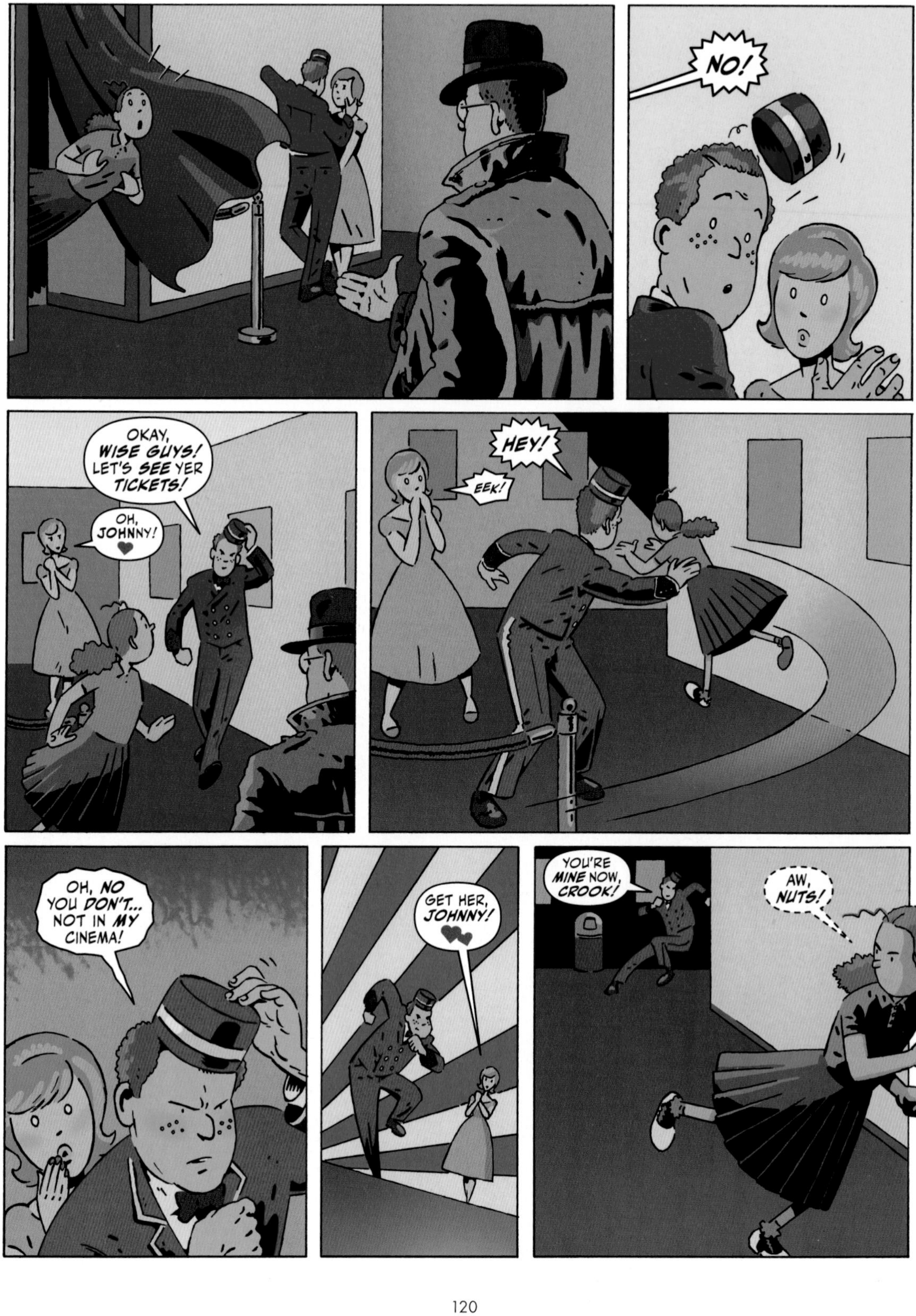

NO!
OKAY, WISE GUYS! LET'S SEE YER TICKETS!
OH, JOHNNY!
HEY!
EEK!
OH, NO YOU DON'T... NOT IN MY CINEMA!
GET HER, JOHNNY!
YOU'RE MINE NOW, CROOK!
AW, NUTS!

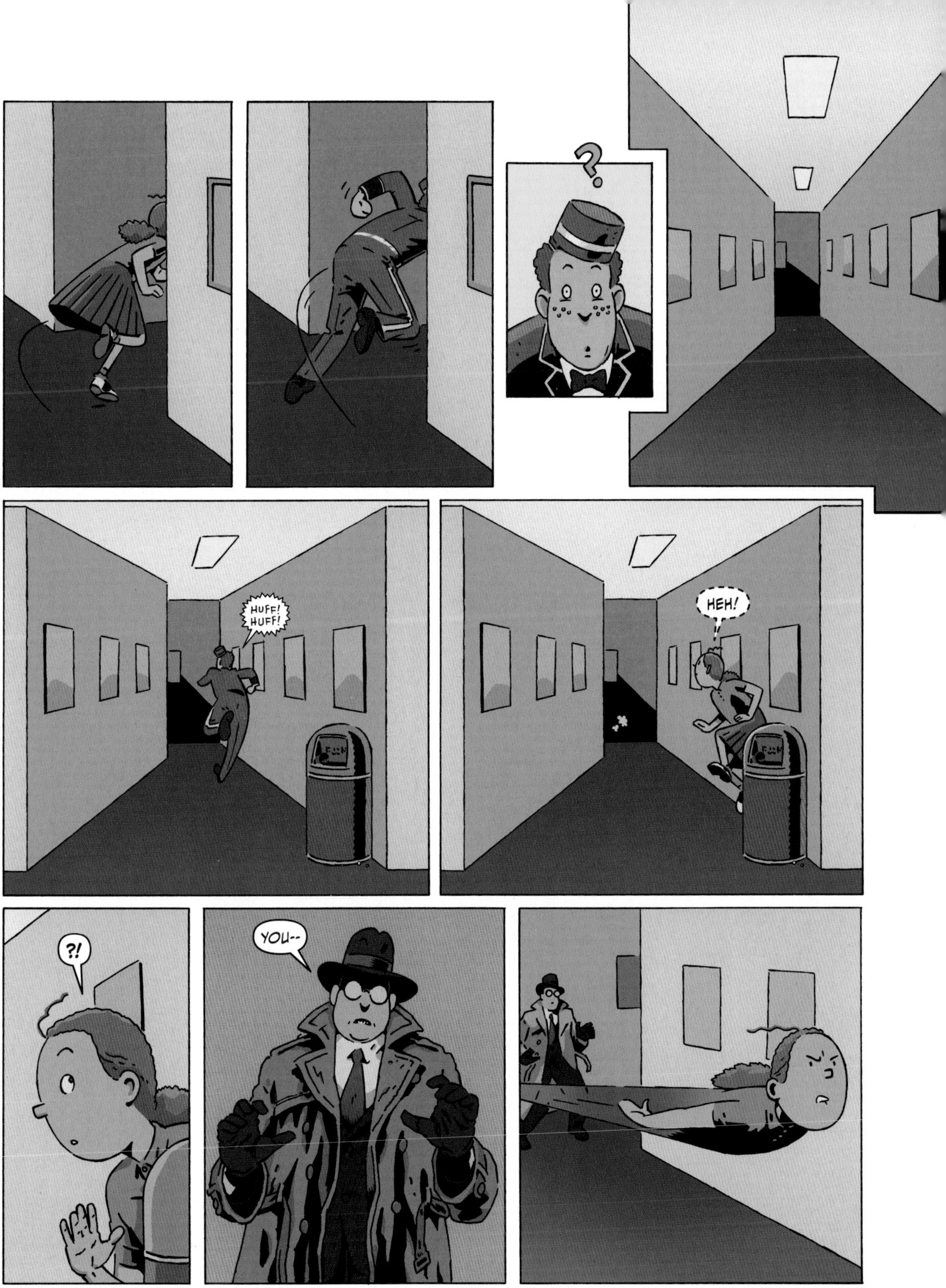
?
HUFF! HUFF!
HEH!
?!
YOU--

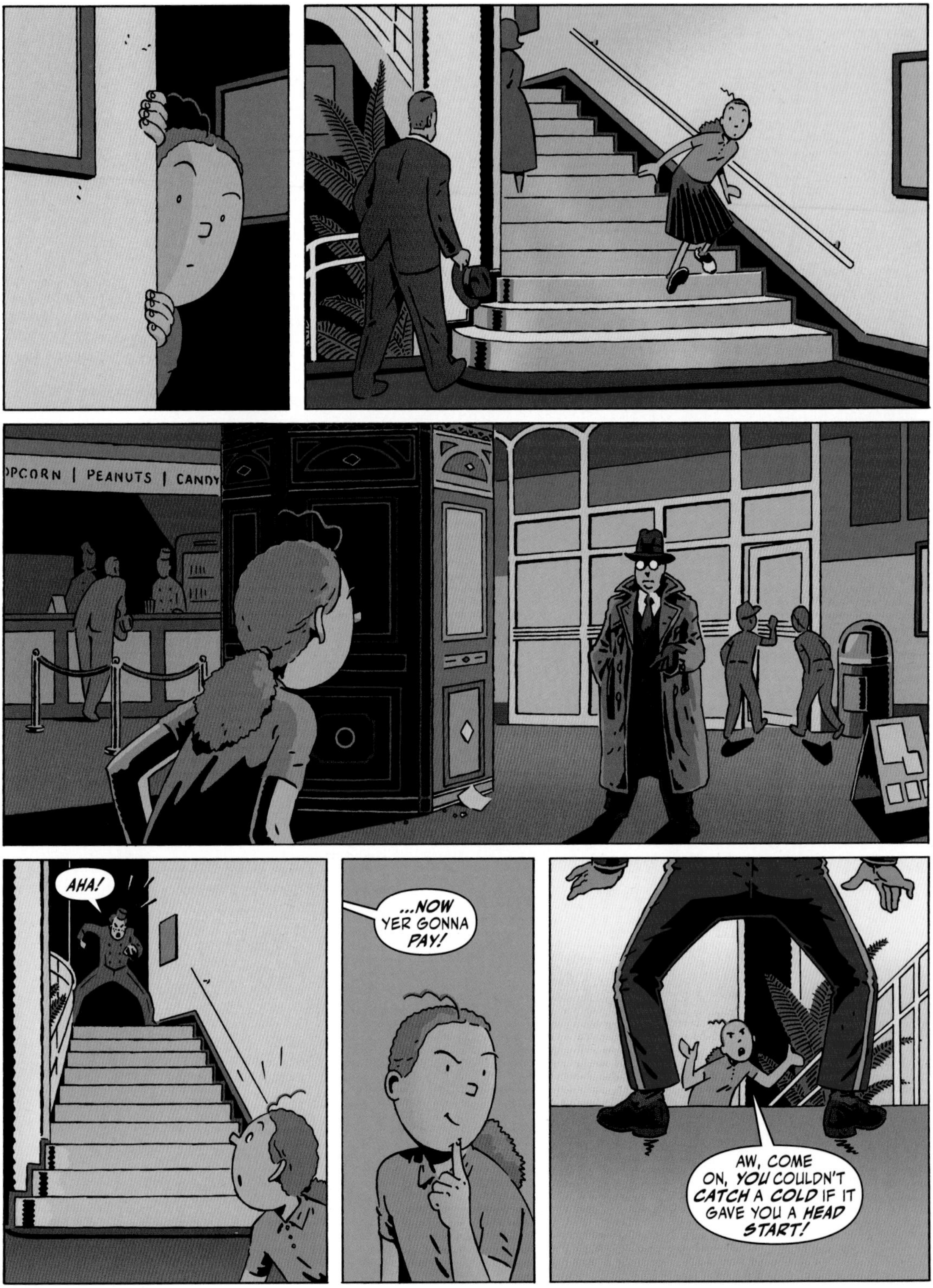

OPCORN | PEANUTS | CANDY
AHA!
...NOW YER GONNA PAY!
AW, COME ON, YOU COULDN'T CATCH A COLD IF IT GAVE YOU A HEAD START!

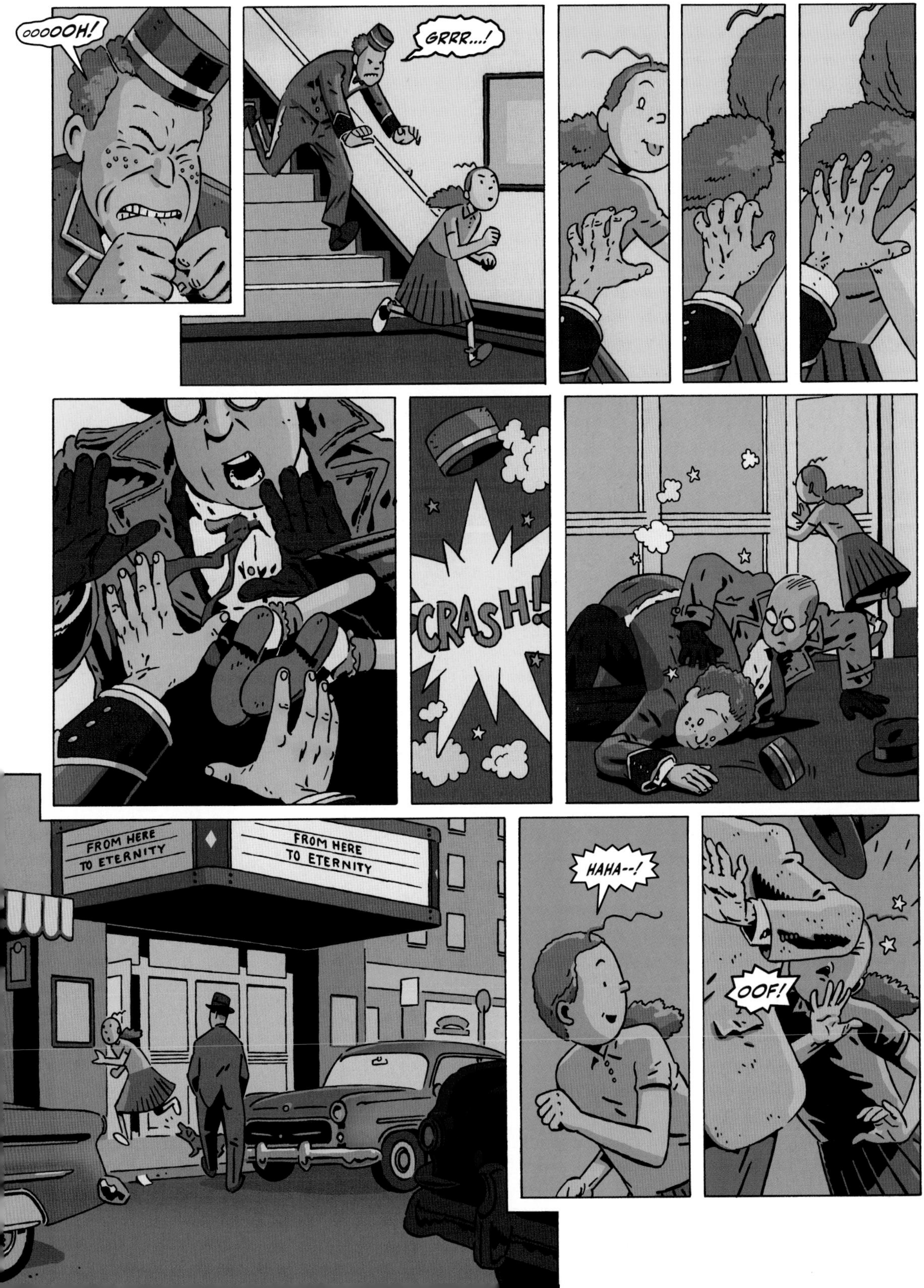
OOOOOH!
GRRR...!
CRASH!
FROM HERE TO ETERNITY
FROM HERE TO ETERNITY
HAHA--!
OOF!

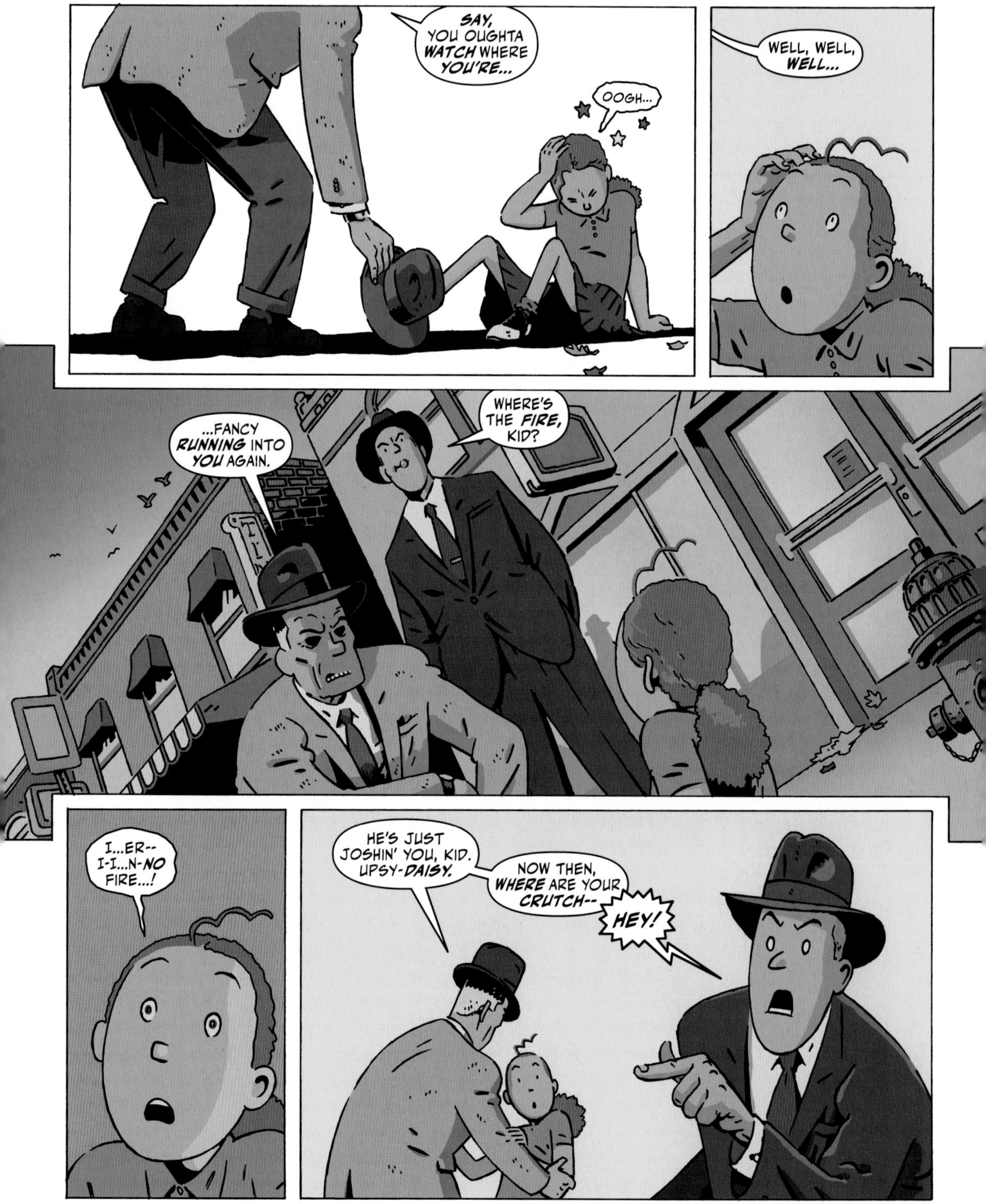
SAY, YOU OUGHTA WATCH WHERE YOU'RE...
OOGH...
WELL, WELL, WELL...
...FANCY RUNNING INTO YOU AGAIN.
WHERE'S THE FIRE, KID?
I...ER-- I-I...N-NO FIRE...!
HE'S JUST JOSHIN' YOU, KID. UPSY-DAISY.
NOW THEN, WHERE ARE YOUR CRUTCH--
HEY!

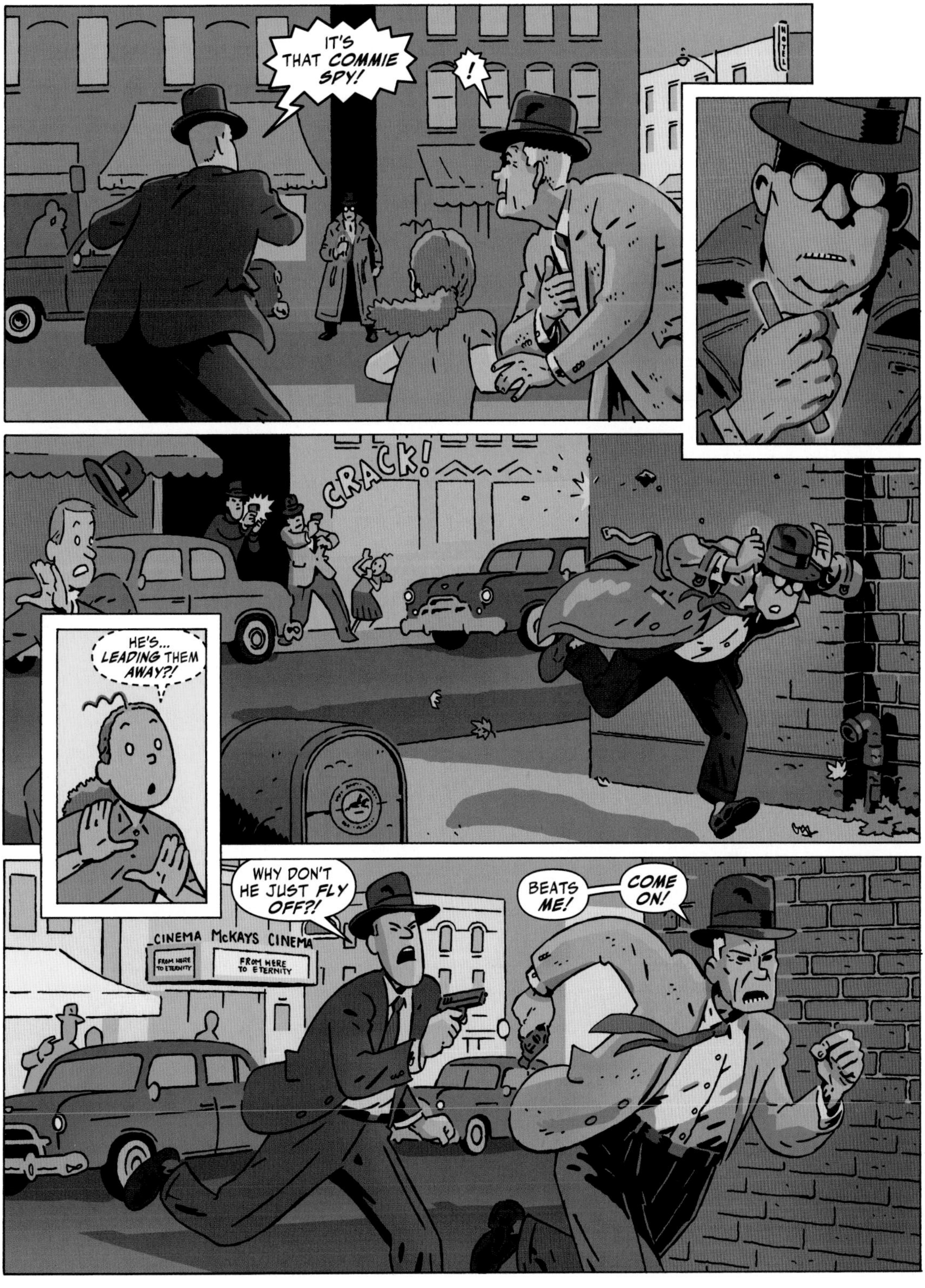
IT'S THAT COMMIE SPY!
!
NOTEL
CRACK!
HE'S... LEADING THEM AWAY?!
WHY DON'T HE JUST FLY OFF?!
BEATS ME!
COME ON!
CINEMA McKAYS CINEMA
FROM HERE TO ETERNITY
FROM HERE TO ETERNITY

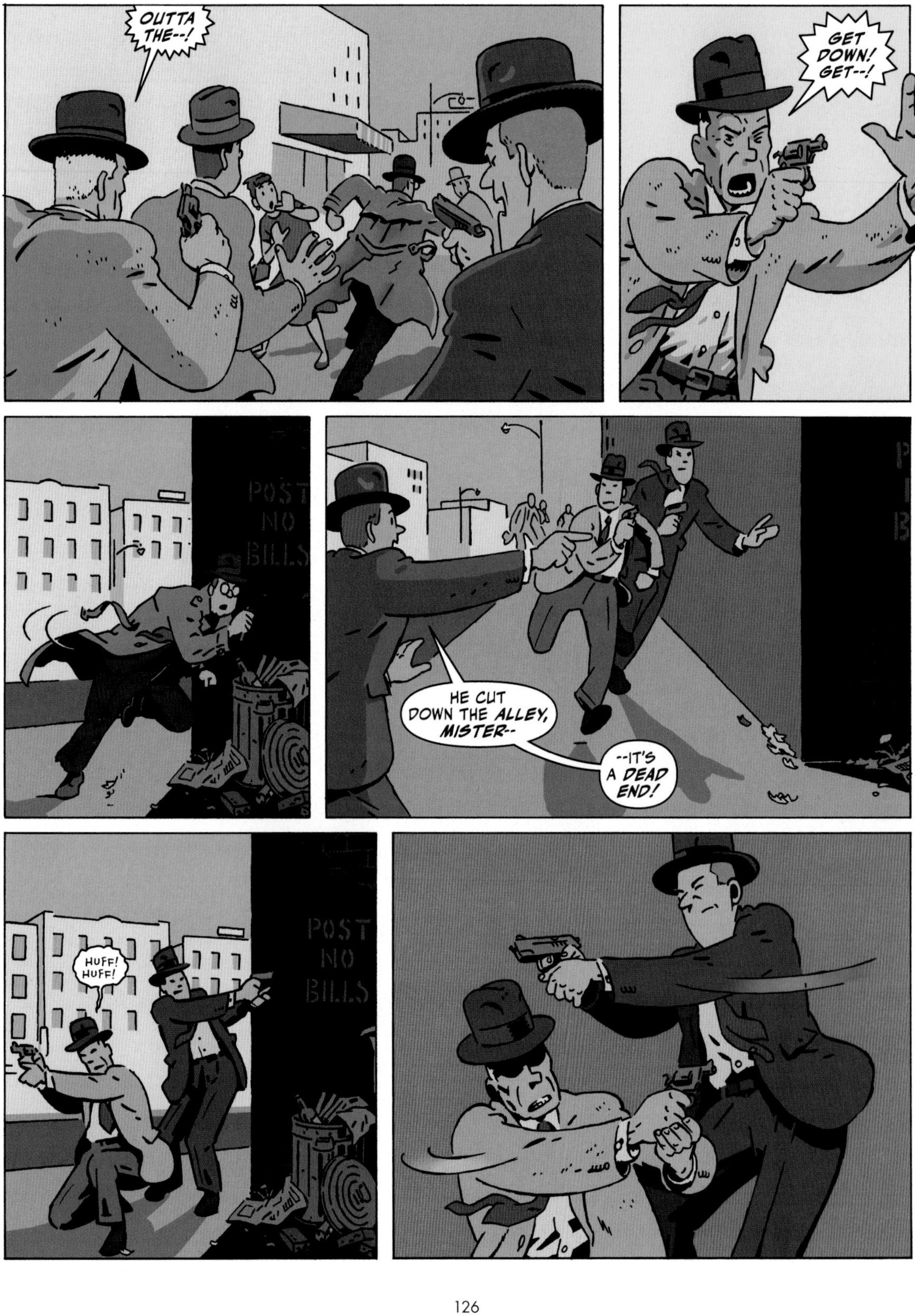
OUTTA THE--!
GET DOWN! GET--!
POST NO BILLS
HE CUT DOWN THE ALLEY, MISTER--
--IT'S A DEAD END!
HUFF! HUFF!
POST NO BILLS

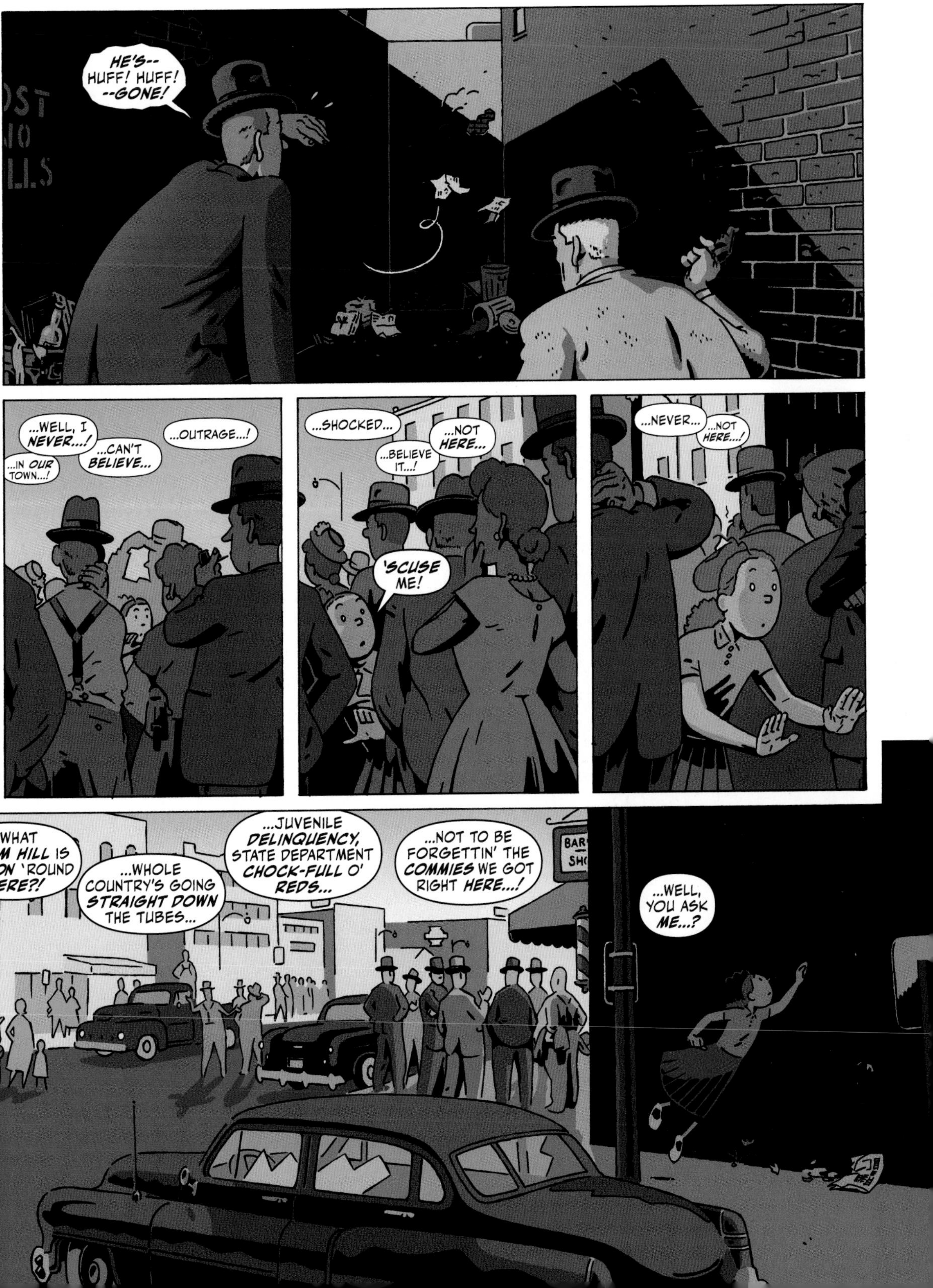
HE'S-- HUFF! HUFF! --GONE!
...WELL, I NEVER...!
...IN OUR TOWN...!
...CAN'T BELIEVE...
...OUTRAGE...!
...SHOCKED...
...BELIEVE IT...!
...NOT HERE...
'SCUSE ME!
...NEVER...
...NOT HERE...!
...WHAT IN SAM HILL IS OIN' ON 'ROUND HERE?!
...WHOLE COUNTRY'S GOING STRAIGHT DOWN THE TUBES...
...JUVENILE DELINQUENCY, STATE DEPARTMENT CHOCK-FULL O' REDS...
...NOT TO BE FORGETTIN' THE COMMIES WE GOT RIGHT HERE...!
...WELL, YOU ASK ME...?

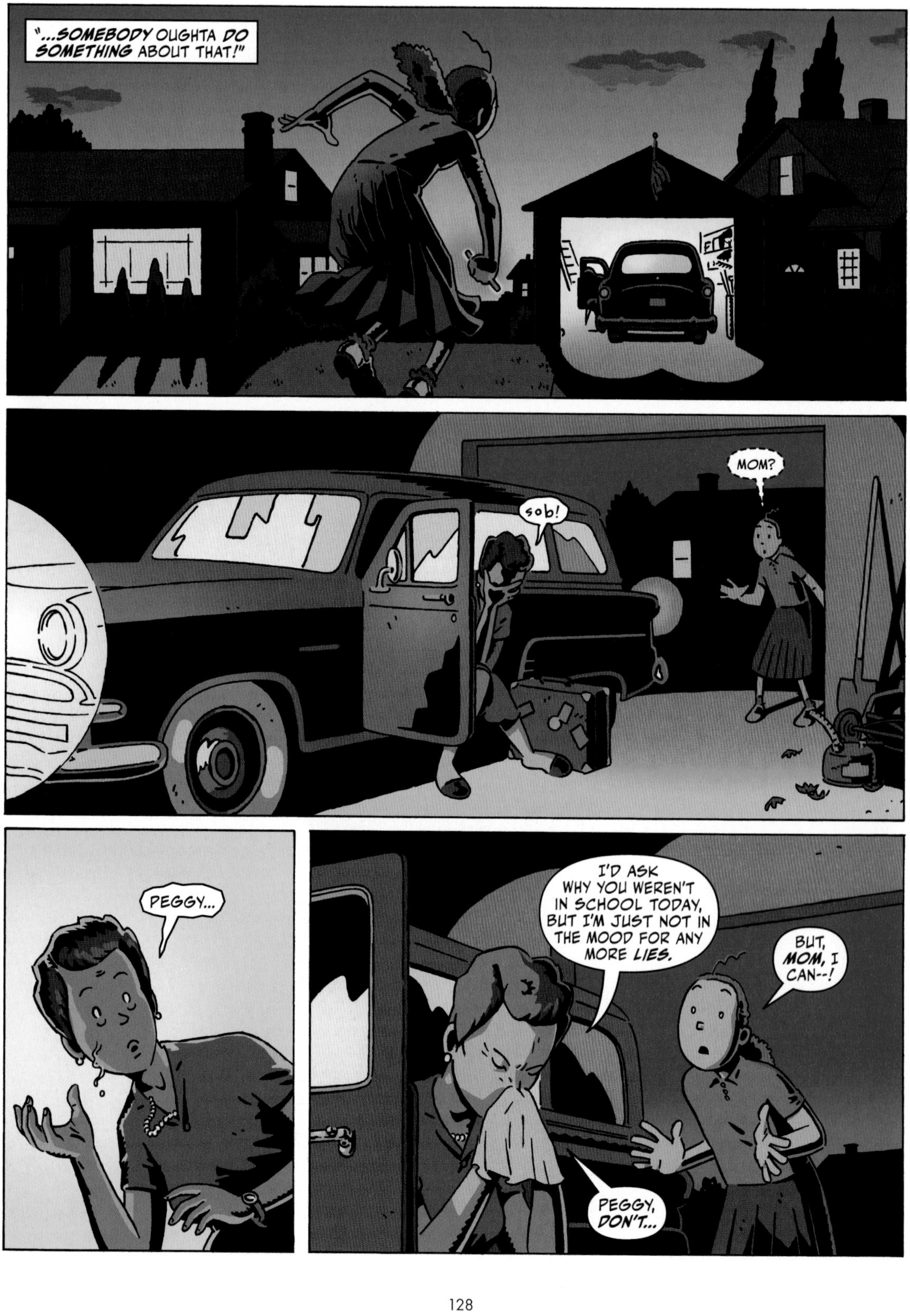
"...SOMEBODY OUGHTA DO SOMETHING ABOUT THAT!"
MOM?
sob!
PEGGY...
I'D ASK WHY YOU WEREN'T IN SCHOOL TODAY, BUT I'M JUST NOT IN THE MOOD FOR ANY MORE LIES.
BUT, MOM, I CAN--!
PEGGY, DON'T...

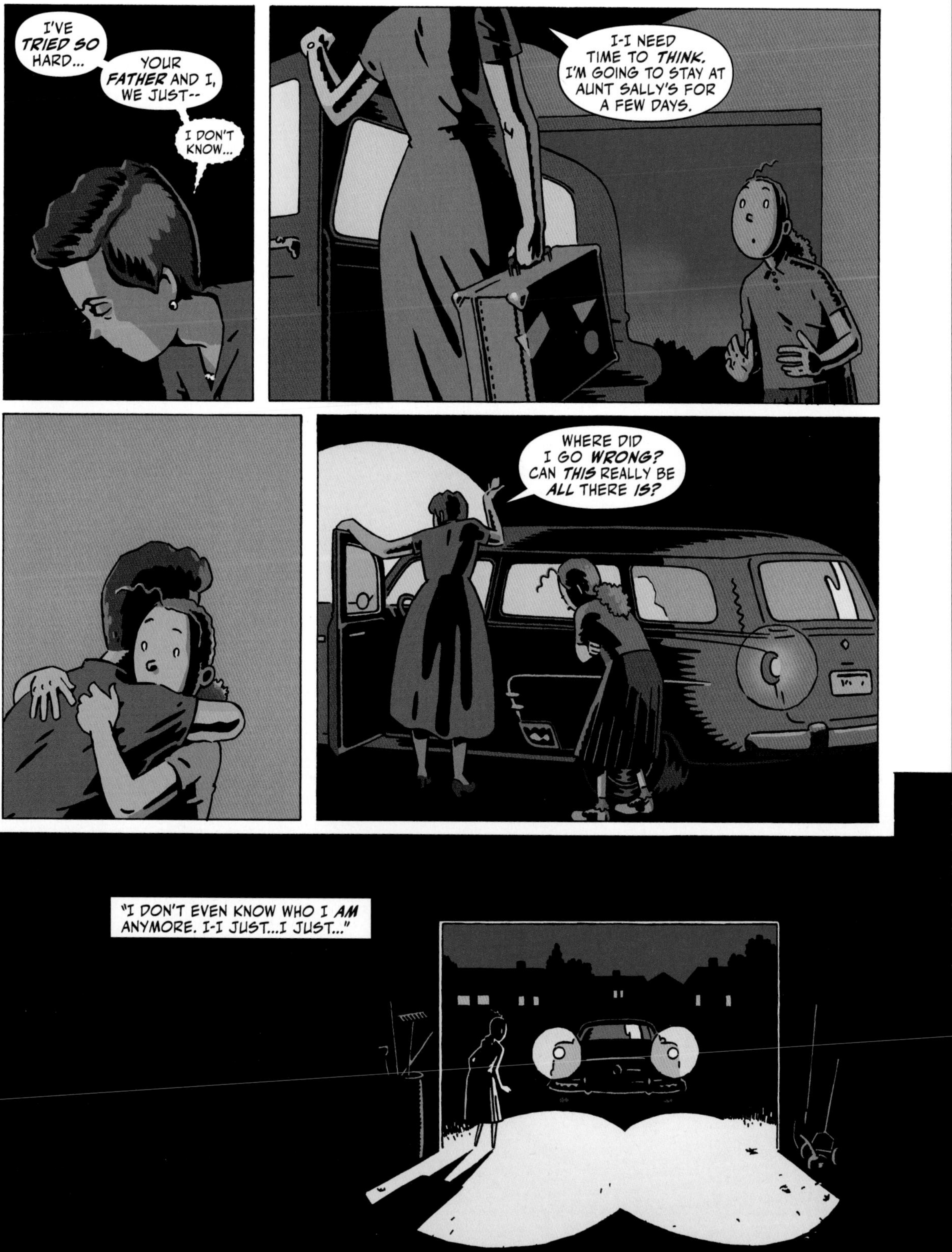
I'VE TRIED SO HARD...
YOUR FATHER AND I, WE JUST--
I DON'T KNOW...
I-I NEED TIME TO THINK. I'M GOING TO STAY AT AUNT SALLY'S FOR A FEW DAYS.
WHERE DID I GO WRONG? CAN THIS REALLY BE ALL THERE IS?
"I DON'T EVEN KNOW WHO I AM ANYMORE. I-I JUST...I JUST..."

"...I FEEL SO ALONE."

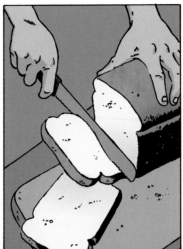

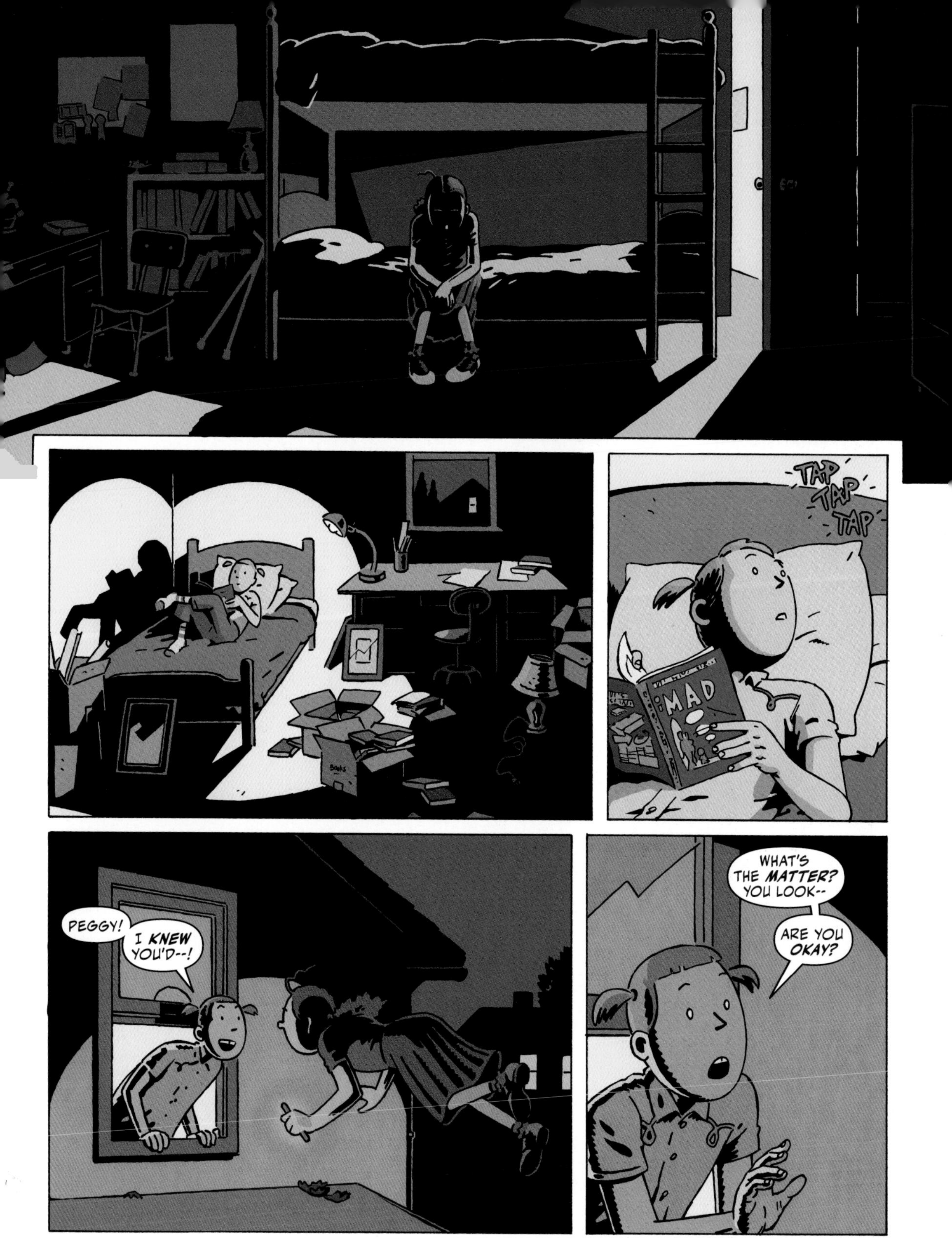
TAP
TAP
TAP
MAD
PEGGY!
I KNEW YOU'D--!
WHAT'S THE MATTER? YOU LOOK--
ARE YOU OKAY?

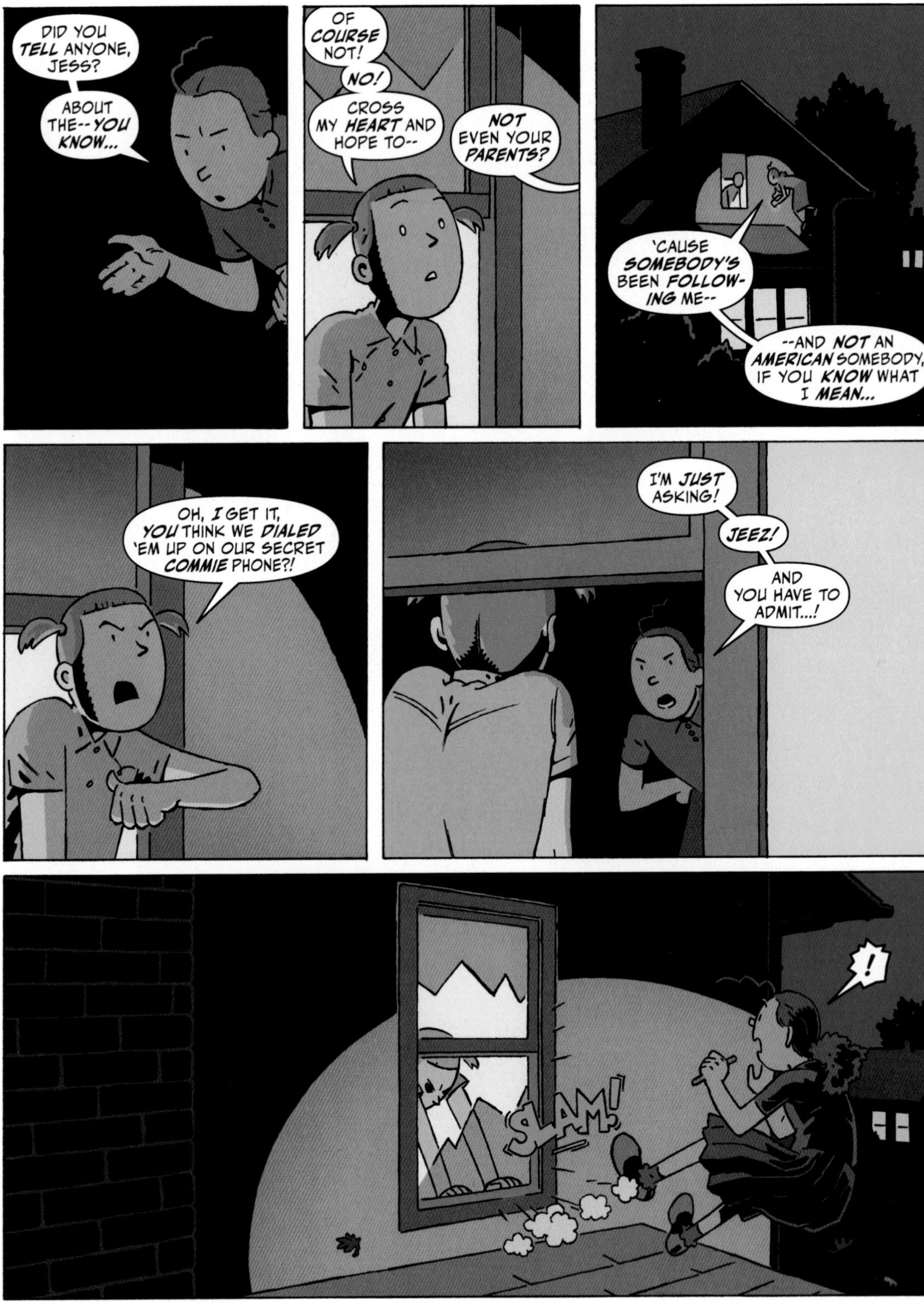
DID YOU TELL ANYONE, JESS?
ABOUT THE--YOU KNOW...
OF COURSE NOT!
NO!
CROSS MY HEART AND HOPE TO--
NOT EVEN YOUR PARENTS?
'CAUSE SOMEBODY'S BEEN FOLLOWING ME--
--AND NOT AN AMERICAN SOMEBODY, IF YOU KNOW WHAT I MEAN...
OH, I GET IT, YOU THINK WE DIALED 'EM UP ON OUR SECRET COMMIE PHONE?!
I'M JUST ASKING!
JEEZ!
AND YOU HAVE TO ADMIT...!
!
SLAM!

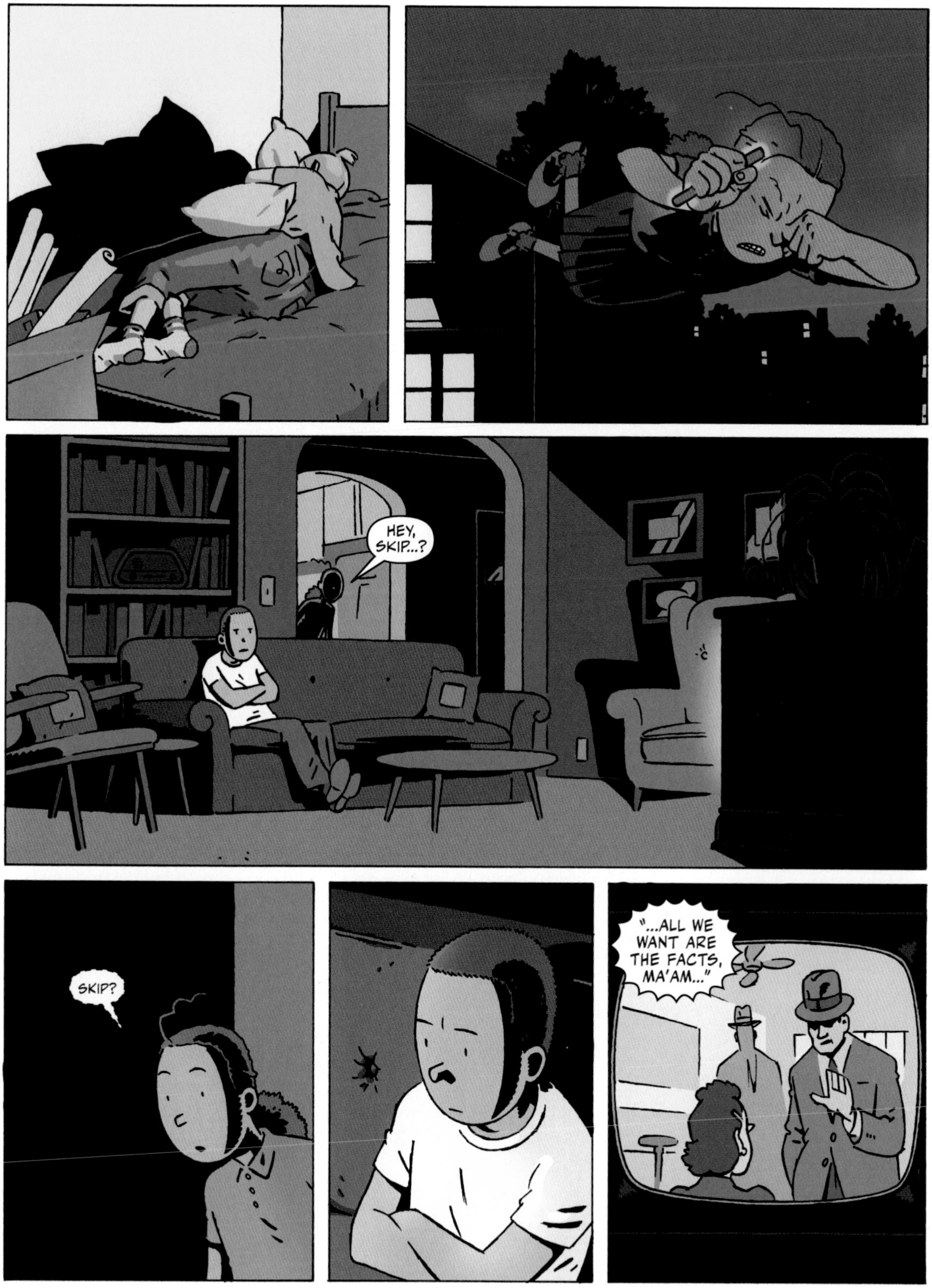
HEY, SKIP...?
SKIP?
"...ALL WE WANT ARE THE FACTS, MA'AM..."

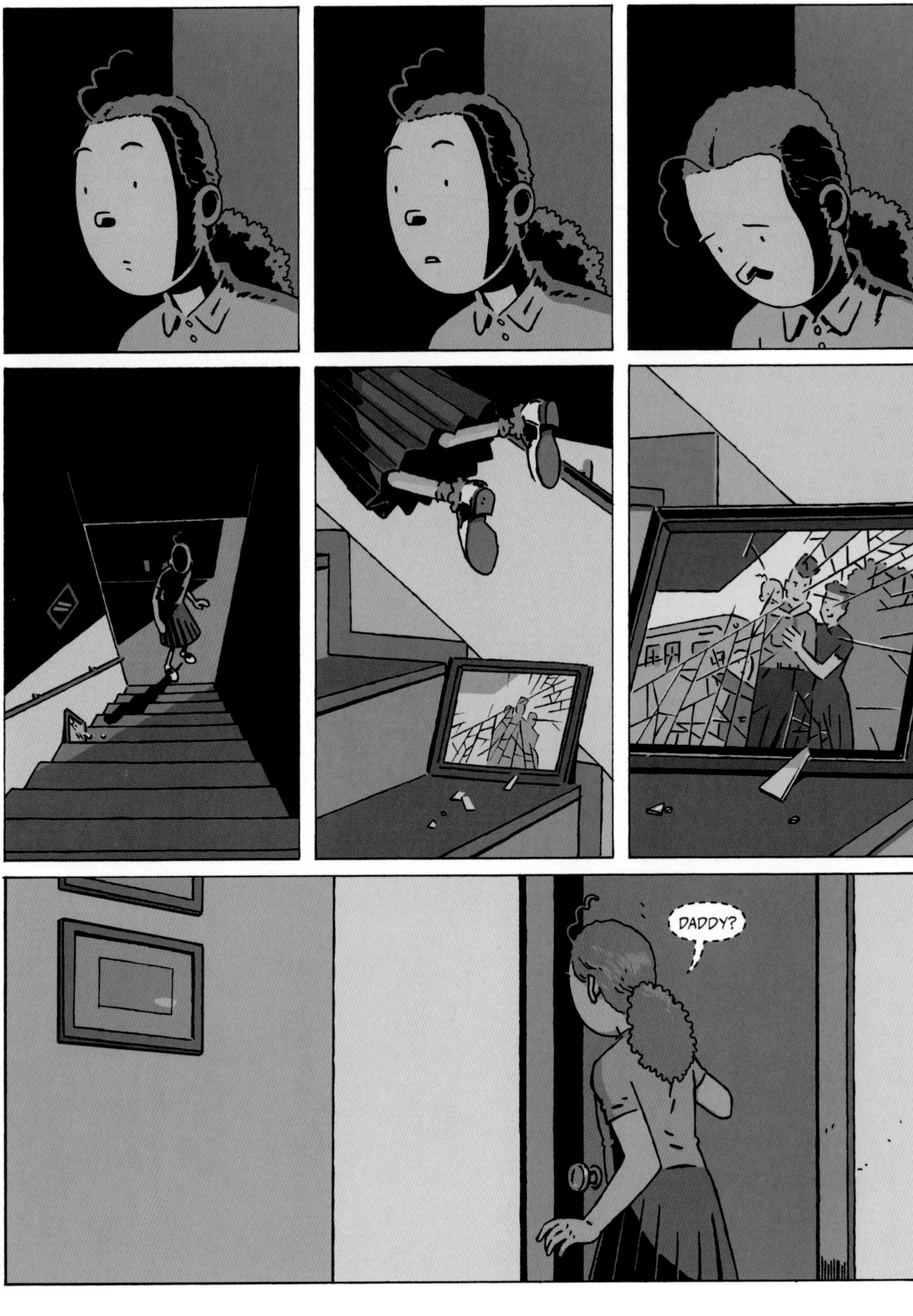
DADDY?

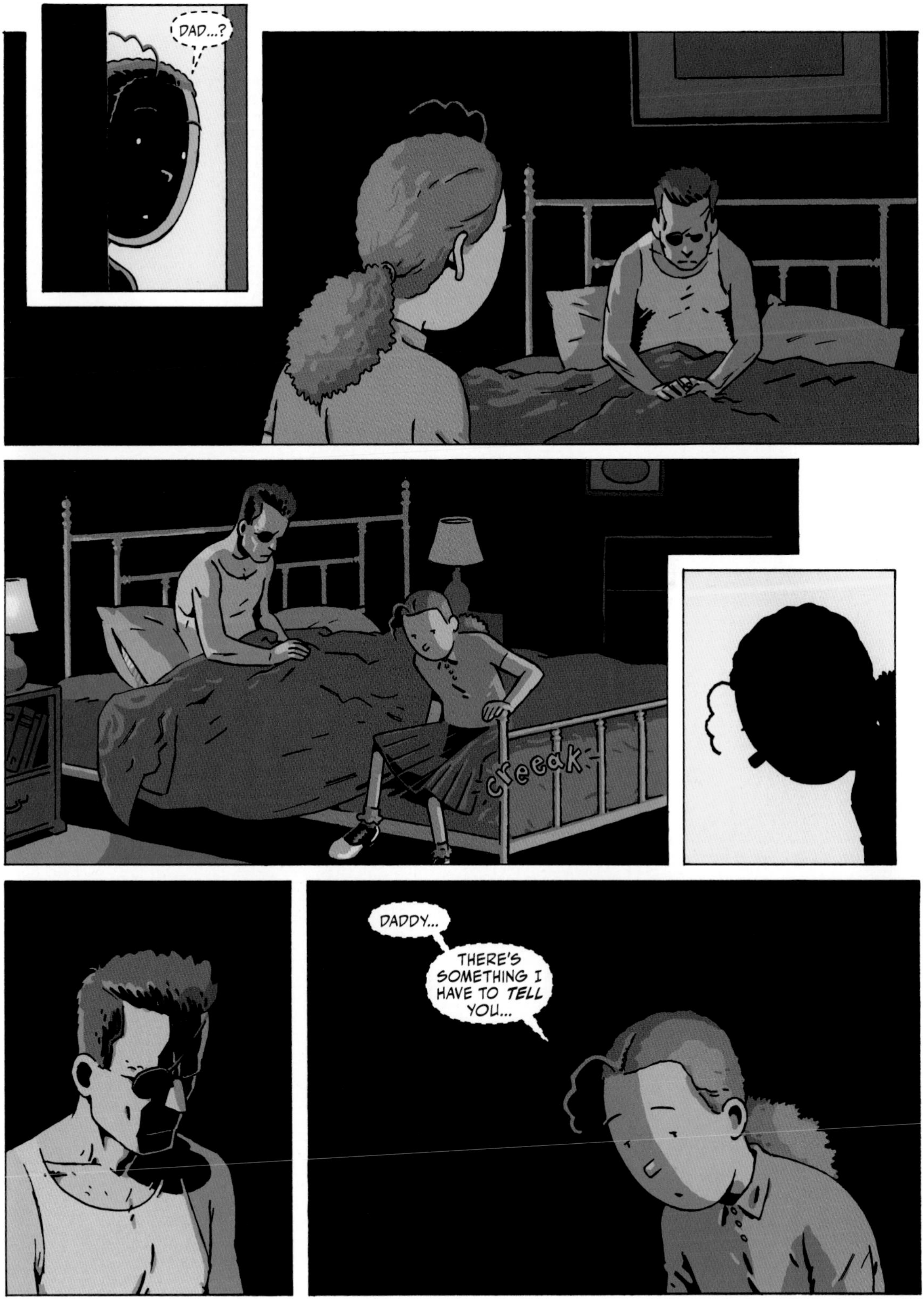
DAD...?
creeak
DADDY...
THERE'S SOMETHING I HAVE TO *TELL* YOU...

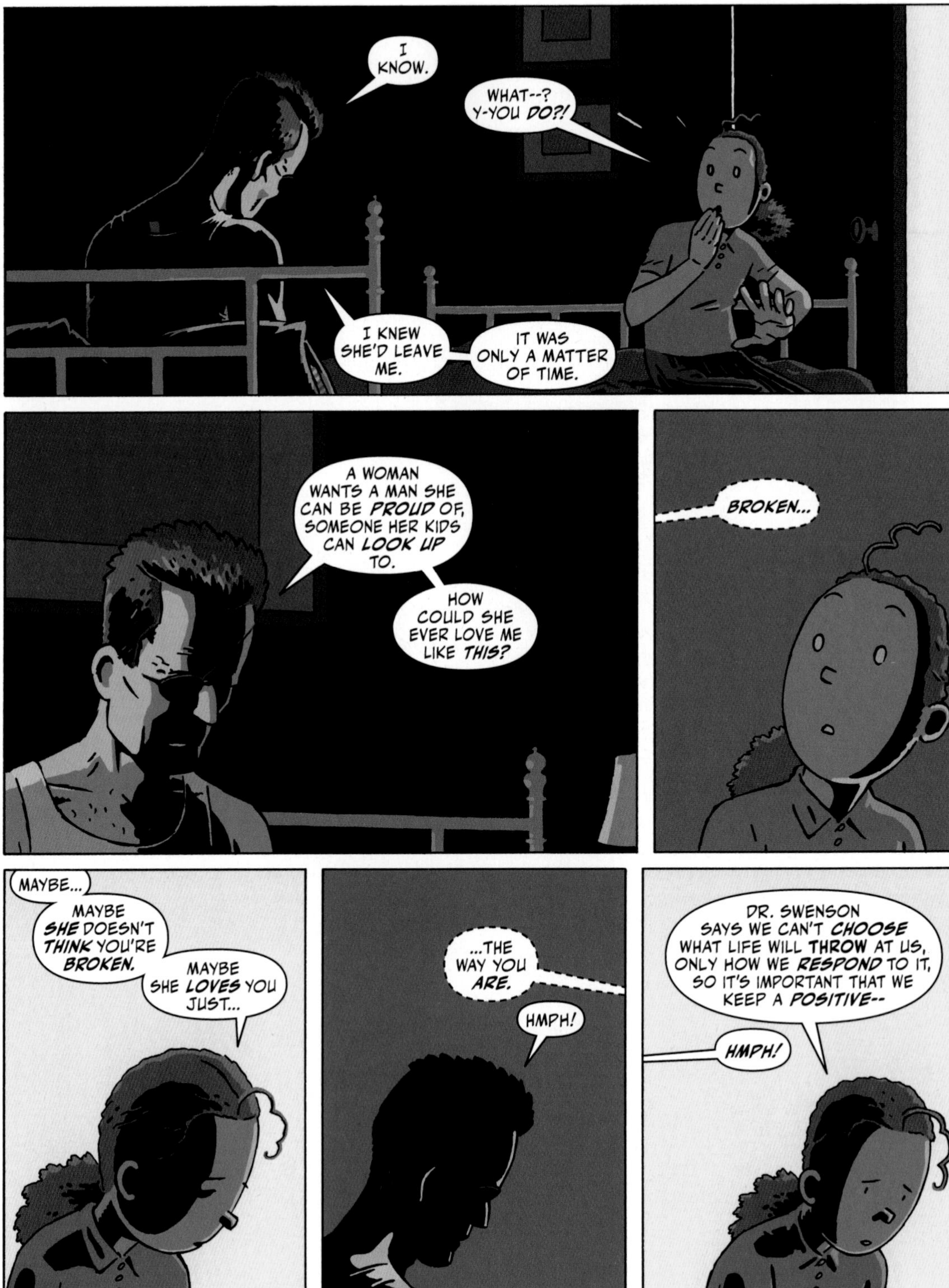
I KNOW.
WHAT--? Y-YOU DO?!
I KNEW SHE'D LEAVE ME.
IT WAS ONLY A MATTER OF TIME.
A WOMAN WANTS A MAN SHE CAN BE PROUD OF, SOMEONE HER KIDS CAN LOOK UP TO.
HOW COULD SHE EVER LOVE ME LIKE THIS?
BROKEN...
MAYBE...
MAYBE SHE DOESN'T THINK YOU'RE BROKEN.
MAYBE SHE LOVES YOU JUST...
...THE WAY YOU ARE.
HMPH!
DR. SWENSON SAYS WE CAN'T CHOOSE WHAT LIFE WILL THROW AT US, ONLY HOW WE RESPOND TO IT, SO IT'S IMPORTANT THAT WE KEEP A POSITIVE--
HMPH!

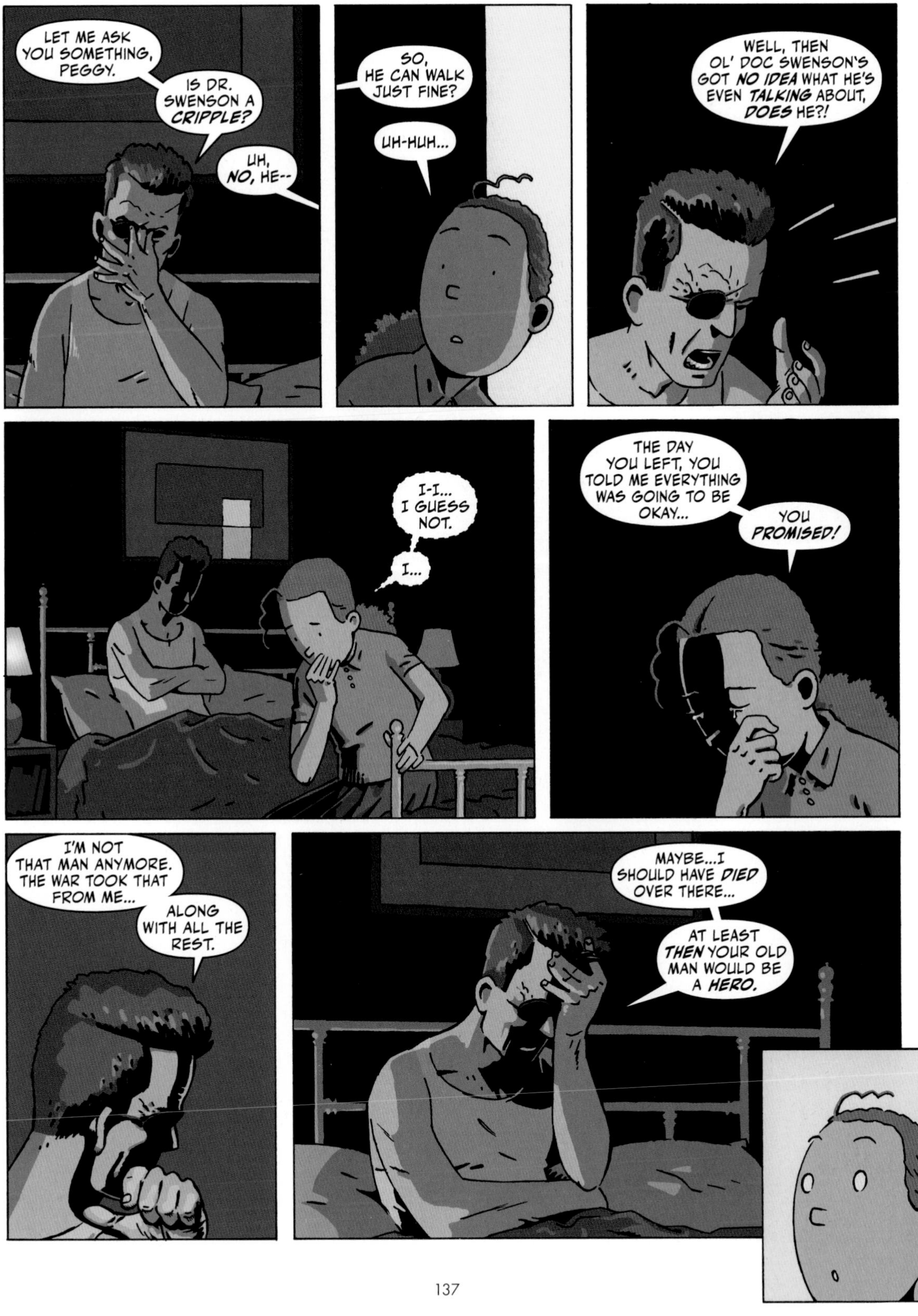
LET ME ASK YOU SOMETHING, PEGGY.
IS DR. SWENSON A CRIPPLE?
UH, NO, HE--
SO, HE CAN WALK JUST FINE?
UH-HUH...
WELL, THEN OL' DOC SWENSON'S GOT NO IDEA WHAT HE'S EVEN TALKING ABOUT, DOES HE?!
I-I... I GUESS NOT.
I...
THE DAY YOU LEFT, YOU TOLD ME EVERYTHING WAS GOING TO BE OKAY...
YOU PROMISED!
I'M NOT THAT MAN ANYMORE. THE WAR TOOK THAT FROM ME...
ALONG WITH ALL THE REST.
MAYBE...I SHOULD HAVE DIED OVER THERE...
AT LEAST THEN YOUR OLD MAN WOULD BE A HERO.

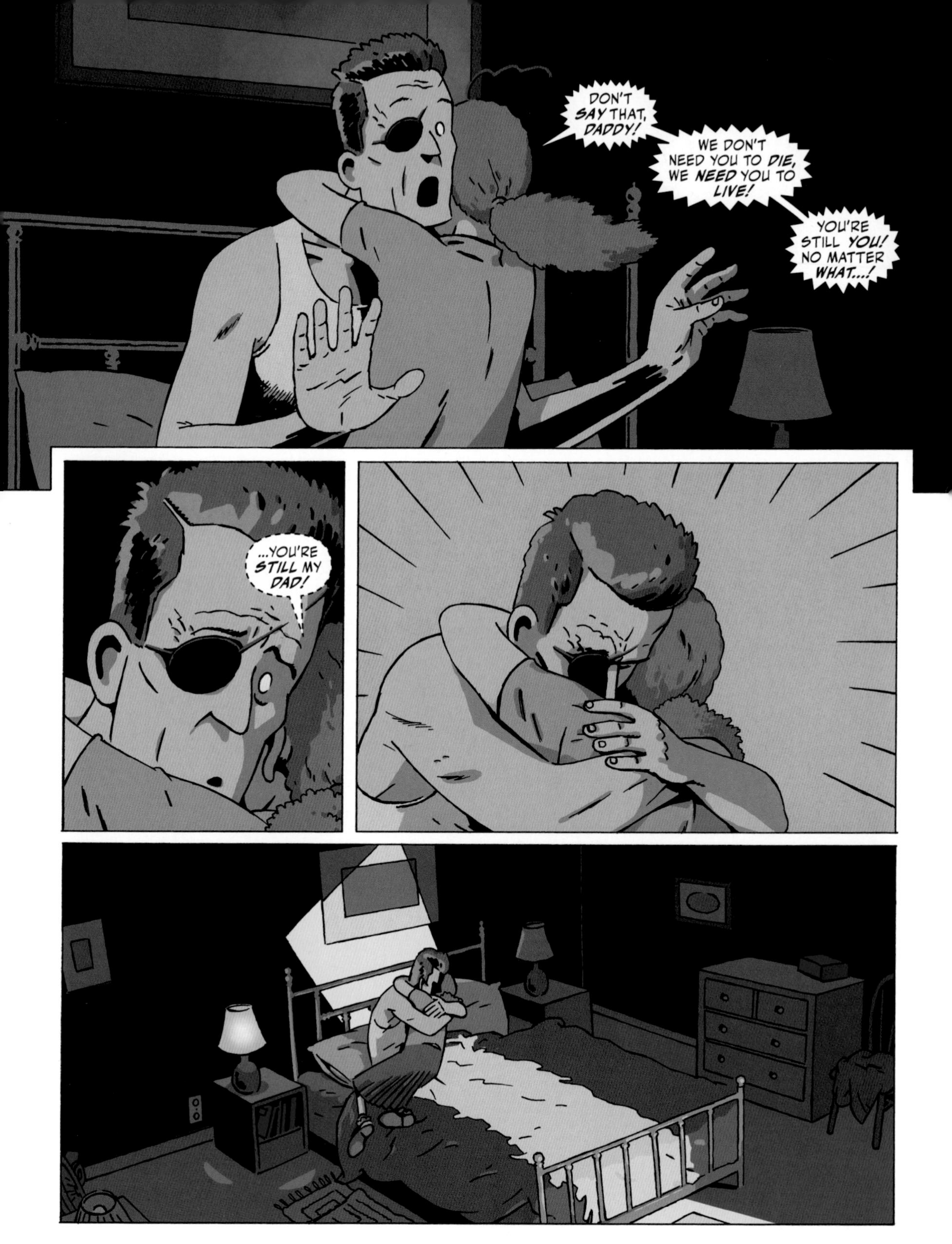
DON'T SAY THAT, DADDY!
WE DON'T NEED YOU TO DIE, WE NEED YOU TO LIVE!
YOU'RE STILL YOU! NO MATTER WHAT...!
...YOU'RE STILL MY DAD!

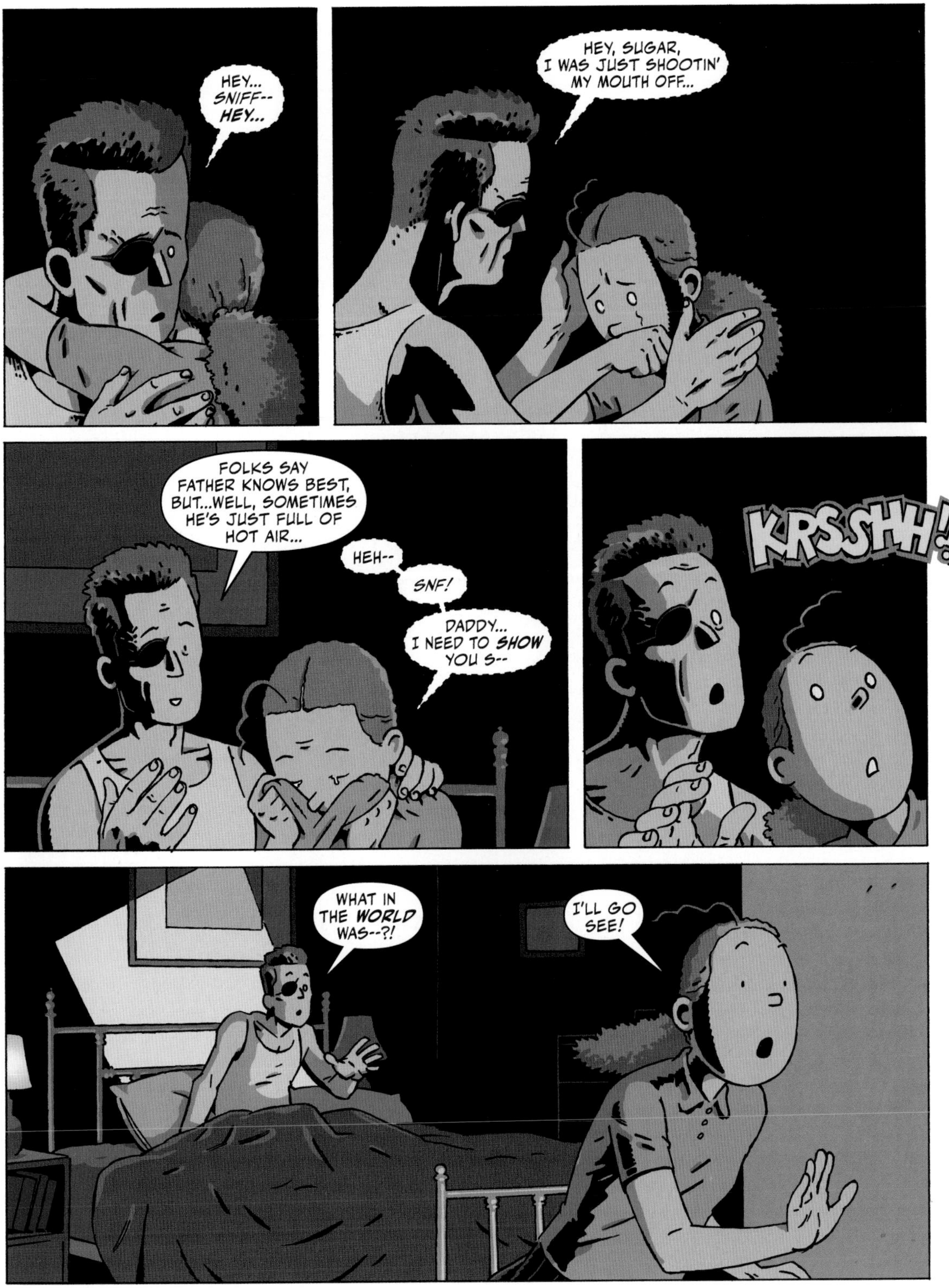
HEY...
SNIFF--
HEY...
HEY, SUGAR, I WAS JUST SHOOTIN' MY MOUTH OFF...
FOLKS SAY FATHER KNOWS BEST, BUT...WELL, SOMETIMES HE'S JUST FULL OF HOT AIR...
HEH--
SNF!
DADDY... I NEED TO SHOW YOU S--
KRSSHH!!
WHAT IN THE WORLD WAS--?!
I'LL GO SEE!

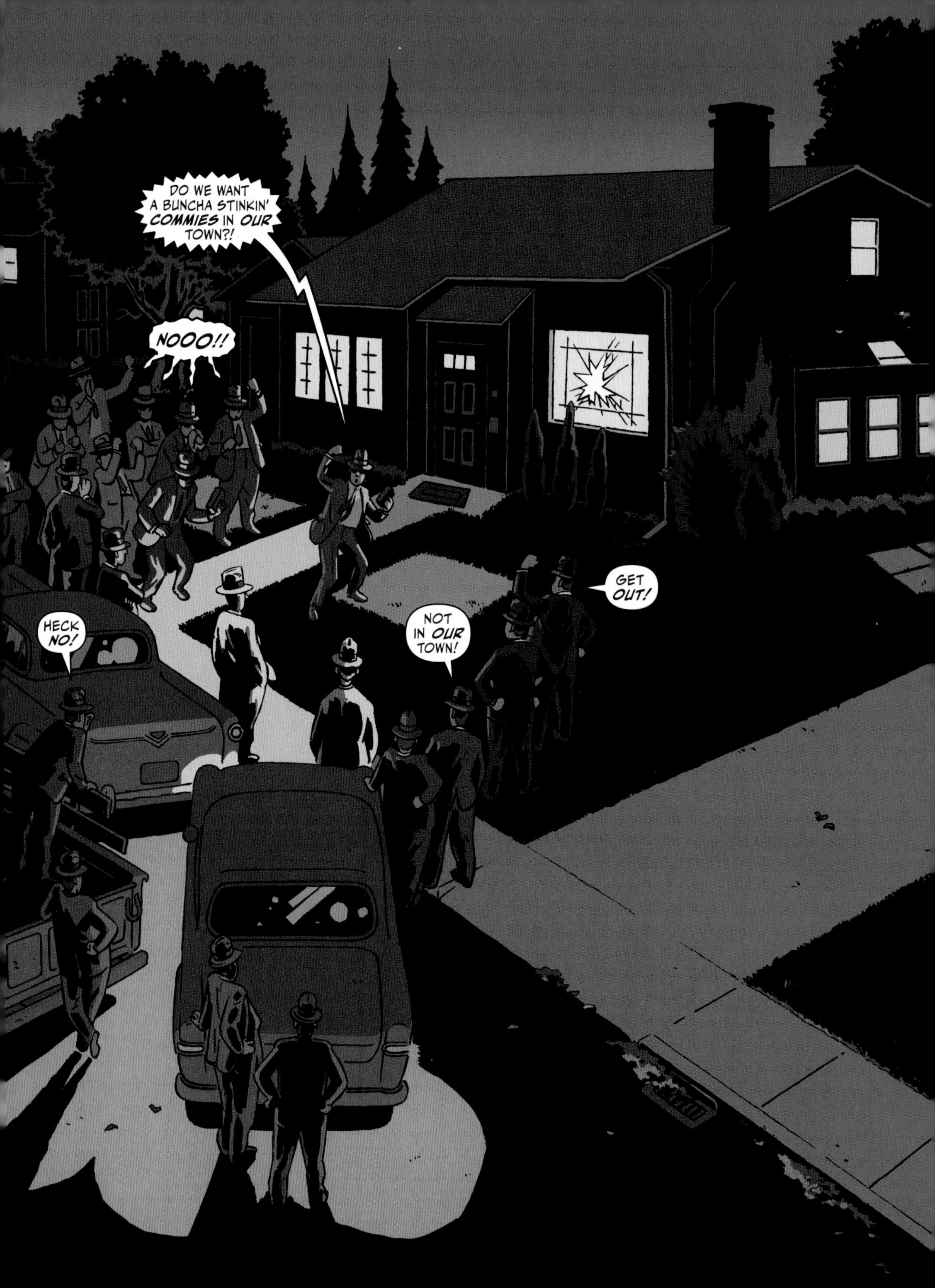
DO WE WANT A BUNCHA STINKIN' COMMIES IN OUR TOWN?!
NOOO!!
HECK NO!
NOT IN OUR TOWN!
GET OUT!

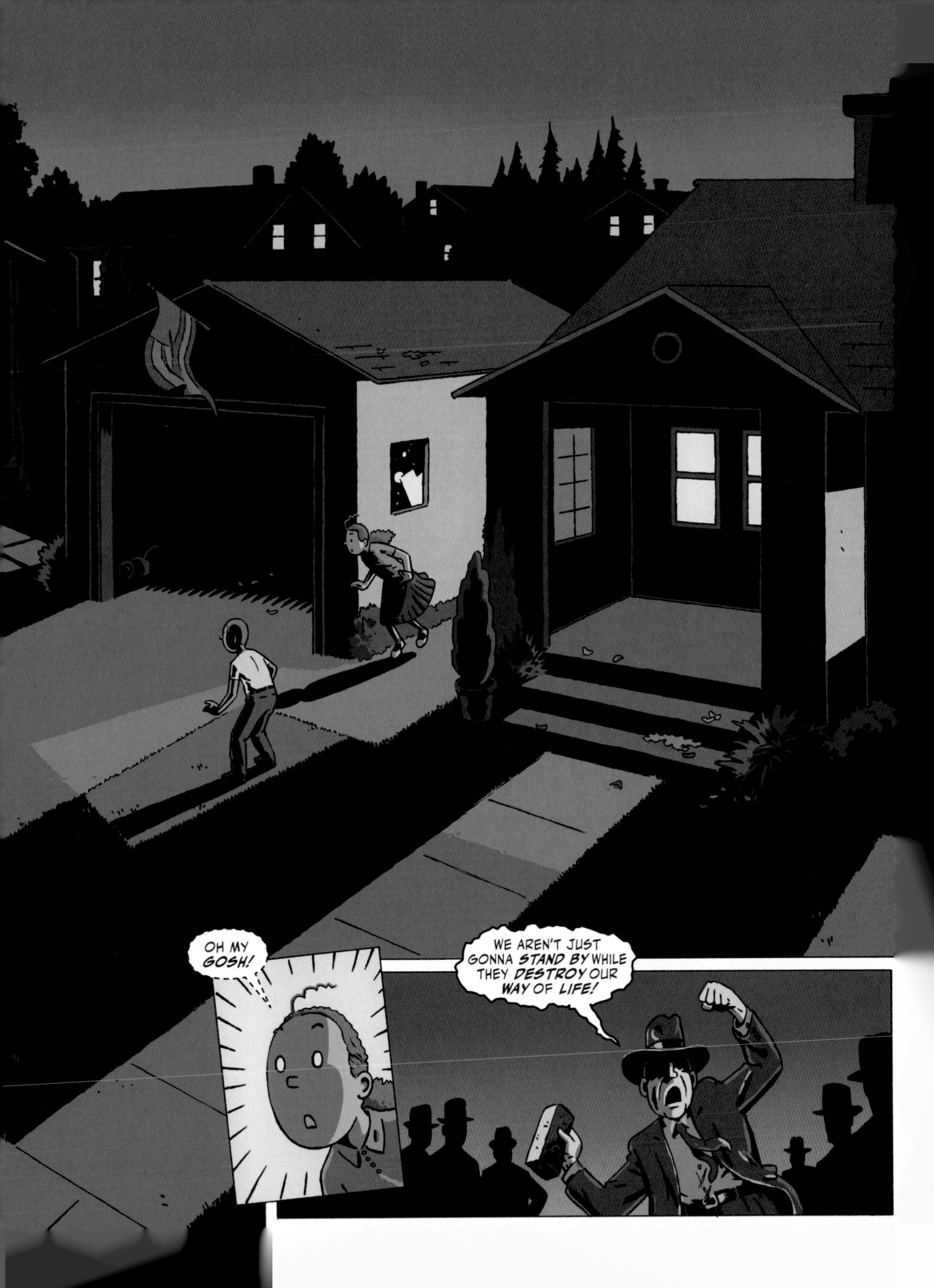

OH MY GOSH!
WE AREN'T JUST GONNA STAND BY WHILE THEY DESTROY OUR WAY OF LIFE!

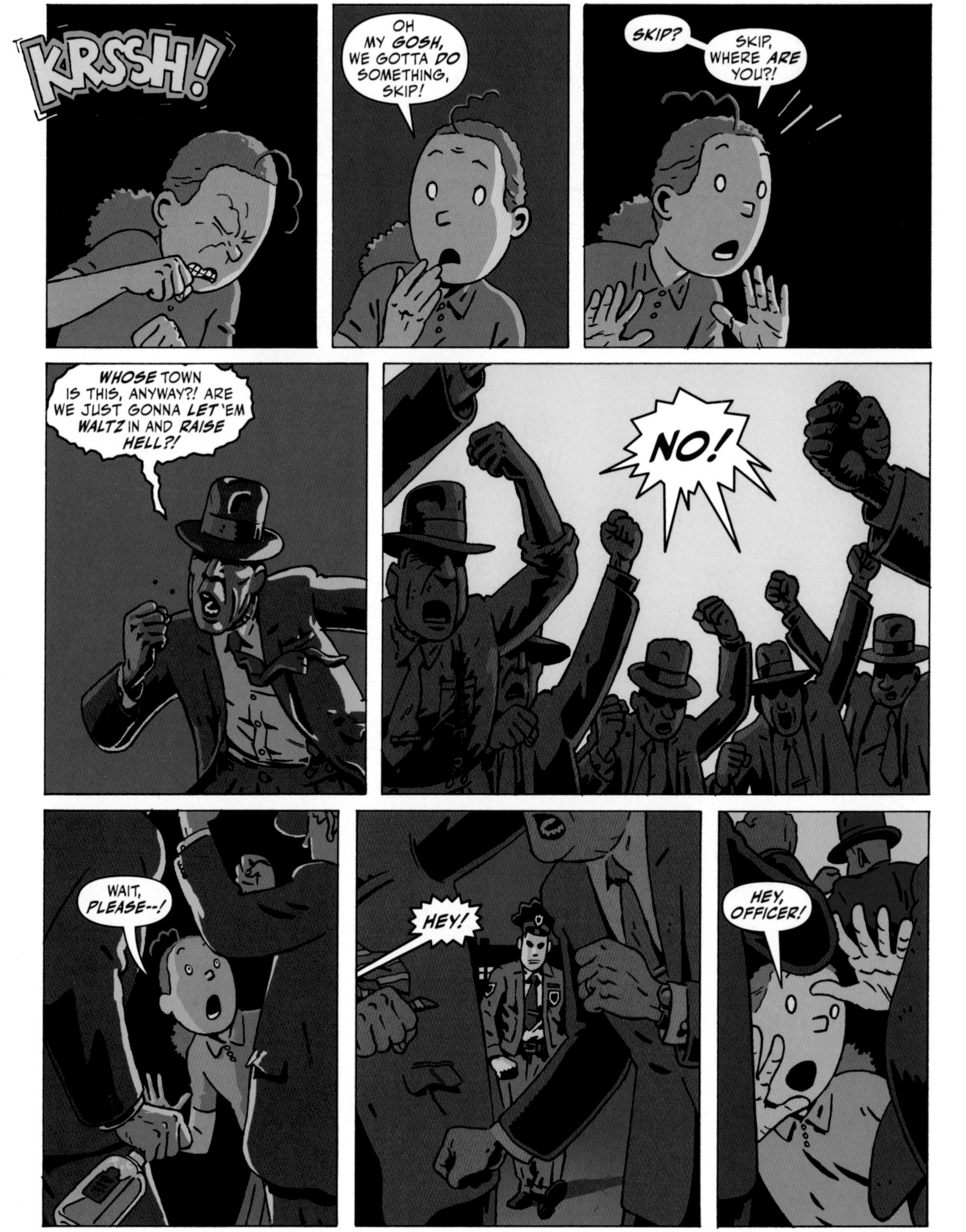
KRSSH!
OH MY GOSH, WE GOTTA DO SOMETHING, SKIP!
SKIP?
SKIP, WHERE ARE YOU?!
WHOSE TOWN IS THIS, ANYWAY?! ARE WE JUST GONNA LET 'EM WALTZ IN AND RAISE HELL?!
NO!
WAIT, PLEASE--!
HEY!
HEY, OFFICER!

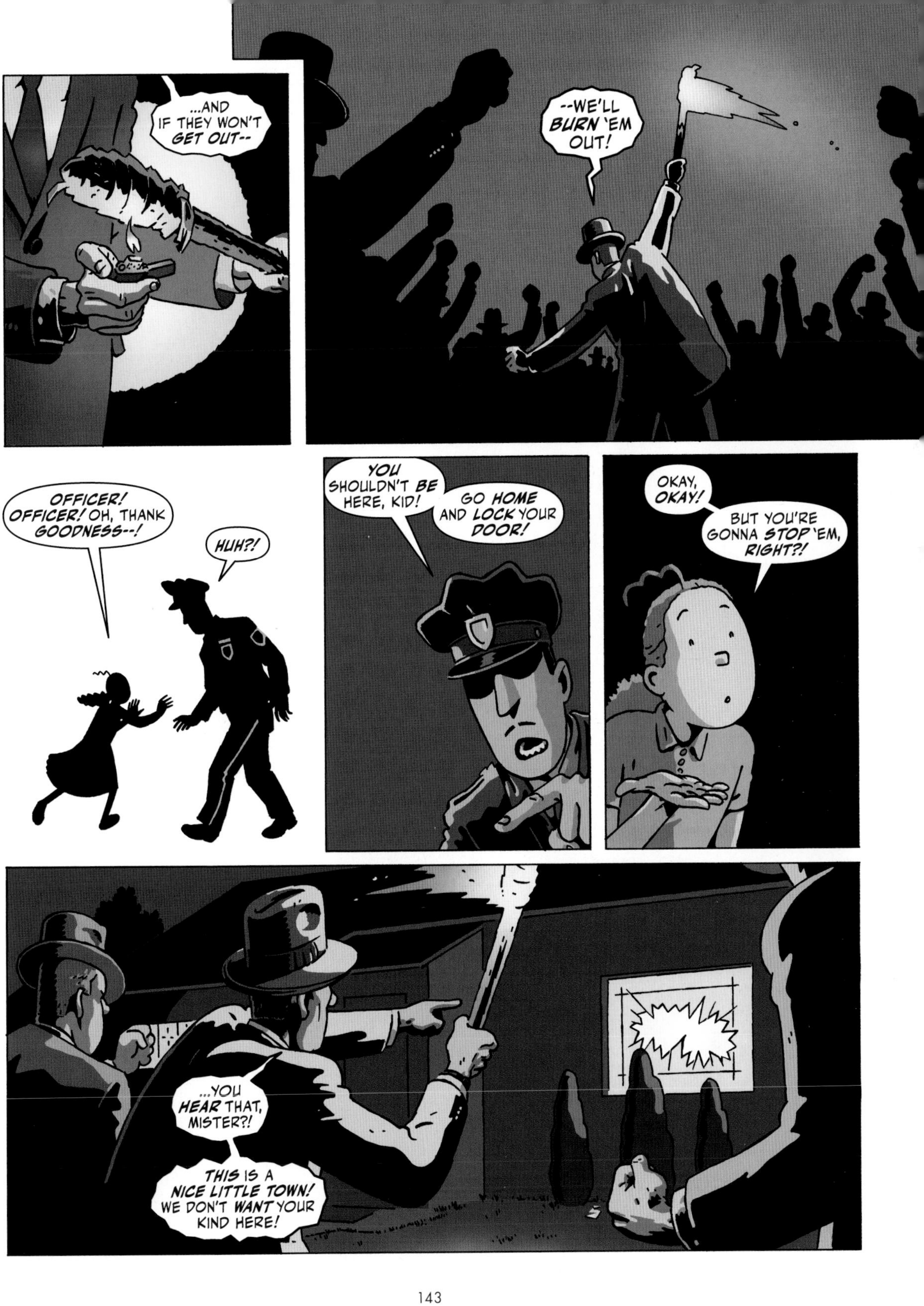

...AND IF THEY WON'T GET OUT--
--WE'LL BURN 'EM OUT!
OFFICER! OFFICER! OH, THANK GOODNESS--!
HUH?!
YOU SHOULDN'T BE HERE, KID!
GO HOME AND LOCK YOUR DOOR!
OKAY, OKAY!
BUT YOU'RE GONNA STOP 'EM, RIGHT?!
...YOU HEAR THAT, MISTER?!
THIS IS A NICE LITTLE TOWN! WE DON'T WANT YOUR KIND HERE!

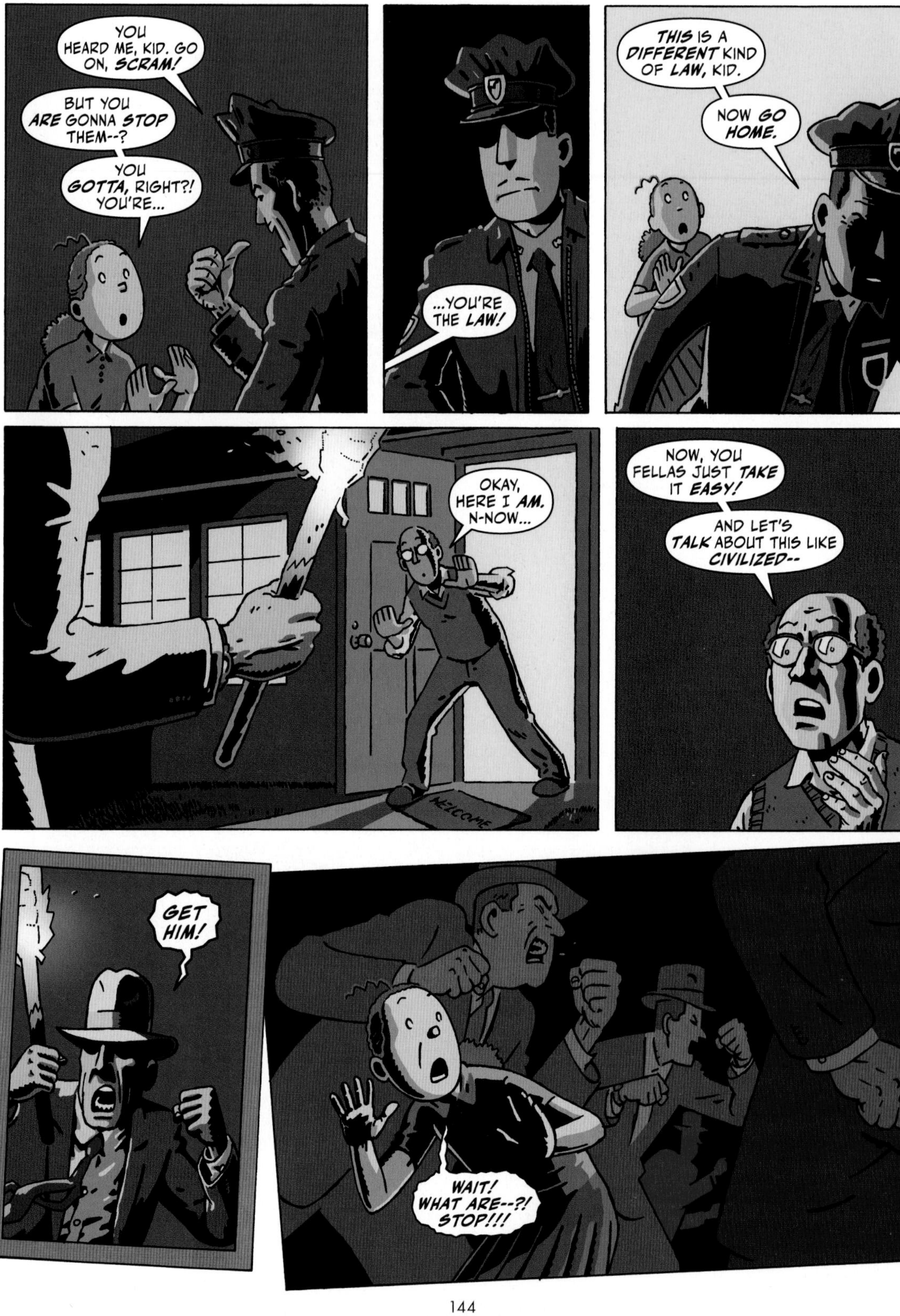

YOU HEARD ME, KID. GO ON, SCRAM!
BUT YOU ARE GONNA STOP THEM--?
YOU GOTTA, RIGHT?! YOU'RE...
...YOU'RE THE LAW!
THIS IS A DIFFERENT KIND OF LAW, KID.
NOW GO HOME.
OKAY, HERE I AM. N-NOW...
WELCOME
NOW, YOU FELLAS JUST TAKE IT EASY!
AND LET'S TALK ABOUT THIS LIKE CIVILIZED--
GET HIM!
WAIT! WHAT ARE--?! STOP!!!

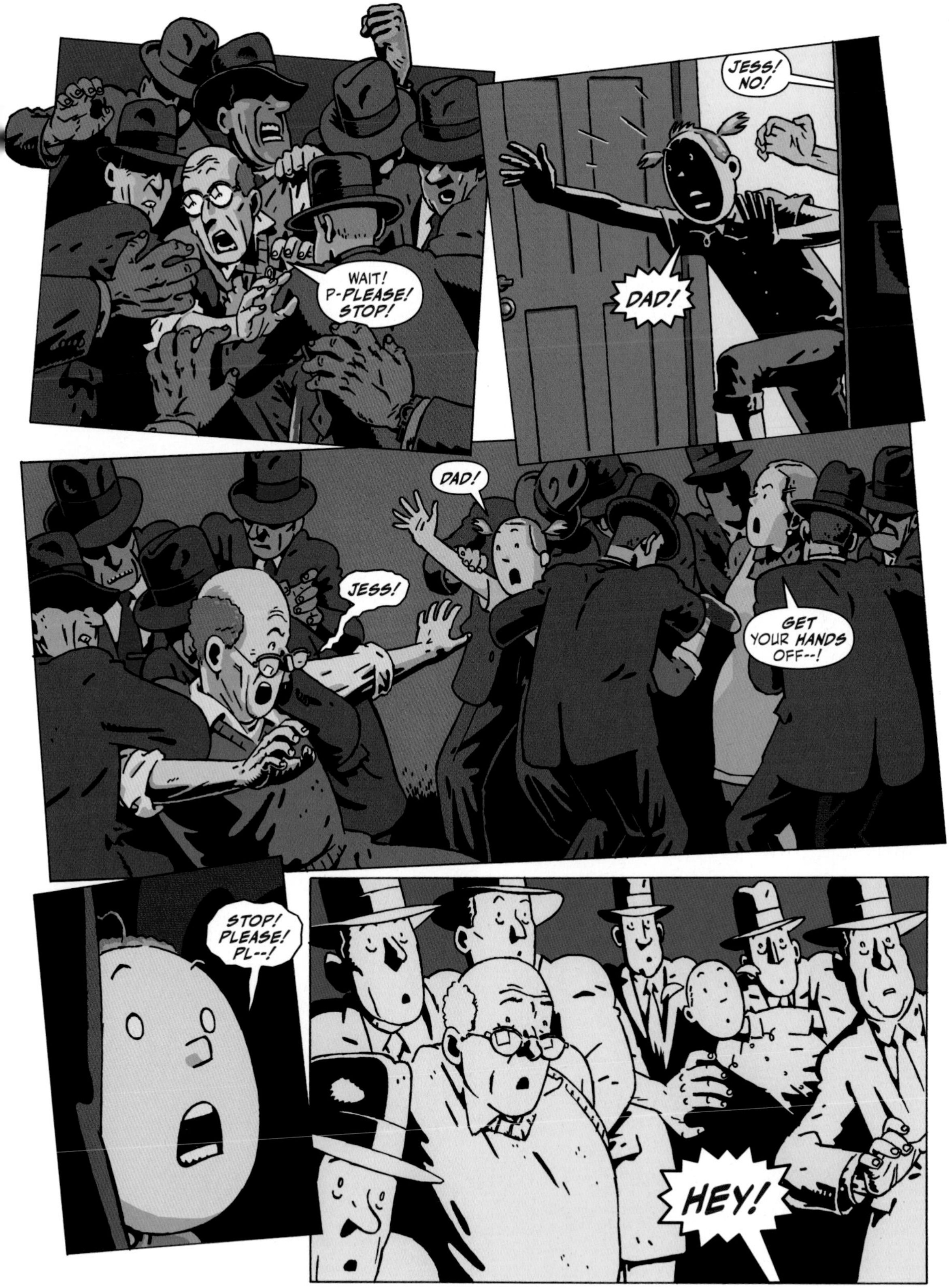
WAIT! P-PLEASE! STOP!
JESS! NO!
DAD!
DAD!
JESS!
GET YOUR HANDS OFF--!
STOP! PLEASE! PL--!
HEY!

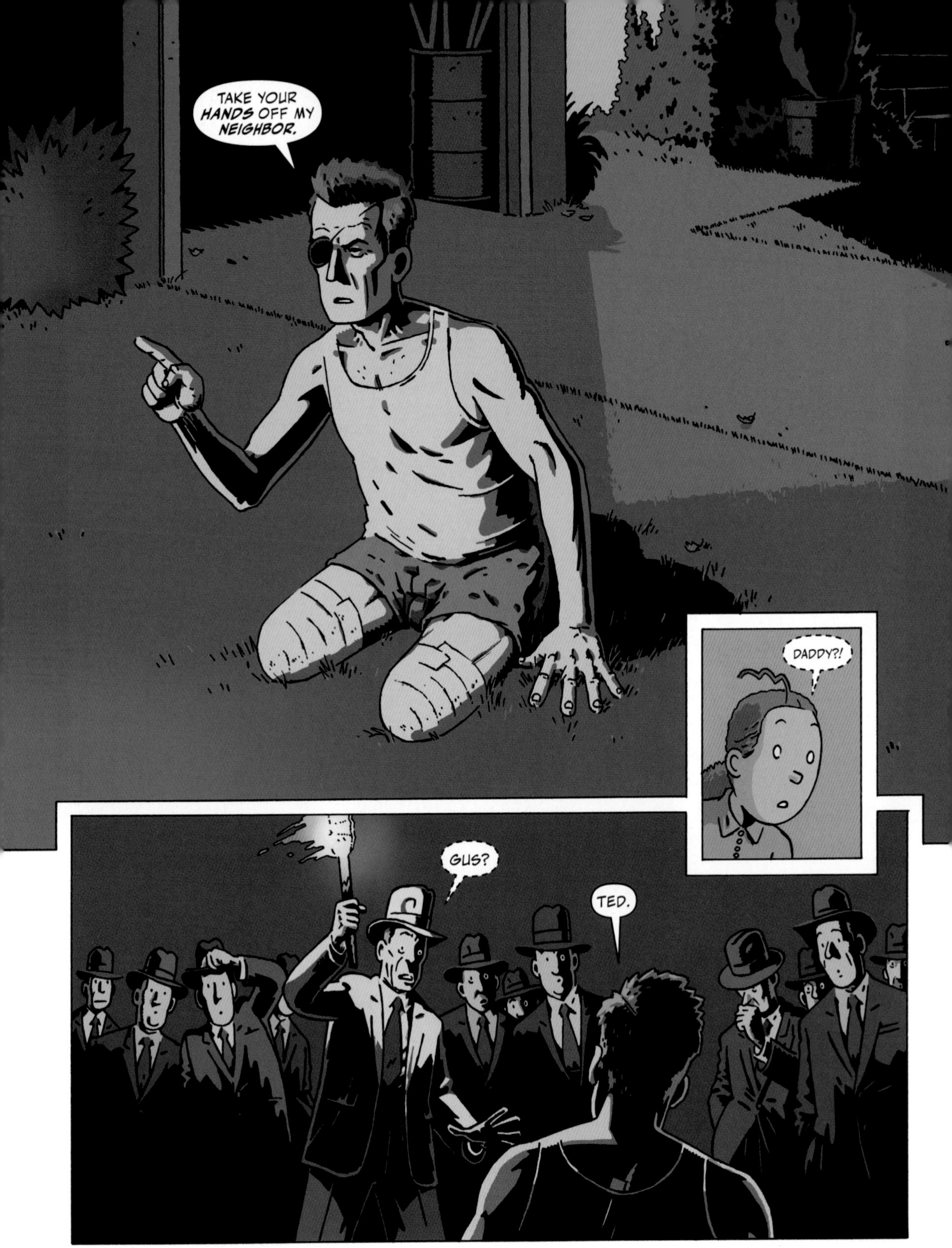
TAKE YOUR HANDS OFF MY NEIGHBOR.
DADDY?!
GUS?
TED.

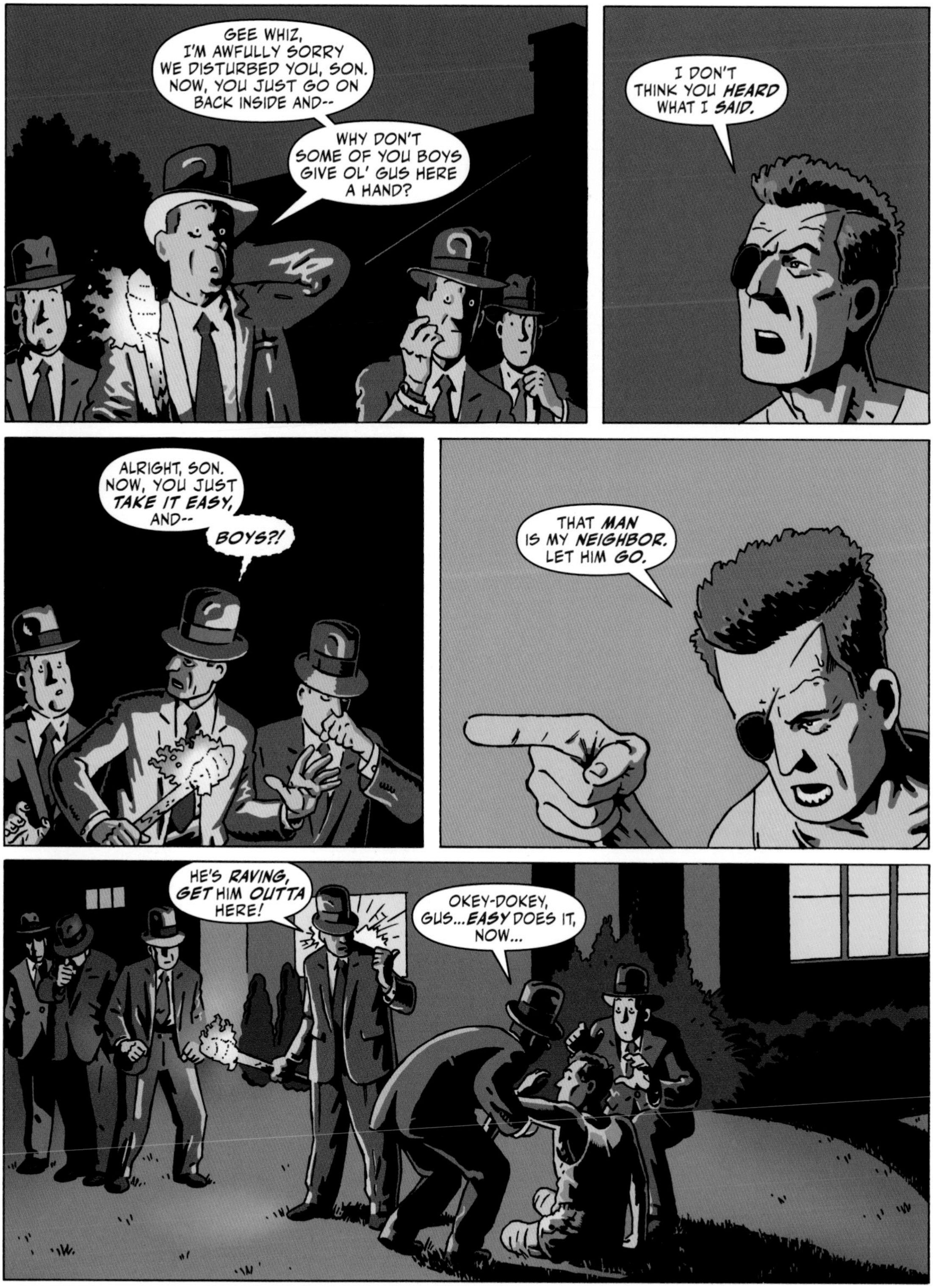
GEE WHIZ, I'M AWFULLY SORRY WE DISTURBED YOU, SON. NOW, YOU JUST GO ON BACK INSIDE AND--
WHY DON'T SOME OF YOU BOYS GIVE OL' GUS HERE A HAND?
I DON'T THINK YOU HEARD WHAT I SAID.
ALRIGHT, SON. NOW, YOU JUST TAKE IT EASY, AND--
BOYS?!
THAT MAN IS MY NEIGHBOR. LET HIM GO.
HE'S RAVING, GET HIM OUTTA HERE!
OKEY-DOKEY, GUS...EASY DOES IT, NOW...

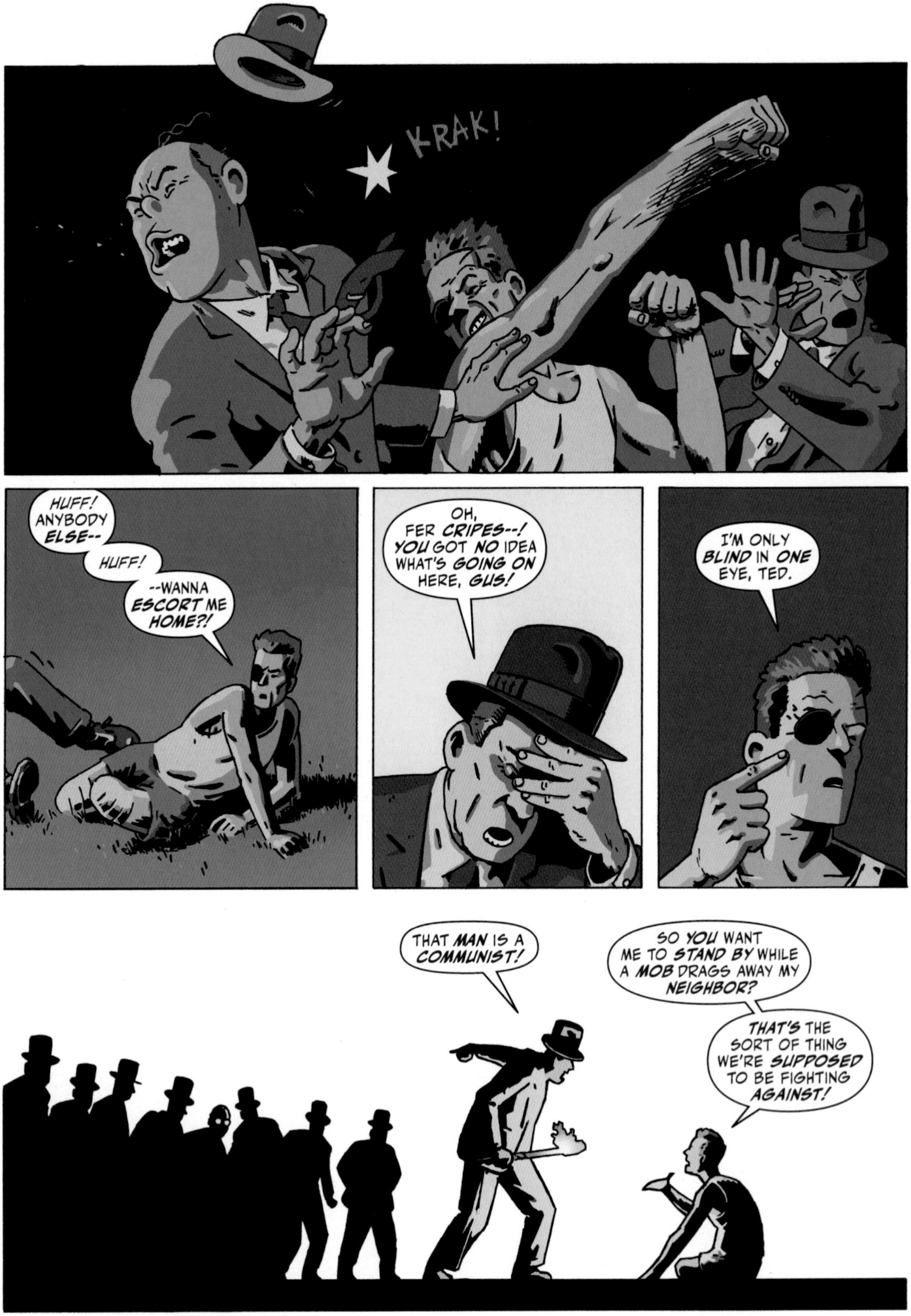
KRAK!
HUFF! ANYBODY ELSE--
HUFF!
--WANNA ESCORT ME HOME?!
OH, FER CRIPES--! YOU GOT NO IDEA WHAT'S GOING ON HERE, GUS!
I'M ONLY BLIND IN ONE EYE, TED.
THAT MAN IS A COMMUNIST!
SO YOU WANT ME TO STAND BY WHILE A MOB DRAGS AWAY MY NEIGHBOR?
THAT'S THE SORT OF THING WE'RE SUPPOSED TO BE FIGHTING AGAINST!

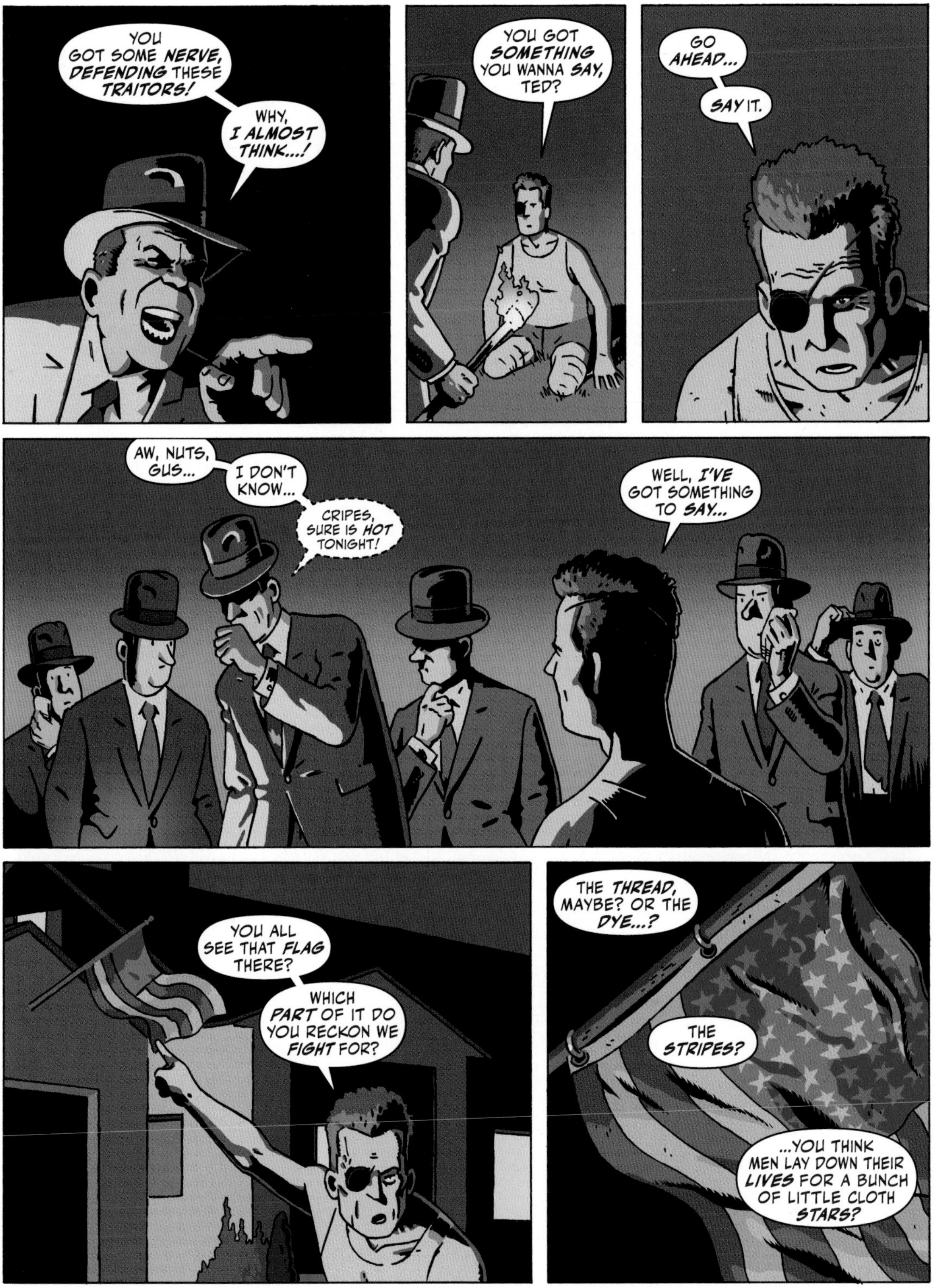
YOU GOT SOME NERVE, DEFENDING THESE TRAITORS!
WHY, I ALMOST THINK...!
YOU GOT SOMETHING YOU WANNA SAY, TED?
GO AHEAD...
SAY IT.
AW, NUTS, GUS...
I DON'T KNOW...
CRIPES, SURE IS HOT TONIGHT!
WELL, I'VE GOT SOMETHING TO SAY...
YOU ALL SEE THAT FLAG THERE?
WHICH PART OF IT DO YOU RECKON WE FIGHT FOR?
THE THREAD, MAYBE? OR THE DYE...?
THE STRIPES?
...YOU THINK MEN LAY DOWN THEIR LIVES FOR A BUNCH OF LITTLE CLOTH STARS?

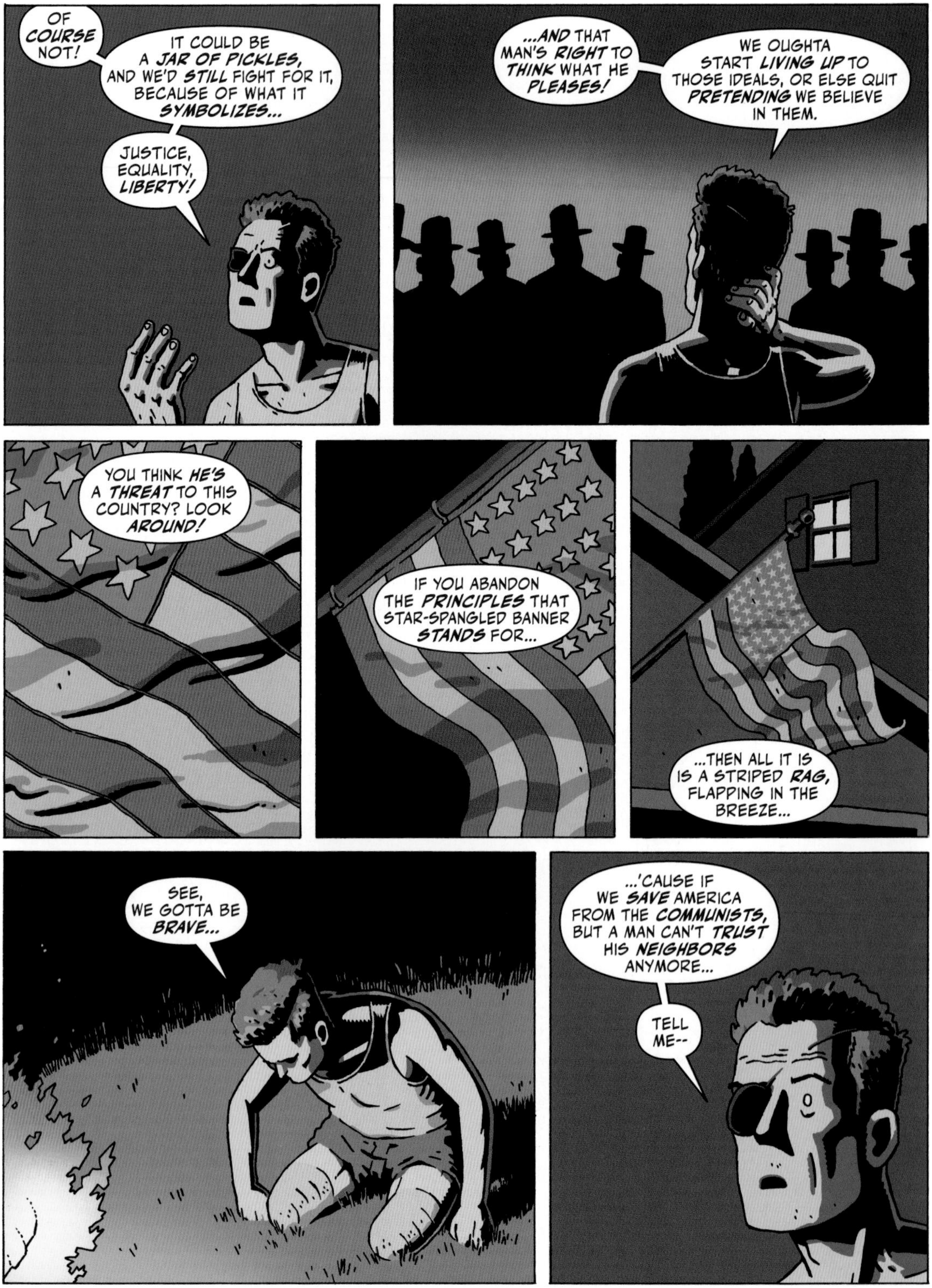
OF COURSE NOT!
IT COULD BE A JAR OF PICKLES, AND WE'D STILL FIGHT FOR IT, BECAUSE OF WHAT IT SYMBOLIZES...
JUSTICE, EQUALITY, LIBERTY!
...AND THAT MAN'S RIGHT TO THINK WHAT HE PLEASES!
WE OUGHTA START LIVING UP TO THOSE IDEALS, OR ELSE QUIT PRETENDING WE BELIEVE IN THEM.
YOU THINK HE'S A THREAT TO THIS COUNTRY? LOOK AROUND!
IF YOU ABANDON THE PRINCIPLES THAT STAR-SPANGLED BANNER STANDS FOR...
...THEN ALL IT IS IS A STRIPED RAG, FLAPPING IN THE BREEZE...
SEE, WE GOTTA BE BRAVE...
...'CAUSE IF WE SAVE AMERICA FROM THE COMMUNISTS, BUT A MAN CAN'T TRUST HIS NEIGHBORS ANYMORE...
TELL ME--

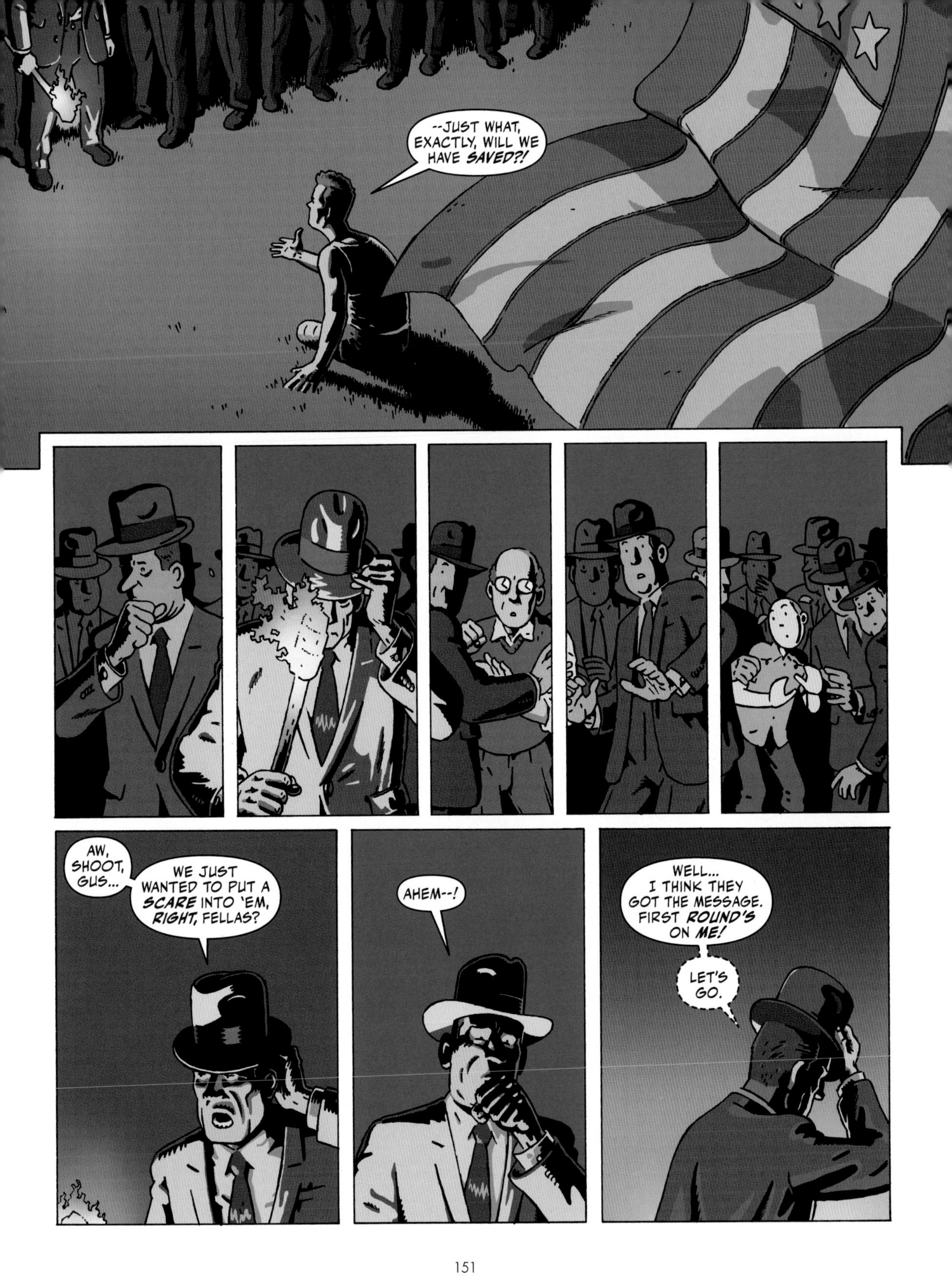
--JUST WHAT, EXACTLY, WILL WE HAVE SAVED?!
AW, SHOOT, GUS...
WE JUST WANTED TO PUT A SCARE INTO 'EM, RIGHT, FELLAS?
AHEM--!
WELL... I THINK THEY GOT THE MESSAGE. FIRST ROUND'S ON ME!
LET'S GO.

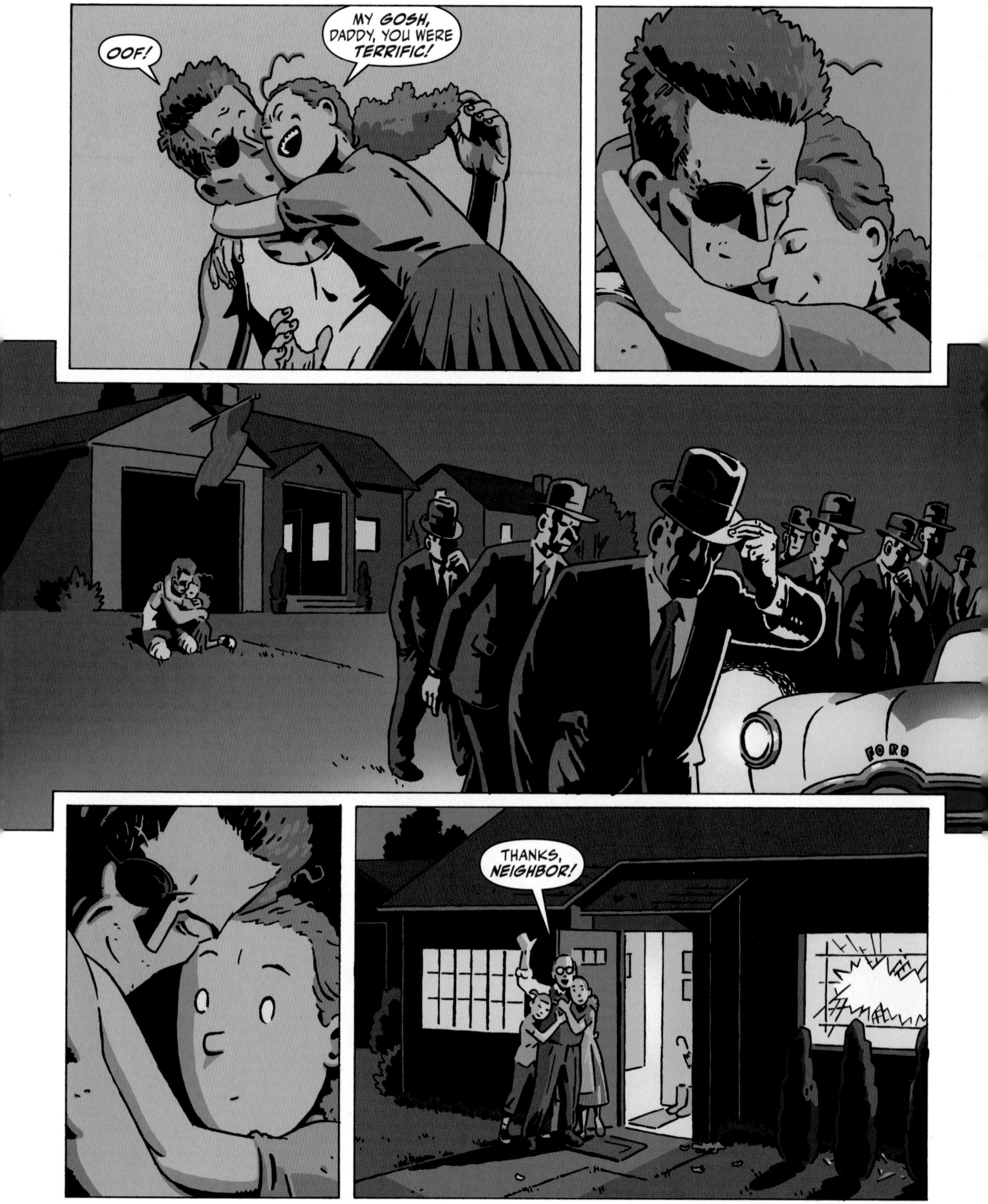
OOF!
MY GOSH, DADDY, YOU WERE TERRIFIC!
THANKS, NEIGHBOR!
FORD

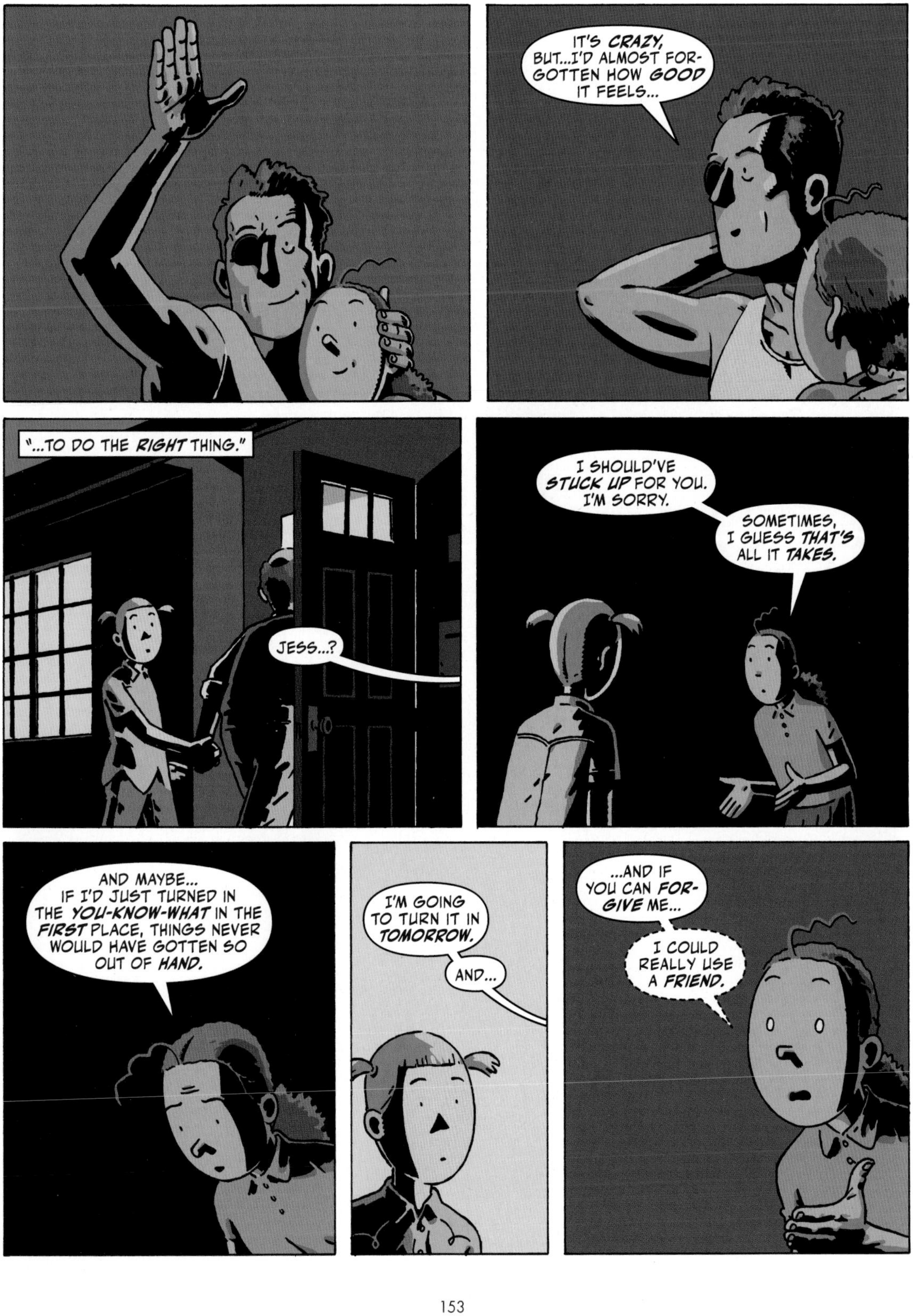
IT'S CRAZY, BUT...I'D ALMOST FORGOTTEN HOW GOOD IT FEELS...
"...TO DO THE RIGHT THING."
JESS...?
I SHOULD'VE STUCK UP FOR YOU. I'M SORRY.
SOMETIMES, I GUESS THAT'S ALL IT TAKES.
AND MAYBE... IF I'D JUST TURNED IN THE YOU-KNOW-WHAT IN THE FIRST PLACE, THINGS NEVER WOULD HAVE GOTTEN SO OUT OF HAND.
I'M GOING TO TURN IT IN TOMORROW.
AND...
...AND IF YOU CAN FORGIVE ME...
I COULD REALLY USE A FRIEND.

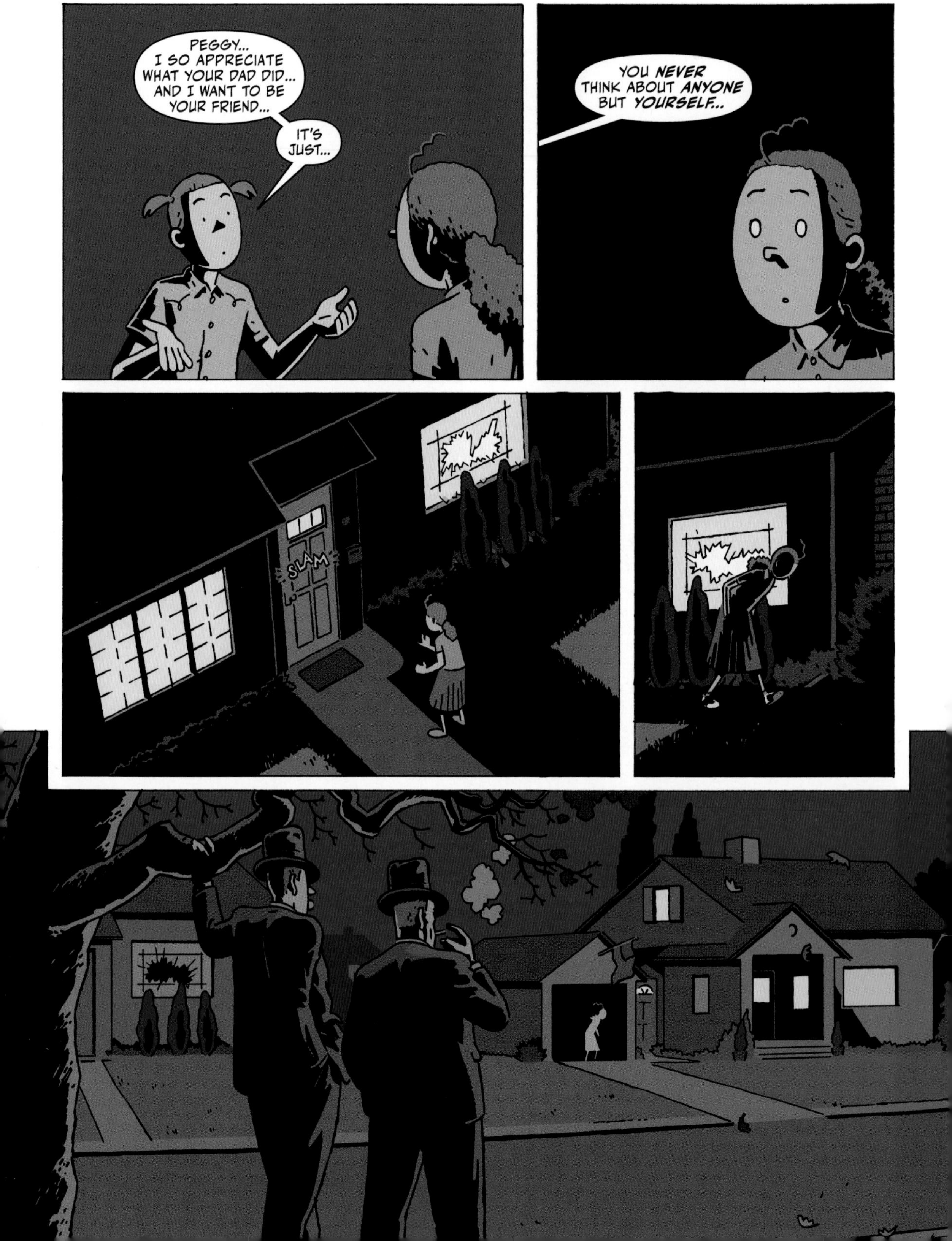
PEGGY... I SO APPRECIATE WHAT YOUR DAD DID... AND I WANT TO BE YOUR FRIEND...
IT'S JUST...
YOU NEVER THINK ABOUT ANYONE BUT YOURSELF...
SLAM

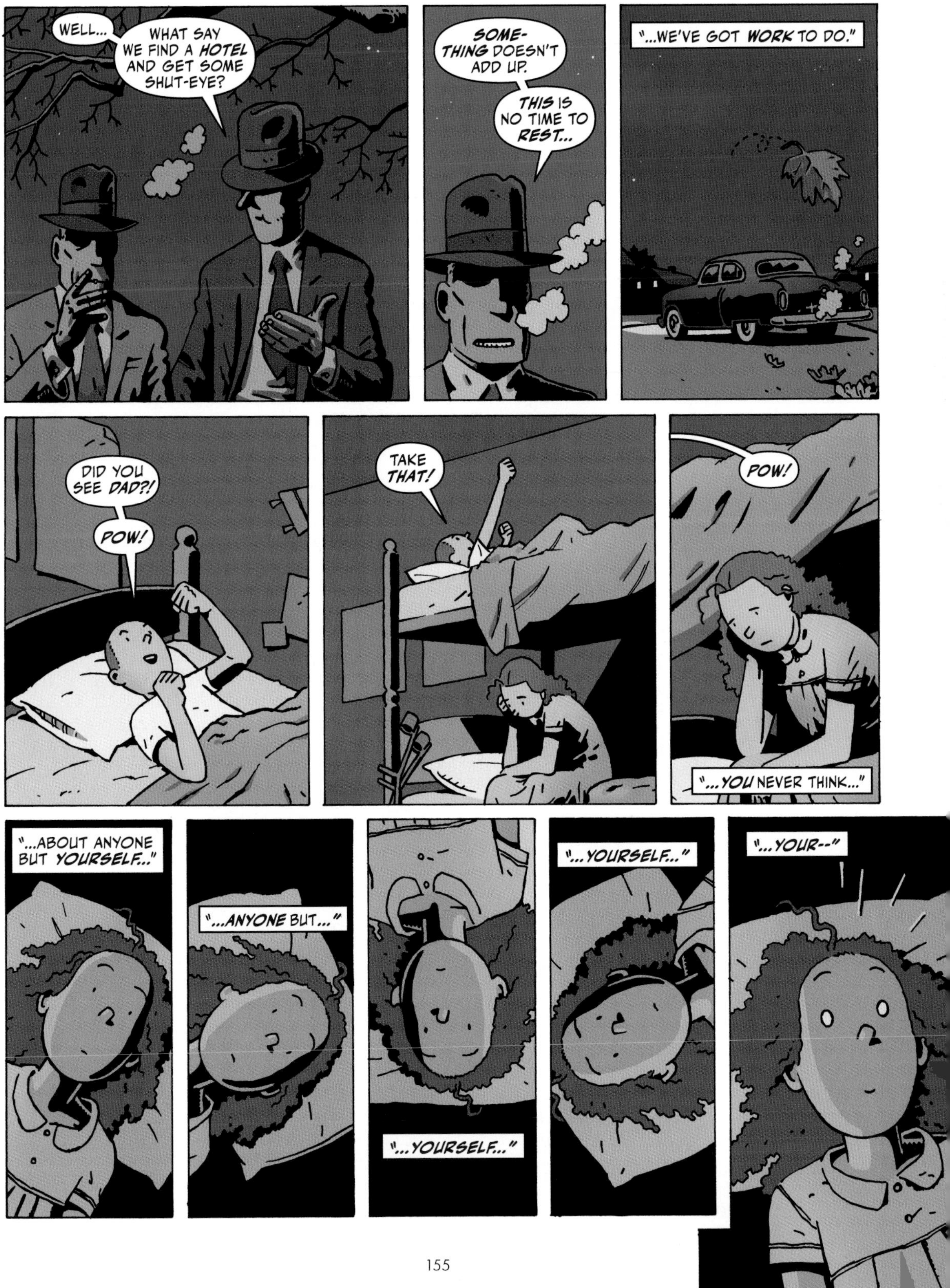
WELL...
WHAT SAY WE FIND A HOTEL AND GET SOME SHUT-EYE?
SOME-THING DOESN'T ADD UP.
THIS IS NO TIME TO REST...
"...WE'VE GOT WORK TO DO."
DID YOU SEE DAD?!
POW!
TAKE THAT!
POW!
"...YOU NEVER THINK..."
"...ABOUT ANYONE BUT YOURSELF..."
"...ANYONE BUT..."
"...YOURSELF..."
"...YOURSELF..."
"...YOUR--"

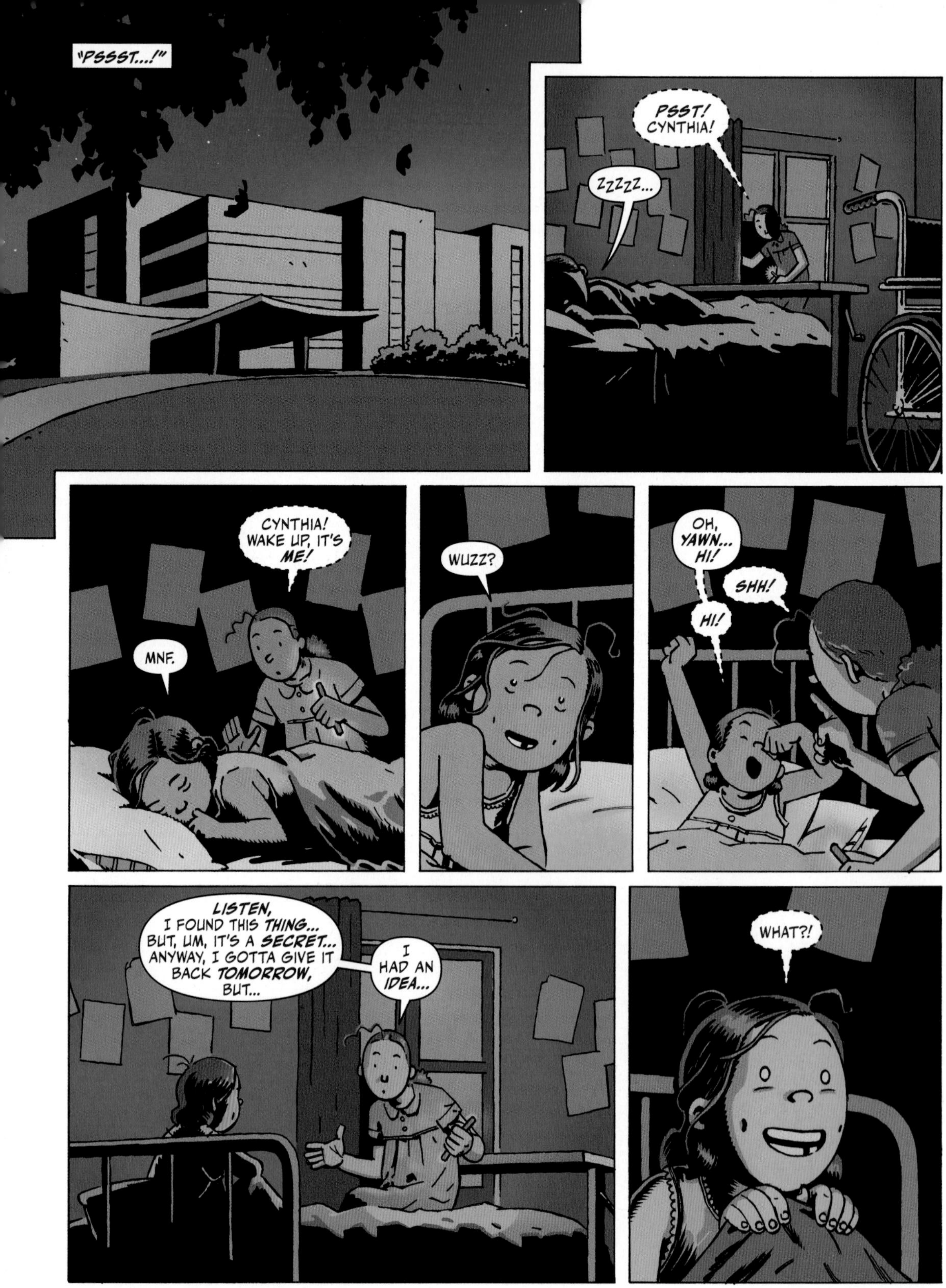
"PSSST...!"
PSST! CYNTHIA!
ZZZZZ...
CYNTHIA! WAKE UP, IT'S ME!
MNF.
WUZZ?
OH, YAWN... HI!
HI!
SHH!
LISTEN, I FOUND THIS THING... BUT, UM, IT'S A SECRET... ANYWAY, I GOTTA GIVE IT BACK TOMORROW, BUT...
I HAD AN IDEA...
WHAT?!

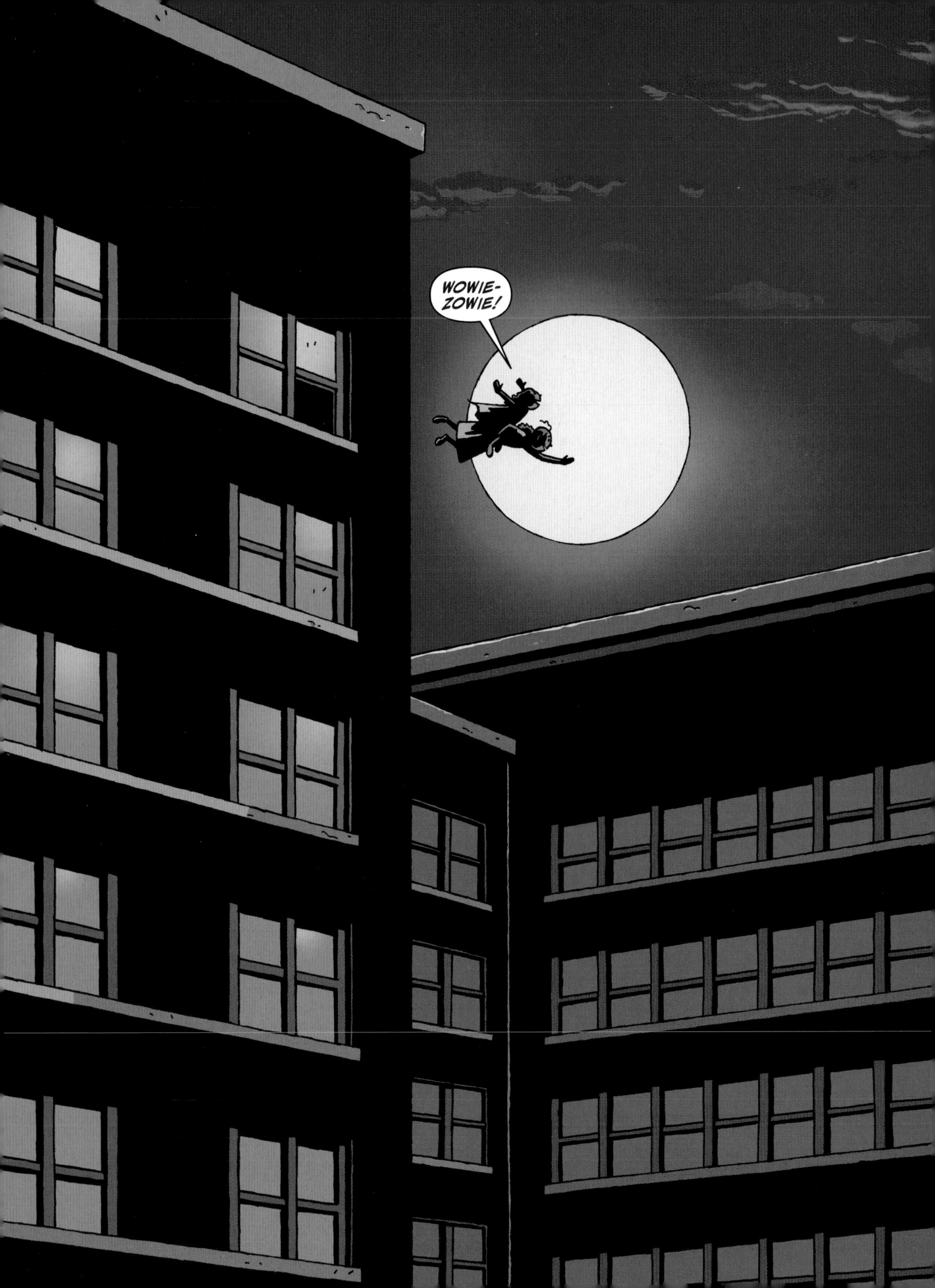
WOWIE-
ZOWIE!

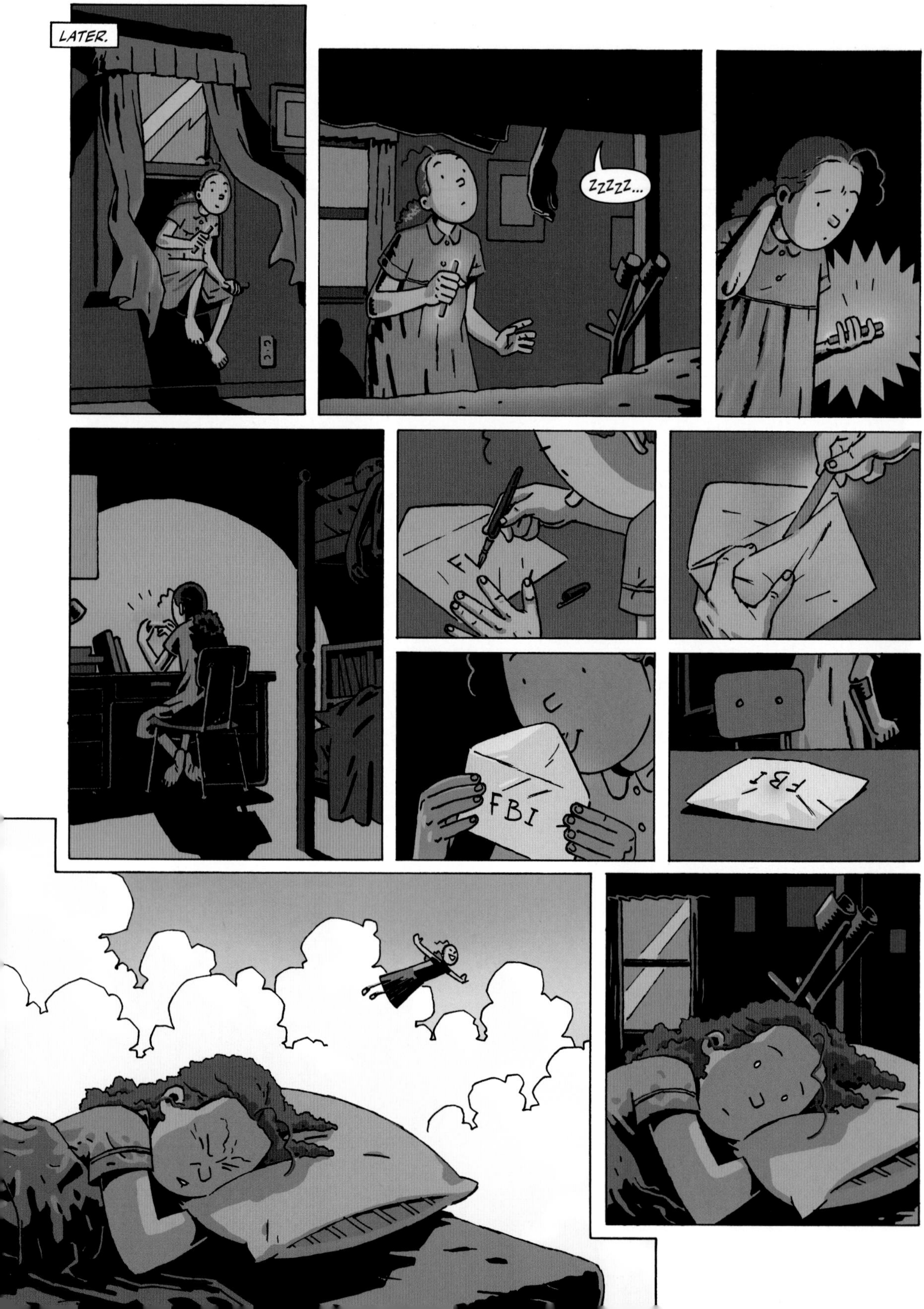
LATER.
ZZZZZ...
FBI
FBI

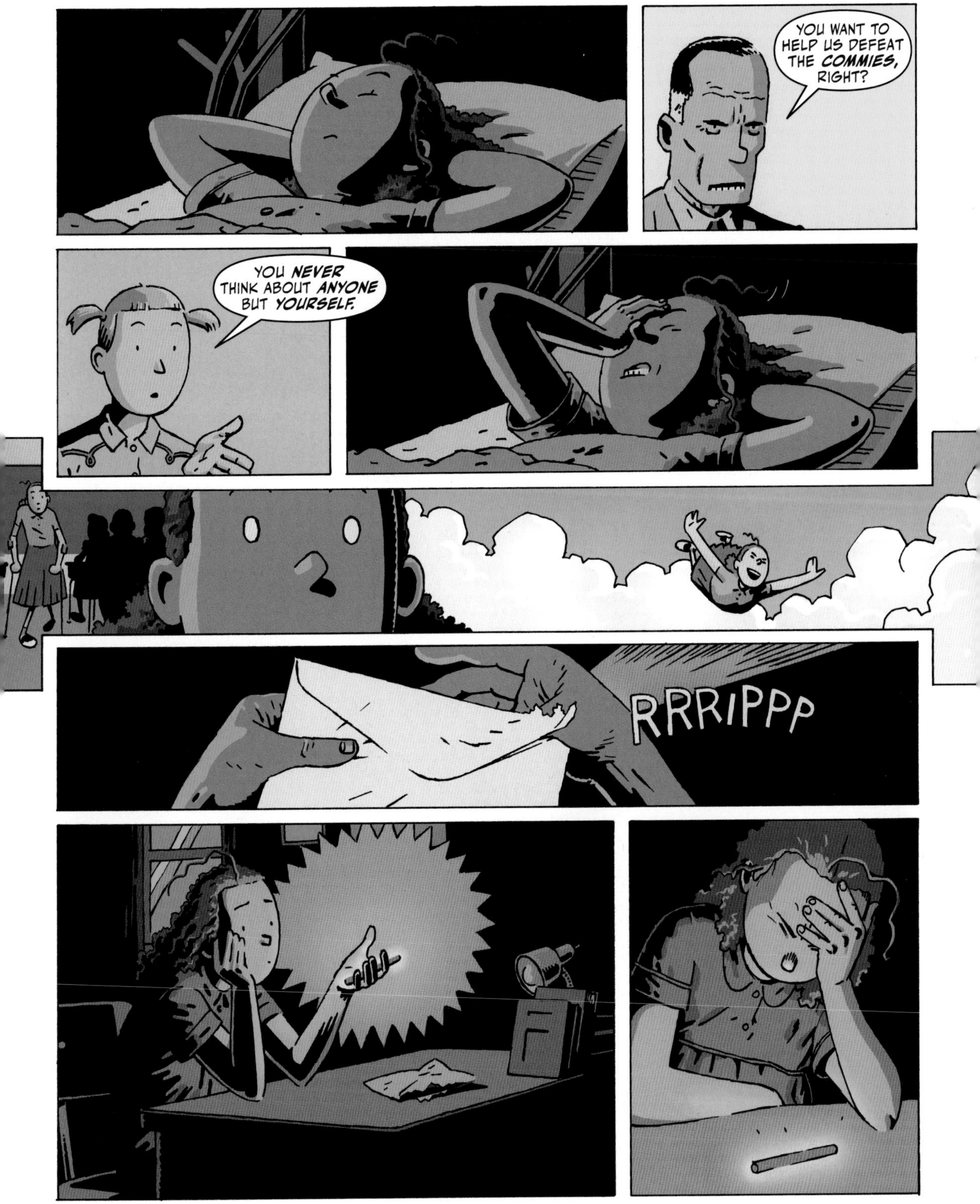

YOU WANT TO HELP US DEFEAT THE COMMIES, RIGHT?
YOU NEVER THINK ABOUT ANYONE BUT YOURSELF.
RRRIPPP

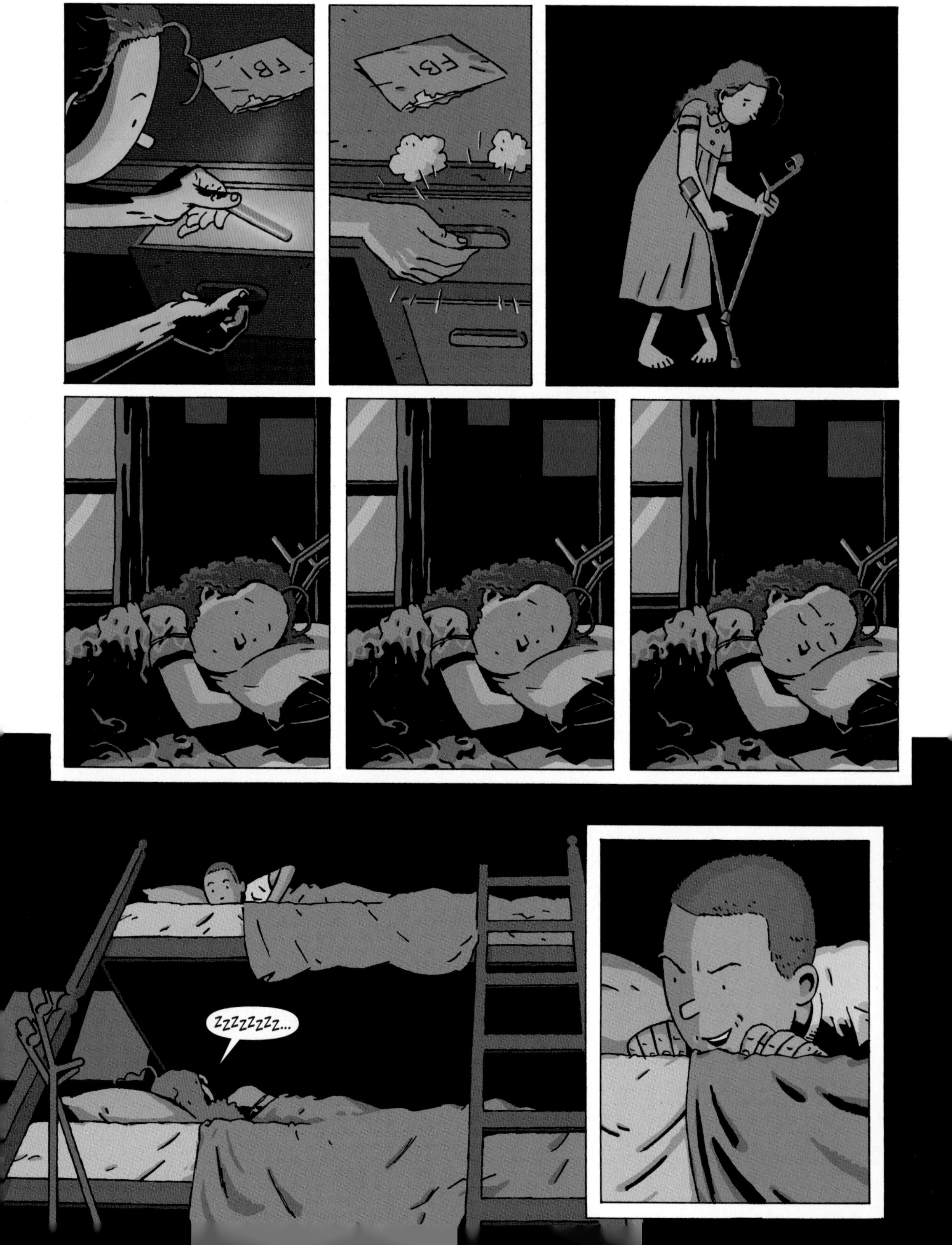
ZZZZZZZZ...

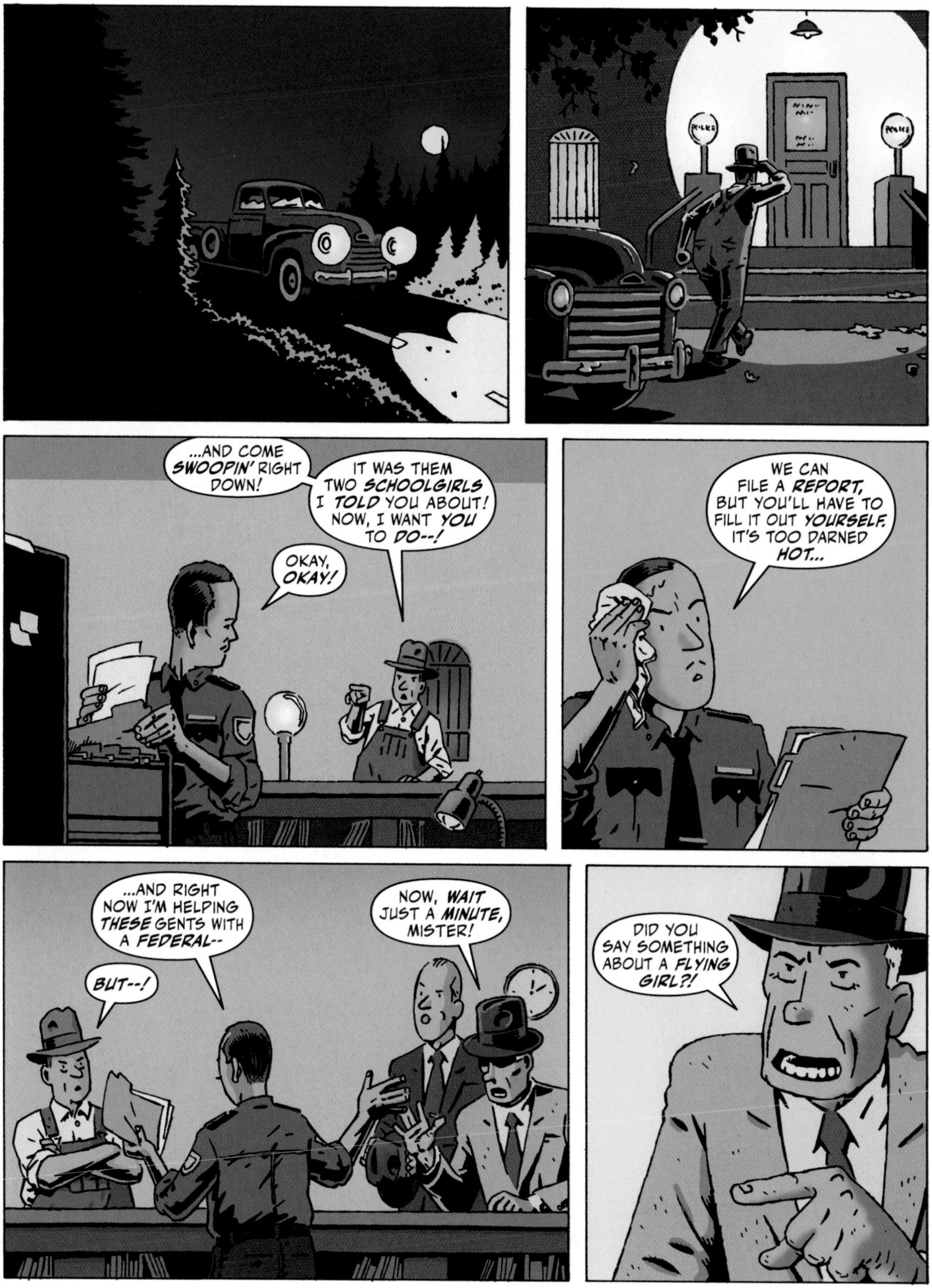
...AND COME SWOOPIN' RIGHT DOWN!
IT WAS THEM TWO SCHOOLGIRLS I TOLD YOU ABOUT! NOW, I WANT YOU TO DO--!
OKAY, OKAY!
WE CAN FILE A REPORT, BUT YOU'LL HAVE TO FILL IT OUT YOURSELF. IT'S TOO DARNED HOT...
...AND RIGHT NOW I'M HELPING THESE GENTS WITH A FEDERAL--
BUT--!
NOW, WAIT JUST A MINUTE, MISTER!
DID YOU SAY SOMETHING ABOUT A FLYING GIRL?!

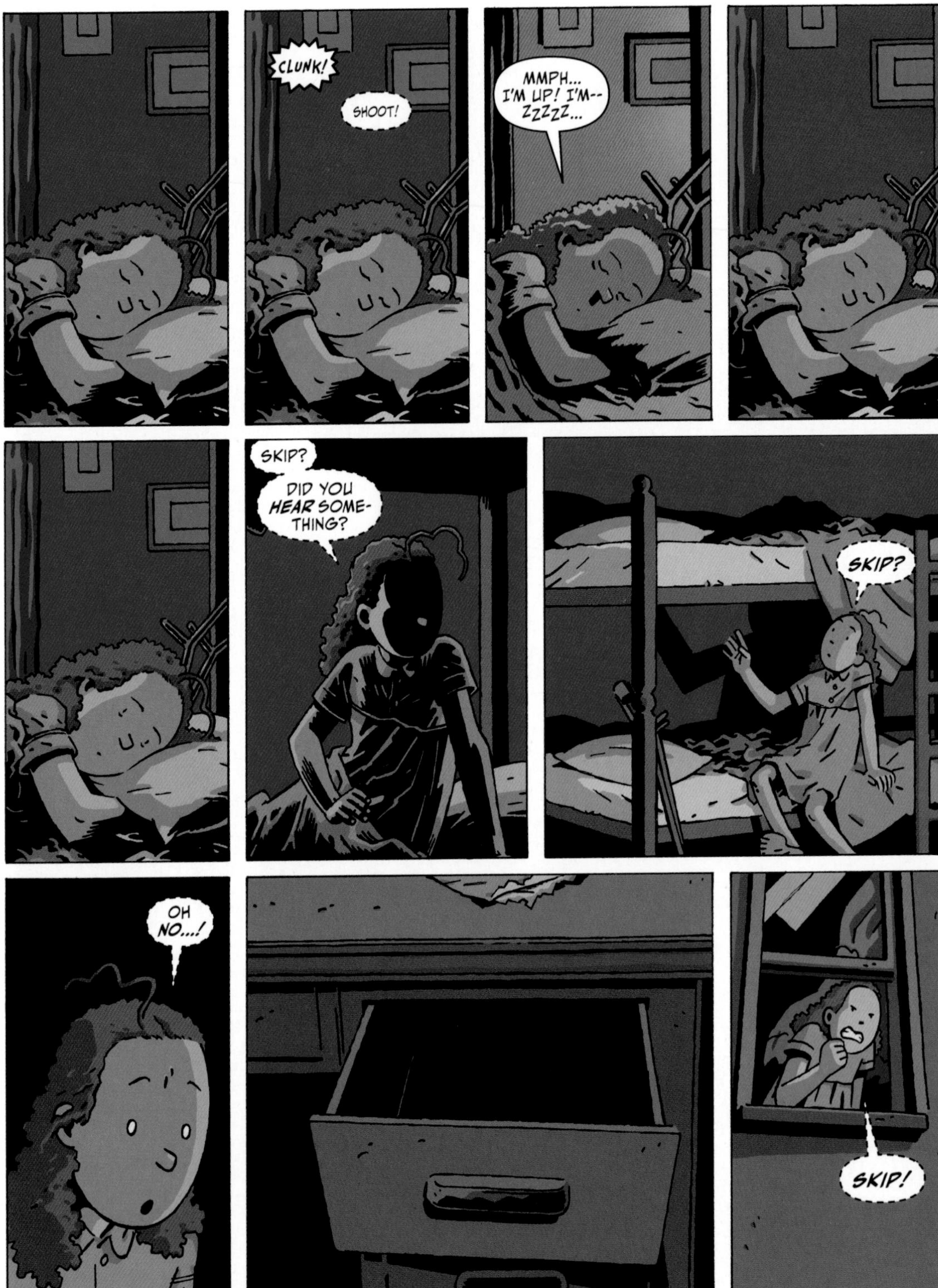
CLUNK!
SHOOT!
MMPH... I'M UP! I'M-- ZZZZZ...
SKIP?
DID YOU HEAR SOME-THING?
SKIP?
OH NO...!
SKIP!

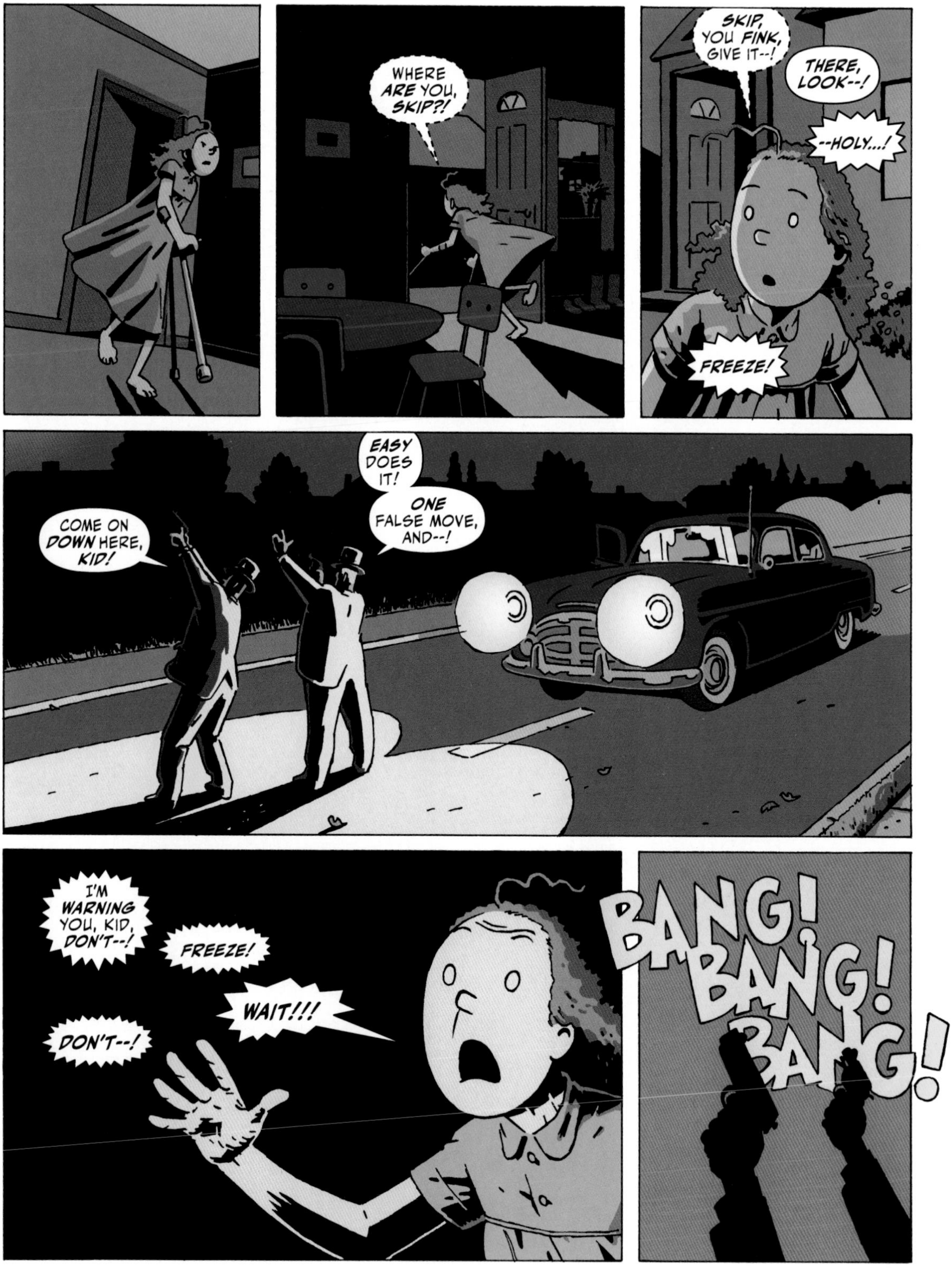

WHERE ARE YOU, SKIP?!
SKIP, YOU FINK, GIVE IT--!
THERE, LOOK--!
--HOLY...!
FREEZE!
EASY DOES IT!
COME ON DOWN HERE, KID!
ONE FALSE MOVE, AND--!
I'M WARNING YOU, KID, DON'T--!
FREEZE!
WAIT!!!
DON'T--!
BANG! BANG! BANG!

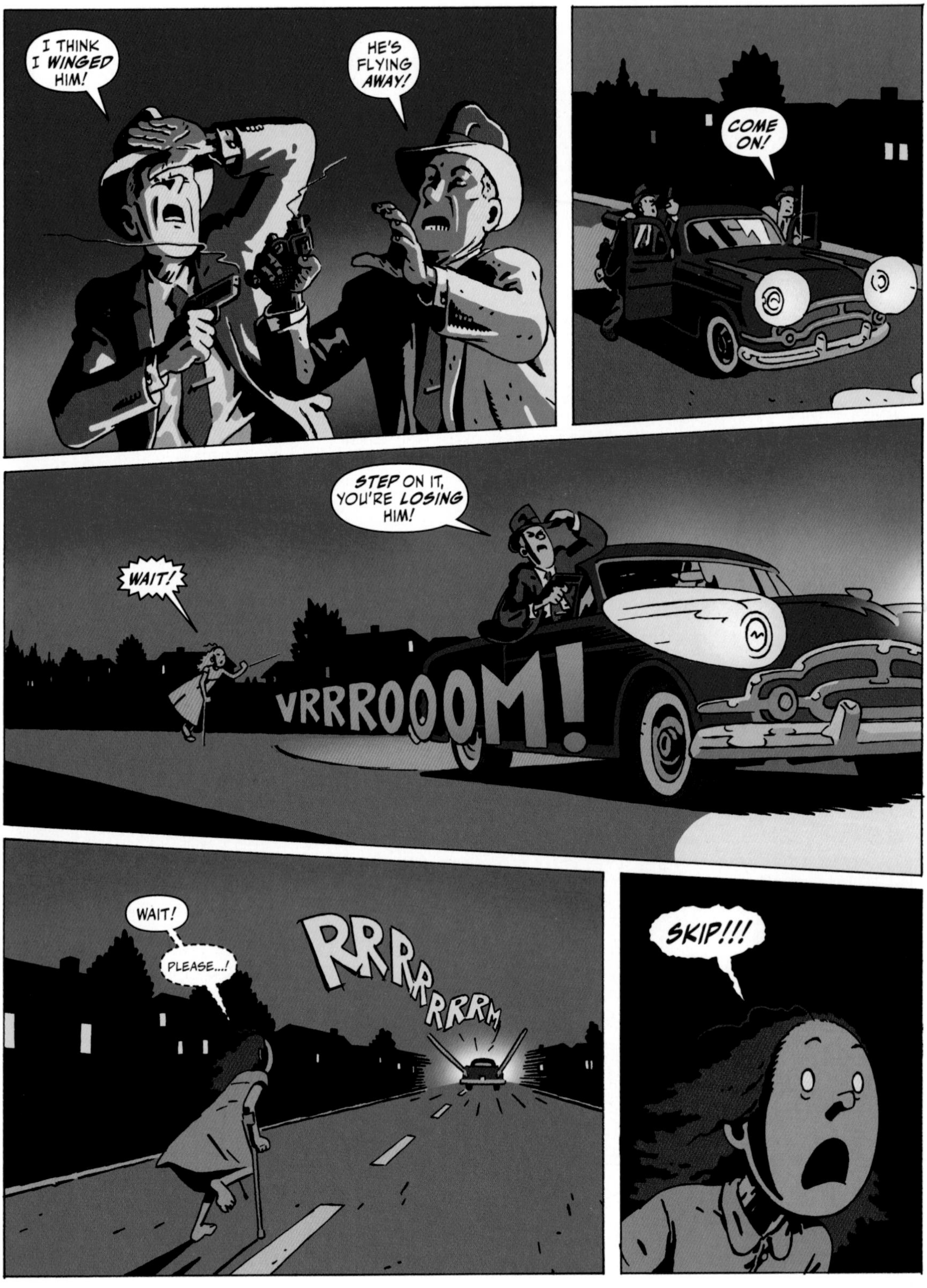
I THINK I WINGED HIM!
HE'S FLYING AWAY!
COME ON!
STEP ON IT, YOU'RE LOSING HIM!
WAIT!
VRRROOOM!
WAIT!
PLEASE...!
RRRRRRRRM
SKIP!!!

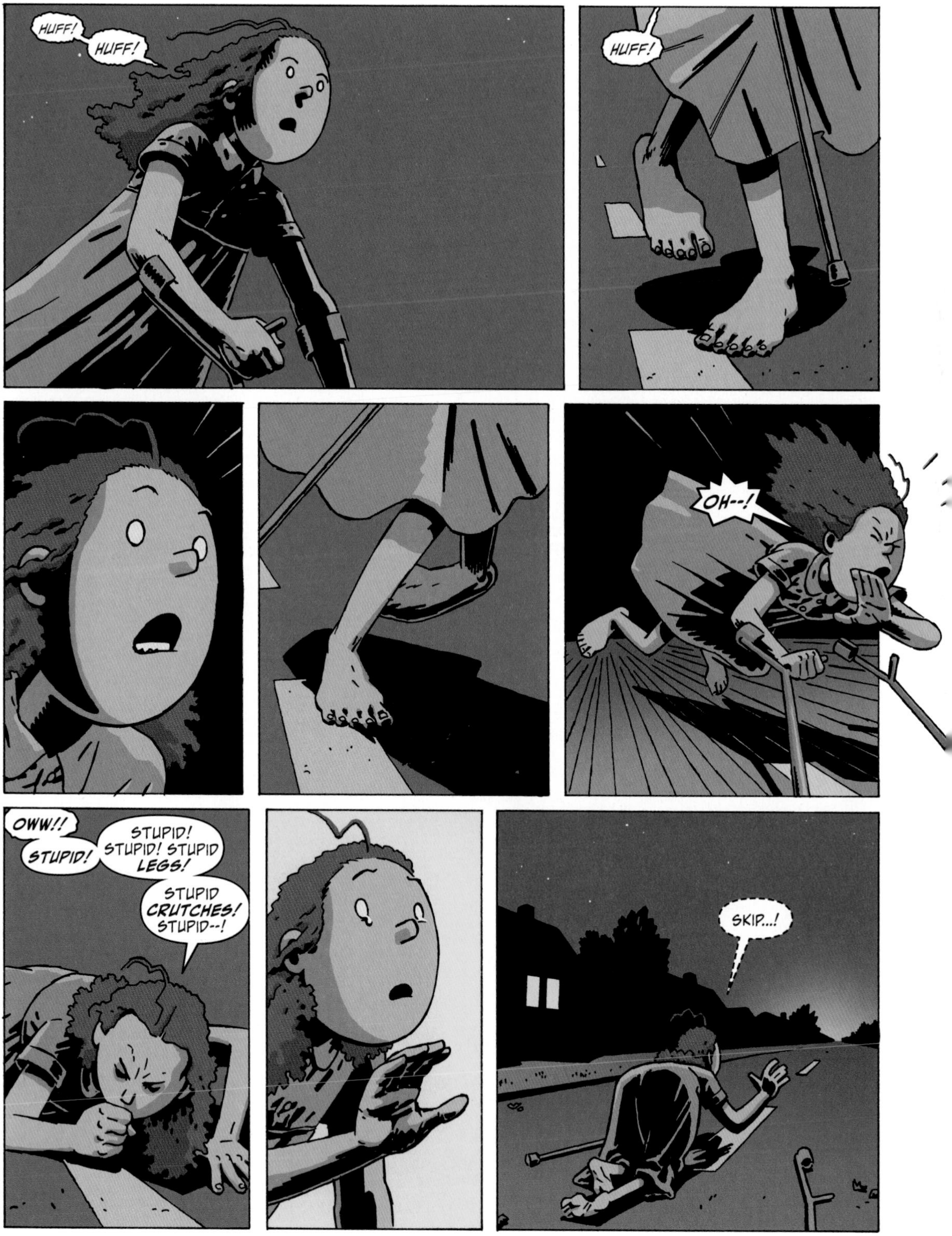
HUFF!
HUFF!
HUFF!
OH--!
OWW!!
STUPID!
STUPID! STUPID! STUPID LEGS!
STUPID CRUTCHES! STUPID--!
SKIP...!

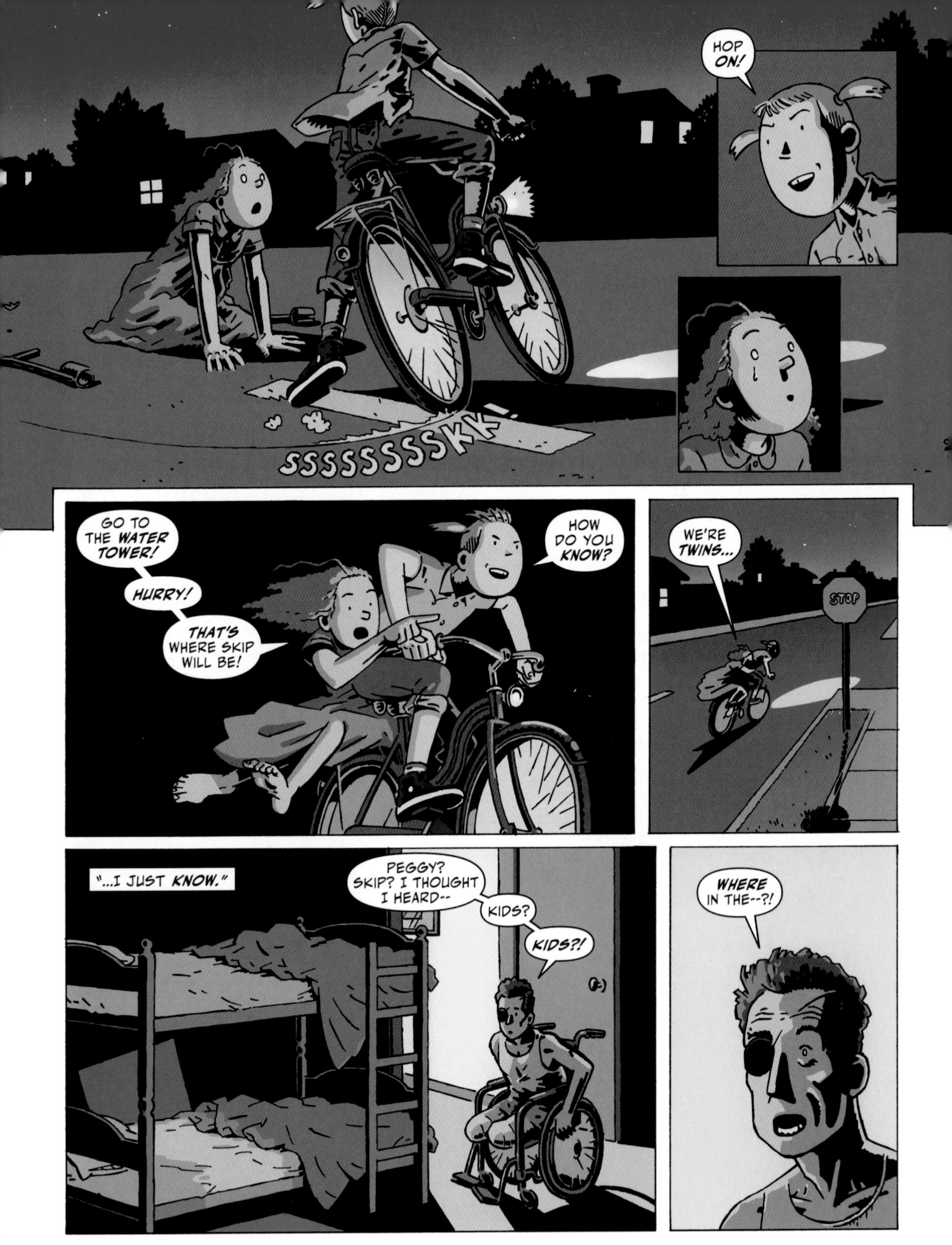
HOP ON!
SSSSSSSSSKK!
GO TO THE WATER TOWER!
HURRY!
THAT'S WHERE SKIP WILL BE!
HOW DO YOU KNOW?
WE'RE TWINS...
STOP
"...I JUST KNOW."
PEGGY? SKIP? I THOUGHT I HEARD--
KIDS?
KIDS?!
WHERE IN THE--?!

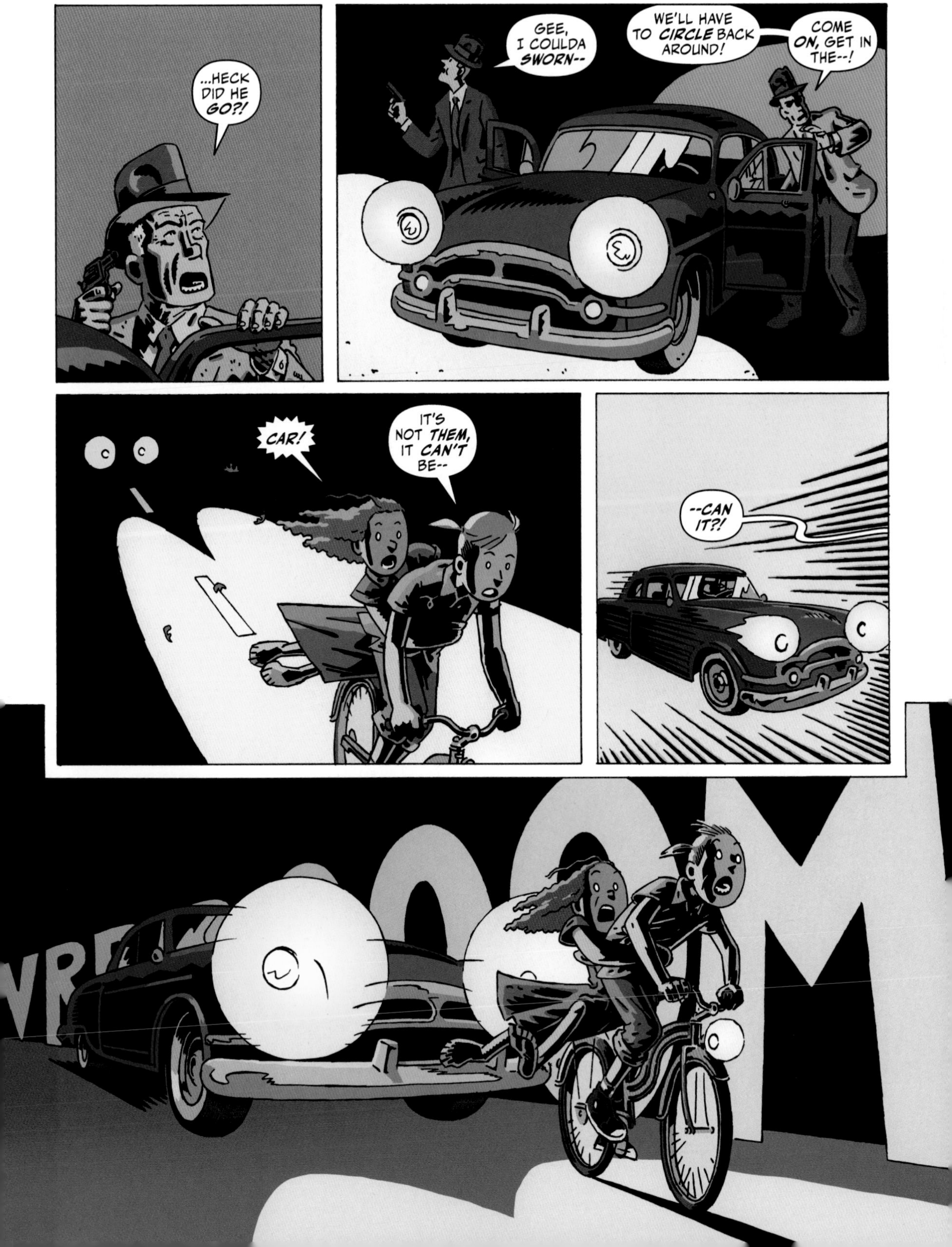
...HECK DID HE GO?!
GEE, I COULDA SWORN--
WE'LL HAVE TO CIRCLE BACK AROUND!
COME ON, GET IN THE--!
CAR!
IT'S NOT THEM, IT CAN'T BE--
--CAN IT?!
VROOOM

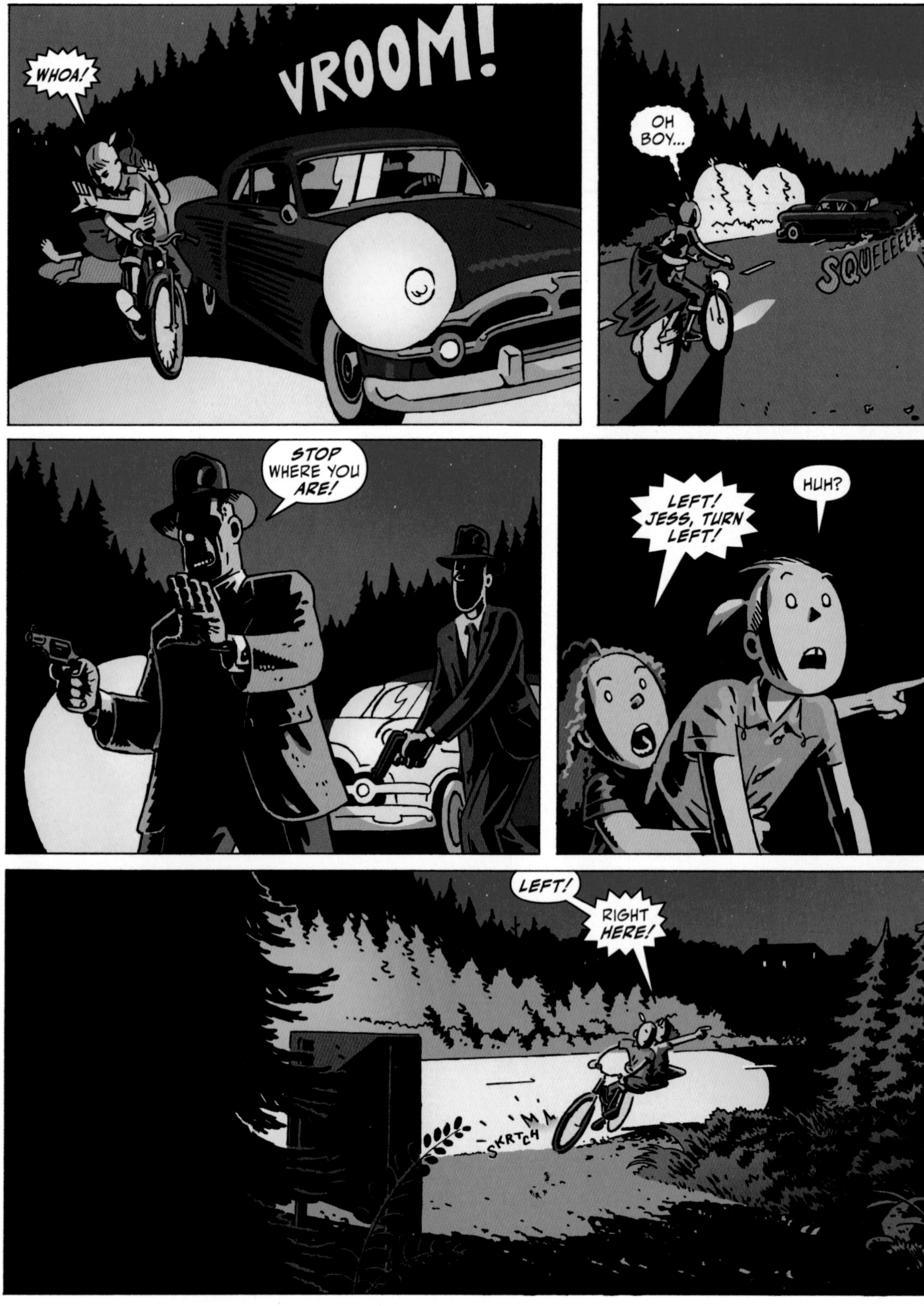
WHOA!
VROOM!
OH BOY...
SQUEEEEEEE
STOP WHERE YOU ARE!
LEFT! JESS, TURN LEFT!
HUH?
LEFT!
RIGHT HERE!
SKRTCHMM

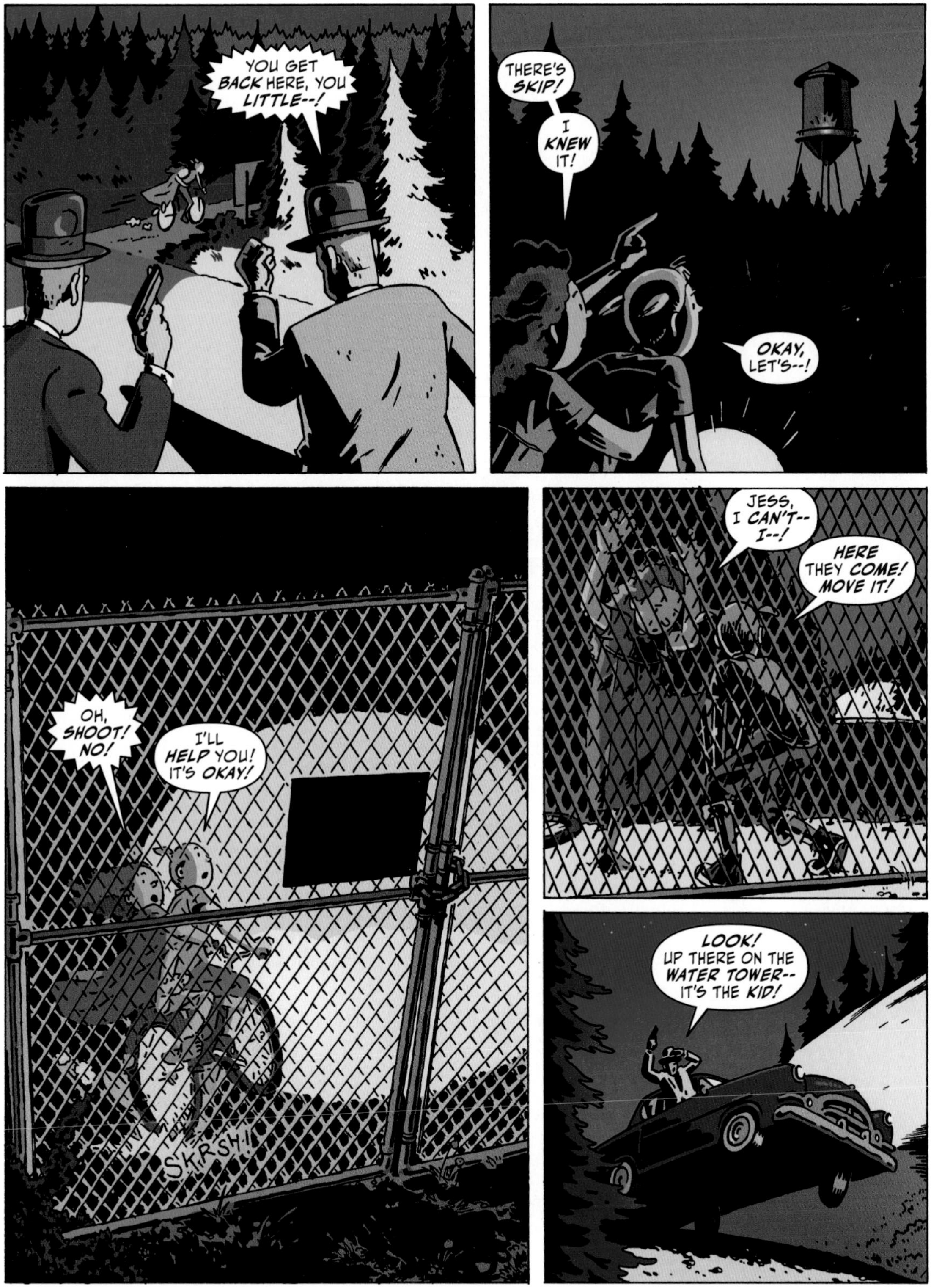
YOU GET BACK HERE, YOU LITTLE--!
THERE'S SKIP!
I KNEW IT!
OKAY, LET'S--!
OH, SHOOT! NO!
I'LL HELP YOU! IT'S OKAY!
SKRSH!
JESS, I CAN'T-- I--!
HERE THEY COME! MOVE IT!
LOOK! UP THERE ON THE WATER TOWER-- IT'S THE KID!

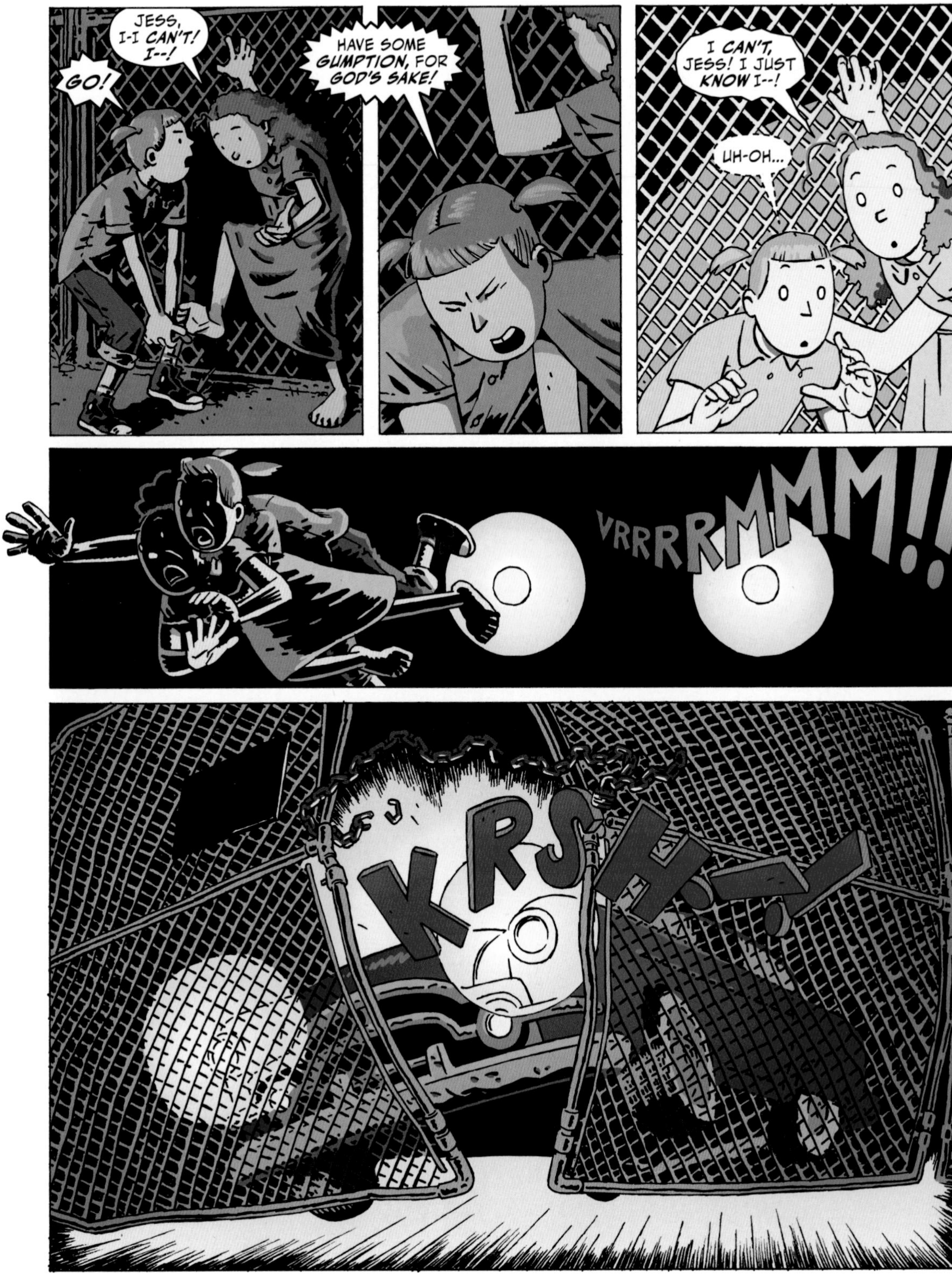
JESS, I-I CAN'T! I--!
GO!
HAVE SOME GUMPTION, FOR GOD'S SAKE!
I CAN'T, JESS! I JUST KNOW I--!
UH-OH...
VRRRRMMMM!!
KRSH--!

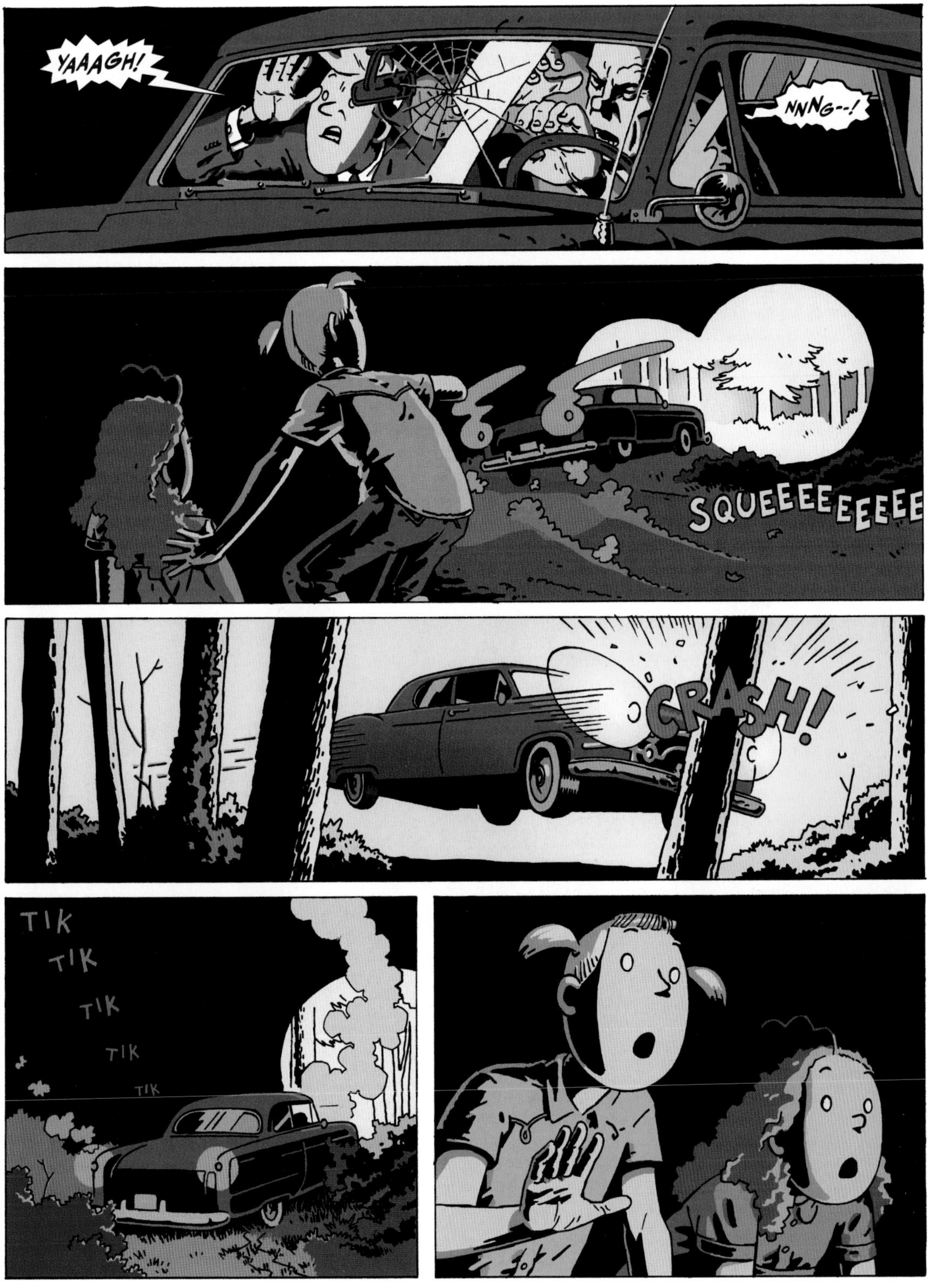
YAAAGH!
NNNG--!
SQUEEEEEEEEEE
CRASH!
TIK
TIK
TIK
TIK
TIK

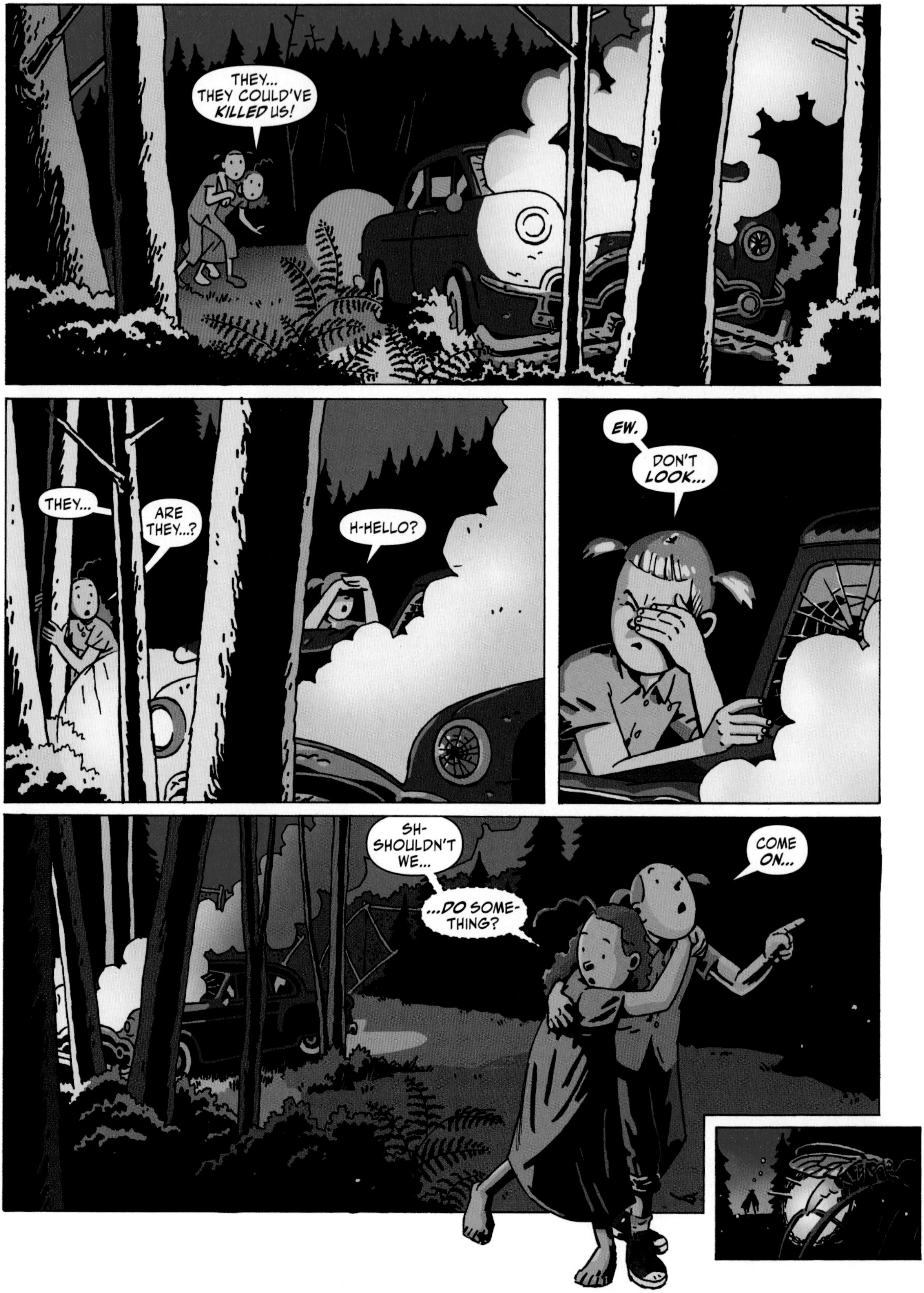
THEY... THEY COULD'VE *KILLED* US!
THEY...
ARE THEY...?
H-HELLO?
*EW.*
DON'T *LOOK...*
SH-SHOULDN'T WE...
*...DO* SOME-THING?
*COME ON...*

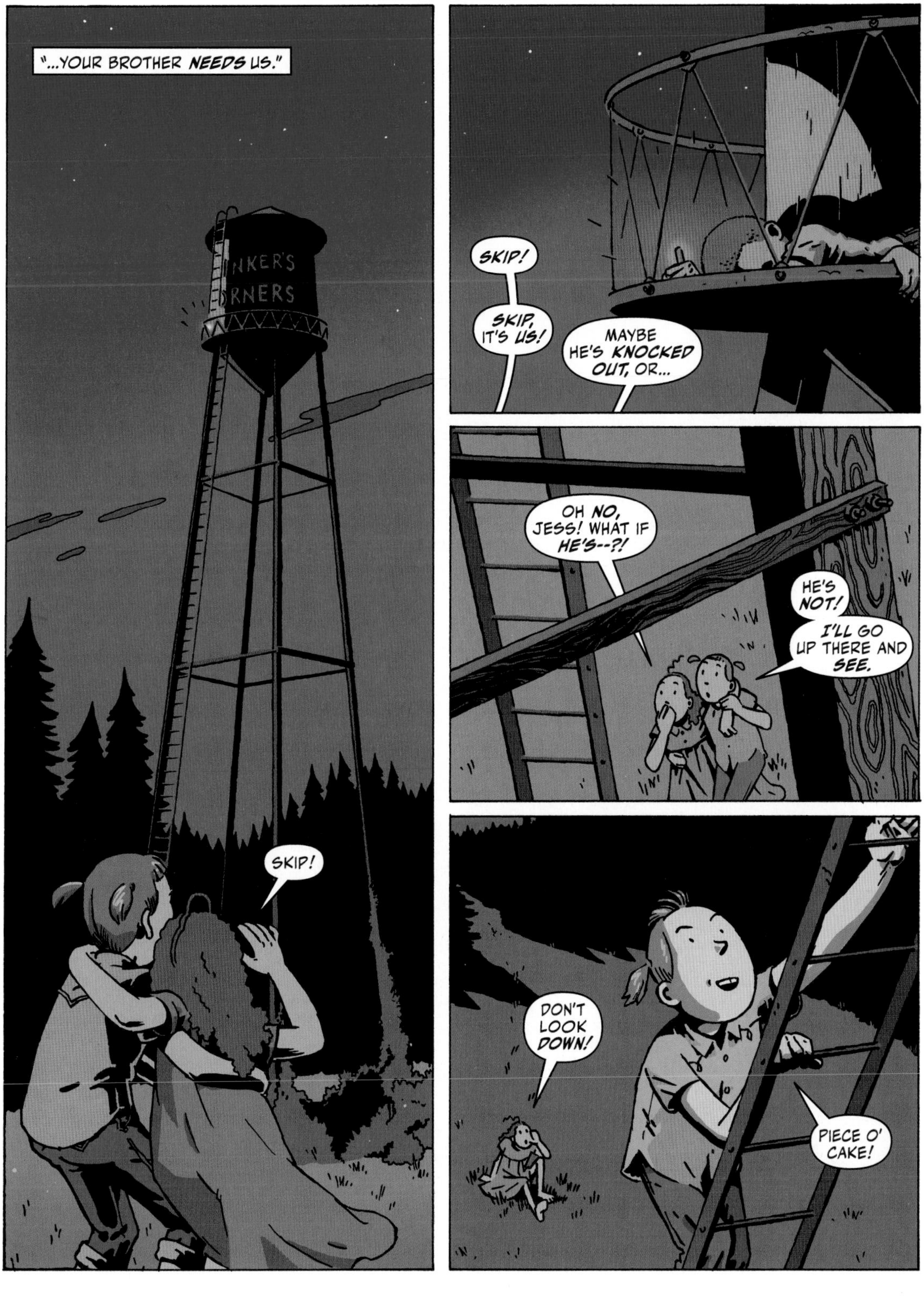
"...YOUR BROTHER NEEDS US."
NKER'S
RNERS
SKIP!
SKIP!
SKIP, IT'S US!
MAYBE HE'S KNOCKED OUT, OR...
OH NO, JESS! WHAT IF HE'S--?!
HE'S NOT!
I'LL GO UP THERE AND SEE.
DON'T LOOK DOWN!
PIECE O' CAKE!

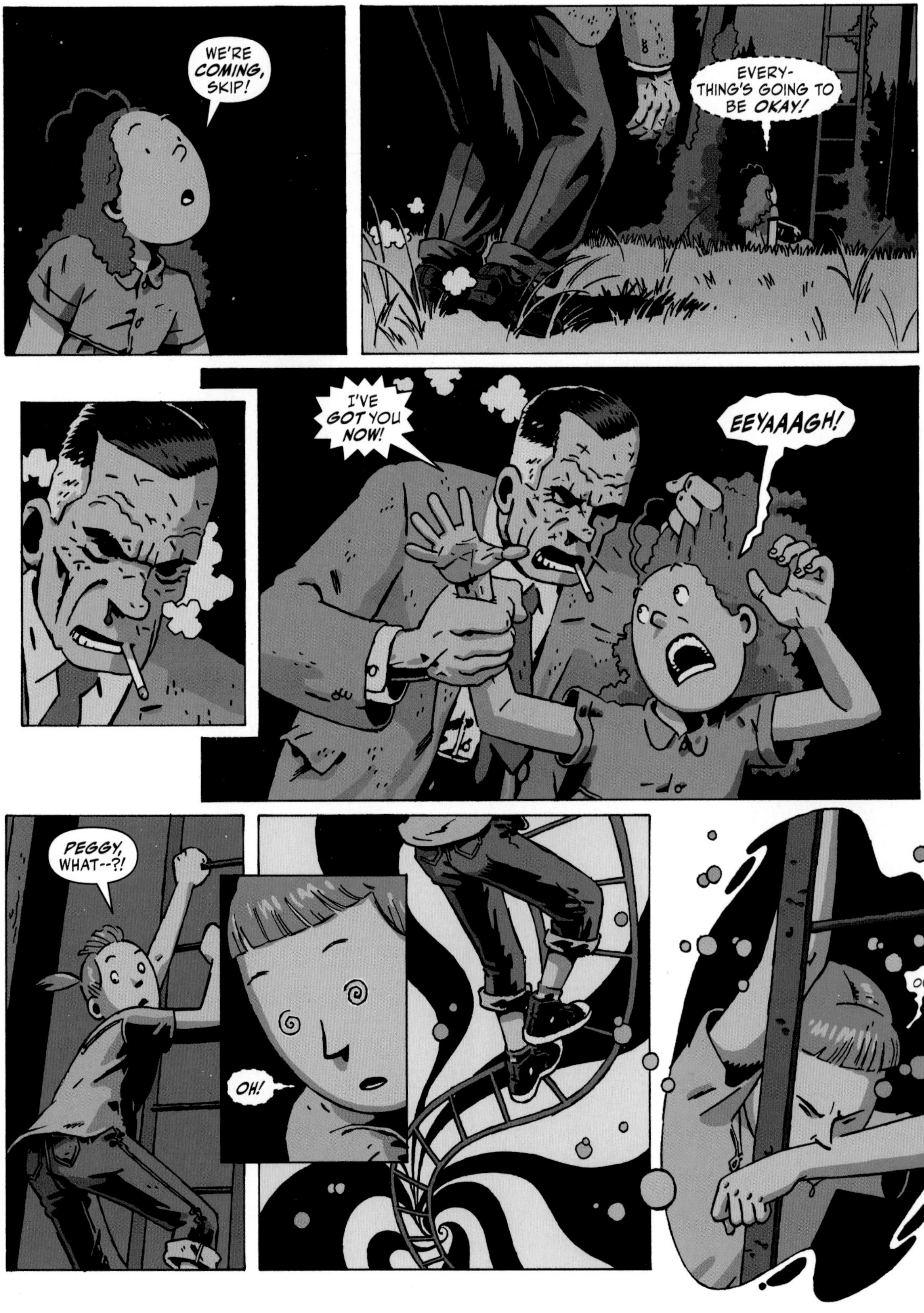
WE'RE COMING, SKIP!
EVERY-THING'S GOING TO BE OKAY!
I'VE GOT YOU NOW!
EEYAAAGH!
PEGGY, WHAT--?!
OH!
OOOGH..

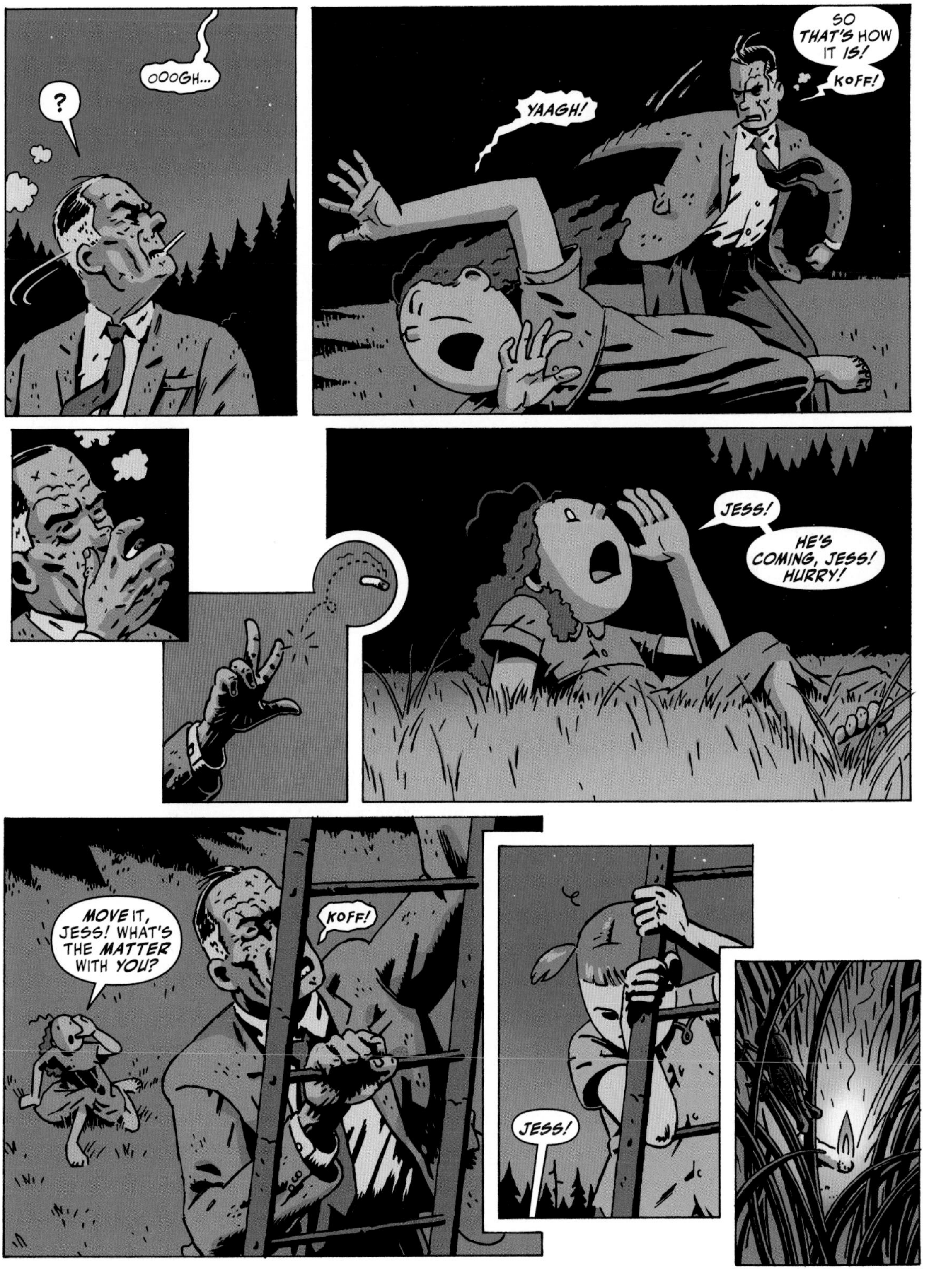
?
OOOGH...
YAAGH!
SO THAT'S HOW IT IS!
KOFF!
JESS!
HE'S COMING, JESS! HURRY!
MOVE IT, JESS! WHAT'S THE MATTER WITH YOU?
KOFF!
JESS!

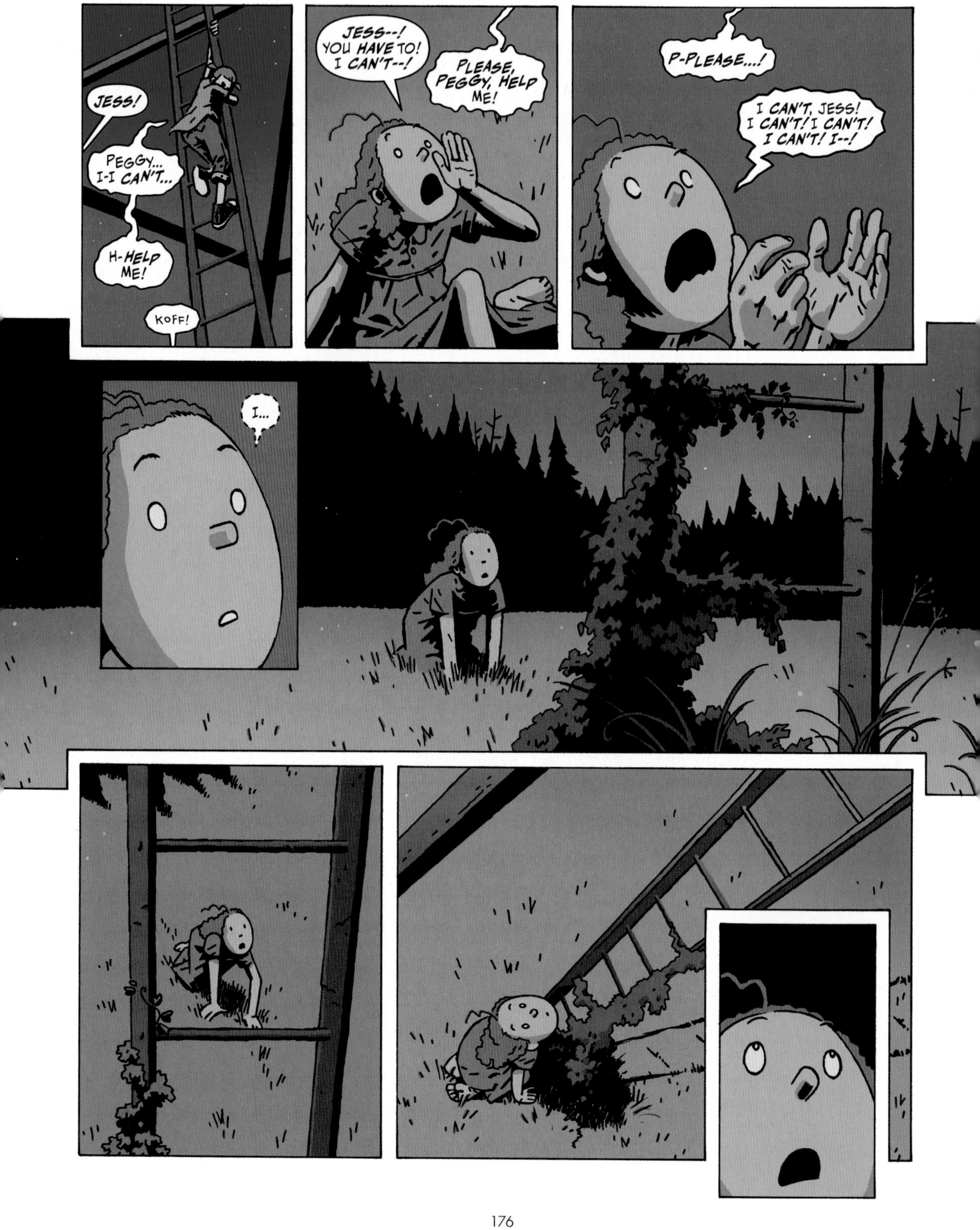
JESS!
PEGGY... I-I CAN'T...
H-HELP ME!
KOFF!
JESS--! YOU HAVE TO! I CAN'T--!
PLEASE, PEGGY, HELP ME!
P-PLEASE...!
I CAN'T, JESS! I CAN'T! I CAN'T! I CAN'T! I--!
I...

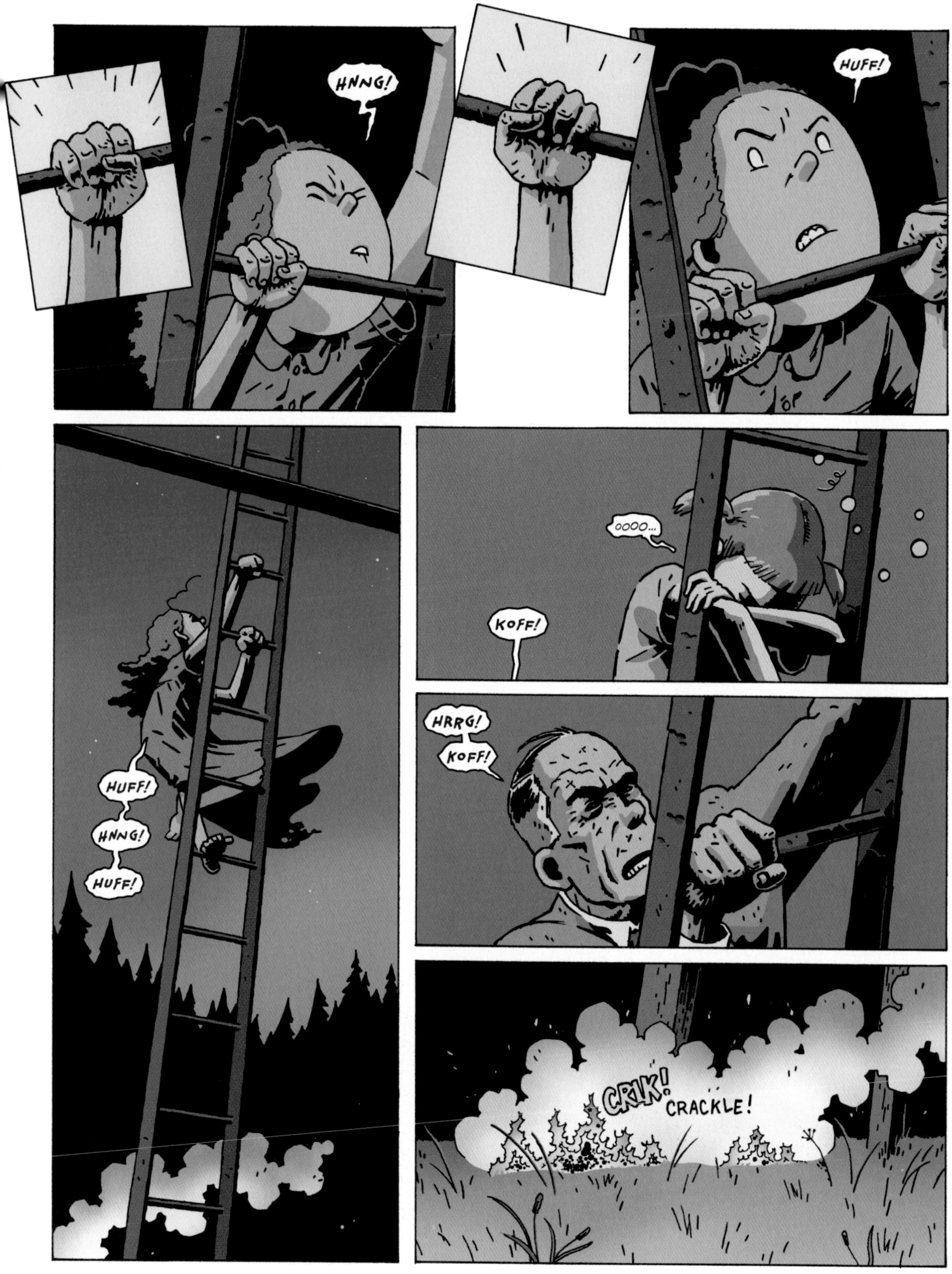
HNNG!
HUFF!
HUFF!
HNNG!
HUFF!
OOOO...
KOFF!
HRRG!
KOFF!
CRAK!
CRACKLE!

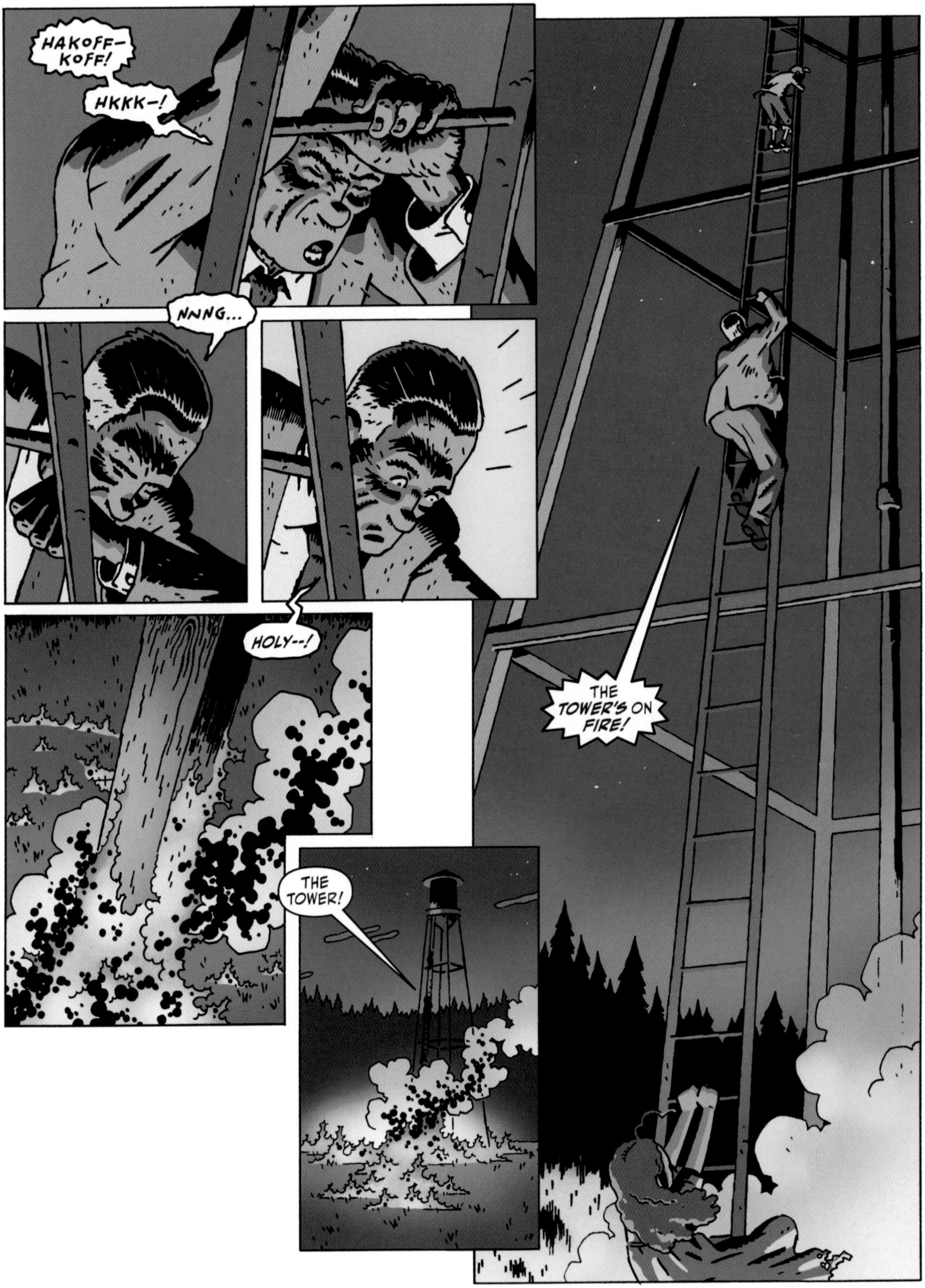
HAKOFF-KOFF!
HKKK-!
NNNG...
HOLY--!
THE TOWER!
THE TOWER'S ON FIRE!

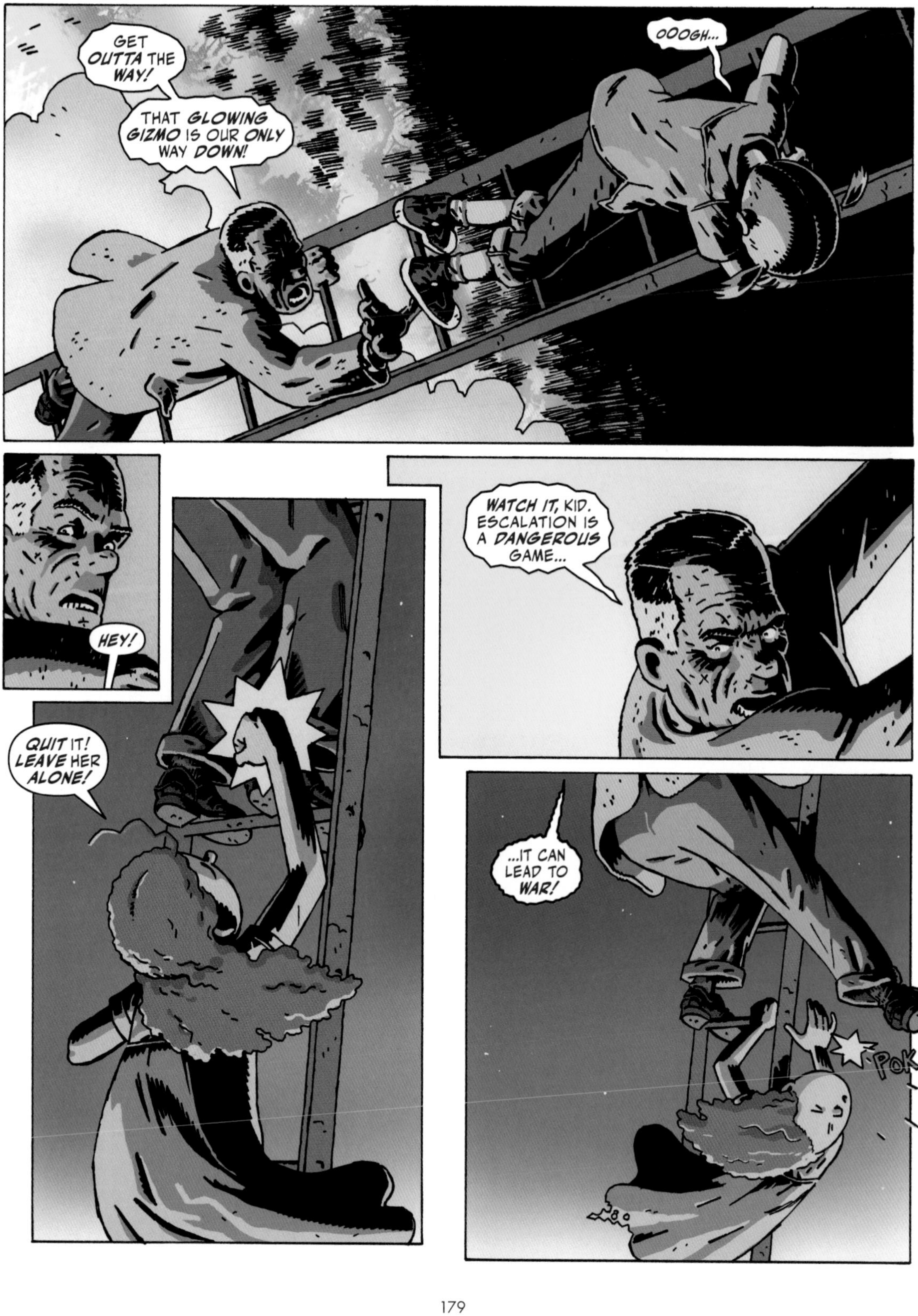
GET OUTTA THE WAY!
THAT GLOWING GIZMO IS OUR ONLY WAY DOWN!
OOOGH...
HEY!
WATCH IT, KID. ESCALATION IS A DANGEROUS GAME...
QUIT IT! LEAVE HER ALONE!
...IT CAN LEAD TO WAR!
POK!

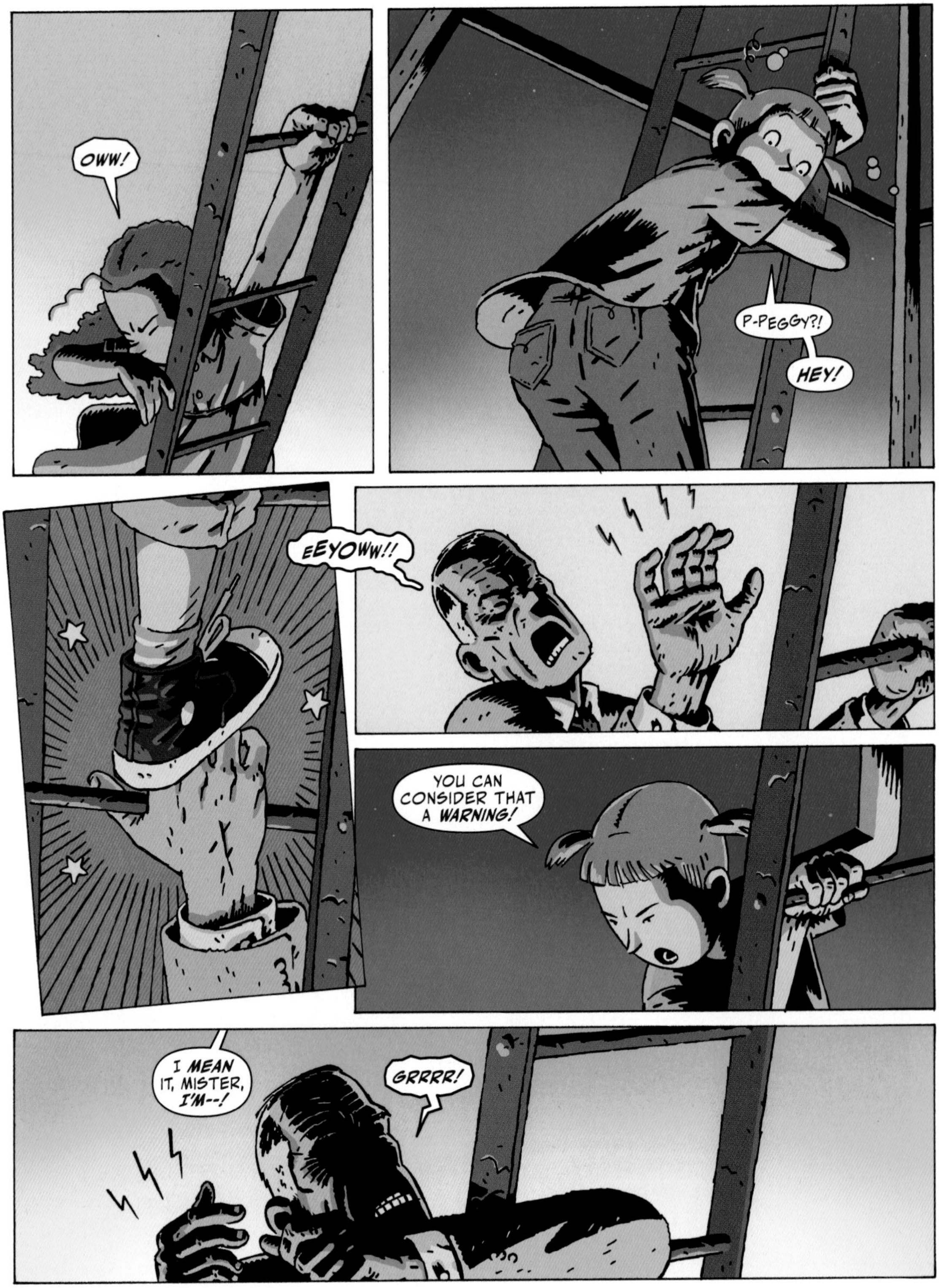
OWW!
P-PEGGY?!
HEY!
EEYOWW!!
YOU CAN CONSIDER THAT A WARNING!
I MEAN IT, MISTER, I'M--!
GRRRR!

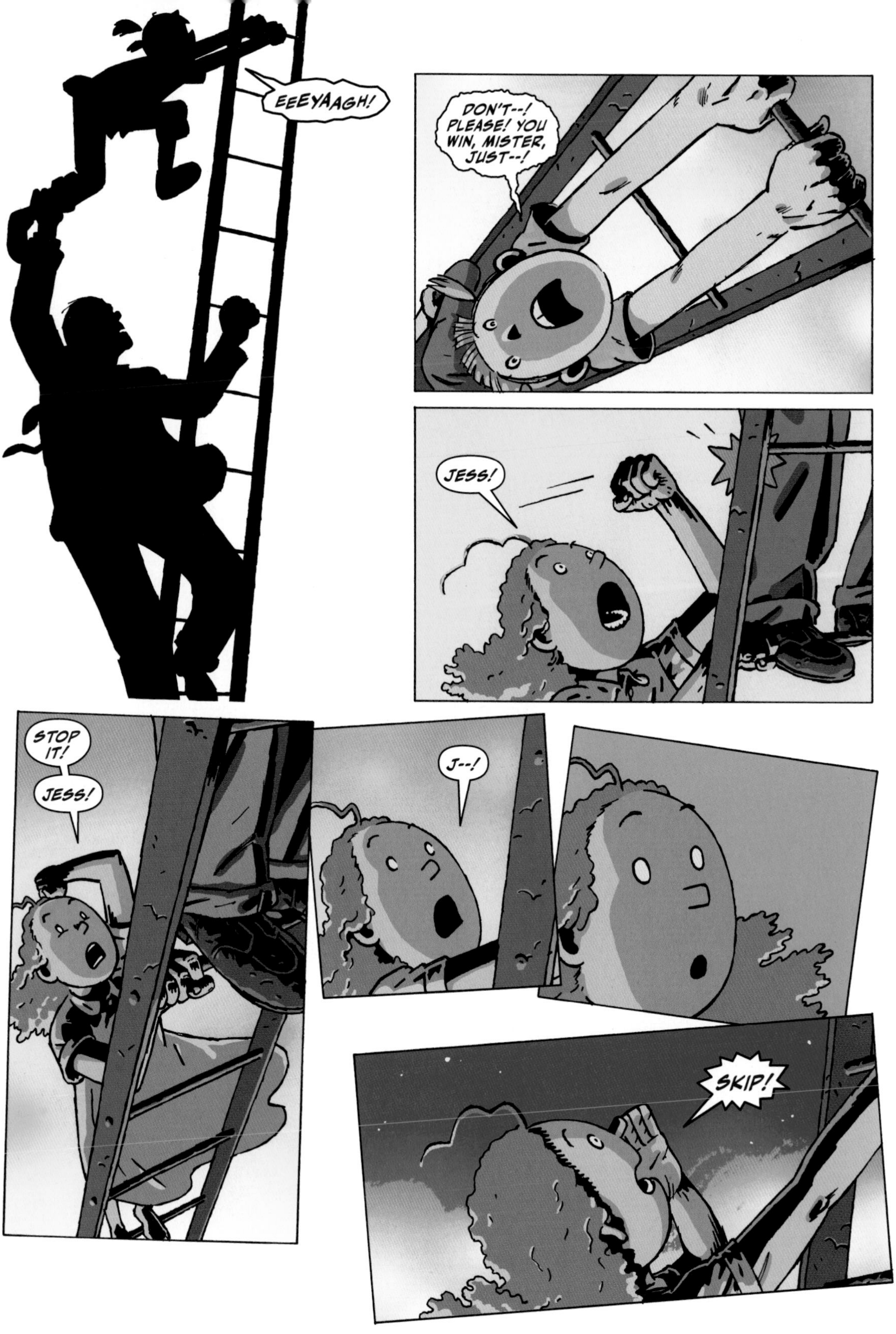
EEEYAAGH!
DON'T--! PLEASE! YOU WIN, MISTER, JUST--!
JESS!
STOP IT!
JESS!
J--!
SKIP!

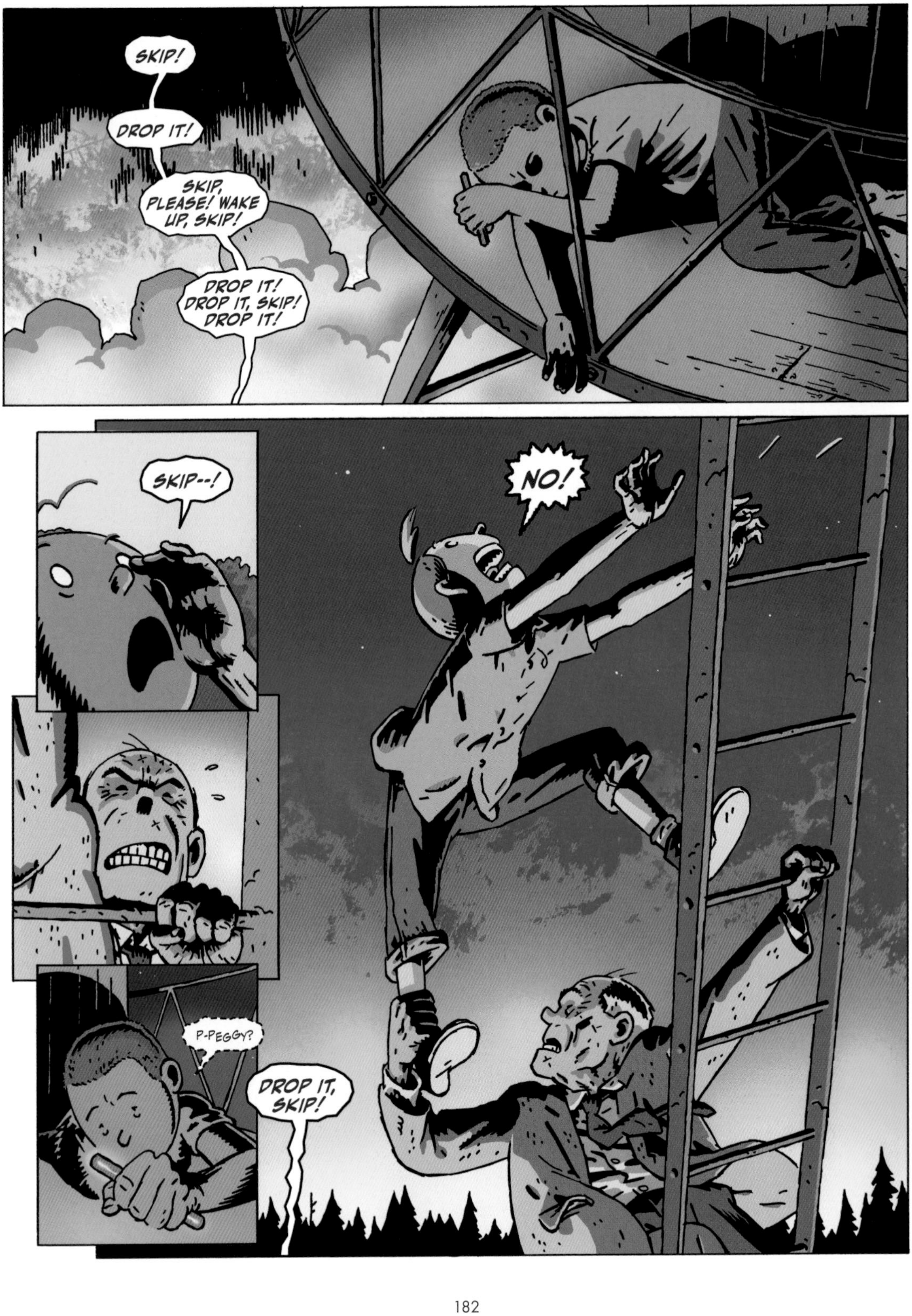
SKIP!
DROP IT!
SKIP, PLEASE! WAKE UP, SKIP!
DROP IT! DROP IT, SKIP! DROP IT!
SKIP--!
NO!
P-PEGGY?
DROP IT, SKIP!

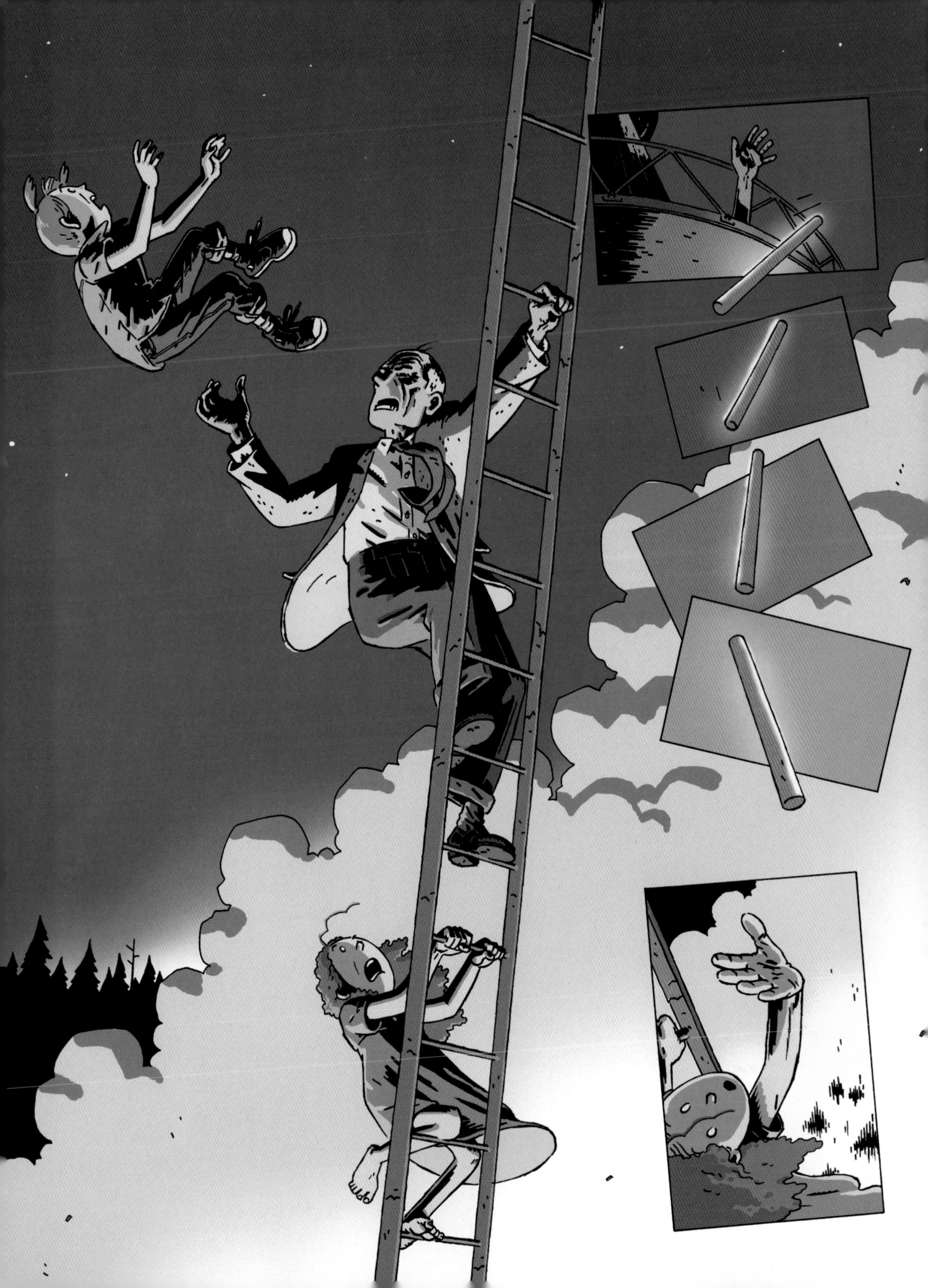

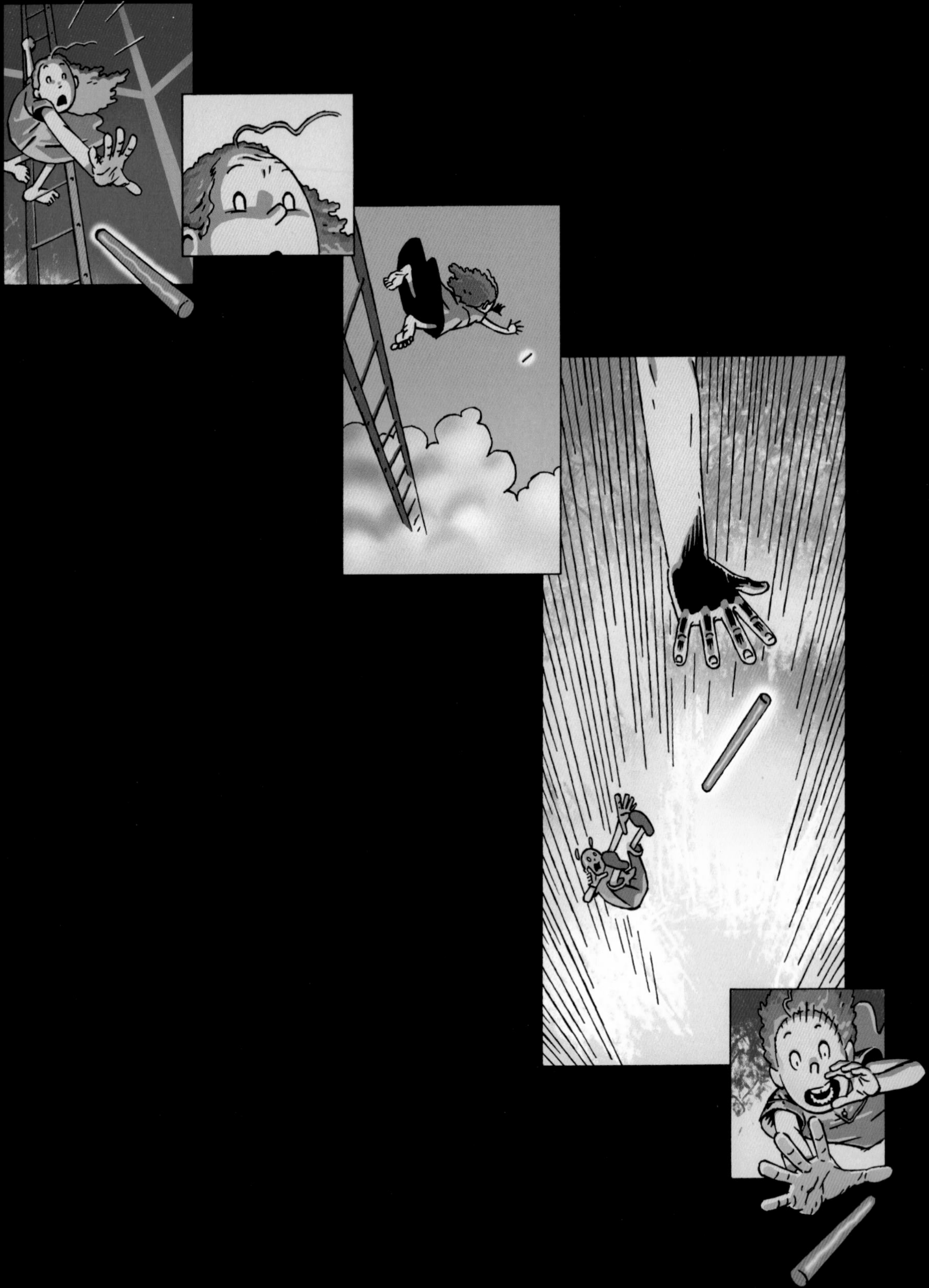

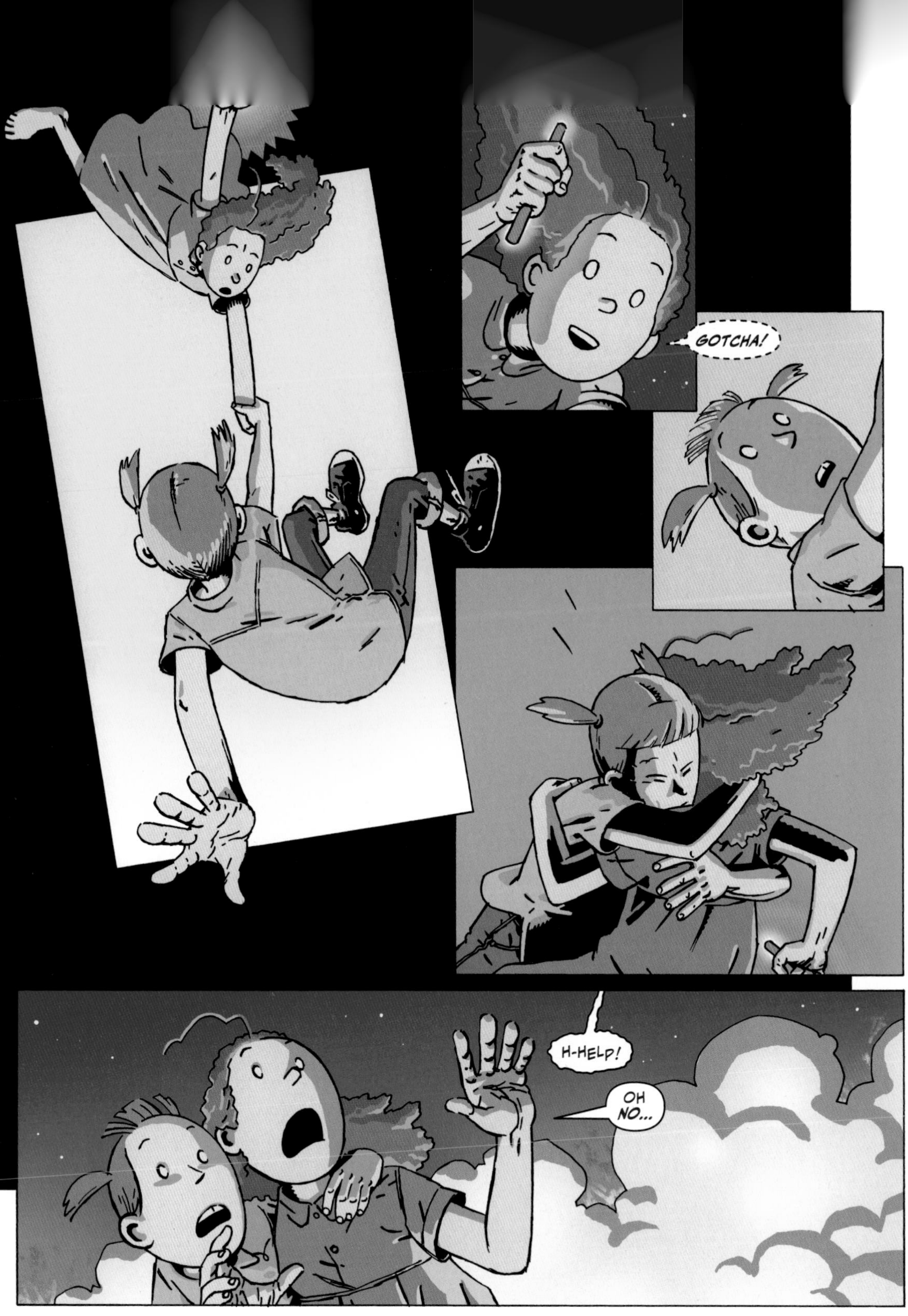
GOTCHA!
H-HELP!
OH NO...

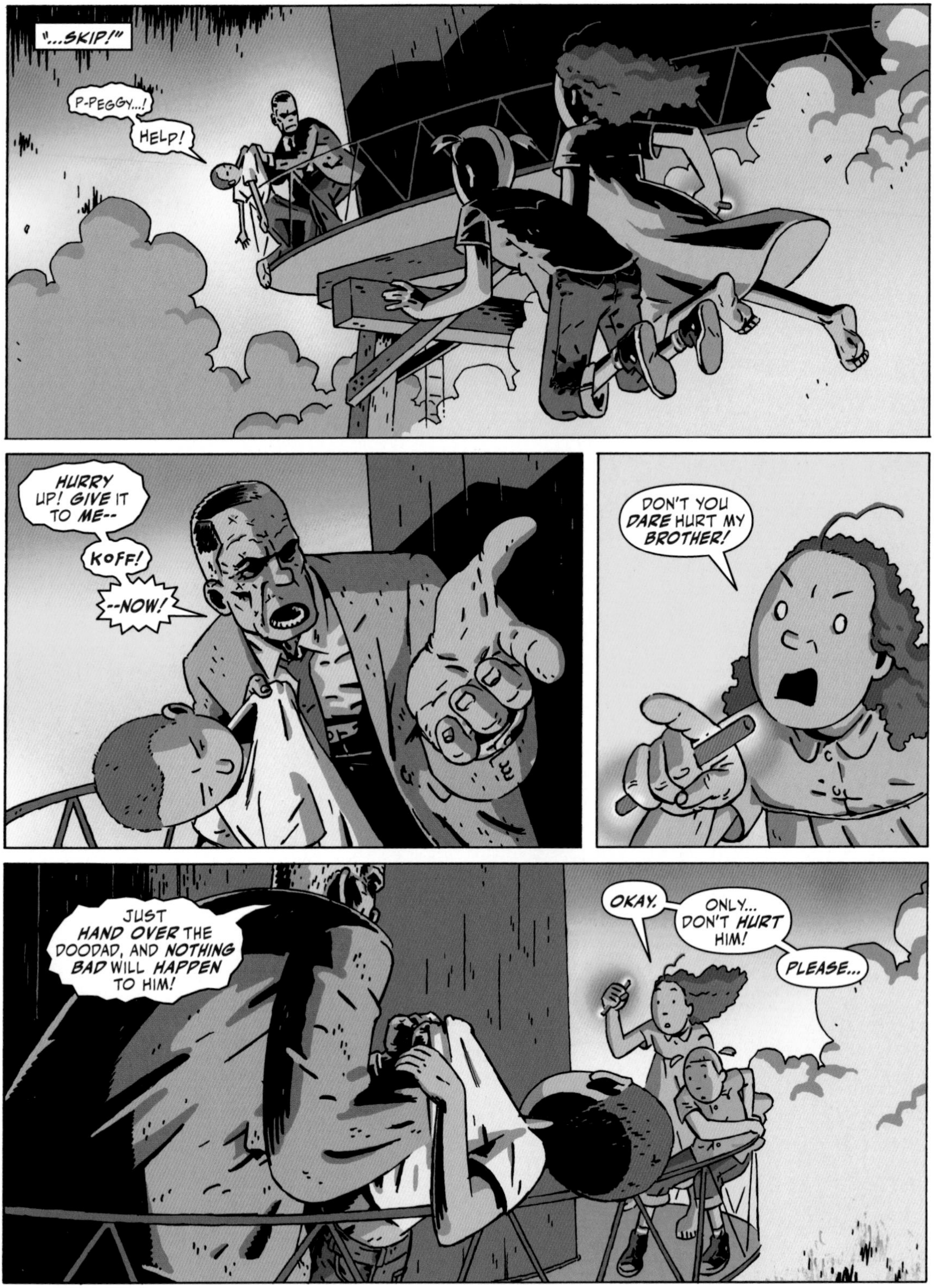
"...SKIP!"
P-PEGGY...!
HELP!
HURRY UP! GIVE IT TO ME--
KOFF!
--NOW!
DON'T YOU DARE HURT MY BROTHER!
JUST HAND OVER THE DOODAD, AND NOTHING BAD WILL HAPPEN TO HIM!
OKAY.
ONLY... DON'T HURT HIM!
PLEASE...

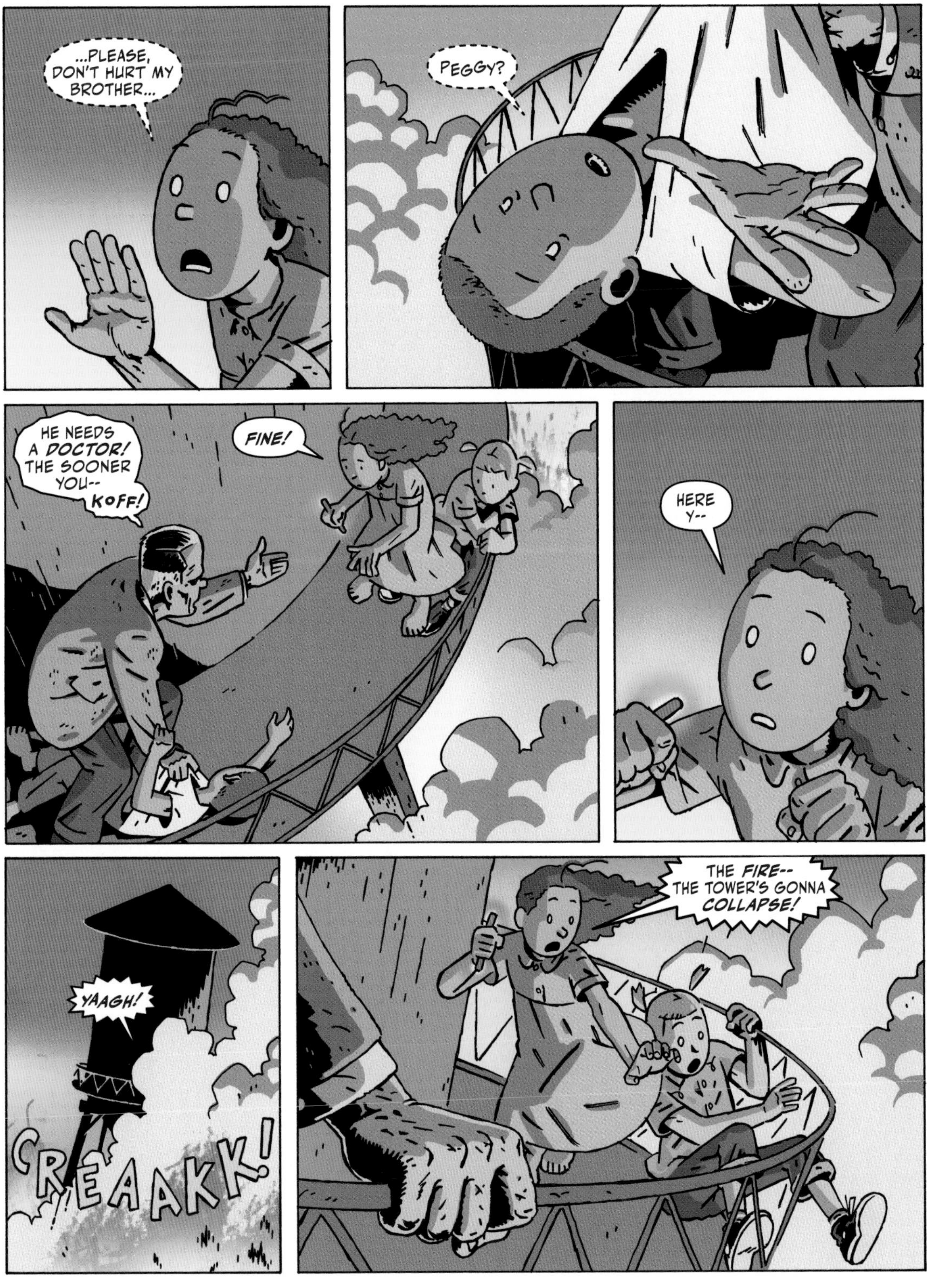
...PLEASE, DON'T HURT MY BROTHER...
PEGGY?
HE NEEDS A DOCTOR! THE SOONER YOU-- KOFF!
FINE!
HERE Y--
YAAGH!
CREAAKK!
THE FIRE-- THE TOWER'S GONNA COLLAPSE!

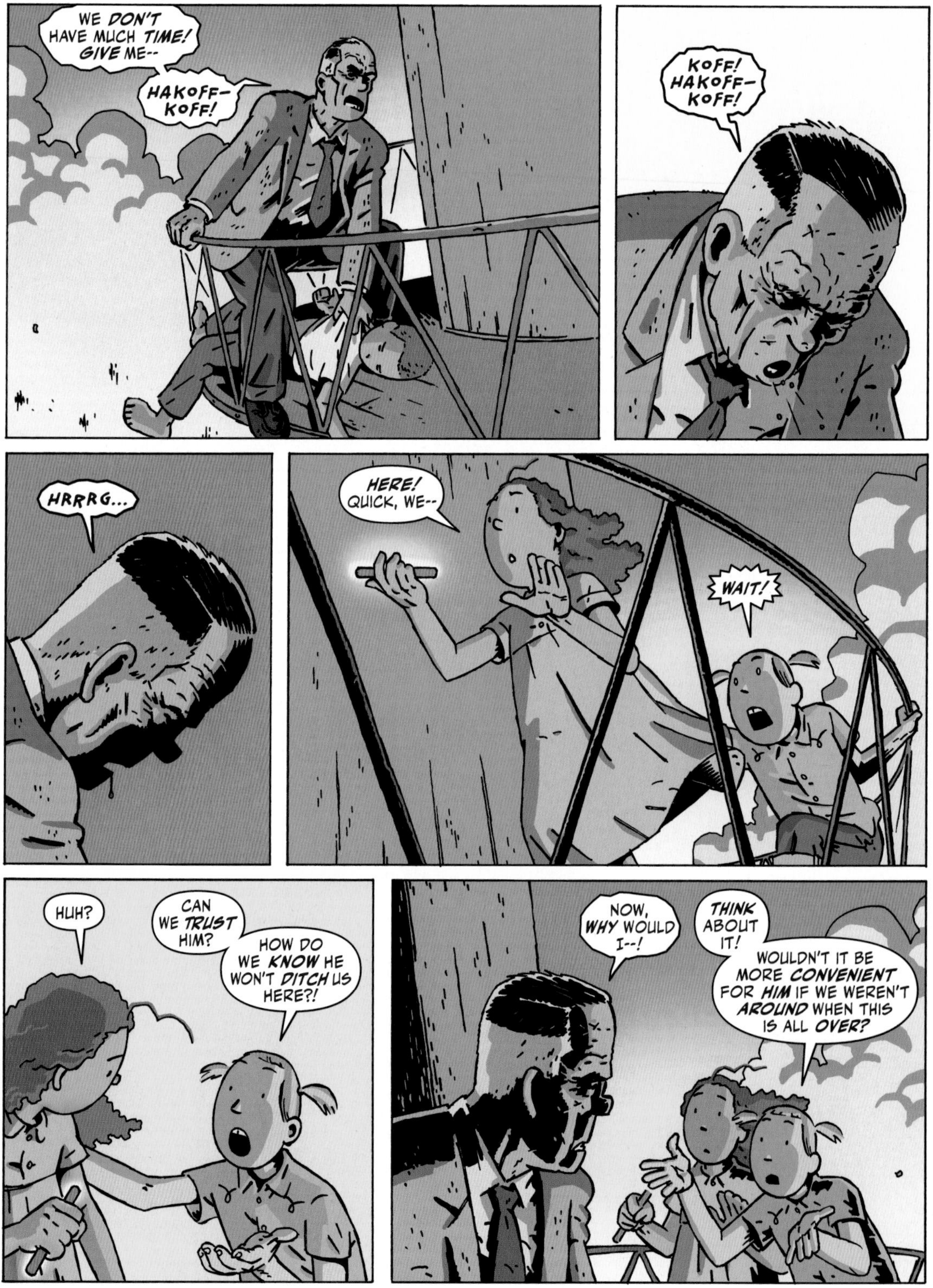

WE DON'T HAVE MUCH TIME! GIVE ME--
HAKOFF-KOFF!
KOFF! HAKOFF-KOFF!
HRRRG...
HERE! QUICK, WE--
WAIT!
HUH?
CAN WE TRUST HIM?
HOW DO WE KNOW HE WON'T DITCH US HERE?!
NOW, WHY WOULD I--!
THINK ABOUT IT!
WOULDN'T IT BE MORE CONVENIENT FOR HIM IF WE WEREN'T AROUND WHEN THIS IS ALL OVER?

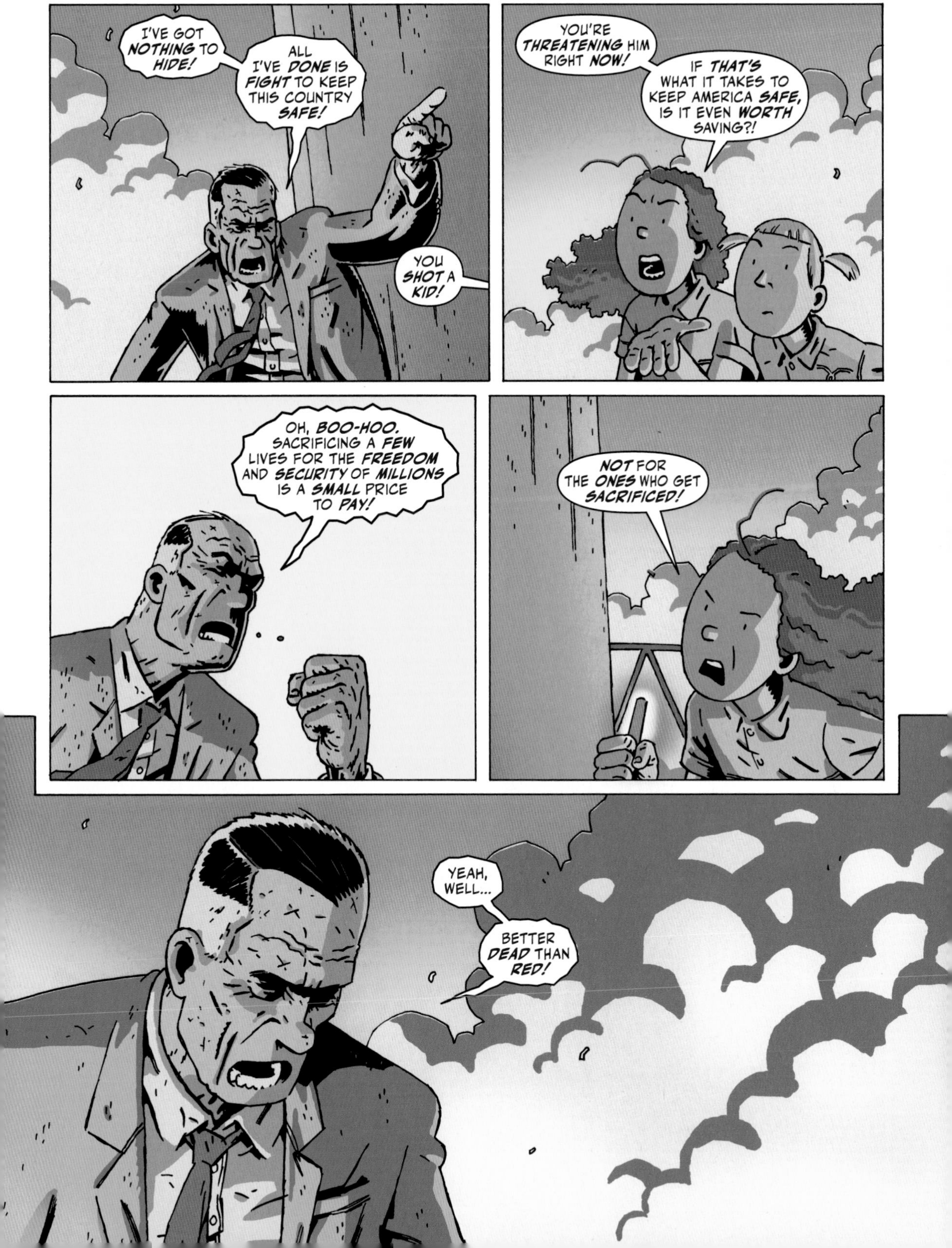
I'VE GOT NOTHING TO HIDE!
ALL I'VE DONE IS FIGHT TO KEEP THIS COUNTRY SAFE!
YOU SHOT A KID!
YOU'RE THREATENING HIM RIGHT NOW!
IF THAT'S WHAT IT TAKES TO KEEP AMERICA SAFE, IS IT EVEN WORTH SAVING?!
OH, BOO-HOO. SACRIFICING A FEW LIVES FOR THE FREEDOM AND SECURITY OF MILLIONS IS A SMALL PRICE TO PAY!
NOT FOR THE ONES WHO GET SACRIFICED!
YEAH, WELL...
BETTER DEAD THAN RED!

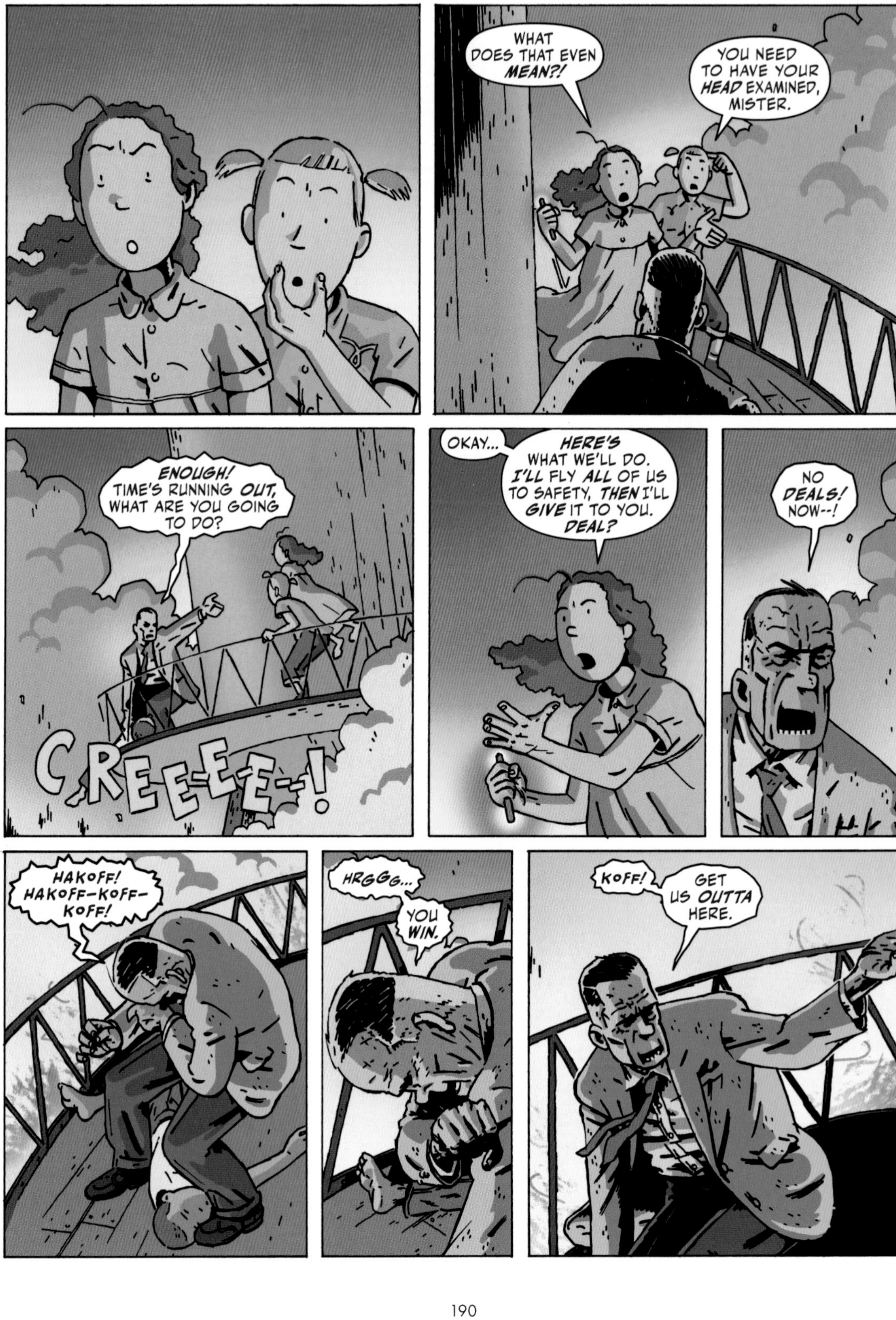
WHAT DOES THAT EVEN MEAN?!
YOU NEED TO HAVE YOUR HEAD EXAMINED, MISTER.
ENOUGH! TIME'S RUNNING OUT, WHAT ARE YOU GOING TO DO?
CREEEE--!
OKAY...
HERE'S WHAT WE'LL DO. I'LL FLY ALL OF US TO SAFETY, THEN I'LL GIVE IT TO YOU. DEAL?
NO DEALS! NOW--!
HAKOFF! HAKOFF-KOFF-KOFF!
HRGGG...
YOU WIN.
KOFF!
GET US OUTTA HERE.

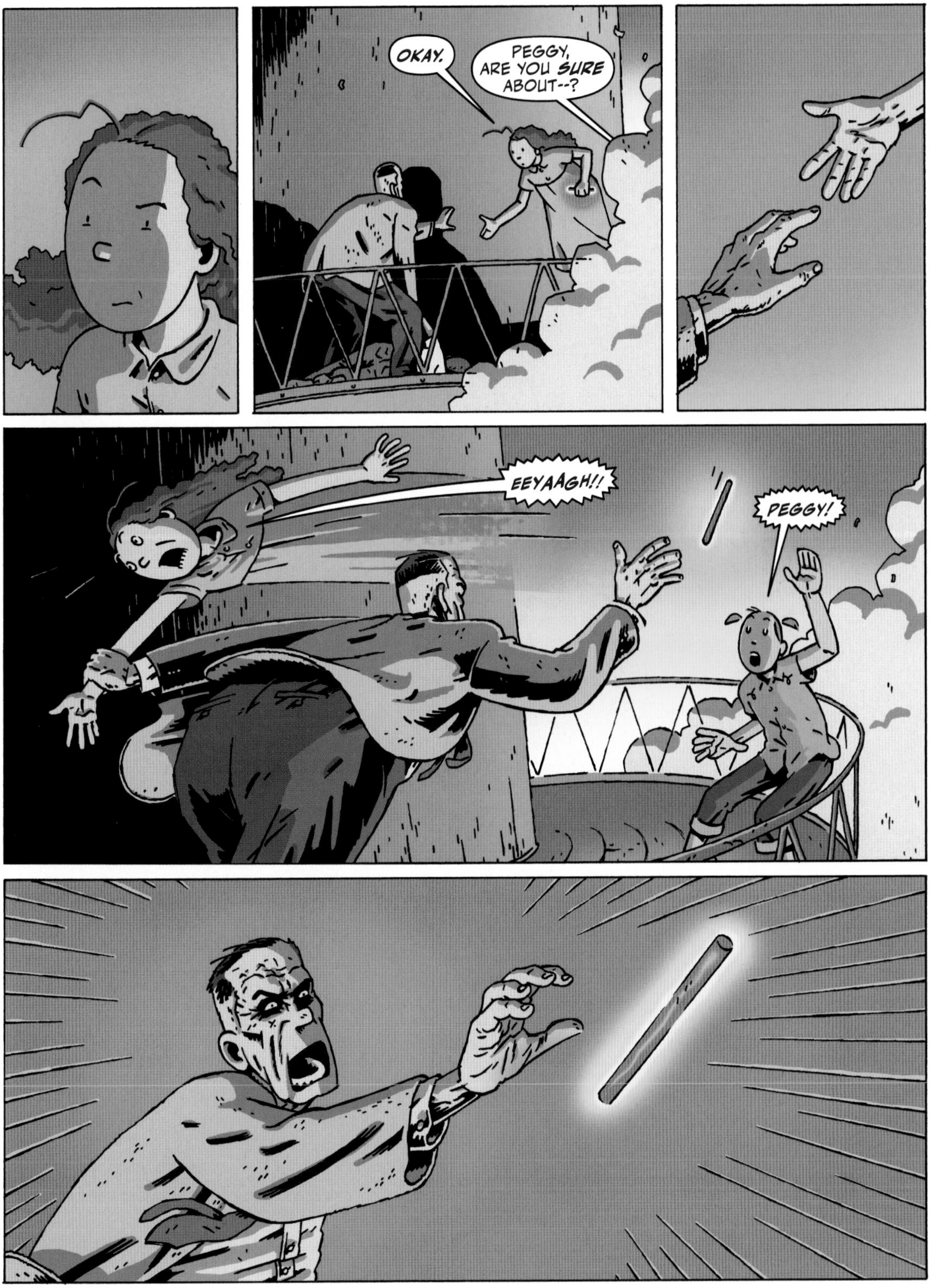
OKAY.
PEGGY, ARE YOU SURE ABOUT--?
EEYAAGH!!
PEGGY!

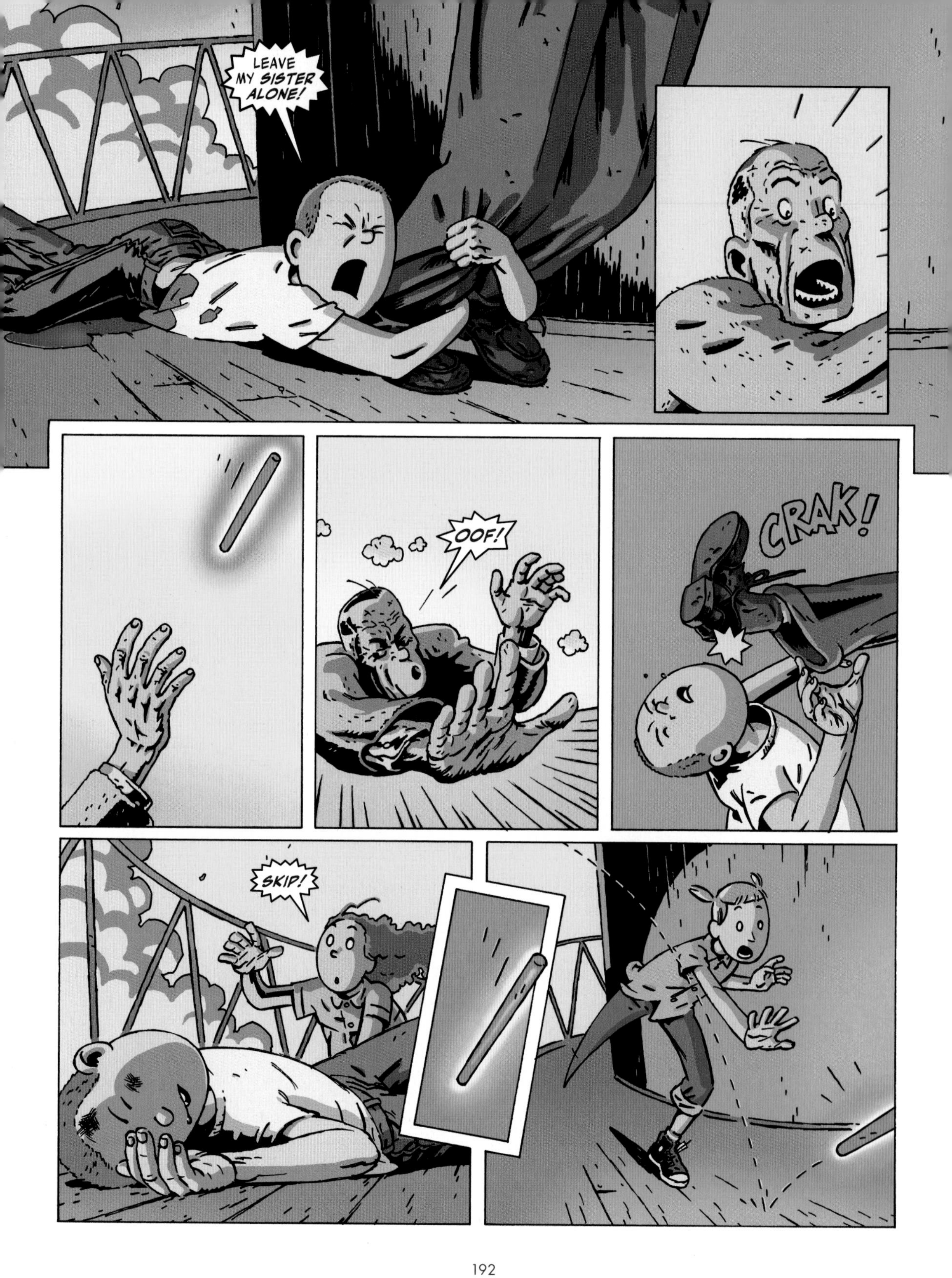
LEAVE MY SISTER ALONE!
OOF!
CRAK!
SKIP!

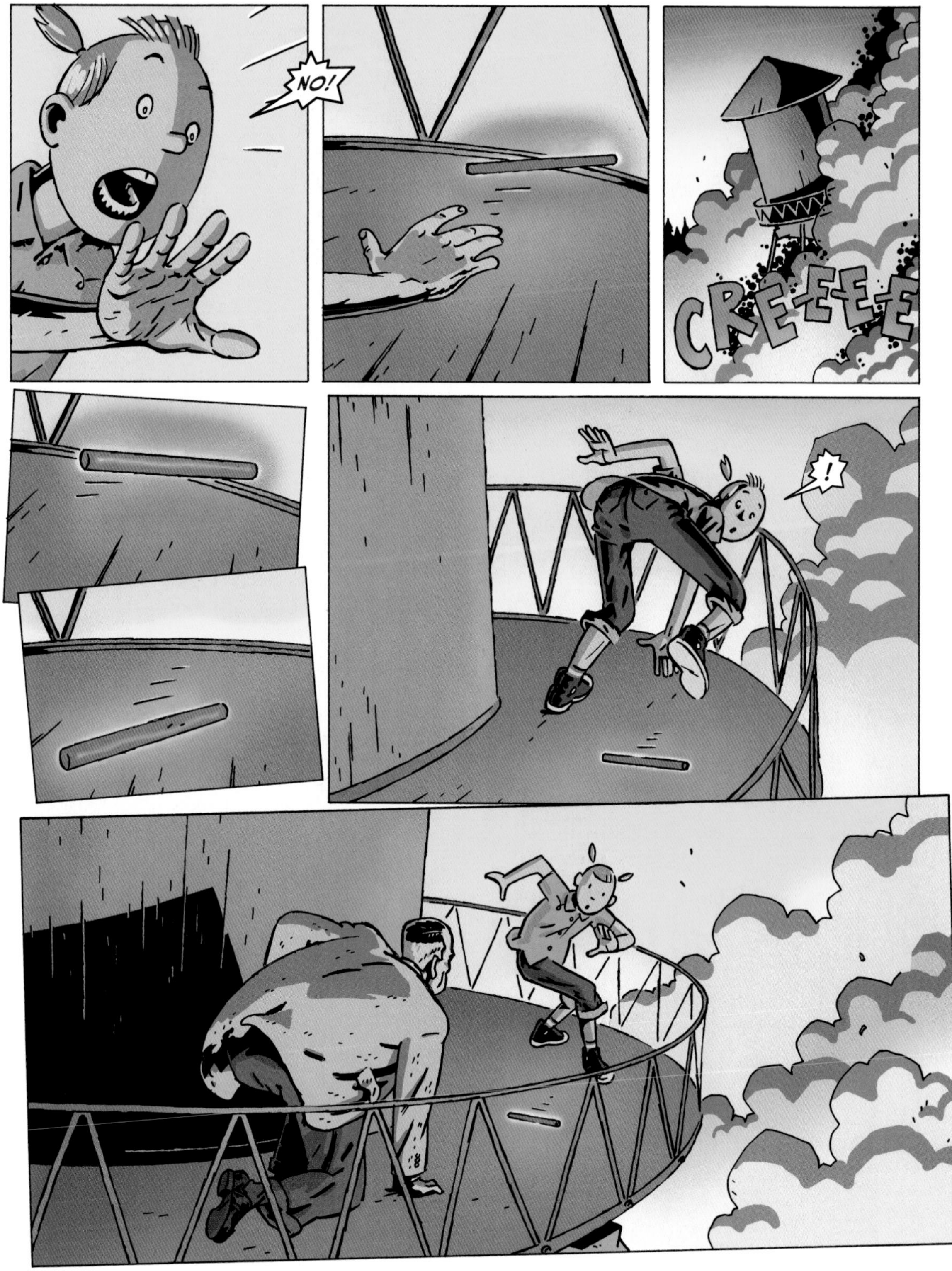
NO!
CREEEE
!

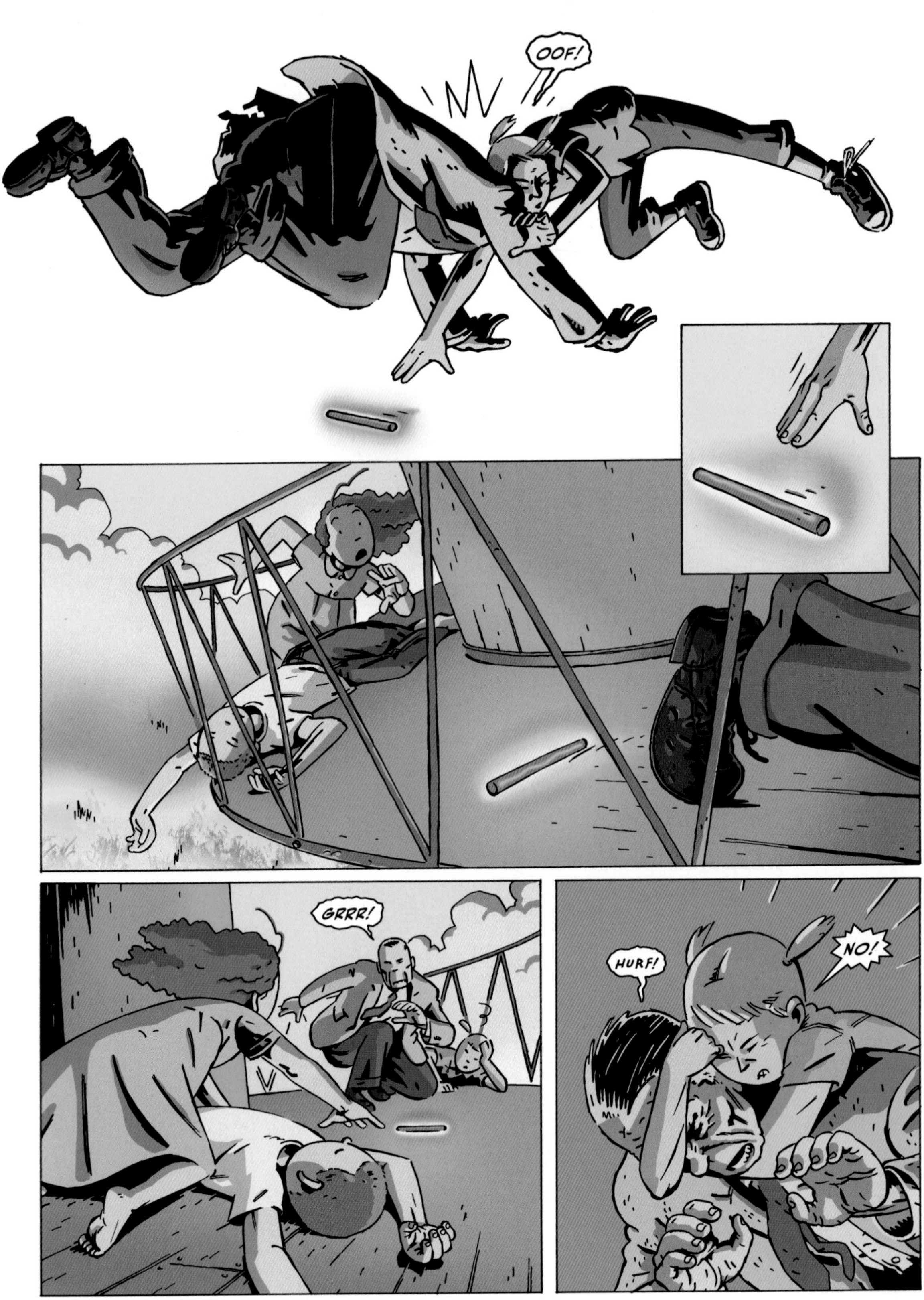

OOF!
GRRR!
HURF!
NO!

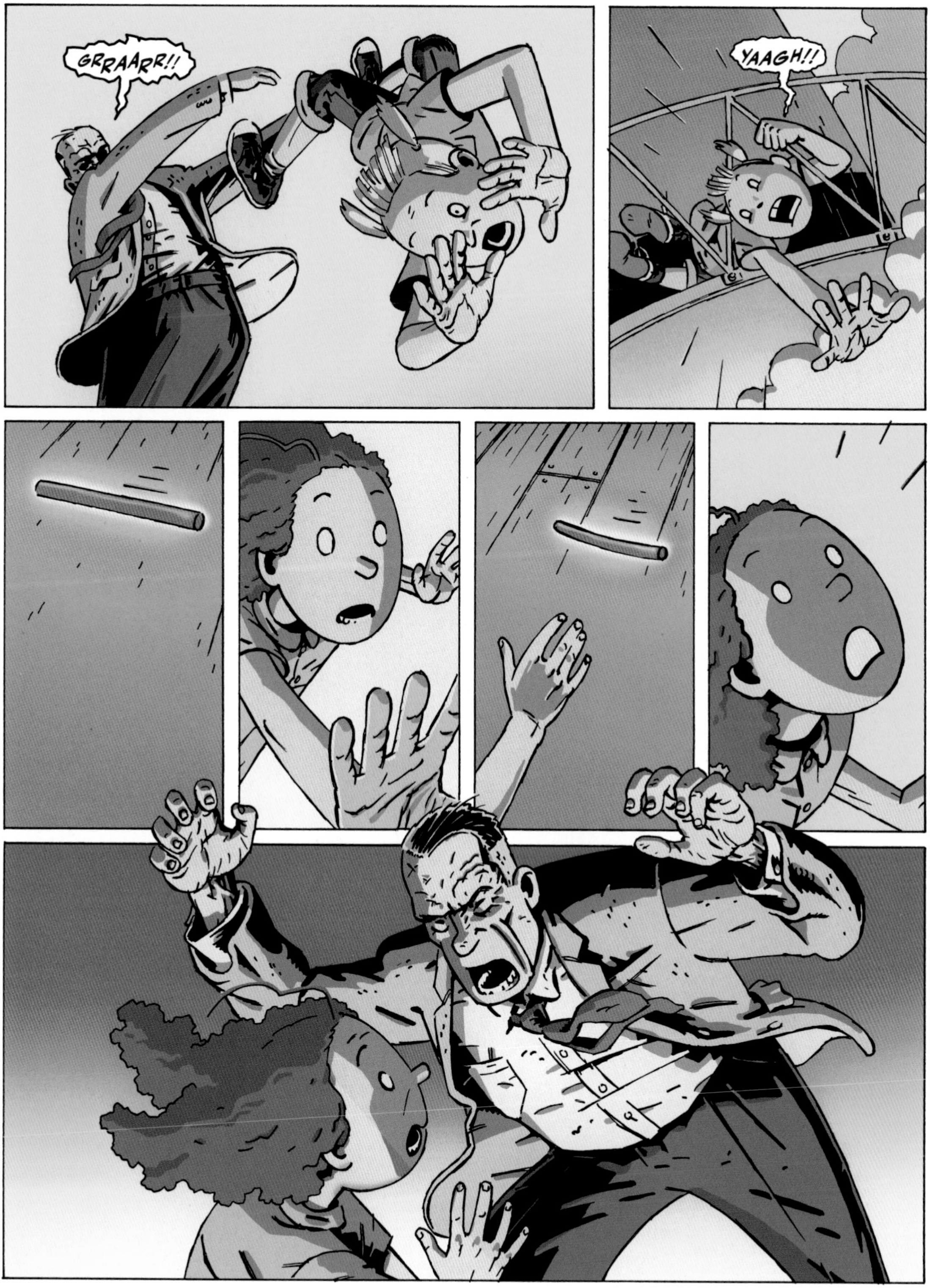
GRRAARR!!
YAAGH!!

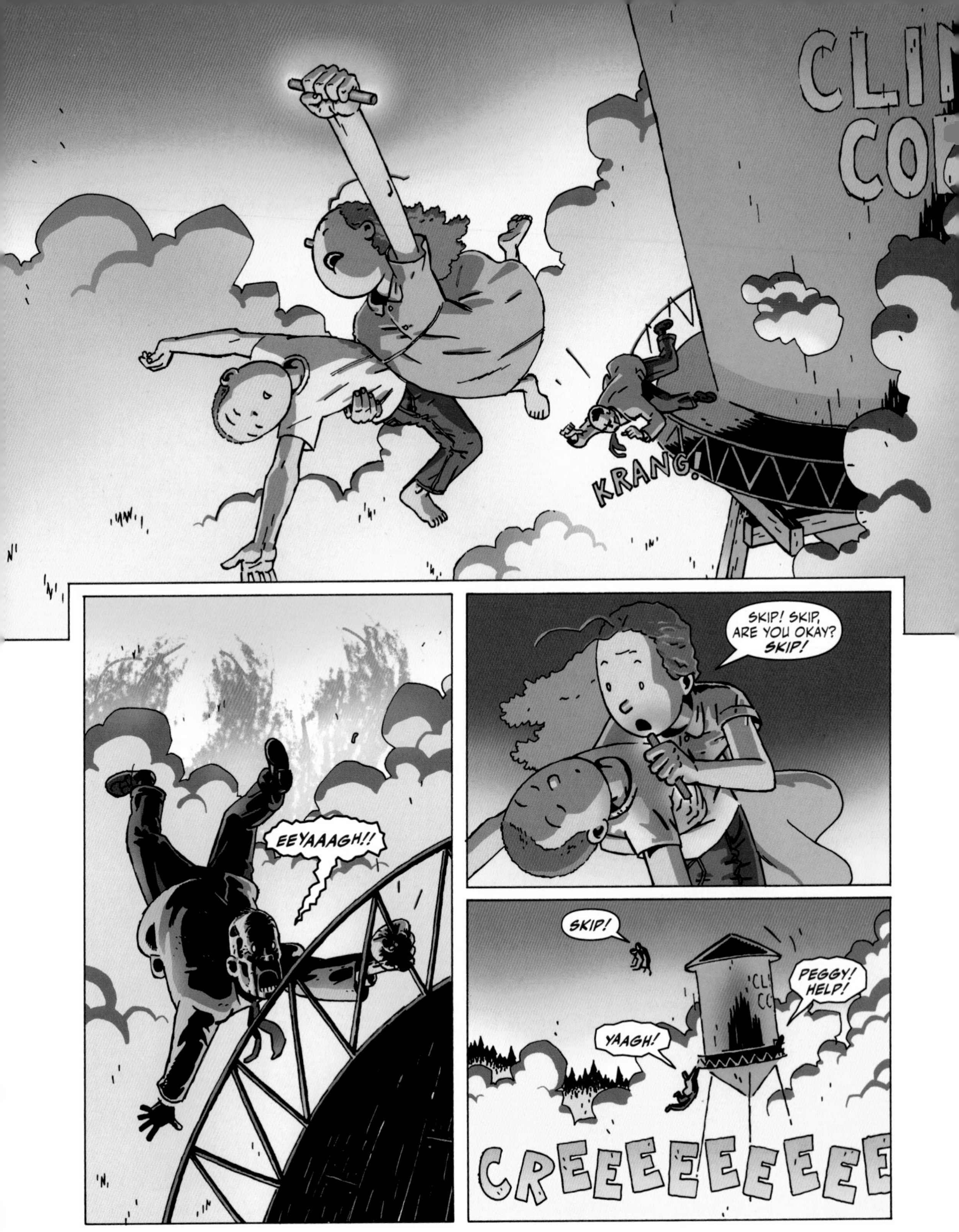
CLI
CO
KRANG!
EEYAAAGH!!
SKIP! SKIP, ARE YOU OKAY? SKIP!
SKIP!
PEGGY! HELP!
YAAGH!
CL
CC
CREEEEEEEEE

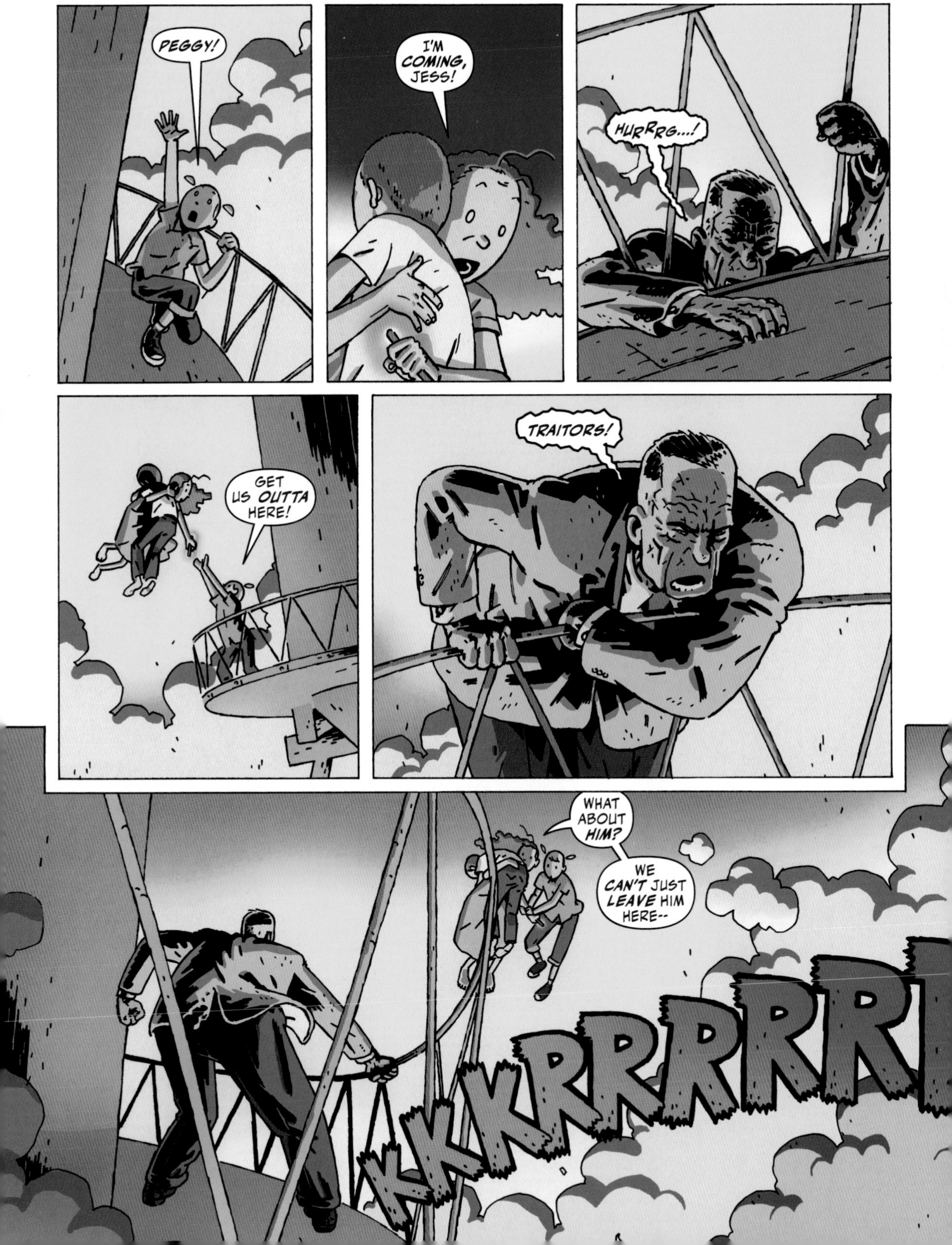
PEGGY!
I'M COMING, JESS!
HURRRG...!
GET US OUTTA HERE!
TRAITORS!
WHAT ABOUT HIM?
WE CAN'T JUST LEAVE HIM HERE--
KKKRRRRRR

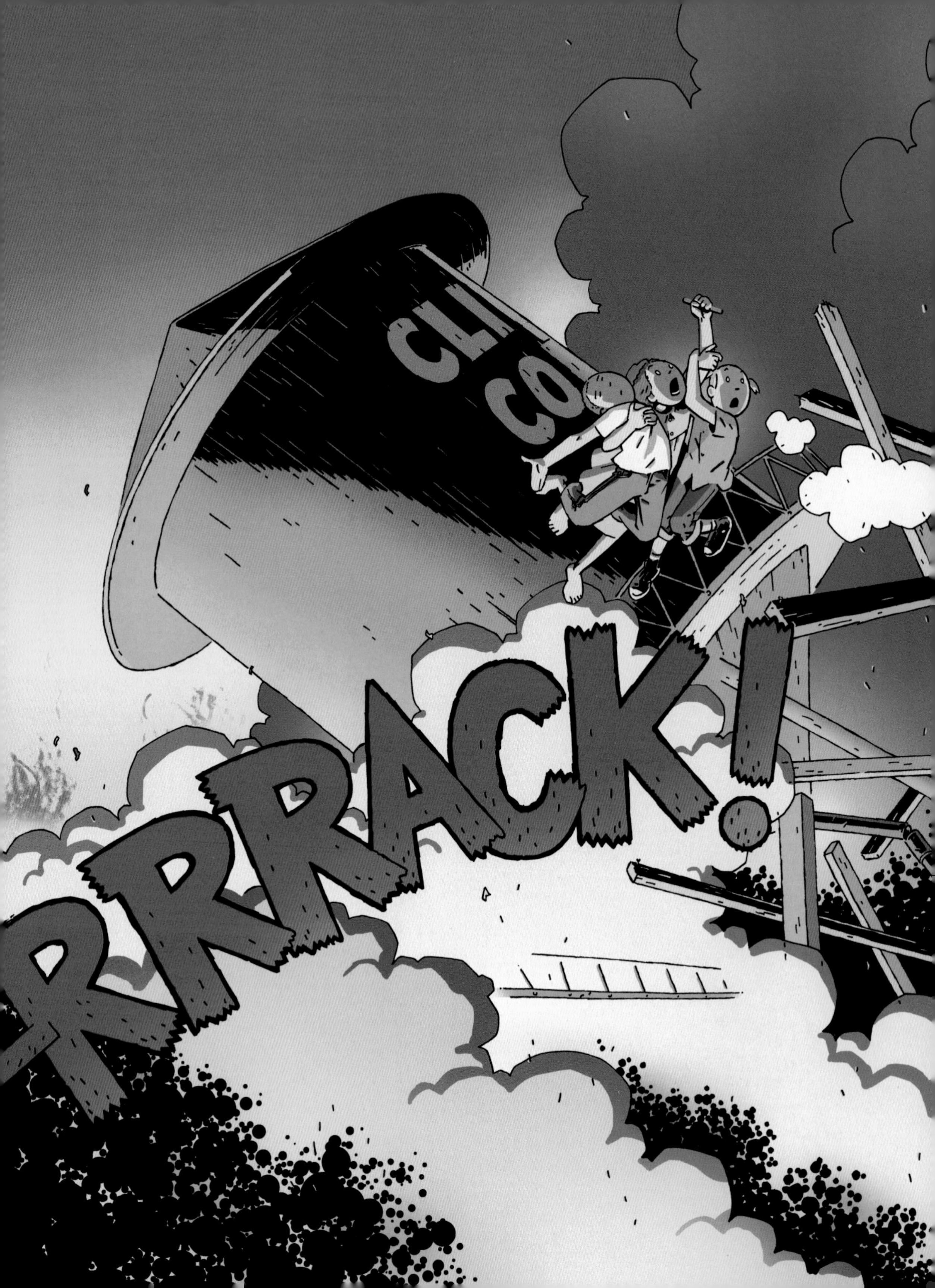
CL
CO
RRRACK!

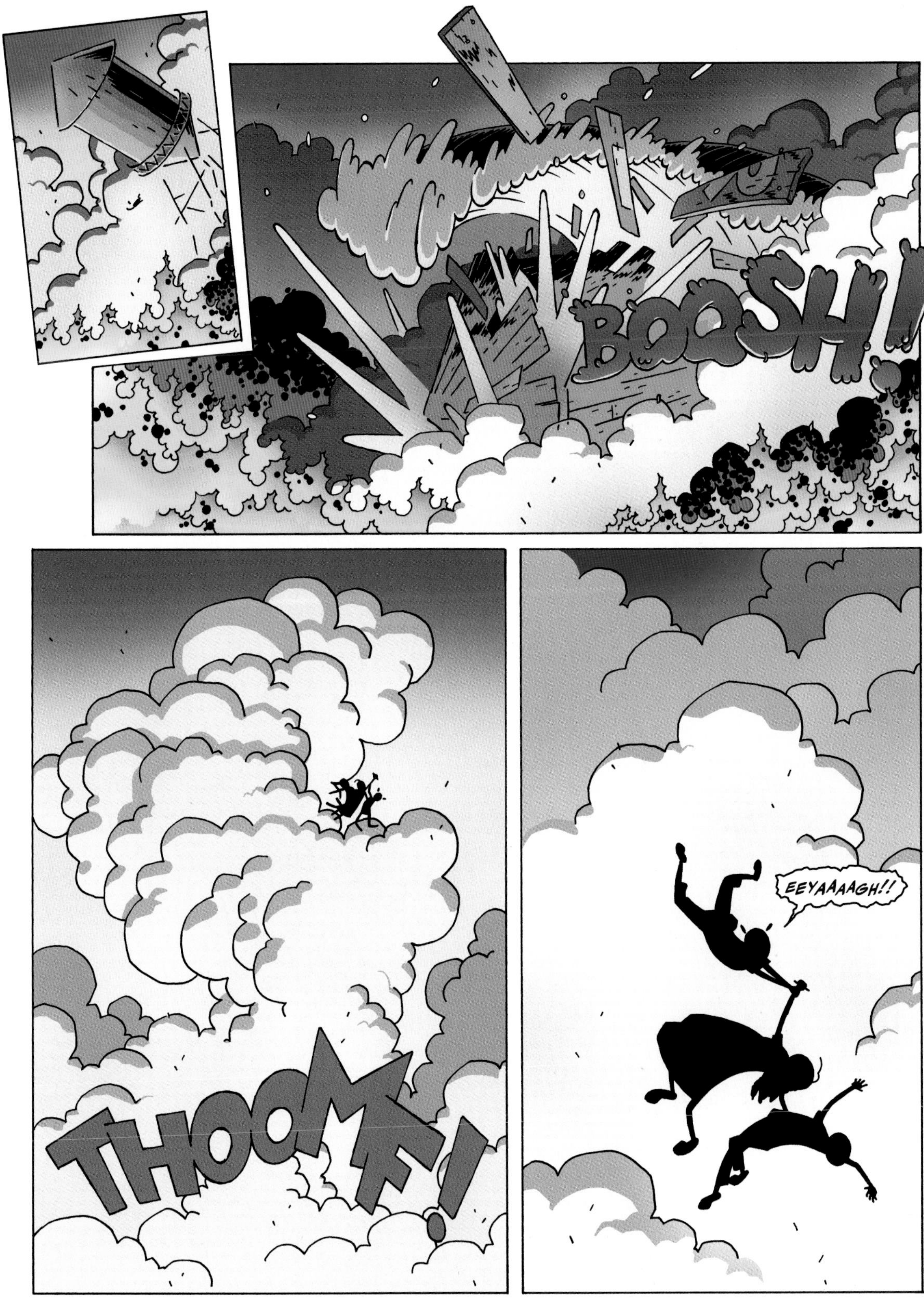
BOOSH!!
THOOMF!
EEYAAAAGH!!

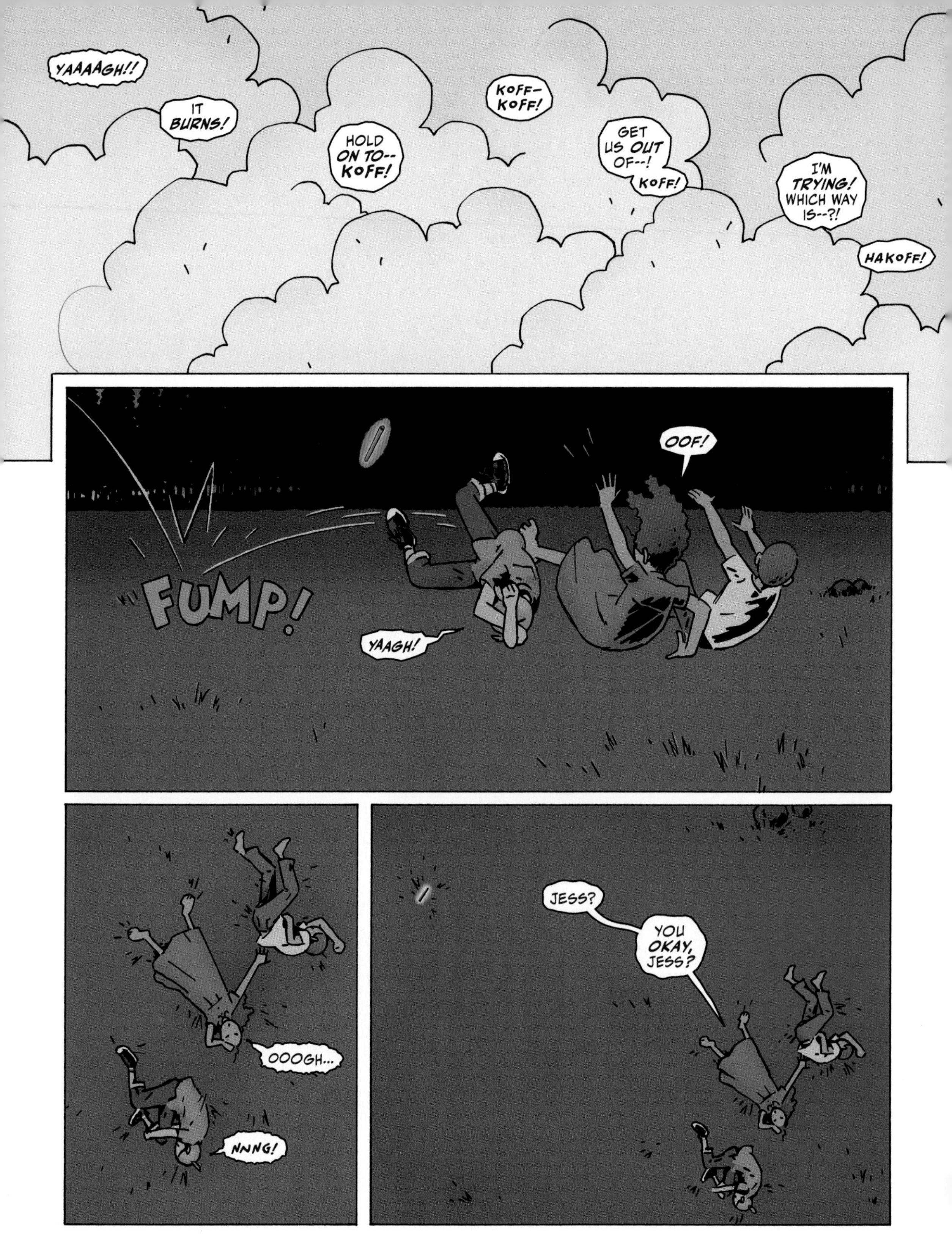
YAAAAGH!!
IT BURNS!
HOLD ON TO-- KOFF!
KOFF-KOFF!
GET US OUT OF--! KOFF!
I'M TRYING! WHICH WAY IS--?!
HAKOFF!
FUMP!
OOF!
YAAGH!
OOOGH...
NNNG!
JESS?
YOU OKAY, JESS?

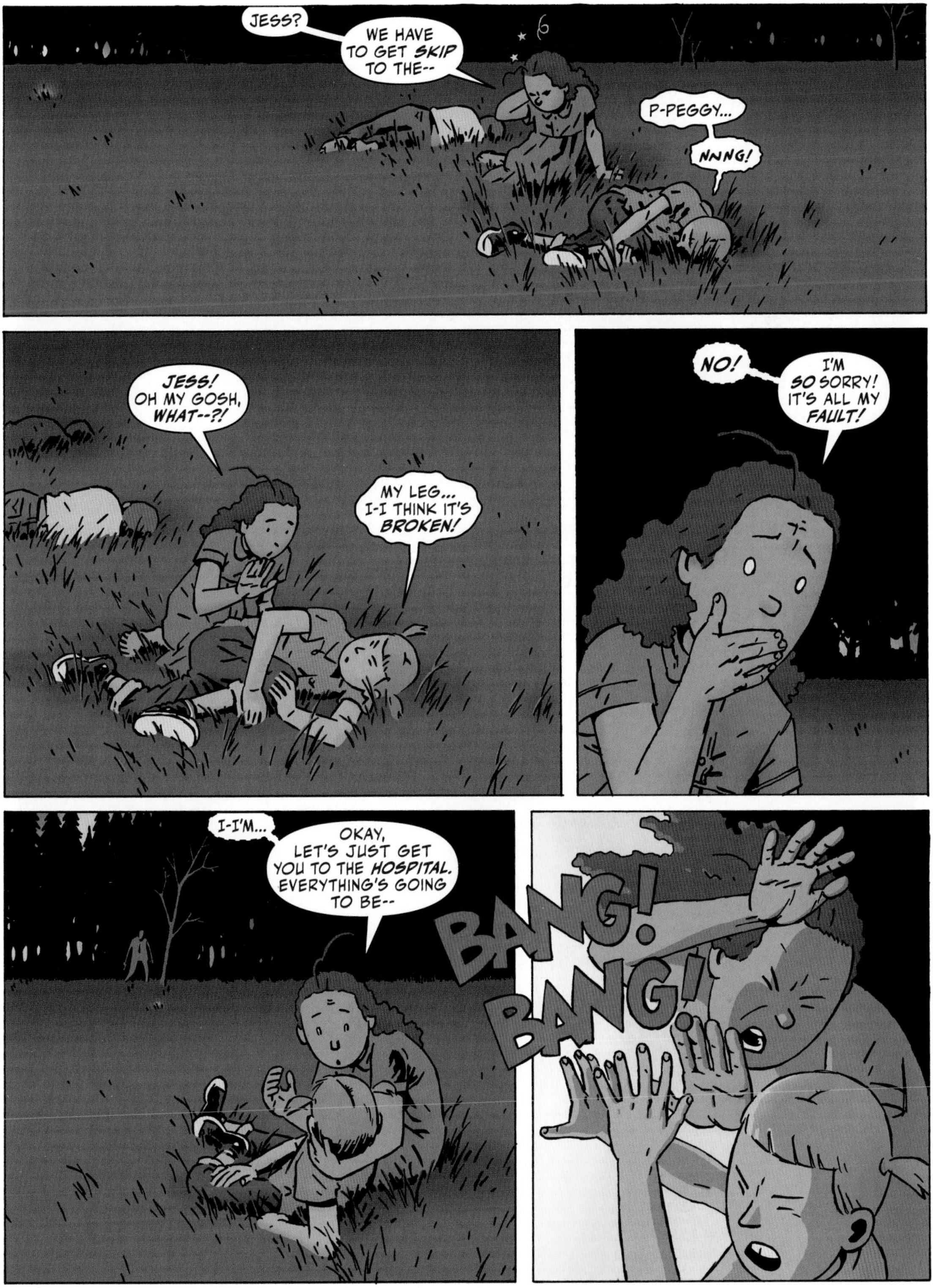
JESS?
WE HAVE TO GET *SKIP* TO THE--
P-PEGGY...
*NNNG!*
*JESS!* OH MY GOSH, *WHAT--?!*
MY LEG... I-I THINK IT'S *BROKEN!*
*NO!*
I'M *SO* SORRY! IT'S ALL MY *FAULT!*
I-I'M...
OKAY, LET'S JUST GET YOU TO THE *HOSPITAL.* EVERYTHING'S GOING TO BE--
BANG!
BANG!

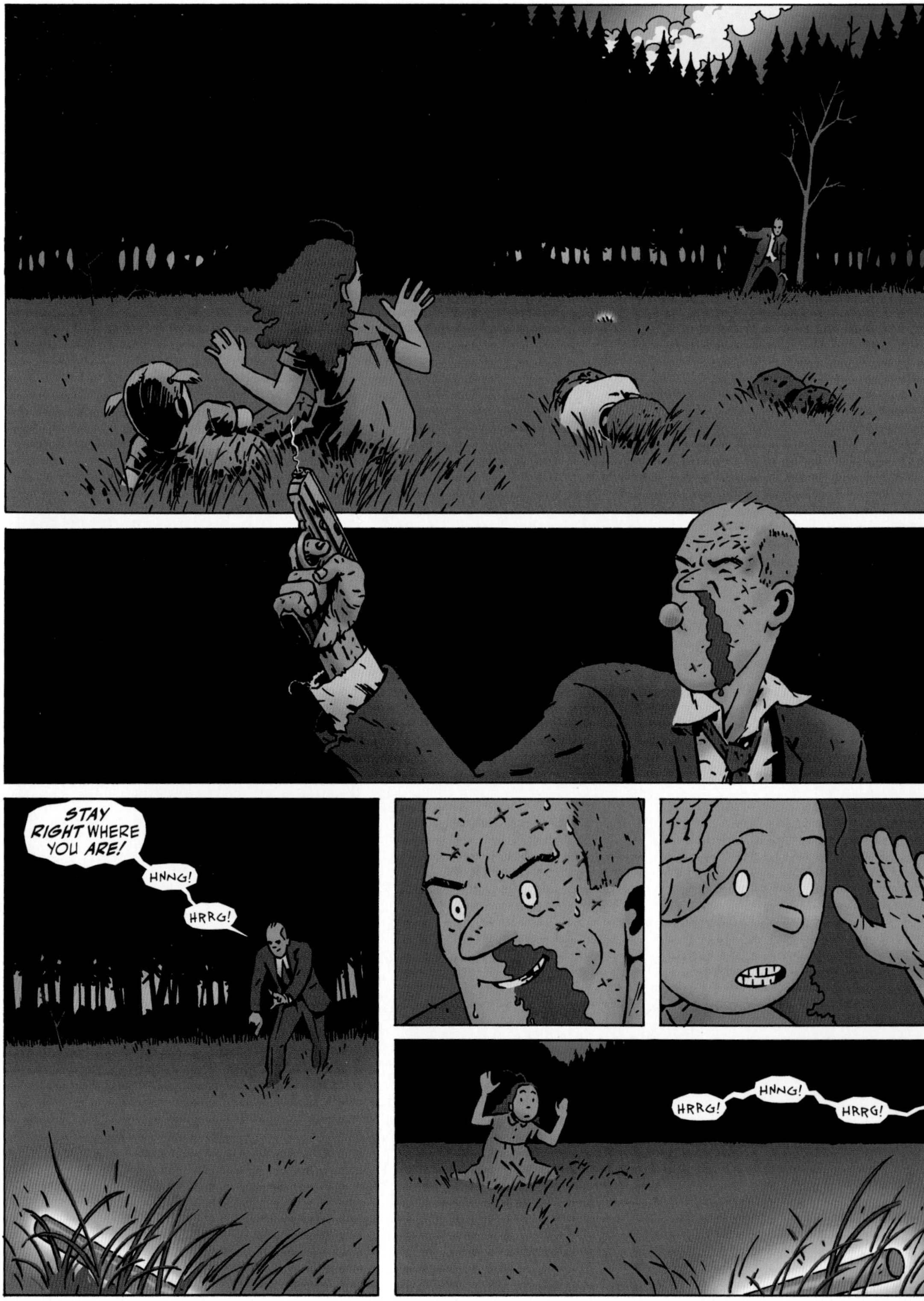
STAY RIGHT WHERE YOU ARE!
HNNG!
HRRG!
HRRG!
HNNG!
HRRG!

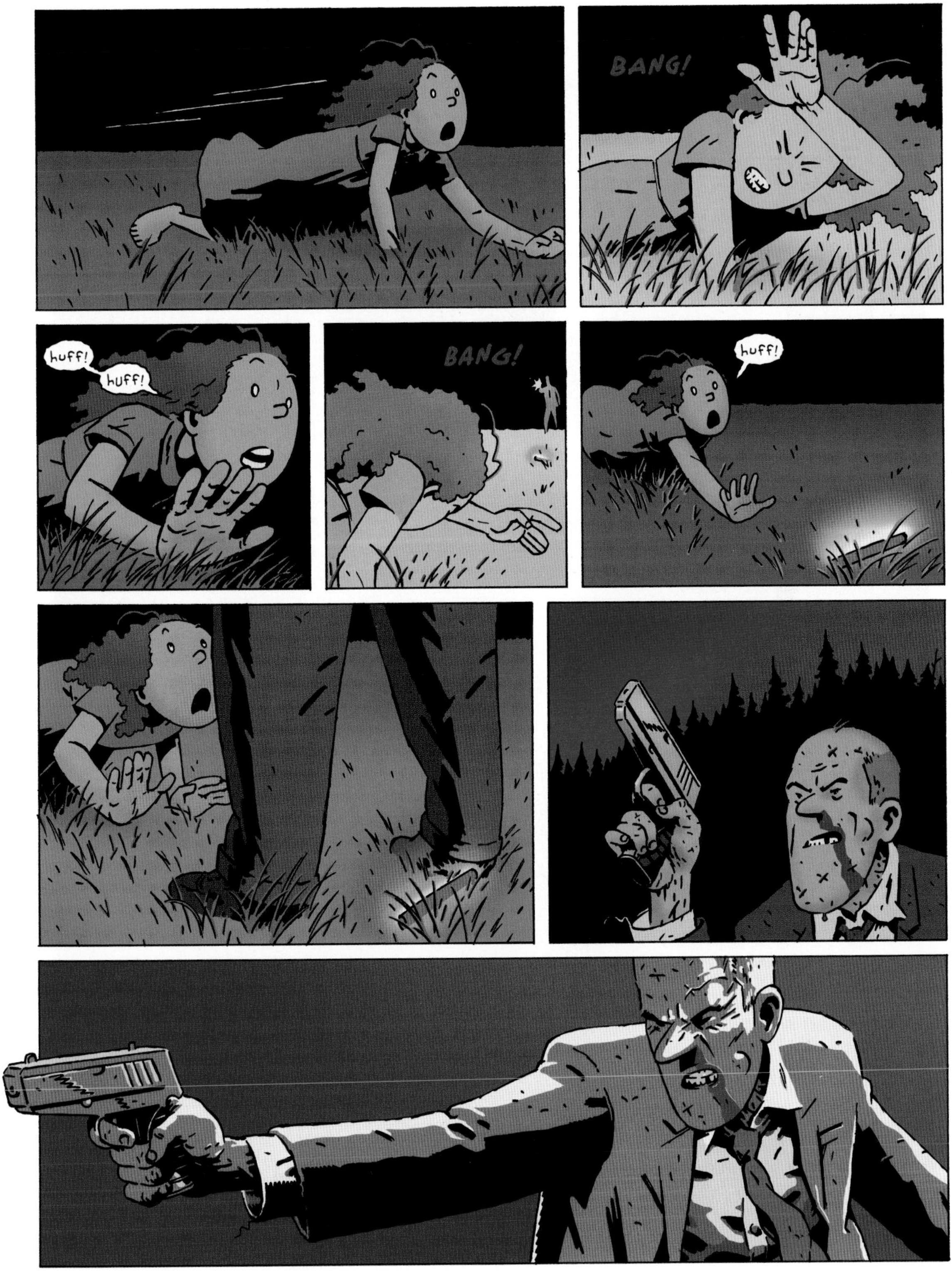
BANG!
huff!
huff!
BANG!
huff!

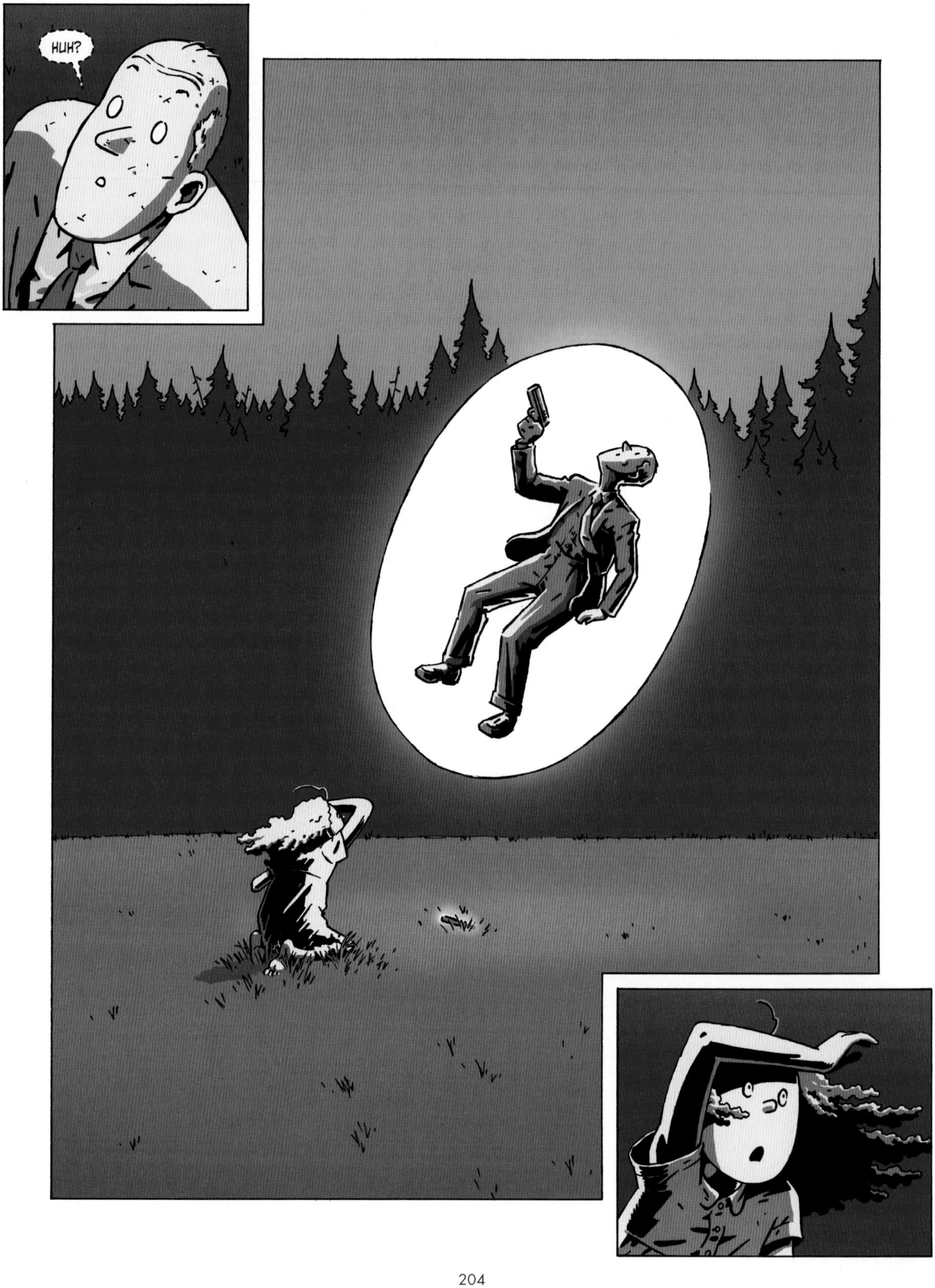
HUH?

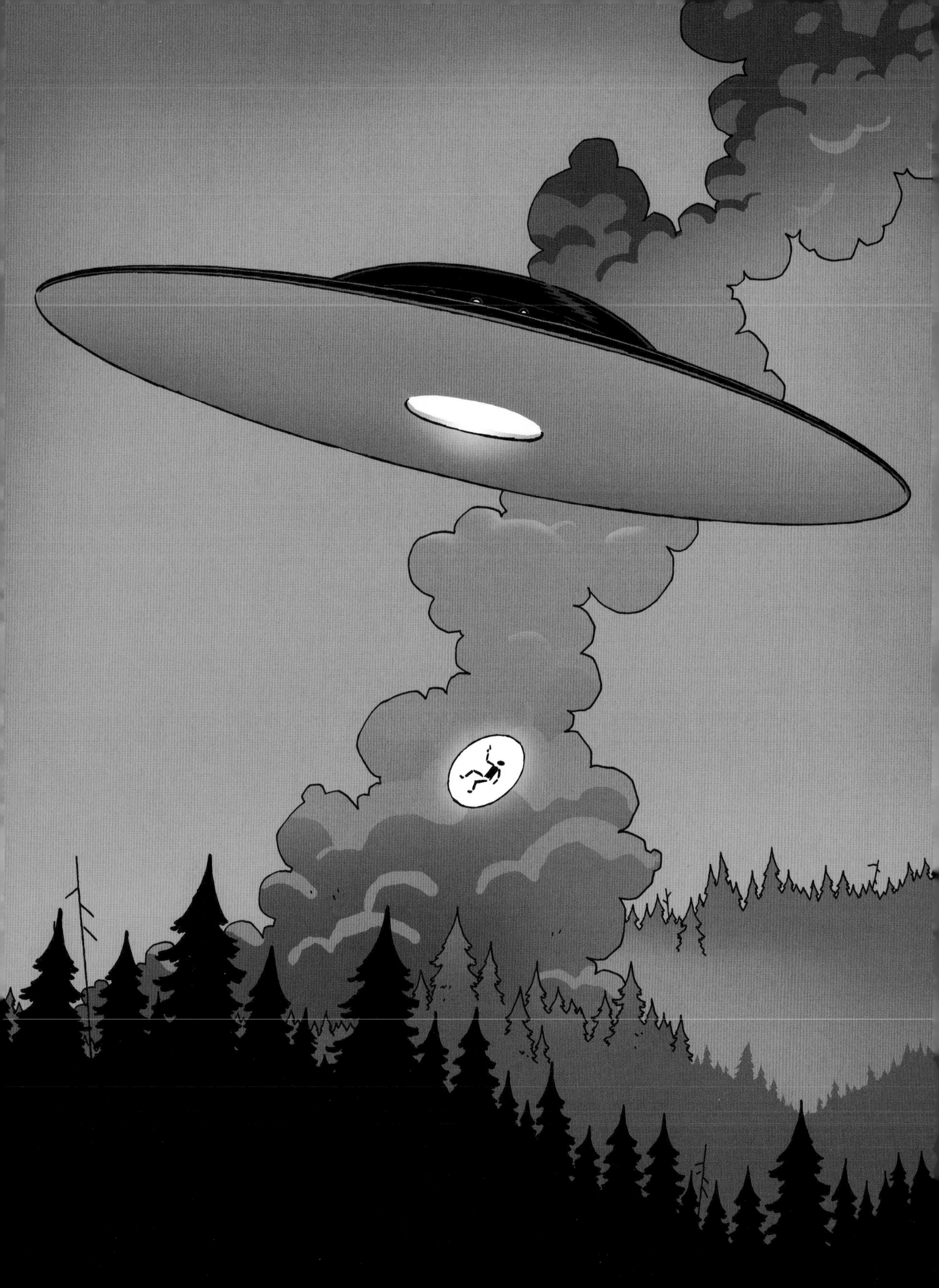

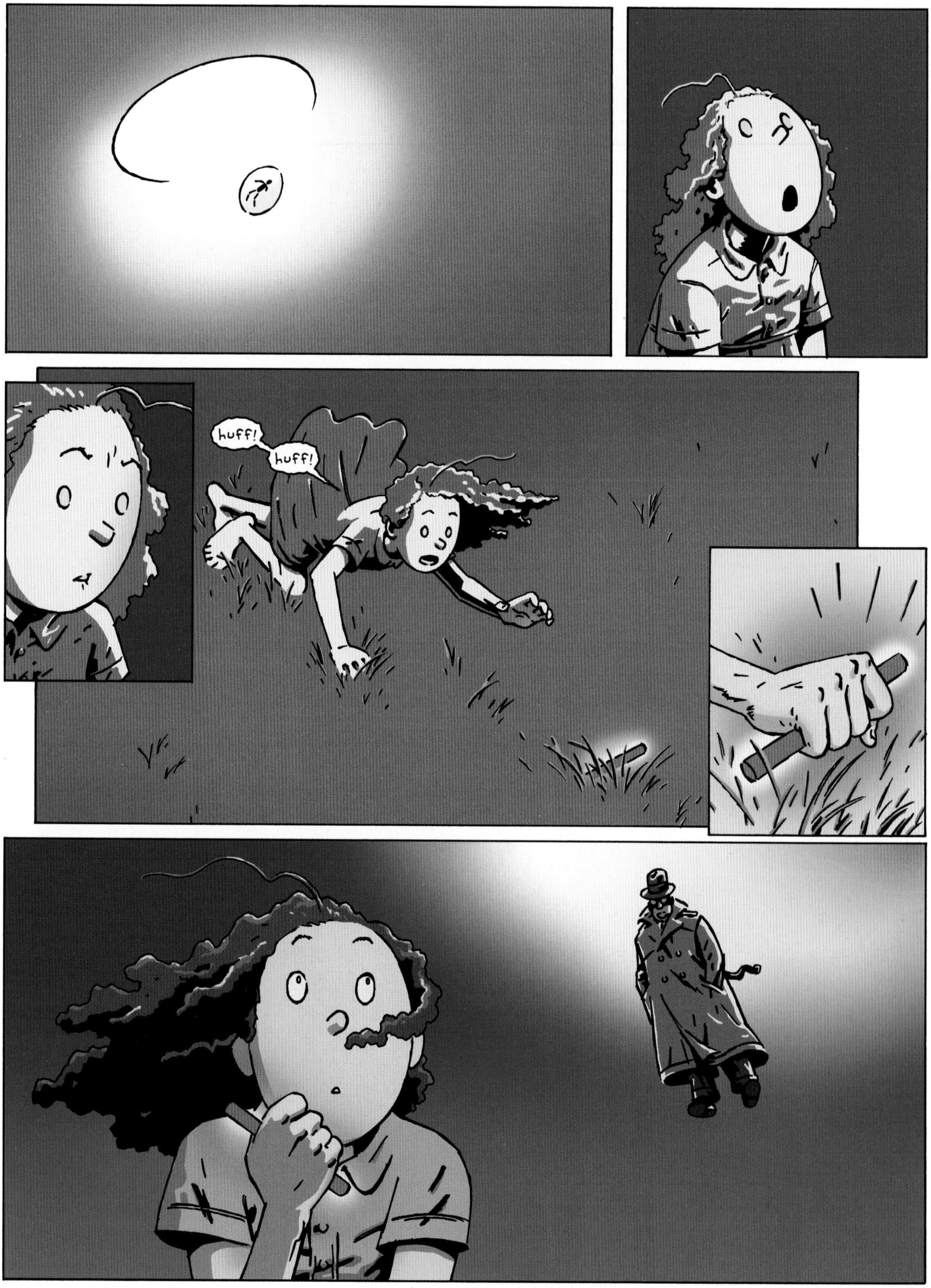
huff!
huff!

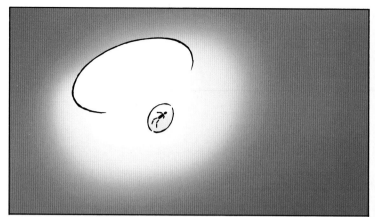

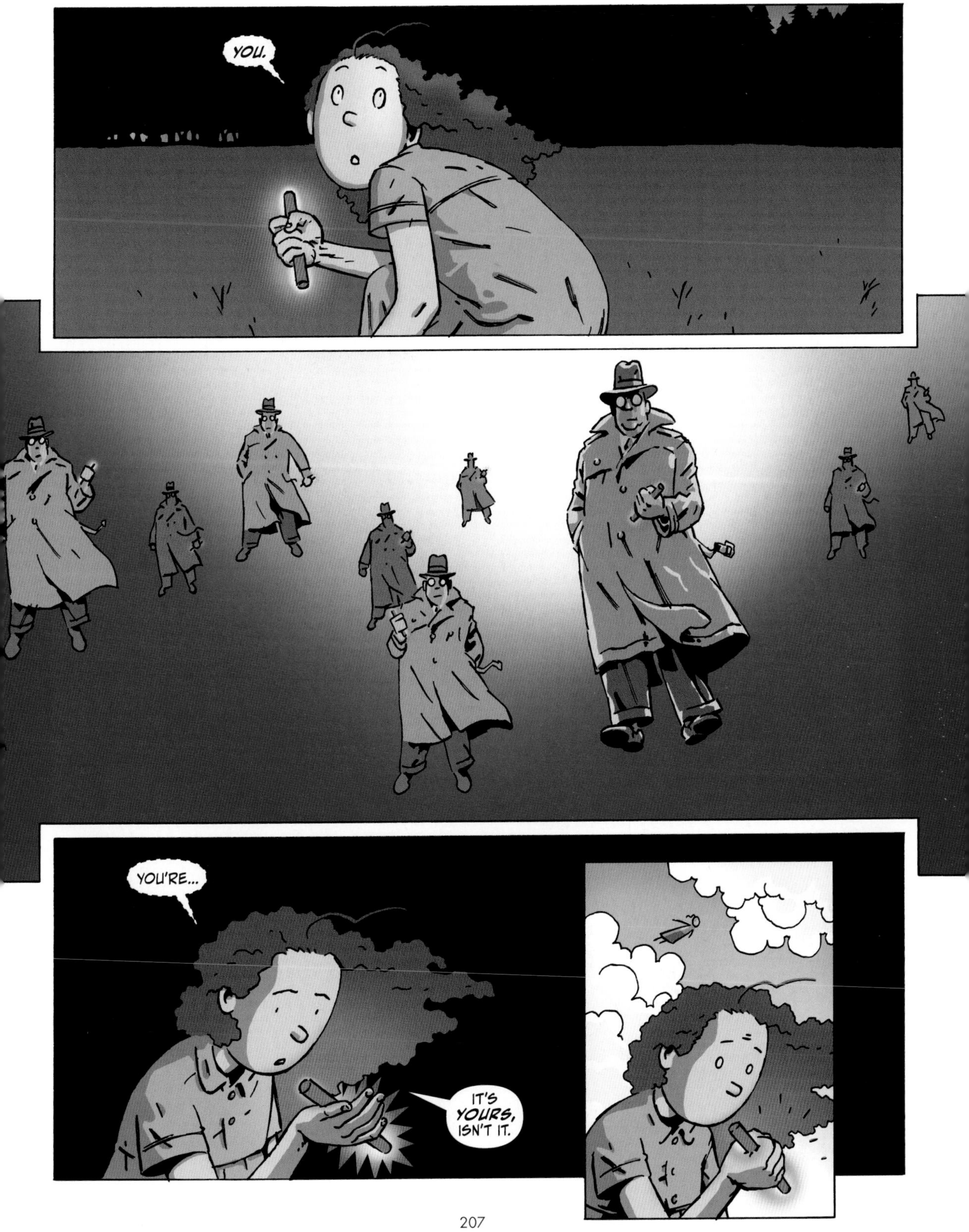
YOU.
YOU'RE...
IT'S YOURS, ISN'T IT.

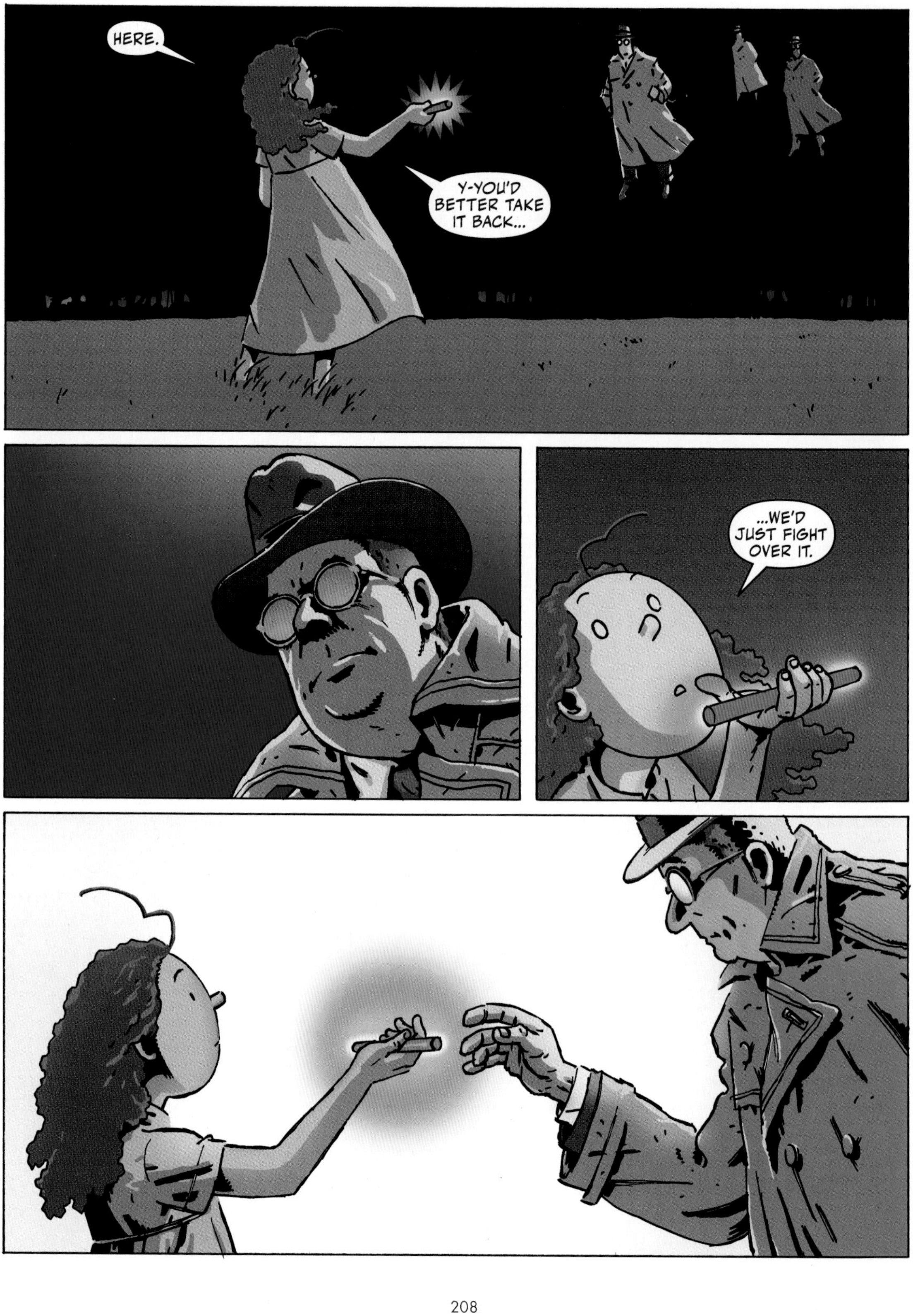
HERE.
Y-YOU'D BETTER TAKE IT BACK...
...WE'D JUST FIGHT OVER IT.

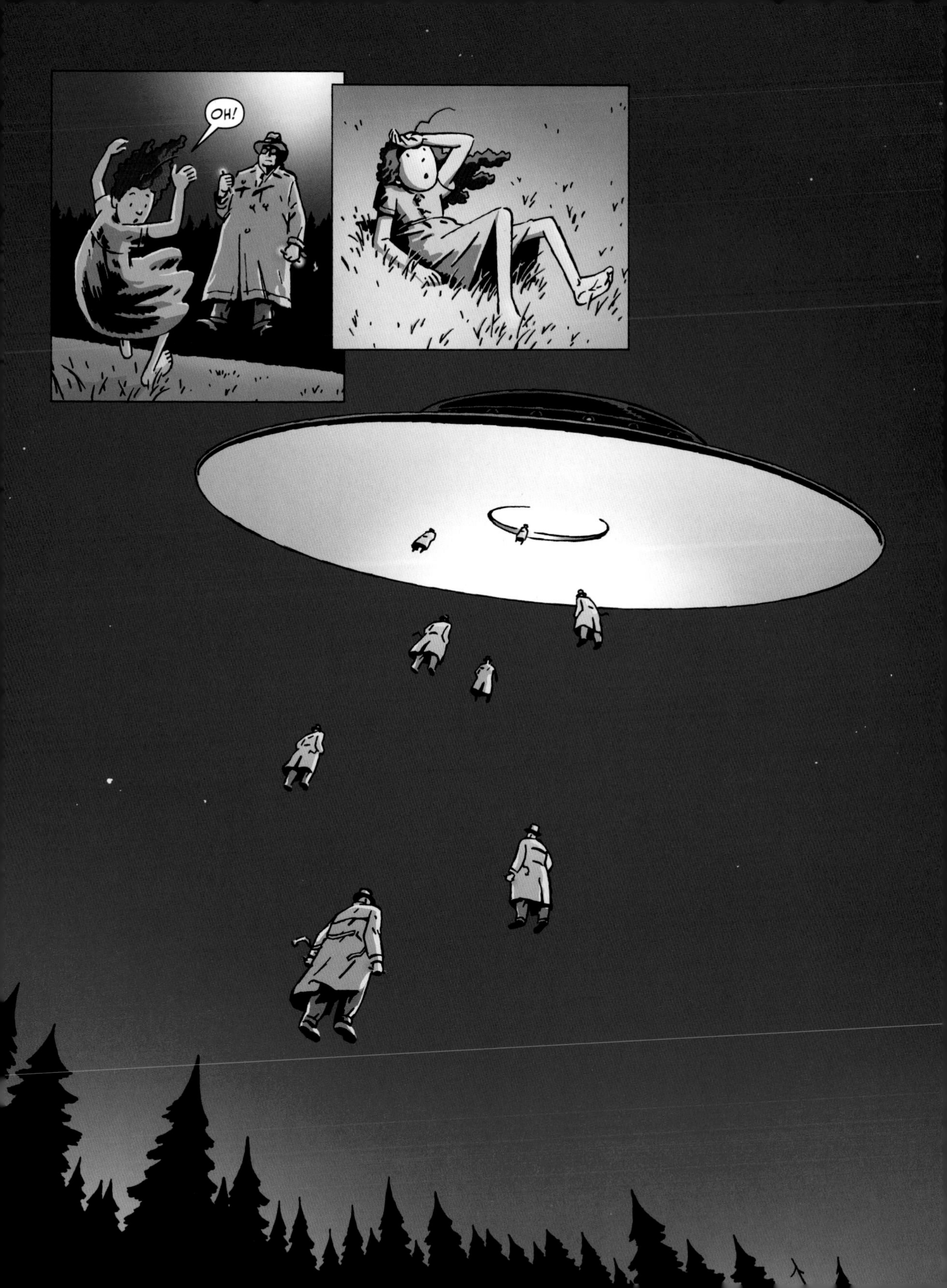
OH!

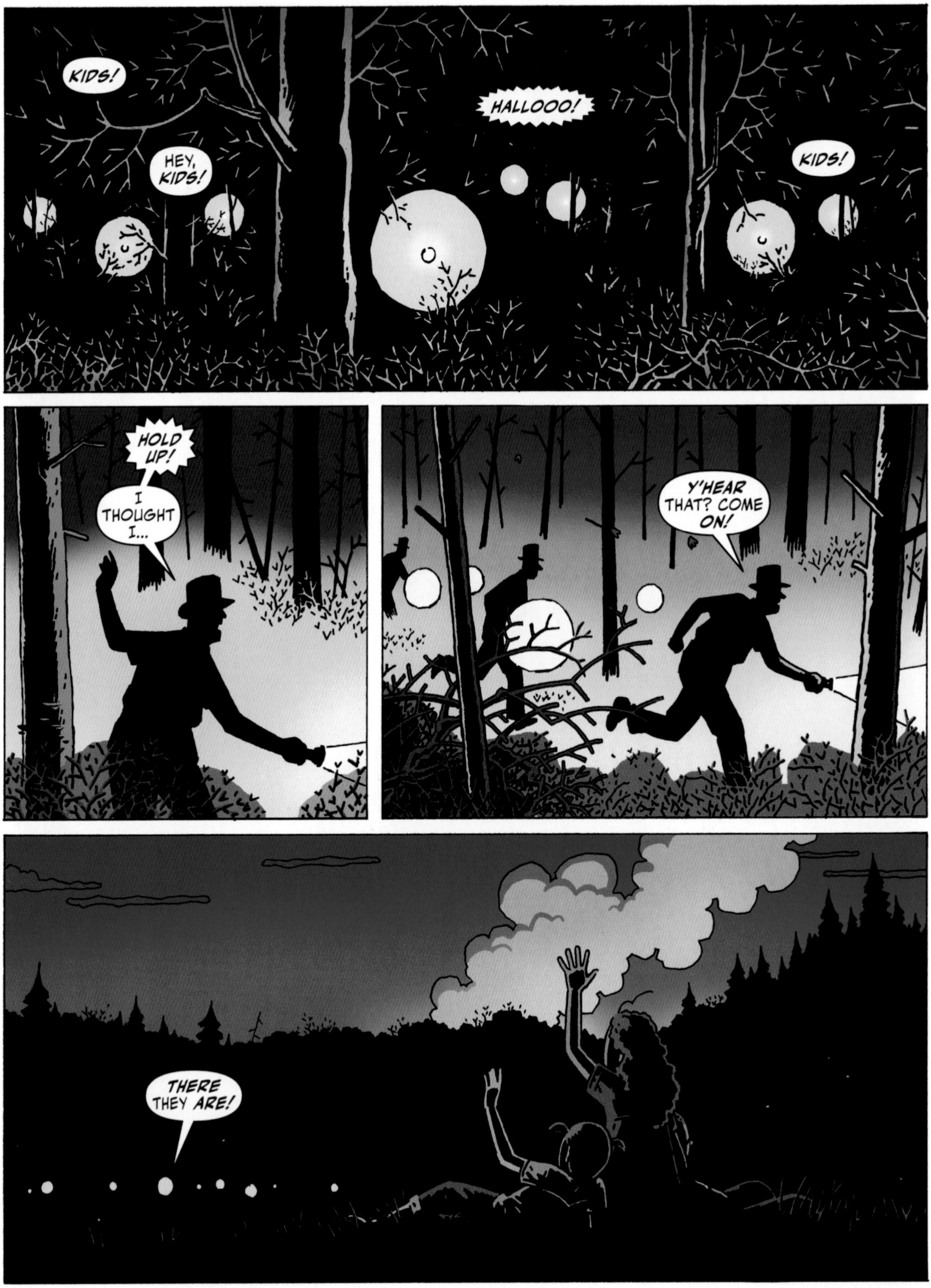
KIDS!
HEY, KIDS!
HALLOOO!
KIDS!
HOLD UP!
I THOUGHT I...
Y'HEAR THAT? COME ON!
THERE THEY ARE!

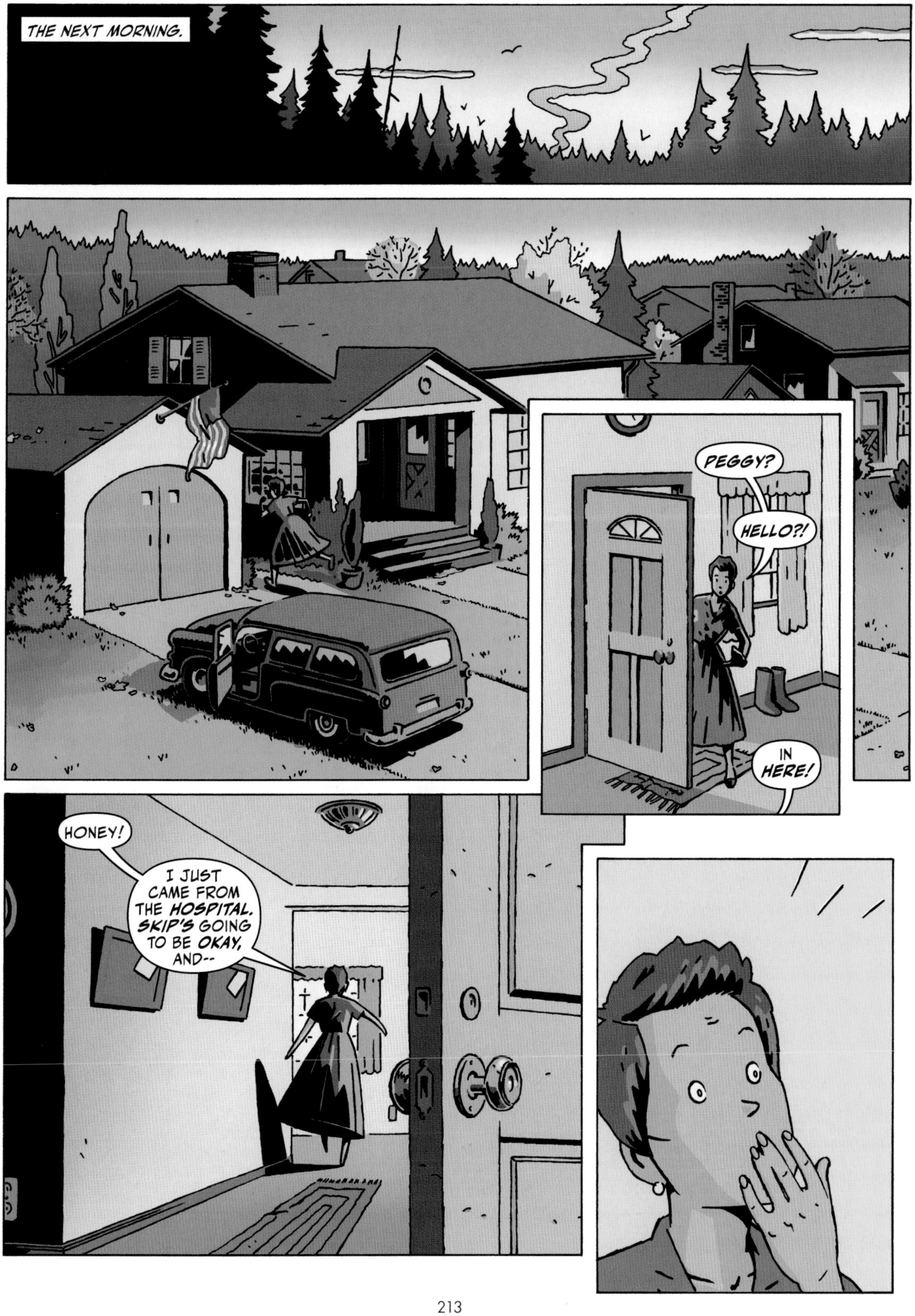
THE NEXT MORNING.
PEGGY?
HELLO?!
IN HERE!
HONEY!
I JUST CAME FROM THE HOSPITAL. SKIP'S GOING TO BE OKAY, AND--

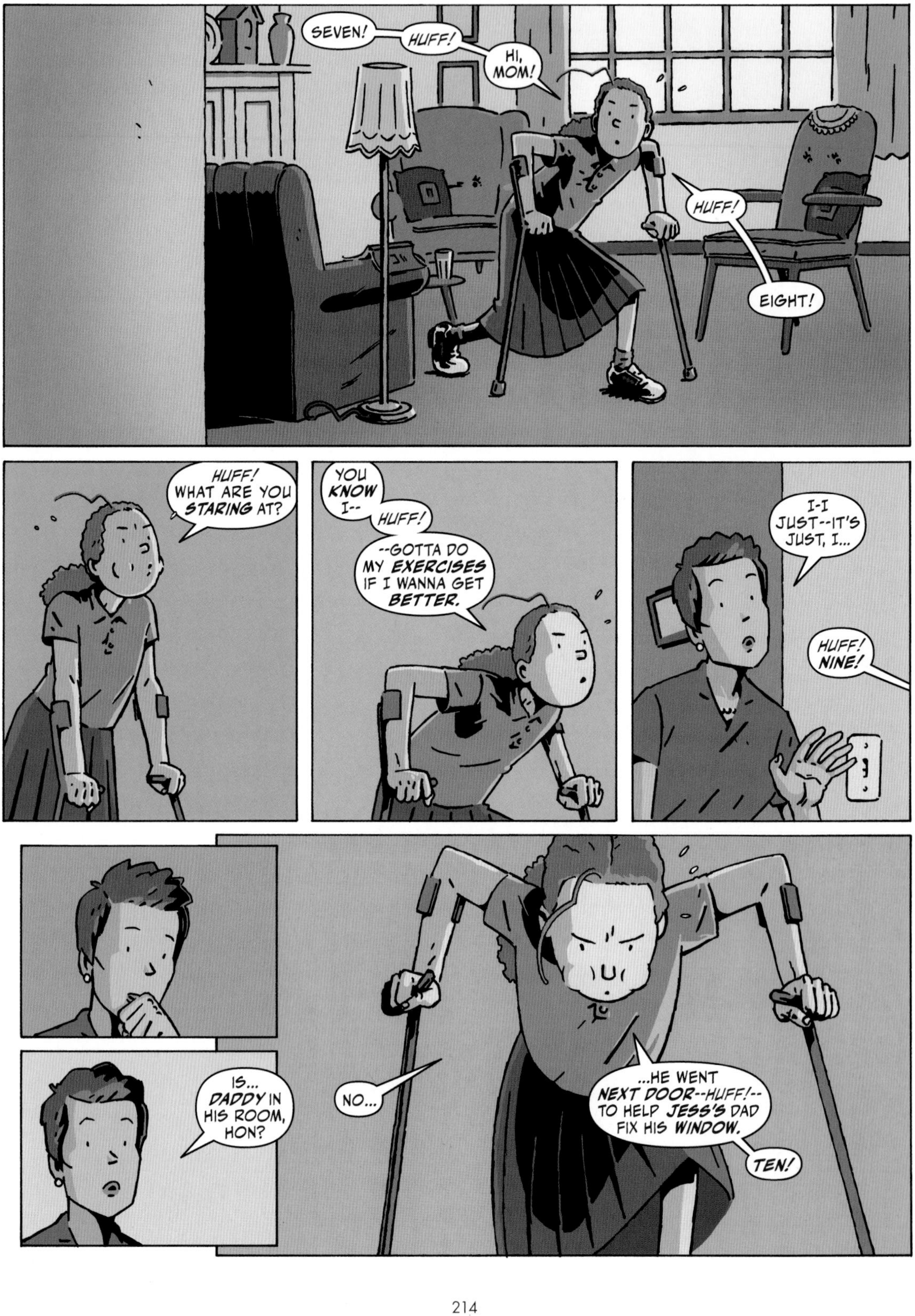
SEVEN!
HUFF!
HI, MOM!
HUFF!
EIGHT!
HUFF! WHAT ARE YOU STARING AT?
YOU KNOW I--
HUFF!
--GOTTA DO MY EXERCISES IF I WANNA GET BETTER.
I-I JUST--IT'S JUST, I...
HUFF! NINE!
IS... DADDY IN HIS ROOM, HON?
NO...
...HE WENT NEXT DOOR--HUFF!--TO HELP JESS'S DAD FIX HIS WINDOW.
TEN!

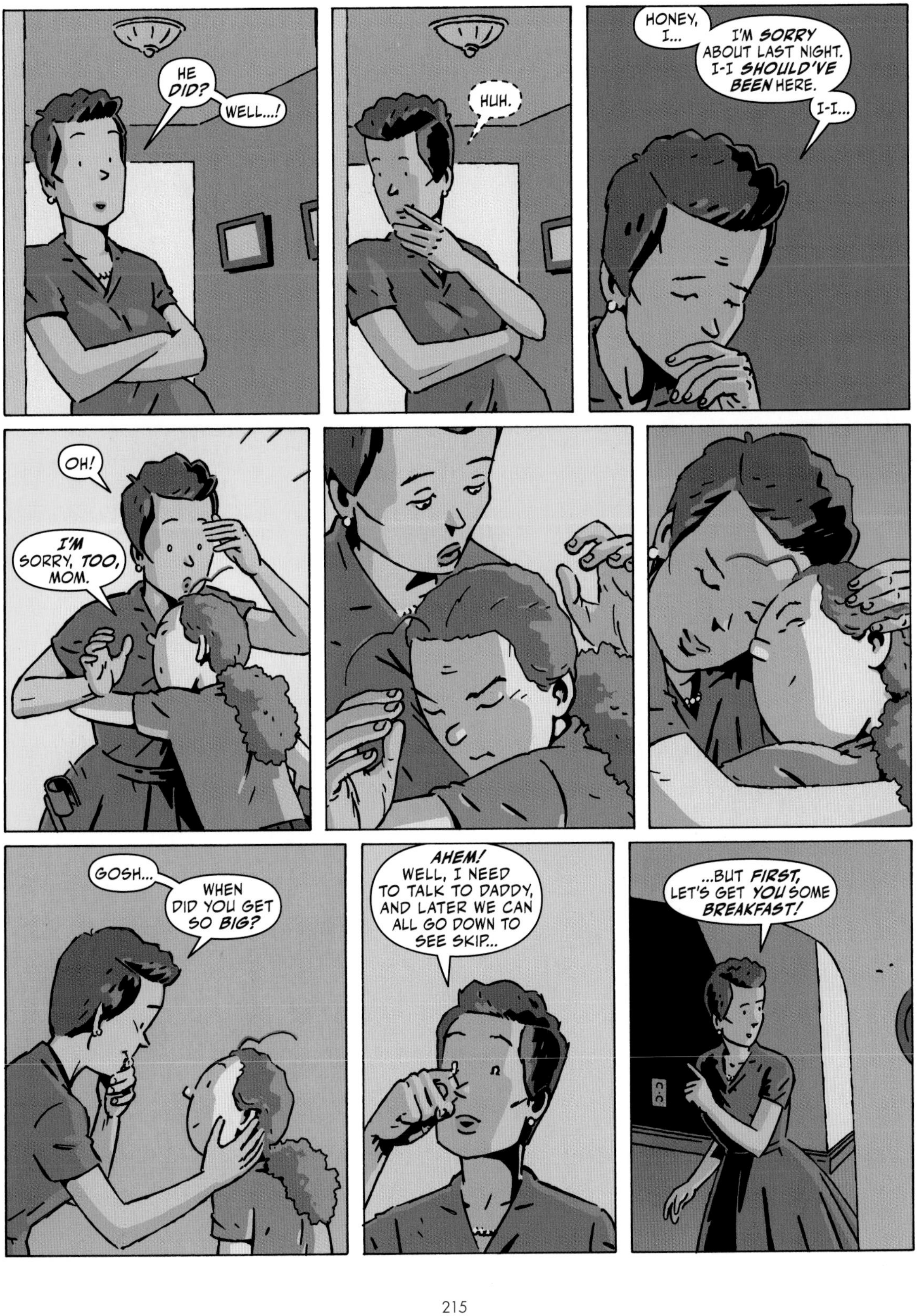
HE DID?
WELL...!
HUH.
HONEY, I...
I'M SORRY ABOUT LAST NIGHT. I-I SHOULD'VE BEEN HERE.
I-I...
OH!
I'M SORRY, TOO, MOM.
GOSH...
WHEN DID YOU GET SO BIG?
AHEM! WELL, I NEED TO TALK TO DADDY, AND LATER WE CAN ALL GO DOWN TO SEE SKIP...
...BUT FIRST, LET'S GET YOU SOME BREAKFAST!

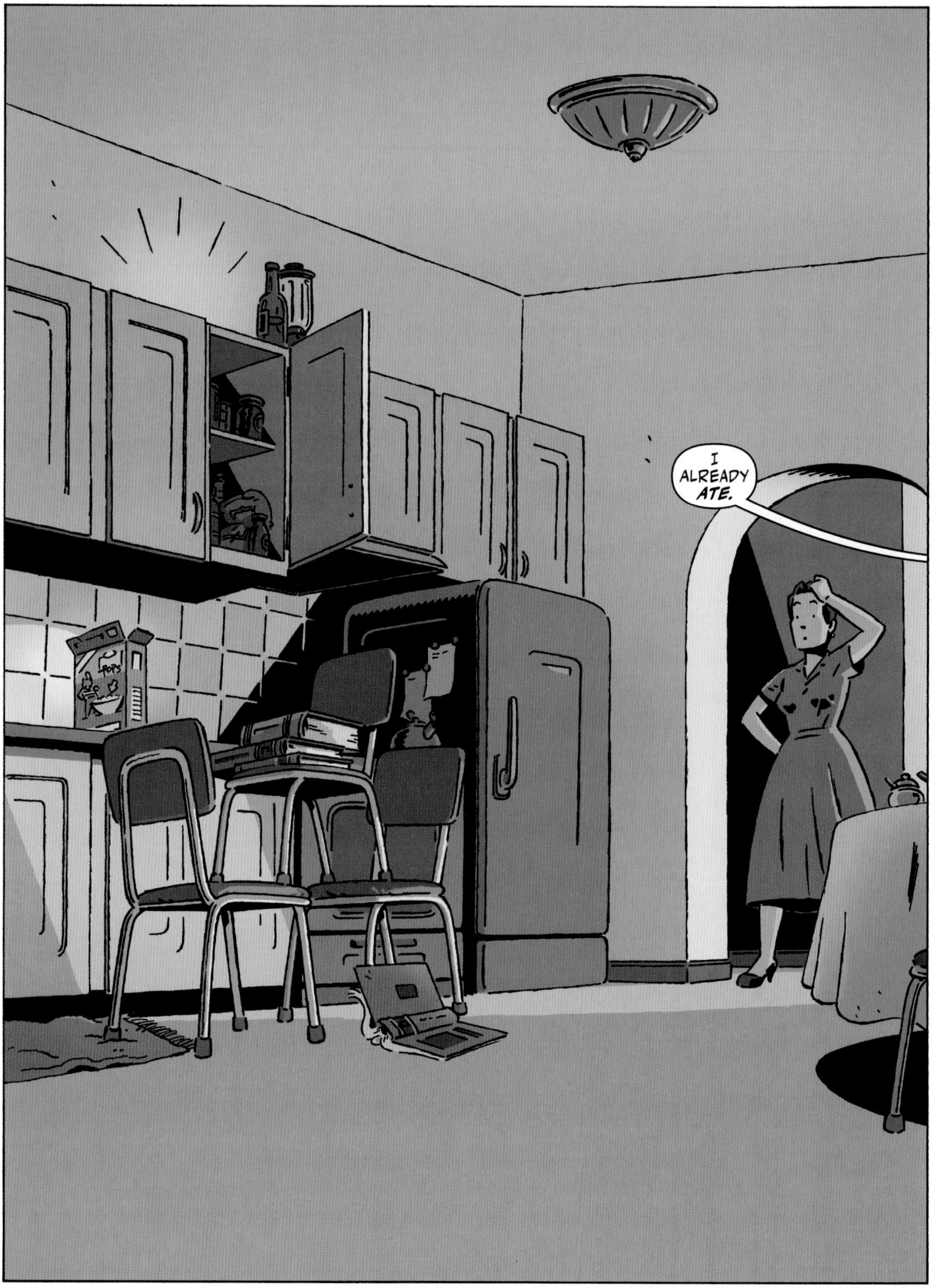
I ALREADY ATE.
POPS

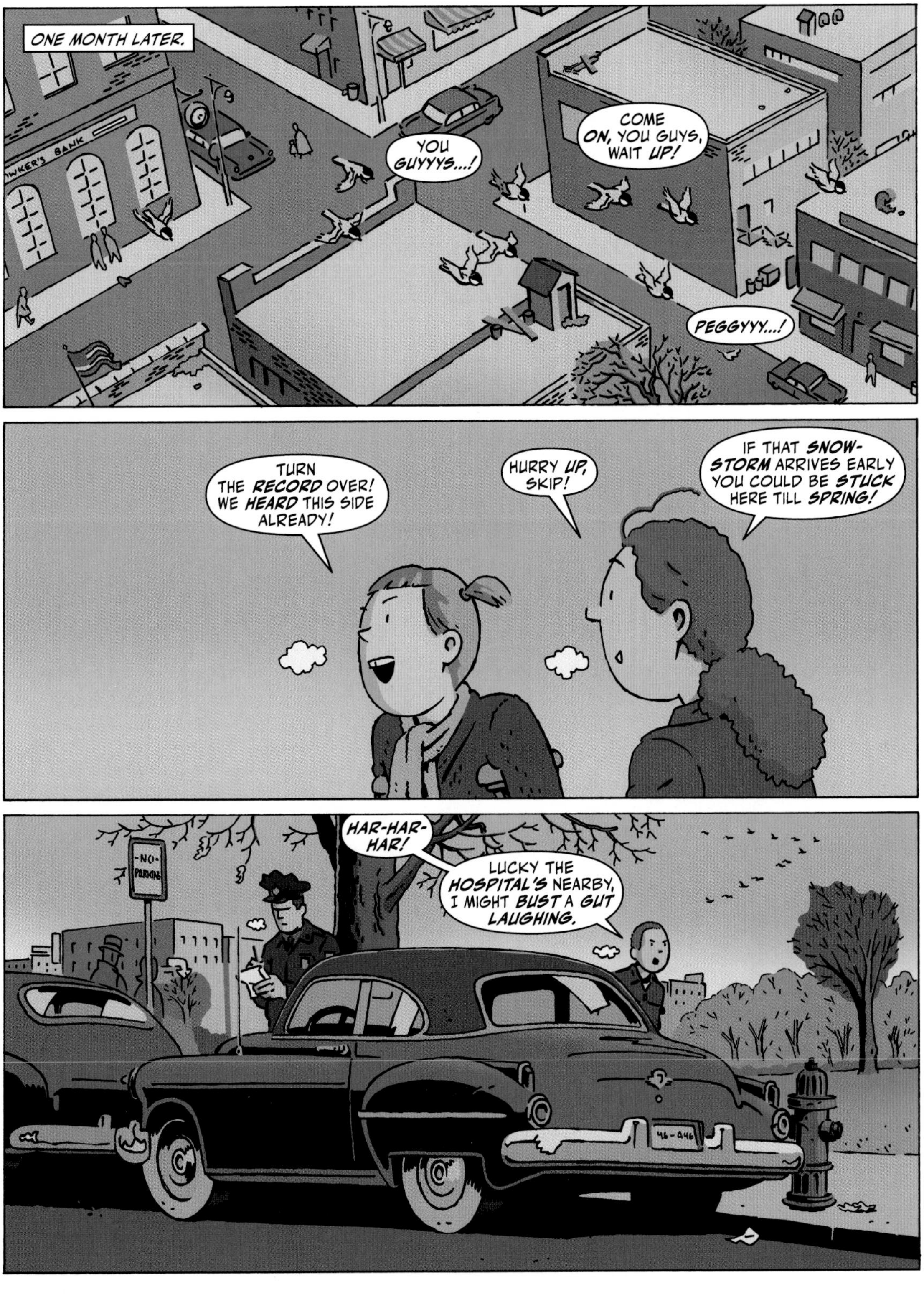
ONE MONTH LATER.
...WKER'S BANK
YOU GUYYYS...!
COME ON, YOU GUYS, WAIT UP!
PEGGYYY...!
TURN THE RECORD OVER! WE HEARD THIS SIDE ALREADY!
HURRY UP, SKIP!
IF THAT SNOW-STORM ARRIVES EARLY YOU COULD BE STUCK HERE TILL SPRING!
HAR-HAR-HAR!
LUCKY THE HOSPITAL'S NEARBY, I MIGHT BUST A GUT LAUGHING.
NO PARKING
46-A46

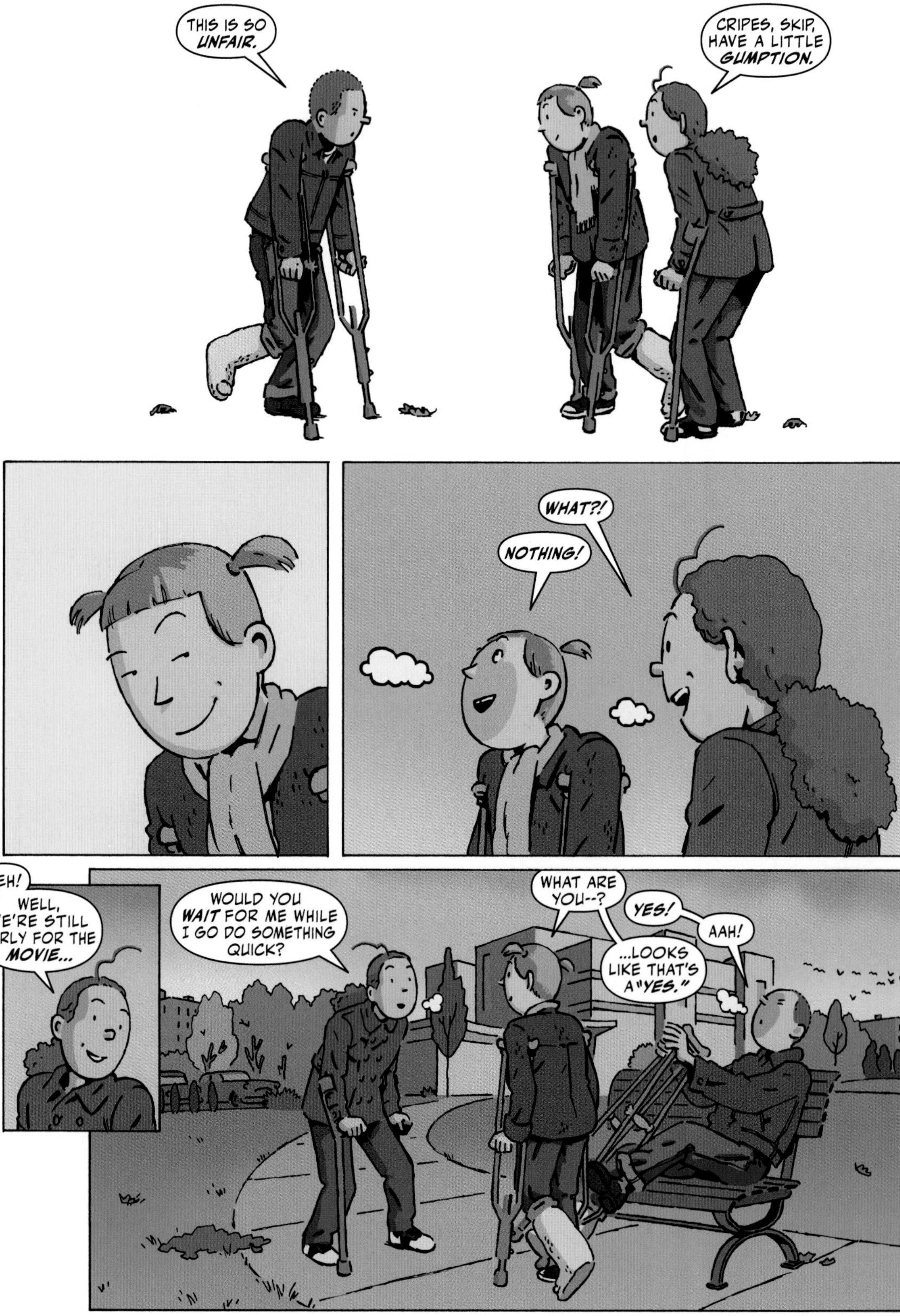
THIS IS SO *UNFAIR.*
CRIPES, SKIP, HAVE A LITTLE *GUMPTION.*
*NOTHING!*
*WHAT?!*
HEH!
WELL, WE'RE STILL EARLY FOR THE *MOVIE...*
WOULD YOU *WAIT* FOR ME WHILE I GO DO SOMETHING QUICK?
WHAT ARE YOU--?
...LOOKS LIKE THAT'S A "*YES.*"
*YES!*
AAH!

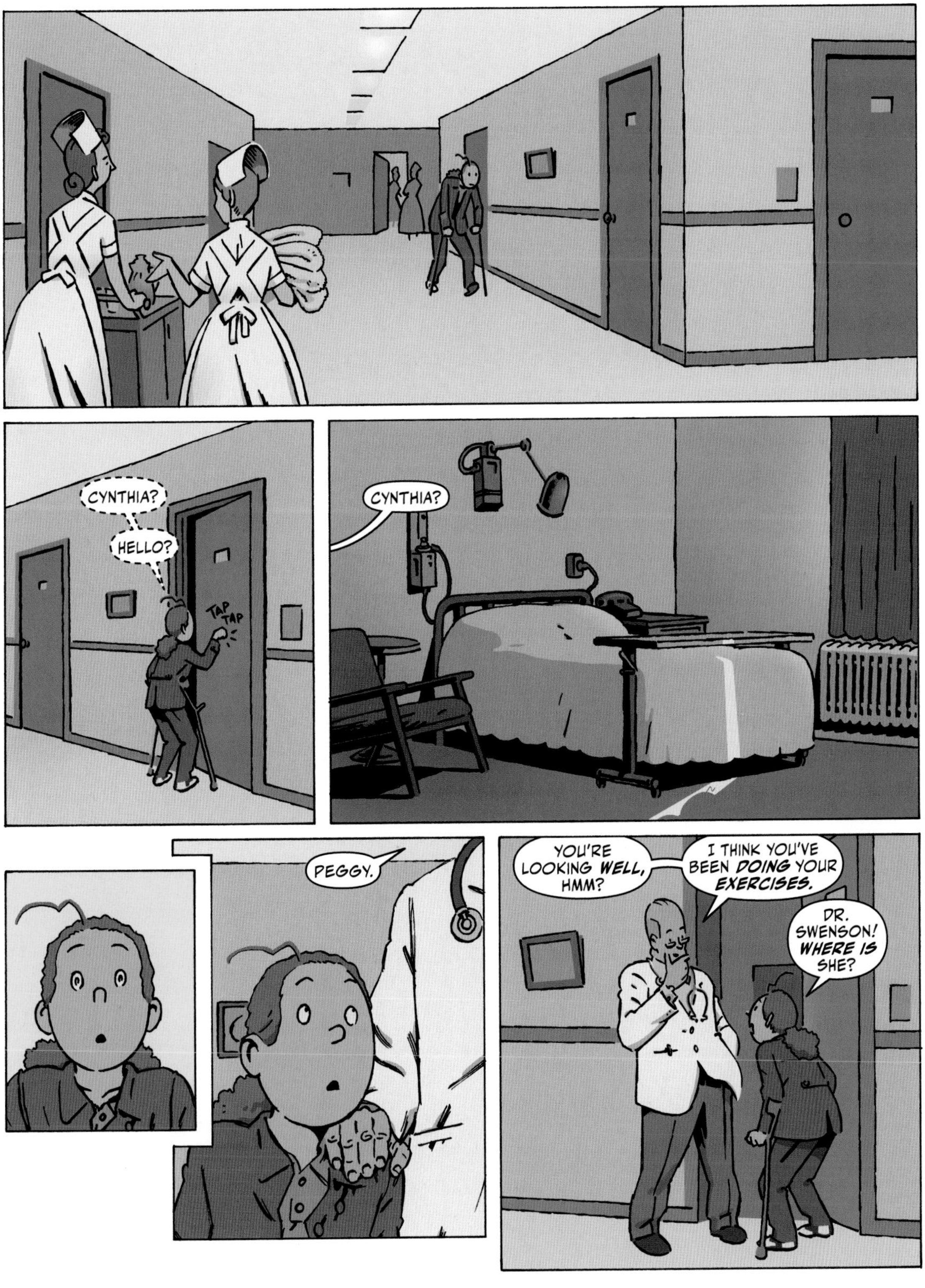
CYNTHIA?
HELLO?
TAP TAP
CYNTHIA?
PEGGY.
YOU'RE LOOKING WELL, HMM?
I THINK YOU'VE BEEN DOING YOUR EXERCISES.
DR. SWENSON! WHERE IS SHE?

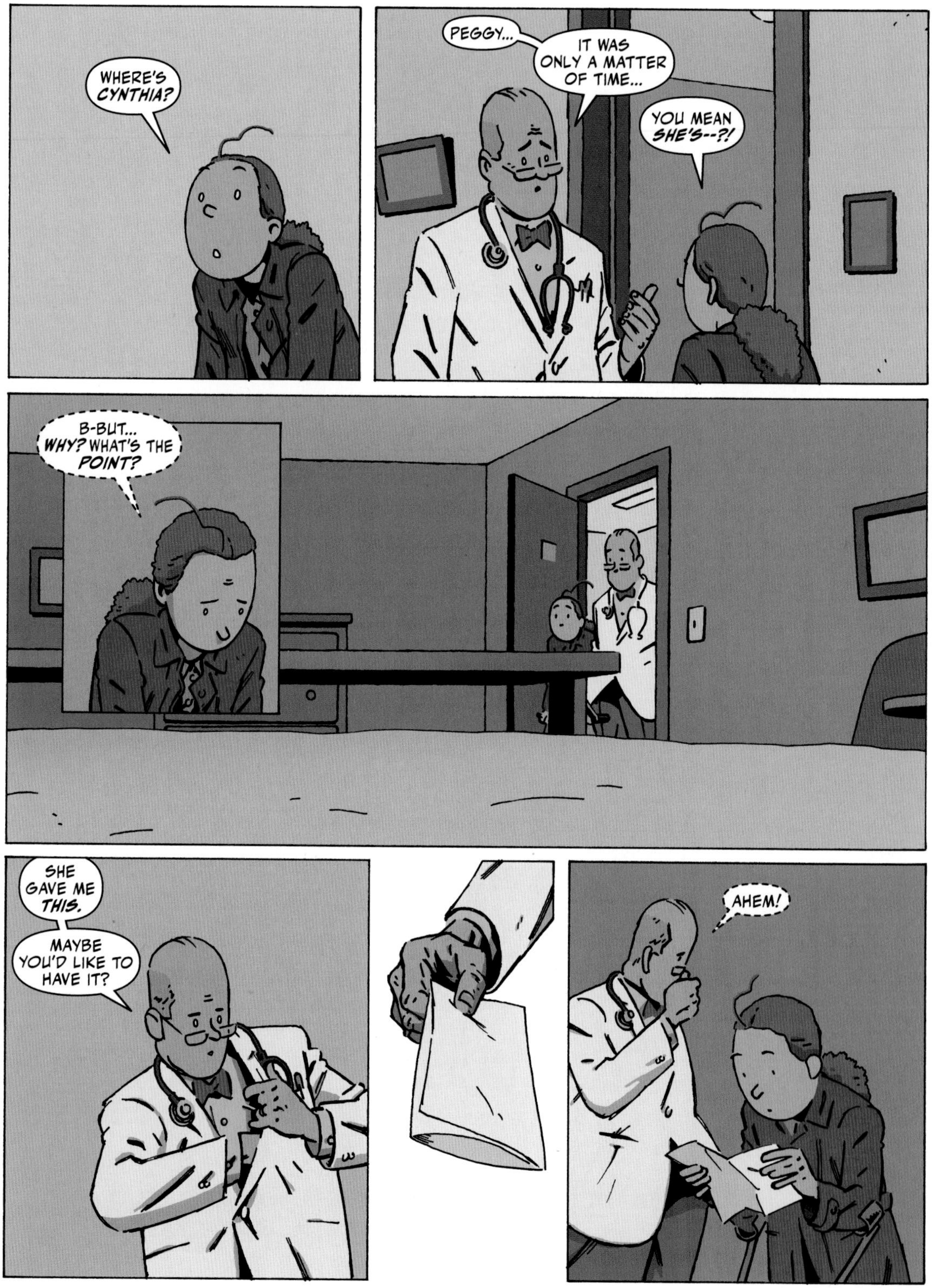
WHERE'S CYNTHIA?
PEGGY...
IT WAS ONLY A MATTER OF TIME...
YOU MEAN SHE'S--?!
B-BUT... WHY? WHAT'S THE POINT?
SHE GAVE ME THIS.
MAYBE YOU'D LIKE TO HAVE IT?
AHEM!

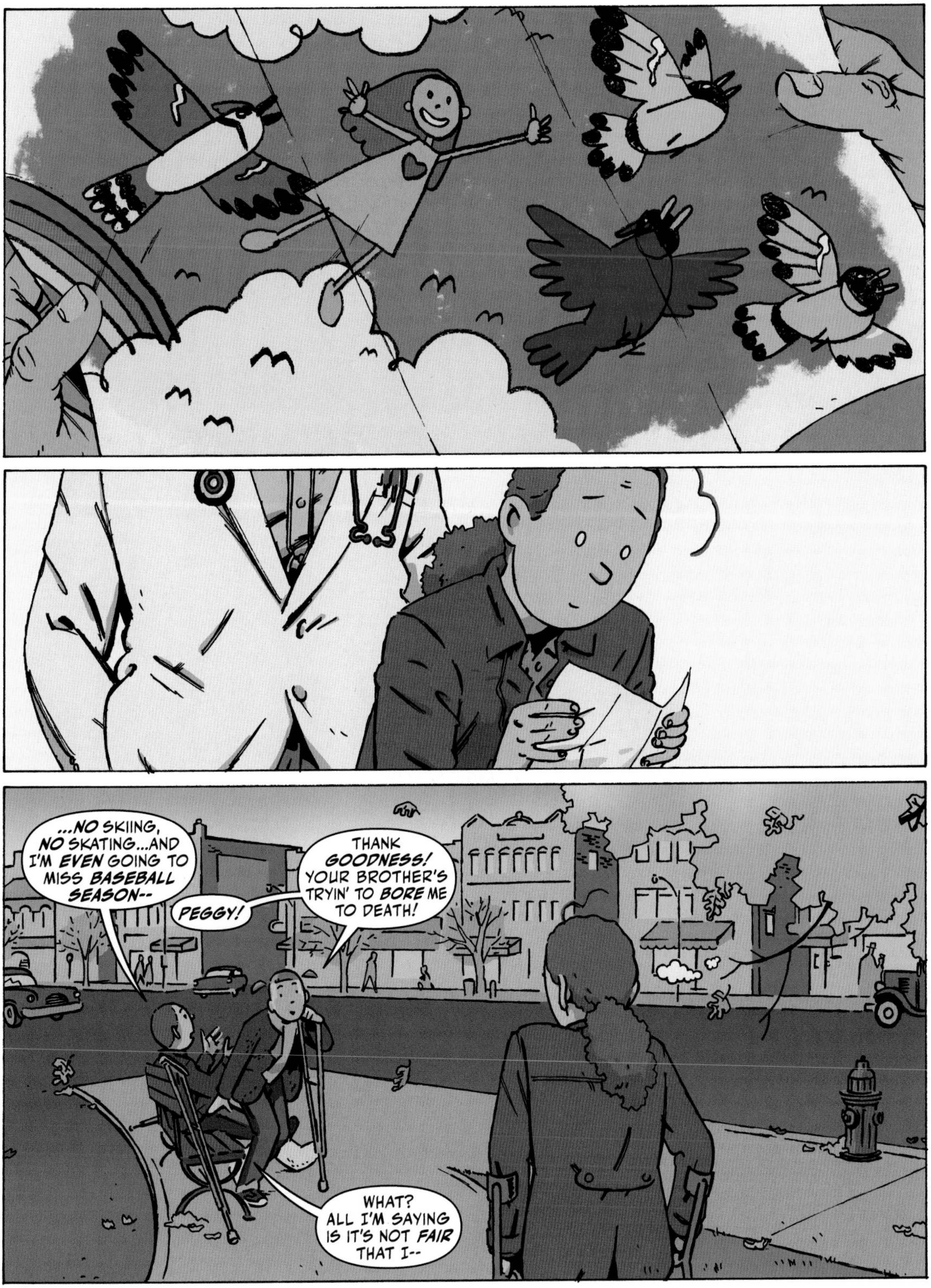
...NO SKIING, NO SKATING...AND I'M EVEN GOING TO MISS BASEBALL SEASON--
PEGGY!
THANK GOODNESS! YOUR BROTHER'S TRYIN' TO BORE ME TO DEATH!
WHAT? ALL I'M SAYING IS IT'S NOT FAIR THAT I--

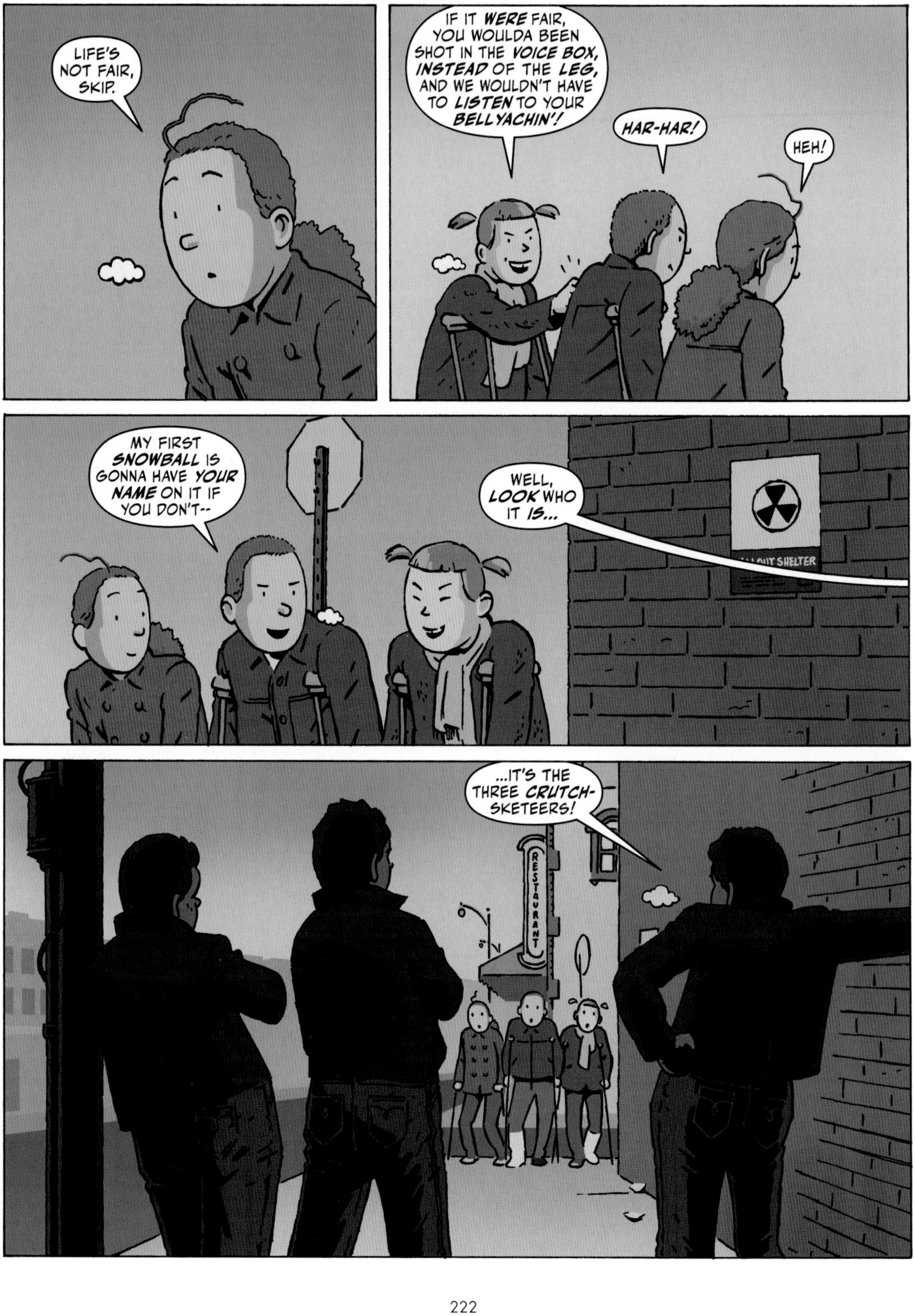
LIFE'S NOT FAIR, SKIP.
IF IT WERE FAIR, YOU WOULDA BEEN SHOT IN THE VOICE BOX, INSTEAD OF THE LEG, AND WE WOULDN'T HAVE TO LISTEN TO YOUR BELLYACHIN'!
HAR-HAR!
HEH!
MY FIRST SNOWBALL IS GONNA HAVE YOUR NAME ON IT IF YOU DON'T--
WELL, LOOK WHO IT IS...
...IT'S THE THREE CRUTCH-SKETEERS!
RESTAURANT

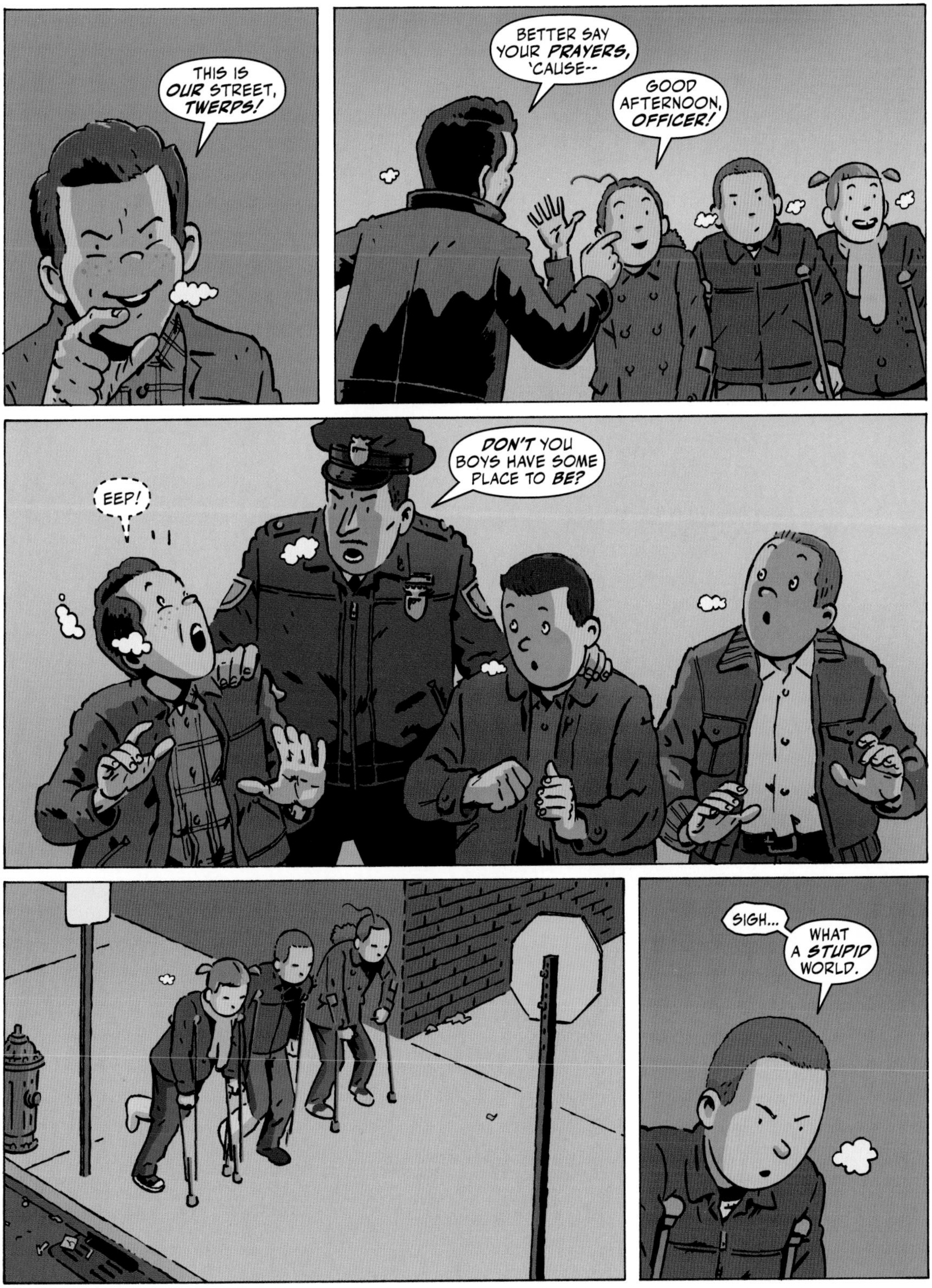
THIS IS OUR STREET, TWERPS!
BETTER SAY YOUR PRAYERS, 'CAUSE--
GOOD AFTERNOON, OFFICER!
EEP!
DON'T YOU BOYS HAVE SOME PLACE TO BE?
SIGH...
WHAT A STUPID WORLD.

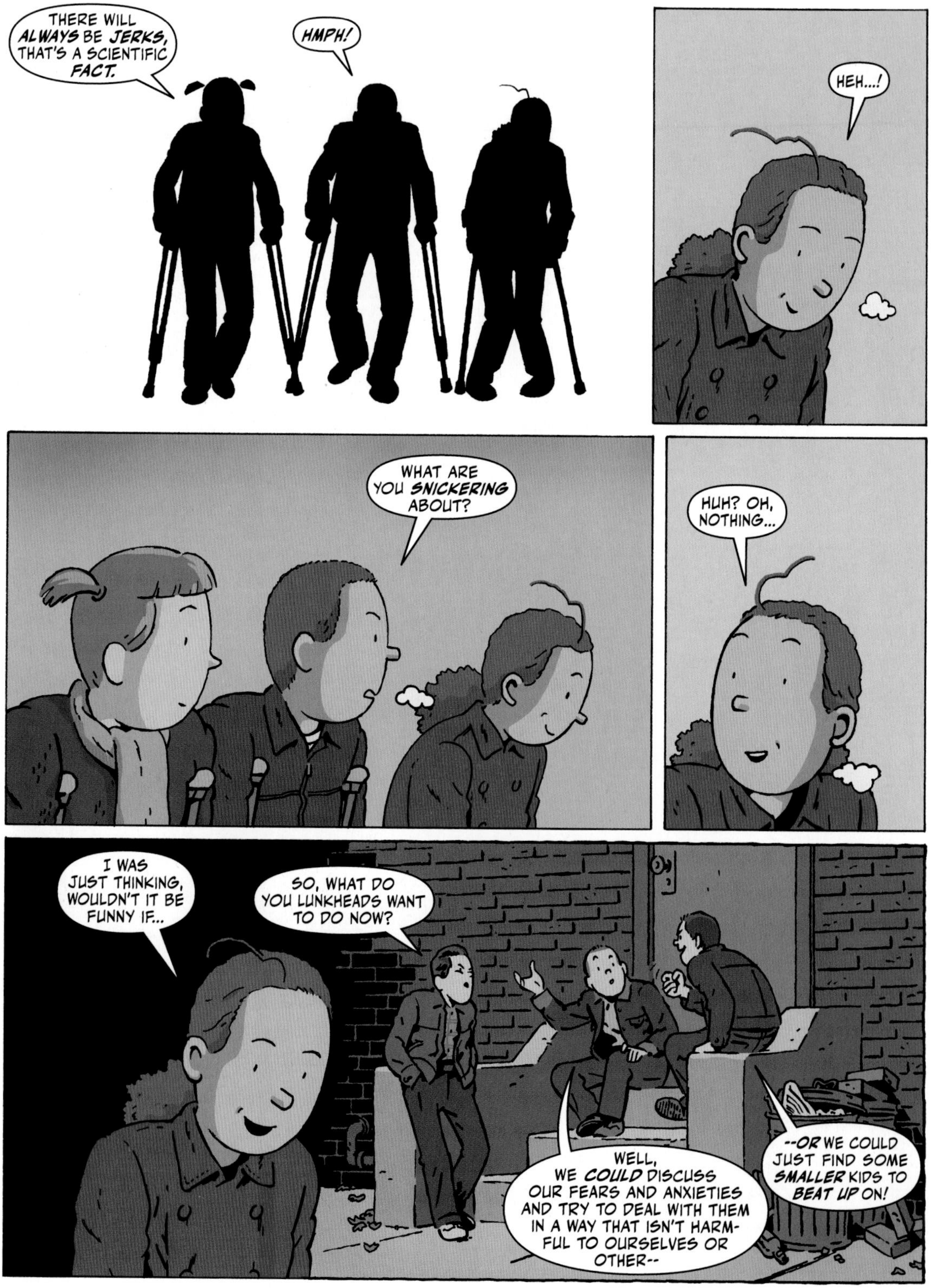
THERE WILL ALWAYS BE JERKS, THAT'S A SCIENTIFIC FACT.
HMPH!
HEH...!
WHAT ARE YOU SNICKERING ABOUT?
HUH? OH, NOTHING...
I WAS JUST THINKING, WOULDN'T IT BE FUNNY IF...
SO, WHAT DO YOU LUNKHEADS WANT TO DO NOW?
WELL, WE COULD DISCUSS OUR FEARS AND ANXIETIES AND TRY TO DEAL WITH THEM IN A WAY THAT ISN'T HARM-FUL TO OURSELVES OR OTHER--
--OR WE COULD JUST FIND SOME SMALLER KIDS TO BEAT UP ON!

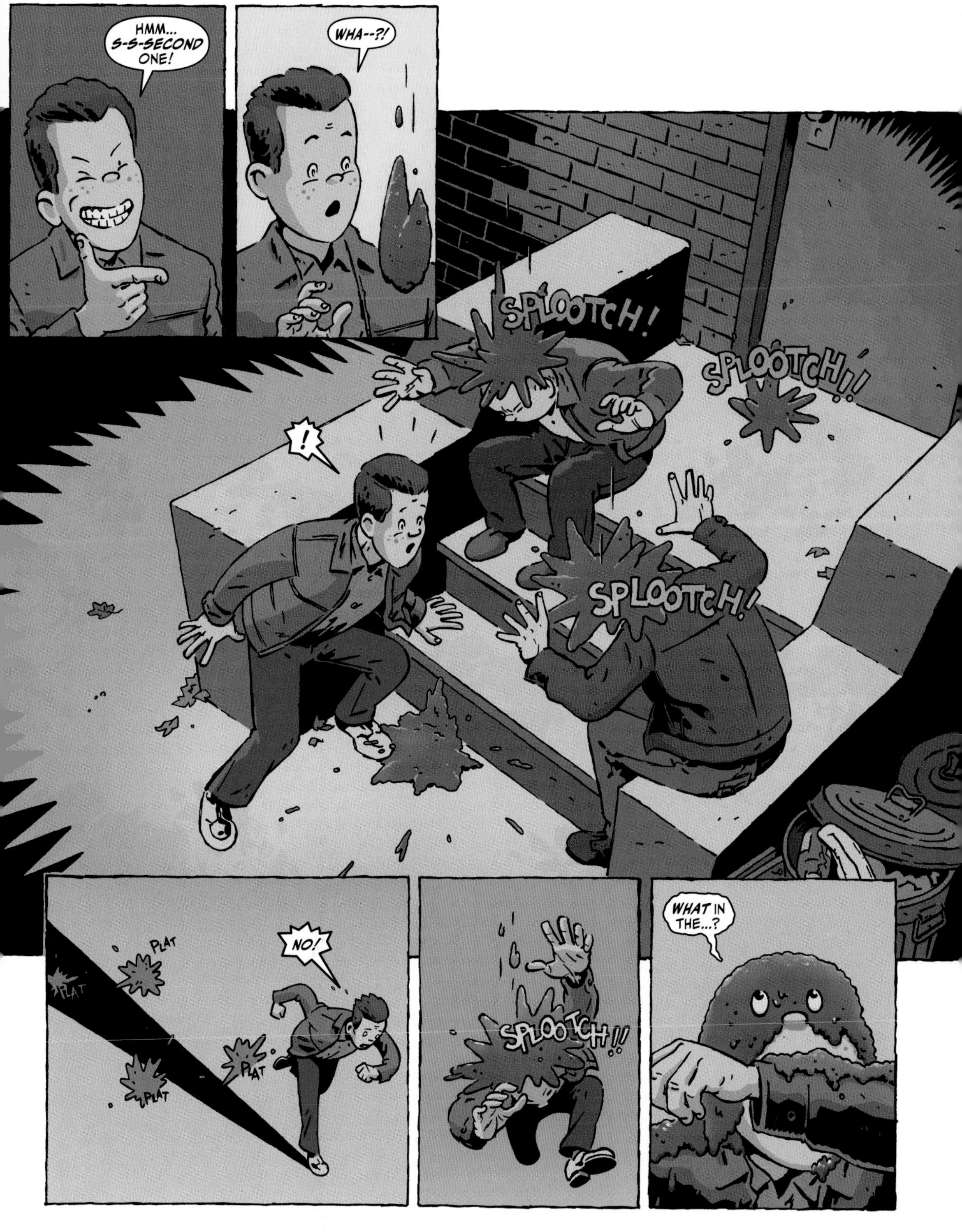
HMM... S-S-SECOND ONE!
WHA--?!
SPLOOTCH!
SPLOOTCH!!
!
SPLOOTCH!
PLAT
PLAT
PLAT
PLAT
NO!
SPLOOTCH!!
WHAT IN THE...?

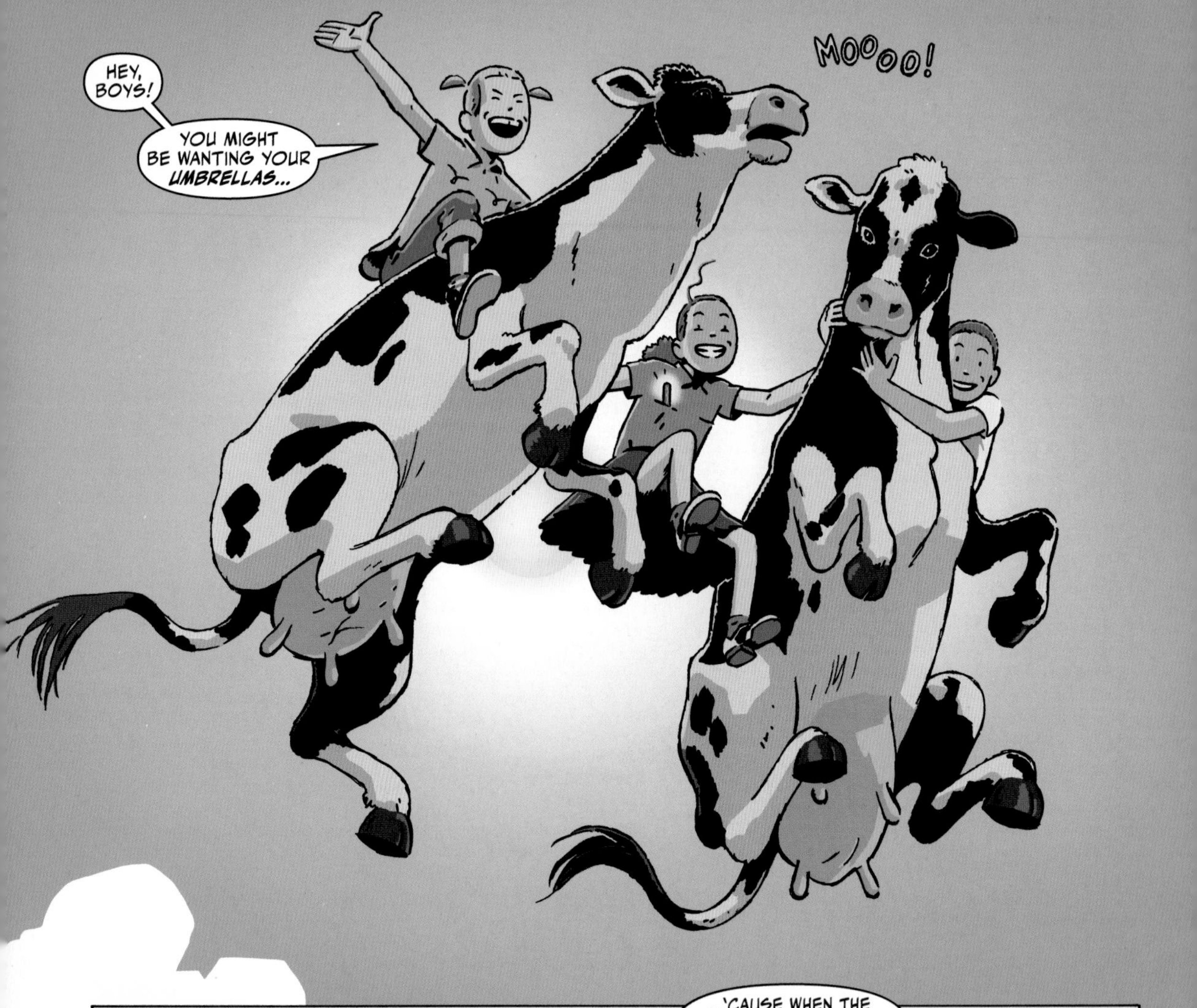
HEY, BOYS!
YOU MIGHT BE WANTING YOUR *UMBRELLAS*...
MOOOO!

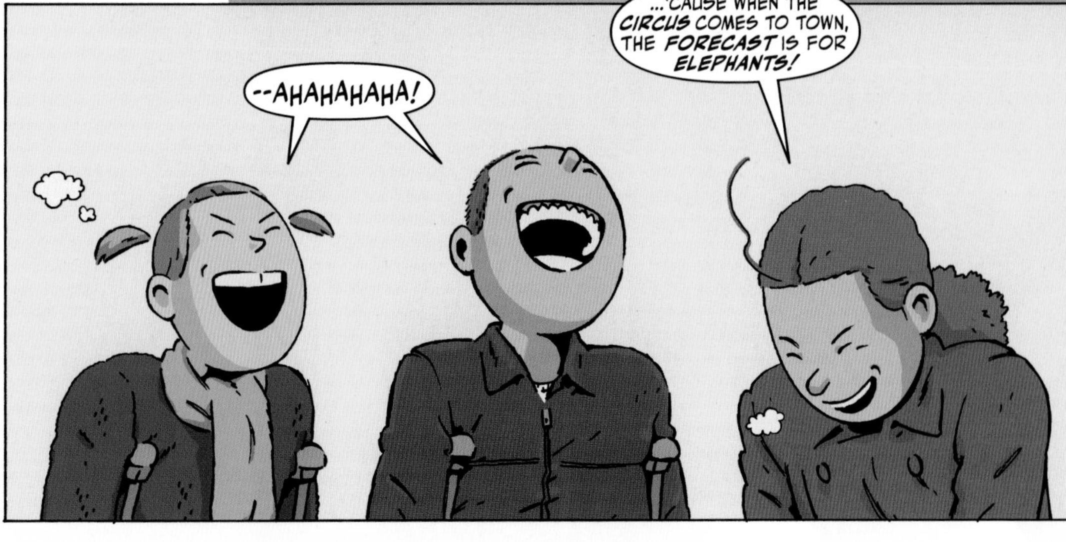
--AHAHAHAHA!
...'CAUSE WHEN THE *CIRCUS* COMES TO TOWN, THE *FORECAST* IS FOR *ELEPHANTS!*

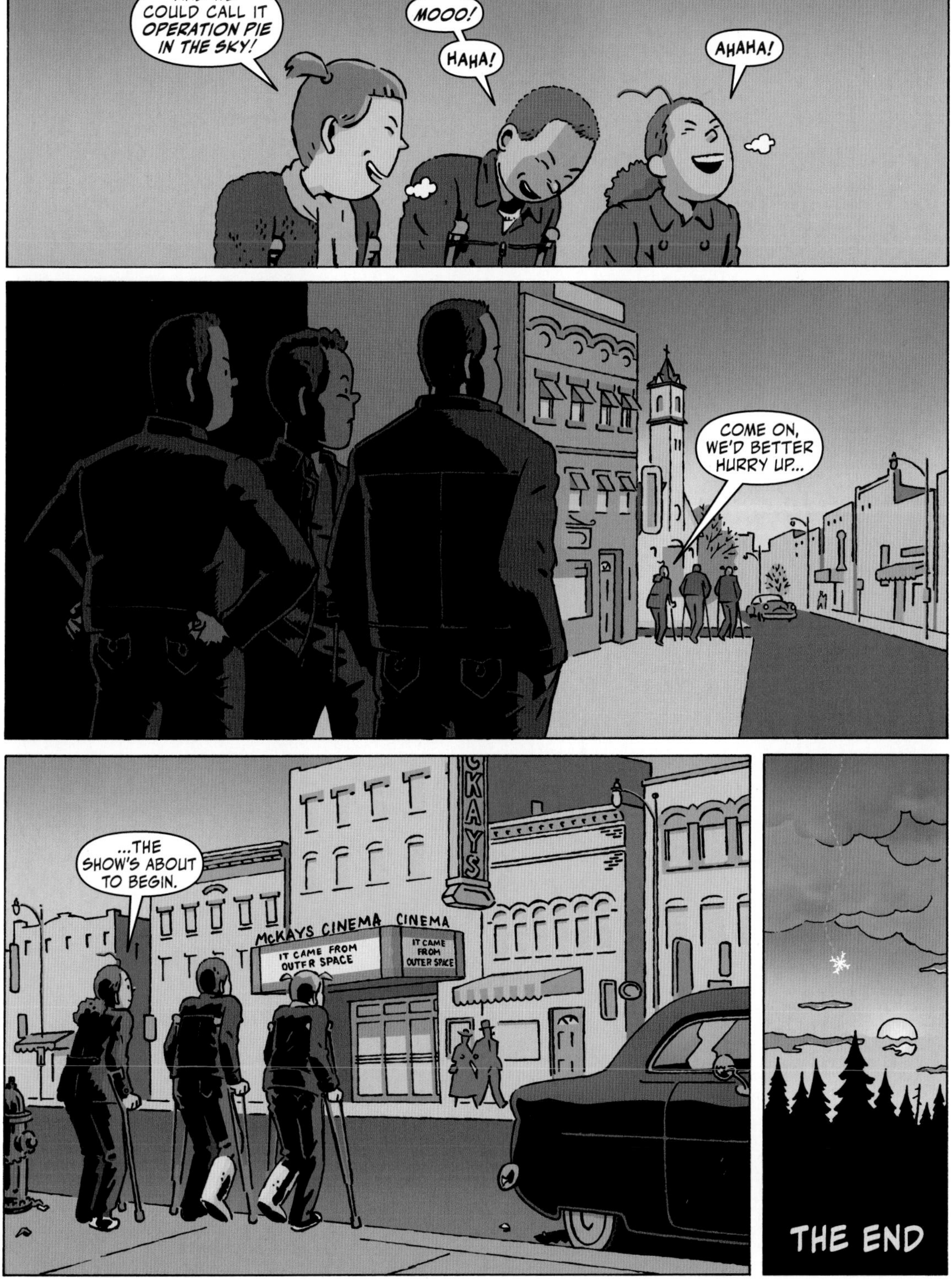
AND WE COULD CALL IT OPERATION PIE IN THE SKY!
MOOO!
HAHA!
AHAHA!
COME ON, WE'D BETTER HURRY UP...
...THE SHOW'S ABOUT TO BEGIN.
McKAYS
McKAYS CINEMA
IT CAME FROM OUTER SPACE
CINEMA
IT CAME FROM OUTER SPACE
THE END

# A NOTE FROM THE AUTHOR

*Red Scare* is a work of fiction that takes place during a very real period in American history. The story was inspired by my love for mid-twentieth-century science fiction films. As I came to better understand history, I realized that those movies often presented an idealized version of life and failed to address many of the important issues of the time. I wondered what a fifties-style sci-fi story set in a more realistic 1950s would look like.

I did my best to reflect 1953 in visuals and language. There are a few scenes that may be startling or even painful for present-day readers.

## THE ATOMIC AGE

Near the end of World War II in August 1945, the United States dropped atomic bombs on two Japanese cities, Hiroshima and Nagasaki. It was the first — and only — time atomic bombs have been used in war, and the devastation they caused left little doubt that the United States was the world's dominant military superpower. Only four years later, however, the Soviet Union announced they, too, had developed nuclear weapons. The thought of the Communist Soviet Union — America's only real rival — armed with atomic bombs raised the specter of a full-scale nuclear war and forced Americans to confront the possibility of having their cities and hometowns turned into scorched ruins overnight.

With both superpowers now in possession of nuclear arms, it seemed humankind's only hope for surviving the atomic age was the belief that neither side would dare launch an attack against the other for fear of being destroyed in a retaliatory strike. The balance of power could only be maintained if each side had the same capability to destroy the other.

## THE RED SCARE

The threat of atomic annihilation was so terrifying to Americans that a sense of "you're either with us or against us" set in, and people whose values or beliefs did not align closely enough with the mainstream norms of the time were seen as enemies. This time period came to be known as the Red Scare. The "red," long associated with the red flag of the Soviet Union, referred to Communists, and the "scare" was the fear that Communists were actively working to undermine the United States.

FALLOUT
FALLOUT
SHELTER

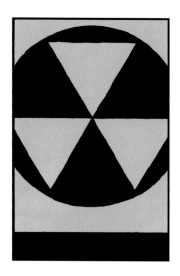

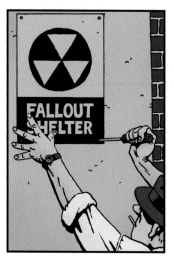

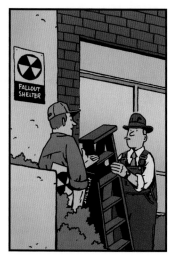

So began the era of backyard fallout shelters, when people built underground bunkers stocked with enough supplies to live for a year or more. And children learned to "duck and cover" in a cartoon produced by the Federal Civil Defense Administration. Shown in schools all over the country, Bert the Turtle taught children to squat down and cover their heads with their arms in case of a nuclear blast. The "Duck and Cover" cartoon can be watched today on YouTube.

During this period several Soviet spies were caught living and working on American soil. Some had even worked on top secret programs like the Manhattan Project, which created the first atomic bomb. Suddenly, Communists were no longer "over there," but in our midst, and it appeared that any seemingly ordinary person might possibly be a spy.

WE'RE GONNA *GET* YOU, YOU *COMMIE!*
I'M NOT--! I HARDLY EVEN *KNOW* WHAT A COMMIE *IS!*
NEITHER DO *THEY!*
*HANG ON!*

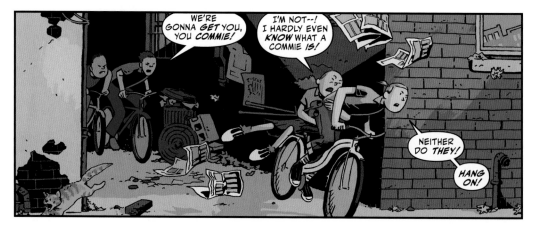

Into this climate of fear strode Joseph McCarthy, a senator from Wisconsin, brandishing a list of hundreds of "known Communists" working in government, people who would side with the Soviets when the nuclear bombs began falling on New York and Milwaukee and Peoria. It didn't matter to the terrified public that Senator McCarthy's lists included little or no evidence to substantiate his claims, or that he gained personally, in power and prestige, from the allegations he produced. "McCarthyism" swept across America.

What awaited those accused of Communist sympathies, be the evidence ever so flimsy, might be dismissal from employment, shunning by friends and colleagues fearful of being tainted by association, blacklisting, and persecution by the FBI. Presumption of innocence and the rights guaranteed by the First Amendment were among the earliest victims of this hysteria, since to doubt or hesitate was to invite suspicion. What followed was a stampede toward conformity, an effort to place oneself above suspicion through sheer normalcy. The Red Scare was on!

As if that wasn't enough anxiety for one decade, there was also a steep rise in reports of unidentified flying objects — the so-called flying saucer craze — culminating in no less an authority than the CIA convening a panel to study the phenomenon. Americans wanted to know: Were those lights in the sky secret Soviet aircraft preparing to drop flaming death on their suburban backyards, or something even *more* mysterious and terrifying?

## POLIO

Polio is short for poliomyelitis and is caused by the poliovirus. The worst outbreak of polio in United States history was in the summer of 1952, when there were 57,628 reported cases. Peggy might have been part of that wave of infections.

While the polio virus has been around for all recorded history (you can see evidence of polio in artwork from ancient Egypt!), in the first half of the twentieth century outbreaks of polio began to reach epidemic proportions, sometimes disabling 35,000 people annually. Fear of contracting the highly contagious disease was rampant, and parents were particularly scared for their children's safety.

Polio often struck in the summer, and children were most at risk. Consequences of catching polio ranged broadly but could include paralysis of the limbs, or even the loss of the ability to breathe without the help of a breathing machine called an iron lung.

The first polio vaccine, developed by Dr. Jonas Salk, was released to the public in April 1955. Since then, the incidence of polio worldwide has fallen by 99 percent and polio has effectively been eradicated in the United States.

THIS FIGHT IS YOURS
JOIN THE MARCH OF DIMES
THIS FIGHT IS YOURS
HMM...

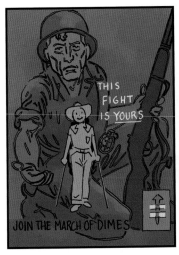

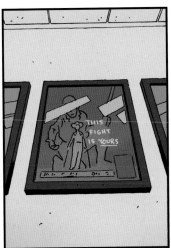

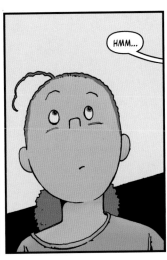

# SKETCHBOOK

Various Character Studies

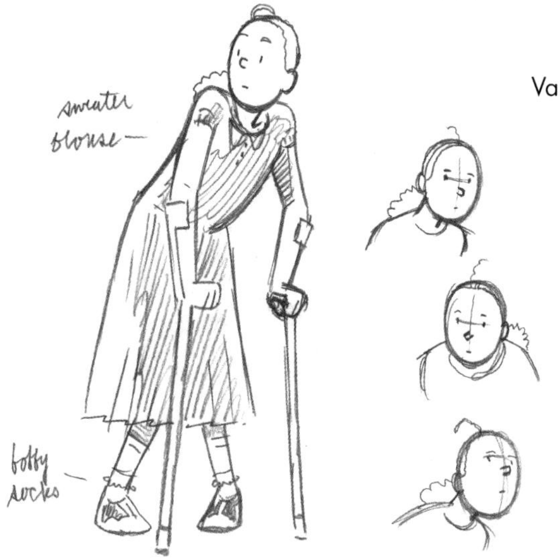

sweater
blouse
bobby
socks


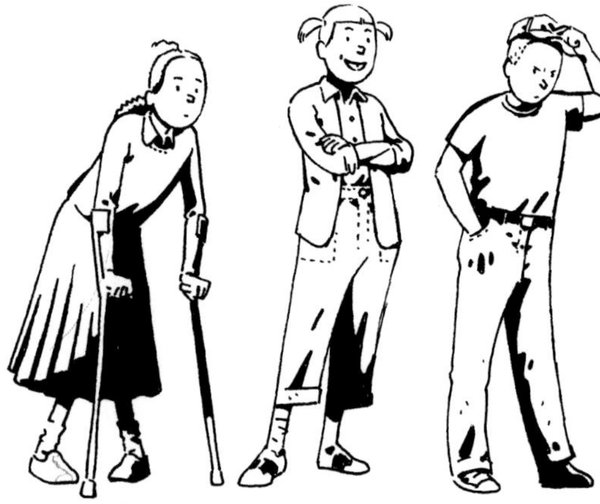

Below is a concept drawing from 2014. The mysterious agent crashing through the window made it from my earliest drafts all the way through to completion.

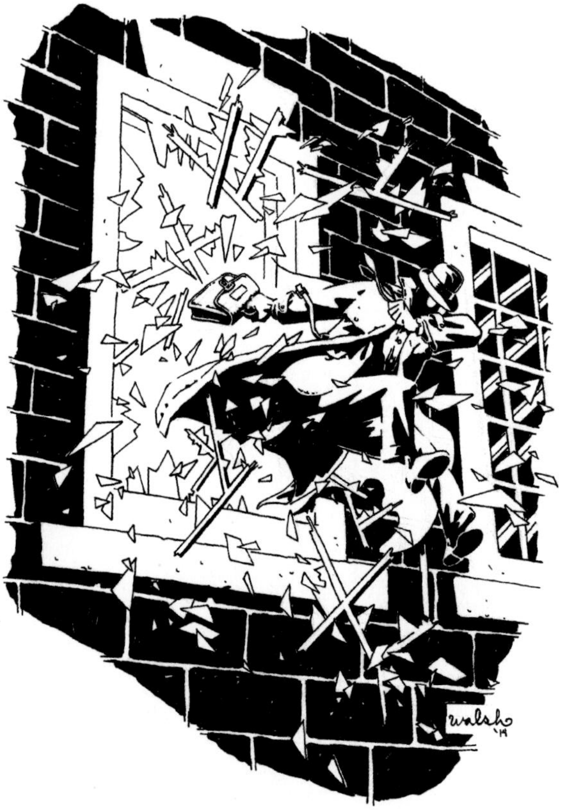

walsh
'14


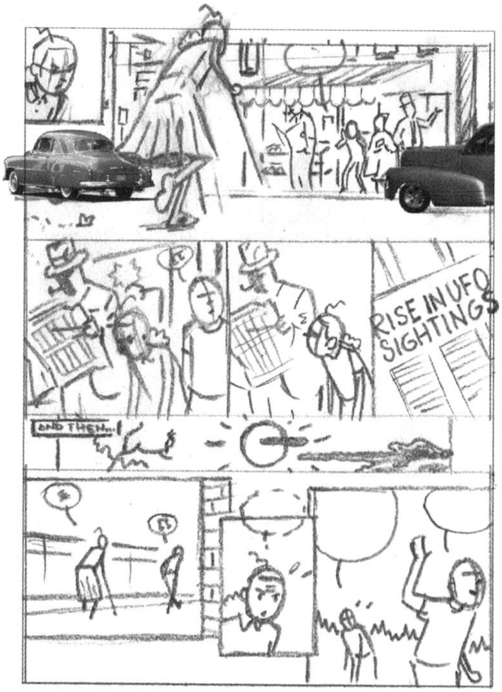

RISE IN UFOS
SIGHTINGS
AND THEN...


Above: I can draw cars but it takes me all day and I don't especially enjoy it, so I stole this idea from the great Sean Philips. I drop photos into my sketch, lower the opacity of the layer and then I don't trace over them, I *draw* over them. It's the same process I use when I refine a drawing by putting it on my lightbox and drawing over it. (Which I do a LOT.)

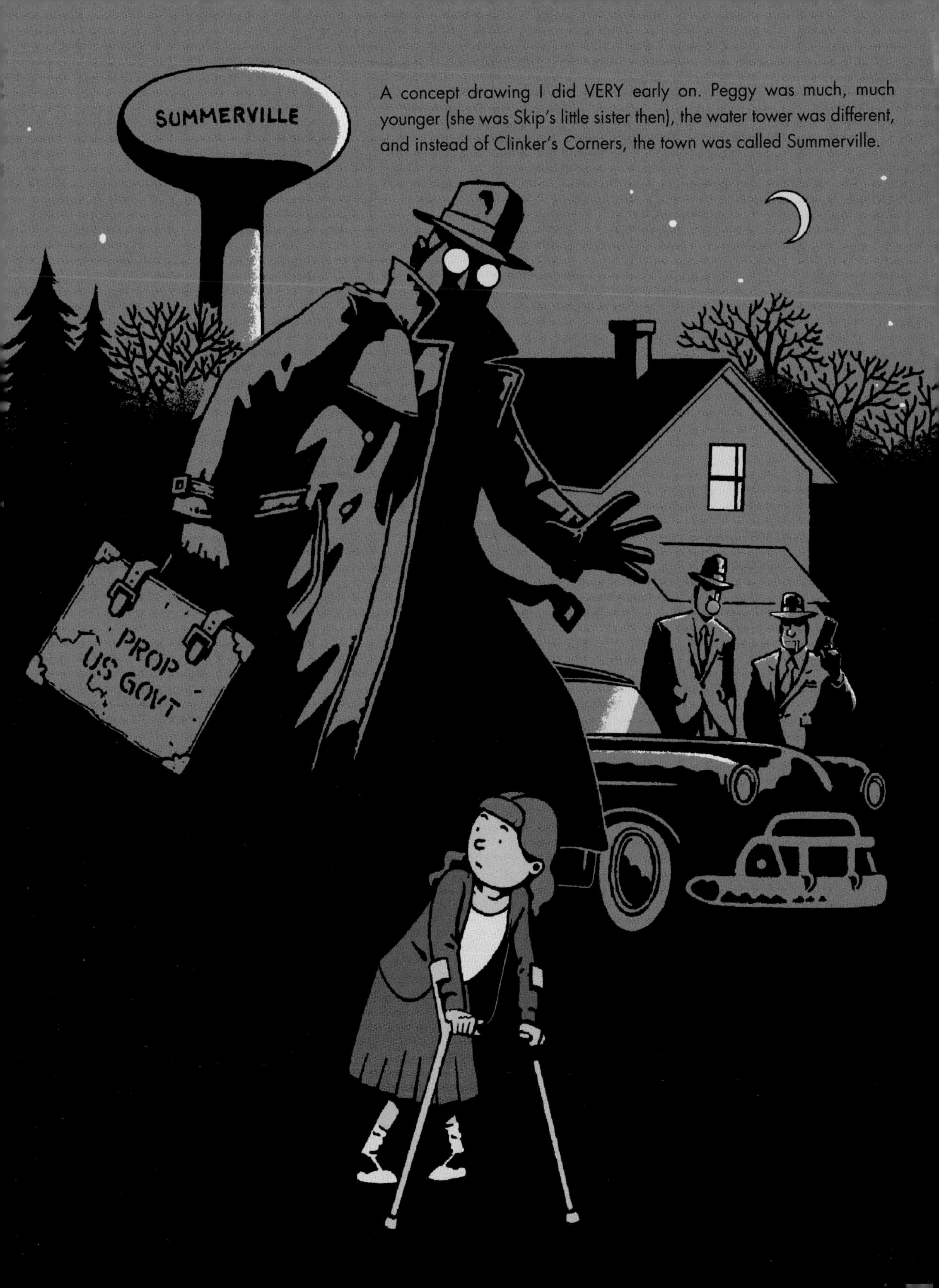
SUMMERVILLE
PROP
US GOVT

A concept drawing I did VERY early on. Peggy was much, much younger (she was Skip's little sister then), the water tower was different, and instead of Clinker's Corners, the town was called Summerville.

Right: While I did write and rewrite a loose prose script early on, a good deal of Red Scare was written like this, in thumbnail sketches. I printed out a template on printer paper and drew out the whole story, two pages of story per sheet of paper. I did this over and over, sometimes with very loose sketches if I felt confident, and sometimes more slowly and pain-stakingly when I was finding my way. When the story was finished in thumbnails, I was often able to blow up the sketches and print them out to give me a starting place for my final artwork.

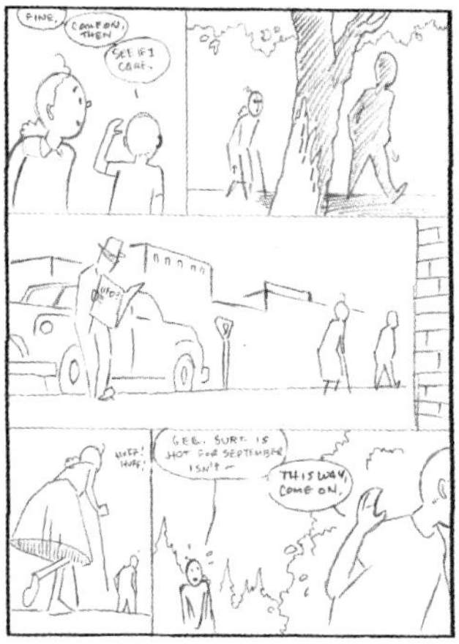
FINE.
C'MON, THEN
SEE IF I CARE.
GEE. SURE IS HOT FOR SEPTEMBER ISN'T —
THIS WAY, COME ON.

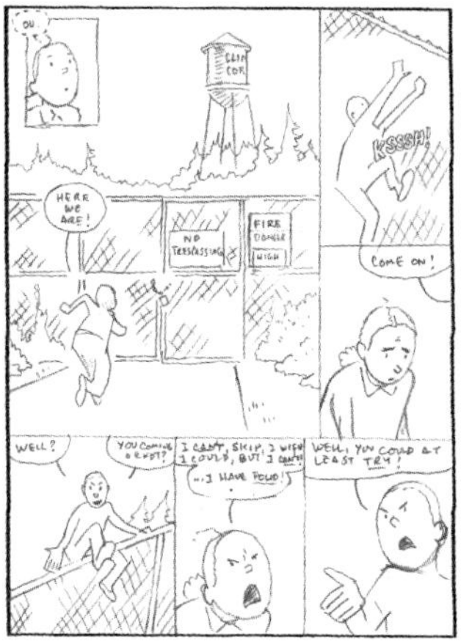
KSSSH!
HERE WE ARE!
NO TRESPASSING
FIRE DANGER HIGH
COME ON!
WELL?
WELL, YOU COULD AT LEAST TRY!

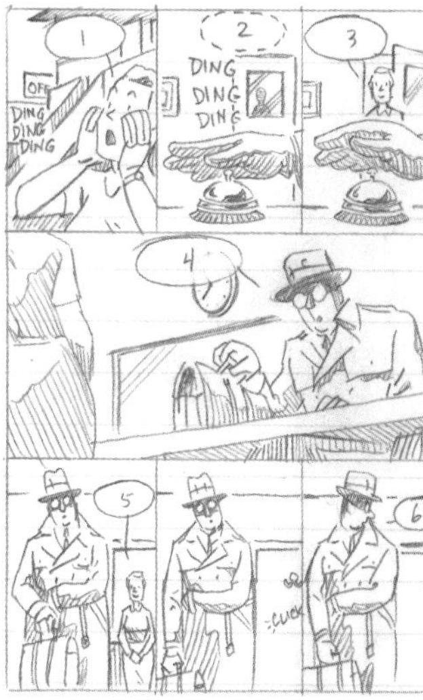
1
2
3
DING DING DING
DING DING DING
4
5
6

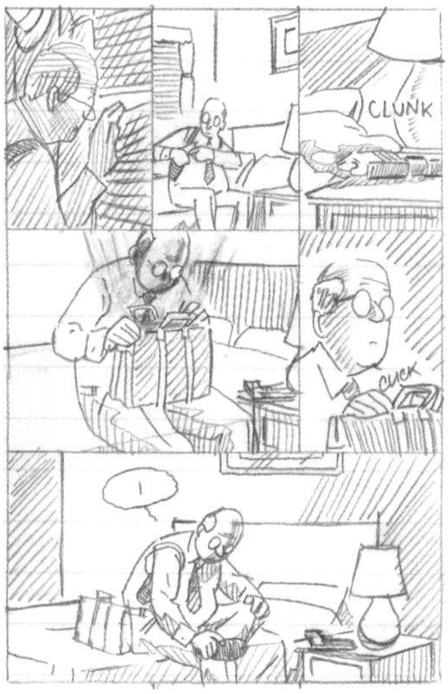
CLUNK
1

To the left are my thumbnails for another early draft. Once again, as you can see, some images stayed in, but many of them were revised or cut altogether.

Thumbnails will often be much sketchier than this, but sometimes I need to see them clearly in order to gauge whether or not the story is working. And I like drawing. Each of these thumbnail pages measures 3" x 4.5".

Below: It sure was a pleasure to finally see this guy get his on page 225. Sometimes getting the pose just right uses a lot of pencil lead!

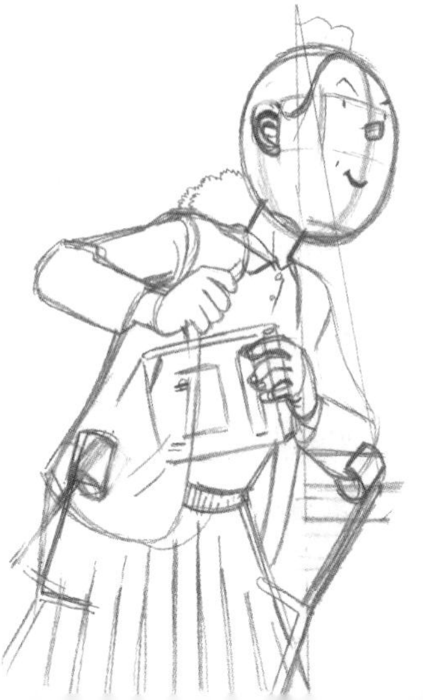

Left: I usually start off drawing free hand, but if the picture's not working, I find that going in and building the structure usually helps, like in Peggy's face here. And I find "drawing through" very helpful. In other words, drawing even the parts that won't be seen in the finished picture.

Gotta keep drawing till you get it right!

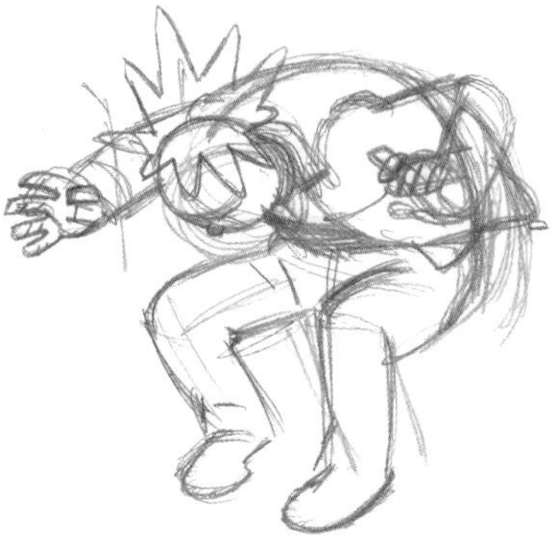

The illustration to the right is one of my favorite images in the whole book. I try to draw using simple shapes and shadow and light. This picture came out just the way I imagined it.

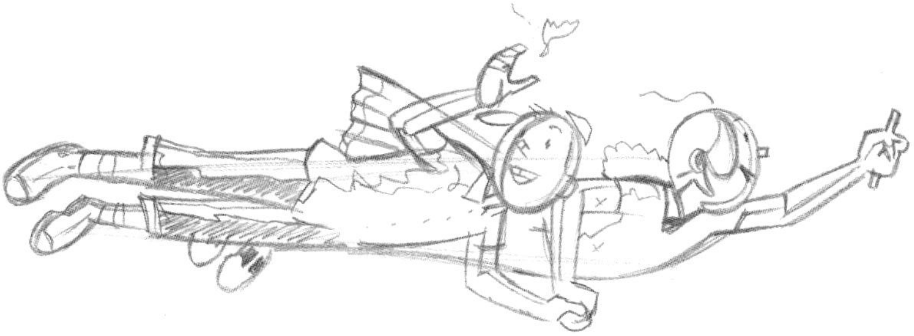

The two panels below, from an early draft of the script, gave more explanation of the origins of Peggy's glowing artifact.

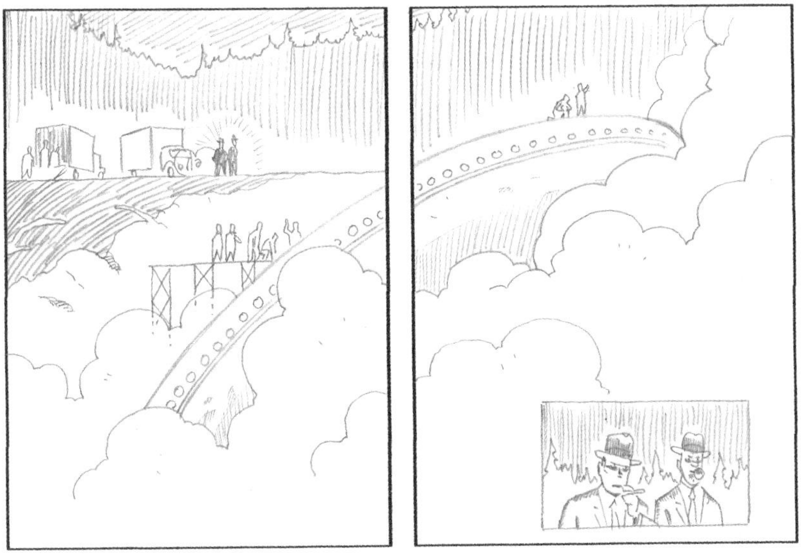

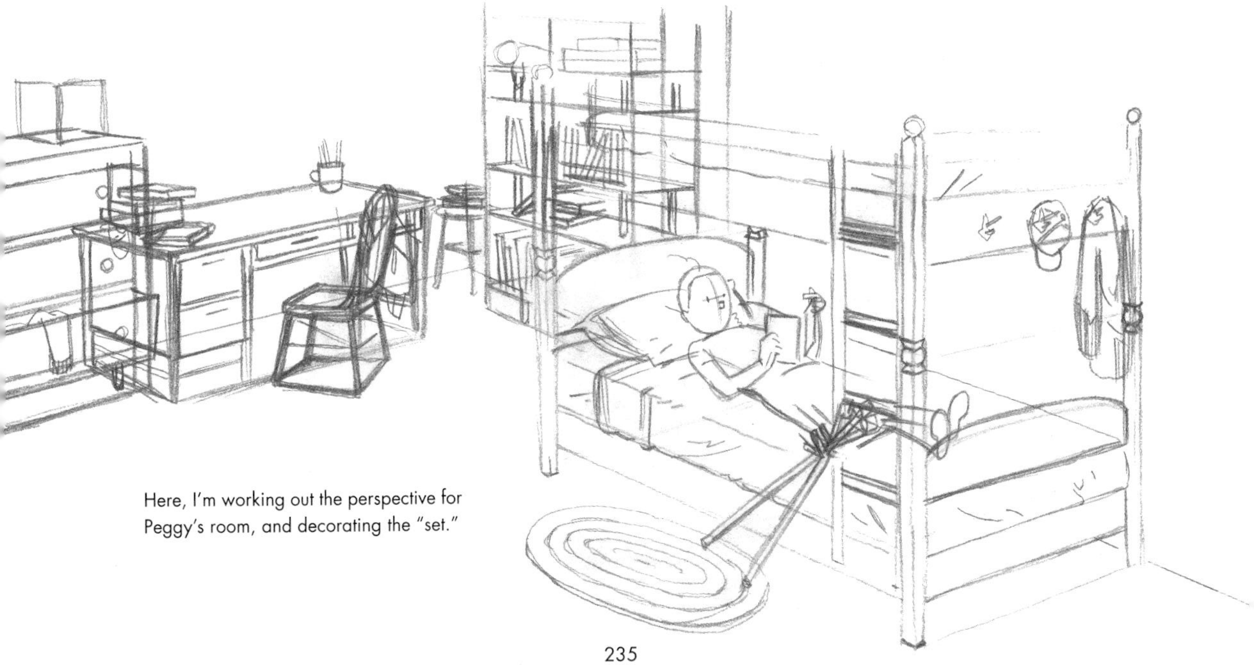

Here, I'm working out the perspective for Peggy's room, and decorating the "set."

Below are the final inks for one of my favorite pages of *Red Scare*. A chase in a library was something I couldn't wait to see come to life. After I scanned the inked page into Photoshop I made some changes to the composition of the first panel – turn to page 115 and compare the final art to this page.

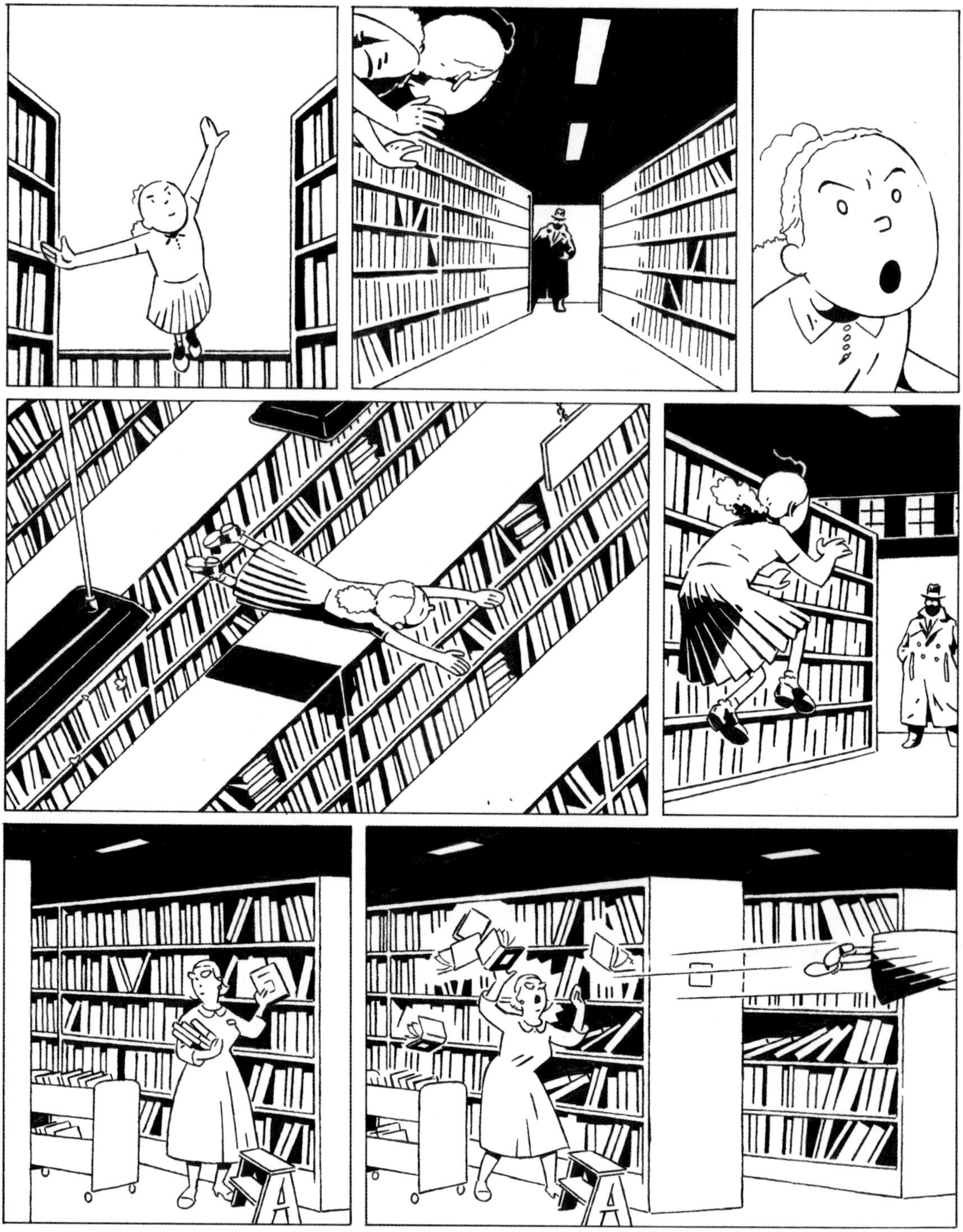

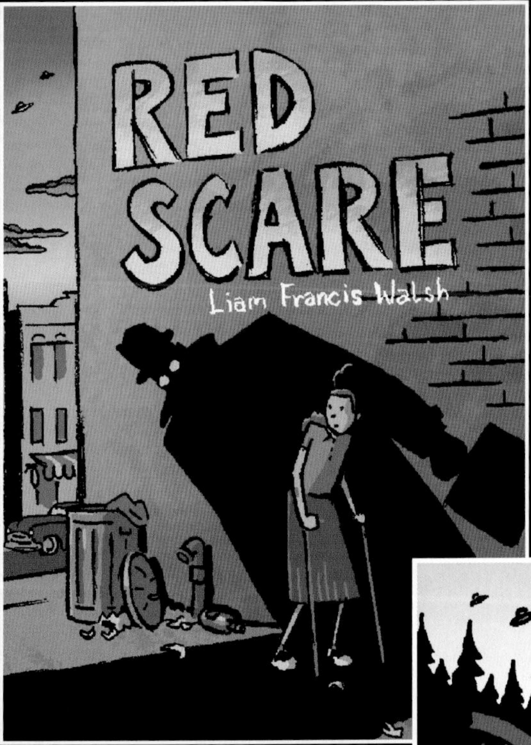
RED SCARE
Liam Francis Walsh

Some alternate covers.

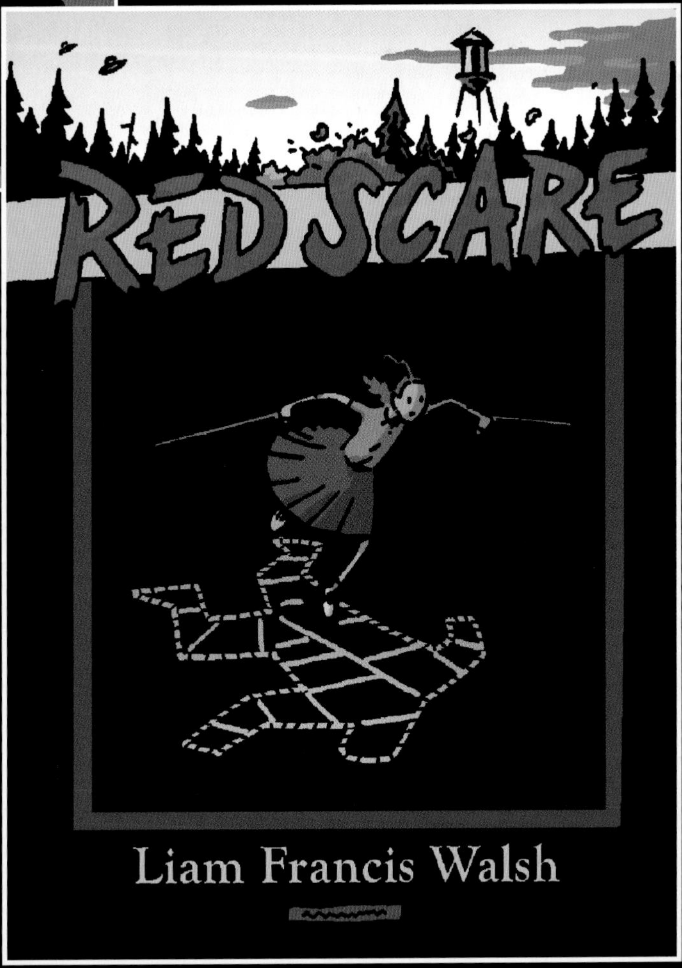
RED SCARE
Liam Francis Walsh

# ACKNOWLEDGMENTS

I owe my thanks to far too many people to list here, but a few I would like to single out are:

Benjamin Schwartz, *New Yorker* cartoonist, doctor, and dear friend, read seemingly endless early drafts of *Red Scare* in teensy, rough thumbnail form and never failed to enthusiastically encourage me to keep at it.

Tom Toro and Liana Finck, both wonderful cartoonists, and Jessica Esch, reader extraordinaire, were kind enough to read my completed manuscript and give me their thoughts.

Special thanks to Wes Dzioba (and co!) who jumped in to help me color when I started to fall behind.

Irene Mastrobattista, my sixteen-year-old next-door neighbor, erased the messy pencil lines on my inked pages in exchange for help with her English homework.

Many thanks to Bob Mankoff, former cartoon editor of the *New Yorker*, who pulled one of my cartoons out of the slush pile and made me a published cartoonist.

Dan Lazar, a wonderful agent and friend, saw one of my cartoons hanging at the Society of Illustrators and helped me become a published author.

David Saylor and Adam Rau, editors and story geniuses, helped me sift through all the ideas and material I'd amassed to find the story at the heart of *Red Scare*.

Phil Falco answered my myriad ignorant technology and design questions and helped me make the book I saw in my head.

My thanks to Donna Lowich for her insights and suggestions about how Peggy manages the effects of polio.

The generosity of my mother- and father-in-law, Luigi and Liliana Della Casa, helped us survive while I worked years past my original deadline.

My own mother and father, and my five sisters and three brothers, support and encourage me every day. I feel very lucky to be part of such a wonderful family.

My godparents, Jerry and Sally Bowker, gave me the best gifts you can give a young artist: attention and encouragement.

The wonderful work of Bill Watterson, Alan Moore, Mike Mignola, and Hergé has fascinated, delighted, and inspired me, and I am endlessly grateful to them.

Spending my days making things up and drawing pictures has been my lifelong dream. I couldn't do it without the love and support of my wife, Alessia, and my daughter, Dora. Thank you — I love you both more than words can say.

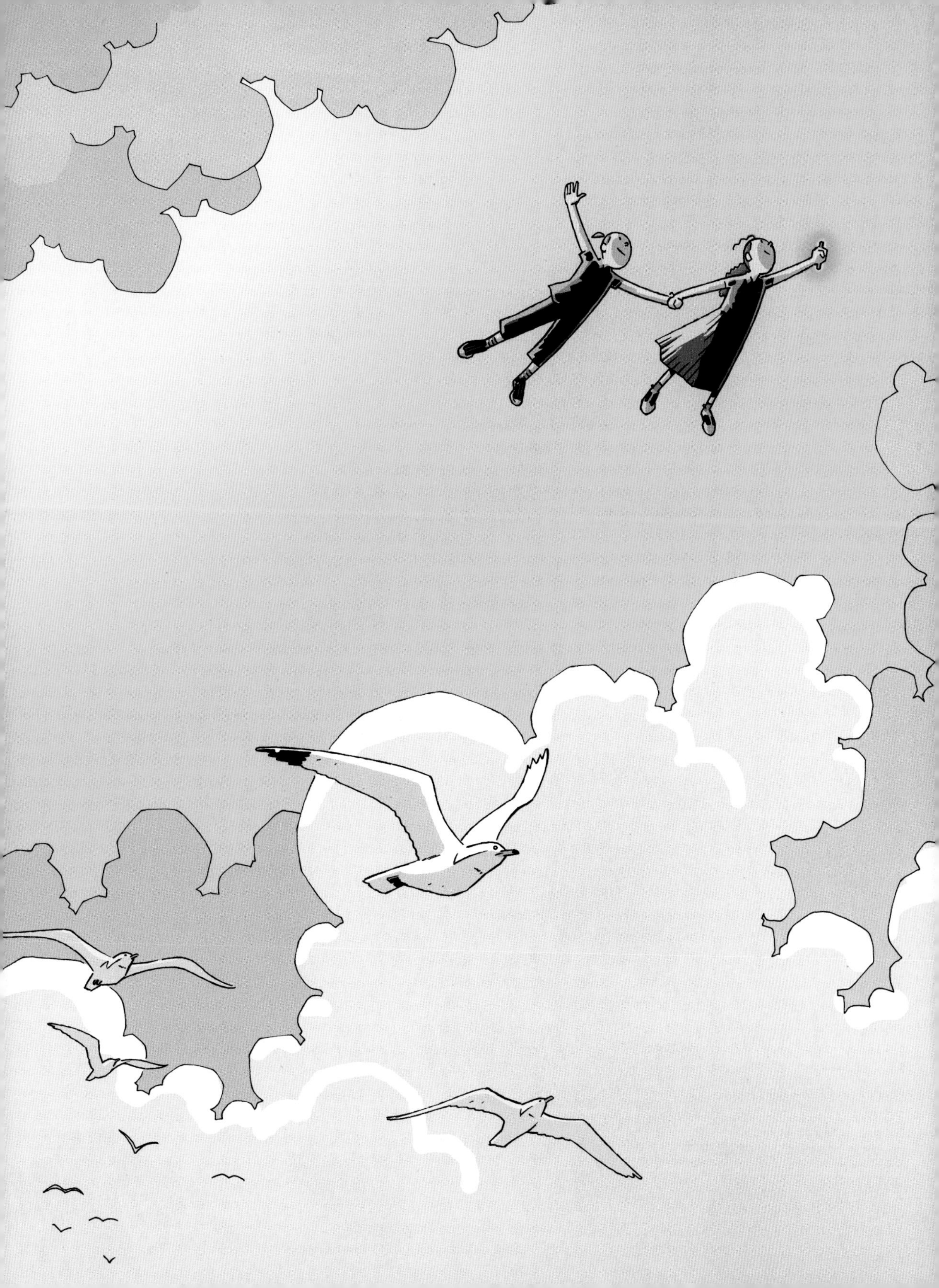

# LIAM FRANCIS WALSH

is an award-winning cartoonist, author, and illustrator. He was born in northern Wisconsin and grew up on a dairy farm with lots of siblings and books and a pet crow. His work has appeared in the *New Yorker*, the *Guardian*, *Esquire*, and *Reader's Digest*, and he is the author of two picture books, *Make a Wish*, *Henry Bear* and *Fish*. He lives in Switzerland with his wife and daughter.

You can learn more about Liam and his work at his website: liamfranciswalsh.com.